Bracken Creek Wolves

Campfires & Canines
Moonlight & Mischief
Secrets & S'mores
Wolves & Watercolors
Snowdrifts and Soul Mates

Aly Hollis

Bracken Creek Wolves Omnibus

Campfires and Canines
Moonlight and Mischief
Secrets and S'mores
Wolves and Watercolors
Snowdrifts and Soul Mates

Copyright 2024 by Aly Hollis

All Rights Reserved

Cover artwork by Nalou Arts

For sunny afternoons
at the creek and cozy nights
by the fire eating s'mores
with our found family.

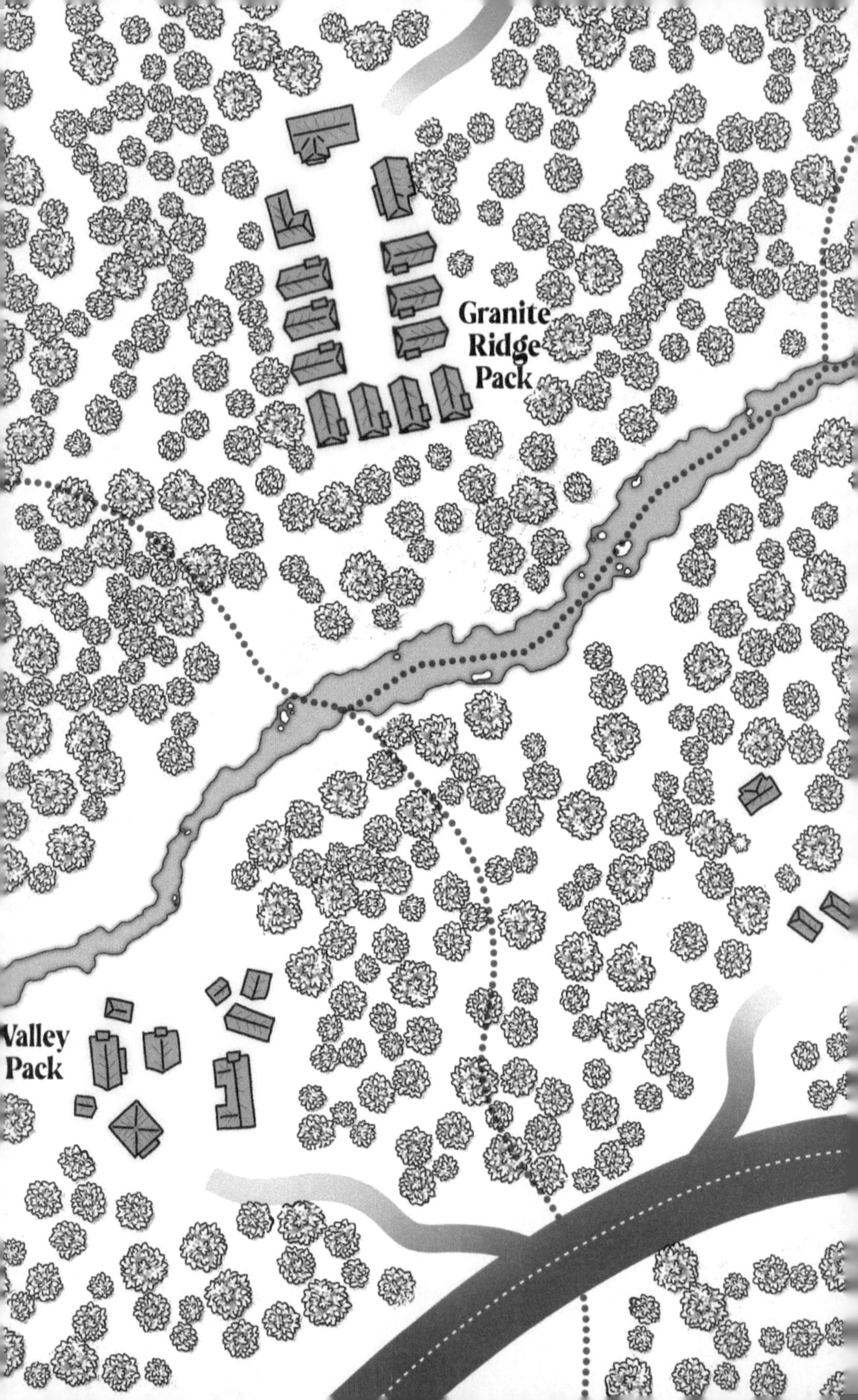

Granite
Ridge
Pack
Valley
Pack

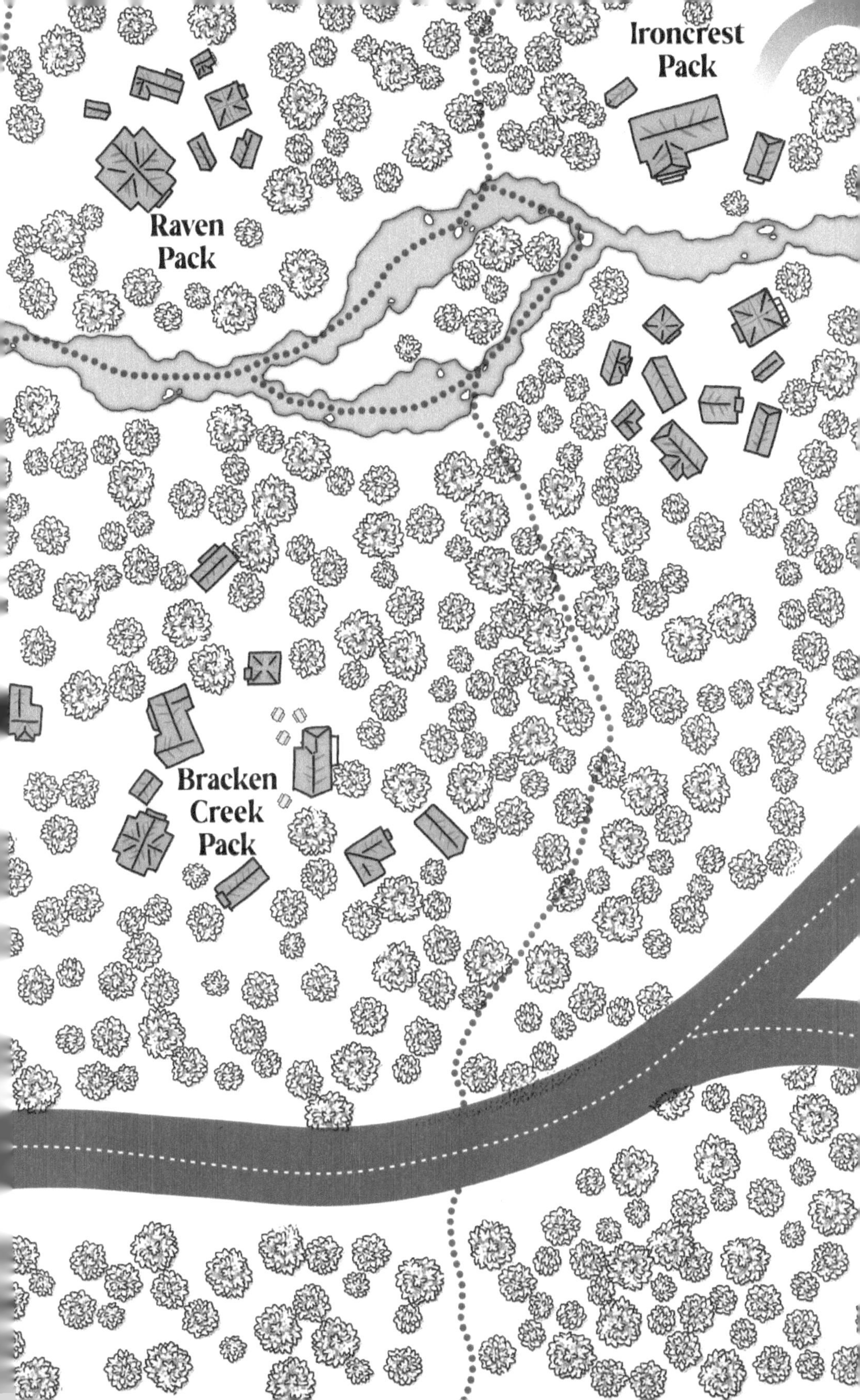

Ironcrest Pack
Raven Pack
Bracken Creek Pack

CAMPFIRES
AND
CANINES

I

COFFEE & CAR RIDES

Hazel

The tiny blue dot is still creeping across the map app, but the coordinating blue line has vanished. Technology has abandoned me in the middle of a forest twelve hundred miles from the familiar freeways of Los Angeles.

The road is blessedly empty, so I slow and pluck my brick of a phone off the holder and reload the map. The pinwheel spins. Schnitzel. I am in trouble. With a frustrated growl, I toss my phone onto the passenger seat where it thuds between a crumbled bag of cheese puffs and my slouching purse. This is going to be so much harder without cell service. I should have known the mountains would be a dead zone. Nothing to do but find some help, but picking a random exit seems like a poor choice.

Leaning into the curve of the mountain road, I scour for any sign of civilization. My uncle's home is still at least a few miles away. I think the app had said twenty minutes left. Hopefully there is something else closer.

Another exit rolls by, but then a larger exit comes into view with a sign for a town. Thank you, baby Cheesus! Now I just need some sort of Wi-Fi and for my brain to work long enough to memorize the route.

The town is tiny, and it feels a bit like a Hollywood set with how the buildings line the street with nothing but swaying trees behind them. I decide it's more of a cute small-town romance than a horror movie, though the forest is ominous. I'll be among the trees for the next week at least, I might as well get comfortable with them.

The gas station probably won't have Wi-Fi. Standing at the end like my mossy salvation is a coffee shop. The brick facade might be crumbling, but every coffee shop has Wi-Fi. I hope.

Tongue sticking out slightly in concentration, I do my best to parallel park. The bumper scrapes the curb. Shit. After growing up in California, I used to be incredible at parallel parking, but it's been a while since I had to do it. Just another skill I've let atrophy. Slimeball Jeremy insisted on being the one to drive us to work so he could show off whatever expensive vehicle he was leasing that quarter. My rusted old Corolla was embarrassing, apparently. I'm glad I never let him talk me into getting rid of it. It was one of the last things I kept belonging to my dad.

How many things did I change because of Jeremy? I bite the inside of my cheek, trying to keep the negative thoughts at bay. But it's a long list of poor choices, everything from bleaching my hair to delaying grad school to work at his family's firm. And look where that got me.

Exhaling, I press my skull into the headrest and squeeze my eyes shut. I'm done beating myself up. The last few weeks have been hard enough without piling guilt on top. Logically, I know it's mostly on Jeremy. My error was trusting a charming, wealthy playboy. Silly me for thinking we were exclusive after he proposed.

Normally after a breakup, girls go home, but that sounds wildly unappealing. I know where that negative, blaming voice in my head comes from, and she's either back home in Los Angeles if she's sober, or who knows where if she's not. At least I had my sister to help me pack up.

Aurora always hated Jeremy and she's not a big fan of our mom either. You could call Aurora aggressive, but I prefer fiery. Unfortunately, she's living with five roommates in a two-bedroom apartment in Hollywood, so staying with her isn't an option.

So now I'm driving through the middle of nowhere, hunting for Wi-Fi so I can find some hidden ranger station in the woods.

My door thuds shut and I take a deep breath of the mountain air: pine resin, musty leaves, and something dusty. It smells almost sharp after a lifetime breathing in smog.

The brick arches above a hand-painted sign with chipped paint spelling out Birch and Brew. Dandelions bob their golden heads along the side of the building, cheerily welcoming me. The thick, wooden door swings open.

Vintage copper equipment gleams behind a stretch of stone countertop below an artful chalkboard menu. Shelves rise up the wall beside the door, holding rows of matte black bags with labels like Evergreen Espresso and Summit Sunrise Roast.

I can't help my smile as I scan the menu. Mountaintop Mocha, Cozy Cabin Cold Brew, Sasquatch Spiced Cappuccino. They're all mountain puns.

"Welcome to Birch and Brew, what can we brew for you?"

"Hi, actually, do you guys have Wi-Fi?" My voice goes high.

The teenage barista raises their studded eyebrow at me. Awfully judgy for someone with green hair and about twenty-three piercings.

"Um, sorry, I do want a drink. Can I get..." Why is it so hard to make a decision when someone is staring at you? "How about a Campfire Chai?"

"Sure. Anything else?"

I shake my head and tap my debit card to the reader. Nothing happens. Oops. Biting in my cheek, I shove my card into the chip reader. "Sorry, do you guys have Wi-Fi?"

They point to a framed sign perched over the mostly-empty glass bakery case. The network name and password are printed in huge, bold text. My cheeks tingle with a blush.

When the barista plunks my drink on the counter, I avoid their gaze, swipe the cup, and slink to the back of the room. Holding my cup in two hands, I take a moment to relax. The first sip is soothing, spices rolling over my tongue. I've always loved chai. Jeremy preferred coffee and pushed me into drinking it. Nope, not going there again!

My chipped emerald manicure clicks against my phone as I plug in the password. The loading dots blinks for ages, but when I'm about to give up, it connects. It's another extended wait for the map to load, but it finally appears and I zoom in. I'm not sure the private road to Uncle Heath's cabin will have a sign, so I zoom in and squint, hoping I can use mile markers or some landmark to identify it. Unfortunately, there is no such detail visible on this map.

Clenching my jaw, I lean back and roll my shoulders. After two days in my rusty car, my hips and back ache. I'm beyond ready to be done with this stupid drive, but I have to figure out this last stretch.

A quiet week or so in the mountains with my favorite, and only, uncle is just what I need. I can't keep couch surfing between friends, and all of my interviews have led to rejection after rejection. It's my fault. My confidence is shot. Being fired from your ex-fiancé's family business will do that to a girl. To be fair, the dickweasel didn't become my ex until after I was fired.

I'm going to hike in the woods, smell the wildflowers, take a nap or two, maybe read a book. Recharge and figure out what to do with my life next. Besides, I've never visited my dad's childhood home. I've always wanted to see it, but Heath always came to visit us, and we never went to him. Something about the faded pictures in my dad's glove box made his home seem magical and mysterious. Heath stood a few inches taller than my dad when they were teenagers, both of them dwarfed by the towering pines.

It took some major convincing, promising to stay out of the way and listen to everything Heath says, but eventually he agreed to let me visit. Now, if I can figure out this map app, I'll finally get to see where my dad grew up.

Glaring at my screen, I toggle the map overlay and zoom in again. Is there a street view setting or something?

"You doing okay?" A velvety voice brushes over me.

I blink up at the person. The man.

He lounges in a chair across the aisle, long legs stretched out like a jungle cat. Bright aqua eyes stare from warm, golden skin and a rugged square jaw. Those eyes could strip my soul bare.

My mouth wants to hang open, but instead I deliberately swallow. I'm not going to drool over the first hot guy that I see.

Our eyes connect and he sits forward, stretching his white shirt across his pecs and biceps. "Hey, is this your first time in Birch and Brew? I don't recognize you."

I pointedly look at his face, that straight nose, full lips - no, not the lips - up to his unfairly long eyelashes. "Do you work here?" I blurt. Smooth. "Sorry, I mean…"

He chuckles, and it's as smooth as butter. "No, just a regular. It's a small town. Easy to spot new people."

"Oh, of course. Um, I'm just driving through." I twist the cardboard sleeve around my to-go cup.

"Cool." He studies me, his head cocked to the side. His blonde lashes glow in the low afternoon light. "Everything okay? You looked kind of upset."

My nose scrunches. "I'm having problems with my map. I lost service and I'm worried I'll miss my next turn."

He maintains eye contact as he slides across the aisle and into the empty seat across from me. His hand extends with a confident smirk. I blink at it. Does he want to shake my hand? "Here, let me see. I know the area pretty well."

"That's okay," I stammer. I'm not showing a stranger my destination. He might be gorgeous, but I'm not that dumb.

"Then tell me the exit. I don't want to leave you stranded. And I promise I'm not a stalker or an axe murder."

"Okaaay," I say, offering him the map.

"Are you going to see Heath Aten?" His platinum hair falls across his forehead as he looks up at me.

My stomach jumps. So much for staying anonymous. "You know him?"

"Yeah, of course. He was friends with my mom growing up. I haven't seen him in a few years, though." His smile puts me at ease.

"Wow, what are the chances? So, can you tell me how to get there?"

"Sure, but it's probably easier to download the offline map. Then your navigation will work without cell service."

"Seriously?" My eyebrows shoot up. How did I not know about this?

He barks out a laugh again. "Here." Warm callouses scrape across my knuckles as he cups my hand and tilts my phone between us, tapping a few settings. In a few seconds, the map is downloading.

"There, that should work great. Why don't you get off the Wi-Fi and try reloading the map?" He releases me, sitting back, the confident smirk back in place like he's some sort of prince charming to the rescue, and I have to admit I'm grateful. I hate needing help with anything, but he just made my day way easier.

The map reloads smoothly, the blue line tracing the path easily. "It worked! Thank you."

"Perfect. Well, it may have a hard time telling where you are, because it's estimating whenever the service gets spotty. So don't worry if your car is off the road a bit on the map. Just make sure to stay on the actual road," he teases.

"Thank you, Captain Obvious." I roll my eyes, and it feels suspiciously like flirting.

"You can call me Jasper," he says, his voice dropping. Cheese and crackers, he is flirting!

"I'm Hazel. Aten. Heath is my uncle."

"Really?" He sits forward, and I look away from the way his shirt stretches again. He really needs bigger shirts.

"Yeah. I haven't seen him in years, though." My shoulders tense and fall in a small shrug.

He cocks his head, his aqua gaze feeling slightly animalistic. "You must be Reed's daughter."

"Oh, yeah, one of them."

"Are you staying long?" I look away again, uncomfortable under his scrutiny. When I glance back, he is relaxed and smiling.

"I haven't made any concrete plans."

"Well, maybe I'll see you again." He winks. I snap my mouth shut, shocked at receiving a wink from this man. Oh, he knows exactly how handsome he is.

"I'm not sure, I'm not planning to come back here. Who knows?" My heartbeat pulses in my throat as social anxiety gets the better of me. "I need to go. But thank you for your help."

He reclines further, a roguish grin across his face. "Have a nice drive. If you get lost, just turn around and come back. I'd be thrilled to see you again."

As I push to stand, my chair makes the worst scraping sound on the concrete floor. Ugh. As I step into the aisle, my hip bumps another chair for a sharper scraping squeal. I'm a hazard. Holding my cup tight to my chest, I navigate out of the cafe with my face burning, too shy to peek back at the blonde charmer.

The moment my car door slams shut, I smack my forehead against the steering wheel. What is wrong with me? I have to get myself figured out, make a plan for my life, and flirting with strange men is not on the agenda! Not that I'm capable of successfully flirting. Clearly. It doesn't matter, I won't see him again.

The afternoon fades, the sun sloping across the horizon as I climb in elevation. Jasper was right about staying on the road. One side leads to a steep drop. Massive pines loom over the road, so I'm driving through a patchwork of daylight and darkness.

My feminine rage playlist cuts out and the map app chirps its instructions. I let off the gas pedal, resting on the brake pedal until the road comes into view. Cautiously, I slow and twist the steering wheel to make the ninety degree turn. Gravel crunches under my tires. I can't see far into the trees. This forest is dense and shadowy, but I'm too relieved and excited to see Heath to feel apprehensive. Not even the red "No Trespassing" and "Private Property" signs dampen my mood as I steer around a curve and lose sight of the highway.

The trees tighten around me in a snug embrace. The road softens into dirt and pine needles, with short, scruffy weeds growing between the tire tracks. Finally, the foliage thins and the drive opens into a dirt parking lot. There are a dozen cars already, and I frown. I knew Heath had a few employees, but I thought he meant one or two assistants, not a huge team. Biting my lip, I pull into a spot between an old pickup and a green Jeep and park.

A weathered office building stands before me. It's one of those trailers, but a really nice one despite the obvious age. An identical one sticks out behind it. If I peer through the trees, I can see a larger building between the trees like some sort of warehouse.

The office door bangs open, making me jump. A broad man steps out, dirty blonde hair to his shoulders framing a short beard that is more silver than blonde now. His weathered skin creases as he grins at me.

"Hazelnut!" he bellows, his voice like thunder.

Leaving my door hanging open, I race to my uncle and fling myself into his arms. "Hi!"

His hugs are just as warm and snug as I remember, and my feet leave the ground for a few seconds. "I'm so glad you had a safe drive! I've missed you."

"It's been way too long!" Familiarity and affection wash over me, easing my tension and heartache.

"I'm sorry, I should have visited," he apologizes.

Shaking my head, I step back from him. "I appreciate you letting me come here. I think I needed a change of scenery." I won't cry. I did enough of that on the phone with him last week. Instead, I fill my lungs with the scent of pine. It smells cleaner out here, almost floral.

"You deserve to take some time for yourself," he rumbles.

A twinge of guilt pinches at me. I feel guilty for imposing, and he was so hesitant to let me visit. But I've wanted to come here for as long as I can remember. His lifestyle intrigued me growing up. He's some sort of director, leader, big boss man, but he never really talks about it and I had no idea it was this big of an operation.

"So this is your office and you live here?" I ask, surveying the landscape.

He nods. "Yes, this is my main office, but the cabin is a ways this way. We should get you settled." His hand waves vaguely to the side, though he looks back at the office. "But first, there is someone I want you to meet."

"Yeah?"

A young man emerges, striding forward. He's nearly as tall as my uncle, but slimmer, all lean muscle and tan skin. Shaggy mahogany hair curls around his ears and brushes his neck, softening sharp features. My brain shorts out. This guy is really, really good looking.

"This is Slate, my second-in-command." Heath claps him on the back.

Slate meets my gaze. His eyes are the shade of a forest after a rainstorm, the deepest evergreen. Mesmerizing. A straight nose leads to full lips that twitch into a perfunctory smile. I thought Coffee Shop Guy was handsome, but this man is otherworldly. What are they putting in the water around here?

He holds out his hand, and I take it. His touch is warm and calloused. Black tattoos circle his forearm: rocky peaks, jagged pine trees, and the outline of foxes - or maybe they're wolves. They disappear under his sleeve and lines peek from his neckline.

I peel my eyes off his body and smile politely. "Hello, Slate," I repeat his unusual name, pleased my voice sounds mostly normal except for jumping in pitch. That can't be helped.

"Nice to meet you, Hazel." His voice is husky and warm. As I stare at him, that polite smile grows uncomfortable. It's nearly a pout.

Pulling back, I cough and look down at the pine needles under my shoes. But who wouldn't stare? Hopefully he doesn't notice the blush creeping up my neck.

"I'm going to take Hazel to my cabin. Can you check with the team before dinner?" Heath rattles off instructions in a tone of such casual authority, I want to jump into action, too. Slate nods and turns. I force my gaze aside. I will not check him out as he walks away. Okay, maybe a quick peek. His waist tapers, showing lines of muscle above dark gray sweatpants. Freaking gray sweatpants.

"Want to get your stuff?" Heath asks, his eyebrows quirking.

My blush deepens, searing my cheek. There was no way he missed me gaping at his assistant. I'd like to crawl into my car and die, but instead I grab my purse and pop the trunk.

Heath slings my duffle over his shoulder like it's full of feathers and not the remnants of my life from the last two years shoved untidily into a gym bag. He sets off into the trees and I have to jog to keep pace with him. After a moment, he slows, matching his pace to mine.

Behind the two office trailers sits a larger building with industrial steel walls and roof. Oversized roller doors face some sort of circle of cleared dirt, marked off like a wrestling ring. Weird.

"Almost there," Heath reassures me. Ahead, an A-frame cabin materializes through the trees. I recognize it from one of the pictures of my dad as a kid, the one where he was hugging my grandparents. Now the cabin has a fresh coat of dusky blue paint. The trim around the windows and the door are still dark stained wood, warming up the entire facade. The little porch covers the entire front of the cabin.

Heath pushes the door open and we step directly into a kitchen. "Hazel, I still need to work while you are visiting. I'll try to be around as much as I can, but if you need anything, you can ask Slate too."

Nodding, I turn to survey the cheery room. "This is the cabin you grew up in right?"

"Yes, of course."

Bumblebee yellow cabinets cover two walls with polished butcher block countertops. One of those oval kitchen tables from the 80's sits in the center with chairs that don't quite match. The wood gleams with use and care. A single coffee cup sits in the center, and Heath grabs it and sets it in the sink. Daisy-print cafe curtains hug the window above the white farmhouse sink, coordinating with the tiny daisies painted across a row of tiles in the white backsplash. It smells like lemon and it's the cutest kitchen I've ever seen.

Heath leads me into a second room. Knotty wood planking covers the floor, stretching into a small living space. Lumpy leather sofas hunch over a shag rug, but that isn't where my eyes are drawn. A huge window takes up the back wall, framed by two bookshelves connected by a cushy window seat. A black cast-iron wood-burning stove perches on a stone slab in the corner. I imagine curling up with a good book while a fire crackles and snow falls outside the window.

"This is the bathroom," he says, pushing open a door to reveal a stretch of ivory countertop and a squat, brass faucet.

"Great," I say. It's small, but that doesn't matter.

"And here is the bedroom." He backtracks and opens a door I missed in the kitchen, leading to a pair of twin beds. He sets my duffle on the antique patchwork quilt of the nearer one.

Heath's expression shifts between anticipation and concern.

"I love it. Thank you for letting me stay." I'm genuinely grateful.

"That was your dad's bed. This one was mine. I've changed a lot, but I kept the bed frames. Solid wood and all. And the quilts were made by your great-grand-mother."

"They're beautiful." I run my finger across the tufted knots dotting the corners of each stitched square.

Heath pauses for a moment, watching me like I might spontaneously melt-down. "Alright, I've got to go wrap a few things up. I'll come grab you for dinner in about an hour."

"Sounds good!" I smile extra wide so he knows I am not some unstable, weepy teenager. Even though I was behaving like one for most of the last two weeks.

With a final nod, he disappears.

I tug open the checkered curtains. The hazy window reveals columns of purple lupine flowers mounding around the base of thick tree trunks. Between swaying branches, another cabin's roof is barely visible.

Shoving off my shoes, I flop back onto my dad's bed. My exhale is slow and cleansing, and when I inhale, I feel my anxiety loosen and a sense of excitement, anticipation, fizzing under my skin. I'm still exhausted, but it feels good to be here. I needed this change.

I was so wrapped up in Jeremy, I forgot about my own life. For two years, I did whatever he wanted, whatever would please him, and look where that got me. Lost. But that is why I am here, to focus on myself and what I want. To finally reconnect with my roots, where my dad came from, and see what that means to me. Hopefully things will be clearer with a few days of rest and some time in nature. And maybe a little more ogling that assistant.

II
FRIED CHICKEN &
NEW FRIENDS

SLATE

We've spent the last two weeks preparing, but now that Hazel is here, nerves and a sense of excitement roars through me. We can handle a few days with a stranger here, and it might even be nice.

Heath is determined her visit will be calm and quiet, without any complications. I'll do whatever I can to make that happen. For her safety and for ours.

In the hour before dinner, I circle our community and check in that everyone is ready for Hazel. The children need to be reminded of what they can and can't discuss. The grumpy elders too. But it seems everyone is set.

Unsure what to do, I hover near the garden and chat with my cousin as he finishes his tasks for the day and goes to wash up for dinner. I don't have to wait for Heath to return with Hazel. But here I am, thinking of nothing but her shy smile. I've never noticed someone's smile like that before.

When they appear through the trees, my chest tightens. Jeans hug her thighs and an oversized sweatshirt drapes over her curves, hinting at what I saw earlier. Wisps of hair have escaped and curl around her heart-shaped face. I'd like to wrap that golden ponytail around my hand to see if it's as silky as it looks.

What the hell? That was creepy.

I don't often meet women my age. The ones that live here, I consider family. My reaction is perfectly normal when a beautiful woman appears, looking like my dreams come to life. I'd have to be dead to not notice the soft cupid's bow in her pink lips or the way her dark eyebrows quirk when she's interested in something. She's stunning. Too bad she's solidly off-limits.

Those lips part as she looks over the people gathered. Half of the community has arrived for dinner already and is milling about, waiting for Heath. From her wide doe-like eyes, Heath didn't tell her anything about what to expect. It's not how I would have handled the situation. We probably seem strange to her.

"Wow, it's like a whole little town." Her silvery voice floats across the clearing.

"I guess you could say that. I've got a team of ten, and they all have their families. There's about forty residents right now." Heath says calmly. That's a decent explanation, I suppose. I watch her lashes flutter as she glances around, probably quickly counting them.

Heath continues to explain, "We try to eat dinner together as often as we can. It keeps the community close. Especially since most of us rarely go into the nearby town." I trail behind them, taking my place as second-in-command but not near enough to spook her.

Her face tilts up to take in Crickett's diner. Its red paint stands out from the soft browns and greens of the landscape, accented with chrome that catches the oranges and purples of sunset.

"So does everyone buy their own and you just sit together?" He holds the door open. "Oh, it's a buffet. So do you pay for it? How does this work?"

Heath chuckles. She's a curious thing, and I remember she went to business school. I wonder what she would think of our finances.

"It's a part of everyone's compensation package. Don't worry, we've been doing this a long time. And there is plenty of food to share with you."

They cross the black and white checkered linoleum and grab plates from the stack. Tonight's dinner is spread across the shiny red bar top - crispy fried chicken, country potatoes, corn, green beans. Classic.

I take my own plate and join them, while giving her a few feet of space. Hawthorne follows with his daughters, and the others form a line down the steps, everyone following the unspoken rules of respect. She doesn't seem to notice, instead breathing in the scent of chicken. "This looks and smells fantastic!"

Crickett pops out from the kitchen with a platter of dinner rolls in her arms. Her apron is dotted with grease spots and her dark hair is piled up on top of her head. The woman can cook - she makes our dinners five or six nights a week plus grab and go lunch items most days. I've taken my turn serving as a kitchen assistant, and she can order her team around like a general.

The moment she spots Heath and Hazel, her entire face lights up. The dish of bread lands with a ceramic clink on the counter. "You must be Hazel!" She rushed around the bar, tugging her apron off. "I've been dying to meet you!"

Hazel pastes a polite smile on her face that widens into a look of shock as Crickett wraps her up in a hug. She awkwardly pats the back of the smaller woman until Crickett releases her.

Heath chuckles. "Hazel, this is Crickett. She's married to my cousin, Hawthorne." He jerks his chin toward the tall man standing beside me.

"Oh! Your cousin. So I've got more family. I didn't realize." Hazel blinks, those doe eyes a swirl of wonder and confusion with an undercurrent of worry.

"You never mentioned us?" Crickett scolds as she steps back, swatting at Heath. She's one of the few who can treat him so casually. "How would you feel if we were keeping family members secret from you?"

Loading chicken onto my plate, I try to smother my smirk.

"Did you cook all of this? That's incredible."

Crickett preens. "Oh, I had plenty of help. Eat up! Once those boys get here, there won't be much left." Her eyes crinkle as she beams at Hazel, circling the counter once more. She pauses at the kitchen doorway and leans back, blowing a kiss to Hawthorne, who is shepherding their daughter forward while balancing a baby on his hip. He winks at her. I swallow and look away from the display of affection. They've been married for about eight years at this point and they're still wild about each other. The PDA doesn't bother me, but the feeling of missing out does. I was a teenager when they met. Crickett is younger than Hawthorne and she came to visit with a friend, and it was instantaneous fireworks between them. I could go searching for that, but I have duties here, so it may never happen.

Following Heath's example, Hazel loads up a plate and grabs silverware and a drink. Heath leads her to a picnic table in the center of the clearing. I hesitate, but once Heath catches my eye and tilts his head in silent approval, I trail after them and slide onto the bench at the end. As more people settle with their food, the sounds of eating and soft conversation fill the meadow.

I watch Hazel tear into the chicken and my worry over her hunger abates. She hums a cute little noise of appreciation that I find far more appealing than I should. Hopefully she doesn't notice me grinning at my drumstick like an idiot.

A strawberry blonde head of curls bounces over and slides into the seat across from me. "Hi Hazel, I'm Marigold!" Her grandmother, Sable, sits beside Heath.

"Hi, it's nice to meet you," Hazel responds politely though her expression has that slight pinch of concern I recognize from earlier. We are overwhelming her. But there is no way to stop Marigold once she sets her sights on something.

"Hazel, Marigold is our school teacher, and this is her grandmother, Sable. She's our nurse of sorts." Heath introduces everyone, leaning back so Hazel can smile at Sable.

The healer's keen gaze appraises Hazel. She wears her long silver hair in a loose braid down her back over the crocheted shawl draping her shoulders. Her stern demeanor contrasts with her hippie grandmother appearance.

"Hello," Hazel responds, shrinking slightly like a wildflower covered in frost. She must meet Sable's requisites because the older woman gives her a curt nod and moves her attention to her dinner.

Marigold is more than happy to seize Hazel's focus. "I'm so excited you're here! How are you liking it?"

Marigold is sunshine incarnate. She looks every bit the teacher with a Hungry Caterpillar t-shirt over bellbottoms. Freckles cover her face, and the only makeup she wears is a bit of feathered eyeliner and some brown mascara to darken her naturally pale lashes.

"Thanks, it's really lovely up here," Hazel says. "So you're the teacher for all the kids here? That sounds like a lot to manage, teaching so many different grades at the same time."

"It's kind of a one-room schoolhouse situation. I only have to worry about the younger kids. The teens do online classes on their own. I've got six students right now. It's busy, but the kids are really sweet."

"That sounds really fun, actually. I bet you're an amazing teacher."

"Aw, thank you!"

The girls exchange niceties, their voices rising. Marigold's grin reaches high-beam intensity, and Hazel's shoulders relax. It makes sense another girl our age would help her feel more comfortable. And Marigold is thrilled to have a new friend, especially a girl. She's been stuck with me and my cousins for our entire lives, so I don't blame her.

Marigold takes a drink and studies Hazel. "You're from Los Angeles, right?"

"Yeah, but I grew up closer to San Bernadino. Not nearly as green. Way more concrete."

"Have you ever been to a movie premiere? Or a talk show? What about seeing a celebrity?" The eager questions tumble out of Marigold's mouth.

Hazel laughs against her corn cob. She sets it down and wipes her mouth with the back of her hand. "No, I've only ever been to Hollywood to see my sister. She has an apartment near there. But I don't go into downtown LA if I can help it. Too much traffic."

"What about the beach?" Marigold asks, her eyes widening until she looks like a burrowing owl.

Hazel purses her lips. "Yeah, a few times. I'm not sure I'm a beach girl. I think I like it up here better."

I shift my weight and Marigold looks over, locking eyes with me. One of her eyebrows raises in suspicion. I refuse to be the one to break eye contact and let on how much I am hanging on every word said at this table. She can already read me too well, so I narrow my eyes into a glare until she looks down.

"How long are you visiting for?" Sable asks, dropping her quiet conversation with Heath.

"About a week, I think." She sounds hesitant like she isn't sure if she wants to stay, or maybe she isn't happy with the limits Heath pushed onto her. He was quite strict, not going out after dark, not wandering far. But it's necessary. We can't take more risks than needed.

"Do you have other destinations planned for your visit?" Sable sips her water.

"Maybe, I haven't figured it out yet. I've got a few friends in Oregon I could visit before heading back to California."

Hazel's tone is reluctant and she didn't say heading *home*, she said heading *back* to California. I shouldn't read into it, but I can't help it.

"Sounds like a nice vacation," Sable says.

"What do you want to do while you're here?" Marigold asks brightly.

"Just relax, I think. Catch up with Uncle Heath. See the scenery." She worries her bottom lip between her teeth like she has more to add but is nervous. "I need to be applying for jobs while I'm here, so I might take some time to do that."

"What kind of jobs?"

"Hazel has a degree in business," Heath says proudly.

"What types of positions are you looking at?" I can't help but ask, butting in. She blinks at me and my stomach jumps at those amber eyes.

"I'm not sure. I didn't really like my last job. I need to see what's available." She trails off. I want to press my thumb between her brows and smooth out the line there. The more we discuss jobs, the sadder she becomes.

"I'm sure you'll find something amazing!" Marigold affirms.

Fisher appears at Heath's shoulder, leaning down and speaking low. Heath glances over at Hawthorne, standing a few yards away, and grabs his plate, standing. "Hazel, I need to go handle something. Are you okay here?"

"Of course, I'll be fine," Hazel says, that small frown deepening.

"We can take care of her," Marigold chimes in with a saucy grin. "Slate can be her personal assistant, tour guide, whatever she needs!"

I look at Heath, silently asking if I need to follow. He shakes his head subtly and turns his back, joining Hawthorne and Fisher.

"Hi Dad. Bye, Dad!" Two lanky figures slip past the trio of retreating leaders. My cousins slide into the empty spots at the table, causing the bench to creak. Great, just what we need when Hazel's already flighty. At least Marigold is sweet and endearing. I can't say the same about Cedar and Onyx. Cedar might be nice, but Onyx is plain annoying.

Hazel puts on her polite smile as Marigold introduces them. "Hey guys, this is Hazel, Heath's niece. Hazel, this is Cedar and Onyx. They're Slate's cousins."

The twins are identical, but easy to tell apart. Cedar, the older twin, is clean-cut with a darker tan from his hours spent outdoors, his hair a brighter blonde as well. Onyx's hair is long enough to shove into a messy man-bun, and he wears mostly oversized band t-shirts and ripped jeans.

"Nice to meet you." Cedar is courteous and careful.

"Hey." His brother stretches out, crowding Sable until she levels a withering glare at him. That causes him to scoot back.

Hazel looks between them. "Cedar, and Onyx?" she confirms. They nod. "You're twins."

"Yup, too bad I got all the good looking genes," Onyx jokes. Marigold barks out a laugh, covering her mouth with her hand. Onyx glares at her, though it's playful.

With a tired sigh, Sable rises, gathering her plate and glass. "Be respectful, boys," she warns before walking toward the diner.

The admonition is applicable. Onyx is a loose cannon at the best of times. I used to see him as fun and spontaneous, the opposite of Cedar. Cedar is the friend you ask to pick you up from the bar when you've had too much to drink. He is reliable and prefers plants over people, so you know he isn't out partying too.

Onyx tips his head toward me, a sardonic grin blooming across his face. "How you doing, Slate?"

Before I can come up with a response that will put him in his place, the twins' little sister stomps up to our table. Briar is balancing baby Dahlia on her hip. It looks like she got stuck with babysitting duty when Hawthorne was called away with Heath.

Dark curls bouncing, Hawthorne and Crickett's youngest daughter is grinning while she yanks on fistfuls of Briar's dishwater-blonde hair. "Marigold, can you take her until her parents are free? Thanks!" She shoves the one-year-old into Marigold's lap and practically runs.

"Oh, she's so cute!" Hazel coos, reaching out and lifting Dahlia's chubby fist with her finger. The baby grabs on and drags Hazel's hand toward her mouth.

"This is Crickett's daughter," I say.

"Oh!" Hazel leans around Marigold to smile at me. Marigold might be sunshine, but Hazel's smile is moonlight washing over me. I would watch it for hours. "So you're my little cousin too!" Hazel's tone modulates upwards and she exaggerates each syllable as she dances her fingers up Dahlia's pudgy belly.

"Second cousin," Cedar adds, doubtlessly without thinking. He's a walking encyclopedia and it tends to slip out. "Technically."

"Want to hold her?" Marigold lifts Dahlia under her armpits and plops her in Hazel's lap.

"Aren't you the sweetest little second cousin?" Hazel bounces her knees, making Dahlia gurgle. Her baby smile is accompanied by a drizzle of drool. Marigold wipes it up with a spare napkin.

The girls fuss over Dahlia, squeezing her little thigh rolls and kissing her sticky hands, until Hawthorne finally breaks off to retrieve his daughter.

"She likes you," Hawthorne says, lifting Dahlia to his chest and patting her back. She reaches for his beard and gives it a tug. He chuckles and tries to loosen her grip. "Let's go help Mama."

"She's adorable." Hazel waves at Dahlia as Hawthorne heads toward the kitchen.

"Hazel, what kind of stuff are you into?" Cedar asks, leaning forward.

"Um, I don't know, creative things." Her vague answer hangs in the air and we all watch her. When she realizes we are waiting for more, her eyes light up. She isn't used to people being interested in her.

"I like taking pictures," she continues, tucking some loose hair behind her ears. "That's probably my favorite."

"Oh, I'd love to see your photography!" Marigold chimes in.

"I'm not any good. I just use my phone." She's apologetic. Who told her she wasn't any good? My jaw clenches, wanting to speak up but knowing it would be out of turn.

"What do you like to photograph?" Cedar presses.

"Anything, animals at the zoo and birds, stuff like that. Pigeons mostly." She laughs awkwardly, that beautiful rosy flush returning to her skin.

"I can think of plenty of animals around here you can photograph," Onyx adds with a suggestive look. I want to grab his throat and yank him across the table. Can't he behave for five minutes?

"Onyx, shut up." Marigold snaps me out of my violent fantasy.

"Like the chickens and our goats," he whines, feigning innocence.

Cedar jumps in. "There's squirrels and raccoons all over the place, too."

Hazel leans in, intrigued. "Oh, you have chickens and goats?"

"Yeah, a few hens. We don't have a rooster – too loud," Cedar explains, "and our two goats are Cheddarbelle and Cheesette."

"Cheddarbelle?" Hazel says, her words breaking into laughter.

"I named them." Onyx puffs up his chest.

"They're Nubian goats. Great for milk," Cedar continues, ignoring his brother.

"Our dad makes cheese with it. Mom bought him a class a few years ago," Onyx says, looking for more of her attention. "He even got a special fridge to age his cheese in."

"That sounds cool. I've never known anyone who made cheese. It seems really difficult," Hazel muses, idly twisting the ring on her right hand around and around. It looks like a vintage wedding band with a few diamond chips that catch the light.

"It's not too hard, just messy," I say. I've helped Fisher with his cheesemaking a few times.

Onyx grins at her. "I'd be happy to give you a lesson any time." The image of Onyx with his arms around Hazel, guiding her as she cuts curds sends a jolt of jealousy through me. I've got to get a grip. Or Onyx needs to leave her the hell alone. Preferably both.

Hazel either ignores him or is oblivious to his flirting. She cocks her head, pursing her lips. "What do you guys do for fun around here?"

"Hang out with these morons," Marigold quips, rolling her eyes.

Cedar smiles at her, a dimple in his cheek. "There's a lot of great hikes around here."

Leaning my elbows on the table, I add, "And there are hammocks around to chill or read."

"That sounds nice," Hazel says.

"I like board games or card games," Marigold chimes in.

"Oh, me too!" The girls grin at each other again.

Onyx waggles his eyebrows. "Want to play some poker?"

I'm going to murder him.

"Don't you dare." Marigold's voice rises, half threatening and half laughing. Hazel laughs, covering her mouth with her hand.

"I wasn't going to!" he whines.

"Onyx, Cedar, you guys are on dish duty tonight." I try to make it sound like it's a planned assignment and not something I decided in the moment. But if Onyx doesn't back off, I am going to seriously injure him. He's doing the exact opposite of what we discussed. Well, maybe not the exact opposite, but definitely not what he should be doing.

"I don't think it was our turn," he starts to argue, but Cedar is already standing and gathering everyone's dishes.

"We'd better get going. Bye, Hazel." He drags Onyx away.

"I'm sorry about him," Marigold whispers, leaning into Hazel.

"They're pretty funny." Hazel shrugs. She's a peacekeeper, I can tell. It makes me like her even more, but it also triggers my protective instincts. She would let others make her uncomfortable just to keep everyone happy, and that's not okay. She shouldn't have to tolerate anyone treating her badly.

The tables around us are clearing. Heath hasn't returned and the sun is dipping below the tree line. Under the canopy, it'll be dark already.

"I'd better get home, too." In seconds, Marigold is bouncing away, leaving the two of us alone. Hazel looks at me and then down, her lips pressing together.

I clear my throat. "Hazel, can I walk you back to your cabin?"

"That's okay." Hazel stands, stepping over the bench. "I remember the way. It's not far." She reluctantly makes eye contact with me again. Flecks of gold drift in her irises, highlighting the warm brown.

"Actually, it's getting dark. The trees look different after sunset and the ground isn't very even. I'd feel better if I made sure you got home safe." I keep my tone even and nonthreatening.

She looks up as if she didn't see the sky darkening. "Okay." Her one-word answer is punctuated by her bottom lip rolling between her teeth. I stare at the small gap between her front teeth and the way her lip pales as she bites it, the color rushing back in as it slides out from under her teeth.

And now I'm staring again. She didn't want me to walk her home. I'm a grade A creeper. Clenching my jaw, I drag my hand through my hair, raking back my wavy curls. "Heath wanted me to," I say awkwardly.

"Sure, it's fine. I don't mind," she says, reassuring me. She's definitely a people-pleaser.

"Sorry," I say, looking into those stunning eyes. "I didn't want to make you uncomfortable. I promise, I'm a gentleman."

She laughs lightly. "Slate, don't stress about it. Let's go."

We walk in silence, the voices of other families drifting through the trees. She steps carefully but still manages to stumble. I offer my hand but she ignores it. From the shy glances she gives me, I can tell she's embarrassed, but she shouldn't be. I warned her. And besides, I can clearly see the brush and uneven terrain her eyes can't. I would never expect her to move through the woods like I do.

I want to touch her, and maybe I should if she's stumbling. She ignores my offered hand. Maybe she doesn't need it and I'm the one desperate for contact. She arrived a few hours ago, a mantra I repeat in my head. She needs space to recover from a bad breakup, not advances from a stranger.

She's off limits and I'm under strict orders to treat her with the utmost deference. I can't imagine what Heath would do if he knew the thoughts going through my head, the urges that keep rising in me, or the way my body sings this close to her.

She reaches the cabin steps and turns to me. For a second, I swear she's gazing at my mouth. I'm too close to her. It would take the slightest step to close the gap.

In the fading light, her eyes grow darker. The gold-brown darkens into the color of earth, rich and deep. I can't seem to step back. She's leaning forward, I think, or maybe it's me.

She gazes up at me and her pupils dilate. My breath catches - she's reacting to me like prey, like I'm dangerous. I've seen the expression on plenty of animals before.

I jerk back and stuff my hands into my pockets, my heart hammering. "Good night."

Her brows crease slightly, disappointment softening her expression. She grabs the door handle and pulls it open. "Night, Slate," she says before closing the door in my face. I stare at the wood for a moment, breathing in her lingering scent.

I have to get rid of this minor obsession that formed when she stepped out of her car and the sun lit her eyes into honey. The problem is, I have no idea how to. In fact, the more time I spend near her, the more it seems to grow. At first, I just wanted to look at her, maybe touch her. Now I feel like I'm about to break if I don't. I need to control myself. It doesn't matter how appealing she is or how sweetly she looks up at me. She's still off-limits.

III
HIKES & HOT GUYS

HAZEL

I nestle into the thick blanket on my uncle's window seat, bringing my hot cocoa to my lips. Its heat slowly radiates through my body, relaxing my muscles and melting away the tension that seems to live within me. This is heavenly.

The night sky outside is almost pitch black, with only the faint golden glow from the cabin windows illuminating the rough trunks of the nearest pine, fir, and maple trees. Leaves quiver in the breeze like black confetti, peppering the trunks with quaking shadows.

Honestly, I feel better than I have in ages. Maybe my ex-fiancé was right about meeting new people. There's something about these friends that feels real. They aren't performing like the social climbers in Los Angeles. Marigold is quirky and charming enough to be an influencer, but I doubt she even has social media.

The twins are hilarious. Cedar is quiet and sweetly nerdy while Onyx flirts shamelessly. With their blonde hair and golden skin, they'd look more at home on a beach in Los Angeles than here in the mountains. They might be handsome, but I hardly noticed when Slate was sitting at the table.

The man was clearly brooding, and it did weird things to my stomach. His lips pout when he frowns, and it seems like he frowns a lot. But something about those emerald eyes draws me in. If he had been the one hitting on me tonight, I would have been a goner. Luckily, he ignored me most of the evening.

I should go to bed, but the unfamiliar scenery keeps me rooted. As I lazily watch the shadows dance, two yellow pinpricks of light blink into existence. Some sort of animal? I can't quite see and as I lean forward and squint, they vanish.

Cedar said there is plenty of wildlife here. If I'm lucky, I'll come across some cute raccoons or foxes tomorrow. After they mentioned the possible creatures to photograph, I have the strongest urge to go hiking.

Finishing my cocoa, I hand-wash the mug and set it on a towel to dry. Heath still isn't home, but exhaustion drags me down. With a yawn, I crawl into my dad's childhood bed and try to picture the wildflowers from today. The riots of yellow and purple are better to dream about than the life in Los Angeles that is no longer mine.

It must work, because I sleep hard and dream of walking in a verdant forest.

I wake up cozy and quiet, too comfy to open my eyes. There's no traffic or muffled thuds of neighbors stomping around getting their kids ready for school. Instead, soft birdsong serenades outside the window.

I'm definitely on vacation. Groaning, I roll and bury my face in my pillow, enjoying the luxury of no alarm clock and having nowhere I need to rush off to. But as memories from last night filter in, I remember all the wonderful things I can do today, and that's enough to get me up.

Rolling out of bed, I find my jeans and pull them on. Heath is absent when I pad across the wood floor and into the tiny bathroom. When I emerge, Heath is sitting at the kitchen table devouring a breakfast sandwich and scrolling through messages. He's getting cell service! I'll have to ask how, but the thought leaves my head the moment I see the plate of baked goods on the table.

"Good morning, Hazelnut!" He practically glows when he smiles, like some Wild West version of Thor.

"Did you get me a chocolate croissant?" I snatch the pastry from the plate. He can keep the danish, but this is mine. After a couple of bites, I pause to accept the tea he offers.

"What's your plan today, kiddo?" He sets his phone down.

I'm too blissed out with my flakey, chocolatey breakfast to be annoyed at being called kiddo. "I was thinking about doing some reading. Walking around in nature. Maybe a nap." It all sounds pretty appealing right about now.

His eyes crinkle in amusement. "I've got to work. But if you want to hike, grab someone to go with you. Cedar shouldn't be too busy, or Marigold if it's after two and her school day is over."

"Sure." I'm not about to argue with his request, even if it irks me. I'm not about to wander off a cliff or even tackle a strenuous hiking trail.

"Be safe, make good choices." Yes, he does think I'm that incompetent. My hackles rise, but I keep my courteous smile. I'll just have to prove to him that I can handle myself.

He stands, setting his dishes in the sink and heading for the door.

"Bye! Have a nice day," I say. He waves one more time and then he's gone. The latch clicks behind him.

I finish my pastry, deliberately taking my time and relaxing, before taking a second look around the cabin.

The kitchen is tidy. A vintage teddy bear cookie jar sits in the corner and I imagine Heath and my dad stealing cookies from my grandmother while she cooked dinner.

In the living room, a collection of spy novels and thrillers pack the bookshelf, their spines all cracked. Some of the titles look positively ancient. Maybe my grandfather loved them. Does Heath read on cold winter evenings? There isn't a television and he can't work twenty-four-seven.

Logs are stacked tidily in an alcove a few feet from the black stove. The whole room smells like cut wood and soap. Distinctly a bachelor pad, but I can see the remnants of a family from when my dad still lived here, before he met my mom and followed her back to Southern California.

Eager to get outside, I yank on tennis shoes and pull my sweatshirt on. My newest book goes into my tote along with a water bottle. Grabbing my phone, I hesitate. It doesn't get enough cellular service out here to fully work, but maybe I'll get some good pictures so I tuck it in too.

While the hammocks I noticed yesterday sound tempting, the idea of seeing the creek lures me northwest. Crisp morning air sends a shiver down my arms, but I know the afternoon sun will warm me.

A squirrel races up a nearby tree, its claws scratching at the bark. The noise makes me jump, but once I see the cutie, I can't help but smile.

I take a deep breath. It's going to be a good day.

My shoes crunch on pine needles. There's an obvious trail here. As I march along, the use of my muscles feels invigorating and the bright scent of pine resin and wildflowers clears my head.

The trees sway overhead, dappling the sunlight. It's somehow energizing but also calming out here. I glance back; the cabin is still visible, but soon it'll be out of view. As long as I stick to this path, I shouldn't get lost.

All sorts of little plants wave as I pass. Even with my jeans, I don't want to touch them and risk poison ivy. I have no idea what poison ivy even looks like, so I step between them, weaving slightly.

The trail slopes downwards and transitions from level forest to rocky mountainside. It twists back and forth, getting harder to follow. Hiking boots would have been a wise idea, but my trusty tennis shoes will do.

A soft rushing sound emerges under the rustle and creaks of the trees around me. I grin smugly - I'm getting close. As the creek comes into view, the hiking trail becomes exceedingly difficult. I have to clamber through the brush to go around a fallen tree wedged between boulders - too high to climb but too low to go under. Locking my jaw, I push onwards, and my perseverance is rewarded.

Scrambling down the rocky slope, I reach the creek. It's got to be thirty feet across, at least. It doesn't seem very deep at this point – maybe up to my waist. I don't want to find out.

Tiny fish sparkle as they swim against the current. Rocks jut out of the water at regular intervals. Some of them are flat, a perfect perch for me.

Pink and purple penstemon flowers cover the shore in a blaze of color. Softer periwinkle forget-me-nots pop up throughout.

I slip off my shoes and socks and roll up my jeans so I can stick my toes in the water. Reaching out for balance, I carefully extend my bare foot until I reach the closest rock. With a gulp, I shift my weight from one foot to the other. I pick my way from rock to rock until I reach the biggest one. It's about ten feet from where I started, not quite in the center of the stream.

The sun is bright here, but the air is cooler. The water makes a delightful babbling sound splashing against the rocks.

Balancing carefully, I turn and lower myself to sit cross-legged. The stone is hot under my hands and warms my ass through my jeans. It feels divine. With a sigh, I savor the success - I made it!

Camera ready, I search for the best angle to capture the white foam curling through the crystal water as rocks disrupt the flow. Then I capture the treetops reaching toward the puffy clouds. I'd love to photograph some animals, but all my little forest friends are hiding.

With a sigh, I trade in my phone for my book.

I skim the next chapter, but the soft splashes of the water are so soothing, I find myself closing my eyes and tipping my face toward the sun. With a shake of my head, I give up and tuck the book away.

Leaning on my elbows, I'm drenched with sunlight and warmth. My soul soaks everything up, feeling fuller and lighter. This is exactly what I need.

The musty smell of the water and plants pacifies my frayed nerves. Thousands of leaves rustling sound like the whisper of a wind chime against the rushing, crashing water as it tumbles around rocks and swirls in the hollows.

There will be times to make big life decisions later. Right now, in this beautiful place, I can be still. I'd bottle this feeling up and drink it every day if I could.

When I start to worry about the sun burning my eyelids, I sit up straight again. Blinking, the stream comes into focus. My gaze drifts lazily along the creek.

Slate stands a ways down the creek and he looks as surprised as I am. He looks like some sort of dryad that materialized from the forest, with his vivid, green eyes glowing and his lips parted.

Shock lances through me.

I spring to my feet without thinking, trying to balance and utterly failing. The rock is slick. With a screeched "Motherfucker!" I slip off and plunge into the flowing water.

My legs and hips hit first and I suck in a sharp breath right before my chest and head go under.

The water's tug is gentle down here. I float along for a second, frozen with shock, before survival instinct kicks in and I start thrashing. If I can get my feet under me, I can easily stand up. Logically, I know I'm not in danger unless I crack my head on a rock, but it doesn't change the overwhelming sensation of needles over my entire body or the ridiculous screaming in my head.

Hands grip my ribcage and lift me up and out of the water. Slate hauls me against him and it's like my soaked chest is pressing against a concrete wall. Gasping, I grip his biceps and push the panic down.

"Don't worry. I've got you." His voice breaks through my chaotic thoughts.

I look up, meeting his gaze. Those dark green eyes are gold in the center around pupils rapidly expanding as he looks down at me. Already, goosebumps cover my skin as my feet settle on the bottom. Did he seriously just rescue me from water that's only three or four feet deep? I would blush if I wasn't freezing.

I manage to step back, grasping at the rock that betrayed me instead of his solid form.

His jaw is tight and his posture is stiff. "Are you okay?"

"I'm fine, just an idiot." My tone is too sharp. We are both waist-deep in creek water. I'd prefer to sink under the surface to avoid this embarrassment.

"Are you sure you didn't hit the bottom or maybe a rock?" He searches me for injuries, careful to not touch me again.

"Seriously, I'm totally okay." I press my lips together, my shame transforming into irritation.

"It's slippery here. You've got to watch for moss." He is trying to make me feel better, blaming my fall on slippery moss, but it feels like I'm being chastised for an accident.

"Oh, the moss. Of course," I say dryly.

Slate laughs, his face transformed. His fine features, straight nose, and high cheekbones go from looking like a tortured artist to an absolute work of art. But then he catches himself and the serious mask falls into place. The loss of his smile is a physical pain in my hollow chest.

"Hazel, what are you doing down here?" He prompts, his voice lowering. If all the hair on my body wasn't already standing on end from my polar plunge, then I'd get goosebumps from the texture of his voice.

"What are you doing here?" A lame retort, but I'm having difficulty thinking clearly.

"Hiking." His answer is automatic. He looks at me, waiting for my answer now that he's given his.

"I was reading." I offer up with a simper. He grabs my bag from the rock. Thankfully, it was safe from my accidental drenching.

He cups my elbow as we step out of the water onto the rocky shoreline. "You shouldn't be this far from the cabins."

"That's not fair," I argue. "It's broad daylight and I'm still close."

Slate peels his wet shirt over his head, revealing a chest that is far more defined than I expected with his lean frame. The tattoos on his arms continue across his chest and around his back - swirls of greenery and wildflowers. I've never seen tattoos like these.

I slam my jaw shut, embarrassed it was hanging open to begin with. But considering the display in front of me, can you blame a girl?

He squeezes the water out of his shirt and then drapes it over his shoulder. Lucky shirt.

"You could have gotten-" He stops as I follow his example and peel off my sweatshirt. He stares. I tug the hem of my shirt, worried it lifted with my sweatshirt, but it stayed safely in place.

Swallowing, I wring the water out of my sweatshirt. "I was following a trail. I wasn't going to get lost."

I make the mistake of letting my gaze drift downwards. His bare chest is dotted with water droplets. It only gets worse. Lower still, his sweatpants are soaked. They hang low over his hips, clinging to his thighs and everything else– I yank my eyes up.

"You need to listen to your uncle. You absolutely could get lost or injured. You've got to be careful," he says.

He isn't even looking at me. He scans the forest around us as if preparing for a bear to leap out and try to eat us.

"You're out here," I argue.

"I live here." The gravel in his voice scrapes against my skin and my breath hitches as a shiver works over me.

"Good thing I have you to keep me safe then." I give him a cheesy smile, hoping to break the tension.

He frowns again, the pout firmly in place.

"Well, I better get back and into some dry clothes." I gather up the hem of my shirt and squeeze it, watching the water drip out of my hands.

"Probably a good idea." He seems to take in my soaked clothes for the first time, his gaze lingering on my tank top for a second. I bite my cheek to suppress a satisfied smile. I'm sure I look like a drowned rat, but it's nice to be appreciated.

Slinging my bag over my shoulder, I shake out my sweatshirt and glare at the heavy thing.

"Give it here," Slate says, plucking it from my hands and tossing it over his shoulder with his shirt. Water trails down his chest. Maybe I should get that for him, since it's my fault. Nope, keeping my hands to myself.

"Thanks," I say, pulling on my shoes. They're dry for now, but water from my jeans will soak my socks soon enough.

Huffing, I slog up the hill. Slate follows, hovering right behind me. It's approximately fifteen seconds before I stumble and his hands are on me again.

"This isn't an easy hike." His voice is kind but I'm frustrated and fairly miserable at this point.

I round on him. "Look, I'm not a child. I've been hiking before. And frankly, I only fell because you startled me. So, it's kinda your fault."

"There's a reason Heath asked you to stick close to the cabins," he starts again.

"Bite me," I mutter under my breath, ignoring the way he stares and starting forward again.

Leaves crunch under his feet as he catches up with me. "There's a huge slope through here, and with all the leaf litter, it's pretty dangerous."

I give him a dirty look and step over an uneven rock in the trail. My ankle wobbles and I slip, my exposed skin scraping across the sharp edge of a rock. Before I can fall, he grabs my hips.

"Shit," I hiss. He releases me with a look of disdain. Whatever, dude. For someone who keeps touching me, he doesn't seem to like the contact.

I angle my calf, observing an angry cut exposed because of my rolled jeans. "You have got to be kidding me."

He presses his lips together. Judgy much? I turn my nose up and continue. But in another five minutes, we reach the boulders I slid down on my way here. Going up looks way more difficult.

Searching for a handhold, I start to haul myself up. It doesn't help that my clothing is now triple the weight it should be. Feet scrambling, I let out a frustrated growl, not caring what he thinks at this point. I look pathetic, might as well sound feral while I'm at it.

Warm hands press to my back, stabilizing me. Before I can protest, he grips my hips and pushes me up. I reach the top ridge and shimmy up the rest of the way.

Slate scales it effortlessly, and I consider smacking him so he falls back down. Maybe he reads my mood, because for once he keeps quiet. The trail evens out and the silence grows awkward. Finally, I can't take it. "So, how long have you worked with my uncle?"

He looks around like he's worried we'll be seen together. "Part-time since I was a teenager, but I've had this position for a couple of years now."

"Do you like it?"

It should be an easy question, but his brows rise and his head tilts as he considers his answer. "Yes, I like helping people and being outdoors all the time."

Generic answers for the win. I'll get something out of him. Adjusting the strap of my bag, I twist to glance at him. "Where did you grow up?"

"My dad worked for Heath's dad, and then for Heath. So I grew up here," he says stiffly, stepping closer until we're side by side.

"So, it's a family operation?" Interesting.

"You could say that." Why is he so cagey?

I press my tongue to my teeth, thinking. "What's the best part about living and working here?" I ask.

"Why all the questions?" He turns to me and raises a single eyebrow.

"I'm bored," I say with a shrug. It's a better answer than explaining I want to peel back his layers and see what lies beneath.

"Tell me about you then," he says, readjusting the wet clothes slung over his shoulder and sending another cascade of rivulets down his chest.

"Answer my question first," I argue. This man brings out my sass, for some reason.

"Fine. I like the community," he says. "Most of us grew up together and it's very supportive. We have fun."

"Do you guys drive into town often?" I ask.

"Not really," he answers, frowning. "I answered your question. You're supposed to be telling me about you."

Sighing, I face forward, stepping over a fallen branch. "What do you want to know?"

"Do you like California?"

"Like in general?" I reply. "It's got great weather and the scenery up north is pretty."

"Not Los Angeles?" he questions.

I cross my arms and scowl at him. "I guess I didn't have the best time there."

"What about where you grew up?" he presses. Nosy.

"We moved a lot. Mostly boring suburbs," I say. "I'd rather have actual nature instead of parks and lawns."

"Yeah? Like this kind of nature?" he asks, the ghost of a smirk flashing across his face.

"Yeah," I echo, trying to think if I can get him to smile again. But his attention is facing forward and he's stopped walking. With a groan, I look up to see the fallen log. It's just as massive as I remember. There's no way I'm trekking through the underbrush to go around it with a scraped up ankle and squishy wet tennis shoes.

"Let me help you."

"What?" I eye his extended hands.

"Hazel, stop worrying." He grabs my waist again, lifting me like a child. His hands are hot against my chilled skin even through my tank top.

"Seriously?" I grumble. "Just freaking pick me up?"

He sets me squarely on the log, and my hands scramble to grip it. Without so much as a second of hesitation, he vaults up as if it's only two or three feet and not almost five.

A real smirk flashes across his face as he perches beside me. He's showing off! I can't even be annoyed; it's impressive and that smile sends my heart speeding. He's so pretty.

"You know, if you want to go hiking, there are some scenic trails around here. I could take you."

I roll my eyes. "So you can keep an eye on me?"

He shrugs, launching himself off the other side.

With a sigh, I push myself off, intending to land on my feet. Instead, his arms close around me, halting my descent until I'm nose to nose with him. His eyes widen, lips parting. My heart hammers, he must feel it where our chests touch. Slowly, he eases me down, and by the time my feet hit the ground, his blank expression is back.

Clearing my throat, I resume our walk. From this point on, the trail is level. Meaning no touching, and I'm not sure if I'm relieved or disappointed. Definitely disappointed. I wouldn't mind being picked up again and getting another up close and personal view of the soft freckles that are almost invisible on his tanned face.

I'm drooling. We need another topic of conversation. Anything to break the tension before I simply pass away. Of course, I say the first thing that pops into my head. "So, do you ever go swimming in the creek? Intentionally, I mean."

"Sure," he says. "Not in that spot."

"Oh? It seems so perfect for swimming."

He smiles at my sarcasm, and it's as stunning as the first. This man is wasted working for my uncle. Someone should call a modeling agency for him.

"There's a nice wide area up the creek a bit. It's deep enough for swimming," he says, his warm tone pulling me from my thoughts.

"Sounds lovely," I murmur.

"Do you want to go? It'll be too cold soon, but it should be okay for another week or two." His brows rise, his expression relaxing. Does he look hopeful?

My heart leaps. "I don't know, the creek was kind of freezing," I tease, although it's a valid concern.

"Are you cold?" He steps closer, brows furrowing and hands reaching out, though he doesn't touch me.

I can't help but grin. "Of course, I am. I'm in wet clothes. But what are you going to do about it? Give me your pants?"

Slate freezes for a second, his lips slightly parted. His bronze cheeks color pink. Good job, Hazel. Nothing like a weirdly sexual joke to make you a new friend.

Turning on my heel, I let out an awkward laugh. "Hate to break it to you, buddy, but you're just as wet as I am. I guess you run hot." Well, that didn't make it better. Laughing, I resist the urge to smack my forehead against the nearest tree.

Thankfully, my uncle's cabin is visible through the trees. "Almost there!" I say, smiling at him as if I didn't just embarrass myself half to death.

He nods, jerking into motion. We don't speak again until we've reached the cabin's porch steps. He hands me my sweatshirt. "See you later." Ducking his head, he turns away from me. He can't get out of here fast enough.

"Bye." My face is burning, the effects of the icy water fading. With a clumsy kick, I send my shoes across the porch and toss my sweatshirt over the railing. It's only a few feet to my bedroom, but I'd rather not drip all over the place. My tank top is almost dry, but my jeans are still soaked. I could take them off, but knowing my luck, Slate would reappear at that exact moment. Chewing my cheek, I dart across the floor and into my room.

After a warm shower and a fresh set of clothes, I curl up in the window seat with my book again. But instead of reading, I mull over my disastrous hike, my fingers running over the edge of my closed book.

What was he really doing out there? He was barefoot, I realize with a jolt. I was distracted by the clinging sweatpants, and his lack of shoes hadn't registered at the time. Didn't that hurt? Maybe he ran around barefoot constantly growing up and it's totally normal for him.

I wish he hadn't treated me like an incapable child, but it was nice to be fussed over. And touched. Those green eyes and that chest swirling with tattoos... The walk back gave me plenty of time to memorize the art inked into the hard planes of his body. They are spectacular, the tattoos and the body. My toes curl.

It was nice to have a real conversation with him. He seems genuine and kind, if not a bit too serious for me. But if he is my uncle's second-in-command, he must have a lot of responsibility on his shoulders. He seems the sort to take care of everything. There's something appealing about that.

I mean, the man is a walking thirst trap. Feeling a bit heated, I lean my head against the cool window. Speaking of thirst, I really should hydrate better after all that hiking... and being manhandled. With a snicker, I unfold my legs and head into the kitchen for a drink and maybe a snack.

IV
CAMPFIRE
CONFESSIONS

SLATE

When I duck into the training room, Heath is leaning against the wall, his arms crossed. He glowers at Fisher and Hawthorne who debate something, gesturing with scowls that hold no malice. They quiet as I approach and lower their eyes. Their display of respect makes me cringe. Both men are father figures to me, especially Fisher who is my uncle, so it's odd to be ranked above them.

"Sir," I address Heath, looking at the ground until he responds to me.

"Yes, Slate?" He pushes off from the wall and uncrosses his arms.

"I have an update for you. Hazel hiked down to the creek on her own." My hands tighten together behind my back, holding my stress there.

Heath frowns at me. "Did she really?"

I control my expression tightly. No hint of worry and absolutely no sign of possessiveness over Hazel. With an even voice, I continue, "She is fine. I walked her to your cabin." I pause, knowing he won't like this. "But she did fall into the water."

He scrubs his face with his hands. "Seriously?"

"Don't worry, I pulled her out and she was uninjured. But on the walk back, she scraped her ankle. It bled a little. I don't think it's serious."

"Understood."

His tone is dismissive, but apparently, I don't use my best judgment when it comes to Hazel so I keep talking. "Sir, I wanted to treat her injury, but she seemed more embarrassed than in pain. I can check on her, or maybe fetch Sable?"

"No, it's fine. She can handle herself. I'll check on her before dinner." He nods, his small sign of approval unraveling my tension. A quiet beat passes and I turn to leave. "Slate?"

"Yes, sir?"

"Thank you for keeping an eye on her. I'd like you to focus entirely on Hazel for the remainder of her visit. I have a feeling she'll continue to take risks and disobey my requests." He smiles, clearly fond of his niece.

"Yes, sir."

Fisher raises an eyebrow, watching me as I dip my chin and turn to leave. He knows me too well and can probably read my relief at Heath's orders.

During dinner, my eyes stay on Hazel. She sits between Marigold and Crickett. It's taco night, cooked by the twins and their mother, my Aunt Clove. At least that keeps Onyx far from Hazel for the time being.

The girls chatter about books, hiking, cooking, recent movies... and Marigold invites Hazel to our campfire night. My heart thuds against my sternum when she agrees to come. I take her plate, relishing the way Hazel smiles and shyly thanks me. Marigold leads her away, and I rush to the kitchen.

"Hazel is coming to the campfire," I say, my chest tight. Before Onyx can make a comment, I drop our plates in the sink. Soapy water splashes across his apron. He lets out a squawk and grabs a towel.

"We'll see you soon," Cedar says, drying dishes and stacking them neatly. Nodding, I launch myself out of the diner's back door and jog toward our campfire spot.

Cedar and Onyx's family home sits southwest of us, closer to the training ring. It makes it easy for Fisher to manage everyone's practices like his father did before him. Unfortunately, the family legacy might end with him. Cedar isn't interested in the role and Onyx can't get his head out of his ass long enough to take anything seriously.

It's a two-story cabin with a balcony extending over the patio. String lights drape from the railing to nearby trees, casting a soft glow. It lights up Hazel's profile as she walks, a golden line along her perfect nose and full lips. Along each wave of her hair.

I can't help but stare. She's utterly perfect.

Her lips part and she lets out a soft laugh at something Marigold says. My long strides reach the fire pit at the same moment. Perhaps I am projecting, but it feels like her eyes light up when she sees me.

We sink onto the split log benches that curve around the stone fire pit. Marigold goes to work crumpling recycled paper to stuff in the center and stacking fresh kindling around it. I stack larger logs nearby, sneaking glances at Hazel.

Once the twins arrive, Cedar flicks his lighter out and starts the fire. It jumps from page to page, growing and licking at the kindling until it catches the wood alight. After a moment, Cedar adds the first log.

Hazel surveys the cabin. "Your home is gorgeous."

"I'd love to give you a tour and show you my room," Onyx flirts. My fists clench. If I have to endure another evening of him flirting, it'll end up in a fist fight. I made it clear he needs to back off and leave her be, but Onyx rarely does what he should.

Hazel laughs at him, flashing her teeth. "Your mom is a baker, right?"

"Yeah, she made dinner tonight," Cedar answers as he steps back from the campfire now crackling happily. With a sigh, he sits beside me, leaving Onyx on his own.

"We helped," Onyx adds, cocking his head as he grins at her.

"Marigold, where is your family's cabin?" Hazel asks, bumping her shoulder into Marigold's. She looks around the darkening forest as if the cabin will magically appear if summoned.

Marigold waves her hand toward the meadow. "Oh, my dad's house is a ways past the diner, you just walk straight. My brothers still live there. But I moved in with my grandma last year so Indigo could have his own room. Cobalt never let him sleep, and he started his internship with our grandmother, plus he isn't done with school. It's just easier for them."

"That's incredibly kind of you," Hazel praises. Marigold's cheeks turn rosy.

"Her house is behind the garden. She likes to have access to all the herbs Cedar grows." Her gaze wanders to Cedar, taking on a dreamy quality. I'm used to Marigold mooning over my cousin, but I'm surprised when Hazel looks between them and smirks. She's perceptive and Marigold fails at being subtle. The only one oblivious is Cedar.

Hazel crosses her arms and rests her elbows on her knees. "Sounds lovely to be right by the garden."

"Yeah, it's great. And I still see my brothers constantly. Indie is apprenticing with my grandma, and I've still got Cobalt in class because he's eleven."

Onyx clears his throat. "Hazel, do you have any siblings?"

"My little sister, Aurora. She's about two years younger than me," Hazel replies, pursing her lips. "She's working on an art degree back in California."

"Are you guys close?" Marigold asks sweetly. Hazel shrugs.

"Not really. She's busy with her own life. What about you guys?" She shifts the attention off herself smoothly.

"It's the two of us and Briar. She's sixteen," Cedar says, rubbing at the back of his neck as he looks up from staring into the flames.

Hazel's gaze moves to me. "Just me," I finally say. It's true enough when I've never met my estranged mother's new family.

Without warning, Onyx hops up. "You know what we need?" he asks over his shoulder as he bolts inside.

Cedar smiles, unperturbed as always. "Hazel, how was your first day here?"

Hazel's eyes flicker to me and then away. A beautiful pink flush rises up her neck. She's definitely thinking about falling in the creek. I'm holding my breath.

"Um, it was nice. I did a little hiking and read my book a bit."

"And now you're going to roast marshmallows, like our forefathers before us." Onyx is back, grinning with his arms full.

Marigold helps him pass out ciders and beer. Hazel accepts a cider and pops the top off. Mesmerized, I watch her bring the bottle to her lips, my own beer forgotten.

Onyx rips open a bag of marshmallows and Cedar produces the long metal skewers we've used to roast marshmallows for as long as I can remember. Marigold spears marshmallows and passes them around.

I take a swig from my beer while holding my marshmallow over the flames. Little sparks float up and away.

"Wow, there are many stars!" Hazel marvels. Instead of watching the fire, she's looking straight up with her mouth slightly open.

"Oh, you can't see them from the city, can you? You have smoke and stuff," Marigold says.

"Smog," Cedar corrects quietly.

Hazel's hair gleams like polished brass in the firelight. "It makes me feel kind of small."

A small blaze catches my attention. "Woah!" Her marshmallow caught fire while she was stargazing. Without thinking, I snatch the stick from her hands and blow it out.

Onyx barks a laugh. "Party foul!"

"Sorry," I murmur, holding the stick out to her.

Her voice chimes at the same moment. "Sorry!" She giggles and accepts the stick and blackened marshmallow. "Thanks." She speaks softly, her eyes connecting with mine. In the firelight, they swim with melted amber. Lost in her gaze, the fire becomes too warm and I have to gulp down the night air to steady myself.

"There, perfect!" Marigold shows off an impeccably golden marshmallow. "This is how it's done, boys."

"Yes, teacher." Onyx is blowing out his own burned marshmallow. He's loved them charred since he was a kid.

"Nicely done, as always," Cedar compliments Marigold, and she looks ready to float away.

"You don't have to eat that," I murmur, leaning toward Hazel. She shakes her head defiantly, pulls the blackened confection off the stick, and takes a bite. She's ornery too. The more I learn about her, the more I like her. Unfortunately.

"So good!" Onyx moans over his marshmallow, causing Marigold to snort and cover her mouth.

"Do you guys do this a lot?" Hazel asks, licking her fingers clean.

"Maybe once a week? Sometimes more." Cedar finishes roasting his marshmallow and spins the stick, inspecting to ensure it's evenly browned.

"It's so relaxing. I'd do this every night if I lived here." She sighs and leans back again to admire the constellations through the swaying branches.

Onyx brushes his shoulder off with a shrug, like he's some sort of rock star. "Campfires are nice, but I prefer more thrilling and impressive activities. Like cliff diving or hang gliding."

I roll my eyes. "You've never done any of those things."

"I could have," he argues, his voice rising with playful outrage.

"But you haven't," I retort.

"You know, for someone who looks like such a bad boy, you're pretty boring yourself," Onyx shoots back.

"I look like a bad boy?" I wonder, amused.

"It's the tattoos," he explains with a sly grin. "But then you open your mouth and everyone knows how boring you are."

I consider chucking a pinecone at him.

"You do have a lot of cool tattoos." Hazel is looking at the flames, avoiding me. "I like the wolf on your back."

A beat of silence stretches between the group. My teeth grind together, waiting for the questions and comments that I know are coming.

"When did you see his back tattoos?" Cedar asks. Onyx's eyes widen like he was just given a gift. Hazel opens her mouth, but no sound comes out.

"She ran into me hiking today," I explain, praying they drop it.

"Oh." Marigold looks from Hazel to me, her eyes brightening with understanding.

Onyx is still grinning like a nitwit and I know I'm going to hear about this later.

"Do you guys have any tattoos?" Hazel changes the subject again, shifting uncomfortably in her seat.

Cedar complies. "I have a few." He lifts one side of his shirt, showing individual stems of his favorite plants in a botanical style down his ribs.

"Oh, that's so cool!" Hazel says. I choose to believe she is admiring the tattoos and not Cedar's six-pack.

Of course, Onyx immediately pulls his shirt off entirely and twists to show off the tribal tattoos across his shoulders and chest, not-so-subtly flexing.

"Put your shirt on, you ding dong," Marigold scolds. She glances at me, nervous. It's fine. I'm fine. I have no reason to be angry that Hazel is looking at Onyx's chest curiously. Marigold jumps in, "Slate, I wanted to add more flowers on my calf. Could we do it soon?"

"Whenever you like," I agree instantly.

"You did their tattoos?" Hazel whips around, surprise widening her beautiful tawny eyes.

"Yeah. It's a hobby," I confess with a shrug.

"How'd you get into it?"

"I did an apprenticeship in town a few years ago."

"Why don't you tattoo for your job?" She frowns at me. I guess we are getting personal.

"I was going to, but the tattoo artist moved away and I had other responsibilities. My dad always wanted me to take over his job someday, and after he died, it just seemed like the right thing to do." I trail off. That answer didn't go according to plan. Bothered, I scuff my heel along the dirt.

"I'm sorry for your loss." Empathy softens her features. It's so genuine that I'm taken aback. Molten gold swims in her eyes as she holds my gaze.

Unfortunately, Onyx butts in. "Way to kill the vibe, dude."

"Fuck off, Onyx," I growl. It's more aggressive than is warranted, but my patience for him is almost used up.

"Chill, guys," Marigold warns in a sing-song voice. Onyx folds his arms behind his head, leaning back with his signature smirk.

Hazel looks between us with her forehead wrinkled, likely trying to interpret the dynamic. "Did you guys all grow up together?"

"Yeah. Slate is our cousin and we're only four months apart, and a couple of days," Cedar answers.

"Who's older?" Hazel asks.

"I am." I say, enjoying the irritated creases lining Onyx's face.

"Marigold is fourteen months younger than my brother and I," Cedar continues.

"But she's pretty cool so we let her tag along," Onyx says.

Marigold leans over and smacks his arm. "So gracious of you."

"I'm jealous. I didn't grow up with any cousins or anything and my sister was always super independent." Hazel hesitates but continues, "I didn't even have many friends until college. And then I met Jeremy." Her voice holds the smallest tremor.

"Jeremy?" Onyx asks. If he makes her cry, I'll destroy him. A quiet growl escapes me.

"My fiancé– nope, my ex-fiancé." Hazel's tone is exhausted. I want to sweep her up in my arms and hold her against me, make her forget him.

"Good riddance. He didn't deserve you." Marigold throws her hands up.

Cedar frowns at her. "You don't even know what happened."

Without missing a beat, Marigold glares at him and snaps, "He didn't make her happy. That tells me enough."

Hazel lets out a laugh, her stiff posture loosening again. I unclench my jaw and exhale slowly, trying to chill. There's no reason to be upset during this conversation, but I can't help the way my heart thuds faster.

"Yeah, I supported him through grad school; we lived together. And then he decided he'd prefer his secretary over me."

Someone lived with her, and then he left her? I cannot fathom a partner doing that, least of all to this woman.

"Men are the worst," Marigold sympathizes. They share a smile full of feminine solidarity.

"Hey! I resent that," Onyx protests.

"Well, I was working for his family's company. Hence, being out of a job." Hazel gives a little bitter laugh. The details fall into place, and anger surges in my gut, hot and bitter.

"What an asshole," I growl, the thought fighting past my teeth.

Marigold nods sagely. "He's not wrong."

"Yeah, probably." Hazel meets my eyes. With a smile lighting up her face, she is ethereal.

I can't help but return the smile. Her face goes slack, her mouth opening a little. What is she thinking? In an instant, she snaps out of it.

"Damn straight!" Onyx offers her a second cider.

"I was kind of overqualified for the job anyway." She twists the top off and takes a long drink.

"Yeah, you were!" Marigold whoops, pumping her fist.

Both of them are getting louder, a mix of alcohol and feminine rage bolstering them. Hazel's face is relaxed, her mouth curved, her cheeks rosy. Absolutely stunning.

"I should have left that job ages ago. I've always played it safe." She takes another swig. "I want to go after what I want, take risks, grab life by the balls."

"Woah there!" Onyx holds up his hands in mock self-defense. "Maybe grab life by something less sensitive."

"Sorry, I think I'm a little tipsy." Hazel giggles, taking another sip of her cider. "Don't worry, I have no intention of going near your..." She wiggles her fingers in his direction.

I snort, almost choking on my drink. Onyx screws up his face in a ridiculous attempt at a scowl.

Marigold holds up her second marshmallow, perfectly golden. "Here, have the Marigold special." Hazel accepts it, her eyes rolling back in her head with a groan as she takes a bite. My breath catches and my blood heats in my veins. Why am I jealous of a marshmallow?

"I meant to ask: do *you* have any tattoos?" Marigold says, grabbing a second bottle for herself.

"Oh, no. Jeremy didn't like them." She pauses, frowning.

"What is wrong with that dude?" I grumble.

"A lot. We established that," Marigold quips, fluttering her lashes at me. She hasn't missed how touchy I'm being.

Hazel purses her lips. "You know, I always wanted one."

"What would you get?" I can't help but ask. I'm greedy for the answer, already imagining artwork across her skin. Something delicate.

She fiddles with her ring again, hesitating before answering. "Um, I kind of like the idea of the phases of the moon."

The group falls into a heavy silence.

"Oh, that's an interesting choice. Why that?" Marigold asks casually.

"I like witchy stuff, like reading paranormal romance books. And Halloween is my favorite holiday," Hazel explains. "I've always wanted to be a spooky bitch."

Even Cedar laughs.

"Yeah, definitely tipsy." She presses her fingers to her eyebrow with a guilty smile.

"Sounds like you need a third," Onyx starts to say, but I cut him off with a raised hand.

"We should call it a night." I set my drink down.

Marigold ignores me and leans forward, catching Hazel's hand and squeezing it between both of hers. "You should get a tattoo if you want to. Slate can do it while you're here."

I'm frozen, my throat closed up. Those golden brown eyes flick over me, judging, considering. "I would love that."

"Yeah, no problem," I find myself answering, as if this is no big deal. "I'm off tomorrow afternoon, or we could find time next week."

"Let's do it tomorrow if that's okay with you?" she says.

Marigold clinks her glass bottle down and stands. "Okay, spooky bitches, I'm beat, and I have to wrangle a pack of little monsters tomorrow."

Hazel sighs. "Me too. I mean, not the monsters part. Oh, speaking of, I'd love to see your classroom."

"Ooh, that would be fun!" Marigold clasps her hands together, smiling brightly. "Want to have lunch tomorrow?"

"Yes, please." Hazel smooths her sweater and stands.

I leap up. "Let me walk you home to your cabin."

"You know, I am capable of getting places without your assistance," she grumbles. I need some way to convince her to accept my help. The trees block out most of the moonlight and she's not familiar with our woods. Besides, I'd follow her home like a puppy anyway to make sure she's safe.

Inclining my head, I lower my voice. "I feel like we've had this discussion before."

It's a little too much like flirting. I pull my little flashlight out of my pocket, click it on, and hold it out to her. "Here, you can even hold my torch."

Hazel giggles. I could listen to her laugh forever. But then she sways a little and I surge forward with open hands. She grabs onto me, our hands twisting together. Her touch is warm, soft.

Her unguarded gaze sweeps down my body. "You'd better keep it. I had a bit more to drink than I realized. Or I'm just a lightweight."

She releases me but I snag her hand and hook it in the crook of my arm. Her fingers grip the muscle, splaying over the treetops of my tattoo. Electricity radiates out from her fingers, running up my arm and across my back, down my spine.

"You're all leaving me! Hazel, can I come too?" Onyx whines.

"No," I answer flatly. She chuckles again, sending more zings through my body.

He doesn't give up. "Oh, come on! Marigold, Goldie, baby!"

Marigold is already walking away, not bothering with a light. "You'll be fine, Onyx. Just don't set anything on fire."

"Oooh," he responds, starting toward the fire pit as his brother dumps sand over the last of the embers. "Party pooper."

"Numbskull," Cedar responds without any venom.

"Bye!" Hazel calls to them as I lead her away.

"Are they always like that?" she asks me. I almost forget to answer her, I'm so distracted by her softness pressing against my side.

"Pretty much."

Her scent teases me, softly floral and warm. I take a deeper breath and try to imprint it onto my memory.

She hums in thought. "Are Marigold and Cedar a thing?"

"No. Why?" I frown. Was she admiring Cedar's stomach after all?

"Oh, I don't know. They seemed cute together," she says, a beautiful flush creeping across her cheeks.

I relax. "Yeah, I think he sees her as a little sister, but I'm not sure. He's not exactly a sharer."

"Seriously?" She raises her eyebrows at me. "You know what, never mind."

"What?" I prod.

"Nothing. I don't know." She tips her face skyward again. "It's beautiful here. I would stargaze every night."

"Yeah, I guess I'm used to it," I admit, pausing to look up. The sky blazes where we can see it between the branches. "I used to sit out and track constellations."

"Why don't you still?" she asks. I pause at the question.

She is so empathetic. She makes me want to spill all my secrets and fears. But she's not a new best friend, she's a guest and soon she'll be gone.

I clear my throat. "Just busy."

"That's a shame," she says. "I took an astronomy class in high school. I don't remember much, but it was really cool."

"Do you recognize any constellations?" I ask.

"I can't see very much here," she complains, scowling at me adorably.

"Here." Keeping her close, I lead her east into the clearing, past the supply building and schoolhouse. "What about now?"

Instead of the sky, she's staring at me with a dopey grin. My chest constricts. We're frozen for a few seconds until she runs her tongue over her bottom lip and finally moves her attention upwards.

"Let's see." She releases her hold on my arm, swaying slightly as she turns in place. My hand automatically goes to the small of her back to steady her, pressing into the thick fabric of her hoodie.

"There." She points. "That's Sirius, the brightest star." She cocks her head, squinting. "Which means, that's Canis Major. Sirius is the chest, and there's the head, body, legs, tail." She gestures at the stars. I can't see it, but I'm not exactly trying. How can I when moonlight washes over her, making her look like a goddess?

"What else? Of course, there's the big dipper, Orion's belt," she continues, "oh, and there's Cygnus the swan."

"That's impressive," I say, loving how her face lights up.

She circles toward me, my hand sliding from her back to her hip. "Thanks." She dips in a wobbly curtsey, making me laugh.

"It's getting late," I say, hating myself for ending this moment.

"Okay." She hooks her hand over my arm again. As we return to the darkness of the trees, she squeezes closer to me. Instinctively, I want to wrap my arms around her, maybe pick her up and carry her. I do neither.

Far too soon, we reach her cabin. She stops on the bottom step and turns to me. I should walk away. This is too intimate, taking her right to her door. Lingering.

"You keep walking me home." Shy, she looks up at me and then back down; her breathing speeds up. If this was a date, I would kiss her right now. I'd pin her up against a tree and taste her until she whimpered. I've completely lost my mind.

"Gotta watch out for our guest," I say lamely, shrugging.

"I appreciate it." Her throaty whisper has me entranced. But she's been drinking and it makes her uninhibited. That might be the only thing that stops me because Heath's mandates are steadily losing their power over me as I stare into the depths of her eyes.

Lips curving, she leans forward. Her fingers lightly touch my arm and skim up my tattoos. I inhale sharply as she reaches the edge of my sleeve and slips under the edge for a second before trailing lower.

She tilts her jaw toward me, silently asking a question I can't answer. Every muscle in my body goes taut. She would taste like cider and marshmallows, which are suddenly the most erotic flavors I can imagine.

Using every ounce of willpower I possess, I take a step away. Her mouth tightens, eyes narrowing in a flash of hurt.

My heart drops. The last thing I want to do is disappoint her. I reach for anything to lift her spirits. "Do you want to come over after lunch with Marigold and we can see about that tattoo?"

Arms wrapped around herself in a defensive hug, she bobs her head slowly. "I'd love that."

"Cool." Cool? Someone needs to put me out of my misery because this woman makes me a fool.

"Goodnight, Slate." My name out of her mouth incapacitates me. I can hardly make my lungs work.

"Night, Hazel," I choke out.

She slips inside and then meets my gaze while she slowly swings the door closed. Even after it's latched, I stand there dumbfounded.

Finally, the sound of crickets pulls me out of my stupor. It's a good thing my feet can wander home without any conscious thought because she's completely shorted out my brain.

I stay up for hours sketching. Moons in arcs, moons with stars in a long narrow piece, moons surrounded by wildflowers. I'm always a night owl, but tonight my blood is electrified and I can't seem to settle. Can't see anything except her eyes. Her lips. Her skin.

Finally, I toss my sketchbook aside and pull off my shirt. I need a run under the stars. The door slams behind me. Lunging forward, I savor the crisp night air and the noisy silence of the forest with all of its creaks and rustling. As my muscles burn, my whirling thoughts fade away.

V

LAUGHS & LEMONADE

HAZEL

The next morning, I sleep in. It's necessary after a long night tossing and turning, my mind obsessing over a certain surly new friend with evergreen trees tattooed across his forearm.

By the time I drag myself up, it's almost lunchtime. No need for breakfast, I'm still full of marshmallows and alcohol. It takes a splash of cold water to wash away the sluggish feeling dragging me down.

My reflection in the mirror is unfamiliar. For the last few years, I straightened my hair to fit a certain image, but now my natural waves stream around my face. Instead of contouring, a natural tan glows in my cheeks. Somehow, I feel more like myself than I have in years. Maybe ever.

In daylight, it's easier to navigate, and I manage to make my way to the clearing and across to the diner without getting lost. The trees are thinner closer to the clearing. The school building, the little store, and the garden create an oval. It's open enough for the kids to play soccer.

The industrial building, which is a training facility of some sort apparently, is barely visible to the south. The obscured offices and parking lot sit past it. They don't intrude on the community space, which is nice.

Marigold's school building gleams with white siding and big windows. Suncatchers blaze a rainbow of color in the upper panes, while paint forms a messy mural along the bottom, picking up the colors of the magenta and amethyst wildflowers bunched along the side of the building.

Marigold waves at me from the school building's yellow door. "Hey, Hazel!"

She is summer, all golden and freckled. Her strawberry blonde hair waves down her back over an olive corduroy jumper with a tiny frog stitched on the front. She's so cute, I feel a bit like a lizard monster next to her. But Marigold has an easy way about her and I've never felt so comfortable with a friend so fast.

She pulls me into a hug. "Come on." Grabbing my hand, she tugs me toward the diner.

"I'm freaking starving," I admit. Since leaving the cabin, my stomach has woken up and started to growl.

"You're telling me!" she agrees. "I wonder what Crickett's got going today."

She pushes the door open. It's quiet, but a few other residents sit at the end of the counter.

"Does everyone eat here for every meal? Is this like the company cafeteria or something?" I ask under my breath. Marigold glances at me, her eyes widening.

"Kinda," she answers slowly, chewing on her lip. "Lots of people like to cook, but Crickett and Clove always handle the community dinners. And then a few of us grab lunch here."

There's pizza, the crispy hand-stretched kind, with an impressive variety of toppings. Marigold grabs three slices of one with at least a dozen kinds of meat on it, but I opt for two slices of a supreme pizza. It's a good balance of meat and veggies so I feel like I'm eating something at least a little bit healthy. I tuck a little chocolate chip cookie on the edge of my plate and use my free hand to pour some lemonade.

Marigold picks a picnic table toward the outer edge in the shade. Crickett waves at us as we pass. She's holding baby Dahlia while trying to convince her older daughter to eat some salad.

"That's Daisy. She's six," Marigold fills in, waving back with a grin. "She's a firecracker. She definitely gives Crickett and Hawthorne a run for their money."

"She's cute. This seems like a great place to raise kids."

"Oh, totally! But I'm a little biased," she says, settling down on the bench and picking up her first slice.

The pizza is as delicious as it looks. We savor a few bites in contented silence. The lemonade is strong, the kind made with fresh lemons. Why is everything better here? Even the sunshine feels like a blessing over my skin.

"Are you doing good today?" Marigold asks. "We didn't scare you off last night, did we?"

I scrunch up my nose. "Nah. It was fun, but the twins are a special kind of hilarious."

"Yeah, Onyx can be a bit much." Marigold sighs like a frustrated mother hen.

"He's fine." I hesitate. "But does he have a problem with Slate? Things felt... I don't know, weird." I chew my cheek, praying I didn't offend her.

"Oh." Marigold frowns, her lips pressed in a thin line. She checks around us - all the tables are empty. "Well, honestly, I think Onyx feels left out right now."

"Yeah?" I knew I had picked up on some personal issues. I want to be friends with both men. More or less. Understanding their dynamics might be useful.

"Onyx and Slate were best friends growing up. We were all close, but they were joined at the hip, you know? I mean, Cedar was always too busy with his books and I was younger and a girl. But Onyx and Slate always pulled all kinds of crazy pranks." She shakes her head, grinning.

"Okay, so what happened?" I'm intrigued, an edge of sadness creeping in as my brain works out possibilities.

"Slate lost his dad as a teenager and he started to get really serious about his life. He wants to live up to his dad's memory, I think. And Onyx hasn't exactly grown up yet, so he got left behind. They don't agree on much these days."

"Oh." I take a breath, sympathy for both of them surging.

"Yeah, but I wish he would just be nice. He isn't going to repair their friendship by being an asshole." Her fingers thread into her hair, tugging it.

"I bet Onyx feels resentful," I muse.

Marigold rests her head in her hand. "You're probably right. And he's too immature to deal with it."

"I wonder if Slate feels like his best friend doesn't support his new choices either..."

Marigold blinks. "Yeah, that would fit. Hazel, you're really insightful!"

Blushing, I duck my chin, studying my plate. "Too bad they can't just talk about it."

"Boys," Marigold huffs, lightening the mood.

"Who needs them?" I grin, eyeing her. "But Cedar's pretty great. Smart, right?"

Marigold blushes. "Yeah, he's brilliant. He grows all of the veggies we eat here. And he's been planting more fruit trees. So far, he's gotten peaches and plums to grow. And more apples. He's also working on more berries too."

"That's super impressive."

"I like to call him plant daddy." Marigold giggles, her nose and ears turning pink too.

"You call him daddy?" I raise one eyebrow.

Marigold bursts out laughing. "Okay, what about you? You're going to tease me about Cedar. Wanna share about hanging out with a topless Slate in the woods?" she bites out between gasps for air.

Blushing, I cringe. "You caught that?"

She finally calms down and levels me with a stare. "Yup. So, what's the deal?"

"He's pretty cool." I shrug, trying to play it off, even though my cheeks sting.

"And hot," she adds. My mouth falls open and I gape at her. She throws her hands up. "If he wasn't like a brother to me."

I narrow my eyes at her. "You know, if he is your brother, then Cedar is your cousin. Right? Isn't that what Onyx was going on about?"

Gasping, she throws a hand over her mouth dramatically. "Oh, no way. I take it back." She pretends to gag.

"Sorry." My smug grin tells her I'm not at all sorry.

"I saw how cozy you and Slate were last night when he walked you home." She takes a big bite of pizza.

"He's clearly not interested. In fact, I'd describe him as wildly repressed."

"He's too serious for his own good," she agrees.

"Major R.B.F.," I add, making Marigold snort and set her lemonade down hard.

"I don't know, he seemed keen on you from where I stood."

I wave it off. "It's because he's worried about me. Pretty sure he thinks I'm a hazard."

She holds up a hand, bidding me wait. "You did manage to fall into the creek on your first day."

The sting in my cheeks spreads to my ears and my scalp. I probably look like a tomato right about now. "He told you about that?"

"Yeah, I needed the whole story on the back-tattoo-hiking situation." Her eyes sparkle.

"What did he say?" I ask too fast.

"Not much, but he did seem kind of, I don't know, flustered?"

Flustered? I can't picture Slate flustered. He seems so calm and collected. "I was the one tripping all over myself. I went down to the creek to commune with nature and all that. But instead, I got a half-naked guy fishing me out of the water. Mortifying."

Marigold's laugh goes silent and she lays her head down on the table. My side aches from laughing and my eyes blur with tears. I haven't laughed this hard in ages, maybe years.

When I find my voice again, I can't stop myself from continuing. "And then he got all wet helping me up. All those muscles. I mean, who has a six-pack like that? Not to mention the fact he was in sweatpants." I bury my face in my hands. Why did I say that?

"Stop," Marigold wheezes. "I can't breathe!"

"Sorry." I give her a moment. "I'll admire from a distance. Because once he opens his mouth, he's a vibe kill."

Marigold takes a deep breath and grips the table edge to steady herself. "Well, you're getting a tattoo from Mr. Vibe Kill right after this."

"Oh my gosh, the tattoo." Last night's plans come rushing back in, sending my heart beating like a butterfly behind my sternum.

"Do you still want to get one?" Marigold asks.

"Totally," I reply. "It was all I could think about this morning. But then we were talking about abs, and I kind of got distracted."

"Don't forget, the hands attached to those abs are going to be all over you."

I glare at her. "You're going to make it weird!"

"I think it's too late for that," she stammers, laughter taking over her again.

"I'm such an idiot," I mumble, burying my face in my hands. How am I going to manage to sit alone with him after this?

Once she's gotten ahold of herself again, Marigold asks, "Where do you want the tattoo?"

"Umm, would it be awful if I got it on my chest?" I blush deeper. It's the only placement that feels right, but it comes with some complications.

"So you want those hands on your boobs?" she quips.

"No!" I open and close my mouth, struggling to answer. "Well, yes, but no."

"Sure." Marigold is positively smug.

"I can't deal with you right now," I say, waving her away. She is the worst and the absolute best.

"Me, or the wet abs?" she presses, a maniacal gleam in her eye.

"You're insane." I bite my lip, failing to suppress a grin.

Marigold sips her lemonade as if discussing the weather. "You're the one getting a tattoo from him. I hope you have the best time."

"I'm going to get you back for this," I grumble.

The trees sway above me as I melt into the hammock. Wavy oak leaves and spiky maple leaves mingle with the canopy of pine and fir needles.

Marigold returns to her students and I wait for Slate to finish whatever work he is doing and join me. It's so peaceful, I'm not full of anxiety for once.

"Hey there." Slate's voice caresses me and my body responds with a lurch low in my gut. Down, girl. "How was your morning?"

He closes the distance between us with all the grace that comes from strength and feeling comfortable in his body. I want to wrap myself up in that confidence.

"Good. You?" I reply automatically, swinging into a seated position with my feet on the ground. My hair fluffs up from static and I flatten my palms over it, trying to tame the poof.

"Quiet. Marigold's good?" he asks stiffly. This is a lot of small talk for Slate. Is he nervous too?

"Yeah. We had a nice lunch. She's... funny." My throat tightens. If she tells him anything I said, I will die.

"She's a great friend. I'm glad you guys clicked." I nod, and he looks away awkwardly.

"Yeah."

"Want to go?" He tilts his head, the hair tucked behind his ear coming loose.

I push up, following him. He's in familiar gray sweats and a soft blue t-shirt. It seems to be his standard uniform. I can't complain about how the muscles in his back ripple under the fabric as he moves. I bite my lip and focus on not falling flat on my face.

He leads me north past the garden and school. We pass a cute stone cottage with a red roof that must be Sable and Marigold's. Another two-story cabin stands to our left, but we keep going into the trees.

"Do you have your phone with you?" he asks.

"Yeah, why?"

He gives me an unreadable look and jerks his head to the left. "There was something I wanted to show you, first."

Wrinkling my nose, I alter my path to follow him. Did he feel like a little hike before tattooing? My stomach flips, remembering our last hike together.

He picks his way through the woods so quietly, I feel like a lumbering hippopotamus beside him. The trees open up to a rocky outcropping, overlooking the creek. Treetops ripple across the landscape across the water.

"Here," he whispers, taking my hand. I mimic his cautious steps. At the end of a boulder, he stops, crouching and leaning against the rock, slowly peering over.

I clench and unclench the hand he had been holding before resting it against the warm stone.

Peeking over, I don't see anything. I raise an eyebrow at Slate. He leans closer and whispers, "See that hole with the grass sticking out? It's a nest."

Blinking rapidly, I narrow my gaze at the spot. A nest for what?

A teeny, furry nose pokes out. I freeze mid-inhale, eyes widening. The creature is a reddish-golden brown, with a rounded face like a mouse, but larger like a guinea pig.

My hand has moved to Slate's arm, and I realize my fingers are digging into his bicep. He doesn't seem to mind. His eyes are fixed on the little animal, and a smile softens his expression.

"What is it?" I breathe.

"A pika."

"What's that?"

He glances at me, his eyes crinkling with a barely suppressed smile. "Just take a picture and I'll tell you about it later."

A photo! I told him I liked photographing animals, and he brought me to see one. I pull my phone out and frame up the pika. It perches on the rock, looking around like it feels our eyes.

I must shift and make some sort of noise because after a moment, it darts away. My breath hisses through my teeth.

Slate stands up and rotates so he's half sitting on the boulder. Joining him, I pull up my photo reel and show him the snaps I took. I have to admit, they're pretty cute. The pika is adorable and it looks even better with the warm afternoon light.

"Those are fantastic," he praises me, tilting his forehead toward mine to see.

"That was so cool," I say. "I wish I lived near wildlife like this."

"Ready to go?" he asks, rising. The lines around his eyes and mouth are tight, like I said something wrong. Swallowing, I nod and follow his lead.

"So what's a pika?" I ask.

"They're related to rabbits," he shares. "They make this high-pitched squeaking noise sometimes that sounds kind of like a lamb. They live with their mates and stay loyal their whole lives. I often see them running around with flowers in their mouths that they use in their nests."

"Okay, that's the cutest thing ever."

He laughs, pausing. Turning, I follow his gaze. A sleek black trailer with dark wood trim stands between trees. It's modern and fits him perfectly.

He holds the door open for me. What a gentleman.

We step into a black kitchen. Dark-stained wooden countertops stretch beneath a brick backsplash. It's utterly masculine and fits the long, narrow space nicely. There's even a bar top with a pair of swivel stools.

"Do you want some water?" he offers, heading toward his fridge.

"Sure." Accepting the glass, I take a sip of water. He leans against the counter, watching me. "Thanks. I love water." Yeah, I am an amazing conversationalist. Totally smooth.

Cheeks heating, I wander into his living room. A leather sofa sits framed with tall bookshelves. Glossy plants drape the window with vines trailing down like a natural curtain.

Framed charcoal drawings surround the TV showing abstract strokes gracefully outlining the human form. I'm fascinated by the chaotic, sweeping lines. The matte texture suggests they are originals.

"Did you draw these?" I ask, sipping my drink.

"Um no, my dad did." He runs a hand through his dark waves. "I know, kind of weird to have your dad's figure drawings."

"No," I rush to say. "They're stunning. I think it's inspiring."

"Thanks." That earns me another small smile. The switch from moody artist to gleaming Greek god is still startling. But I happen to like both versions of Slate.

"Is this where you grew up?" I ask. Stupid. It's way too new and small.

"I got it a few years ago. My dad's cabin is bigger, but I felt weird staying there without him, so I closed it up. For some day."

"Sorry," I whisper. I lost my dad as a child, but for Slate, it's more recent. It's obvious in the tightness of his jaw and the tension of his shoulder blades. I may have learned to live with it years ago, but he hasn't. Not yet.

"I barely remember my dad, but my mom still talks about him. She has so many stories, I feel like I know him." I'm not sure it helps, but it's my truth.

"My mom left when I was a baby, so it was just him and me. I'm lucky I had him," he reflects.

"He must have been great."

His expression softens, his lips curving into a whisper of a smile. There's a warmth in his eyes, love despite the loss. I'm desperate to hear more, and to share my own story with him.

I want to tell him how my mom never recovered from losing my dad, and how chaotic it made my childhood. It was the opposite of an idyllic upbringing in this forest community.

Instead, I change the subject. "Your friends' tattoos were amazing. How much can I pay you for this?"

His eyebrows shoot up, his relentlessly green eyes flashing in surprise. "Don't worry about it." He takes my glass and sets it in the sink beside his own.

"Slate." I prop my fists on my hips, ready for an argument.

"Hazel, don't worry about it." His voice quiets. "My friends pitch in for supplies, but I've already got more than enough. I'm just happy I still get to tattoo sometimes."

"At least let me buy you lunch." I have to do something, but I realize how silly that sounds. "Or whatever. Maybe a gift card?"

He laughs as he walks past me. The sound rolls over me, causing goosebumps to prickle down my arms. He disappears through an archway into his bedroom. I spy the corner of a gray comforter, tucked in military style.

He returns with a bin of equipment and sets it on a small wheeled side table. With practiced motions, he pulls the ottoman closer and gestures for me to sit on the sofa. I obey.

We're so close. This won't be weird. I won't let it be.

He lays out plastic wrap, paper towels, his tattoo machine, and a variety of other little items. Without looking up, he asks, "What are you thinking?"

I'm distracted by his smooth motions and the way the tattoos on his forearms twist. "Um, what?"

"For your tattoo?"

I flush, squeezing my knees together. "How about moon phases, like we talked about? I don't know what else. Sorry."

"How about some little vines with them? Or stars?" he suggests.

"Sounds beautiful."

"Okay, I've got a few ideas. Where are you thinking for location?"

I hesitate, gathering my courage. "Uh, could we do it here?" I trace my fingertips between my breasts. I wore a soft, stretchy bralette and a loose shirt today, trying to plan ahead.

Slate looks up, going very still as he sees my hand. Fascinated, I watch his throat work as he swallows. After a tense moment, he answers, "That's a sensitive spot. Somewhere like your shoulder would be less painful." His voice is suddenly hoarse.

Too painful? I am a woman. We are made of tougher stuff. Suggesting it's too painful solidifies my decision. I'm done being cautious.

"I think I can handle it."

Now he's mentioned little vines twisting around the phases of the moon, I can't imagine it anywhere else.

He nods. "Look, we can start with one small piece of it, so if we need to stop, you'll still have something pretty. Then we could come back later to finish, whatever you want."

Warmth blossoms in my chest. He respected my choice but also offered alternatives so I have plenty of options. Jeremy would never.

He leans forward with a marker in hand. "Here, lift your shirt. Let's draw it out and you can see if you like it."

"Oh yeah, about that. How are we going to do this?" My cheeks flame.

"I've never done a sternum tattoo before. What would be comfortable for you?" He asks, eyes on my bust. My next breath comes in shaky.

Why did I decide on this again? No way am I making it through this unscathed.

"Um..." I tug on my neckline, glad I picked the clothes I did. I can pull it down to expose almost the entire area while keeping my boobs mostly covered. "Here, and I'll pull my shirt up the other way if you need to go down further."

He scoots closer, reaching out to wipe down my skin. One hand goes to my ribs and the other lowers the marker. He bites his full bottom lip as he skates the felt over the delicate skin between my breasts, sketching out his idea. I'm so entranced, my eyes go unfocused. After a moment, he finishes and straightens.

"Go check it out and tell me what you think," he says, capping his marker with a click and jolting me back to reality.

I stand, legs shaky. The bathroom is all white penny tiles with a black mirror and black faucets. Very modern. Biting my lip, I study my chest in the mirror. A slim line of moons, starting from an upturned crescent, down to a round full moon, and back again, ends level with the bottom of my breasts. A fine line twists between them with a few tiny leaves. Opposite the vine, little stars dot the skin. It's one of the prettiest things I've ever seen.

With a whoosh of breath, I plop back on the sofa and meet Slate's expectant gaze, grinning. "It's perfect."

"Okay. Feeling ready to get it done today?" He asks, pulling on gloves.

"Yup."

"You can lay down." Grabbing a pillow, I slide sideways, still gripping my shirt out of the way.

With confident motions, he finishes prepping all the equipment and wrapping plastic around everything. The machine buzzes as he tests it.

Turning back to me, he glances at my face. "Deep breath. Let me know if it's too much." I nod.

The needle hits my skin and I close my eyes for a moment, refusing to flinch. It's like a deep scratch, worse than a nail but less painful than a cat scratch. Definitely manageable.

He starts with the crescent moon at the top, pausing when he completes those first two lines. "Doing good?" he checks.

"I'm fine. Let's do it," I say, working to keep my voice even, though my heart is racing with how close he is leaning over me.

His left hand presses at my collarbone, stretching the skin. Lowering the needle again, he pulls the line for the waxing moon.

I relax my muscles, watching his expression of deep concentration. It's easy to lose track of where he is tattooing. The whole area hurts like hell, but I'm distracted by the curve of his lips and the way they part in concentration.

His dark brown hair curls over his cheekbones and around his ears so artfully, it's a shame to not take a picture. His eyelashes are unfairly long. On any other man, I would think they're wasted, but nothing is wasted on him.

I relish this chance to stare at him without being caught. His jaw is sharp, dusted with stubble like he hasn't shaved since I met him that first day. I'm aching to reach out and feel the roughness.

He smooths a wrinkle of fabric flat against my breast. My stomach lurches and I fight to stay still. This little tattoo is going to take forever this close to him.

SLATE

Slowly the designs take shape on her skin. I finish all five moon phases and pause, straightening my back and taking a deep breath. Her skin is an expanse of pale gold marred only by my art. It's sinful and exquisite.

"How are you feeling?" I check her unruffled expression. The girl has a high pain tolerance, I'll give her that. It's not a complicated design, but it's definitely a sensitive spot for a tattoo, and she's sitting like a rock.

"Told you I'd be fine." She quirks up half her mouth in a pleased smirk. It's adorable.

"Okay, let's get this done." I drape my cord out of the way, leaning in.

The hand holding her shirt shifts, showing me her dark green painted nails again. They're almond-shaped, a bit like claws. I imagine them digging into my skin.

Nope, not appropriate.

Inhaling sharply, I pull my machine away until I'm focused. This has to be perfect for her. Adjusting my hold on her skin, I lower the needle again, gently tracing the vine running the length of the tattoo.

"So what's your favorite thing to tattoo?" she asks.

I grab a paper towel and wipe off the excess ink.

"I guess natural things. Anything botanical or even animals," I finally respond. "I like designing art that matches the person."

"Like plants for Cedar because he loves gardening," she says.

I pause. "Yeah, exactly that."

Working my way up, I add clusters of little leaves.

"So why the trees and mountains for yourself?" Her voice is hesitant.

I shade the leaves, unsure of what to say or how to say it. "I feel like it's part of who I am," I answer, "like I only am who I am because of where I am from, and I wouldn't be me anywhere else."

Her lips pucker into a surprised O shape.

"Sorry, is that weird?" I try to backpedal.

"No," she says softly, "It sounds lovely. I can't imagine feeling that way."

"Why?" I ask without stopping to think.

Her lashes flutter and her cheeks hollow while she considers her answer. "I've never lived in the same place long enough, I guess. After my dad died, we moved around a lot. My mom had a really hard time dealing. She's not very good at taking care of herself." Her voice is low, but every word pierces into my chest as if it was me and not her with a needle sinking into skin.

"I'm sorry." It's all I can manage. Grief and anger roll through me. Her father was one of us. After his death, we should have cared for his family. He may have left, but it didn't change that she deserved so much better. If her mother couldn't cope, then surely Hazel was left to fend for herself.

"It's okay," she reaches out with her other hand and lightly presses her fingers against the exposed skin above my gloves. Is she trying to comfort *me*? Surprised, I look from her hand to her beautiful face, and she pulls away.

I can't begin to express the injustice now eating away at me. It's acid in my lungs. But words don't change the past and she doesn't need my sympathy.

"Is there a lot left to do?" she asks, redirecting me.

"The stars and then some shading," I answer. She burrows down a bit more and stills, looking up at me patiently.

Back to the business at hand. Cautiously, I add the fine-line star clusters. Each array is so precise, I have to move slowly. It's worth the extra effort because the delicate starbursts are the perfect detail to complete the design.

Hazel is watching me, her honey eyes staring up at me. At this angle, her lips are pillows, her nose upturned the smallest amount. Her golden waves fall across the sofa cushion on either side of the pillow. The roots are dark - she must bleach her hair. I bet she's stunning as a brunette too.

Keeping my eyes on my work instead of her glorious face, I clench and relax my hands several times to keep them limber and steady.

It only takes about five more minutes to shade in each of the little moons. The entire tattoo only took twenty minutes, not counting set-up time. I was so focused, hours could have passed and I wouldn't have a clue.

Setting my machine aside, I drag a final wipe up her sternum, followed by a thin layer of gel.

Done! I sit back and pull off my gloves. She starts to sit up and my hand shoots out to press on her stomach and keep her flat. She freezes. My bare skin against her thin t-shirt shocks me.

"Hold up. I need to wrap it," I say. She takes deep breaths, her chest rising and falling more than when I was tattooing her.

I finally locate the clear bandage I want and smooth it over the skin. "There. Good to go."

She pops up and heads right to the mirror, and I hear her squeal. The sound makes my brain go blank. Not a thought.

"It's perfect. Thank you." Beaming, she drops back onto the sofa, perching on the edge, as near to me as she can be.

"Should we have added more?" I ask, second-guessing my design. I lean closer, getting a better look at how the tattoo looks now she is sitting up.

"No, it's everything I wanted. I can't wait to show it off." She wrinkles her nose at my scowl. "Just to a few people, like Marigold."

She releases her shirt and it settles into place to cover her. The top of the tattoo peeks out - the curve of a crescent moon and a tiny star, right in the valley of her cleavage.

Her arm is on my bicep, burning me. I glance up. My stomach tightens. She's inches away. With the height differences of our seats, she's nose to nose with me for the first time. Her eyes are molten, flecks of citrine in warm brown.

My hand is already on her ribs, though I'm not sure when it moved there. I drag my eyes down, over the tattoo again, and up to her parted lips. I'm a moth and she's an inferno. I can't help but lean in, drawn by her warmth and scent.

Hazel blinks at me, her pupils huge. Her tongue darts out, wetting her lips. She's going to kiss me, I realize with a thrill. I know I shouldn't, but those reasons are distant, and unimportant when she has me ensnared. And I can't bring myself to care.

My eyes close on instinct. Her mouth connects with mine and fireworks go off behind my eyes. She is so sweet. Her lips slide across mine, tentative. I press into her, intoxicated by the sensation. I need more.

Her fingers thread into my hair and twist into the strands. The light tug sends sparks down my spine. I groan and she answers with a soft, sultry noise. Without thought, my hands grasp her waist, pulling her into me.

She deepens our kiss, her tongue in my mouth. She is wild honey and jasmine. Her nails lightly scrape my skin and I go feral. Surging out of my seat, I cover her with my body. She arches under me as I run my thumb across her jaw and down her throat.

Every inch of skin is lustrous. I can't get enough. I want to touch, taste, feel every part of her I can. Desperate, I kiss the side of her mouth and then her jaw, working my way down. She melts in my hands. Everything in me screams to claim her, make her mine forever. Every touch surrenders more of me to her.

"Slate." Her voice is shaky, begging.

I'm jolted back to reality, remembering who I am and who she is. Releasing her, I jump up, trying to gain some distance. Every cell in my body is lit up, my breath uneven and my heart racing. Avoiding her gaze, I deliberately look down at the ground.

She's panting. The noise echoes in my ears and I want to feel it on my skin. I'm feverish, the loss of her warmth a physical ache.

What was I thinking?

"I'm sorry, I shouldn't have done that," I grind out.

"What?" Her voice is breathy. "I kissed you."

There's a silence while I calm myself before I can safely look at her. When I do, it guts me. Her lips and cheeks are deliciously pink, but her eyes are humiliated. I can't stand that expression especially when I am the cause.

"No." I search for words to make it better. "You're perfect. Incredible."

"But." Her lips thin, her embarrassment flaring into anger.

"It's just, I don't date." It is the only way I can think to explain.

Her expression hardens, lines forming around her mouth as she frowns. "Gotcha." With sharp movements, she picks up her phone and bag.

"I mean, I don't plan on being in a relationship. I don't do dates or anything. But if I did..." I'm an idiot.

She stands. "It's fine. I'm sure you're busy, I'll go." Her tone is breezy. She betrays nothing of the hurt that I saw.

"I'm sorry."

"Slate, I appreciate the tattoo." She sets her shoulders, determination glinting in her beautiful eyes. "And you're gorgeous, so I don't regret kissing you. But if you don't date, that's fine. Don't stress it. I'll see you later." She is smooth and confident. Indifferent. It has to be a mask.

With a brittle smile, she marches past me. The door slams behind her. Thunderstruck, I walk through the bathroom to my bedroom and faceplant into my bed.

I'm a worthless slug.

She was recently cheated on and dumped, and then I let my little obsession get the better of me. Now she feels rejected again.

Unfortunately, I don't see any solutions. I let things go too far and this is the consequence. There's no universe in which I can have her.

Heath is going to kill me if he finds out I kissed her.

VI
GIRLFRIENDS
& GARDENING

HAZEL

Thankfully, Slate sits elsewhere at dinner. Heath isn't busy and we sit together under the trees. We're joined by Marigold's family - her father, Elm, grandmother, Sable, and her two brothers, Indigo and Cobalt.

Her father is about Heath's age, and I wonder if they grew up together like Slate and the twins. Indigo is his copy with reddish-brown hair cut short and ocean-blue eyes. He has a calming energy that reminds me of Sable. I understand why Indigo would be the one to work for her.

But the youngest brother, Cobalt, is more like Marigold. His bright strawberry-blonde hair is always in his eyes and he never stops talking. He's all light and laughter.

Marigold gushes over my tattoo. Her warm energy soothes away my jagged edges, calming the storm in my chest. For the first time in hours, I relax.

Heath and Elm recount old adventures for us, including a time they were camping with Hawthorne, and Elm accidentally answered nature's call in front of a hunting camera. Heath retrieved the feed and presented him with a framed picture for the holidays of him squatting against a tree - fortunately a bush was covering the crucial bits.

Marigold's heard the story before and she starts laughing before the end, her face cherry red. She confirms the photo is still hanging in the bathroom of their family's cabin.

I picture my dad, Heath, Elm, and Hawthorne running around between cabins, getting into all kinds of trouble as young teens. The previous generation doing all the same things we did as teenagers. Or rather, the things I would have done, if I had been raised here instead of a thousand miles away.

A strange mix of longing, grief, and happiness aches in my heart. Marigold must notice, because she draws me into her storytelling and makes me laugh so hard my eyes tear up again.

After dinner, Heath and I share some hot cocoa in his cabin and he tells me more about my dad as a kid. Even though Heath is younger, he was the natural leader. My dad was the one keeping the peace and making sure everyone was cared for. They were a team. I can feel how much he misses his brother as if his emotions are soaking into me from across the living room.

I go to bed smiling, feeling closer to my father than ever before. My sleep is peaceful and I wake up with my mind already buzzing with an idea. While I brush my teeth and wash my face, I meticulously fold up my disastrous and glorious kiss with Slate and tuck it into the farthest corner of my mind. There's so much to be excited about and I won't let him deter me.

The pine air is brisk and I tug my flannel around me. I love the slower pace and the peacefulness the forest brings, and I have never felt so accepted as with this new group of friends. In three days, they've burrowed into my heart. It's time to be honest - I don't want to leave.

Los Angeles seems dull in comparison with the vibrant community, even though it's tiny. The idea of going back makes me sick. Here under the swaying branches, I feel more alive than ever before.

I imagine having dinner every night at the picnic tables, laughing with Marigold and the twins, even Slate. It wouldn't be too shabby. I could even flirt with Onyx and Slate would be jealous. Nope! Slate does not factor into this. If anything, he's a drawback.

I'll need an income. I can't mooch off my uncle forever. And a place to stay. He might prefer to not have a roommate. In my head, I'm already assembling a checklist.

The trees thin and Crickett's diner comes into view across the clearing. It's mid-morning, so it's mostly empty. The kids are all in class with Marigold.

Halting, I prop my hands on my hips. Where do I start? I don't want to bother my uncle in his office, so I turn left. There's a small building beside the school. Heath said it's a store. A bell jingles as I push the door open.

It looks like an old convenience store with wood floors, sturdy shelves, and a selection of household and personal items. There's everything from soap to clothing to snack foods. There are even tools and batteries on the far wall.

"Hey, Hazel!" A petite woman with dark skin and bright rainbow braids rests her elbows on the counter, a laptop open beside her.

"Hi." I give her a lame half-wave. I don't remember being introduced to her.

"I'm Fern. Do you need anything? I can put it on Heath's tab." She offers with a wink.

I shrug, shoving my hands into my pockets. "I'm just checking stuff out, but this is cool."

Wandering toward the counter, I peer down a couple of aisles. Toothpaste, shampoo, bandages, and basic medication in one aisle; the next holds cleaning supplies, trash bags, and toilet paper.

"Well, let me know." Fern turns to her computer.

I don't need anything, but it feels silly to decide to live somewhere without thoroughly exploring it. And it's nice to know I won't have to drive into town every time I need to restock shampoo.

The store is small and I've seen all of it within minutes. I should leave, but Fern's eyes are on me. "How are you enjoying your trip?" she asks.

"It's been stupendous." Could I have picked a weirder word?

She seems unbothered. "Planning on staying much longer?"

"Um, maybe." I rock my weight from my heels to the balls of my feet. Why do people keep asking how long I'm staying? Am I inconveniencing them somehow? Then they're going to be very disappointed at my new decision.

"What's the deciding factor?" she asks.

"I'm sorry?"

Her eyes crinkle and a gem glints in the ring through her lip. "What's influencing whether you stay longer or leave?"

"Oh, well, I was originally planning to leave early next week." I hesitate but decide to open up. "I just really like it here. I was thinking about hanging around longer." Close enough.

"Glad to hear it." Fern stands up, arching her back in a stretch. "You fit in nicely."

My lips twitch upwards. "Thanks. I'll see you later."

Content to watch the goings-on, I settle in a hammock. A couple of older men stroll past, chatting about some repairs. A few minutes later, the twins' mother, Clove, leaves the diner and heads toward their cabin. She waves at Cedar as he pops up in the garden. He's got gloves on and a trowel in hand.

Just as I'm dozing off, a handful of kids burst out of the school. Marigold doesn't follow them. I hesitate, not sure if I should wait for her. But maybe she could use my help.

The school interior is one large space, save for some bathrooms off to the side. Marigold is gathering up artwork and sliding it into a drying rack.

The ceiling is wooden beams and planking, like Heath's cabin and the diner. The floor is a colorful linoleum pattern and the tables are all glossy pine smudged with lines of marker. The entire space is a riot of color and smells like wax crayons and chalk.

Huge windows on every wall alternate with bulletin boards covered in the kids' artwork and various charts - multiplication tables, world maps, and an outline of basic grammar rules and sentence structure. An illustrated alphabet spans the windows, close to the ceiling. Opposite, a historical timeline mirrors it. Dozens of little hand-written notes mark out all sorts of important events.

I circle, amazed at all the work she must have put into the space. It's as happy and welcoming as Marigold herself.

"Hi!" She crosses the room to hug me. "What's up?"

"Need any help?" I ask.

"Sure. Can you gather up those markers?" She wastes no time, moving from the artwork to some wayward papers. By the time I've gotten the markers into their bin, she's spraying each table and wiping them down with practiced efficiency. I busy myself by tucking in each chair.

"Okay, looks great. Those little pups are going to be cleaning the chicken coop this afternoon so I left them off easy this morning. Wanna grab some lunch?"

"Sounds good."

A few minutes later, we sit down with grilled cheese sandwiches and pickles. "So, what's on your mind?" she asks. How can she read me so well already?

"Um, yeah, I wanted to talk to you about a few things." I stall. What if she is only kind because she knows I'm temporary? The intrusive thought crashes in, stealing my confidence.

"Of course, anything." Her sandwich crunches as she takes a huge bite.

"I was wondering what kind of jobs might be available here." I hold my breath, counting. I will not let my anxiety spiral.

"Really?" She drops her food onto her plate, her eyes wide and her grin messy. She wipes the back of her hand across her lips, chewing fast so she can speak. "Are you thinking of moving here?"

"Yeah, at least for a while." I smile hard enough my cheeks hurt. It's the best reaction I could have hoped for.

She squeals and throws herself over the table to hug me fiercely. "I'm so excited!" Her hair drapes over my cheek, catching on my nose as she squeezes me and sways happily.

Laughing, I pat her arm. "Me too."

She plops down, absolutely glowing with excitement. It makes my heart soar. "Why the change?"

"It's so peaceful here. Everyone is kind, and I love that you guys are all close. I've never had that." Now I've opened my mouth, it's pouring out. "I don't remember being this happy in a long time. There's something about being here. It feels right."

"You belong here." Her hand squeezes mine.

"I don't know about that, but I think I'd like to."

She looks over the meadow where some of her students are playing soccer, their lunch forgotten. "I don't think I'd want to live anywhere else either."

After a moment, I remember my itinerary. "Okay, I need a job and I need to figure out where to live."

"I bet Heath would let you stay. He's got the space. Otherwise, you can stay with me until you can get your own place. I mean, it's pretty tight. I already sleep in a sofa bed 'cause there's only one bedroom. But you're always welcome!"

"Oh, geez, I can't do that to you." I cringe. "But we could get a new place together and be roommates, and then you wouldn't be sleeping in the living room."

Marigold gasps, "I love that idea."

"Are there cabins available?"

"There's an empty guest cabin we could ask to rent. Or we could look into getting a trailer like the one Slate owns. A lot of the single people have them, actually: Aven, Ewan, Linden."

"I don't know who those people are," I remind her.

"Sorry." She covers a laugh with her hand. "You met Linden, right? He's your uncle's office manager. And then Aven is a few years older than us. She keeps to herself, but you'd recognize her."

"I guess I still have a lot of people to get to know." Anxiously, I pick the crust off my sandwich. I try to picture myself with a whole community around me, arm in arm with Marigold and surrounded by friends. But instead, a sleek black trailer appears in my mind. And a pouty frown and soulful emerald irises. Not helpful.

"I think you know almost everyone. Don't stress it," she reassures me. "Ewan is a biologist-type. He's been on a research trip for the last two months. I think he'll be home soon."

"A research trip? That sounds interesting."

"Probably, but who knows." Marigold takes a bite of her pickle. "So what's next? A job?"

"Yeah. I have enough savings to last a while, thankfully, but I can't be a bum."

"I'm sure it won't be a problem."

"It's what I'm most concerned about. But I guess I can always apply for remote jobs," I say, pulling my hands into my lap before I completely destroy my lunch with my nervous fidgeting.

"Of course, you can if you want to." Her unwavering confidence bolsters mine. "I'm not sure exactly what, but there's always work to do. Heath will know. He helps people find their place." My uncle, the boss.

"He seems to run everything around here."

"You have no idea," Marigold quips with a happy sigh.

I raise one eyebrow at her. "Sometimes you guys sound an awful lot like a cult."

She wrinkles her nose. "Not like that."

"I mean, my uncle has a personal assistant. I didn't see that coming."

"Slate's more like a protégé," she says. "Speaking of, you didn't tell me anything about yesterday."

I stare at her, unsure of what to say. There's so much to tell but I don't want to think about any of it. It's simultaneously delicious and agonizing. "Yeah." My fingers spin my ring absently.

"I don't like how that sounds." She frowns, pushing her plate aside and resting her forearms on the table so she can lean closer conspiratorially.

"Well, I got a super cute tattoo," I say brightly, cocking my head. The smile feels false.

"You did." She nods along, her brows rising expectantly. "And what about the moody artist?"

"Not great." I flatten my lips between my teeth. "I'm kind of embarrassed."

Marigold is quick to soothe me. "You don't have to tell me. But I promise, I'll blame him entirely."

That works. The damn breaks. "It was terrible."

"I'm sure it's not that bad. There's no way it's worse than some of the stuff I've done." She's so kind, but I doubt it.

"Okay, everything was great while he tattooed me, right? And I love it. But then afterward he was right up in my space, and he was staring at my lips, I swear. I mean, he's so cute. I thought we were having a moment so..." Cringing, I force the words out. "I kissed him."

Marigold throws her hands over her mouth with a dramatic gasp. Cheeks burning, I hang my head.

"And then?" she demands.

I take a deep breath. "Honestly, I swear he was into it. He stuck his tongue in my mouth, for fork's sake." I pause, the memory lighting up my nerves. "But then he jumped back like he suddenly discovered I was a frog."

"Are you serious?"

"Yup."

"No!"

"He said he doesn't date." I shrug, trying to remain cool.

"What an idiot," she groans, dragging her hand down her face.

"He was trying to let me down gently. I'm glad he told me after a kiss and not after... whatever."

I can almost feel the sensation of his hands on my waist, demanding, pulling me against him. The heat of his mouth. I would have gone along with anything at that moment. Unable to show my face, I rest my forehead on my crossed arms.

"Look, I know this doesn't help, but he is totally into you. I've seen how he looks at you."

"Kinda makes it worse," I try to joke, but it comes out more of a whine.

"This is a Slate problem. Maybe he'll get his head out of his ass, maybe not," she says, "but you definitely shouldn't wait around for him. You're better than that."

I straighten. "You're right."

"Of course I am."

Deep breath. This isn't the end of the world.

"This was more fun when we were talking about moving in together, and not about, you know." My fingers wiggle as my cheeks scrunch.

"That tool?" she fills in. "I agree. I'm one hundred percent on board with the roommates idea."

"It would be so fun." My mood lightens and my shoulders relax. No reason to worry over Slate when Marigold is on board with the moving idea.

"We can bake, craft, play cozy games, talk shit about boys."

A giggle escapes me. "You know, I met this cute guy in town. Maybe I should take him up on his offer of a coffee date."

"You totally should! Screw Slate. You deserve all the coffee dates."

"Or I'll be a spinster. When I'm old, I'll live in your basement after you marry Cedar."

Marigold snorts. "I think the basement is reserved for Onyx."

"I'll live there with him. It wouldn't be so bad. We could play video games and I can be Auntie Hazel to your kids."

"You'll be Auntie Hazel to them no matter what." She squeezes my hand.

"Thanks."

"Incoming," she murmurs.

Cedar, Onyx, and Slate are all approaching. Slate looks away, markedly showing he doesn't want to be here. Marigold was right – screw him!

Onyx throws his arm over Slate's shoulder, jostling him. "Look who we found lurking." Slate pushes him off.

"How was your morning?" Cedar asks Marigold, sitting beside her.

"Good, thanks. You?" She blushes. I wonder if he notices.

Cedar launches into some explanation about ladybugs. Marigold is fascinated, but I tune him out. Slate is smiling at Cedar and Marigold, but when he glances at me, he stops. My stomach plummets.

"Gotta get back to the kids. We're going to be helping with the coop, remember? See you guys at dinner." Marigold's hand lingers on Cedar's shoulder before she jogs away, her long braid swinging behind her.

Onyx has an easy grin. "Want to hang out, Hazel?" I glance at Slate. He's glaring at Onyx, his jaw tight.

"Sure." I don't mind irritating him and I have a feeling Onyx will be on board with it too.

Slate gathers up our two plates. "I'm going back to work too. See you later."

"You don't have to do that." Scowling, I reach for our plates.

"I'm going to go grab some food anyway. It's no trouble." He strides away. Clearly, he can't tolerate breathing the same air as me after my blunder last night.

"I'm heading to the garden," Cedar says.

"Oh, can I see the garden?" I jump at the chance.

"I'll give you a tour." Onyx offers his arm as we stand.

I'm impressed he's being such a gentleman. The jokes seem to wane after Slate leaves. We walk along in silence. I enjoy the closeness, but it's not the same as with Slate. We follow Cedar through the trellis archway covered in little white flowers.

I glance between the brothers. They're an interesting contrast. Cedar's hair is lighter and his skin is a darker golden tan. He could pass as a surfer. Onyx looks more like a gamer, like maybe he wore eyeliner in middle school. He's got that grungy look. To be clear, he's objectively handsome, they both are. But they're too broad, too blond, like Prince Charming. Not my type. There's something about Slate's sharp features I can't resist.

"Let me know if you have any questions," Cedar offers before heading to his supply shed.

The air hums with bees. A vibrant patchwork of garden beds spreads out in front of us. The midday sun lights up fiery tomatoes and glossy zucchini hiding under plate-sized fuzzy leaves.

Trees dotted with peaches and plums line the far side. To the left stands what I thought was a shed, but I realize now it's the chicken coop. Marigold directs a group of kids as they scoop out dirty litter into trash bags. I can smell the manure now that it's being stirred up, but I don't mind.

To the right, another shed opens to a pen with a couple of goats standing atop a log. They're almost hidden by the bramble of blackberries growing along their fence.

I spin in a circle. "I can't believe your brother grows all this."

Onyx smiles, and it's the most genuine one I've seen from him. He's proud of Cedar. "We all help and Tansy is really in charge. She's been the gardener for years, but Cedar's so good with plants, she's been handing more and more over to him."

"I think that's the most you've ever said without teasing someone," I observe, patting his arm.

He rolls with it, grinning. "Then I'd better get a joke in right away."

My pats turn to a smack on his arm.

"Shit, I can't think of any," he says in mock horror.

A real laugh escapes me. I'm enjoying his company. Maybe the rude comments are hurt stemming from his broken friendship with Slate, and he's kind hearted on his own. As I study the set of his shoulders and the curve of his mouth, I know I'm right. He's a sweet guy under the sass and humor.

We stroll along the stone-lined path. Barrels cut in half serve as containers for basil, rosemary, and mint. I breathe in the herbal perfume.

"Have you seen these suckers?" Onyx crows, yanking a massive, misshapen carrot out of the ground.

Cedar appears at his shoulder. "Oh good, you can harvest those for me." He shoves a basket into my hands and disappears again.

Onyx slings the carrot into the basket and takes it from me. Without complaint, he squats down and starts picking through the carrot greens to find the biggest ones.

I join him, relishing the feel of the crumbling dirt and the smooth carrots.

"So." Onyx breaks the silence. "You and Slate?" He leaves it hanging.

"Nope." That's all I'm going to say. I tug another particularly huge carrot out of the ground and toss it into the basket

"Oh?" He cocks his head, frowning.

"Why? Are you planning to make a move?" I tease.

He throws his head back and laughs. "As much as I would love to, I'm pretty sure he would skin me alive if I tried that."

"Cheese and rice! Are you kidding me?" I grumble. Slate doesn't have some sort of claim on me.

"Sorry, babe," he apologizes.

Irritation prickles. "He and I aren't a thing, and we aren't going to be. He's made that really clear."

"Geez, if you want me to make a move on you that badly-" he jokes.

"I don't need to be looking for a date right now. I literally broke off an engagement a few weeks ago." Humor and frustration collide, rolling into chest-constricting grief in a millisecond. Tears threaten to fall, damn it!

"I'm sorry, Hazel. I didn't mean–" He grabs my hand, clasping both my fingers and the carrot I'm holding.

"This is ridiculous!" It's all I can manage. The first few tears escape.

"It's fine. Everything is fine." His voice is gentle. I've never heard him use this tone before. His eyes are so dark blue, they could be navy. The sea at night. "We all adore you. Slate is being his normal asshole self. Don't worry about it for a minute."

He makes me giggle as a few more tears manage to drip down my face. I wipe them on my sleeve. "He's trying to make sure no one is disrespecting you or whatever. Even if he's too much of a douche canoe to realize." He stands, brushing the dirt off his pants.

I'm still confused, but I'm tired of discussing my issues. Tired of the self-pity party that still rears up unexpectedly. I'd rather focus on anyone else.

"You're sort of pissy with him," I note cautiously.

"I guess I don't like the guy." Onyx shrugs. "Anymore."

If he can butt into my personal business, I can do the same. Besides, I want to help. "I heard you used to be super close. And then he kind of went to do his own thing. I'm sorry, that sucks."

Onyx rolls his eyes. "Doesn't anyone keep their mouth shut around here?"

"Sorry, it kind of came up."

"He's the one missing out. I'm fucking delightful." He grins, confident as ever. "I've still got Marigold, and my brother, and now you."

He tugs me to him, wrapping me in a hug. He makes me feel safe. I wrap my arms around his waist.

In my ear, he whispers, "Should I make a move now?"

I pull away and slap his chest playfully.

"Don't go!"

"Why don't you get back to work?" I huff in exasperation, smothering my smirk. He doesn't need the ego boost.

"Probably should. But this is more fun." He scoops up the basket.

"I'm going to go find a shady place to read. You go do whatever you're supposed to be doing, and I'll see you at dinner."

"You're abandoning me." He grabs his chest, dramatic as always.

"Weirdo." I chuckle, walking away. His friendly laugh follows me, warming my heart.

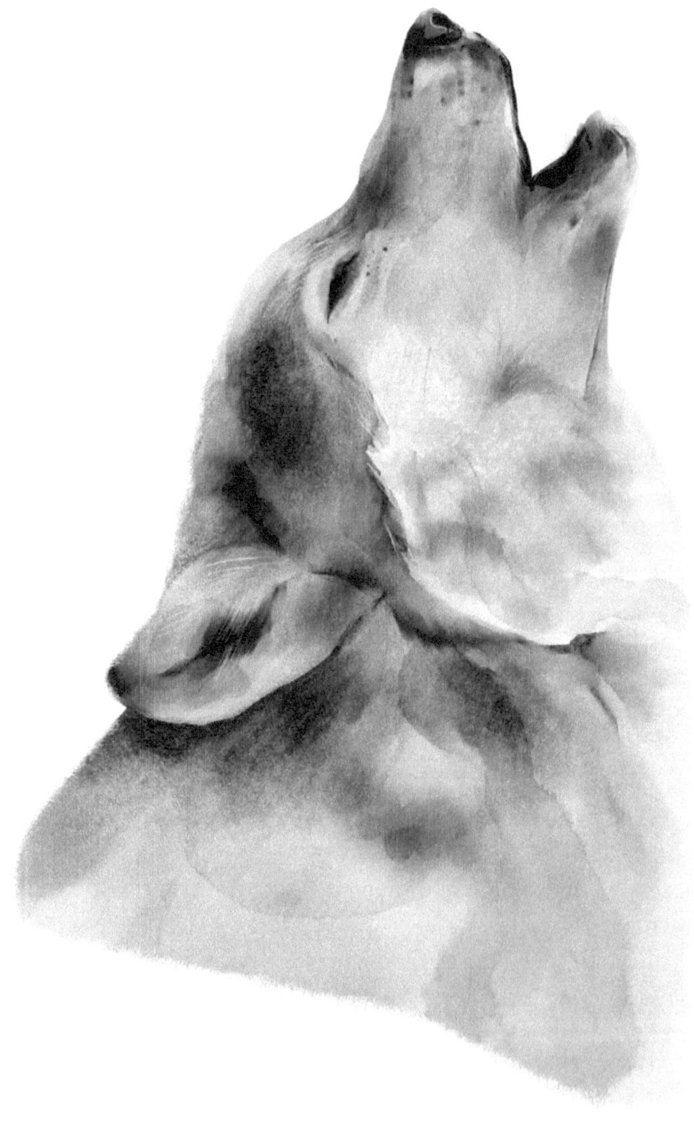

VII
TENSION & THE TRUTH

HAZEL

Dinner conversation is light and the twins head off to help their mother prep tomorrow's baking. Marigold agreed to babysit earlier, so that leaves me and Slate. He's still avoiding me and he disappears as soon as he can. I decide to call it a night early.

Getting ready for bed, I carefully peel off the bandage and wash my tattoo. Gingerly, I pat it dry and smooth on the gel he gave me. Despite how the evening ended, I love the little line of moons. It makes me feel more like myself.

To be safe, I set an alarm to get up in time to talk to my uncle. Otherwise, I won't see him until dinner, and even then, it's hit or miss. He likes to move between tables, talking with everyone.

Luckily, I'm early enough to catch him this morning.

"Good morning!" I reach for my customary croissant and am disappointed. Today it's muffins. Sighing, I pick up one studded with blueberries.

"You're up early, Hazelnut." He sips his coffee, ignoring my pout over the baked goods.

"I guess I'm all caught up on sleep."

Lines form around his eyes as he smiles at me, setting his phone face-down. "Good. I'm glad you're resting up."

"I wanted to talk to you," I say cautiously, picking at my muffin. Little crumbs accumulate on the table in front of me. "I've been thinking. You know, it's wonderful here. I had no idea you had this whole little community." I'm rambling.

"Thanks," he answers, waiting for me to continue. His attention is a pressure filling the room. Stifling me.

"Okay, so I really like it here and I think I want to stay longer," I say. Not as direct as I would like, but at least I said it. Nausea rises up my chest, my anxiety clawing up and trying to take control.

"How much longer?" His expression melts from an easy smile to a frown, his brows lowering and mouth downturning.

Swallowing thickly, I suck in a shaky breath and continue, "Like months. Or maybe long-term?"

His frown deepens. "I'm not sure that's a good idea. You can't put your life on hold. I know what happened was tough, but-"

"That's not it!" I cringe, rushing to correct his impression. This is going all wrong. "I want to live here, get a job and my own place to live."

"Oh." He tilts his head, eyes on me with such intensity, my skin itches, my anxiety threatening to take over.

"Marigold and I talked about being roommates. And she said you might know where I could work. I'm not going to just mooch off of here, and I don't expect to stay here."

He studies me, the silence eating away at my resolve. "Hazel." His tone is gentle, but I know where this is going.

"I'll do just about anything. Maybe you need help in your office? I'm good at that stuff. HR, bookkeeping, anything." I scramble to convince him I'm worth keeping around.

"I have people for those things already." My stomach, somersaulting near my heart, suddenly drops.

"I can always find a remote job and work online." My voice is weak. I know I've lost, but I can't stop.

Heath sighs, sitting back in his chair. Sympathy softens his face. "Hazel, you can't stay here."

My entire body sways back, the declaration feeling like a physical blow. Heat prickles in my eyes, so I grit my teeth and ask, "Why?"

"This isn't your home. You'll be better off back in California."

If anyone has the right to tell me where I belong, it's my uncle, but I'm sick of men deciding where I go. Irritation burns through my fragile feelings of failure, kindling the desire to fight back.

"I don't feel like that's true," I say reasonably.

As if he senses my rebellious anger, Heath raises his chin, his eyes widening a fraction. "I'm glad you like it here. But it's not the most comfortable or safest place for you."

Comfortable? As if I was some princess who tantrums over seeing a bug in her bathroom. It's not like they're camping in Antarctica out here. I decide to ignore the *comfortable* and focus on the *safest*.

"Safety? I'm not a child. I'll carry a flashlight and some bear spray. I can learn whatever," I argue, my teeth grinding together.

Whatever Heath sees in my determined stare, he doesn't like. Brows furrowing again, he stands and tucks his phone in his pocket.

"I'm sorry, Hazel. You need to move on. It's what's best for you."

Tears burn in my eyes but I suppress them. I've always cried when I'm angry. Being treated like a child and told I'm incapable of living out here like all these people do, it's humiliating. Especially coming from Heath, who has always been my biggest supporter.

"You didn't want me here in the first place," I say softly. It's more of a realization than an accusation. I remember his reluctance to allow me to visit.

Heath grips the back of his chair, looming over me. "No, Hazelnut. Listen, you are my family. I wish we lived in the same area. But this isn't the place for you. You wouldn't be happy here in the long term, and I want you to be happy."

I shake my head. "I-" I can't come up with another reason, but I can't stand the idea of someone else making these decisions for me. Not after wasting the last two years. But my fire is burning out, leaving a bitter emptiness behind.

"I'll come visit you more often. We can make it a yearly thing, every summer. But you deserve a city life. Like your dad." He reaches out and squeezes my shoulder. "I love you."

I can't make my voice work, so I nod and try to smile.

Glancing at his watch, Heath straightens. "Look, I have to go to work. Why don't you go see your friends?"

I take a deep breath. "I think I'm going to head into town. I'm supposed to call my therapist and this way I can do a video call. There isn't enough service out here to do it."

"Great plan, kiddo. Take care of yourself."

"Of course." I trace the wood grain of the table until he disappears out the door, the weight of my failure pressing down on me.

A few tears fall as I drive into town. But by the time I park outside Birch & Brew, I feel drained, leaving a hollow sickness that I intend to fill with some sugary drink. Anything for a little dopamine. Flipping the visor down, I check my face, brushing hair back from my splotchy skin.

The coffee shop is quiet, not surprising for late morning on a weekday. I order from the same barista and hover near the end of the counter as they make my drink. Three paintings hang on the far wall, a swirl of black and gray that reminds me of Slate's father's artwork.

"Hey, stranger." A rich voice wraps about me.

Jolting, I spin. "Oh, hey!"

Jasper's blue eyes are glittering gemstones, his pale hair artfully swept back. It looks like bedhead, but I have a feeling he put significant effort into the style. He smiles, his teeth white and straight. His sculpted features look so similar to Slate, my stomach does a flip.

"Fancy meeting you here." He reaches for a coffee mug already waiting for him, giving the barista a bro nod.

"You know, this is only my second time visiting, and you've been here both times. You're making me think that you live here."

"It's got the best Wi-Fi in town," he explains with a shrug. "Come join me." It's not an order, but his confidence draws me in. He's the distraction I need while I wait.

"For a bit. I've got a video call in like twenty minutes." I grab my cup and follow him.

Jasper settles at a little cafe table. His laptop is already sitting open, but he closes it and gives me his full attention.

"So, are you still in college? Or working remotely?" I ask.

"Maybe I'm moderating my wildly successful social media channels." He raises an eyebrow.

"Seriously?"

"Hell no." He laughs.

Wrinkling my nose, I tilt my head and look him up and down. "I don't know, you could pass for an influencer."

"Oh really. What makes you think that?" He might be asking for compliments, but I'm not sure how else to answer.

"Everything, the hair, the eyes." I wave my hand.

He leans forward, his sly smile splitting into an amused grin. "Now you have to let me take you on a date. Or at least let me buy you your next coffee."

"I think I'm good." I deflect, lifting my cup. The idea of a date makes my insides squirm and not in a pleasant way. He isn't the one I want asking me out, unfortunately. That thought sours my mood.

"Next time," he insists, his smirk disappearing into his coffee cup as he takes a long drink.

"So what are you doing?" I ask, eyeing the computer. "Sorry, you don't have to answer that."

"No, it's cool. I'm taking online classes." He rests his free hand on top of his computer, tapping his fingers lightly.

"So I was right about college."

"Yeah, I'm taking my sweet time finishing up my bachelor's degree. Should have been done a couple of years ago."

"What are you studying?"

"Environmental studies."

"Sounds interesting," I say, surprised it's not business or something else common like psychology or communications. He seems like he could be a marketing guy.

"Yup, I'm going to save the world." He crosses his arms, the snarky smirk in place.

"Sounds like a good plan." Relaxing, I lift my coffee in a little cheers before taking another long sip.

"What did you study?"

"I graduated last year with a business degree," I admit, feeling silly.

"What are you doing with it? If I can ask."

"At first, I wanted to do leadership development, " I admit. "You know, like helping managers be better. Making improvements that actually help people. But there aren't a lot of jobs like that and I've been doing all sorts of random office jobs."

"Is that what brings you to town today? Working remotely too?"

"Uh, no. I've got an appointment with my therapist." I grimace, all the difficult things I need to discuss with my therapist rushing back in.

"Cool. Good for you." He smiles. When I can't manage a genuine smile in return, his lips curve downwards. "Are you okay?"

"Yeah, totally." I say, pressing my lips together tightly.

He studies me, that keen stare breaking down my resolve. My fingers grip the sleeve around my to-go cup, twisting it around and around. After a moment, I can't take the silence.

"It's just that I kind of wanted to move here. I like it a lot. But my family isn't on board. They want me to go back to L.A." Shame heats my cheeks. I'm hunched over, subconsciously avoiding this uncomfortable discussion topic, but when I straighten, the freshly-tattooed skin on my chest stretches and I wince.

Jasper leans forward, concern ferocious in his gaze. He reaches out but doesn't quite touch my wrist. "Are you hurt?" His voice is low.

My blush deepens and I press my hand to my cheek. "No. I'm sorry. I got a tattoo and it's healing."

His eyebrows shoot up. "Can I see it?"

"Um, maybe next time." I figure that's a better answer than, *no way, it's tucked between my boobs. You gotta buy me dinner first.*

"I can't wait." He sits back. With a grin, he pulls out his phone. "Can you put your number in my phone? Or let me text you?"

Remembering Marigold's delighted response when I mentioned my coffee friend, I oblige and text him my name. My stomach squirms, excitement warring with a sense of wrongness. I don't want to mislead Jasper. He seems really nice.

"Hey, I've got to go," I blurt, realizing the time on my phone. "I guess I'll see you sometime soon?"

He stands up at the same time as I do, stepping closer and opening his arms. "Hazel, you're doing the right thing by following your instincts. I'm sure it'll work out and your family will understand."

I blink at him, mumbling, "Thanks," as he pulls me into an embrace. His warmth wraps about me, his arms squeezing around my shoulders as his face presses into my hair. It's a very good hug.

"You smell..." he murmurs, "Good." He finishes the sentence slowly as if he isn't quite sure of the right word.

"Thanks, I guess." I squint at him. "I'll see you later."

He waits until I'm halfway across the coffee shop to sit down and open his laptop.

Settling in my car close enough to still access their internet, I open the video call link. My therapist's face smiles back at me. We begin our comforting routine of checking in on how I am doing. She is supportive as I recount my tentative decision to change my plans and stay and all the turmoil over my uncle's reaction. She doesn't have any answers, but it helps to work through my anxious thoughts with her. It leaves me feeling regulated and calm.

As we are wrapping up, a tall figure ducks out of the coffee shop. If he sees me, he doesn't react. Jasper strolls down the sidewalk, the sun lighting his hair into a white-gold blaze against his tawny skin. I watch his retreating back.

I don't want to go back and face my uncle yet, so I get out of my car and stroll down the street. A matching brick building houses a tiny clothing store and I duck inside. They share the space with an outdoor supply store, and I toy with the idea of getting some hiking boots. It's an enjoyable distraction. That is, until my mother calls.

My phone vibrates in my back pocket and the screen says Mom. With a deep breath, I accept the call.

"Mijita!" she warbles.

"Hi, Mama," I answer, forcing a smile and praying for patience.

"I heard you took a little trip! Why didn't you tell me?" she sweetly accuses.

"Mama," I start.

"Did you bring Jeremy with you?" she interrupts. "Are you eloping and not telling me?" Her voice rises hysterically. Is she serious?

"Mom."

"I can't believe you'd do that!"

"Jeremy and I broke up!" I blurt.

She gasps dramatically. "What?"

"Yeah, he was a jerk," I say lamely, really not wanting to get into details.

"Oh, it's okay to have some little fights," she says. "You shouldn't throw your relationship away because of it. You don't want to end up alone."

Anger flares and I snap, "It wasn't a fight. He cheated on me."

The line is quiet. I think it's the first time in my life she's been speechless.

"So yes, we broke up." A bitter little laugh slips out.

"Oh, Mija, how could you let this happen?"

I choke. "I'm not sure," I mumble, "how could..." I can't bring myself to endure her special type of torture today. "Look, Mom, I can't talk."

"You need to come home, baby."

"I said, I can't talk right now." This call just needs to end.

"Come home tomorrow," she demands.

Time for some boundaries. "That's not going to happen."

"Excuse me?"

"I'm sorry," I spew, an automatic reaction, "but I don't want to."

She cuts me off again. "How could you speak to your mother like this?"

"I need to go."

"How could my daughter be such a disrespectful little-"

"I love you," I say, right before ending the call.

Within seconds, my phone pings with incoming texts. Exhaling slowly, I mute my messaging app. My therapist would be so proud.

By the time I'm back at my car, it's later than I planned. Unless I want to be driving in the dark, I'd better get moving.

SLATE

I'm pacing the border of our property, using patrol as an excuse when everyone knows I am waiting for Hazel to return. The sound of gravel crunching under tires and the soft rumble of an old engine filters through the forest. I wait until I see a glimpse of her through the trees and then head toward Heath to report.

He greets Hazel at the parking lot and walks her to a table. I don't like this. Her body language is rigid and reluctant.

Across the clearing, everyone is already eating dinner. I can't fathom eating while Hazel is distressed. I hover far enough away, Hazel doesn't notice me, but close enough I can hear everything.

They make small talk for a moment. Hazel shares about her afternoon in town.

Heath rests a hand on her shoulder. "I think we should have a going away party soon. How about tomorrow or Sunday?"

"What?"

"Everyone's gotten pretty attached to you the last few days. I'm sure you'll want to head back to California on Monday or Tuesday. They'll want to say goodbye before you go."

I can't believe he is telling her to leave like this. I clench my fists.

"So, I'm leaving in three days?"

"You'll want to get started on the job search. And I'm sure your mom is anxious to see you again." He is warm and reassuring, but her breathing is speeding up. Tension tightens her shoulder blades, pinches the corners of her mouth, and curls her fingers.

"You called her, didn't you?" She's so quiet, I almost miss it.

"She misses you. Besides, from home, it'll be easier to apply for jobs and get interviews."

From her defeated slump, I can tell Hazel won't stand up for herself. She stares blankly into the distance. "I need some air before dinner."

"Sure, but stick close. It's getting dark." His eyes flick to me and he nods slightly. I don't need his command to follow her. Nothing could keep me away.

"Fine, whatever." Crossing her arms, she trudges through the trees, heading directly into the forest - exactly what Heath said not to do. The sun is setting and under the canopy, it's already dark.

Silent tears track down her cheeks. I can't stop myself from intercepting her path. She whirls around, her pinched expression snapping to a glare.

"Are you okay?" I ask. Dumb question. I shift my weight uncomfortably.

"Did he send you to babysit again?" Her voice is venom.

"No." Okay, maybe he did, but I would have come anyway.

"Go sit on a cactus," she growls, turning away from me and stomping a few more steps before halting. The only sound is her shuddering breaths and the fluttering leaves. When I don't answer, she glares. "Why are you even here then?"

"You might not believe me, but I do care if you're okay or not," I confess.

"Whatever. I should just leave. My family doesn't want me here. You certainly don't." Anger saturates every syllable.

That's wildly false, but I don't argue. She digs her fingers into the sleeves of her sweatshirt, tugging the fabric tighter around her. Her expression fades, her anxious thoughts claiming her again. Cautiously, I step closer, waiting for a reprimand that doesn't come. If anything, she drifts toward me.

Gently, I wrap my arms around her, pulling her close. She presses into me, her cheek on my chest. Tears soak into my shirt and her body slumps against mine. I breathe in her sweet scent. The smell of coffee and gasoline clings to her, and under that, something familiar I can't quite identify.

"Of course, I want you here," I finally say.

"No, you don't." Her argument is muffled against my shirt.

"You have no idea what I want," I mutter, my voice scraping and raw.

She lets out a scornful laugh. "I don't think *you* even know what you want." If only she knew. I'm holding the only thing I truly want. She looks up at me through her lashes. "You're an amazing artist. And yet you just abandoned it based on someone else's dream."

With a deep sigh, I tip my head up and search the streaks of purple and navy through the leaves. If I'm asking her to be honest with me, I have to do the same. "I love tattooing. But I also love taking care of everyone here. Sure, it's not as enjoyable, but it's the most valuable thing I could do with my time."

She turns her head, pressing her face directly into my chest and muffling her words. "I want to stay. But my uncle won't let me."

"I'm sorry." It's all I can say.

We linger in that quiet moment. Her distraught breathing slows and steadies. "I don't want to leave. This feels like home," she whispers.

This feels like home. Home.

I pull back so I can see her expression. Her tears have subsided, leaving her lashes glossy and her nose a charming shade of pink. Gently, I wipe the lingering moisture off her cheeks with my thumbs.

Taking a deep breath, I cling to the words I think will help her, refusing to speak the confession threatening to burst from my mouth. "I can't speak about the rest of your family, but Heath loves you. He is always going to put your well-being and safety first."

Her jaw juts out and her eyes narrow in determination. There's that spark. She hasn't given up, not really. "I don't understand. You live here, Marigold does, even children, what's wrong with me? Why can't I?"

And we can't give her a good reason. Damn. I search for any response that won't make things worse. "It's not that simple."

"That's not fair," she argues, her hands gripping the fabric of my shirt sleeves.

"No, it's not," I agree. "You should be the one to decide where you live. Nobody else." I shouldn't speak against Heath, but something about Hazel makes me forget the rules and expectations. She takes over my thoughts, leading me to think and do things I never would have otherwise. It's another reason I shouldn't be holding her here in the forest.

"I don't want him to be disappointed in me." Her quiet admission punches me in the gut.

I tip her chin up so she has to meet my gaze. She needs to hear this and know I mean it. "Your happiness is worth more than his approval."

Her eyes are russet, dark and deep, in the fading light. My hand moves until I'm cradling her face. She hasn't moved, her face tilted up toward me, mouth slightly open.

My father's voice echoes a warning in my head, *Put your duty first. Pack above all.* But then she's reaching for me and I'm lost to her.

Her hands press against my stomach, sliding around my ribs to my back. Everywhere she touches sparks electricity. I smooth her silky hair, my fingers tangling in the waves. So soft. I can't resist her a second time, now knowing what she tastes like. I lower my face until our breath mingles. She only needs to move an inch and our lips will touch.

A twig snaps.

My muscles tense and I slowly raise my head, my instincts screaming inside my head. Not wanting to scare her, I take a slow breath, looking for confirmation. It was probably an animal. The faintest scent of an enemy reaches me. No!

Hazel pulls away, a frown furrowing her brows and wrinkling her nose. Thankfully, she stays quiet. Spinning, I grab her arm and haul her behind me. I have to keep her close. I can't see anyone, but it doesn't mean they aren't there.

My head swivels as my ears catch subtle noises. The smell is unmistakable now. We don't have long. I have no doubt they're closing in. We are minutes from the compound. This shouldn't be happening.

Another soft rustle sends my heart racing. I can't protect her if it's more than one. Glancing around, I drag us sideways.

"Hazel, can you climb this tree?" I demand.

"What?" Frightened, her voice pitches high.

"Right now." Eyes wide, she nods. "I'm going to help you up." I lace my fingers together to boost her up. "As fast you can. Get up at least ten feet."

For once she doesn't argue. I push her as high as I can. She hooks her arms around lower branches and heaves herself up and out of reach. It won't keep her safe long, but it should be enough time for help to reach us.

A dark shape moves between trees. I follow the movement, every muscle tense and ready. Stepping from behind the foliage, a gray and brown wolf slinks into view, fifty yards out. I bristle. He could close the distance in three seconds. I bare my teeth at him. He snarls back.

A second wolf, darker gray and black, emerges behind him. Together, they stalk toward us, slowly spreading further apart to attack from both sides. We are in trouble. I hope the breeze turns and Heath or Hawthorne can sense them too. I'm not sure how long I can hold them off.

"Holy shit!" Hazel shrieks. "Slate, get up here!" I pray someone hears her.

The gray and brown wolf gathers on his haunches and springs. I won't let him get near Hazel. Darting forward to meet him, I shift into my canine form, leaving torn clothing behind. My paws hit the leaf-strewn ground, propelling me up to meet the intruder's attack.

"What the fuck?!" Hazel screams.

The wolf snaps at my throat, but my thick ruff of fur protects me. I'm bigger and my momentum knocks him back. Before I can press my advantage, the second wolf is on me. Her teeth slice into my shoulder as she rams into me. Snarling, I twist and clamp my teeth down on her ear. Blood hits my tongue and I push toward, trying to force her to the ground. She stumbles sideways, a pained yelp ringing in my sensitive ears. Hearing a growl from the first wolf, I let her go and brace myself for his attack.

He's fast, using his smaller frame to his advantage. I don't turn fast enough, and his teeth sink into my neck on his second attempt. He doesn't rip and tear, but pushes me down. Growling and snapping, I shove back. My natural instinct is to pull away, but training overrides it. Using my weight against him, I push and he loses his balance and stumbles, his teeth loosening the fraction I need to pull free. I ignore the rip of my skin and the bright, blooming pain.

The gray and brown wolf recovers from his blunder and lunges, while his partner attacks from the other side. Her paws hit my shoulders and ribs, and with all of her weight and momentum, I'm forced to the ground. Tensing, I keep my legs under me to protect my belly and throat. Their jaws snap like bear traps, and I prepare myself for whatever injury they will inflict, but I will not give in. Not when Hazel needs me.

The darker female wolf growls, preparing to strike. Gathering my strength, I look for any angle to exploit, any chance to turn the fight.

A steel gray blur crashes into her with a snarl that echoes in the trees. Fisher knocks her aside, Aven flanking him. My pack made it.

Hawthorne drives the male wolf back, his hackles raised to make him look massive. His ears press forward, tail curled in an aggressive display. Lazuli is right behind him, his white chest making him easy to distinguish.

Heath follows, standing taller than the rest of us. His posture is rigid and a deep growl resonates from his chest. Dominance rolls off of him, urging me to stay on my belly.

The rogue male scrambles back, but then leaps for Fisher in a feint. Both intruders dart away, disappearing into the trees. My four packmates race after them, leaving our Alpha standing over me.

Heath raises his golden muzzle, eyeing Hazel in the tree. She's still letting out a stream of quiet curses and clinging to the branches with white knuckles. He looks from her to me, and I sense his intentions through our pack bond.

While Hazel's terrified eyes are on Heath's hulking wolf form, I move to the base of the tree and shift back, pulling on my abandoned sweats as fast as I can. My shirt is destroyed, so my chest is bare, blood streaking down one shoulder.

With a swish of his tail, Heath turns and trots away. Hazel watches him go, her mouth ajar.

Facing her, I reach up, speaking slowly like she's a terrified animal. "Hazel, you're okay. It's okay now." She stares at me and I beckon to her. "They're gone. Come down; I've got you." After a moment, she starts to release her grip and climb down. Clumsy with fear, she slips and slides down the trunk. I grab her, lowering her to her feet. She's pressed against me and I don't let go.

"Why are you shirtless again?" she asks, her voice scratchy from screaming.

"Everything's okay," I repeat.

"Slate!" she screeches, seeing the bloody tear running from my shoulder blade up to the base of my neck. Yanking her sweatshirt off, she presses it to my wound.

"Don't worry, it's nothing. Looks worse than it is."

"We need to get you to the hospital." Am I her biggest worry right now?

She's shaking. I scoop her up, bridal style, and she presses her sweatshirt against my neck as I walk. Slowly, I pick my way through the trees, trying to not jostle her too much. Blood drips down my back and I hope she doesn't notice in the darkness.

VIII
HIDDEN HERITAGE

HAZEL

My uncle stands in the meadow, waiting for us. He is also shirtless and my brain knows it means something, but it can't quite process it. He's ordering different people in various directions, and it looks like the entire little community is rushing around.

He watches us even while speaking rapidly with Hawthorne. Slate reads his expression and veers toward Heath's cabin. Through my blurry vision, I see strawberry blonde hair and a heart-shaped face bobbing by Slate's side. It's the first time I've seen Marigold silent, or maybe I'm not absorbing sound.

A third set of hands opens the door for us. Slate sets me down. Marigold tucks a blanket around me. She hovers, wanting to be close. Why doesn't she sit next to me? Oh, Slate is occupying the seat already. His warmth soaks into my thigh.

Marigold presses a mug into my hand and encourages me to lift it and take a sip. The cocoa warms my belly and settles my nerves. We sit in silence and gradually my breathing calms. The room comes into focus.

The kitchen door squeaks and I jerk. Sable shuffles in, an oversized carpet bag hanging from her elbow. Marigold opens her mouth but then closes it with one glance from her grandmother. Sable lifts my chin, studying my eyes. She wipes my palms down and applies a pungent cream to the abrasions I haven't noticed until now.

Slate won't let Sable tend to him until she's thoroughly inspected and washed all of my cuts and scrapes. He sits forward so blood doesn't stain Heath's cushions. Deep gouges curve along the base of his neck toward his spine. Finally, Sable cleans it and he isn't even bleeding anymore. How is that possible?

Slate turns his head and smiles at me. "It's nothing, see?" His voice is barely above a whisper and it makes my stomach flutter. It's a euphoric relief, as if I've been in pain for days and it's finally lifted. He's okay.

Heath strides in, Fisher behind him. He tips his head, the motion almost imperceptible if I hadn't been staring right at him. Marigold reaches over and squeezes my hand, before walking out.

Heath perches in the armchair, steepling his fingers and focusing on Slate. "What happened?"

"We were just walking and talking. Only fifty or sixty yards out. Even with cabins. And two unknowns approached, hostile," Slate reports calmly.

"What did you do?

"Hazel climbed a tree. I defended us when they attacked."

"Did you?" Heath's mouth is tight. I sense more meaning behind their conversation, but I'm not privy to it.

"Yes, sir."

"Okay." Heath nods.

I am so exhausted, emotions ripping through me all day followed by a massive dose of terror. I'm at my limit.

"What the hell is going on?" I snap, my voice clogged up.

Heath pauses, assessing me. "Did I tell you we have a coyote problem around here?"

I shake my head. "I don't think so. Didn't look like coyotes." I press on. "Pretty sure it was wolves."

"Ah, yes, we have wolves in these woods. Which is why I've tried to keep you from going out alone after dark."

"You could have told me," I grumble half-heartedly, my mind still spinning.

Sable clears her throat. "What did you see, Hazel?"

Her tone is gentle and my anger cools. I chew my lip, willing myself to go back in memory. "Um, two wolves came at us. And then Slate was there, and then he wasn't and there was another wolf, and then a bunch of them, and they ran off. And Slate..."

I look from Sable to Heath. His face is pensive. I wish I could read his thoughts, to know what he is keeping from me. The memory and my own words keep turning over in my head.

At the risk of sounding truly unhinged, I turn to Slate. "Please tell me you didn't magically somehow turn into that wolf. 'Cause that would be ridiculous." My attempt at a joking tone fails. "But it kind of looked like it. I mean, where were you?"

Slate's face is stone. He doesn't reply but instead looks to Heath. There is something challenging in his expression.

"Never mind, I was so freaked, I couldn't see straight. Sorry, I'm out of it." I force a weak laugh. No one responds.

Sable breaks the silence, addressing my uncle. "Someone needs to reassure this girl."

Heath sighs. "Alright." He gives Slate the slightest nod.

"Hazel." Slate's voice is cautious and gentle. My skin prickles with apprehension. "You saw right. I shifted into my wolf to protect you."

Suspicious, I narrow my eyes. They had to be pranking me. I try to come up with a joke or snarky response. But after seeing those two predators racing toward us, I've got nothing.

"I would never hurt you. I'd only ever protect you." Those green eyes are wide and sincere. Is he concerned I'm scared of *him*?

I slowly inhale. "So, is this something you do often?"

The corner of Slate's mouth quirks up the smallest bit. "Yeah."

"Oh." He sounds more like he's admitting he strips on the weekends, not that he's some sort of supernatural. "For how long?"

"Since I was eight," he answers without missing a beat.

"Cool." I need a second. I squeeze my eyes shut, pressing my fingers on the bridge of my nose. "Okay, does anyone else do this?"

Heath answers, "Everyone living here is a wolf shifter."

To learn an entire small community I'm hoping to join turns into canines on the weekends is next-level bonkers.

"Are you kidding me?" I grind out, swallowing.

"I'm sorry." Heath rests his forearms on his knees, leaning toward me.

"You're telling me I've been staying in a literal fucking wolf pack?" I can't decide if I'm hysterical again or simply amused and exhausted. Or some mix of all three.

"Hazel." Heath's tone is severe. "This is our biggest secret. Absolutely no one can know; you can't tell even your mom or Aurora."

"Of course, I would never."

"I appreciate that." Heath runs his hand through his hair, looking as tired as I feel. "I would have trusted you with this secret years ago, but humans are not allowed to know." His mouth tightens. "If the other packs find out you know, there will be consequences."

"Oh."

"That's why I wanted you to go. So something like this couldn't happen. It endangers you." All of his protectiveness and concern over safety starts to make sense.

"Wait." I shift my weight, tugging my blanket around me. "Does this mean my dad could...?"

Heath hesitates, a sad smile curving his mouth. "Yes. Your dad was a wolf shifter."

"Am I part *wolf shifter* too?" The term feels foreign to my tongue.

"No." A sense of loss washes over me for something I never had, something I don't even want. "That's why I visited so often when you were about seven to ten, to make sure."

My brain has run out of bandwidth. I open my mouth and close it again.

"She needs rest," Slate insists, his brows drawn tight in concern.

"Good idea. We can talk about it tomorrow." Heath stands, offering me his hand. Tentatively, I take it and allow myself to be pulled up. Slate shadows me.

"Hazel, I need to handle some things. We need to find those rogue wolves. Someone will stay with you, just in case. Try to get some sleep."

I nod, numbly plodding to my room, the blanket trailing behind me.

SLATE

Hazel looks smaller curled up in bed, her arm tucked on her head. I'd give anything to comfort her, but instead I latch the door to give her privacy.

Fisher stands by the door and Heath walks to him, exchanging quiet words. They arrange a guard rotation, but the idea of someone else watching over her feels wrong.

"Alpha, I would prefer to stay with her." My voice is quiet, but he knows it isn't a request. I rarely ask for anything, but after fighting two rogue wolves for her, he cannot deny me.

Heath's jaw ticks. He isn't happy with me, but he is a skilled leader and knows when his people are reaching their limit. With a curt nod, he leads Fisher out.

I rest my forehead against Hazel's door for a moment, grounding myself. Her addictive scent wraps around me as I listen to her uneven breathing. She isn't asleep yet. Maybe she's hungry- - she didn't have dinner. The only thing I can find in Heath's cabinets is bread and peanut butter, so I make her a sandwich. I lightly knock on her door and hear a soft, "Yeah."

Easing the door open, I take in her disheveled hair, as if she had been turning over in her bed unable to get comfortable.

"Thanks." She takes the plate, relief softening her features. "Are you going to watch me eat?"

Sure, I'd watch her eat, but I should have some food too. Shrugging, I return to the kitchen and slap together another sandwich. She watches me as I sit on the bed across from her, a half-smile on her face as she takes a bite.

"I still can't even comprehend this," she murmurs. I don't know what to say. "No one was going to tell me?"

"No," I say.

"That sucks." She sounds more sad than petulant.

"Humans who find out about us either have to stay, like if we find a human partner. Or they are killed."

She jerks up, eyes wide. "Seriously?"

"We can't risk the world knowing. We'd never be safe again," I try to explain. As her face pales, I know I shouldn't have told her - it's too much. Heath omitted these details for a reason.

"So does that mean I'm stuck here and I can't leave?"

"No, of course not."

"I hope you guys aren't planning on killing me then." She laughs weakly.

My lip curls into a snarl. "I'd kill anyone who tried."

"Woah, but thank you." She tucks her hair behind her ears.

"You can leave whenever you want to. We trust you to keep it secret. But we need to make sure no one else finds out you're aware of what we are." I need to stop talking. I'm scaring her, but she deserves to hear the truth. Standing, I take her plate and stack it on mine.

"Are you leaving?" She squeaks, surprising me.

"I'll stay outside your door until Heath comes back," I reassure her.

"Could you maybe stay in here?" Her words are slow and faltering.

I can't refuse her. Nodding, I step out long enough to set the plates in the sink. Then I'm heading for the second bed in her room. She grabs my hand as I pass. Against my better judgment, I let her pull me down beside her. Her eyes search for permission and I gladly give it to her. I'd give her anything.

It's incredible she trusts me, even after discovering I'm not quite as human as she is. She nestles into my chest, curling into me. It feels so right to wrap my arms around her. I've wanted to hold her like this from the first night at the fire when she looked at me with the stars reflecting in her eyes.

"You know, my mom always said I was weird like my dad," she whispers. "It always made me proud. I barely knew him, only vague memories." She quiets. "She loved him so much, but he wasn't even honest with her. She has no idea about this huge part of who he was. And it turns out I'm nothing like him."

I squeeze her tighter for a second. "You are, though. Everyone talks about how kind and compassionate he was. You are the same."

Hazel's breath wavers. I tuck my chin and I can see tears welling in her eyes. Reaching up, I brush them away as they fall.

"Our dads were friends. He talked about him a lot. How great he was," I share.

Hazel raises her face toward me. "Your dad?" She asks, her question tentative. I never talk about him to anyone, but suddenly I want to share with her. Somehow, I know she'll understand.

"He was the Beta. I wanted to live up to his example."

"You do." She speaks against my chest, the vibration like butterflies. "You're a protector. He would be so proud."

"He raised me by himself. He was a great dad," I share, my grief surging for a moment before it ebbs again.

"I was only five when my dad died," she shares, her voice rasping. "My mom has her own demons. She's fought addiction my whole life. But she's been doing good the last few years."

"That's tough." My chest aches for her. I can't imagine the struggle of your only parent being an addict. She's resilient.

"I had to grow up quickly and take care of my sister."

"You should never have had to do that. You deserve to be taken care of," I growl, not trying to hide the animalistic noise under my words now.

She shivers. Worried she's cold, I rub circles down her back. "I wasn't lucky enough to grow up here." Her tone is a little bitter.

"I wish you had."

"Me too. But I don't belong here." She untucks one of her arms and snakes it around my waist, underneath mine. Heat blooms where her hand presses.

"It doesn't matter you aren't a shifter. You're still from here. You belong here if you want to." Heath would be furious, but I believe it.

A soft, contented noise comes from her throat. "Thank you for watching out for me, even when I was a bitch about it."

"If that was you being bitchy, I think I like you," I murmur, freezing when my words echo back to me. Feeling shaky, I try to continue, "Besides, you didn't know what was going on. I'm sorry." I kiss the top of her head, giving in to the urge.

"I like you too." Her sleepy voice is almost inaudible.

My breathing slows to match hers as she drifts off. I wait as long as I dare before untangling myself and returning to the isolation of the kitchen. I can still feel her heat against my chest and across my ribs.

IX
TOURS &
TRANSFORMATIONS

HAZEL

I wake up on top of the quilt still fully dressed. Someone took off my shoes at some point. I feel the ghost of another person as the memory of Slate's embrace drifts back. Smiling, I bury my face in my pillow as my cheeks heat. It's silly to be excited about our cuddle time - he was merely comforting me.

In daylight, the memories of wolves feels false, like it was CGI. Maybe I'll go into the kitchen and everyone will jump out and yell "Surprise!"

No such luck. Marigold sits in the kitchen, sipping apple juice with her feet propped up on the chair next to her. Her freckled face is adorable with twin braids framing her bright expression. "Good morning, sunshine."

I sigh, glancing at the clock on the stove. 11:36 A.M.. That's late, even for me.

"Did you need to teach today?" I ask, guilt edging my words.

She smirks. "It's Saturday."

"Oh." I've lost my sense of time completely. With a grunt, I drop into a kitchen chair opposite her and rest my forehead on my arms. A plate scrapes as Marigold slides it across the table. The smell of chocolate croissants is the only thing that can pull me from my muddled confusion.

"Thanks," I say, grabbing one. "Thanks, these are my favorite," I say between bites.

"Slate brought them over." She winks.

"He did?" After guarding me all night, he got up early to get my favorite breakfast. "Where, how?"

Marigold giggles. "Clove makes a ton of pastries at once, and then freezes most of them. She keeps them under lock and key so he must have begged."

"That's sweet," I say, losing myself in the flaky pastry.

"So Heath asked me to keep you company today and answer whatever questions you had." She rubs her hands together. "I was thinking we owe you a proper tour."

"Sounds good." Finishing my breakfast, I head to the bathroom and change clothes. After yesterday's chaos, I opt for a workout set of leggings and my softest hoodie. Instead of sandals, I grab my old tennis shoes.

"You doing okay?" Marigold asks as we leave the cabin.

"I mean, I found out the little community I wanted to join is actually a pack of magical wolf-people." I laugh awkwardly. "Totally not a big deal."

"I can't even imagine," she empathizes. "I mean, I've known since I was a kid. It's my normal. But it's all new to you."

"I could have grown up here if my dad hadn't left," I say softly.

The conversation with Slate last night rattles around in my head. The unfairness needles at me.

"Hazel, he left because he loved your mom and didn't want to put her in danger," Marigold says.

"Of course, but she could've lived here. He didn't give her the option." I know it isn't entirely logical, but it still hurts. "Like they're going to make me leave."

Marigold frowns at me, her feet slowing. "Hazel, we're on your side. I'll support you in whatever you want. But you need to listen to your uncle and try to see the big picture."

"Ouch." She's right. I'm navigating a world I don't understand, and I need to listen and learn. For today, I can at least get my bearings and stop the pity-party.

"I'm sorry." She pulls me into a hug.

"Thanks." I squeeze back. I've never had a friend like her and I don't want to let her go, or any of them.

She spins, throwing her arms out. "Welcome to your official tour of Bracken Creek Pack. First, the training room." She points behind us.

"Oh?" I frown. "What's the deal there?"

"We learn defense and offense, both in human and wolf form."

The strangeness hits me again and I want to laugh in disbelief. "I guess that makes more sense for a wolf pack than a group of forest rangers." Her laughter echoes in the trees.

As we walk, she points out the other buildings. "You know the supply store and the school, of course."

The red and chrome diner gleams from the opposite side of the meadow. Shaking my head, I say, "Now everyone eating free dinners together every night makes a bit more sense too."

She grins at me. "What you probably didn't realize, is that everything in the store is free too. We only take what we need, but it's pretty cool."

I pause, propping my fists on my hips. "Okay, so what is my uncle? The king?"

"He's our Alpha." Marigold raises her chin, meeting my gaze with confidence.

"What about everyone else?"

"Slate is his Beta, which is like his second-in-command."

"What?" My face scrunches up in bewilderment.

"Yeah. Heath has been mentoring him for a few years." She nods. "And then Hawthorne is third in command, called the Gamma. He is considered the Mediator and helps with disputes within the pack and our relationship with other packs too. It's a pretty important job."

"You've got the whole Greek alphabet going on." I say, trying to keep track of everything.

"Let's see. The twins' dad, Fisher, is Delta. He is like a trainer. And my dad is a Zeta, which is like a guard or a fighter, along with Lazuli and Cassia. Remember the cute couple with the new baby?"

"That's a lot of positions." Already the information is swirling around, getting confused. Hopefully there won't be a quiz later.

Marigold shrugs. "It keeps everything organized and running smoothly."

"Anything else, while we are at it?"

"There's also Thetas. They guard and fight too, or whatever, but they're more like scouts. It's a step down from Zeta."

"Who is that?" I glance around like they might all pop out to surprise me.

"Aven. She's older than us and keeps to herself. And then the newest is Vale. He's seventeen."

"Seventeen?" I raise an eyebrow.

"Yeah, we usually start training for a position around fifteen. Trying different work skills. And usually, everyone is done with their school credits by sixteen or seventeen anyway. "

"That's why you only teach the elementary kids?"

She nods. "Like my brother, he started an apprenticeship with our grandma."

The image of Sable tending to Slate's shoulder flashed in my mind. "She's not exactly a nurse is she?"

"Healer." She smiles proudly.

"Of course, why wouldn't you have a magical healer?" I joke.

"I don't know about magic or not, but she's great with fixing people up. We heal faster than humans and we respond better to natural remedies like herbs and stuff like that. That's what she is really good at."

"Makes sense. Slate wasn't even bleeding last night by the time she checked him out." Shaking my head, I try to clear the image of his bare chest and the blood dripping from the wound. My absolute terror at seeing him hurt.

"Hungry?" she asks, leading me toward Crickett's diner.

We grab plates and tacos with various toppings. I devour my first taco, savoring the spicy beef filling. Crickett is an incredible chef. It's impossible to stay upset with good food in my stomach and a sunny day with a friend. Things seem much better already.

Mentally, I review what she's told me. "So you're a teacher, Slate is Beta. What about the twins?"

"Oh, same as they said." She sips her drink. "Cedar is a gardener, and Onyx is trying to become a Theta. He's stuck doing odd jobs at the moment. But aside from those rankings I mentioned, everyone else has normal jobs."

"Normal, except you turn into wolves?" I shoot back, a smile tugging at my mouth.

"You're stuck on that part, aren't you?" she teases.

"I think that's very reasonable."

Two matching figures slide onto the benches beside us. "I heard you're in the know now." Onyx grins, shaking his dirty blonde hair off his forehead.

"How are you handling everything, Hazel?" Cedar's clear blue eyes are concerned.

"It's starting to sink in, I think. Not completely freaking out anymore."

Onyx raises his eyebrows. "Anything else we can do to help?"

"Any questions?" Marigold presses.

Everything about this experience is strange. A whole new world has opened up, one I had no idea existed. Now that I've had time to process, I'm curious about the actual transformation. Shifting, they call it.

"How often do you do the wolf thing? Do you have to change at the full moon? Is there a limit?" I blush, the questions tumbling out of me. It feels too personal to ask.

"We can shift whenever we want to. It's a little tiring, but not too bad," Marigold explains. "Not something you'd want to do several times in the same day though."

"The moon being full makes our urge to shift somewhat stronger, but we are still in control," Cedar adds.

Marigold scrunches her nose. "You know how kids get kind of crazy at the full moon? It's like that."

"Okay, is it instantaneous? Or does your body, like, morph and change?" I chew my lip, feeling awkward.

"Oh, totally instant. Can you imagine? That would suck." She laughs.

"One more question. I'm sorry," I preface, my face burning. "What's up with the whole sweatpants and no shirt thing?"

Onyx barks out a laugh. "Clothes don't change with us. Unless you want to be all tangled up, you've got to strip. We can basically leap out of our sweats at least, but the shirt has gotta come off or it'll tear or you'll get caught up in it."

"You jump out of your pants? I might need to see that," I joke, picturing sweats falling around a wolf's ankles.

"I'll take my pants off for you any time," Onyx flirts.

"Careful. Slate will definitely rip your throat out now," Marigold warns, voice low.

Scowling, I look between them, mouth open but silent.

Cedar tilts his head. "Are you and Slate-"

"No," I cut him off.

"Someone needs to tell him that." Onyx snorts.

Marigold squeezes my wrist. "We shouldn't have said anything." She glares at Onyx.

"Why, though?" I ask gently, hoping for an actual answer.

She purses her lips, thinking. "He is kind of acting like you're his girlfriend. He won't let any other guys even look at you."

"Seriously?" I huff, irritated Slate is acting like a caveman. "You know what? It doesn't matter. I'm supposed to be leaving."

"You can't leave," Cedar says, like it is the most obvious thing in the world.

"I don't think I have a choice."

"Fuck that. You're part of the pack now." Onyx crosses his arms.

Affection blooms in my chest as sadness balls up in my throat. "I'm not."

"I don't think Slate will want you to leave," Marigold muses, staring into space for a moment. "And if you want to stay..."

"Oh, he wants me gone," I insist. It's easier to focus on the times he's pushed me away, and not on the heat between us last night. Right before the wolves attacked, when I was sure he was about to kiss me. And afterward, he held me so tenderly. My skin heats thinking about it.

"Hazel." Cedar's tone is firm. I snap up, listening. "He doesn't want you gone. The opposite, actually. But ultimately it's up to you and Heath." I nod, mutely.

Marigold has had enough of the somber topic. She claps her hands together. "This is her welcome tour. What else can we show her, boys?"

"What do you want to see?" Onyx asks, smirking.

I take a breath, gathering my courage. "Could I see someone turn into a wolf? Shift? Is that weird, I don't want to offend anyone." My words get away from me as I lose my nerve.

"No, it's cool," Onyx reassures me.

"We better not do it here. Heath is still maintaining she doesn't know anything," Marigold cautions.

"Training gym. Everyone is patrolling for the day. It'll be empty," Onyx suggests, leaping up. He cleans up our plates and jogs to catch up.

We duck into the industrial-style building. The walls are metal as well, with a huge rolling door that's currently lowered. A selection of staffs, crossbows, and a row of increasingly large daggers line the far wall. I'm a little surprised, expecting a typical gym.

A small collection of gym equipment huddles in one corner, mostly weights. Benches span the right wall, and in the center is a collection of sparring rings marked with paint on the floor.

"This is really something," I whisper.

Cedar turns, opening his arms wide to indicate the room. "This is our dad's domain. He is very serious about everyone being capable and ready for anything."

"Okay, boys, show her what you've got!" Marigold croons.

Suddenly nervous, I bounce between my heels, twisting my ring around my finger. "How do you do it?" I ask.

Marigold winks and motions to the twins. Onyx tugs his shirt off his head, tossing it to the side. My gaze traces the dark tribal tattoos across his shoulders and chest, curling around his ribs. It makes me think of Slate. I drag my eyes up, seeing Onyx grin at me.

In an instant, he is gone and a dark gray and black wolf is trotting forward. He's larger than I expected, especially up close. I react on instinct, leaping back as my brain screams danger. Marigold grabs my arm and holds me steady.

"It's only Onyx. It's okay," she soothes. I take a shaky breath and repeat her words in my head until I am reasonably calm.

The dark wolf, Onyx, freezes, watching me until my breathing slows. He creeps forward, his ears flat against his head. As he gets close, the fear rises up my throat, choking me, but I steel myself and stay still. He bumps my hand with his nose. It's cool and dry.

He does it again, nudging my hand up and over his fluffy head. From years of petting friends' dogs, I automatically curl my fingers into his fur and scratch under his ear.

Onyx cocks his head, his mouth opening to reveal an impressive array of teeth over which his tongue lolls. He looks like a giant puppy.

"Seriously, dude," Cedar mutters.

"You too, Cedar," Marigold prompts. Her mouth curls into a devious smile. She watches closely as Cedar folds his shirt and sets it on the closest bench.

In an instant, he is replaced by a reddish-brown wolf with gold dusting his back. I'm less startled this time. He simply sits, staring at me with familiar aqua eyes. Behind him sits a crumpled pair of sweatpants, making me giggle.

Squatting, I study Onyx. His fur is thick and around his ears, it's super soft. "Can they understand me?" I ask Marigold.

Cedar nods. The human gesture is unnerving on a wild animal.

"But you can't, like, talk?" I ask stupidly.

Marigold light laugh floats around me. "No, but we can kind of sense each other. Like a general feeling of their emotions and rough location."

"Cool." I look from Cedar to Onyx again. "Can they turn back any time?"

Onyx shifts, still grinning and now completely nude. He's sitting on the floor facing me.

"Oh my gosh." I throw my hand up and turn away. He cackles.

Marigold scolds him, and when I dare to turn around, Cedar is pulling his shirt down over his botanical tattoos. Onyx is still bare-chested but at least he put his pants back on.

"Really?" I ask, wrinkling my nose.

"We're all used to it, sorry." He shrugs, not looking one bit apologetic. "Your turn, Goldie."

Marigold slips her dress over her shoulder and I look away. Cedar and Onyx both politely avert their eyes, but I can't resist spying on Cedar to see if his eyes wander. They don't.

Marigold is a pretty reddish-golden wolf, like Cedar but much lighter. She wags her tail and it's precious. Her dark eyes against her light fur make her look like a puppy.

"You're so pretty." I crouch down, looking from her paws to her fluffy ears. She ducks her head as if embarrassed, but her tail wags faster.

Standing, I rub my hands over my arms, tugging at where my hoodie is snug at my wrists. "I appreciate this, guys. Makes me feel less like I'm being pranked."

Marigold shifts, shimmying into her dress. "That's all there is to it, no big deal."

I raise an eyebrow. "No big deal? I'm pretty sure you guys are freaking magic."

"Magic is merely a phenomenon scientists haven't figured out yet," Cedar says under his breath.

Onyx bumps into him and coughs in a way that sounds suspiciously like, "Nerd."

The twins produce granola bars from a nearby bin and we all settle on the benches. They tell me about their first time shifting and how much fun it is. That feeling of unfairness rears up again, but I breathe it out and smile. They are sharing a huge part of who they are, and I love them for it.

The door clangs open and Fisher strides in. His posture is tight and his expression alarmed. Cedar, Onyx, and Marigold jump up. He closes the distance, his lips a thin line. I expect to be told off for using the space or something.

"We have a problem. Hazel, I need you to come with me. Cedar and Marigold, stay to each of her sides, Onyx behind." Orders given, he turns and heads to the door.

Frowning, I look between my friends. What the hell? But they don't question Fisher, but stand and square their shoulders. Marigold takes my arm and urges me forward. I blink at her.

We file out and step into formation. Marigold takes my hand and squeezes it. "It's going to be okay. Heath's got it," she whispers, but I don't miss how tight her expression is. My lungs constrict, anxiety rearing up and causing my heart to pound.

"Shit," mutters Onyx. I look past Fisher's back. There are more people in the meadow than there should be. Strangers in groups with expressions ranging from angry to bored.

Slate appears, taking Cedar's spot beside me. He ducks his head, his breath ghosting over my ear. In any other circumstance, I would be thrilled with the attention, but from the tension in his shoulders and the tightness of his jaw, this is not flirting.

"I'm so sorry, Hazel. Another pack knows you're here." He looks furious, but his voice is soft. "I'm not going to let anything happen to you."

Instinctively, I cling to his arm. His lashes flutter as his eyes flick down and back up to my face, something determined in his eyes.

Heath stands in the center, his thumbs hooked in his pockets and his stance wide. He exudes confidence. Hawthorne and Elm stand on either side and others continue the formation. It must be the Thetas and Zetas.

Clove takes Fisher's hand. Fern and Crickett assemble a line on either side of us. The energy is volatile and my heart speeds up.

Slate snakes his arm around my waist. The heat of him is grounding. He looks down at me for a moment. "Stay right with me. It's going to be fine."

"You're freaking me out," I whisper. "What's going on?"

He presses his lips together in a worried frown. "Those two wolves got away. They must have been from another pack. Now the other local packs are coming to investigate, but Heath will keep you safe."

Looking into his eyes, I can see the unspoken, *I'll keep you safe*, but I'm afraid he can't. Not if all these wolf shifters have shown up wanting to enforce their rules since I know their secrets.

With his free arm, Slate rubs his palm along my other arm and pulls me into him.

"It's going to be okay," Marigold reassures.

"Doesn't sound like it," I hiss. Marigold eyes Slate and a small smile flickers across her face. "What?" I demand.

"He's getting his scent all over you," Marigold whispers.

Slate grips my waist and pulls my back into his front. His cheek rests against my hair for a second. I twist, frowning at him. He doesn't budge, touching as much of me as he can. I squirm. He's not subtle.

"So they know you are protected by him," Marigold explains, angling closer to my ear. My skin flushes.

Slate glares at Marigold. "They're not getting near her," he growls, and it vibrates through me. I can't help but shiver.

Clove glances over at us and tips her chin up in approval. My friends cocoon around me, but their concern is so thick, I'm nauseous.

Heath opens his hands as if in an invitation. Three men step forward, their people behind them. The center man is tall and lean, with dark gray hair cut short. "Zephyr, Alpha of the Ironcrest Pack," Slate murmurs in my ear. "To the left in the leather jacket is Ferris. Alpha of the Granite Ridge Pack" I can't miss the disdain in his voice.

I narrow my eyes at Ferris. He looks like a biker with a short beard of blonde and silver, and angry brows drawn low over his pale blue eyes.

A thin woman with red lipstick steps up to stand his shoulder. Her dark hair, sharp jaw, and full mouth look oddly familiar. Slate goes very still against me. My eyes go wide at a flash of platinum behind her. It's the boy from the coffee shop. Jasper stands among Ferris's cronies.

"What the hell?" I gasp, reaching up to grab Slate's forearm across my chest.

Jasper stares ahead blankly. Does he know *I'm* the human they're here to deal with?

Marigold squeezes my wrist. "That's Ferris's mate, Sienna, and their son, Jasper is the blonde one." I tear my eyes away and glance at Marigold. I can sense there is more she wants to share. She presses her lips together for a second. "That's Slate's sorry excuse for a mom."

My mouth drops open. Slate tightens his hold, his hands clenched over my shoulders. Twisting in his arms, I reach up and gently touch his jaw, tracing my fingers down his neck.

"Hey, it's okay," I mutter. He breathes out, the spell broken as he leans into my touch and dips his head. Pressing his face into my hair, he breaths in slowly. We stand that way for a moment, my hand on his neck and his lips in my hair.

Another man steps up, his skin and hair darker. His irritated looks seem to be directed at Ferris or Zephyr, not Heath.

"That's Cashel. Alpha of the Valley Pack west of us. They're friendly." Slate identifies the third group.

"When was the last time four packs met?" Heath sounds casual, but I know him well enough to hear the underlying threat. "I would have appreciated some notice. I am not prepared to host you properly."

Zephyr clears his throat. "Alpha Heath, good to see you. We won't be here long, but we were told you have an unclaimed human girl living with your pack."

Me, the human girl. I take a breath but it doesn't help. I can't get enough air into my lungs. I'm grateful Slate is holding me upright.

Heath's reply is smooth. "Our only visitor is my niece."

"Is she one of us?" Zephyr's question cuts in.

Heath pauses. "She is a human born of wolves. She is part of my pack and under my protection."

"She's human. Doesn't matter who her parents were," Ferris accuses.

"Alpha Ferris, I suspect the two rogue wolves who attacked my pack last night were your minions," Heath responds casually, leveling his own accusation.

Ferris waves his hand in dismissal. "I was not aware you had any problems with rogues. My pack is all accounted for."

"Regardless. My niece is not just a human. Our law does not apply to her in that way." As Ferris opens his mouth, Heath continues, "We can discuss this as a full tribunal of Alphas if you insist. But we need to set a date and gather Nyx as well."

Cashel is nodding, but Ferris looks murderous. "There is no need. Our laws are clear and I will happily enforce them if you fail to." His words snake toward me.

"I don't think so," Heath replies.

Ferris steps forward. Everyone's posture changes minutely. They're getting ready for a fight; I realize with a jolt of panic.

"Heath, I'm sorry, but I believe our laws are clear in this matter," Zephyr weighs in.

Marigold and Slate both go rigid. I can feel the energy rapidly escalating toward violence. I latch onto Slate, digging my fingers into his arm. He takes a deep breath and opens his mouth.

"She's claimed." Slate's voice is clear, carrying over our front line. It's met with silence. Then several voices all speak at once.

"Who has claimed her?" Ferris demands.

"Excuse me?" barks Zephyr.

And I swear I can hear Jasper say, "What the hell?"

"That went from zero to a hundred real quick," Marigold mutters. Everyone turns to look at us. Slate is undeterred, loosening his hold on me and raising his chin.

"I have." Slate steps forward, tucking me behind him. Our friends move with us, keeping me surrounded.

"Prove it," Ferris snarls.

Slate's eyes narrow, his tone sharp. "We haven't completed the marking yet. Since she is human, we want to be cautious. But we will do it very soon."

"See, Ferris, we have no problem," Cashel retorts.

"I want it verified."

Zephyr sighs. "Fine, send someone to check on them tomorrow. Boy, you'll have to complete the claiming tonight. She'll be fine, I'm sure."

Ferris glares, his eyes are slits.

"I've been away from my pack long enough" Zephyr raises his hand and his team moves out.

Heath nods. "Good to see you, Zephyr. Cashel. Have a safe journey home."

"Be well, my friend." Cashel smiles and then leads his people away.

"You have until noon tomorrow," Ferris growls.

"I look forward to greeting your representative tomorrow and sending them back to you with confirmation. Now get off my land." Heath's tone is pleasant, but it's clear he's lost his patience with Ferris.

"Gladly." Ferris turns with a flourish of his leather jacket. I spot Jasper ducking into the group. How could he be the charming friend from town and also stand with the family threatening me? It doesn't matter - I'll never see him again, especially if I never set foot in that coffee shop again.

As Fisher and Hawthorne escort our visitors out, Heath turns to us with an unreadable expression. "Meeting, now."

SLATE

Hazel pulls her knees up and hugs herself, perched in a rolling office chair. She looks so delicate, I can't peel my eyes off of her as I settle beside her. My hand grips the back of her chair as I keep my expression carefully neutral. Inside, chaos swirls. Hawthorne eyes me, his brows furrowed. Heath paces along the wall.

"What are our options?" Heath asks.

"We have about twenty hours. We could transport her away. Or Slate can claim her," Hawthorne muses, "I don't think a deception is likely to work."

Heath nods, pausing. His palms flatten on the table, his hulking form leaning forward. "I think getting her out of the area is our best choice."

Hazel digs her nails into her arms hard enough to leave a mark. No one is considering what she wants, nor do they seem to be taking my offer seriously.

My teeth grind together, anger cutting through the sense of disorientation. She deserves better, and it's ultimately her decision, not theirs.

"They'll hunt her." My voice is hoarse.

"And they'll try to take sanctions against us for letting her go," Hawthorne adds thoughtfully.

Heath narrows his eyes and I realize how angry he is. Somehow he suppresses the rage from filtering through our pack bond, but it glitters in his eyes. "Hazel does not have to be claimed and have her life upended just because of some rogue wolves and Ferris making threats." He says Ferris like someone would mention rotting garbage.

"Don't I have a say in this?" she says, her voice shaking, "I've said all along that I want to stay."

My muscles tense. She wants to stay now that she knows what we are? If so, I'll do what is necessary to allow her to stay. Frankly, I can no longer imagine my pack without her in it. She might only agree to my proposal so she can stay or to keep herself safe. Whatever her reasoning, I'd still offer it to her.

"This is exactly why I didn't want you staying very long. In case something like this happened. All it took was one mistake and your life is now forfeit," Heath growls at her and she shrinks in her seat.

I want to launch myself across the table at him. I've never gone against my Alpha before, but for Hazel, I would without hesitation. "I am ready to claim her. I will keep her safe," I say, looking boldly into Heath's eyes. His will presses back against mine, but I hold my ground.

"I want to stay with Slate," Hazel murmurs.

"You don't know-" Heath argues.

She interrupts him, her voice rising, "Then tell me!"

Heath slumps into the seat beside Hawthorne with a rough sigh. "Claiming is what mates do. It's our version of marriage. And it's permanent. No divorce."

Hazel glances at me. I'm waiting for her to change her mind, but she's studying me as if trying to read my mind. Resolute, I keep my face placid. This will be her decision and I'll submit to whatever she wants.

"What's involved?" she asks.

Hawthorne folds his hands on the table. "A bite. It leaves a permanent mark."

Her voice shakes. "A bite? Like he'll bite me? Where?"

"Here." I press my thumb to her shoulder muscle right where it connects to her neck, above her clavicle. My voice is soft, just for her. "I'll be as gentle as I can, but it'll scar. That's kind of the point."

My fingers rub circles at the base of her neck, trying to comfort her. I can see a thousand thoughts and emotions in those honey eyes. It's so intimate, we could be the only two people in the world.

Fidgeting with her ring again, she opens her mouth, her eyes never leaving mine. "Yes."

Yes she understands? Or yes she wants to be with me? There is no room for misunderstandings.

"Do you want to be mated to me?" I ask.

She tenses. "It's like being romantic partners? Permanently?"

"Yes, but I won't require anything from you. This is for your protection."

"Are you sure you want to be stuck with a human for the rest of your life?" Her smile is self-deprecating.

"I'd do anything for you." The words are spoken without thought. Her mouth opens slightly as she gazes at me.

Heath sets an elbow on the table and pinches the bridge of his nose. "Are you absolutely sure, Hazel?"

She flinches, a blush spreading across her face.

"You need to understand that if you decide to leave, it'll cause Slate pain to be apart. It's more than a promise or commitment. You're tied together on a deeper level."

"If she wanted to leave, I'd endure it for her to be happy," I say quietly. "I watched my dad handle it for years."

"Your father was in agony," Heath snaps, his careful control slipping.

I don't care if I'm risking the same pain he lived with, pain that ultimately killed him. For her, I'd be damned.

Hazel hesitates and I watch the facts connecting in her mind. "Your mom left. Didn't she? For that other Alpha. And it hurt your dad because they were mates?" My jaw clenches. I don't like to think about my mother and I never wanted my deepest wound exposed to her. She reaches out and rests her palm on my thigh. "I would never do that to you. If we ever leave, it'll be together."

My heart stutters. "If that's what you want," I say.

Heath scrubs his face. "I can't convince you otherwise, can I?"

She shakes her head. "This is the safest option, isn't it?"

"Yes, most likely," Hawthorne says.

"Then that's my choice."

Heath scrubs his face. "I can't convince you otherwise, can I?"

"You're the one who always worries about my safety." She raises her chin, daring him to argue.

I can't help but smirk. She's been so frustrated with rules and the constant concern over her safety. Even though it was necessary and valid, I love seeing her throw it back at him.

Heath sighs, resigned. "Fine. Get to Slate's cabin. Stay out of sight until tomorrow."

"Thank you," Hazel says, her voice fading. "I know this isn't what you wanted for me. But it feels right."

"I'm glad." Heath leans back in his seat, crossing his arms. "Be careful."

"Thank you, Alpha." Rising, I dip my head in respect. Hazel stands, her hand slipped into mine as naturally as any mates. My chest squeezes with something akin to affection as I lead her to the door.

"Slate?" Heath stops us. "If you guys don't go through with it, it's fine. We'll figure something else out."

Hazel squeezes my hand and leans into me as if saying she's made up her mind and it's me. I nod briefly and let the door close behind us. She clings to me, allowing me to guide us home.

X

KISSES & CLAIMING

HAZEL

Marigold and Cedar delivered to-go containers of dinner, but I hardly taste it. I set aside the half-eaten casserole and sit quietly watching Slate finish his portion. His mossy eyes stare back, but our silence is not uncomfortable. It's thick, apprehensive, full of questions waiting to be spoken.

He makes swift work of cleaning up while I slip into the bathroom and wash up. Cool water on my cheeks soothes my racing pulse. What am I doing? Agreeing to essentially marry a stranger - one who has been hot and cold, protective, reclusive.

When I return, Slate holds out a glass of wine. The weight of the glass in my hand feels good, and I take a tentative sip. It's crisp and earthy. Smiling, my next drink is longer, allowing the alcohol to soften the edges of my anxiety. Slate is watching me like I'm a skittish animal.

The silence suddenly feels uncomfortable, like we should have started speaking long ago. "This feels weird. Like we're having a shotgun wedding. But not..." I'm rambling. "Sorry."

"It's okay."

I need him to do something to distract me or I'm going to start spiraling. "Do you guys normally do some sort of ceremony or something?"

"Not really, unless you're the Alpha or heir and it's an arranged-type thing." Shrugging, he sets his glass down. "But people usually ask someone to be their mate in a nice way. Kinda like a proposal, I guess. It's common to have a party afterward. We can do that if you want."

"I'm good. I don't like that much attention." I twirl the stem of my wine glass, watching the remaining liquid slosh as a way to avoid his intense gaze.

He steps closer, the motion fluid. I'm vividly aware he's a predator. It's undeniable. I should have known the first time I saw him. His lissome movements never seemed totally human to me.

"Hazel," he says, his husky voice drawing me in. "Do you want to be my mate and my partner? I have to know without a doubt."

I shouldn't. It's one thing to want to kiss him. But to want to commit to him for life? That's idiotic. But I do. I'm scared to admit how much I want him, or the fear I feel at the idea of being separated. Nothing outside of here makes sense any longer. He's my center of gravity. No boyfriend before was like this. The pull between us is cosmic, incapacitating, irrefutable.

He waits for my answer, still as a stone. Swallowing, I force my voice to work. "Yes."

Something in his expression flickers, a hint of worry or fear. "We have to be intimate for me to claim you. After today, you don't owe me anything."

"Are you doing this out of loyalty?" I ask, interrupting him. Cocking my head, I try to read him. "Is this you being a hero? Or do you actually want me as your girlfriend? Mate?"

As the light outside fades, his evergreen irises darken. My heart thrums in my throat and my skin warms until I feel feverish, burning and freezing simultaneously.

"I want you in every way you'll have me. Romantic partner, friend, protector."

"Oh," I say, my throat thick. "So romance it is."

He takes the glass from my hands and sets it on the counter. My stomach somersaults at the domineering move.

"I promise to be devoted to you," he murmurs as he closes the distance between us. Heat radiates off his body, washing away the ice prickling in my veins. I'm drawn to him and his irresistible words as his voice lowers, scraping against my ribs. "I'll do everything I can to make you happy."

"I'm pretty happy right now," I say in a breathy whisper. He hasn't even touched me and I might implode.

"Can I kiss you?" he asks.

Nodding, I reach for him, unable to restrain myself. His cotton shirt is worn soft. I glide my palms upwards over his pecs to hook around his neck and thread into his hair.

Adoration fizzes through my veins. He didn't hesitate to claim me in front of everyone, making this huge commitment to keep me safe, and he meant it. Not just fulfilling a duty, but offering me his heart.

I tip my chin up. Achingly slow, he bows his head. His cheek brushing mine is like fire. And by the time his lips finally meet mine, I'm desperate panting, on the verge of whimpering.

His touch is explosive. I press my body into him, my soft curves against his lean muscles. His hands grip my waist, fingers splayed to feel more of my stomach and hips as his tongue slips into my mouth.

I break the kiss off with a small gasp, trying to get enough oxygen to slow the pulse pounding in my ears. My fingers twist in the fabric of his shirt as I lean into his chest and steady myself.

"Are you nervous?" he whispers in my ear.

"No," I lie, shivering.

"Really?" A wicked grin lights up his features and I'm overwhelmed by how handsome he is. It's wildly unfair. He's so cool and confident. I want him ruffled, desperate, needy like I am.

Feeling deviant, I slip my hands under the edge of his t-shirt, against his bare skin. He's blazing hot to my touch.

"Are you sure you want to tie yourself to me? There's no undoing it." Each word is precise.

"I'm very sure."

He searches my face, concern softening his mouth into that pout I love. I can't help but rise on my toes and kiss him. His hands run up my back and tangle into my hair and I suck in that full bottom lip. He groans, sending spirals of desire through my stomach.

"You shouldn't," he murmurs against the crook of my jaw. "You should have left."

I tip my head to give him more access, and he rewards me with a rumbly growl while he nibbles the soft spot right below my ear.

"Don't tell me what I should want," I grind out, the words broken. It's hard to string words together when his tongue is on my skin. "I want you, I already did, and if you want me…"

I can't explain it, but from the first time we met, it's been this inevitable, unavoidable slide toward utter devotion. The threats from the other packs may have sped up the timeline, but I have no doubt we would have ended up here in the end. I know it in my bones.

"You're stuck with me now," he replies.

Irritated, I wrinkle my nose. "Maybe I want to be stuck with you," I growl, shoving him backward to emphasize my point. He allows me to push him onto his sofa, dragging me down with him.

I straddle him, my hair falling around us. He lays back, admiration all over his face as I lean over him.

"This is my home. I couldn't bear leaving now. I've never felt like I belonged anywhere, and then I met you and the pack." Tears prick my eyes. "When Heath told me to leave, I felt like my heart was being cut out. I know I shouldn't have, but there is something about it."

He cradles my face, his thumbs wiping away a tear that escaped. He listens with rapt attention, making no move to interrupt me.

"You were in the center of it," I finish.

"It's because you're pack," he whispers. "That's why it feels like home. You belong here."

I press a hand against his chest. His heart beats steadily against my palm. "Are we completely ready to be mates and make that commitment? Probably not. But I have no doubt it's where we are headed. I couldn't keep my hands off of you.

"I should be worried about *you*. You're the one tying yourself to me," I say, my voice raw.

He sighs. "I never stood a chance." His fingers thread through my hair. Tugging me down against his chest, he wraps me securely with both arms. When he speaks, I feel the vibrations in my ribcage. "I've heard pack members talk about meeting their mate. We don't date often, because when we finally fall for someone, that's it. It's like something clicks into place, or a bond that becomes unbreakable before you even realize what's happening."

"Do you feel like that?" I'm scared to ask, but I have to know. What if I'm depriving him of a true mate?

"Couldn't you tell?" His grip loosens and I sit up, trying to interpret his expression. "I was obsessed with you from the first time we met. I stayed outside your cabin at night." His eyes crinkle, amusement curving his beautiful mouth.

My cheeks burn. "Seriously?"

"The things I wanted to do to you. I thought I was going crazy." His fingers dig into my skin and heat floods my body. I'm suddenly very aware of my position straddling him.

"Yeah?" I whisper hoarsely. "Like what?'

He closes his eyes, his smile turning bashful. "Well, last time you were here, I desperately wanted to strip you down right here on this couch."

"I thought about you constantly, too. You kept taking your shirt off," I say.

"Like this?" Pushing himself to a seated position, he pulls his shirt over his head in one motion.

"Very distracting," I agree, enjoying my new position in his lap. I mirror him, pulling my shirt off and tossing it on the floor.

His green eyes are bright. Not bright, almost glowing – like an animal's eyes reflecting moonlight in the darkness. I gape at him, stunned. He frowns, cocking his head. "Um, your eyes..."

Slate falls back, his hand coming up to rake through his hair while his lips curve into a wry smirk. "Yeah, that happens," he says nonchalantly.

I lean forward to get a closer look. His dark lashes frame those captivating irises, now almost uncomfortable to look at.

"I was pretty worried you'd notice," he admits, "Before, when we first kissed."

"That's why you wouldn't look at me." I assumed it was out of embarrassment. "I definitely would have noticed."

"Do you think it's weird?" he asks, his tone vulnerable.

"I think it's incredible," I breathe, bringing my hand up to graze his cheek.

"You're amazing," he says reverently, and then it's like he can't stop praises from tumbling from his lips. "You're creative and funny and I can't get enough of you," he says, his words slow and heavy.

"I just thought you were super hot," I whisper, my lips tracing against his skin. "Look at you."

He barks out a laugh. "If I start talking about how beautiful you are, we won't get anything else done," he says darkly.

My breath is sharp, my insides going liquid. "I believe you were telling me all the things you imagined doing to me."

"Was I?" Looking thoughtful, he slides my bra strap off my shoulder and kisses the exposed skin. "When we were out by the creek, I could have bent you over one of those rocks." I don't let him finish that thought.

Our mouths crazy together in a searing, out of control, all-consuming kiss. Heat surges in my core as his tongue strokes mine. I can feel how he is hard beneath me. Those sweatpants don't hide anything. I can't resist rocking against him. He growls, his abs tightening, his fingers digging into my hips.

Gently, he rolls me over onto my back. The feel of his weight against me is luscious. Unable to stop, I kiss and suck my way down his neck.

"Hazel," he rasps and I feel it like a caress. He stares down into my eyes for a moment. "We don't have to do anything tonight if you don't want to. You're in charge."

"If we're doing what I want to do, don't plan on sleeping," I manage to say, ignoring the burn of a blush in my cheeks. There's no room to be embarrassed when his hands trace over my bra.

"Perfect." The reverberation of that single word runs down my neck to my stomach, leaving a trail of molten.

"I want to mark you. Claim you." He licks up the column of my throat, causing my whole body to shudder. "May I?"

"Please," I whimper, not even embarrassed I sound so desperate.

He groans, lowering his mouth again. I'm mindless against the barrage of sensation from his teeth and tongue and lips.

I wait for the feeling of teeth sinking into my skin. But instead, his hand caresses lower, drawing swirls across my skin. I release my hold on him, hoping we are about to shed the rest of our clothes.

"Do you want this?" he teases, his voice a rough whisper.

I can barely answer. "Yes." His hand slips lower, lightly skimming over me. It's maddening. "Please," I beg again.

I reach for his waistband, but he grabs my hand. Weaving our fingers, he presses them above my head.

"Patience," he says.

His kisses journey down my chest and he tugs on my bra with his teeth, pulling it the rest of the way down and covering me with his mouth. Unable to move, I writhe against him, all rational thought lost. He pauses, eyes lit from within. "Tell me what you want."

"I want you to take off your damn pants," I growl, shocking myself, but I can't stand any more teasing.

He smirks but lifts off me. I unbutton my jeans, but falter when he eases his sweatpants down. Wow, just wow. If I knew what these wolf shifters were packing, I wouldn't have bothered with the California boys.

My mouth goes dry, and I can't help but stare at him while he tugs my jeans down. He pulls my ass out from under me so I'm flat on my back. Then he's over me, skin to skin, only my underwear between us.

"You are so beautiful," he hums. I can't tell if the hammering pulse in my skin is mine or his.

He rocks his body against me, his length pressing hard against my last bit of clothing, and I swear I will stop wearing undergarments from this point on.

I want to tear them off, reach for him, anything, but my hands are locked around his biceps like I'm drowning and he's the only thing keeping me afloat. Somehow I know he'll guide me through this storm.

My nerves are on fire. I'm pretty sure I'm being electrocuted as he grinds against me. Everything is wound so tight, my nails dig into his muscles.

With a growl, he scrapes his teeth down the side of my neck, from the sensitive spot under my jaw down to my collarbone, as his hips rock against me, hitting the perfect spot. Unable to help myself, I lift my hips and press back, prolonging the delicious contact that has my eyes rolling back in my head. His hand grips my thigh, lifting my leg over his hip. My gasp echoes in the small space. I'm not going to be able to hold out much longer, and we've barely done anything.

"I'm, um, yeah," I sputter.

His hand slides between us, brushing over my panties. I can feel his smile against my skin when he feels how wet they are. There's no hiding it.

"Please," is the only word I can say. After a beat, he moves under my underwear and repeats the movement, gentle, exploratory. But as his fingers trace upwards, that's the last straw.

Stars explode behind my eyes. I try to hold on, but there is no resisting. I'm dragged under, and I can't help but moan out his name like a curse, my back arching and hips bucking against him involuntarily.

I scarcely notice his mouth moving lower or his teeth sinking into muscle. I'm too blissed out.

Chest heaving, my senses start to return to me. I smile at Slate, only to see his eyes wide. His hand presses to the spot he marked. "Are you okay?" he asks, voice tight and words clipped.

"I'm fine," I say, brushing his hair back from his face.

"I'm sorry," he mutters. "Hold on." He places my hand over the spot and presses my fingers down before scrambling up and darting toward the bedroom doorway.

Trying to not panic over his reaction, I scoot back and pull myself upright. Only then do I feel the wetness. I run my fingers down my neck and over the shoulder muscle and they come away bright red.

"Oh," I say dumbly.

Slate's back, pressing a towel to the spot. I flinch at the pressure. A throbbing pain blooms from the spot, as if my awareness was the cause of the hurt.

"Shit, I'm so sorry," he says.

"Don't be."

"I should have thought about this."

"Thought about what?" I lean my head back, closing my eyes as the discomfort heightens.

"You're human. You don't heal as fast. Fuck, that's a lot of blood."

"It's all good," I mumble, trying to stay still.

"Hazel, should I get Sable?" He sounds truly panicked now.

"No, it's okay," I reassure him. "I'm fine, it'll stop in a minute, I'm sure."

"If it doesn't, I'm getting her."

"Sure," I say, replacing his hand with my own.

He stands again, returning shortly with medical supplies in hand. Unfortunately, he's pulled his pants on. Those should be banned when we're alone together.

Cautiously, he replaces the towel with a bandage and wraps it tightly, twisting the gauze under my opposite arm. "You should rest. I don't want it to start bleeding more."

I scowl at him. "I'm pretty sure we were still in the middle of something."

His pouty frown kills my hope of any more action tonight. I huff. "Let's go to bed." He grabs my hand, leading me toward his bedroom.

"Sounds good to me," I say, trying my best to flirt. No reaction.

We pause in the bathroom. He leans me against the sink, grabbing a warm washcloth to wipe down my still-healing tattoo.

"Thank you," I say. He reapplies the moisturizer. "Does this mean I get tattoos whenever I want now?"

His mood stays somber, but he answers, "You get anything you want."

"Oh?" I lift one eyebrow.

"Starting tomorrow." The corners of his mouth start to bend. Cautiously, he checks the bandage, and seems satisfied the bleeding has slowed.

Happiness bubbles up in me. Tonight may have gone a bit awry, but we have tomorrow. And the next day, and the next. With that warm feeling bubbling in my chest, I follow him into the bedroom and allow him to tuck me under his comforter.

"Rest," he says.

"It's cold," I say. Without hesitation, he slides in behind me and wraps his arm around me. Sighing, I nestle into his warmth. "Promise me something."

"Anything." He nuzzles into my hair, kissing behind my ear.

"Don't leave me," I whisper, feeling silly. "I don't like waking up alone."

"I finally get you to myself all night. I wouldn't miss this for anything."

It's worth one last attempt, so I wiggle my ass against him. He's hard against my backside. Unfortunately, he loops his arm over mine, pinning me down thoroughly before I can reach for him.

"You agreed to rest," he purrs.

"I want to touch you." I try to sound sultry and it must work because he twitches against me.

"I'll happily let you. Tomorrow."

"You're going to have to make this up to me."

"I can't wait." He presses a final kiss to my temple.

His hands stroke down my arm and back up, soothing me. I relax into the mattress, relishing the feel of his fingers gently massaging my scalp and then caressing down my spine. I'm asleep in minutes.

SLATE

We're twisted around each other. She's using my arm as a pillow with her leg draped over mine. As soon as I move, her eyes pop open. A languid smile spreads across her face. It's moonlight hitting my skin. I'm drawn to her like my own personal gravity.

She hooks her leg higher over my hip and nuzzles into my neck.

"Good morning, gorgeous," I murmur. "How about some breakfast and we check your new mark."

She whimpers in protest, her fingers feathering down my abs.

I catch her hand and kiss it, looking into her eyes and asking, "What's the ring you always wear?"

She twists her hand to display the tiny silver band. It may have been ornate at one point, but time has worn it smooth. "My grandma's. On my mom's side," she answers.

"It's beautiful."

"Thanks." She looks like she wants to ask me something, but she doesn't.

I click my tongue and roll away. "Come on."

Grabbing clothes, I head into the bathroom. When I emerge, she's got her back turned to me and she's slipping one of my shirts over her head. My mouth waters. To my delight, it doesn't quite cover her perfect ass.

Like she can read my mind, she smirks over her shoulder and slips into the bathroom. It's tempting to follow her, but the urge to provide for my mate drives me into the kitchen. After tossing some bacon into a pan, I set about washing and slicing up peaches.

"A balanced breakfast. You take such good care of me." She kisses my bare back and I'm suddenly pleased I didn't bother with a shirt.

"Gotta keep my girl fed." I offer her the plate of bacon.

She's looking at me like she'd prefer to devour me instead of her breakfast. But instead, she takes a bite of bacon, closing her eyes and groaning.

"You shouldn't do that," I warn. Slowly, she spears a slice of peach and brings it to her mouth, closing her lips around it while making eye contact.

"You're something else." My voice scrapes. As much as I would love to throw her over my shoulder and carry her to bed for the entire day, we have responsibilities.

I wash my hands and softly tug the neckline of her shirt aside to inspect my bite mark. She curves her neck, presenting herself to me. I bite my cheek. Doesn't she know what she's doing to me?

She winces as I peel the bandage off and swipe antiseptic over the marks. Her beautiful smile is back when I look up from taping fresh gauze over the wound.

As I wash up, she picks at her fruit. "So, is it always the men who claim women?" she asks, breaking the silence.

I shake my head. "Sometimes it's women who ask. Most couples, both claim each other when it comes down to it."

"Oh." She sits back. "Can I claim you?"

Smiling, I reach out and run my thumb over her bottom lip. "With these little teeth?"

She bites at my thumb, her blunt teeth grazing it as I pull back. "How are yours any different? I mean, you're human unless you wolf out, right?"

"You think so?" I can't keep the challenge out of my voice.

Her eyes go wide and then narrow. "You're going to have to prove it one way or another," she dares me.

I've never been one to walk away from a confrontation. Grabbing her chair, I spin the barstool to face me and step between her thighs. My palms hit the countertop as I loom over her. She looks up at me, her pupils blown out. I haven't even touched her yet. "I like you wearing my shirt," I purr.

In a smooth, sudden movement, I grip her hips and lift her onto the countertop. Shoving the barstool aside, I press right up against her. She parts her legs for me. So compliant.

A squeak escapes her mouth before I cover it with mine. This is no gentle good morning kiss. I delve deep, our teeth and tongues clashing while my hands roam over her bare thighs and soft stomach.

Her hands go around my neck and fingers, twisting into my hair. She wraps her legs around my hips, hooking her ankles at the small of my back.

I stroke the silky skin at the bottom of her breast. "Perfect," I murmur against her lips.

Her breathing is rapid and shallow. She's as turned on as I am. I break off our kiss and lean back, letting her see my eyes lit up again.

Her mouth falls open, mesmerized. I grin wide, running my tongue over the edges of my teeth. It's not a huge change, not noticeable unless you know what to look for. They're slightly longer and sharper.

We stay there, both breathing hard. She reaches up like she's going to touch my teeth, but hesitates.

"You're stunning," she says.

Flushing, I pull her against my chest, needing to just feel her against me. She's content to snuggle against me for a moment, and everything feels perfect.

"Don't forget, we need to show your mark to whatever representative they send. And I'd feel better if Sable took a look," I murmur, kissing her hair.

"Sure. We also need to hit up my uncle's cabin." Her words are soft and satisfied, sending a thrill through me.

"Whatever you want. I can help you pack."

She tips her chin, her eyes connecting with mine. "You want me to move in with you?"

She had any doubt? "Of course. Unless you don't like it here."

"I do." She says, running her teeth over her bottom lip. "I guess I didn't think about it. I'd love to move in. But for today, we can just grab a few clothes, a toothbrush, and my meds."

"Whatever you want."

"Slate," she says, her tone dropping, "I'm on the pill, so we don't need to worry about that. But I also take an NDRI. I've been on it since college."

I keep my voice casual. "I don't know what that is, but it's fine."

"It's an antidepressant."

My chest tightens realizing she was nervous to tell me this. "Okay, no big deal."

"Yeah, of course not. I just wanted you to know."

She rubs her hand across her face. Did I react wrong? Or is that regret? Everything happened so fast. Now in the light of day, is she realizing she made a mistake?

I brace myself. If she regrets it or is unhappy with me, I'll face it. I'll do whatever she needs. She opens her mouth. "How are you feeling about seeing your mom yesterday?" Her question blindsides me.

"Fine," I answer automatically. It's a lie. An accidental one, but I still feel a twinge of guilt.

"Do you hate her?" she asks tentatively.

I sigh. She deserves nothing but honesty from me, even if it's uncomfortable. "I never knew her. She left when I was a baby. I mean, her son is only a couple of years younger than me."

"Jasper," she clarifies.

"Yeah." Something about how she says his name bothers me.

She hesitates, taking a deep breath and letting it out slowly. "So, I recognized him," she admits. My mind goes blank. How is that possible? "Yeah, I met him at the coffee shop in town."

"He does classwork there, I guess," she explains, her voice rising. "He was nice. Welcomed me to town, gave me his number."

"That fucker." My vision spots for a second, an overwhelming sense of protectiveness washing over me, stronger than before.

I'm growling, low in the back of my throat, anger bubbling up. My possessive need to protect her rears up, overwhelming me. My fingers dig into her soft hips, and I take a slow breath and unclench my hands.

"I don't think he knew who-"

"If he ever touches you, I will kill him," I interrupt her. She has to understand, I can't tolerate an enemy anywhere near her.

Her eyes widen. "Did you just threaten murder?" she questions.

Would I murder someone who tried to hurt her? Absolutely. Just the thought makes my heart slam into my chest.

"Look, I need to go check in with the Alpha." I bristle, stepping back and walking past her. I have to get outside, out of this small space. I read it in her face – he did touch her. They spoke, he probably flirted. I don't want her to witness the rage this triggers in me.

"Slate!" she splutters.

"Hazel, I need a second," I say, closing my eyes. I'm not going to speak to her unkindly despite the fact I want to snarl. It's almost impossible to string words together. "My emotions are a bit out of control today with what we did last night. It's an instinct thing. I need to cool off and talk to Heath."

"Okay." Her voice is tiny. I am an asshole.

My mind searches for any way to make this right, but the desire to hunt my brother down and murder him still fogs my vision. I pull open the door. "I'll make sure someone is outside if you need anything. I'll be back soon."

The door slams shut behind me and I drop my hands to my knees, sucking in air like I'm drowning. It's a struggle to not shift into my wolf right there on the steps.

Onyx stands outside. His smile vanishes. "You okay, dude?"

"Keep her safe," I demand, stalking off to find Heath. I knew the scent on her two nights ago, the night the rogue wolves attacked, was familiar. I should have realized.

The pieces start to fall into place. My instinctual anger is justified.

That piece of shit met her. He knew about her. He would have smelled our pack on her skin. He tried to sentence her to death.

I'm shaking. I steady myself, attuning to my pack. Their steady presence takes the edge off. But I need to report to my Alpha, right now.

XI
HEARTACHE &
HELPLESSNESS

HAZEL

Slate isn't back quickly.

Worry and then irritation slowly builds in me. I settle myself by snooping. Slate is surprisingly organized. Nothing tucked in random drawers, nothing in the back of his closet.

I find a few photos on his bookshelves. Young Onyx, Cedar, and Slate laugh at the camera. Slate with a man who must be his father with lighter hair but the same brooding eyes.

After a while, I head to the bathroom and peel up the edge of my bandage. The bleeding has stopped and now a collection of thin scabs form an oval across my shoulder. I tenderly touch them, relieved it's looking better.

Laying across the couch, my unoccupied mind spins. All of Slate's little hesitations. The way he stopped things from going further physically. His dramatic reaction to our discussion about his mother and half-brother.

I have no idea how he feels about anything for sure. His words of devotion begin to sound hollow the more times I replay them in my memory.

Huffing, I push up and begin to pace. I need to talk to him. Or a friend. The best choice would be my therapist, although I'll need to spin this a bit. She will be concerned if I start going on about werewolves and mates.

After shooting her a text, I dress properly with my bra from the night before, tucking his oversized t-shirt into my jeans.

My therapist returns my text almost immediately. She'll be available in about thirty minutes.

The door squeaks as I step out. A familiar head of dirty blonde hair swings around to look at me.

"Hey, Hazel." Onyx's easy smile relaxes me.

"How long have you been out here?" I ask.

His smile morphs into a distinct smirk. "A while."

"Don't be weird. Please."

"Nah, Lazuli got the night shift." He shrugs, laughing at my pink cheeks. Noticing the glossy edge of the bandage visible under the neckline of my borrowed shirt, his expression sharpens. "Are you okay?"

The question yanks all of my anxious, swirling emotions to the forefront. I swallow and focus on staying calm.

"Yeah, I'm good. I'm a bit overwhelmed by everything. Could we head to my uncle's cabin and get some of my stuff?"

"Of course." Onyx nods. He looks like he wants to hug me, but he keeps his arms at his sides. The times everyone joked about Slate getting upset with him play in my mind. Is my mate that possessive?

Scanning the trees, Onyx leads me south toward the little blue cabin that was my temporary home until yesterday. Heath is gone, so it's empty.

Rushing, I grab my backpack and stuff in a change of clothes, my phone, and my medication. Lastly, I head to the bathroom and grab a few toiletries.

"Ready to go?" Onyx asks.

"Yeah, but I've got a call scheduled with my therapist," I say.

Onyx bobs his head. "Cool."

"But I don't get enough service here," I say. "Usually, I'd go into town, but considering…"

Onyx nods. "Okay, let's get you some bars. There should be more service down by the parking lot."

He stays on my heels as I wander toward the road. The meadow is eerily quiet. Holding up my phone, I see one tiny bar of service. We pass Vale, who is standing in the parking lot.

A short distance down the road, Onyx halts. "We shouldn't go any further. How is it here?"

I hold up my phone, seeing another bar appear. "Not quite, but almost." I take a few more steps down the road. Onyx follows, apprehension tightening his face. He scans the trees continuously.

"Can I get some privacy?" I ask, knowing it's probably in vain.

"No can do," he responds. "Sorry."

"Are we worried about something?" I ask, his serious expression scaring me.

"It's cool. Like half the pack is patrolling. No rogue wolves are getting through today. We're safe."

"Okay. This'll only take like ten minutes." I dial, and it rings once, twice. Without warning, Onyx grabs my arm and yanks me into the trees. The crunch of gravel grabs my attention. A black car is swinging around the curve of the road.

I end the call before she can answer. I'll call back as soon as possible, but I don't want to be caught on the phone when the representative shows up to verify my mark.

"Smells like Ironcrest," Onyx mutters, his brows creasing.

The car slows as it approaches. Onyx pushes me behind him and we move further into the safety of the forest.

The window rolls down, and a tall man I vaguely recognize from yesterday stares out at us. He's got a wide jaw with a chin cleft like a butt.

I smile, trying to make a good impression, but it falls off my face when he levels a gun at us. "Get in the car or I'll shoot." The driver's voice is harsh and grating.

"Not a chance," Onyx growls.

I gape, my brain going blank at the sight of a pistol pointed at me, or rather, at my friend who has placed himself between me and the danger.

Onyx hisses to me, "Get ready to run into the trees."

"What?" I grip his shoulder, a wave of dizziness hitting me. Am I still breathing?

To the driver, Onyx snarls, "What are you doing?"

"Hey, stop!" I yelp, tugging Onyx back a step.

For a moment, everything is frozen, but then Onyx's head jerks to the side. Two wolves are approaching from behind us. So much for running. Snarling, they flank us.

"They won't shoot you," Onyx says. "As soon as I shift, you need to run."

Is he going to take on two wolves while someone shoots at him? Are you kidding me?

"No!" I hiss.

"Sorry, babe. It's my turn to be a hero." He grins at me, looking like himself again for a split second.

"Get in the car!" the driver yells again.

Onyx shoves me and throws himself toward the wolf blocking my way. He shifts before hitting the ground.

Gasping, I stumble before I get my feet under me and take off sprinting.

A gunshot echoes around me, stinging my eardrums echoing off the trees. Twisting, I peer over my shoulder.

Onyx is on the ground, his dark fur glistening red. The two wolves bound after me in flashes of teeth and gray fur. Paws hit my back and I go down hard. Stones embed into my palms. I'm wrenched up, a large man gripping my upper arm. My throat is raw from screaming as I'm dragged toward the vehicle.

The driver holds the door open while the naked man climbs in and hauls me into his lap. I screech, flailing and scratching. The other nude man slides in beside us, grabbing my wrists to restrain me further. They wrest my backpack off. I gulp in the stale, stinking air and almost choke.

Another door slams and we're reversing. I'm thrown forward and then slammed into my attacker's bare chest. The burly man beside me cinches zip ties across both wrists. I try to ram my heel into their shins, but I can't get any leverage.

As we hit the highway, I realize I can't escape this moving car. The next chance will be when they stop to bring me indoors or transfer vehicles. Against every instinct, I go quiet and stop thrashing, instead sitting stiffly. I don't want to be touching these men. I'm going to be sick.

We race down the road and I'm too overwhelmed to tell which direction. Trees blur. Maybe seconds later, maybe an hour, we pull onto a dirt road obscured by the forest, our speed barely lowering.

When we finally screech to a halt, I'm yanked out by my bound wrists. I stumble as soon as my feet hit the ground. The stranger lets me fall into the dirt and I hiss at the pain stabbing my hip and elbow. There's another black sedan ahead. These men have masks and are dressed in loose black clothing.

Two men grab my arms and drag me toward the car. I hear the others arguing behind me.

Everything goes dark as a black pillowcase is shoved over my head. Panic overwhelms me and I start fighting again. With everything I can muster, I swing my zip-tied hands, balled into fists, and manage to hit a solid form. The flesh doesn't yield.

A huge hand grips my throat over the baggy pillowcase. My panic turns to ice, every shred of survival instinct I possess is screaming at me to submit.

Cruel laughter shames me. I'm stuffed into another car, smacking the side of my head against the frame. I bite down a whimper. A hand grips my forearm, keeping me from trying to pull the pillowcase off.

The remaining car doors close and we lurch forward. My arm is bruising where he grips it. I try to tug away, but he must enjoy squeezing it harder. A small cry escapes my throat.

Someone in the front of the car growls, and the man finally releases me. I double over, not attempting to remove the pillowcase, just trying to get some space to breathe and not throw up.

Breathe in, breathe out. I missed one chance, but they'll have to stop the car again. I want to tug at the pillowcase, but I need to bide my time.

The car slows and finally stops. Doors open and even through the fabric I can smell clay and sulfur. Brutal hands pull me out of the door.

The second my feet hit the ground, I duck my head and tear off the pillowcase. Everything around me is brown and gray, with my captors looming.

I'm slammed against the car door. The hulking brute snarls down at me. "Grab her," shouts another man.

"No!" I fling myself sideways, but he's already wrapped his sausage hands around my waist. With one heave, I'm over his shoulder, potato-sack-style.

"Let me go!" I screech, banging my fists against his lower back. He grunts and slaps my thighs. Tears spring up in my eyes.

"Hit her again and I'll kill you," another voice threatens. It's familiar and smooth, but I'm too foggy to place it.

The man climbs a few steps. I blink, getting a view of mud and concrete, and then are over a threshold onto glossy black tile. His grip on my legs hurts.

We take a sharp right and pass through another doorway. It's dim, and my hair blocks most of my vision. After descending dark, carpeted steps, I'm flung down on the floor, knocking the air out of me.

Gasping, I roll over and curl into a protective ball. By the time I can suck air into my lungs and sit up, I'm alone.

Tears streak my face, and I wipe them away with the hem of my shirt. They keep coming. Every time I blink, I see the vision of Onyx splayed out and bleeding.

Slow breaths. In, out. Panicking won't help me. There's nothing I can do for Onyx from here. Our pack will take care of him. They must have heard his howl and were probably seconds away. He'll be fine, I have to believe it.

I'm in a basement. It's a fancy basement, with crown molding circling the ceiling, but still terrifying considering the circumstances. An old, faded suede sofa sits behind me, and to my left is a thick flat-screen television. Past the television, a kitchenette occupies the corner. Twisting behind me, I can see two open doors, one to a dim bedroom and one to a bathroom.

The entire basement smells damp and dusty, but at least it doesn't smell like a serial killer works down here.

So, where the hell am I, and who would kidnap me?

The door at the top of the stairs clicks and swings open. A willowy woman saunters down the stairs - Ferris's mate, Sienna. Slate's mom. My muscles tense at the sight of her.

"Hello, Hazel." Her voice is rich and charismatic. Her chocolate hair falls in a perfect blow-out and her cheeks are carved out like a movie star. She's glamorous. And she's the woman who abandoned her child, my partner. I hate her instantly.

"I'm glad I finally get to meet my son's mate," she croons.

Irritation cuts through me. "You don't deserve to call him your son. He doesn't call you a mother." She smirks, crossing her arms. Now that I've opened my mouth, I can't help but continue. "When he finds me, you're going to seriously regret this."

"Maybe." She shrugs. "Please, take a seat."

My instinct is to refuse, but standing seems too difficult and the sofa is better than the floor. Scowling, I push up with my hands and wince at my aching wrists. I'm not graceful, but I manage to make it to the sofa and plop down. To my dismay, my jeans tore in the struggle, gaping open to reveal my inner thigh.

Sienna sashays closer.

"Leave me alone," I growl, raising my chin.

She reaches for me, her fingers tipped with crimson stiletto nails. Pinching my shirt, she tugs the neckline to the side to see my claim mark. The bandage ripped off during the struggle, so she has a clear view of the new scabs. I jerk to the side.

"Pity he marked you." She sighs. "But don't worry, those will fade."

The words don't make sense. "Excuse me?"

"Oh, you didn't complete the claiming," she casually answers, like mentioning what's for dinner.

"What do you mean?" My teeth grind so hard my jaw clicks.

"Did you have sex with him?" she asks, her cold eyes meeting mine.

"None of your business." I curl my lip. It's not exactly a normal topic of conversation to have with your boyfriend's estranged mother.

"You didn't," she responds curtly, flipping her dark waves over her shoulder. "Your mark will be gone within a few days."

She's lying. If more was necessary, he would have told me.

But if she isn't... we could still complete it. Or if the worst happens, he could be free of me. A sick sense of relief weighs down my chest. He won't live in unavoidable pain from losing me.

A few tears escape and drip down my cheeks. My teeth sink into my bottom lip. I won't grieve. Not when I can still get back to him.

"I think you can do better," she suggests with a shrug. "Jasper was certainly taken with you."

I go rigid. Did she kidnap me to set me up with her other son? Right after she threatened my life, which prompted her first son into claiming me?

Clearing my raw throat, I say, "Not interested."

"Well, once this mark fades, I'm sure he can win you over. Or there are other ways to motivate you. But I'm sure that won't be necessary."

"Why?" I ask. "I'm just a random human."

"You have Alpha blood. You're the heir to Alder's line."

But how am I an heir? I'm not even a shifter. It makes more sense to go for someone like Hawthorne or his daughters. But thank goodness she didn't. I can't stand the thought of those sweet girls in danger.

She continues, her voice musical, "Your blood has rights to that pack. It has power."

"Okay, that's creepy," I say.

Her hand shoots out and slaps me across the face, knocking me over onto the arm of the sofa. The shock lances through me a split second before the pain.

"Be respectful," she commands.

In my head, I'm screaming profanities at her, but I manage to clench my jaw shut. My skin burns where she struck me.

"I'll leave you to settle in. It'll be a quiet week waiting for that-" She waves her hand at me. "To fade."

I jerk the zip ties around my wrists. They're cutting into me. It hurts enough I'm willing to trade my remaining dignity for some relief. "Can you cut these zip ties?"

She shrugs. "We learn through pain." So that's a no.

She glides up the stairs without glancing back at me.

Queasy, I close my eyes and slow my breathing, keeping my wrists stationary to try and minimize the pain. When I can't stand it any longer, I start searching the space. Maybe there's a way out. Unlikely, but I have to try.

There are no windows. The only door is the one at the top of the stairs, and it's locked. I can't even hear anything through it. Hopeless, I flop on the sofa. How am I going to get home to Slate? Tears drip down the sides of my face, soaking into my hair. The shock of the situation is starting to fade and depression settles over me like a weight.

I jolt awake to the sound of the door swooshing open. Scrambling to an upright position, I rub the crust from my eyelashes. I'm not ready to go head-to-head with Sienna again, but maybe this time she'll cut these awful zip ties.

Instead, an athletic figure with bright blonde hair ducks down the stairs. Fury surges through me, sending me to my feet despite my aching body.

"What the absolute fuck, Jasper!" Not my best opening, especially when I need to ask for something. But I thought he was my friend. Or a casual, friendly acquaintance. Not someone who is pure evil.

He tilts his head, a cocky smile pasted on his face. I want to beat it off him. "Good to see you again, Hazel," he says, setting my battered backpack down on the tiny table near the kitchen.

"Go to hell," I spit.

"Already there, love," he mutters, so quietly I question if I heard correctly.

He reaches me and tries to grab my wrists. I jump away.

"You kidnapped me, you twatwaffle," I growl.

"My mother kidnapped you," he says flatly.

"Are you kidding me?" The exhaustion and rage are making me woozy, but I am not done with this fight.

"You need to calm down. Getting upset will only make things worse," he chides me.

"Did you tell me to calm down?" I snarl, my voice rising into the hysterical zone.

"I'm trying to help you," he promises, pulling a small pair of scissors out of his pocket. I've never heard this sober tone from him before. His trademark cockiness is gone. Now, worry lines his eyes.

He takes my wrists and snips the zip ties. I eye the scissors as he slips them into his pocket. Do I think I could wrestle them away from him and use them to escape? No. But I'm desperate at the moment.

My breath hisses out as I rotate my wrists.

"Hazel," he begins.

I ignore him, grabbing my backpack and rifling through it. My phone is missing, but everything else is there. Grabbing my spare leggings, I hold up a finger. "I need a minute."

He pauses, his brows furrowing. I head straight to the bathroom and slam the door between us. He can wait.

Purple bruises bloom down my hip. After changing out of my ruined jeans, I take extra care to wash the raw skin around my wrists. And then, in an attempt to delay dealing with Jasper, I drag my fingers through my mess of hair. It's ridiculously tangled, but bedhead followed by a kidnapping will do that to a girl.

"I'm sorry," he says as soon as I open the bathroom door.

"Are you?" I ask, resting my hand against the door frame. I have no desire to get closer to him.

"Yes."

"Your mother said my mark will fade and I'll be your mate instead." I jump right to the point. I need to know where he stands.

Jasper stands stone still, clasping his hands in front of him, studying me. No reply.

"I said yes to a coffee date, not to being your mate," I growl. "In case you forgot, I'm taken."

He shrugs. "It's not what I planned either."

"Then tell her to eat a shit sandwich." I sweep my palms out as if this is the most obvious thing in the world.

His shoulders droop. "You don't know my mother. We don't have a lot of choice here."

"I don't know you either."

He blinks, hurt flashing in his expression before his mouth thins as anger sparks in his eyes. "You realize, without my protection, she'll use you against Heath and then kill you." His voice is a low warning.

I try to not cringe away from him. "Look, that doesn't make it okay."

"I can't help you any other way," he says. So that's it.

I want to storm off, but my only option is the bedroom and I don't want to risk him to follow me in there. But tears are filling my eyes and I know I'm seconds from an ugly, uncontrollable cry.

"Asshat," I choke out, spinning and slamming the bathroom door behind me.

He knocks. "Hazel, I left some soap and stuff for you." When I don't respond, he continues, "I'll come check on you later. Get some rest."

"You planned for this?" I ask, my voice hollow.

There's no reply.

There's a toothbrush and tube of toothpaste in the vanity drawer, along with a hairbrush and an organic floral deodorant. I guess this is Jasper's idea of a woman's basic toiletry kit. There's expensive shampoo and soap in the shower too.

I wait until I'm sure he's left and start to investigate the bedroom as well. The dresser in the bedroom holds a few pairs of leggings and soft t-shirts. There aren't any undergarments, but I know shifters aren't big on underwear.

Despite how cliché it might be, I fling myself down on the bed and let the sobs overtake me. The idea of being forced to accept Jasper in place of Slate makes me want to scream. How is Jasper okay with this? Why would he want a mate who is a prisoner, fighting him every step of the way? And would the bond even work in these circumstances? I dig my nails into the comforter until my ragged breath evens out. The sobs leave me feeling empty. Numb.

Unfortunately, I won't find any solutions lying here. It'll be easier to cope when I'm not hungry. Slate would want me to take care of myself.

Moving robotically, I move my backpack to the bedroom and try to tuck it away. I leave my personal items so they're easier to grab in an escape, but I grab my medication and take the morning doses I should have had hours ago.

Searching the kitchenette, I discover some frozen meals, a few apples and grapes, and a pack of sandwich cookies. With a microwaved entrée, I settle on the sofa.

The morning replays in my mind over and over. The rough hands digging into my arms and ribcage, dragging me backward. The way Onyx dropped to the ground. The rage in Slate's eyes as I told him I recognized Jasper. What if that was our last conversation?

Curling up into a ball, I hug myself as my tears turn into body-shaking sobs. I thought I was drained of sadness, but it wells up again and again. What if Slate or Heath gets hurt trying to rescue me? What if Onyx isn't okay?

Exhaustion drags me under and I fall back asleep on the sofa, the throw pillow under my head soaked.

XII
FRACTURES &
FRENEMIES
Slate

As soon as the gunshot sounds, I know she's gone. I bolt out of the meeting. Packmates are in motion around me, but I don't hesitate as I race past the parking lot, searching frantically. Instead of finding Hazel, there's only Onyx on the ground. Vale is already trying to stop the bleeding. I see him struggle to sit up. He's okay, and Hazel is far more vulnerable.

Exhaust from a vehicle forms a trail in the air that I can track. I shift, letting my shirt rip. In seconds, I'm down the road, following the sounds of tires and the lingering car fumes. Running alongside the road, I cut through the trees. The car must be barely out of view.

I can run fast, but not as fast as a vehicle. I'm forced to rely on smell, following it down the road until the scents around me change abruptly - it's our border. If I keep going, I'll be invading the Ironcrest Pack territory.

I pace for a moment. Was someone else driving through? Or was it Ironcrest who took her?

Although I can't enter as a wolf, I could drive through as a human. With a snarl, I turn back the way I came. My lungs burn as I push to my limit.

Onyx has been moved by the time I hurtle down the gravel road. I shift back and start jogging toward the clearing, only pausing to pull my sweats on.

Heath steps out of Sable's cottage across the clearing. Hawthorne reaches him before I can, but I don't hesitate to interrupt.

"They took her east," I shout. "To Ironcrest." I finally stop, bracing my hands on my knees and breathing hard. Blood rushes in my ears.

"East," Heath repeats. "Did you see the vehicle?"

Shaking my head, I explain, "I only smelled alcohol and exhaust fumes. The wolves must have shifted and gotten into the car because I couldn't smell anyone along the road."

"Damn," Heath mutters.

"We should take a car to Zephyr, immediately. Intercept them before they can move her again," I demand.

Hawthorne raises his eyebrows at Heath. "I doubt they'll let us in."

Heath nods. "Gather enough wolves for an exit strategy." He strides toward our trucks.

Hawthorne and I gather seven other wolves, as many Thetas and Zetas as possible, and we all pile into two vehicles. Hawthorne insists on driving my truck. My blood is still full of adrenaline, so I want to argue, but I know he is right. I'm shaking.

"It's going to be okay," Hawthorne maintains.

"You don't know that," I say through gritted teeth.

"They could have killed her right there on our lands. But they took her, so they want her alive. And we are going to get her back," he reassures me.

My rage isn't quelled. "Zephyr betrayed us."

"Maybe, but they could have only driven through Ironcrest. It's still the high-way."

"They sided with Granite Ridge." There is no doubt in my mind.

"We'll see. I hope you're wrong."

We roll onto Ironcrest land, stopping when we reach the dirt road leading to their compound. Hawthorne rolls down the window. Heath drives the second car behind us, but Hawthorne is our Gamma. This is his responsibility.

Three Ironcrest members stand by the road, arms crossed.

"Gentlemen, we need a word with your Alpha. Following up with yesterday's business. It's urgent." Hawthorne's tone is diplomatic.

One of them steps away with a handheld radio. I grind my teeth together, trying to wait.

We are waved through. She could be here. Or we could be too slow. I will never forgive myself if she gets hurt.

We pull into an open area. A small group waits for us, led by Zephyr. At least he has the decency to come meet us himself. We unload, Hawthorne and Heath stepping forward. A warning look from Heath keeps me at the back of the group.

Closing my eyes, I breathe deep, trying to catch any hint of Hazel. Nothing.

"Unfortunately, rogue wolves have invaded our land again, and they targeted my niece. She's been taken." Heath gets right to the point.

"I'm sorry to hear it. Please let us know how we can help." Zephyr's words are kind, but his rigid stance contradicts them.

"May we walk through to check for any sign of where they may have gone?" Hawthorne says.

"I'm afraid my pack isn't up for that much of a disruption."

There's a stretch of silence and I clench my fists. Elm steps closer to me, placing his hand on my shoulder.

"We need to investigate this. We tracked them to your border," Heath insists. "How can we make this unobtrusive for your people?"

Zephyr stares him down. He's older, with silver hair and deep lines across his forehead. He's always been a respected alpha, but my instincts are roaring: he is untrustworthy.

"Perhaps a small party, two or three of your Thetas? They can walk the road, but nowhere else."

Heath nods. He arranges for Hawthorne to take Elm and Vale. Elm has the experience and Vale has exceptional senses. Rationally, I know this is the right choice. But I cannot tolerate him sending others instead of me.

I push forward. "Alpha. I need to go." My voice is rough.

He levels his stare at me. "You know that's not a good choice."

"Why?" I demand. I'm aware my tone is disrespectful but I can't help it.

"Get in the truck." He dismisses me. I glower and climb into the truck, imagining disemboweling the Ironcrest Zeta watching me.

A few minutes later, Heath climbs in to sit beside me.

"I know you're barely keeping it together. I understand," he says, quietly.

"You should let me go," I protest again.

"You wouldn't respect their guidelines. We both know that."

I can't argue. It's the truth.

"Trust your packmates. There are times as a leader you have to let others handle things, even when you desperately want to handle it yourself." He is trying to focus me on my position and duties. I can only think of Hazel.

"That's not acceptable when she is at risk," I growl.

"I know. But you could make this situation worse," he responds, still patient.

I bury my face in my palms, trying to force away the dull ache behind my eyes. The same horrible images of Hazel hurt and scared cycle through my mind.

Heath leaves me to my thoughts.

Eventually, Hawthorne's team returns. We load up. I can see from their faces that nothing substantial was discovered.

On the drive home, Hawthorne fills me in. They found absolutely nothing. No hint of Hazel. No trace of any Granite Ridge pack scent.

Our best chance of tracking her has slipped past us.

I choke down my rage layered over absolute terror. Fear I won't reach her in time. Fear of what might happen to her. Fear of a life without her.

HAZEL

No one visits me the next morning.

I'm sure Heath and Slate are searching for me. They won't stop until I'm safe. I trust them. But every passing hour spikes my anxiety. I need to be patient.

Laying on the sofa, I stare at the ceiling. When I'm hungry, I scrounge some grapes and cookies.

As I'm setting my plate in the sink, the door opens. Turning, my heart jumps as I recognize Jasper. His face is cold and distant. My frown transmutes into a glare when his mother follows him down the stairs.

Her hair is in a single thick braid today, draped over her shoulder like a sexualized video game character. Blood red lips and a cat-eye complete the look.

She strides forward confidently and I can't help but note how Jasper's posture is lowered, his shoulders slumped. She has him beaten down, probably for years. The dynamic between them is clear. Somehow it triggers fresh rage. My hands curl into fists.

"Feeling more cooperative today?" she begins.

"I should rip out your eyes with my nails," I hiss before I can think better of it.

Sienna's laugh is shards of ice. "I appreciate the passion. Don't you, Jasper?" She smiles at her son and then turns her sinister expression back on me. I step away, gripping the countertop.

"But you won't. If you raise a hand against me, I'll break you and enjoy it." Her soft voice is brimming with threat. She looms closer.

She pinches my shirt and stretches it, the neckline revealing the healing claim mark. At least I hope it's healing, not lightening.

"Fading already," she smirks. My stomach drops. As she retreats, she murmurs. "Just like his dad, couldn't get the job done."

I'm on her before I realize it. I have no idea what I think I can accomplish, but I'm clawing at her face like a crazed housecat. She catches my right hand. I kick her in the shin and try to pull free.

With a smooth, practiced movement, she twists and snaps my wrist. My snarl becomes a scream.

Agony shoots up my arm. She releases me and I collapse to my knees, cradling my wrist. My heart is racing and every beat throbs down my arm.

Jasper stands beside me, and I hear his apathetic voice. "You made your point. I'd appreciate it if you didn't do that again; I don't like my things broken."

"Feeling possessive?" she sniggers.

"Didn't you say she's mine?" he counters. "I'll handle breaking her. I'm happy to keep you informed of our progress." His voice is haughty. Nausea rolls over me, fear heightening my pain.

"Of course. I look forward to it. I'll see you both at dinner."

I try to stand, but my vision goes spotty and I sink back down with a grimace. The door shuts with a dull thunk. I suck in a ragged breath and slowly let it out.

Jasper runs his hand down my back, and I hunch lower, snapping, "Don't touch me!"

"Hey, let me help you." His soft tone is so at odds with the heartless man he was a moment ago, I feel whiplashed.

Jasper grips my waist and supports me as I painfully hobble to the sofa. I can't help but curl over my right arm, a low whine accompanying each exhale.

He grabs a first-aid kit from the bathroom and crouches down in front of me. As he reaches for my arm, he makes low shushing noises. It takes all my self-control to allow him to handle my wrist. Gingerly, he wraps it to form a sort of soft cast.

Biting my lip, I unsuccessfully will the tears away. After a few long moments, the pain starts to subside to a tolerable level, as long as I don't move.

"She is foul," I growl, glancing down at my wrist. He did an impressive job. "Why do I get the feeling you've done this before?"

Tension creases the corners of his mouth.

"What did she mean about dinner?" I ask.

"She's decided you're joining us for family dinner," he says.

"No, thank you," I quip without thinking. But maybe it's an opportunity. "I guess I could," I amend my answer.

"Not optional." He turns his back to me, heading into the kitchenette. I focus on my yoga breathing for pain management while he hand washes my glass and fork from last night that I stranded in the sink.

"Doing okay?"

I narrow my eyes, refusing to reply to stupid questions. My wrist still feels like it went through a meat grinder. Besides, it's time he provided some answers.

"I need you to answer a few things, please."

"Sure." He slouches beside me and folds his hands behind his head.

"Do you know if Onyx is alive?" I bite my lip.

"What?" He sits forward sharply.

"He got shot," I say, a sarcastic edge sharpening my words.

"Are you serious?" Grabbing his phone from his pocket, he types, his lip curling into a snarl. "I'm sorry, I didn't know. That shouldn't have happened."

"No kidding," I bite out, but my throat is tightening now I'm thinking about my friend. The sound of the gun echoes in my head for the hundredth time.

"Tell me exactly what happened," he requests quietly.

I shudder. "A car pulled up, and the driver had a gun pointed at us. And then two wolves attacked, and he was defending me. He was a wolf when they shot him. And then the guys grabbed me."

"Where did they hit him?" He asks.

"I don't know, by his shoulder. Above his leg."

Jasper's face is closed off. Finally, he says, "Shifters are really hard to kill. As long as they didn't get his neck or head, I'm sure he's okay."

"He'd better be," I growl.

For a beat, I fight back tears and he pretends the carpet is interesting. "What do you know about your mom's plans?"

Jasper shakes his head. "I don't. She wants you to join the pack and for us to be mates. She's decided you're the ideal addition to the bloodline because you have a claim to Bracken Creek." I grimace. "My turn. Why did you go stay with Heath and his pack?" he asks.

I raise an eyebrow. "He's my uncle."

"I know. But did you know he was a shifter?"

"No." Biting the inside of my cheek, I decide to be honest. "He used to visit us in California, but I had no idea what my dad was either."

"I'm sorry." He reaches out, his hand covering my knee. I pull it away and he lets his hand drop. "Have you ever been to Bracken Creek before?"

"No."

"Why now?" He presses.

"I got let go from my job." I'm humiliated, but maybe it'll make him feel bad. Humanize me. "And broke off my engagement. Seemed like a good time for a road trip."

"Ouch. What happened?"

I scowl at him. "He preferred his new assistant over me."

"Asshole," he growls. I raise my eyebrows.

"What's your family like?" I ask.

"You met my mom." The muscles in his arms flex as he tenses up.

"What about the rest?" I press. I need to know who I'm dealing with.

"My dad is always busy with pack business." He hesitates. "He focuses on our finances and territory, business stuff. But my mom is in charge of the people."

"Seems like a bad choice."

"You would be correct," he mutters.

"Jasper, where are we, exactly?" I lower my voice, hoping he will trust me and share something useful. I need to escape this hellhole before they break me.

"My family's basement," he answers without hesitation.

"Your family's house?" I echo and he nods once. "Do you live..." Pointing up, I shrug.

"I moved out a couple of years ago. Needed some space."

"Can't imagine why," I say dryly.

"This used to be my room," he says, leaning against the cushions.

"You had a whole suite down here," I say, hoping he'll keep talking and let something slip.

He shrugs. "My sister still lives here. Up there."

I had no idea he had a younger sibling. "How old is she?"

"Ember is sixteen."

"What is she, evil like you?" I say with narrowed eyes.

He sighs. "Ember is a lot like my mom, unfortunately."

"Oh, no," I breathe out.

His eyes are almond-shaped, decidedly unlike Sienna and Slate. I see the similarities, but there are more differences.

"You look like your dad," I say without thinking.

"So do you," he replies.

"What?" My stomach flips. I inherited his tan skin, Greek nose, and wide-set eyes. But how does Jasper know that?

"I saw pictures. From when my mom was a teenager. Her, your dad, Clay, Heath, a few other friends," he explains.

"Do you still have them?"

He shook his head. "Sorry, I saw them in my mom's things before I moved out."

"I wonder why she kept something like that," I muse.

Silence stretches between us again. Jasper looks apologetic. I don't care. He is holding me hostage and I won't let him win me over like his mother wants. But if he is truly a good person, maybe he can be persuaded to help me.

"What am I going to do?"

"Hazel." He turns toward me. "If you start acting like you like me, I can probably get you out of this basement."

"Like I can go home?" I ask.

"Sorry, no," he answers.

"What's stopping me?"

"About fifty wolves with anger problems," he says. "They wouldn't be gentle." His tone isn't teasing or even sad, it's resigned. Like he's already accepted this reality.

I chew my cheek, trying to think.

"The only way I can keep you safe is by keeping you with me," he reasons. "If you're mine, no one else will touch you."

"You sound a lot like your brother right now," I say.

He scowls.

"Have you met him?" I have to know. I can't imagine Slate and Jasper in the same room, but surely the packs have met up at some point.

"We've been introduced," he says coolly. "He wasn't a fan."

I can't help but smile. "He is a bit intense sometimes."

He scoffs. "That's one way to put it."

"I miss him," I say. Jasper ignores my comment and checks his watch.

"We should get ready for dinner. I'll have to grab a dress from Ember for you."

"I'd prefer not."

"Again, not optional. I'll be back in a bit."

XIII
DINNER DISTRESS

HAZEL

"This is ridiculous," I mutter under my breath as he leads me up the stairs with a hand on the small of my back.

Ember's dress is black at least, but it's about three sizes too small, showing off the rolls of my stomach and cutting into the skin under my arms. But it was mandatory apparently.

"You look fine," Jasper says.

I glare at him. "Fine?"

"Yeah."

"If you thought I looked decent, you'd say good. Fine means you agree it's awful."

Jasper grinds his teeth, his jaw shifting. He tilts his head toward me. "Is this your biggest concern right now?"

I take a beat before responding. "Fine."

He rolls his eyes and we step from the hallway into a dining room. The house's aesthetic seems to be modern luxe meets mob boss. It's cavernous and cold.

A massive black stone dining table stretches the length of the room with three bulbous chandeliers reflecting on its polished surface.

The table is set for five. Everything is fancy, from the crystal wine glasses to the gleaming silverware. Including knives. They're confident I'm already submissive, or they aren't worried about what I could do with a blade.

Sienna stands at the window, looking out at the sunset. She turns and sips the red wine in her hand while judging my appearance.

"Glad you're here. Come sit down." Her voice is silky sweet, like corn syrup laced with poison.

She settles at the seat to the right of the head of the table. Jasper heads toward the other side and pulls out the second seat for me, leaving the spot across from Sienna for himself.

"Lovely," Sienna says. Her skimpy dress shows off two matching sets of pale scars. Claim marks. One from Slate's dad, and one from Ferris. Nausea washes over me.

The alpha strides in, followed by a teenager with short pink hair and an upturned nose.

"Father," Jasper greets him.

"Darling!" Sienna kisses him and runs her hands down his arm. He settles at the head of the table and she sinks down beside him. "I'm so glad you could break away. You've been working so hard," she simpers.

"As have you," Ferris responds without any inflection.

"You remember Hazel," Jasper says.

Ferris studies me with those cold, gray eyes. "Happy to have you here."

"So, how's the wrist feeling?" Sienna turns her siren eyes on me, turning my blood cold. I press my tongue to my teeth. She ignores my silence. "So unfortunate. I hope you'll be more careful."

Ferris grunts in agreement. I wonder if he even knows what happened.

"Hazel, this is my sister, Ember," Jasper says.

"So you're the human." A scathing sneer sharpens Ember's features.

What do you say to that? Sorry to disappoint you.

The silence stretches, and Sienna's smile becomes murderous as her eyes narrow and her perfect, straight teeth flash. "How are you liking everything?" Sienna asks, the threat in her tone unmistakable. I hold my ground, raising my chin.

"She's just-" Jasper starts to say.

"She can speak for herself," I snap, "But considering I'm here against my will, I don't feel like making small talk."

Sienna's pinched glare transforms into a spiteful grin. She must be thinking of all the ways she'll hurt me after this.

Jasper's hand moves from the back of my chair and brushes under my hair to grip the nape of my neck. He leans close. His breath is warm and I shy away, but his hand on my neck holds me in place. "Please, play nice," he whispers, "I don't want you to get hurt."

Two servers step through the other doorway. They set plates before us. Slices of roast, a dressed baked potato, and a stack of baby carrots.

The conversation pauses while everyone is poured wine and takes their first few bites. I angle my fork with my left hand awkwardly. The meal is bland compared to Crickett's cooking, but I keep my opinion to myself.

Jasper squeezes my neck, his expression prompting.

"Dinner looks lovely," I say. I want to gag.

"Thank you, dear," Sienna responds.

There, I managed some small talk. I look at Jasper as if to say, *Happy?* His hand stays in place but the pressure eases.

"Hazel, tell us about yourself," Ferris asks.

"She earned a bachelor's degree in business," Jasper offers.

"What a boring subject to study. At least with economics or finance, you get something specific," Ember drawls. Those are big opinions for someone who probably hasn't finished high school.

"What are you going to study?" I ask her.

"Psychology."

"Isn't that pretty general too?" I can't help myself.

Ember's brown eyes are darker than mine, almost black. She looks down at my chest and back up, raising an eyebrow at me.

"I mean, Jasper picked environmental studies, didn't he?" I continue. I'm not letting a teenager bully me.

Jasper grins into his wine glass and his hand under my hair has started to stroke down my spine from the middle of my neck to between my shoulder blades.

"We're very proud of him," Sienna says, still playing the adoring mother. Jasper's smile turns brittle. He's barely touched his food, and now he sets his drink down with a clink.

"So, tell me about your pack," I ask Ferris. If I am forced to sit here, I might as well gather information.

Ferris's head tilts in a purely animalistic way. No one would think this male was human. His voice is hoarse. "We are the largest pack with the most territory."

"Wow," I say. "Where do your borders extend to?"

"You'll have to study some maps," he answers.

Sienna jumps in, "There will be a lot to learn."

"I'm sure she's up to it," Jasper says.

The second their eyes are on each other instead of me, I slip the steak knife into my lap and under a cloth napkin.

"Our lineage has ruled Granite Ridge for four generations. Ferris is a powerful Alpha, and Jasper will be, too. It's essential we uphold the highest standard." Sienna drones on.

"Excuse me, I'm not feeling well and I would like to be excused."

"Jasper, why don't you take care of her," Sienna instructs.

"I'm happy to escort her." Ember pushes her chair back as she stands.

"Absolutely not," Jasper growls. He pulls my chair out and offers his hand. I ignore it, instead using my left hand to subtly shift the knife along my thigh and keep it out of sight.

"Thank you," I murmur.

His hand is at the small of my back as we walk toward my prison. As we exit the hallway into the entryway and out of view, I press my lips together firmly. Do or die.

I suck in a deep breath and rotate, holding the knife in my left hand with the blade down. Using my closed hand, I shove Jasper hard.

His eyes widen and he stumbles back a step before catching himself. I dart toward the door, but he's on me. I swipe the knife at him, hoping to keep him at bay.

His face is a mask, the charming boy gone. He surges forward, reaching for my uninjured wrist. I slash at him again, catching his ribs with the tip of the blade and nicking his pressed shirt. Red blooms from the spot.

I grab the door handle and twist. Something heavy hits my back and I slam into the door. My weapon clatters across the tile and I land in a heap.

A huge silver wolf stands over me, a row of fangs bared in my face. With a flick of his tail, he strides away, leaving me curled over my broken wrist.

"That was stupid." Ember's voice cuts through my panic. She's flipping my knife over in her hand with an acidic grin across her face.

"I thought you knew better," Sienna tuts.

Jasper grips my upper arm and tries to pull me upright.

"Jasper, don't be an idiot," Ember snaps.

He steadies me as I rise, keeping my eyes on the floor. My wrist is screaming at me. Nausea rolls over me, turning my vision gray for a second.

"If I can't handle my mate, then I don't deserve her," Jasper snarls.

Ember halts, raising her hands in surrender. "Fine." The knife is gripped lazily between her thumb and palm.

"Come on," Jasper rasps, his grip on my bicep firm. Maybe to the point of pain, but I can't feel anything but my heartbeat in my wrist.

We slow on the stairs, but he follows me all the way down. Someone else closes the door behind us and I hear the lock click.

He drops his hand and trudges to the bathroom. I follow him in. He unbuttons his shirt and pulls out the familiar first aid kit.

"I'm sorry," I mumble.

His cool aqua eyes regard me for a moment before he returns to cleaning the small cut.

"Here, let me." I can't help it. I take the butterfly bandages from him and apply one end below the cut. Pressing the skin down, I place the other end, so it holds the wound shut.

He follows it with a large Band-Aid.

Finally, he speaks. "That stunt is not going to help our case."

"So I should lie down and be a good girl?" I say with venom.

He looks exhausted. "You'd prefer to spend the rest of your days locked down here?"

"No, I want to get home to my real mate," I say. I look for any hint of sympathy, but he's closed off.

"I'll let you get some rest," he says, turning away.

He drops his ruined shirt into the trash can and trudges to the living space, flopping onto the sofa and throwing an arm over his eyes.

"Aren't you leaving?" I ask.

"No."

Great.

"I'd prefer you left," I argue. "Aren't you worried I'll try to kill you in your sleep?"

With a groan, he sits up and looks at me over the back of the sofa.

"Really?" He smirks at me, though the warmth doesn't reach his eyes. "If we want to convince anyone you're warming up to me, we need to spend more time together."

"Ugh." I wrinkle my nose and pull the bathroom door closed.

I clumsily comb out my hair and brush my teeth. Then I change from the dress into a t-shirt and leggings, sighing as I ease the overly tight fabric off.

In my temporary bedroom, I carefully lock the door and tug the handle to make sure it's secure. Exhaustion weighs my movements. I settle on top of the covers and wince. It takes ages to position my wrist in a way that isn't agony. But I'm exhausted, and I sleep like the dead.

SLATE

Heath stands in the center of the training room, his arms folded and his frame tense. The Thetas and Zetas stand loosely around him.

"Elm, Cassia, Aven, take the outside border. Vale and Lazuli, go over the trail again. See if we missed anything."

They bow their heads and head toward the lockers to stow their clothes before shifting.

"Hawthorne, contact Cashel and Nyx again. I need to talk to them as soon as possible."

He eyes me. "Slate, take internal patrol."

"Send me to the border." It escapes my mouth before I can think better. "Or let me take a car and follow the trail past Ironcrest. I know I can track her."

We both know it isn't true. There's no unique scent to follow. They used a car, something we weren't prepared for. It's not how wolves operate. And wolves certainly don't use guns.

"No," he admonishes me. I bristle. "Slate, you're going to get yourself killed if you try."

After a sleepless night, my control is nonexistent. Every part of me aches, and I let my anger show. "She's your niece. I thought you'd be a bit more concerned about her," I snap.

Hawthorne looks between us and heads to the door, giving Heath privacy to put me in my place. I'm reckless, the chaos inside my head drowning out logical thought.

"It's going to be okay. We will get her back, without losing anyone else." His soothing tone does nothing to calm me.

"She's worth more than that," I spit.

The line between his brows deepens. "How would Hazel feel to come home and learn two of her friends died when it could have been handled peacefully?"

He's right, but I can't stop. "We don't know if that's possible. We don't know what's happening to her right now."

"She'd be devastated," he warns.

"I'm not asking for a team. But let me go after my mate!" I'm shouting. I've never raised my voice at Heath or even seriously disagreed with him before.

"You're not the only one here with a mate." His voice is low.

"How'd that work out for you?" I snap. It's so far over the line that he can't let it slide. I welcome any pain he'll inflict. I deserve it for letting this happen to her.

Heath advances, his movements liquid. He looks down at me.

"I'm going to let that go because I know you're exhausted and blaming yourself. I know you're newly mated. But if you ever speak to me in that manner again, you will lose your position in this pack." His voice is deadly.

His dominance presses down on me, pushing me into the floor. I want to snarl, but I also want a home here for Hazel and me when we get her back. Begrudgingly, I drop my eyes and bow my head.

"Go, run it off. Where I assigned you."

This time, I hold my tongue. But I don't obey.

Tearing off my clothes and shifting, I spring toward the southern border. I won't cross any boundaries unless I catch a trail.

Ahead I spot three wolves - Lazuli's white and gray form, Vale's solid black wolf, and Onyx's charcoal one. A snarl builds in my throat. He was supposed to be protecting her. I trusted him.

I'm not in control of my own body as I leap at him. Onyx twists, baring his teeth even as I pin him to the ground.

Lazuli is yelling at me. It's muffled by the blood rushing through my ears. When did he shift back?

Onyx stops growling and lays his head down, submitting. He shifts, his bare chest under my paws. His eyes are bloodshot.

Suddenly ashamed, I step back and shift, kneeling beside him with my knees in the dirt. "You were supposed to keep her safe," I growl.

Onyx sits up, grimacing. His hand grips his shoulder, steadying the place where a bullet ripped right through him. Purple bruising radiates out from the dark scab.

Lazuli pulls me back, his words finally clearing my fog. "She should have been safe. They were a hundred feet from the office! They would have snatched her right out of your house if they had to."

"I'm sorry, man." Onyx's midnight eyes meet mine, looking as angry as I feel, with the same edge of devastation.

"You should have died before you let them take her." Part of me knows I'm being cruel, but I don't care. I can't bring myself to forgive either of us.

"Believe me, I tried," he says, motioning to his bandage. "But it didn't stick."

"We are going to get her back," Vale says, sounding overly confident for a gangly teenager.

"Whatever it takes," Onyx says firmly.

I want to believe them. I need to trust Heath as he works with the other Alphas to figure this out. But every instinct I have is roaring for me to do something. Track, hunt, fight, defend. I can hardly think. And what if they're too late, or all his efforts fail and we've lost precious time trying to be diplomatic instead of tearing apart the Ironcrest and Granite Ridge territories?

We failed to solidify our bond. If we're separated too long, her mark will fade away. Then she's just a human who knows our secrets, and she loses what little protection I was able to give her.

"Come on, join us on patrol. It'll help to be doing something," Lazuli says before shifting into his wolf.

"Do you want me to?" I ask Onyx.

He's staring unfocused, as lost to his anxious thoughts as I am. At my words, he snaps back. "Yeah, come on. Maybe we'll find something we missed yesterday."

I close my eyes, allowing my wolf form to emerge. It feels grounding to dig my claws into the earth and focus on picking apart all the scents on the breeze.

Lazuli leads. I shouldn't be with them, so I don't pull rank. But he's right, it helps to be doing something and to be with my packmates. Onyx stays near me, and I sense his concern and guilt. Somehow, it makes me feel less alone in this.

XIV
MEATLOAF &
MANIPULATIONS

HAZEL

The next morning, Jasper wakes me up by knocking on the bedroom door. "Hazel?" I sit up, my head pounding. I'm dehydrated. "I'm making breakfast and then we need to talk," he says.

Groaning, I head into the bathroom, cleaning myself up the best I can with my left hand. My wrist feels decent and I want to keep it that way.

It takes a few minutes to awkwardly pull my shirt over my head with one arm. I rinse a washcloth and start to dab at my tattoo. The lines are no longer raised and angry-looking. Confused, I wipe my finger down the tiny black moons. It's completely healed. How many days has it been? Three? Four?

Dragging the brush through my hair, I'm surprised to see my brunette roots are getting long. It's only been a few weeks since my last highlight. I'm looking less and less like the polished Los Angeles girl I was pretending to be for so long.

He's waiting for me at the card table in the corner of the kitchenette, looking far too relaxed for someone sitting in a fold-out chair. He takes a huge bite of a waffle and waves his fork at me. Sighing, I settle into the seat across from him and stare down at the waffle he brought me.

"Ready for some fresh air?" He sounds hopeful.

"What do you mean?" I ask.

"How's a pack tour and then lunch sound?" His grin is lopsided. He's back to being confident and charming.

"I don't know."

"How's the wrist?" he asks, eyeing the bandage. "Need me to redo it?"

"It feels pretty good. Let's leave it alone," I say. "So we're going out there? With your packmates?"

He nods. "It'll be fine."

I hesitate. I want the chance to escape, but I'm terrified of his mother and her minions. My attempt last night didn't go well, and it could have been so much worse.

"Look, Hazel, I've been thinking," Jasper begins.

The door clicks open. "Knock, knock, lovebirds." Sienna's voice drifts in. She doesn't wait for an invitation.

Jasper drops his head, his hand massaging the nape of his neck.

Reflexively, I move to stand behind Jasper's chair so my back isn't to the wicked witch. He reaches up and takes my uninjured hand.

"Good morning, Hazel." Sienna is positively cheerful. The hair on my arms raises.

"Mother," Jasper responds coldly. He pushes his chair back, standing and wrapping his arm around my waist.

"Just checking up on our newest pack member." She draws closer. "I heard you two spent the night together."

I hate the implication and the way her glittering eyes rove over me. It's easy to tell who the real predator is here.

As much as I hate it, her thinking we are bonding is what keeps me safe. I grip Jasper's shirt, wishing I could disappear.

"How's that mark fading?" The memory of our last encounter is still fresh in my mind, so I freeze when she reaches for me. She tugs my neckline and inspects the ring of soft pink scars. "Very good. You're about ready for a replacement, don't you think?" she murmurs, not letting go of me.

"I asked you not to touch my things," Jasper growls.

Sienna turns her cat-like gaze on him. He doesn't back down, his stare level and his chin high.

She strikes without any warning. Her open hand slaps him hard enough to knock him down. He tumbles into me, but Sienna has my shirt in her grasp, so as I sag, I'm choking on my shirt collar.

She releases me and I drop beside Jasper. Knees stinging, I pull him up. He rubs his hand over his jaw. "Don't touch him," I snarl.

Sienna cocks her head, sinking into a crouch. She grips my broken wrist. I freeze, barely breathing. She deliberately pauses, her eyes boring into mine. Unexpectedly, she drops my wrist and instead pinches my chin, tipping it up and down, studying me. Her mouth pinches, and then she releases me and stands. "Excellent. I'll leave you guys to it."

Jasper rises and holds his hand out for me.

She pauses at the base of the stairs. "I expect a new claim mark by tomorrow morning."

"You can't make me do this," I stammer.

Sienna takes a step toward me, her eyes narrow and her smile terrifying. "Girl, I've been very kind to you so far. You've been our guest. I've treated you like a daughter. If you two can't cooperate, then we can resort to other measures." Her eyes flick down my body. "You don't need all your fingernails to be a good little mate."

As fear washes over me, Jasper pulls me against his chest. He wraps his arms around me protectively.

"Very good." Sienna says, closing the door behind herself.

"Are you okay?" I ask in a hollow tone.

"Fine. Don't worry about me." His voice rumbles through his chest. Shivering, I push his arms away. My panic spirals higher, threatening to overwhelm me.

A new claim mark by tomorrow? Time is up. "What am I going to do?" I exhale a ragged breath, my throat clogging up.

If she tried to take Bracken Creek, it would be destroyed. My friends would never submit to Ferris and Sienna, and Heath would never allow it to happen while he was living. The idea makes my skin icy.

Jasper turns his back to me, cleaning up our breakfast.

I imagine returning, now mates with Jasper, standing beside Sienna as she orders her wolves to subdue my friends. Slate would be betrayed again. I don't even notice I'm crying until it builds into a sob.

Jasper is there, rubbing my back. I want to hate him. But he's had over twenty years under Sienna's dictatorship; can I really fault him for obeying her?

"I won't do this," I choke. "I can't do this to them."

"We'll figure it out," Jasper murmurs.

"I can't be responsible for this." The tears come faster now. I'm shuddering, hands shaking, body freezing.

Jasper guides me into a seat and lets me cry it out until my cheek is flat on the vinyl table and my tears are spent.

He sits across from me. "Look, I'm going to get you out of here."

I sit up so fast pain shoots through my arm. My breath is a hiss but I can't be bothered. "What do you mean?"

"I don't exactly want to be tethered to someone we…" He trails off.

"Abducted?" I supply.

"Yeah," he says.

"You're seriously going to help me?" I whisper, scared Sienna might hear through the ceiling.

He looks at the table. "I want to. But it's going to be hard."

"I don't care. I'll do whatever I have to," I emphasize.

He smirks wryly. "We'll see about that."

We stand before Sienna and Ferris, who are holding court in a pair of armchairs before the sleek marble fireplace. Modular seating wraps the cold room. They sent away the attending pack members so we could have privacy.

My left arm supports my right, and Jasper's hands are heavy on my hips.

"So you've decided you prefer Jasper, after all." Sienna's face pinches in suspicion.

I inhale slowly. "I would prefer a strong partner and some sort of autonomy over a life locked in a basement." It's technically true.

"I am going to take her on a tour of our territory and then get her settled into my house," Jasper says.

"And?" Sienna asks.

"We would like an official claiming celebration since we are alpha heirs," he requests. I try to keep my breathing even though my heart is racing.

"Of course," Ferris answers. He lifts Sienna's hand and kisses it. They're the picture of magnanimous leaders, even if it's a façade over rotten teeth and claws.

"I think it's an exceptional idea. I'll get the team started right away," Sienna says. "Do you have any preferences?"

I shake my head.

"Hazel has never attended one before, so we will trust your decisions," Jasper says smoothly.

"Perfect. Let's say nine o'clock for your little party?"

"Nine is good." Jasper steers me away. The moment we are out of sight, my muscles slacken.

"Well done," he murmurs in my ear.

Jasper guides me to the left into a foyer. With a heave, he pushes open an ornate ivory door, and I step through and get my first real view of Granite Ridge Pack.

The sky is gloomy, casting the entire compound in a gray light. It's so entirely different from Heath's pack, I'm shocked. Concrete buildings line up on either side of a dirt road.

I want to relax, but the show isn't over. Jasper's plan is clever, but it's risky. But I meant it when I said I would do whatever's necessary. Step one was requesting a celebration for our official claiming. Step two, convince everyone we're genuine. My stomach clenches with guilt.

Jasper takes my hard, guiding me down the main road. Sickly-looking weeds grow up around the sides.

Jasper shows me their training building. It's all cinder blocks and steel. Their cafeteria sits directly opposite, maintaining the uniform look.

Inside, a dozen men are lifting weights or sparring. Weapons line the walls here too, but there are a lot of guns out in the open. The suspicious looks the pack members shoot at me make my stomach churn. I'm relieved when Jasper leads me outside again.

There's no school or store, only a few utility and storage buildings. Two or three dozen identical homes extend down the lane. It's odd that his family enjoys a sprawling luxurious manse while their entire pack lives in matching utilitarian housing.

"That one is mine." He points to the third house on the right.

"You guys don't have a school?"

"Nope. Not a lot of kids right now," he says.

"That's kind of sad."

"I hadn't thought about it." He shrugs.

As he walks me around the perimeter of the compound, I try to spy out anything that might provide an opportunity to get away later, but I can't even tell which direction is north or south. I don't even know where Granite Ridge is in relation to Bracken Creek.

My wrist starts to ache with the motion of walking. I bite my cheek. There's nothing I can do about it.

We ended up at the cafeteria for an early lunch. It's more like a school lunch line than the delicious buffets at Crickett's. I'm handed a tray with dry meatloaf, mashed potatoes I'm sure was made from potato starch and sawdust, and some corn and spinach devoid of any salt. We sit at a folding table and I try to eat a few bites of the food, but it's so bland, and I have no appetite.

"Can I see more of your territory?" I ask. "Maybe a little hike?"

"Maybe next time."

His eyes are scanning around the room, reminding me of his brother again. I rub at my claim mark with my uninjured hand. As of this morning, it's nothing but shiny pale pink scars, far too light for my comfort.

Jasper stills. "Hazel, finish eating," he says quietly.

Four men amble across the space, taking up positions on either side of both of us.

Jasper's pose is casual, but every muscle is taut. I sit very still and grip my fork.

"Hey, Jasper," one of them croons.

"Flint," Jasper responds, "Aries."

Flint is rough and wiry and looks like he would like to eat me. Aries is a massive man with black hair in a ponytail. The other two are teenagers, following their role models, no doubt.

"Is this your little human slut?" Flint asks. His friends guffaw.

"Apologize." Jasper's voice is low.

"Why?" Flint challenges. "She was your brother's bitch and now-"

Jasper slams him down on the table so fast I didn't even see him reach up. My tray bounces with the impact. His shoulder is inches from me and I cringe away as far as I can without touching the greasy kid next to me.

Aries pulls a switchblade and snaps it open next to Jasper's head. My heart accelerates. I fight to keep my breathing steady. Don't show fear.

"Give me a good reason," Jasper growls, ignoring the blade.

"Jasper, please," I whisper. I'd prefer he doesn't become a human pin cushion.

"Apologize to her," Jasper reiterates, his voice so low it vibrates in my bones.

"Sorry," Flint mutters.

"Don't worry about it," I rush.

Jasper releases him, glaring at Aries. "If you look at her again, I will cut off your dick."

I choke, somewhere between a gasp and a laugh. Jasper stalks to my side, scattering their sidekicks. I take his hand and we abandon our trays on the table.

He leads me across the road toward his cabin. We reach the front and he stops. "I have to kiss you." His voice is barely audible. It's a warning, not a question.

"Not a chance," I growl. But the eyes of half his pack are on us, with varying expressions from smirks to hunger.

"I have to show that I'm claiming you." He pushes my back against the door.

"I can't," I argue. He rests his forearm above my head and leans into my space. A lithe form with red lipstick is standing behind the gaggle of jeering idiots. Watching, judging. "Fine." The word feels like a betrayal.

I rest my head against the door and close my eyes, resigning myself to this compromise. Praying Slate will forgive me.

Kissing Slate is like grabbing a live wire, full of sparks and electricity. Kissing Jasper is like curling up with a warm blanket. He is gentle, tipping my face up with his hand on my chin. His lips are soft, pressing to mine and not demanding more. He holds me still until we hear cat calls from his packmates.

When he releases me, his sea-blue eyes softly glow. Pushing the door open, I stumble inside. The door slams and I leap away from him.

"You okay?"

"Obviously not." I'm at my breaking point. I miss Slate so much it's like a physical wound, worse than my broken wrist. And now I've kissed someone else. It might have been for my own survival, but I feel like slime. My voice is shrill. "Your packmates threatened to stab you."

Jasper grabs my shoulders, keeping me at arm's length. "Hazel, breathe. You're okay."

"Okay?" I repeat. My breathing is shallow and quick.

"I'm going to keep you safe," he murmurs.

I try to glare at him, but the room has started to spin. My cheeks are wet. "I can't handle this," I gasp.

Jasper drags me to the sofa and I collapse. My body shakes with another uncontrollable sob. He presses a cup to my lips. "Drink." I manage to obey. The cold water pulls me out of my spiral and my breathing levels out.

"I'm sorry my pack is full of assholes," he says. I focus on his face. His lips are a thin line.

"Does that kind of thing happen a lot?"

"The disrespect?" he asks.

"The violence," I clarify.

Jasper shrugs. "My mom encourages it. Keeps us strong." I stare at him. "It's how things are." He turns away, face closed off.

"It doesn't have to be," I say weakly. "Jasper, this is insane. The cruelty and ruthlessness - none of that is normal. My uncle's pack isn't like that at all."

His back still to me, he throws his hands up. "Look, I can't change anything. I've tried."

"Seems to me that you're adding to it," I argue weakly.

He spins, anger flashing in his eyes. "Do you have any idea what they would do to you, given the chance?" Breathing heavily, he narrows his stormy blue eyes. "I should check your wrist." His voice is dull.

At the little kitchen table, he unwraps and examines my wrist. The swelling is gone but an angry bruise wraps around the circumference. He gently rewraps it. Once he finishes, he cradles my wrist and meets my eyes.

"Would it be so bad if it was me?" His soft voice pleads with me. He is alone here. It breaks my heart, but I can't save him by sacrificing myself.

I sigh. "But it's not. Honestly, it never could have been you. Slate and I were drawn together from the first day. I've never felt that with anyone else," I try to explain.

He rests his forehead in his hand, slumping in his seat.

"Why don't you leave?"

He looks tortured. "I'm the heir. Next in line to be Alpha."

"So?" I press.

"Where would I go? No other pack would have me. I'm too dominant. I would be a threat to their heirs, whether I wanted to be or not."

I have no words. I don't understand their world.

"I can't be a wolf without a pack. Hazel, you have to understand that for us, our pack is everything."

"Wouldn't it be better to be alone and free than endure the abuse here?" I whisper. I want to take the words back, but I still believe them.

Before my eyes, he shuts down. "Let's just watch some TV and wait for tonight."

He has one of those projectors and a white screen that unravels from the ceiling. While he looks through options, I microwave a bag of popcorn from his snack cabinet.

"How's this look?" He's selected a superhero movie.

"No, thank you."

"Okay, what do you want to watch?

"We could find a true crime doc since your family is so murder-y," I quip.

"Or a comedy," he says, good naturedly.

"I've got an idea." Wrenching the remote away from him, I navigate to the search bar and start punching letters. A few moments later, I've queued up a ridiculous old horror movie - featuring werewolves.

Jasper laughs. "Fair."

As we eat and he laughs at the movie, I find myself slowly relaxing. Everything is going to be okay. But as the sun sets, my nerves surge.

He turns the volume down while the credits roll. "Doing okay?"

"Yeah, I'm okay," I lie. There are so many ways this could go sideways.

"I'm going to get you a dress to wear and see about that wine."

Jasper disappears into his bedroom and reappears holding a mason jar with translucent pink liquid inside.

"Is that-"

"Concentrated rowanberry juice," he supplies. "It blocks our shifter abilities for an hour or two." He grins, sloshing the contents of the jar. "No wolves to worry about."

"You've just got that lying around?" I ask, raising an eyebrow.

"Yep. Usually, I use only a little at a time to dose people I'm pissed at. But I think it'll take the whole batch this time. To be safe."

"You won't overdose them or anything?"

"Nah, might make them puke at the worst," he says shrugging, "I'm off to go poison the beer!"

"Be careful."

He smirks. "It almost sounds like you care about me."

While he's gone, I poke through his drawers and closet. The man has a lot of knives and he didn't bother locking them away. My heart softens, some shred of trust solidifying. But the house is only so big, so I end up back on the sofa. I want to peer out the window and watch his packmates, but I'm too worried about them seeing me.

Nerves escalating, I pace from the kitchen to the living space and back, over and over. It's going to be fine. I'm going to make it through this. Slate will be fine, Jasper will be okay, and Onyx is probably healing. I'm not going to break down again.

"Baby, I'm home!" Jasper hollers.

He leans around the doorframe and holds out another black dress. It looks shorter, maybe above the knee, and is thankfully closer to my size.

"Looks great," I say, taking it from him.

"And you'll need this." He holds out a knife in a strappy sheath. The blade is short but wicked looking. "It should fit under your skirt without showing."

"Thanks." I take the weapon and test out the strap around my thigh. It's perfect.

"You can keep that. Consider it a mating present." He winks at me and I shove him, rolling my eyes.

"One more thing," he says, holding out my cell phone. "I nicked this for you. If she notices, I'll just tell her I wanted to go through your messages."

"Oh my gosh!" I press the power button, but only a red empty-battery icon flashes.

"Sorry, I don't have that kind of charger," he says.

Swallowing back my disappointment, I say, "Let me change. You need to make yourself look decent too."

"You know I already look incredible," he replies with a cheeky grin. I respond by shutting the door in his laughing face.

XV
FLIGHTS & FOES

HAZEL

The party is in full swing by the time we arrive, intentionally late. Sienna and Ferris stand on a small platform in the center of the road, between the cafeteria and the training facility. Folding tables and chairs outline the space with the center left empty.

Beer is flowing and several pack members seem pretty drunk already. Is the rowanberry affecting them?

I smooth down my skirt and tuck my hair behind my ears.

"You look fine," Jasper murmurs. I scowl at him. "Sorry," he amends. My nerves have nothing to do with my appearance.

Taking my hand, he leads me toward his parents. We step onto the platform, our steps making a hollow sound. Jasper kisses his mother's cheek. His father grips his shoulder and nods stonily.

Someone shoves mugs of beer into our hands. I wrinkle my nose at the smell.

Ferris raises his mug, and the shifters around him fall silent. The quiet ripples out until every mouth is shut and all eyes are on him.

His deep voice carries, but he makes no effort to raise his voice. The entire pack listens intently, worshiping every word.

"My pack, we are here to celebrate a mating bond between our heir and the heir of another alpha line. Their offspring will lead Granite Ridge forward. Some day we will not only be the biggest pack in the state, we will be the most powerful pack on the continent!"

The crowd roars, but it cuts off the second Ferris opens his mouth again.

"To my son and his new mate!" He raises his mug and takes a swig. The entire crowd echoes their alpha, everyone chugging their beer. Jasper takes a drink too, but I guess he has to if he wants to avoid suspicion. The fact he is now hobbled too makes my stomach churn.

Now the real party begins. Music pumps through old speakers. There are only a handful of female shifters in the pack, and the men shove each other and jostle for a chance to dance with them. Most of the women have two men grinding up on them.

"Want to dance?" Jasper murmurs in my ear. His thumb rubs over my knuckles.

I grimace. "Rather not."

He chuckles. "We have time. At least get a drink and eat something."

"No offense, but the food here is terrible."

He pulls me into his chest, his hair brushing my temple as he leans over my shoulder. "We still have to show off how we are a couple," he reminds me.

"Gross," I mutter.

"Just what every man wants to hear," he retorts with a chuckle. Exhaling dramatically, I turn my head and place a kiss on his cheek. "That's not going to sell it," he warns.

"I hate you," I whisper as he drags me toward the center. I'm joking, mostly.

We halt in the middle of the throng. The music vibrates in my bones. Ignoring everyone around us, Jasper pulls me close and we start to sway. As the pop vocals race through the chorus, he spins me. His smile is genuine, and I can't help but return it.

Softly, he murmurs, "We've got a lot of eyes on us."

"One time." I hate this part, but it'll be worth it.

With a sigh, I take Jasper's face in my hand and kiss him, mouth closed. Holding my waist, he presses forward, bending me backward. It's an effective show and over quickly, fortunately. It takes all my willpower to repress the urge to wipe my mouth as he tugs me out of the spotlight. Hopefully, everyone thinks we are seeking out privacy to cement our bond.

The moment we close his front door, he drops my hand and hurries to the window. "Okay, let's give it ten minutes." Without glancing at me, he crosses the room, heading toward the bedroom.

Lurching forward, I catch his arm. "Jasper, thank you for this." Swallowing, he nods curtly and steps past me.

It takes only minutes to change into a dark t-shirt and leggings and strap my knife on my thigh again. I'm tightening the laces on my tennis shoes when Jasper leans around the door frame. "I think it's been long enough. This will take me a minute or two and then you run like hell."

"I'm ready." Slinging my backpack over my shoulder, I follow him to the bedroom window. He slings a leg over and slides out, turning to catch me as I jump after him. My breathing aches in my chest as I press against the concrete wall and watch him creep around the corner.

The minutes stretch as the raucous party reverberates through the dim. Drunk men shout and jeer, and it sounds like at least one fight has broken out.

All at once, the overhead string lights and the safety lights cut out. Darkness overtakes the commune. Shouts rise, but I don't wait to listen. Heart thudding, I take off, racing forward into the blackness of night. There's scarcely enough moonlight to see the tree line, but I have to reach it before anyone thinks to look into the night. My eyes aren't as sensitive as a wolf's, and I'm terrified they won't adjust in time. As the trees loom, my vision brightens, and I gasp in relief.

Plunging into the trees, I splutter as my chest splinters. I'm not meant to be running like this. The border is not that far - the steady downhill slope reassures me that I'm going the right direction.

Just as a sense of near victory gives me a second wind, the crunch and snap of a pursuer echoes around me. Blind terror washes over me, making my steps clumsy. I'm going to fall, and they'll catch me.

A body hurtles into me, nails scraping along my back as they clutch at my shirt. I roll once and then spring up, ignoring the pain shooting through my arm.

Ember is crouched a few feet away. Her dark eyes glow like liquid copper. I fumble with the straps around my leg and yank out the knife a second before Ember leaps at me.

I slash wildly. She hisses, twisting to avoid my blade.

"You can't make me go back," I snarl.

Ember straightens and begins to prowl in a wide circle. The knife in my hand is shaking.

"Don't worry, frail little Hazel. You're not going back to my brother." Her teeth gleam in the darkness.

"What is wrong with you?" I mutter.

She launches and I strike, slicing into her arm. But she is so fast and isn't deterred by the blood streaming down to her elbow. She grabs my left wrist and twists it. I hold onto the handle with every ounce of strength I have, but she wrenches my arm around and brings a knee up into my gut.

My ass hits the dirt hard. I can't hesitate, not if I want to live. Scrambling back, I crawl away from my attacker.

Her lean form advances, now gripping my knife. With a smug laugh, she tosses it between her hands. "I don't know what my mother was thinking. You aren't even a wolf. And Jasper is clueless."

She's faster than I am. But what's my other option? Pushing myself up on my feet, I turn and run with everything I've got, waiting for the blade to embed into my spine.

A screech splits the air along with the sound of two bodies colliding. I turn to see a flash of platinum hair.

"Don't touch her!" Jasper roars.

Ember uses her momentum to roll onto her feet in a smooth movement. "I think you should take off with your little mate while you can. I'm going to be the next alpha and we both know it."

"Run, Hazel!" Jasper yells.

My feet stumble but I right myself and tear through the undergrowth. Bursting from the trees, I stumble down the steep hillside leading down to the creek. Fog rolls down the gorge, reflecting the silvery moonlight. I could cry with relief.

Slate sprints toward me, the calf-deep water soaking into his gray sweats. I meet him in the shallows and he scoops me up. Water sprays around us and I latch onto him, clawing at his shirt. I'm desperate for him. He carries me toward Bracken Creek territory. I'm never letting go of him again.

Chest heaving, he pulls away to study my face, but I press forward and crush our mouths together. It's not a gentle hello kiss, it's fear, relief, and need all rolled together.

I could kiss him forever, but I don't know who is emerging from the forest behind us. The entire Granite Ridge pack could come racing from the trees at any moment. We need to move. He slides me down his body and onto my own feet, his hand tight around mine.

Onyx steps from the shadows, flanked by two reddish-gold wolves, Marigold and Cedar. My breath rushes out, at the sight of him, pale but very much alive. I launch myself at my friend. He lifts me in a hug and spins us once.

"I'm so relieved you aren't dead!" I blurt out, tears pooling in my eyes.

"I barely needed a Band-Aid," he jokes, shoving his unruly hair from his eyes.

Slate lets out a low growl and I whip around. Jasper stumbles from the forest, trying to slow his descent down the hill. Blood splatters his shirt, and I have no idea if it's his or Ember's.

"Are you okay?" I yelp. Jasper nods, stepping into the water.

Onyx grabs my arm and pulls me against him, backing us away.

Slate stalks forward, closing the distance in two strides. Jasper takes a step back, raising his hands defensively. Without waiting for an explanation, Slate draws back and swings. Jasper makes no attempt to block him. His fist connects with Jasper's jaw, sending the younger brother reeling.

I let out a strangled cry and start toward them, but Onyx catches me around the waist. He holds tight, murmuring apologies into my hair.

"What the hell are you doing?" I look between Slate and Onyx, begging for someone to stop this.

Slate looks at me, his face hard. "He's the one who sent the rogues after you and betrayed you to the other packs."

Jasper's lips thin, but he doesn't argue or deny it.

"It wasn't his fault," I protest, "and he made it right."

"So he suddenly has a conscience?" Slate fumes.

"No," I plead with him.

Jasper meets my eyes, shaking his head.

Does he want Slate to hurt him? Maybe coming home injured is the only way his mother won't blame him for my escape. I stifle a sob.

Marigold and Cedar pace the edge of the water, ready to leap forward and defend Slate. Shaking out his hand, Slate steps back and I sag with relief.

Jasper's face hardens. "Is that all you've got?"

"You're not worth it," Slate says over his shoulder.

"Doesn't she taste like berries when you kiss her?" Jasper taunts.

Slate snaps. He rounds on him, and I turn my face into Onyx's chest, unable to watch. But as the sound of fists striking flesh echoes around me, I can't help but peek. Slate grips Jasper's shirt as he lands a blow into his gut. Jasper gasps for air. Slate releases him and he crumples into the water.

Without glancing back, Slate stalks toward me, his eyes dark. Onyx releases me and steps back. I peer past Slate, tears wrecking my vision.

Jasper rises, water dripping from his black clothes. He wipes blood out of the corner of his mouth.

Unable to stop myself, I push past Slate, I start toward Jasper, but he holds up his hand. His expression is resigned. "Go back to your mate." The disdain in his voice is like a knife. He turns and walks away, clutching his ribs.

I stand there, stunned, the icy water rushing around my ankles.

"What happened?" Slate asks gruffly, grabbing my forearm to get a better look at my wrist. "Hazel, who hurt you?" His voice is so low, goosebumps break out over my arms.

His eyes work their way down me, searching for other injuries. I ignore him, watching as Jasper trudges up the hill and into the trees.

Slate stands beside me. "Did he touch you?"

My stomach drops. I asked him not to, and he hurt Jasper anyway. Anger curls within me, hot and bitter. Scowling, I face my mate. "He protected me."

Slate's lip curls.

"Not very well," Onyx growls.

"He shielded me from his pack and then risked himself to help me escape." A shiver racks my body. Slate wraps his arms around me, his warmth seeping into my chest.

"I'm sorry," he says. "I should never have left you."

I can't even answer. I can barely see through the blur of tears. I let Slate sweep me up in his arms. His woodsy scent washes over me, the promise of safety and refuge, and I am so very tired.

He scales the hillside effortlessly, and I press my face into his chest. I could fall asleep like this, except I'm filthy and he is damp. As he walks, Slate murmurs apologies and promises, and slowly my heart thaws.

He sets me down as we near his cabin. His hand stays around my waist, and he grips Onyx's arm with the other. Marigold and Cedar are already gone. "Thank you, man."

Onyx nods. "I'm glad we got you back. Slate was getting pretty unbearable." His familiar grin in place. Slate lightly shoves him. Onyx laughs and jogs off toward his family's cabin.

Slate lifts my arm again, just below the wrap. "We should take you to Sable to check your arm."

"Yeah," I agree, but we don't move. He takes slow, deep breaths.

I missed this man so much. Leaning my head back, I look up at those evergreen eyes, almost black in the night. Under the trees, where the stars can't reach us, he is a silvery outline.

His hand rubs up and down my back, tangling in my hair.

"I tried to run. They locked me in a basement. Sienna thought she could beat me until I agreed to be Jasper's mate, and he didn't even want that either. We poisoned everyone so they couldn't shift, and Jasper's sister attacked me..." The words rush out.

Slate starts to respond, but I suspect it's going to be threats of violence against anyone who even looked in my direction during this ordeal, so I stop him the best way I know how. Grabbing his shirt, I yank him down and cover his mouth with mine.

Heat races through me, my skin tingling. I might be angry with him, but I need him more. He grips my ass and lifts me, my legs looping around his waist. Turning us, he presses my back into a tree. A thrill zings in my blood and I scratch my nails down his ribs.

He kisses down my neck. I recognize now that he is replacing the scent of his brother with his own. Claiming me again in this small way.

"Take me home," I rasp.

A throat clears, the noise cutting through my fog. Slate sets me on my feet so fast I almost fall, but his grip on my waist is steel.

The Alpha, my uncle, stands there. His hands are in his pockets and his eyebrows are the highest I've ever seen them. "Hazel, you're home," he acknowledges.

My face is on fire. "I'm sorry. Yeah."

A smile creases his face. The joy at my homecoming is stronger than my embarrassment. I dive toward him and he wraps me in one of his massive hugs. "You're safe." His voice falters. Is he crying?

"Jasper decided to help me escape," I fill in, "and Slate met us..." I turn to my mate. "How did you know to be there?"

"Someone texted me." He shrugs. I give him a pointed look.

"You should have told me," Heath warns, glowering at Slate.

Slate dips his head. "I'm sorry. I didn't want to risk anyone else if it was a setup."

Heath's jaw ticks. "We can talk about this later."

"Sir? Her wrist was injured," Slate interjects.

"Sable is probably still awake. She's a night owl," Heath says.

Great. Now it'll be hours until I can get Slate alone again.

SLATE

Sable's home looks older than the other cabins. It's built of rough stacked stones instead of timber. Growing up, I imagined it was some sort of witch cottage here long before our pack arrived.

Hazel sits on a raised bench, the warm light of overhead lanterns turning her skin and hair a shade deeper gold. I hover nearby. Sable wants me to leave, but it's not going to happen.

Sable gently unwraps the filthy bandage and turns Hazel's wrist over. She makes a thoughtful humming noise which means she finds something interesting.

Hazel is distracted by the shelves of glass jars and bundles of herbs hung from the rough-hewn beams across the ceiling. I love seeing her face relaxed like this. Sable cocks her head, causing her long braid to slip over her shoulder.

I can't stand waiting a second longer. "Is she okay?"

"Of course," Sable murmurs.

"I'm fine." Hazel chimes in, rolling her eyes. As if she wasn't just held captive by our enemies for three days.

Heath looms in the doorway, his arms crossed. The muscles in his forearms twitch and his hands clench. "What happened to your wrist?"

Hazel bites her lip, her mask slipping and showing her exhaustion. I want to hold her, sweep her away to rest. "Um, Sienna. She broke it, or tried to." She shrugs as if it is no big deal.

It hasn't occurred to me how the injury happened, or I assumed it was during the kidnapping. Hearing it was my own mother who intentionally hurt my mate, my breath hitches. A growl rumbles from my chest without my permission. My eyes are likely glowing green.

"I, apparently, disrespected her," Hazel adds.

Heath's face is stone. I can feel his rage pouring off him in waves through our pack bond. He is as angry as I am, and I find it comforting.

"I'm going to kill her," I snarl. It's out of turn, but I can't help it.

Hazel frowns. "No, you aren't."

Sable smiles at her indulgently. "Hazel, you couldn't stop him if you wanted to. She hurt his mate."

"She's his mom," she argues.

"No, she isn't," I snap. I take a slow breath to steady myself. I need to shift and run. I need to fight and tear and draw blood. But I can't leave Hazel. Look what happened last time I left her alone.

Sable shushes us. "When did this happen?"

"Two days ago?" Two days. She spent three days total with these monsters. I will never forgive myself.

Sable exchanges a meaningful look with Heath. Apprehension prickles across my shoulders. Patting Hazel's hand lightly, she says, "It looks good. You're healing quickly." She pulls out a structured brace and slips it over Hazel's wrist and between her thumb and fingers, tightening the Velcro straps.

"Thank you." Hazel bends her arm, testing out the range of motion.

"Were you hurt in any other way?" Sable's voice softens.

Hazel shakes her head. I'm not sure I believe her. She puts everyone else first, and I know she will minimize her pain.

"Okay, you two should sleep for a few hours. We can discuss everything properly in the morning," Heath instructs. He says sleep a little too forcefully. My neck flushes again and Hazel turns a gorgeous shade of pink.

She nods and pushes off the bench onto her feet. I can't help but reach for her hand, but she pulls away. "Could you guys give me a minute?" She looks from me to Heath.

Icy fear sinking into my stomach, I follow Heath outside. He continues to walk, surveying the meadow bathed in starlight. We have three hours at least until sunrise.

I lean against the doorway, waiting for her. Hazel doesn't understand wolf senses and I can distinctly hear every word of their discussion. I feel guilty for a moment, but I can't bring myself to move. With instinct demanding that I protect her, I couldn't go further from her if I wanted to.

Her worried voice drifts through the door. "Sienna said my mark was fading."

Fading? So soon? I thought we had time for our relationship to progress. I didn't want to rush her. And then we were torn apart.

Sable murmurs her answer. I can only pick out the words *decide*, *Slate*, and *committed*.

"So if we, you know, it'll become permanent?" Hazel asks, her voice faltering with an awkward laugh.

"Yes," Sable answers. She's shuffling around tidying up.

"What if it fades? Can we claim each other again later?"

"Yes."

"Okay, just wondering." Hazel's footsteps near the door. I pull myself together.

"Talk to your mate," Sable instructs before Hazel opens the door. Her shoulders slump and her eyes are glazed. I loop my arm around her waist and lead her home.

The words repeat in a loop, mixing together in my thoughts. Fading. Later. But the way she looks at me, I dare to hope she is picking me and our future together.

She presses into me and I kiss her. It's brief and sweet. A promise.

The moment the door to my trailer closes, she spins, grabbing my hands. She pulls me past the kitchen and toward our bedroom. Ours. Everything I have was hers the moment I first saw her.

She closes the door, soaking us in darkness. I'm glad I can still see her, even if she can't see me. I don't want to miss a single expression on her perfect face.

Her delicate fingers trace my jaw, hook behind my neck, and guide me to her. Her lips hover over mine and I can feel her hesitation. I wait, restraining myself.

"All I wanted was to get home to you," she whispers. Warm affection blooms in me. I can't begin to express to her how badly I wanted her back. How incapable I am without her now.

I brush our lips together, pulled in by her gravity. "I would have found you, no matter what."

"I know," she answers against my mouth. Her eyes drift closed. She runs her nails down my shoulder blades and the world falls away.

Her kisses are needy. We find our rhythm, her tongue in my mouth and my hands slipping under her shirt and across the smooth skin of her stomach.

I back her into our bed and settle between her legs when they fall open. I can feel her pulse racing, matching my own.

She is a goddess, with her golden hair splayed out around her like a halo.

She pulls my mouth to hers and softly bites my lip. Her kisses are rougher, frantic. Her chest heaves and I feel my nose brush against a tear.

Pulling back, my heart shatters. Her eyes squeeze shut, her lashes dark. I brush my hand down her cheek. "Hazel."

"I'm so scared this isn't real," she whispers.

I kiss her brow. "This is the only real thing. And I'm never letting you go." She releases a shuddering breath. With fluttering lashes, she looks up at me.

Her honey eyes are glowing like a wolf.

I gape at her.

"Sorry," she says. Her breasts press into me as she takes a deeper and slower breath.

"Eyes." It's all I can manage to blurt.

"What?"

I ease off her, kneeling on the bed beside her. She sits up, frowning.

"Slate, what's wrong?" She's more concerned this time. The glow fades and her light brown irises return to normal.

"Your eyes." I blink. "They were glowing."

She stares for a moment. "What do you mean?"

"Your eyes looked like mine do sometimes."

"How is that possible?"

"I don't know." I stammer.

She grips her shoulder, right where I marked her. "Is it because you claimed me?"

"Maybe." I've never heard of anything like this happening, but it's so rare for a wolf to take a human as their mate.

"What else could it be?" She touches her fingertips to the corner of her eye as if she could feel something different in her anatomy. "Are they still?"

I shake my head.

"Are you sure?" she asks, flopping down on the bed and staring at the ceiling.

I stretch out beside her and tug her side against my front. "Did they do anything else to you?"

She shakes her head.

"Other than breaking your wrist?" I prompt.

She huffs. "No. I would have told you."

"What if Jasper put something in your food?" She stiffens.

"I know you don't believe me." I expect anger, but she sounds sad. "But he took good care of me and kept me safe like you would have."

"Because he wanted you," I argue, despite knowing better. I'm not very reasonable when it comes to my mother and her new family, and not remotely reasonable when it comes to my mate, either.

"He wouldn't have." Her brow creases.

"How can you know?" My voice is soft, betraying my fear.

Her frown melts away. She sighs, rolling to her side and reaching up to run her hand through my hair. "He's your brother. And he's a lot more like you than you know."

"Okay." I want to trust her.

Mollified, she presses against me, sliding a leg between mine and tucking her head against my neck. I stroke my hand down her side in long, comforting strokes. She needs rest.

"I'm sorry all this happened," she mumbles into my shirt.

"You didn't do anything wrong. And they'll regret coming for you," I rumble, pressing a kiss to her hair.

My world feels whole again. I need her softness, crave her warmth. I don't know what I would have done if she was truly gone. It would have destroyed me. "I can't lose you," I admit.

"You won't. Jasper-" I don't need her reassurances. Not now.

I stop her words with a kiss. "I don't want you saying another man's name in our bed," I growl.

With a smirk, she slips her hand under my shirt again. Her fingers draws a path of down my stomach and across the edge of my waistband. Forget rest, I want to pin her down to this mattress until we are both spent.

"Then make me say your name," she whispers.

I groan into her neck. It takes every last shred of self-control I have, but I tug the blanket over us.

"Hazel. You need to rest."

I don't think I could resist her a second longer, but her exhaustion finally overtakes her. She slurs half a sentence about needing me, and then stills. Her breathing evens out.

I close my own eyes, taking a slow breath. I'm not going anywhere - I'm not sure I can sleep without holding her. Never again.

XVI
SHOCKING SURPRISES

HAZEL

Birdsong yanks me from sleep. For a second, I'm disoriented, panic freezing my lungs. But the heavy weight of Slate's arm across my ribs brings me back to reality.

I'm okay. I made it home.

I close my eyes for a moment, letting myself sink into the warmth of our bed. Memories of his body pushing mine into the mattress make my stomach clench. We still haven't finished what we started.

His touch relaxes me. Even when I don't understand the dynamics and dangers of wolf shifters, he is my safe place. That affection pushes away the lingering fear from my involuntary visit to Granite Ridge.

Slate is still sleeping. I'm used to his dazzling smiles and his dark brooding, so this soft expression is fascinating. He's completely relaxed. I indulge myself, staring at his beautiful face.

His hair falls over his brow and his long lashes are dark against his tan skin. A dusting of barely-there freckles cover the bridge of his nose and his cheekbones. They speckle his shoulders too.

After a minute, his breathing picks up as he wakes.

The moment his moss-green eyes open, his lips curve into a sweet smile that turns my organs to goo.

Tentatively, I brush his silky hair out of his face. "Good morning to you." I bite my lip. I want to kiss every inch of his skin, but his emerald eyes hold me captive.

They gleam playfully. Without warning, he pushes me back and rolls over me. I shriek, giggling as he nibbles my neck. His dark hair brushes against my jaw. I squirm under him, his erection nudging my thigh. My knees fall open wider automatically.

He kisses my cleavage before biting there too. Not hard enough to break the skin, but hard enough to make my eyes roll back in my head. I hope it leaves a hickey.

"Slate," I say.

He hums in return, his mouth hot on my ribs, working his way lower.

"I'm filthy. I got mud in your bed." Cringing, I tug the edge of my shirt. Spots of dried mud have soaked into the fabric.

"Don't worry, I have other sheets," he says with an amused smirk. "But how about we get you cleaned up?"

Taking my hand, he leads me into his bathroom and flips the shower faucet to hot. "I'm capable of showering on my own," I protest.

"Yes, but maybe I don't want to be away from you," he responds, dragging my shirt over my head and placing a kiss on my shoulder.

I grip the sink, a bolt of excitement running through me as he pulls his shirt off, followed by his pants. With a kiss to my stomach, he slides my leggings down, lifting each foot to tug them off.

When he stands, I can't help but launch myself at him. It's the first time we've been entirely bare with nothing between us. His kisses are scorching as he walks me backward into the shower. We're crowded together in the small space, hot water sluicing between our bodies.

Steam billows around us, and I groan in pleasure when the scalding water hits my shoulders and soaks into my hair.

Slate lathers shampoo through my hair, gently untangling it with his fingers. His nails scrape across my scalp, making me shiver. I rotate to see his shaggy hair slick on his neck, water dripping over his cheekbones and lips.

Entranced, I frame his face with my hands and draw him to me. My body is aching for his, and I show him with slow, sensual kisses. I struggle to breathe, I'm so overwhelmed by the feeling of him. It washes away the last three days, leaving room for nothing but our connection.

My hands slip down his wet skin, loving the tapered shape of his back muscles as he shifts under my touch.

"I love your hair," he says, twisting it around his fist while he drags his teeth across the fading claim mark. Electricity sparks everywhere he touches. My hands wander lower and he sucks in a breath as I wrap my fingers around his cock, stroking down and up. "What are you doing?" he rumbles.

"You don't want me to?" I ask innocently.

"Of course I want you to." He tugs my hair, angling my head so he can capture my mouth again. His kiss stills as I stroke his length again. "But I can't do everything I want to do to you in this shower."

"Want to get out then?" I purr, anticipation swelling within me.

"In a minute," he says, his rough voice caressing me even while his calloused hands grip my hips possessively.

He spins me, hauling my ass up against his cock. Startled, I fling my hands up against the tile walls on either side of me to balance. "Good girl, just hold still," he murmurs against my neck. This man will be the death of me.

I shiver even in the hot water, trying desperately to obey as one hand cups my breast, water running over his hand, while the other hand wanders lower.

"I can't believe I waited this long to get my hands on you," he says, grazing the skin below my ear with his lips while his fingers skim the apex of my thighs. I jolt at the contact and his other hand tightens across my chest, holding me flush against him.

"Sorry," I mutter.

He nips my ear lobe. "Don't be."

Each breath is heavy, the air thick with steam. His fingers sweep lower, teasing my core, before slipping one inside. My body arches, and his grip tightens. "I told you to stay still." The hand on my breast glides higher, stroking my neck and sending sparks down my spine.

A second finger joins, and he starts to pump them in and out until I moan. His thumb presses against my clit. Panting, I scramble to anchor myself, hands slipping over his slick skin.

"I can't..." I whimper, words dropping away as the pressure threatens to send me over a cliff.

"Do you want me to stop?" he asks, and I can hear the smirk in his voice. I shake my head, my hair falling heavily around my shoulders as the water drips over them and runs down my stomach.

His motions begin to accelerate, and can barely stand, leaning heavily against him for support. "Let me see you come again," he says, his voice scraping over me. It flings me over the edge and I gasp, throwing my head back. Water hits my cheeks and parted lips. His adept fingers draw out the shaking tension until I am about to lose my sanity entirely. Without his hand across my stomach, I would collapse. Heart racing, I gulp down air. When I finally open my eyes, he's watching me with a satisfied look on his face.

"You've ruined me," I mutter. "You are a sex god and nobody will ever compare."

His glowing eyes flash as he growls, "If you're my mate, no one else will touch you ever again."

I blink at him. "Yes," I promise. His intense broody expression softens as he calms down. I've noticed when his eyes glow, he is far more possessive. His wolf instincts push to the forefront.

Slate flips the shower off and wraps a towel around me before grabbing one for himself. Gently, he uses a third towel to dry my hair. He's so tender, tears prick in my eyes. "Good?" he asks.

"Great." I lean up and kiss him briefly.

"Let's go," he urges, never releasing his hold on me. But before we can take more than two steps, his phone buzzes. Grabbing it, he scrolls through a few messages and his face falls.

I tighten my grip on my towel. "What's up?"

"Heath will be here in a few minutes. We'd better get dressed."

"Tell him to wait," I say, desperate to see what this man will do to me naked in a bed.

He chuckles, shaking his head. Water droplets spray me. "I don't think that'll work. But after we see him, I'm yours to do whatever you wish."

"Anything?" I say, grinning.

"Promise," he says, kissing my cheek.

Sighing, I start picking through Slate's clothes for anything that might fit me. He pulls open a drawer, showing a selection of my clothing. "I got these from Heath while you were gone. Wanted to be ready when we got you back," he says thoughtfully, pulling on his clothing.

Reluctantly, I pick a soft pair of joggers and a dark t-shirt, and then take my medications. While we wait for Heath, Slate pulls out some fruit for us. I peel a banana and take a bite.

Far too soon, a knock sounds. When my uncle steps into our trailer, he somehow seems larger in the narrow space.

"Alpha," Slate greets Heath, his eyes on the ground. It's a sign of respect, I now recognize. How many little gestures did I miss before?

"Slate, Hazel," he says.

"Hi," I respond, taking my last bite and setting the peel aside.

Slate returns to my side, wrapping an arm around me. "What's the situation, sir?" he inquires, all business despite his possessive hold on my waist.

"We are safe for now. Granite Ridge will want to avoid the other packs learning what they did." He crosses his arms and leans against the door frame.

Slate frowns. "Didn't we contact them while searching for her?"

Heath nods. "Yes, but that wasn't an accusation, nor did we have any proof of anything. Now that we have Hazel's testimony, we have insurance against Ferris. I've only notified Valley Pack of Hazel's return and what we know about who is responsible."

"They should be held accountable," I interject, surprising myself.

"Yes, and they will be." Heath steps closer and places his hand on my shoulder. "But you are more important, and I won't risk you or our people unnecessarily."

"Of course," I say, feeling self-conscious.

"Alpha," Slate says, "we noted something unusual."

Heath freezes, looking not-quite-human.

"Hazel's eyes were gold," Slate says simply.

"Are you sure?" Heath asks.

"Yes."

"I didn't feel any different," I add, worrying over Heath's grim expression. "I'm fine."

"Thank you for telling me. Please notify me of anything else you discover. I'll have some food delivered for you." Heath heads out, a preoccupied expression creasing his brow.

A thought strikes me and I jump off my seat. "I'll be right back. I want to ask him something." Before Slate can protest, I slip out the door and jog after my uncle.

"Hazel?" His face is lined, exhaustion and worry weighing him down.

"I wanted to ask about his mom. Both his parents actually." My tone is hushed, hoping Slate's sensitive hearing won't pick up my words.

"Why?" Heath asks.

I purse my lips. "Sienna was obsessed with me joining her pack. I need to tell you about some of the things she said."

"We can talk about it when you're recovered." Heath tucks his hands in his pockets.

"I'm fine," I lie. He knows. His eyebrows rise slightly.

"She wanted me to become mates with her son. He said it was so she could try and take over our pack. Since I'm related to you, I guess?" Everything comes out in a rush. I bite my cheek.

Heath nods slowly. I hold my breath. "She always wanted to be an Alpha. I thought Granite Ridge would have been enough for her," he muses. "I guess not."

"What do you mean?" I press. I need to understand why she would go to such extreme measures.

Heath sighs. "When we were young, Sienna wanted to be mates with your father. She pursued him even when they were kids. When he rejected her, she settled for Clay. He was in line to be beta. She wanted him to challenge for Alpha, which never would have happened."

"Oh."

He doesn't mention himself. I'm curious if Sienna went after him too, but I don't want to make him uncomfortable.

"Around the time she had Slate, Ferris's first mate passed away. She left for his pack within a few weeks." He speaks so calmly, but I can sense disgust under the surface.

"Could they just come in and try to take us over? Why did they need me?" My attempt at indifference fails as my voice shakes.

Heath straightens his arms out and grips my shoulders. "The other packs wouldn't let them do that. You don't need to worry about anything happening. None of this is your fault, and we're more than capable of dealing with them."

I force my mouth into a smile, despite the fear still churning in my gut.

"Are you really okay?" He asks.

"Yeah. I'm going to go back to Slate." Slate's presence is the only place I feel safe. He is flame, chasing away the shadows.

Heath nods and strides away. I go straight into my mate's arms. He holds me tight and I feel my worries dissolve. We can tackle anything together.

SLATE

Hazel looks up at me. "Okay, what do we do now?" She raises an eyebrow suggestively. but I can sense worry and anguish swirling beneath the surface.

"I don't know if we have ten minutes or two hours." As much as I would love to take her to bed, it isn't a good idea.

She absently rubs at her claim mark and I resist the urge to ask to see it. Instead, I busy myself with tidying up. She wanders to the bookshelves and starts pulling out random books and skimming the back of them. I'll need to clear out space for her book collection. This is her home too.

By the time I'm done washing up, she's curled up with a pile of my sketchbooks. My face heats. "Is this okay?" she asks, closing the book in her lap.

"Of course." I scoot the pile over and sit next to her. She nestles into me. I can't help but wrap my arms around her and haul her into my lap.

She eases the book open again and flips to the middle. I appreciate how delicately she turns the pages, careful to not smear the pencil. "I love this," she murmurs, pausing on a drawing of a wolf.

"That's Clove," I say. She tilts her head, waiting for more. "She was the closest thing to a mother that I had growing up."

"That's why you're so close to Cedar and Onyx," she concludes.

"Did you have anyone who was a father figure, growing up? After your dad died?" My words are faltering, worried I will upset her.

"Heath." Shaking her head, she turns the page to a landscape of the mountain. She runs her finger over the edge of the paper. "What was your dad like?"

I take a moment, thinking of my dad with his easy smile and messy reddish-brown hair. "He was steady." It's the best way I can describe him. "He loved this pack. He was always helping people, even outside his beta duties."

"And he liked to draw too?"

I nod. "Charcoal and ink. He wasn't a huge fan of my tattoos, but he would still get me equipment and supplies."

She smiles at me. Her affection is like an energy inside of me, bubbling up and making me feel light. "He sounds amazing." She squeezes my hand.

"He was," I agree. "I try to be like him. Everyone depended on him, and I'm afraid I'm not as good." I rest my cheek against her hair and breathe her in.

"You are," she says. "I can tell how much everyone loves you. I think you do way more than you realize."

"You're amazing," I say, nuzzling against her neck.

"Are you doing okay with the whole mom situation?" she asks.

I pause again, but this time it's not because of thought, it's because of the spark of irritation thinking of my mother brings up. But I don't want her to think I'm upset with her. I run a finger through her hair, reveling in the silky strands.

She studies my face. "Not really." My voice cracks. "I'm so angry. It feels like she wants to destroy everything in my life."

"She could never do that." She sets the sketchbook aside and turns, wrapping herself around me, arms around my shoulders and head in the crook of my neck.

"She betrayed my pack, caused my father pain every day for almost twenty years, and then abducted my mate." She squeezes me tighter.

"She failed." It's only two words, but it breaks some of my fears. Hazel is so much stronger than I knew. I'm so in love with her.

I grip her waist as if she's my life preserver and I'm drowning. Without even considering what I'm doing, I'm kissing her.

She slides one leg over so she's straddling me and kisses like I am her air. Her hands trail down my neck and shoulders, burning me.

Slowly, I slide my hands down her waist and over her hips, loving the curve. She hums her approval as I squeeze her plump ass. The vibration raises the hairs on the back of my neck.

She swivels her hips and I can't breathe. I try to get more air while she kisses my cheek, my jaw, my earlobe. She nips my neck and electricity sparks from the point of contact.

I need her so badly. Even if we only have five minutes, I'll take whatever I can get.

She grabs the hem of her shirt. Before she can pull it off, my phone pings. I let out a frustrated growl and she giggles.

Another message pings. I grimace. I'm desperate for her, but also anxious to get any news. I reach for my phone and unlock it.

I have to clear my throat to speak. "We're needed for a meeting in the training room."

"When?" she asks dismissively, tugging her shirt up to show the soft curves of her stomach.

I hate myself. "It's right now."

She drops her hands and groans. Even this sound resonates through me. I take a slow breath, reaching for neutral.

"Let's go see our friends. I'm sure everyone is excited to have you back," I say. She rolls her eyes at me. So I lean in, whispering into her ear, "And then I'm going to take you back here and fuck you against every surface in our home." She shivers and I grin, loving her reaction.

We take a few minutes to arrange ourselves, and then I take her hand and we head toward the training building.

Heath and Sable are waiting for us. Heath clasps his hands behind his back like he is facing a difficult discussion. I can sense their apprehension across the room.

We stop a few feet from them and I pull Hazel against me, looping my arm across her chest. Even with her uncle and our healer, I feel the instinct to protect her. Or maybe to keep her to myself.

She looks up at me, frowning. "Sounds like a lot of people outside. Is something going on?" she whispers.

I freeze. Sure, I can hear several familiar voices in the meadow. It's the kind of quiet noise I tune out most of the time. But Hazel shouldn't be able to hear them at all.

"Hi, Hazel, Slate." Heath smiles at her, loosening his shoulders in a visible attempt to appear non-threatening. He hasn't missed my possessive hold.

"Alpha," I answer.

Hazel looks between us. "What's going on?"

Sable gently takes her wrist and removes the brace. She examines the skin, now free of bruising. "How are you feeling this morning?"

"Fine. Tired," Hazel answers with a small laugh.

Sable bends her wrist inwards slowly. "Does this hurt at all?" Hazel shakes her head. "Well, your wrist is healed. Normally it takes humans about four to five weeks to heal simple broken bones."

Hazel stares at her. "Um, maybe it wasn't broken, just sprained?" Sable purses her lips.

"Your eyes turned gold when you were feeling strong emotions, correct?" Heath says.

"I guess."

Heath drops his voice. "Hazel, I'm sorry you have to face something else after what you just went through."

"What?" Her chest rises with quick and shallow breaths, and I hold tighter to stabilize her.

"We believe latent genes from your father are now manifesting," Sable explains. "Most likely triggered by joining our pack paired with being under significant stress."

The meaning slowly sinks in. Hazel hasn't moved. "I'm sorry, what?" She blurts.

"You are a wolf shifter," Heath confirms.

"Are you sure?" I ask. Sable nods.

"That's not..." She pauses, her face scrunching into a confused frown. It's quiet for a moment. Heath and Sable are patient.

"Hazel, you could hear everyone outside the building, right?" I ask gently.

"So?" She blinks at me. "They're loud today."

"A human wouldn't be able to hear them. They're pretty quiet right now, actually," I say.

"Oh." Hazel leans heavily into me.

"We need to prepare for your first shift," Heath says.

"Are you serious?" Hazel asks. "I'm going to turn into a freaking wolf?" She looks between us as if waiting for someone to yell *Surprise!*

"We're sure," Heath answers.

"We looked into it, and there is some record of this happening, but it's rare." Sable soothes her.

"Did you know this could happen?" Her voice rises two octaves.

"No. I had no idea it was possible," Heath answers.

Hazel is pressing into me as if trying to escape the situation by burrowing into my chest.

"How are you doing?" I ask her, running my hands down her arms.

"I need a minute," she mutters, closing her eyes.

"Why don't you guys take a moment to process everything?" Sable smiles, looking expectantly at Heath.

"We need to plan, but we can spare ten minutes," he concedes and follows her out. The door shuts and I listen to their footsteps retreat. The room is silent. Her heartbeat pulses against my skin, or maybe it's my own.

"Are you okay?" she asks.

I blink at her. "Of course." Why is she worried about me? I'm not the one who had their world turned upside down.

"You signed up for a human mate, and now apparently, I'm not." She keeps her eyes closed, resting her cheek against my chest.

"Hazel, I would love you if you were a giraffe. I would love you if you were a worm." I punctuate my words with a kiss on the top of her head. "I would love you if you were a loaf of bread."

She giggles and the sound melts the ice in my chest.

Her eyes go wide. "Hold up, does this mean I can't have chocolate anymore?"

I bark out a laugh. She opens her mouth and closes it again, her cheeks coloring.

"How do *you* feel about being a shifter?" I prod.

"I don't think I've got a choice," I frown at her, but she continues, "but I wanted to belong here, and now I guess I do."

"You already did," I say.

She sighs and I can feel her relaxing against me. "Well, now I'll somehow figure out how to be a wolf. Nothing we can't handle."

"I love you," I say without thinking.

The warmest smile spreads across her face. "I love you too. I couldn't deal with any of this without you."

I grin. She's okay. We're going to be okay.

She kisses me sweetly. It's not the desperate kisses we usually have. It's soft and affectionate.

"You can handle anything. You don't need me." I speak against her lips.

Brushing her nose against mine, she speaks slowly, her voice heating. "I very much do need you. Even if it's just because I want you. So badly." I am considering finding us some privacy right now.

Unfortunately, the click of the door opening interrupts us. She turns toward the doorway, looping her arm around my lower back and settling against me in a casual pose, not a we-almost-ripped-our-clothes-off pose.

Our friends and family file in, Marigold, Cedar, Onyx, Clove, Cassia, and Heath.

"There's a lot to discuss and plans to be made," Heath announces, taking his place as we join the group loosely circling him.

Everyone waits expectantly. "Let's get down to it. Hazel is a shifter and it's manifesting now. We need to prepare for her first shift."

The rest of the group is frozen, staring at him.

Marigold breaks first. "Hazel!" She squeals. She pulls Hazel away from me and squeezes her. Hazel hugs her friend, tears starting to form. She wipes them away as Marigold releases her.

I can't help but pull her into my arms, wiping away the lingering tears as everyone crowds her.

"Congratulations," Clove says. "Glad to hear it."

"Happy for you, Hazel," Cedar adds. Onyx's face breaks into his shit-eating grin. I can't even imagine what is running through his head.

Hazel blushes.

Heath clears his throat. "We need to plan for your first shift."

"Okay?" Hazel says, more of a question than confirmation.

"If we don't, you will shift at some point soon when your emotions are high. And we want to make sure it's a safe environment. So facilitating your first shift is wise," Heath explains.

Hazel still looks confused.

Clove tips her chin up, silently asking permission from Heath. He gives it.

"Hazel, when our children first shift, they're usually eight or nine. It's an overwhelming experience. But they already have a ranking in the pack, at the bottom. There are safe boundaries in place." I am endlessly grateful to Clove for stepping up as a mother to Hazel in this moment.

"However, when an adult wolf joins a new pack, they don't have a ranking to start with. They have to find their place. It's based on age, ability, power, and personality. We call it dominance. And sometimes that can involve challenges or fights. But since they are experienced adults, they usually know how to navigate the process without injuring anyone."

Hazel nods. "So I have to find my ranking?"

"You will naturally," Clove reassures her. "We want to make sure you can do it safely."

Hazel blinks, eyebrows rising. "I'm sorry, are we worried I'm going to hurt someone? How?"

Heath shifts his weight. "Your first shift is intense. Your new instincts might overwhelm you. If you're dominant, that instinct might be to fight another wolf in order to establish your position."

I see understanding in our friend's faces. Marigold has a worried little smile. Cedar is nodding.

"We don't want to risk anyone's safety. So by guiding your shift to happen sooner, we can create the ideal environment," Heath explains.

Hazel chews on her lip. "Are we seriously worried I'll go crazy and attack someone?"

"For the most part, we can sense who is more dominant or submissive than we are. It's a hierarchy," I reassure her. "If you are particularly dominant, you may challenge other dominant wolves in a struggle to find your place. But most likely you'll sense who is more or less dominant than you and everything will fall into place."

"Since you come from a line of alphas, you may be quite dominant," Heath adds. Hazel's pulse speeds up. She digs her fingers into my arm.

"What if I challenge someone?" she asks.

Heath continues, "I won't let anyone get injured. But you also need to establish yourself with a position in our pack, so it's okay if you do challenge someone. For example, Cassia is one of our most dominant Zetas which is why I asked her to join us.

"Most likely, you will either submit to her or challenge her. And I will be there as a safety net if things go wrong," Heath reassures her.

Hazel looks to Marigold and then to Clove.

"Honey, I am very submissive. You don't have to worry about challenging me," Clove says kindly.

Marigold nods along. "We're here for support."

"I don't think anyone should be there. Until I can get a handle on things," Hazel argues.

"If it's not now, it'll be the next time you shift," Heath warns. "But facing two or three wolves at first should make things much easier. An accidental shift in the middle of a crowd is what we want to avoid."

"It'll be okay," I say softly in her ear.

She looks up at me. "You're second-in-command, the beta. Does that mean you are the most dominant wolf aside from my uncle?"

I stand a little straighter. "Yes." She grips me a little tighter. I suspect her wolf instincts are riding her hard at the moment.

"I'm sure everything will go smoothly. But I would rather be over-prepared instead of risking someone getting injured," Heath summarizes.

Hazel shakes her head. "I can't imagine I'll be dominant."

"We will see. Now we need to decide when and where," Heath says.

XVII
METAMORPHOSIS

HAZEL

Twelve hours later, we stand in a dark forest. I admire a full moon through the swaying branches. Supposedly, it will make this easier for me.

Bugs hum and something bigger rustles nearby - a raccoon, I think. But I keep my eyes fixed on Slate.

His cheekbones are highlighted with starlight and his dark hair gleams like gunmetal. I want to anchor myself to him and listen to his soft reassurances. But everyone is counting on me to handle this transition. This isn't exactly what I imagined my first evening back with my mate would include.

"Marigold, Cedar, keep your distance. Clove and Cassia, forward." Heath directs his team.

"Ready?" He asks softly, just for me. I nod.

Heath and Cedar turn their backs. Everyone is waiting on me.

I suck in a shaky breath. My mind is racing and I can't recall any of the instructions they had provided earlier.

Awkwardly, I pull off my clothes. Maybe someday I can shift right out of my clothes like my friends, but not today. My face is burning even while the rest of me is shivering in the cold night air. What if we're wrong? Maybe because I'm half-shifter, I only get a few of the benefits like sensitive hearing and glowing eyes, and nothing will happen when I try to wolf out.

"What exactly do I do, again?"

Clove's warm voice floats over me. "Do you feel anything? Any sensations in your body or strange perceptions?"

"Um, I don't know. Maybe?" I close my eyes.

All I can feel is my pulse. But there is something else. Something buried, that now I lean into. An urge to explore and run through the forest. It's a wildness I've possessed all along. But now it's pulsing strong with each beat of my heart.

A strong sense of possessiveness rocks me. I tune into Slate in a whole new way. I want to claw at anyone who even looks at him. I want him all to myself.

My eyes pop open. "Guys, I have no idea what I'm doing," I complain.

Slate comes closer. He slips his hands around my waist and leans our foreheads together. "You can do this. I'm sure it's strange, but let those instincts take over. It's the desire to be free and the feeling of being one with the forest."

I take a slow breath. I can do this. His hands fall away, but I can still feel his warmth close to me. I try to focus on the sensations and emotions again.

This sense of wildness grows as I let myself fall into it. It's throbbing inside of me. I want to crawl out of my skin.

The intensity surprises me. My eyes pop open and I look to Slate to ground me.

His full mouth curves. "Your eyes are glowing."

"I feel like I want to take off running," I whisper.

"Keep going," he replies. He flexes his hands at his side as if he wants to reach for me but is stopping himself.

I focus inward again. The wildness pulses stronger until I feel like I could be lost. Swept away until no one even remembers me.

My skin prickles and I feel as if my entire being is shimmering. It's like electrical current and wind.

My body feels different, stronger, and tingling with energy that has nowhere to go. I want to tear at my skin to release some of it.

A wave of scents hits me all at once - the warm smell of Slate that also lives on my skin. The herbal scent that makes me picture Cedar. Clove smells like yeast and cinnamon. Heath smells like salt and grass.

The forest around us is lit up with spotlights. I can see every twitch of my friends and movement of the tree branches. I can see bats dancing across the clouds past the treetops. My field of vision is wider and the trees look more gray than green now.

Slate's huge wolf is before me, but now I can see he's not mostly black. He is the darkest gray-brown, with a dusting of cream along his chest and up his muzzle. His evergreen eyes meet mine, the moon lighting them up into lanterns.

I freeze. He's a wolf, and he is at my eye level. I look down at my feet. They're paws.

No amount of preparing, imagining the experience, and expecting it to happen can lessen the absolute shock flooding my system.

My fur bristles and it's like when my arm hairs stand on end.

Slate moves forward, bumping his snout into mine. I can feel pure joy radiating from him. I want to leap and run and play with him. I've never felt someone else's emotions this strenuously.

I sense anxiety from my packmates. They've all shifted and we stand in our lopsided circle, everyone looking at me.

Movement grabs my attention. Clove's cream and reddish-brown wolf is lowering to her belly, her ears flat against her skull. One look at her and I know I am more dominant than she is. She's submitting to me. I could stand over her and make her roll over. But my human side remembers I respect this woman. She is like a mother to my partner.

The strange impulse startles me. I look for my friends. Marigold's golden wolf paces a few yards away and I can instantly recognize my place above her as well. Her anxious excitement brushes against my mind, just as I can sense a nurturing warmth from Clove.

A gray and brown wolf moves diagonally to me and my attention focuses on her. My ears press forward. It's Cassia. I'm not sure how I know, but I have no doubt.

The confidence blooming within me is shocking.

I take a step forward. So does she. Her tail curls higher instead of swishing down low like my friends. Irritation spikes in my chest. I can feel defiance from her. She is dominant. And apparently, so am I.

She holds her ground as I advance. Slate hovers behind me. Will he stop me?

A few feet away, Cassia warns me. Her lips curl to show a row of very sharp teeth. I'm not concerned. My instincts instill a strange confidence.

She rushes me, ramming into me to force me back, snapping at the thick fur at my neck. I stagger, but instinct surges within me. I twist while also rearing up. She's thrown to the ground by our momentum.

I'm on her, snapping at her shoulders. She scrambles away, staying low to the ground. Someone is growling - it's coming from me.

My hackles raise and I'm a huge ball of fur. My tail is stiff and high, my shoulders rigid. I hold my ground. Cassia's eyes follow me, her lips pulled back in a snarl.

I take a step forward, glaring at her. She growls but sinks to her belly. Another step and she quiets. Her tail wraps around her haunches and she lowers her head in submission.

Respect emanates from her. I challenged her and won. It was more of a contest of willpower than an actual fight, despite the snapping teeth that would have terrified me as a human. My surprise is overridden by the pride and admiration seeping into me from the wolves around me.

I turn to Heath, my Alpha. He sits, watching me. There's no urge to challenge him. On instinct, I lower my head.

Something strange is happening, like I'm using unfamiliar muscles. I realize my tail is wagging.

Slate brushes against my shoulder. Affection flows between us. He licks my cheek. I lean into him, unfamiliar bodies with fur and sharp edges.

The intense urge to run and explore surges again. I have to move. I tilt my head like a puppy, a silent invitation. With a sudden burst of energy, I tear away from him, the pine needles churning under my paws. My tail whips behind me.

I can see every divot in the earth, every rock and stick. Confident, I leap forward, picking up speed. Slate hurtles along behind me, his mouth open and tongue lolling like a dog.

I have no idea where we are going, but I can smell my packmates all over these woods so I am pretty sure we are safely within our boundaries. The ground rolls downhill.

The scent of petrichor, moss, and minerals surrounds us as we reach the creek. The trees are open here, and the moonlight is so bright. Slate's golden-green eyes are reflecting the light at me. He is magnificent.

I stop. I want to return to my human shape, but no one instructed me how to. Maybe it's the same process as shifting. I close my eyes and push away my wolfish instincts. I grasp onto my human feelings and the desire to take that shape. Nothing happens. I search inside my emotions, digging out the uniquely human emotions like worry. The magic shimmers across me again.

Relieved, I grin at Slate. He follows me, shifting into his human form. His naked human form. My words drop out of my mouth as I take in his powerful body.

"You okay?" he says softly, reaching for me. He runs his palms down my arms.

"Better than okay." I can't stop grinning.

"Did you mean to shift?" I bite my lip, watching his gaze wander down my body too.

"I wanted to talk to you," I say.

He nods, patiently waiting.

"That was kind of incredible." I breathe out, exhilarated.

"You are amazing. You did so well," he praises me, "but I'm sorry, I don't have any clothes stashed around here."

A giggle escapes me. I cross my arms over my chest. "Maybe I don't care about getting dressed."

"You're running high off your first shift," he murmurs.

"I'm pretty sure my current feelings have more to do with you," I tease. He slides his hands to my waist and around to my back. I shiver. Greedily, I touch his bare chest, running my fingers down his pecs and tracing the creases of his abs.

"Hazel," he whispers, "your mark is almost completely gone."

Craning my neck, I try to catch a view of the pink scars. I can see the very edge, and they're barely visible. Grief over losing this sign of our relationship wells up, choking me. But we can still solidify it or even redo the claim marking, I remind myself.

"It's okay," he says. "You're a part of this pack. You don't need to be claimed." He lowers his head and kisses my cheek. I stay still, his words echoing in my head.

"Are you serious?" I blurt. "We are mates, aren't we?"

Slate drops his hands like I've burned him. "You get to decide that."

"I'm your mate," I repeat, thickly. Why is he bringing this up again? I tried to be extremely clear that I want him. I choose him.

His hair falls over his forehead as he ducks his head and stares at the ground. Maybe it isn't that he doesn't believe me. What if he's the one who wants out? My throat catches. "Why don't you believe me?" I ask.

"What do you mean?" He frowns.

"Why are you saying we don't have to be mates? After everything we've been through and how we feel about each other?" I can't stop myself and it's no longer euphoria I'm feeling.

"Hey, it's going to be okay. We can talk about this later, not right after your first shift," he says. I want to strangle him and also climb him like a tree. He's right about emotions running high.

My mind spins, and I struggle to put together a coherent response. The sounds of wolves approaching interrupt me.

I freeze, eyes wide as I look to Slate. "What do we do?"

Slate shrugs. "Nudity isn't a big deal in the pack. But generally, we try to keep clothes nearby to put on. We don't exactly all hang out naked."

Back to my wolf form it is.

Before our friends reach us, my eyes drift shut and I call up the wolf instincts swirling right below the surface. Shifting is easier the second time. Their emotions wash over me and I relax into them. I let their joy carry me along.

Slate is already bounding toward our friends as they burst through the trees. Onyx's black wolf is massive, beside his reddish-brown brother. Marigold looks like Cedar's match, with her coat a lighter version of his. She dances around me, brushing against me and circling again.

The wildness I am becoming so familiar with is heavy in the air between all of us. It's coming from within me, and also emanating from them too. I don't know who moves first, but suddenly we are all running along the creek.

We weave through the trees, coming closer together and spreading out again. It's the freest I've ever felt. I can't believe I've gone my whole life without this.

Slate

I can feel Hazel's irritation across the room. She stands by Cassia and Aven, the furthest apart we have been since her return.

Last night after our run, she was exhausted. I held her close and listened to her breathing until I couldn't stay awake myself.

Shadows smudge under her eyes and she is pointedly not looking at me. Maybe she's taking my suggestion seriously. She is free for whatever future she wants. She doesn't have to be chained to me.

The claim is over. The mark was completely gone this morning. I have no right to her. And she doesn't need my protection any longer. Never mind that I could never give her up. But I'd willingly love her from a distance if it meant she was happier.

"Aven and Fisher, take the west side. Vale, take the east border with Hawthorne. I want eyes on Zephyr." Heath directs his wolves like the general he is.

"Cassia, Lazuli, Elm, I want you on the north border and hang toward Granite Ridge. Slate, take Hazel west. Teach her how to recognize our borders and how to identify other packs."

He turns, not waiting for confirmation. Everyone else moves toward the exits, but I'm hung up on his instructions.

"Sir, is it wise to take her so far from town?" I blurt.

Everyone halts on their way out the door. I know I've spoken out of turn, but I can't seem to keep my head straight where Hazel is concerned.

"You're safe near Cashel's territory," Hawthorne reassures us.

Heath's eyes narrow, the silent warning clear. "Do you have concerns, Slate?"

"No, Alpha." I lower my eyes. I'm far more respectful than in our last conflict, and he seems satisfied.

Everyone's attention lingers on me for a moment before they obey Heath's silent dismissal and head to their assignments. Thankfully, Heath lets it go and leaves us.

"That was awkward," Hazel says, sidling up to me. The distance she leaves between us stings. My instincts demand I reach out and touch her, draw her close.

"Yeah, we're not exactly supposed to question our Alpha. Especially not in front of everybody," I mumble.

"Why did you?" she asks.

"I'm not exactly reasonable when it comes to you," I answer simply. I don't feel like explaining, so I pull off my clothes and shift.

I lead her west, along the road and out toward Valley Pack. We slow, and she lowers her nose to the ground. The pack scent fades as we reach the unclaimed land that creates a wide ring between us and our neighbors. Their scent wafts across and I can spot when she catches it because she pauses and cocks her head.

I can feel her curiosity through the pack bond. Her ears relax and her tail sways.

Time for some education. I rub the side of my face against her neck and shoulder. She repeats my motion, the sway of her tail speeding up.

Turning back to the edge of our territory, I approach the tree trunk closest to us, rubbing against it to transfer our scent. I scratch at the base, further marking the landscape with my scent.

Hazel looks at the tree and back at me, and then she leans in and sniffs it. She's so intelligent. After a moment of hesitation, she copies my motions.

We wander the border, heading generally northwards toward the creek. I won't take her past it. I don't want to bring her anywhere near Ferris and Sienna's territory, even though there is a huge stretch of Valley Pack between our current position and our enemy's border.

On this western edge, the creek cuts deep into the land, leaving us on the precipice of an outcropping. Late morning light paints the treetops along the opposite rise. It's one of my favorite views.

I locate our clothing stash. She pads behind me and shifts seconds after I do. Unzipping the knapsack, I pull out some shirts and sweats for us. She raises an eyebrow at me but accepts them.

Giving her privacy, I spin and dress myself. When I turn back, she's dressed with her hands gripping the hem of her shirt. Her gaze rakes over the mountainside and the creek fifty feet below us. It's fast and deep at this point, resulting in white foam swirling around the rocks.

"It's gorgeous." She stares for a while and then reaches for my hand. "I'm sad I didn't grow up here with you."

I shrug. "What if we wouldn't have gotten together in that case? Maybe you'd be with someone like Onyx."

She wrinkles her nose at my suggestion and I can't help but smile. "Or we would have been childhood sweethearts and hooked up as teenagers."

"I would have wanted that, for sure," I admit. She admires the landscape, but I admire her. I'm entranced with the slope of her nose and the curve of her cupid's bow. The way her eyelashes frame those captivating eyes. "But you would have had so many other options, being the heir of an alpha."

She lets out a small frustrated noise, air hissing through her teeth. "Why are you still doubting what I want?"

"I don't want you to feel obligated because of everything that happened. You are entirely free now to stay with our pack or leave entirely. You don't need me. No one will mess with you now that you have your own fangs," I say, tipping her chin toward me.

"I want you." She levels her full attention on me, her golden-brown eyes grasping my very soul. For once we aren't drunk on lust or exhaustion. "Do you want to be my mate?" she asks quietly. My blood heats.

"You were forbidden," I finally say. "You were my dream, and then suddenly you were mine. It felt too good to be true. But the next day, it all crashed down around me." I want to pull her against me, but I keep myself still, my hands flexing. "I would do anything for you. Give up anything if it makes you happy."

"Slate," she says, taking a step closer, "you make me happy."

I hate myself in this moment, but I have to be sure. Because if we do this again, it'll be permanent. I'll be sure of it.

"If none of this had happened, and I hadn't taken away your freedom like that, and you could go anywhere without limitations, what would you want?" I need to know.

"I would want to be right here with you." She presses her chest into mine. I can't help my hand going to the small of her back.

She tilts her head, looking quite wolfish. "What about you? Given total freedom, what would you want?"

I pause. "To be here. And if you were a random shifter that showed up, with no family saying you were off-limits..." I lower my lips to her ears. "I would have pursued you, immediately, completely."

"And now that I am one of you?" she asks, her cold fingers sliding under my shirt. My breath hitches.

"You're incredible."

"You want me?" The words are loaded - do you want to be my mate? Do you want to stay together? Forever?

"Desperately." My hoarse whisper scarcely makes it out of my mouth before she's on me.

She kisses me, and I haul her up against me, stepping away from the edge. I need her in a feral way and I don't want to be worrying about falling off a literal cliff.

She wraps her legs around my waist and grip her ass, squeezing her soft flesh. Between kisses, she bites my lip and I growl. She likes that, her thighs tightening.

I kiss her lips, her jaw, her ear, her neck.

"Don't talk about me leaving you. Never again," she snarls, her nails digging into my back. I murmur my agreement into her skin.

As we are pulling off our clothing, a howl wrenches us apart. "Shit," I growl. I'm starting to believe we are cursed.

"What?" She chews her lip. Her instincts are probably telling her it's a warning, but she hasn't heard this kind of communication before.

"Something is wrong. It's an emergency. We need to go back." I toss our clothes in the bag and stash it away. She's already shifted and I join her. Quickly, she leads the way to our meadow.

XVIII
CLAIMS & CHALLENGES

HAZEL

Fear cuts through me as I fly toward our home. So many things could go wrong. I refuse to lose my new family. We slow at the back of the training building, shifting and pulling our clothes from earlier on.

Cassia, Lazuli, and Elm arrive seconds after we do. As a group, we jog toward the meadow where several voices are yelling over each other.

Standing by the parking lot are the last people I want to see ever again. I grip Slate tight to keep my hands from shaking. To his credit, he doesn't pull me behind him. He stays by my side. I'm not the fragile human I was last time.

Ferris stands in front of a line of sleek black SUVs. He looks bored. Sienna, beside him, looks irate. On his other side is Jasper, a black eye blooming over his cheek. I frown. Slate hadn't hit higher than his jaw, and with how fast we heal, this had to be newer.

Aries, Flint, and a few other Zetas I recognize are flanking their Alphas. All of them look ready for blood.

Slate and I take our places beside Heath. Hawthorne stands on his other side. The normally peaceful Gamma looks ready to fight, his stance low and loose.

Cassia steps up to my left side and I give her a grateful nod. A deep sense of loyalty aches in my chest. I would die for these people, and they would for me as well.

"What are you doing on our land again," Heath demands.

"Where are your manners, Alpha Heath?" Ferris drawls.

Heath cracks his wrist, hands in fists. "Considering the last time wolves trespassed on my territory, my heir was kidnapped, I am not feeling particularly polite."

Ferris shrugs. "That's unfortunate." It's not an admission of guilt, but not a denial either.

"What do you want?" Heath's voice is deadly.

Sienna's lip curls in disgust. "We are here to retrieve a wolf from our pack."

My muscles go cold. Heath growls, "There is no one here that is yours."

"But there is," Sienna says, her contemptuous smile opening to show fangs between her blood-red lips.

Ferris sighs as if this is all tedious for him. "We gave refuge to Hazel, and she came into her wolf while a resident of Granite Ridge Pack."

The entire crowd erupts in snarls and growls. I dig my fingers into Slate's arm to anchor me. The emotions bashing against me are overwhelming. My own emotions alone would be difficult, but the weight of the pack, dull as it is while I'm not a wolf, is too much.

"She is the intended mate of our heir," Sienna claims.

"I recommend you rethink that statement very carefully," Slate threatens. He looks ready to gut her.

Ferris motions to his son. Jasper's platinum hair is disheveled and he looks pale. "Jasper, testify to this Alpha."

His voice is defeated. "Hazel was living with me in our pack lands. She pledged to be my mate."

"Like hell, she did," Slate shouts.

"Leash your Beta," Ferris growls.

Heath is unconcerned. "You are laying claim to his mate. You're lucky he isn't ripping your throat out." Heath glances at Slate. "Yet."

"They were in the middle of a ceremony when she was stolen away from us," Sienna says.

"Stolen? You're the one who stole me!" I find my voice. This entire situation is ridiculous. How can they stand here and make these claims?

"Hand over our wolf and we can avoid any violence," Ferris says, his voice smooth.

"Go fuck yourself!" Onyx shouts from over our shoulders.

Heath holds up a hand. The pack goes quiet. Calmly, he turns to me.

"I never agreed to anything, and Jasper never even asked," I say savagely. Eyeing Sienna, my rage overflows. "This pathetic excuse for an Alpha threatened us, tried to force us to become mates against our will. She abused both of us. "

"One more word about my mate, and I will direct an attack." Ferris's sharp voice cuts me off. He might not care if I'm forced to rejoin his pack, but he certainly cares about Sienna. Movement ripples through the line of Granite Ridge members.

Heath chuckles. "That will not end well for you."

He is trying to diffuse the situation, but violence and rage are bubbling up through the pack bond. We are seconds away from an explosion.

Slate releases my hand and takes a step forward. I want to grab him, but Cassia touches my shoulder.

"You want to take her? I challenge you for her." His voice is clear, every syllable clipped with anger.

"Not necessary," Heath snaps.

"I think it's a great solution. Let's see how he stacks up against Jasper," Ferris says. His cocky grin reminds me of his son. But on him, it is petrifying.

"Are you kidding me?" I protest. Slate keeps his focus fixed on Ferris and Jasper. I follow his gaze to Jasper. He is frozen as if waiting for violence from beside him instead of from us. An idea sparks.

"If Slate wins, Jasper joins our pack," I interject.

Slate bristles and opens his mouth to argue, but Heath stops him with a hand on his arm. My uncle takes a moment, looking between me and Jasper.

"Why would we do that?" Sienna spits.

I bare my teeth at Sienna. I haven't forgotten the pain of her claws in my arm.

"As it stands now, you'd have to drag me out of here and I'll fight you the rest of my life. I'll never accept Jasper." It's the truth. I could never live under this woman's control. "I'm proposing, if you wager Jasper, that I will come willingly to your pack."

It makes me sick to say, but I need to convince her.

"It doesn't matter. Jasper won't lose." Ferris crosses his arms.

"Or I could just break you," she hisses.

"You missed your chance for that," I say.

Ferris nods. "Fine, I'll accept those terms. When Jasper destroys your boyfriend, you come willingly and accept him as your mate. No need for violence." Sienna huffs, as if violence is exactly what she wants.

"Give us a moment," Heath says tersely.

Our Zetas and Thetas stay facing the enemy pack, but Heath leads us away. Slate walks stiffly, tension in every line of his lean frame.

Heath turns to us, his arms crossed.

"Sir, I saw the opportunity to end this without fighting," Slate says, his eyes on the ground.

"You can't sacrifice yourself like that," Heath cautions.

"Yes, Alpha. But I can beat him," Slate reassures us.

"He will lose on purpose. He wants to be free of them," I whisper. Slate's eyes narrow in disbelief. "Believe me, Jasper is as much a prisoner there as I was. I wasn't lying when I said she mistreats him."

Heath studies me for a long moment. "I understand, but I don't like any of this. If you're sure, I trust you. But if things go sideways, we can't let them walk out of here. We outnumber them now, but we won't if they get reinforcements."

He's talking about destroying another pack's leadership. Contingency plans. I admire the strategy even as fear lodges in my chest like ice.

Heath returns to deliver the news.

Slate stays rooted. I gingerly touch his arm. He shakes his head like clearing away thoughts. "You said you were my mate minutes ago," he says roughly. "I don't like hearing Jasper laying claim to you."

"I'm sorry, I didn't see another way," I say, frustrated. He needs to see the bigger picture. "Slate, he is your brother, and that makes him my family too now."

He shakes his head rougher, a scowl darkening his eyes.

"I know this is hard for you, but we have this chance to save him from Sienna. He's the one who had to grow up under her rule."

He meets my gaze, his expression softening. I'm getting through to him.

"He needs to get out of there, or she will turn him into our enemy for sure," I push. "But it's not about me. I'm yours. Nothing will ever change that." I wrap my arms around his waist. "It's only you. I need you to know that, especially before this fight."

Slate still doesn't answer, but he returns my embrace. His thumb runs over my throat, angling my mouth toward his. His searing kiss crackles through me down to my toes.

We break away. "Okay. I trust you," he finally says.

"I love you," I murmur. "Don't get hurt, and try to keep him in one piece." I kiss him one more time as he grumbles.

He hesitates. "Does he for sure know you aren't going to be his mate?"

I roll my eyes. "Of course. But maybe try to tell him the plan. That we are trying to free him. Just to be safe."

He rolls his shoulders and exhales, turning back to the gathering.

SLATE

"An heir for an heir," Heath announces.

I face Jasper in the training ring. It's an outdoor space for sparring. The entire crowd has moved around us, the Granite Ridge pack on the southern side closest to the road.

We have both taken our shirts off so we are ready to shift. I'm taller but Jasper is more muscled.

We are evenly matched, except his exhaustion is written into every movement. It's not the kind of exhaustion from a sleepless night. It's the soul-deep exhaustion from a life slowly killing you. It's what I saw in Hazel when she first arrived.

Hazel grips Marigold's hand tightly. Sienna paces back and forth across the circle. Heath and Ferris stand stoically opposite of each other.

I focus on my opponent. I hope he isn't too stupid to realize we are trying to help him. I have to figure out how to tell him our plan. It'll be impossible once we shift. All of this is a huge risk.

He starts to circle so I move too, keeping distance between us.

He darts toward me, feinting to the right and swinging with his left. I block easily. But he follows up with a jab on the right which hits my ribs. Pain radiates from the impact and I snarl.

I react with a quick swing which he ducks. Lightning fast, I follow with a kick. As he jerks away to dodge, I strike again and connect with his chest. He reels back.

Sienna screeches instructions at him. I can't process the dissonance of yelling from all sides.

He comes in for a second attack. I block his first blow, but he surprises me by ducking and ramming his shoulder into my gut. I slam into the dirt, his weight on top of me. Gasping, I manage to grab his arm, keeping him from punching my kidney.

His free hand swings for my face, but he's angled all wrong.

"She wants to rescue you, jackass," I hiss.

"And be a slave to your pack?" He grunts, finally breaking free of my hold. "No, thank you."

I shove him away. We both roll to our feet. He's managed to push me toward my pack and away from his.

"We don't keep people against their will," I say.

"That would mean more coming from someone I could trust," he grunts, surging forward with another punch I block.

"This wasn't my idea." I bare my teeth.

"You don't have a lot of those, do you?" he taunts.

"Hazel wants you to lose," I growl, dodging a kick. "Otherwise, she could have just come with you."

He pauses, and I restrain myself from landing a hit.

"I don't lose," he hisses.

He advances with a barrage of swift, hard blows. I block everything I can, but blows litter my ribcage. He is well trained and he has a few pounds of muscle on me. But he never goes for a knock-out.

As he comes in close, I try one last time. "Then you're condemning Hazel to belong to your mother."

He jerks back as if I landed a punch. He meets my gaze and the smallest nod lifts his chin. I hope he is truly cooperating and not tricking me. Regardless, I'm on guard.

We circle each other for a moment before he shifts into a magnificent white wolf and I follow his lead. Normally, this is when the fight really begins. We meet in a clash of snapping jaws and snarls, my umber against his snow.

He rears up, trying to get above me, and I take the opportunity to dive underneath to his throat. His fur is thick and I can't get purchase. But he stumbles as he tries to avoid my teeth and regain his footing.

I surge forward. He catches my shoulder, teeth sinking into my skin. I snarl and sacrifice more blood for the opportunity to pin him. Instead of pulling away, I push forward, and he goes down.

I twist, my skin tearing, and am able to close my jaws over his neck. My weight presses down on him. He should be able to throw me off, but he doesn't.

His struggles are weak, and I growl as I ram him into the dirt. Finally, he goes limp. He lowers his tail and head, acknowledging me as the victor.

I release him and step back. My chest heaves, heart pounding, blood from my injury wetting my fur. Everyone around me is roaring. I don't care. I need to see Hazel. I shift and pull my pants on.

Jasper lies in the dirt looking thoroughly defeated and humiliated. Blood is splattered across his chest and it's mostly mine. It was worth it. I kick his pants to him.

Hazel runs toward me, throwing her arms around me. She barely spares a glance for Jasper. I'm not sure if it's because he's still naked or because she isn't concerned about him. I don't care. She is showing everyone she picks me and it makes my heart soar.

I lift her a few inches in a tight squeeze. She kisses me sweetly.

"He is no heir of mine." I hear Ferris snap.

Heath shouts, "Lazuli, Hawthorne, please see the Granite Ridge Pack out."

"Are you okay?" Hazel slides down me to her feet and gently touches the bloody laceration cutting across my shoulder.

"It's nothing." I can't feel it.

Jasper stands, wincing. "I see how it is," he grumbles.

Hazel shoots him a glare. "Shut up, Jasper. You made my mate bleed, and he was trying to help you." I grin.

"Jasper, please visit our healer, and then let's talk," Heath says. Aven and Elm step forward to escort Jasper to Sable.

"You need medical attention too," Hazel says, eyes still on my injury.

I shake my head. It'll heal fine on its own.

I pull her closer, speaking into her ear. "I did what you said and didn't rip his throat out," I joke.

She smacks my arm, but then kisses me again. "Thank you. But seriously, you need Sable."

"I'm fine for now," I argue. "I want to go home."

She opens her mouth to protest, so I scoop her up and carry her toward our cabin. I want her all to myself. I need reassurance of our bond after what she asked of me.

Slamming the door behind me, I set her down and peel off my shirt. I reach for her clothing, but she stops me. "Slate, that looks awful. Let me help," she says.

Taking my hand, she leads me into our bathroom and starts to wipe the blood off my chest. The wound is already healing, but I'm covered in blood. With gentle strokes, she washes away the fight and soothes my soul.

I watch her work, transfixed by the soft expression on her face and the way she moves. Her hair grew at least two inches in the last week - her dark roots are to her ears. I hope she keeps growing it out because I love the warm, rich color.

"Thank you for doing that," she murmurs, "Thank you for trusting me."

Figuring I'm clean enough, I gather her to me and press a hard, needy kiss to her mouth. "You're my equal. I trust you and I want you to lead just as much as I do."

She sighs happily. "I love you."

"I love you," I barely manage to say before we're kissing again. I taste her, lost to the feeling of her tongue while her hands dip under my waistband. Breathing heavily, I tear my mouth off her skin. "What I want to do to you is going to take much longer than the few minutes we have right now." She bites her lip, giving me a devious look. "We need to check in with our Alpha, and then I want you all to myself, for at least a few days, if not a whole week."

For once she doesn't argue.

XIX
ADMISSIONS &
ADMONISHMENTS
HAZEL

We meet Heath outside the office trailers. He's quietly discussing something with Fisher.

"Slate, Hazel, I'd like you to join me for our discussion with Jasper," Heath instructs. He fixes his gaze on me. "Since you were the catalyst that brought him into our pack."

My stomach flips. Is he angry? I can't tell. His perfectly neutral expression holds while he ushers us into the building.

As I pass him, I pause. "I'm sorry," I whisper. His eyebrows furrow and he raises a hand to stop me. Fisher brushes past us and follows Slate into the room.

"What are you sorry about?" Heath asks.

I fidget, trying to pull my words together. "For Jasper, making you take him."

Heath nods. "Hazel, if anyone else tried that, I wouldn't have allowed it to happen. Any of it." I bite my lip. He continues, "But you are my heir now. You're next in line to be Alpha and that's why I let you make that choice."

Heir? I swallow, regretting this conversation already. I should have questions, but I can't process what he's saying.

"You did the right thing." He guides me forward.

Jasper sits at a conference table, his head in his hands. He's got dirt smudged across his cheek and his hair is sticking up to one side. Not his typical polished style.

Elm stands against the wall behind him. Beside him is Aven, the younger Theta. She's polite but reserved, and right now she's watching Jasper like he's an interesting bug she's considering squishing. Fisher and Slate stand on either side of the door, waiting for Heath. He takes a seat opposite of Jasper. Slate holds out the chair to Heath's right for me and then sits beside me. Fisher sits on Heath's other side. Jasper watches us, his expression wary.

Heath folds his hands on the table, finally breaking the silence. "I would like to ask you about your old pack."

Jasper nods. "Of course."

I press my lips together, trying not to smile. Jasper's outlook is changing before my eyes. It's more than I hoped for.

"First, should we be concerned about a rescue attempt from your parents?"

Jasper shakes his head. "When Ferris disowned me, he meant it. They'll consider me dead."

"Sounds like Sienna to me," Slate mutters. Heath ignores him.

"How many wolves does Ferris have now?"

Jasper rubs the back of his neck. "Um, I think they are at about seventy-five."

Fisher and Heath don't react, but Elm stiffens. Granite Ridge is almost double our size.

"What can you tell me about Ironcrest?" Heath asks.

"Zephyr and Ferris meet regularly," Jasper confirms grimly. "I don't think they like each other. But they've worked out some deals. I don't know any details."

"What was their role in abducting Hazel?" Heath's voice is lower. He looks calm, but I can sense his anger simmering.

"They are the ones who grabbed her. I went in the car to pick her up from them on the edge of Raven territory."

"Were they involved?"

"No, Nyx doesn't have the resources to watch the north end of her territory. I believe Ironcrest has all but taken that land."

"Interesting," Heath says, "How did Granite Ridge even know about Hazel?" Jasper swallows. He looks to me, an apology in his eyes. "They knew you had a visitor. They have security cameras along the road." The tension in the room ramps up.

"I met Hazel in town. And the second time I ran into her, I identified your pack." He looks away, a slight slump to his shoulders. "I told my father. And I regret that."

Closing my eyes for a second, I let the betrayal sting and fade.

Heath's mouth is a thin line. "The rogue wolves?"

"Ours. But I didn't even know about it until after we came to confront you about Hazel."

"Why abduct her?"

"My mother wanted to induct her into our pack." He folds his hands in his lap, his gaze flickering toward Slate. "She wanted us to be mates so we could claim your pack someday. I didn't know what to do to protect her. I was trying to find a way out of it, but then my mother was demanding I claim her immediately. So we acted the part to keep her satisfied, and planned her escape."

Tension holds Slate's frame stiff, but his head is still inclined toward me, and his grip on my thigh hasn't wavered.

"What happened after you let her go?" Heath's voice is soft.

Jasper looks away. "They beat the shit out of me. I had to fight my sister so I told them that Ember was trying to kill Hazel, and that Hazel managed to escape while I was defending her. If you think I look bad, you should see Ember right now."

I never thought I'd feel bad for his psycho sister, but the idea of her own parents punishing her physically makes my stomach roil.

"I'm sorry. I didn't make the decision to take you, but it's my fault any of this happened," he says, his aqua eyes meeting mine. He slouches in his seat. I want to forgive him, but now isn't the time.

Clearing his throat, Heath folds his hands on the table. "I expect loyalty from my pack, without exception. And I expect absolute honesty, no withholding information. Or the consequences will be serious."

Jasper blinks at him. "Yes, Alpha."

"Then I'd like to welcome you to our pack," Heath begins. Jasper's eyes widen. "I'm sure we can find a place for you. But do you want to join our pack? You are free to go otherwise."

"Alpha, I didn't expect this," Jasper stammers.

Frowning, Heath studies Jasper. "What did you think would happen?"

Jasper looks over at me, his expression still confused. "In Granite Ridge, any wolves we take from other packs are used for labor only, if they are allowed to live. They don't have any sort of freedom."

Heath's jaw tightens and he lets out a slow breath. "That's not how we operate here. What would you like to do in our pack? You can work toward being in our rankings or take a community role."

Jasper wavers and I see tentative hope bloom in his eyes. "I enjoy patrolling and protecting, sir. But I'll take any role offered."

"Alright, why don't you train with Fisher for a few weeks and we can go from there?" Heath says and Jasper nods, still looking shocked. "Elm, would you take Jasper to our guest cabin and make sure he has what he needs?"

Heath stands, effectively dismissing us. Slate's hand is steady on my back as we pause at the doorway. I want to hug Jasper or maybe strangle him. He frustrates me, and I still feel betrayed by him, but I choose to believe the Jasper in front of me is the real one.

"I'm glad you're okay," I say. He dips his head in respectful acknowledgment. As he meets Slate's gaze, his feet halt.

My mate bridges the gap. "Thank you for getting her home," he says. They still have a lot to sort out, but it's a start.

XIX
FIREWORKS & FOREVERS

SLATE

While Hazel checks in with our friends, I take some supplies out to my favorite spot. She's waiting in our home when I return. Her wide, concerned eyes meet mine, and my heart nearly bursts.

"Hey," I say, going to her.

"Where were you?" she asks softly, resting her cheek against my shoulder. I love how she always reaches for me.

"I want to take you somewhere special to me," I say, loving the smile she gives me. "Come on, let's grab some food and head out."

We bypass the normal dinner gathering, and I snag the picnic basket Clove and Crickett put together for us. They were enthusiastically supportive of my plan.

As we walk hand in hand through the forest, Hazel tips her head back, gazing at the pink streaks of sunset darkening to dusky purple above us.

The silence is comfortable. But there are things I need to say. I swallow, gathering my thoughts. "Hazel, I'm sorry." She turns, surprise arching her eyebrows. "I'm sorry for doubting you. I'm sorry I tried to get you to move on." I pull her to a halt and look directly into her eyes. They're melted gold. "I would never have moved on. If you left or met someone else, I would have continued to live for you."

Her mouth parts and I can't resist running my thumb over her bottom lip.

"When we were apart, I was terrified I'd never see you again," she whispers. "That was all I cared about."

"You are everything to me," I murmur, pulling her closer.

She searches my face, her long lashes framing those beautiful, expressive eyes. Reaching up, she rakes her fingers through my hair, brushing it out of my face.

"Thank you for fighting for me." Her soft form melts into mine.

"I'd do anything for you." My voice is husky.

"Maybe less violence next time, please," she teases, winking at me. She starts walking, tugging me along.

"Next time?" I question.

"You're right. No next time." She laughs, the sound washing through me, leaving me warmer.

"No one would dare disrespect you again. You're got your own fangs now," I say. She laughs, throwing her head back and causing her hair to ripple. "You're a powerful wolf. It's a good thing we're mates, or you'd take my position as Beta."

"Oh!" She blinks at me. Did she not consider rankings?

The earth slopes as we start descending toward the creek. The water is wider here and the flow is gentle.

My favorite swimming spot is a basin with trees curving over the water. It's quiet, dark, and private. I've already set up a tent for us on the shore, safely away from the water.

"It's perfect," she whispers. "Can we go swimming?"

"Sure." I follow her down to the water's edge. "Don't fall in," I tease.

She raises her middle finger at me. I start to laugh, but it dies in my throat when she pulls her shirt up over her head and drapes it across a rock. She drags her pants down next. The bare expanse of skin is bewitching.

She squeals at the cold but slides into the water anyway. Her hands drag through the water, sending ripples out from her like she is a buoy. My eyes trace the black vine and moons of her tattoo between her perfect breasts. I can't believe I got to mark her in that way, before claiming her for my own.

Setting the food beside the tent, I wade in after her. When she was human, I'd have worried about her getting too cold. But she isn't human, and besides, I have plans to warm her up.

She drifts backward, letting herself sink until the water sloshes over her shoulders and soaks her hair.

I push forward, aching to reach her. She smirks, gliding back and keeping a few inches out of reach. I narrow my eyes. So this is the game.

Sucking in a breath, I duck under the water and propel myself forward, grabbing her around the waist and pulling her under too. She doesn't fight me, just brings her hands to my shoulders as bubbles cascade around us.

With an arm wrapped around her soft form, I effortlessly rise up out of the water, clutching her to me. Her legs wrap around my waist on instinct as she shrieks in laughter. She's higher than me, and I gaze up at her gorgeous honey eyes and delighted smile. Her brown and blonde hair drips over us.

I continue wading forward until I press her against one of the boulders edging the pool. She gasps, the sharp intake of breath sending a jolt of desire down my spine.

Starving, I run my tongue up the center of her chest, across the tattoo I inked into her skin, before nuzzling one of her breasts and closing my mouth over her nipple. So soft and perfect. She arches into me.

She groans, "I need you, now." Her command shoots straight to my cock, but I restrain myself, moving to her other breast. I want to take my time with her.

"Want to go into the tent?" I murmur, sliding her down until I can reach her mouth. Her kisses are like swallowing coals, searing against the cold water.

She reaches between us to grip my shaft. "When I say now, I mean now," she bites out between kisses, dragging her hand down and back up. She's stripping away my self-control, making me frantic.

I kiss her hard, her tongue diving into my mouth. With one hand against her ribs to hold her in place, I guide myself to her entrance. Her legs clench around me, pulling me closer. Our hearts beat together. Two souls fusing. Slowly, I push into her, watching her eyes flutter closed and her teeth pinch her bottom lip in ecstasy. She's magnificent. As I fill her, she lets out a guttural moan that makes my eyes roll back in my head.

Placing a hand on my chest, she blinks at me with hazy eyes. "Mark me," she demands. Her throaty voice is intoxicating. "Claim me."

I nod, unable to form a response other than to worship her body. The little sounds of pleasure I draw from her with each movement are the most erotic thing I've ever heard. "You feel so fucking good," I growl. The choppy water crests over her breasts.

I slam into her harder, earning a gasp. Tension coils between us, almost unbearable. Hooking my hand under one soft thigh, I tilt her, pressing deeper. Her nails scrape my back, her hips rolling to meet mine. We are wild things among the trees where we belong.

My instincts are riding me hard, and I can't wait any longer. She arches her neck to present herself to me, making me nearly come from the sight. Giving in to the pressure, I sink my fangs into the muscle where neck meets shoulder. This time there's no fear, no doubt, no guilt, just a deep sense of devotion.

She cries out my name, her fingers digging into my skin. The flood of pleasure from our completed bond compounds the sweet feeling of her orgasm pulsing around me. I drive into her, the rush of my release extinguishing my thoughts. Mindless, I nip at her neck and catch her mouth for another scalding kiss.

She pants against me, her body pliant. We stay connected, the magic of the claiming buzzing between us.

"Wow," I blurt, my thoughts scattered.

She lets out a hoarse laugh. "That was unbelievable." I smile against her skin.

We disentangle. Her eyes are glazed so I carry her to the shore. She clings to me, her wet body plastered to mine.

I gently set her on the rocky bank and wrap her in a towel. While I'm grabbing my towel, she runs her hand over the bite mark. Wiping off the blood, she reveals nearly healed marks underneath. Unlike her first set, which healed into nothingness, these are glistening, shining scars against her skin.

I can sense her emotions clearer now, more than the pack link. Her well-being is like a beacon inside my soul.

"Can you feel that?" I ask.

"What?" she asks shyly.

I grab our picnic basket and sit beside her. "How clear our connection is now."

"Maybe."

She rests between my bent legs, her back to my front, and we take turns feeding each other bites of meats and cheeses. I learn she prefers green grapes over red and salami over prosciutto - all these little mundane facts we missed and can now spend our lives discovering. I kiss her neck, adoring every piece of her I unravel.

Full and satisfied, I urge her into the tent and crawl in behind her. I've unrolled thick sleeping bags and zipped them together. We slide in and I pull her to my side. She drapes an arm and leg over me.

With a grin, I reach into the corner and grab a gift bag.

"What is that?" She giggles.

"Open it," I urge her.

She props herself up and tugs the box out of the bag. She turns it over and gasps.

"Are you serious?"

"You deserve it," I murmur.

She studies the box. It's a digital DSLR camera I ordered for her the first night we kissed. It was a stupid choice at the time, but now I can't help but think somehow I knew she was mine.

"Thank you." She leans over me and kisses me.

"You deserve everything. You are the most compassionate person I've ever known." I press a kiss to her new claim mark. "I love you."

She giggles and stops my compliments with another kiss. It's slow and languid, lips brushing against each other with no end in sight. I twist my fingers in her hair and she runs her hand down my neck, across my chest. I could do this with her forever.

HAZEL

Slate kisses like he loves, thoroughly, sometimes rough and urgent, sometimes soft and slow. I want to live in this moment forever.

I trail my hand downwards, across his abs and lower. His relaxed body goes taut. I skate my hands back up, admiring the lines of his muscles.

My leg is tossed over his and it's all too easy to slide over him until I'm straddling him. He's hard again.

"I want to claim you too," I declare before I lose my nerve. My stomach flips waiting on his response.

A soft smile curves his mouth. I'm taken aback again by how his features go from handsome and broody to ridiculously gorgeous.

"What do I do?" I ask, shaky. He sits up and I'm across his lap.

"When it feels right, you just bite," he explains, although it's not exactly helpful.

"Um, feels like what?" I press, a blush warming my cheeks.

He pauses, absently tracing from my ribs over my stomach to my thighs with his fingers. "I guess it feels possessive and like you would cease to exist if you didn't. It's instinct."

"Alright, I can try." He watches me warily as if he thinks I'm about to lunge and bite him any second. Giggling nervously, I reach up to frame his jaw with both hands. We kiss sweetly, but I grind down onto his cock to get the message across.

"Do you really want to do this?" he murmurs. I answer by running my tongue up the column of his throat, like he's done to me so many times before. It's like I've flipped a switch. He grabs my hips roughly and flips me onto my back.

"I'm never going to get enough of you," he murmurs, his mouth against my thigh. His hot breath against my chilled skin triggers a shiver down my spine. "You are so tempting." He licks my inner thigh, making me squirm. "You make me lose my mind," he growls before running his tongue up my core and swirling it around my nub. My hips buck, stars exploding behind my eyes, and he has to hold me down so he can continue.

"I could feel how much you enjoyed that through our bond," he says. I can only moan in response. "I can feel how aroused you are."

I'm going to climax from this man's words alone. I suck in the cold air, my entire body on fire. My stomach clenches as he lowers his delectable mouth, now lavishing his attention at the apex of my thighs. One hand releases my hips so he can slide one finger in me, and then two. I grip the cotton of the sleeping bag, my eyes squeezed shut.

"Look at me," he commands, and I force my eyes open, my heart racing at his salacious grin. "I need to know what you like." I gape at him. Those glowing green eyes watch me intently as his fingers curl, rubbing against the front of my inner wall. I moan, my back arching. "There it is," he murmurs, repeating the motion. Without stopping, he lowers his mouth and resumes using his tongue in ways that make the rest of the world cease to exist.

He lets out a dark groan and withdraws, leaving me aching. "I'm going to come on our bedding from how much you're enjoying this." My stomach clenches at his words.

I let out a laugh. "I have a solution for that," I say, reaching for him. He kisses me hard, and I push his shoulders until he lays back. I'm so slick, I line us up and sink onto him smoothly. Every sensation narrows to that exquisite stretch and ache. He's watching me, heavy-lidded with a lazy smile.

Feeling like a goddess, I rock against him. His hands grip my waist and guide me as I roll my hips. Pressure builds, pushing out rational thought. He tugs my mouth down to his, folding me over him. Then he's driving up from beneath me and I'm holding on, my breathing ragged.

Urges rise up, and I run my tongue across his shoulder muscle, toying with the idea of marking him. Can I really do this?

Slate is close to finishing, a look of concentration sharpening his beautiful features. I watch, fascinated, as he slows, his expression softening as he comes. I can feel it through our bond, a surging pleasure. I curl over him, experiencing his pleasure, when my lips brush his skin. An overpowering instinct swells in me, and I sink my teeth into his muscle.

The claiming snaps into place, and the feel of his orgasm hits me in full, causing my own body to shatter. I cling to him, waves of euphoria overwhelming me. He shouts, my release hitting him just as his ends. Intense possession and love wash over me, shocking me as I come down.

I can taste his blood. I wipe my mouth with the back of my hand. "Baby, that was so hot," he says and I can feel his pride. It's like our connection is turned up to max volume, incomprehensible and all-consuming.

"That was intense," I gasp, collapsing down beside him.

"That's one way to put it." Laughing, he wraps his arms around me, and I nestle into him. We stay like that, our breathing slowly returning to normal.

Slate drags his fingers through my hair, staring at the ceiling of our tent. "Do you want to move into my family's cabin?" he asks, surprising me.

"Yeah?" I ask, trying to sense through our bond if he wants to or not. I only feel anticipation and satisfaction.

"We don't have to. I just thought, because it has a lot more room," he rambles.

"Really?" I laugh. "Tell me about this additional room."

He sighs, squeezing me tight. "Let's see, it's got an actual kitchen, like with a dishwasher."

"Good start, I like dishwashers," I say, kissing the nearest skin I can reach, in this case, his collarbone. Honestly, I hadn't noticed his kitchen lacked a dishwasher.

"And it's got three bedrooms. So we could have an office or whatever you wanted."

"Or an art studio?" I murmur. It's too dim to see if he blushes, but I can feel his pleasure through our bond.

"Do you want to?" I ask.

"Yeah, I think we should work on making it our own. We can stay in our trailer until we're happy with it. I'll fix it up however you like."

"I'm sure it'll be perfect. I can't wait to see it."

"Tomorrow," he promises.

I answer by him leaning in to brush my lips against his. It's not a soft good-night kiss, because I'm not done with him yet. My tiredness fades away as he tangles his hands into my hair and kisses me like I'm his oxygen.

"I hope you weren't hoping for a good night's sleep," he rasps, making the air on my arms stand on end.

EPILOGUE

HAZEL

We tumble back into our trailer, hands all over each other. We have sawdust in our hair and we're smudged with wood glue and stain.

We've developed a routine in the last few months. After Slate leads the morning patrols and I spend a few hours shadowing Heath, we grab lunch and head to his family's cabin. Currently, we're refinishing the wood floors.

I fell in love with the cabin the first time I saw it. The walls and ceilings are all wood planked, and multi-pane windows span the kitchen. We plan to order new appliances soon.

The closet hides a stack of original art by Slate's father, Clay, and by Slate as a teenager. I'm looking forward to finding a place for them.

The cozy living room still held an antique rug, now safely rolled up, and some beautiful brass lights. Two little bedrooms and a bathroom are tucked under the stairs. Slate's childhood room will be a guest room for now and the extra room will become an art studio for him.

Up the stairs is our private space. Slate has been installing floor-to-ceiling shelving along one wall for all of our books. Our bed will face the small balcony. I love the view of the foliage and all the birds who fill those branches.

The tiny bathroom holds a claw-foot tub and more brass fixtures. I'm grateful his dad never got around to updating the cabin because the vintage style is perfect.

We work until the light starts to fade and then we close up the cabin and head home.

I am deliriously happy. Slate made good on his promise to christen every surface in our trailer, and I'm looking forward to moving into our new home and repeating the process.

We shower together with a few kisses sprinkled in. It's too easy to miss dinner if we let ourselves get too lost in each other.

He traces his fingertips over my second tattoo, one he gave me two weeks ago. It's a trailing design of curling fern leaves, tiny mushrooms, sprigs of blackberries, and a wolf's paw print down my left arm. It's his paw print to be exact. My paw print is inked on his ribs to match.

I pull on fleece-lined pants and a thicker coat. Slate tosses on a hoodie and follows me out, his damp hair falling over his forehead. I toss my shoulder-length brunette hair into a messy bun. I was able to chop off the remaining blonde within a few weeks of my first shift. My hair still grows insanely fast and I understand why Slate's hair always looks a bit shaggy.

"You cold, baby?" He gently teases.

"Duh! It's colder than a penguin's ballsack." I say, earning a laugh from my mate. Even with my warmer shifter body, I still haven't acclimated to this cold. And it hasn't even snowed yet.

Everyone is busy eating already. We grab our dinner and slide onto the benches of a picnic table with our friends.

Marigold and Onyx bicker over some game, and Cedar is explaining to Jasper how he is sprouting the plants for spring in his little greenhouse.

"Hey, guys." Onyx grins.

"How's the house coming along?" Jasper asks.

"Good. I need to start picking out curtains," I joke.

Marigold gasps. "Can I help with the decorating?"

I nod, smiling at her.

"Any word from Granite Ridge?" Slate asks Jasper.

Jasper has been helping Hawthorne and Heath with a border negotiation involving the Raven pack for the last few weeks, but Ferris is decidedly uncooperative.

He shakes his head. "No one will answer my messages. They're too afraid of upsetting the alphas."

"Why would they be upset?" Marigold cocks her head. She's sitting between Cedar and Jasper, and I don't miss the weird push and pull between them.

Jasper laughs. "I'm sure they don't allow anyone to talk about me. I mean, my parents probably think I'm either dead or being treated like a slave."

"I told you we don't do that here," Slate adds dryly.

"Thanks, dude." Jasper shoots back, sarcastically. "Sienna would shit herself if she could see me now."

"Hope so."

Marigold giggles. "Look at you guys, getting along so nicely."

Onyx reaches across the table and pats Jasper on the back, a little too hard because he lurches forward. He rolls his eyes.

"He isn't too bad. He's a lot like you, Slate. But without the stick up his ass." Onyx taunts.

"You're sure fixated on my ass, Onyx." Slate teases right back.

Onyx lets out a huge laugh. "You wish!"

Jasper groans. "Dude, that was the lamest reply ever. You've got to step it up."

"Don't encourage him," Cedar deadpans. Marigold bursts into a huge fit of giggles, clutching her side.

I place my hand over Slate's and squeeze his fingers. I love our group. Jasper fits in perfectly, though Slate won't admit it.

"Campfire tonight?" Marigold proposes.

"I'm in!" Onyx answers. Cedar and Jasper nod.

I glance at Slate. He grips my thigh possessively. I want to drag him home and ravage him, but I also don't want to miss out on time with our friends.

"Your choice," he murmurs, his face calm. But I can tell my need has bled through our bond because his pupils are blown out and his hand is slipping higher up my thigh.

"Let's go for a while. Then I want you to myself," I answer. His green eyes shine back at me and his Adam's apple bobs. I stare at the column of his throat for a second, letting out a slow breath. I need to calm down.

Jasper gathers up our plates and takes them to the kitchen. He's still trying to earn his place here, though we've all accepted him.

Slate takes my hand and we wander toward the twins' cabin. I pull him closer and he kisses my temple.

I revel in the darkness. While not as keen as my vision as a wolf, I still can see surprisingly well now. It's almost pitch black in the trees, but I can make out each root and rock in our path.

We grab an Adirondack chair and drag it closer to the fire pit. Slate pulls me down into his lap and I nestle my forehead against his neck, my cheek on his claim mark.

Cedar is feeding the flames and coaxing them to grow. Marigold perches on the nearby bench, watching him.

Jasper arrives, unfolding a thick plaid blanket. He offers it to Marigold, and she smiles sweetly as he sits beside her and drapes it around both of them.

I don't miss how Cedar glances back and his gaze lingers on them. Marigold's cheeks flush as Jasper quietly speaks to her.

Onyx arrives with his bag of marshmallows and a stack of graham crackers and chocolate. I've started to insist we make full s'mores instead of gooey marshmallows alone. Any chance for more chocolate.

I hold both of our sticks while Slate's hands slide into my jacket, hot against my stomach.

The boys argue over anything and nothing. Marigold has us all howling with laughter over the escapades of her students. Jasper and Onyx inexplicably start a competition to see who can fit the most marshmallows in their mouths. When Onyx gags and spits out a whole handful of wet marshmallows, I decide we've had enough.

I don't have to say a word. Simply the thought of taking my mate home sparks enough heat between us, Slate tells everyone goodnight and carries me bridal-style northwards toward our trailer.

He sets me down once we reach the kitchen, and we start mauling each other. We stumble past the plate of lopsided chocolate croissants from our recent cooking lesson with Clove. Slate's attempts usually turn out better than mine, but I'm determined to learn.

We barely make it to the bedroom. I'm desperate, every bit of my desire is reflected back through our bond.

Later, I'm draped across Slate's chest, sweat sticking our skin together. Snow is drifting past our window.

"It's your first snow," he says, his eyes on me instead of the window. I nip his palm as he brushes my hair back from my face and then turns back to the mesmerizing snowflakes.

"It's so beautiful," I say.

"See if you still feel that way in February," he mutters.

I grin at him. "Want to go for a run?"

I know what he likes. "Yes, please."

We don't even have to strip, since our clothes are already scattered in the living room. Within seconds, we burst out into the frigid night. My wolf eyesight can see the snowflakes so clearly, I'm tempted to sit and stare. But Slate is already bounding ahead, joy flooding my emotions. With a huff, I tear off after him. As I get close, he darts forward in a sprint, and I give chase.

We speed through the trees, that sense of utter freedom lifting my soul until I could fly. There's nothing else I'd rather be doing, nowhere I'd rather be, and no one else I'd rather call mine.

MOONLIGHT
AND
MISCHIEF

I
WOLF PUPS & WRESTLING
Marigold

"Did you have to stick a crayon up your nose? Really?" Suppressing a smile, I tip Daisy's chin up to get a better look. The end of a broken green crayon peeks out of her nostril. "Goddess help us when you start shifting," I mutter under my breath while stretching to reach the nearest tissue box.

"Hold one side closed." She pokes at her nose on the wrong side, wincing. "No, baby, this one. And then blow your nose hard. If it doesn't come out, we'll have to get your mama."

Leaving the tiny menace to her task, I survey the rest of my class. My job isn't difficult with such a small class, but these students are a bit wilder than typical human children.

"Wrap it up, friends! It's almost two," I command, gathering spare art supplies from the closest table.

Buttery light streams in the massive windows. The walls of my one-room schoolhouse are wallpapered with their paintings and drawings between multiplication charts and historical timelines, handmade by yours truly. Students sprawl across benches, paint brushes and markers in their hands.

"I'm serious, I'm not cleaning up after you pups. Five minutes!"

At the sound of my scolding, a dishwater blonde head leans around the door frame. "Doing okay, Goldie? Need me to teach any of these kids a lesson?"

"Hey, Onyx," I plant a hand on my hip, a wry smile curving my lips. "I think we're good, but thanks."

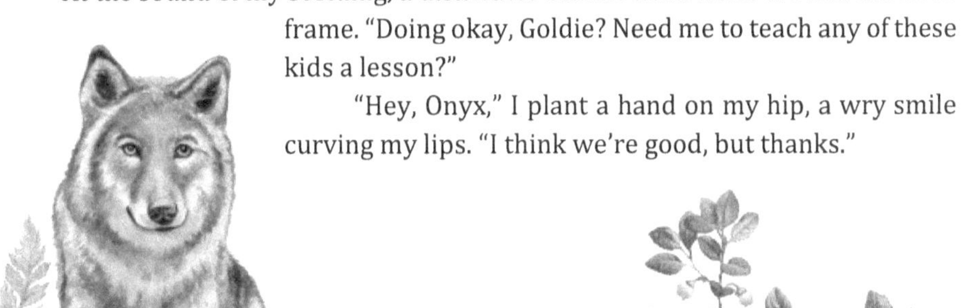

"Got any more of those cookies you made for your class?" he asks.

"They're for my students," I say, rolling my eyes. Wandering to the back table, I wrap a napkin around one of the remaining chocolate chip cookies and bring it to Onyx.

"You're the best!" He says, a grin lighting up his face.

Leaning past him, I wave at his twin.

"You want a cookie too, Cedar?"

"I'm good." The afternoon sunlight streaks his hair amber, contrasting with the deep tan from his hours outdoors. He's handsome in a golden-age movie star way.

Onyx is more of a rebel, always dressed in grungy band shirts and ready with a joke or prank, but he's a sweetheart under the shenanigans.

"You guys busy?" I ask, hearing a chorus of giggles behind me. Nosy little stinkers.

Cedar nods, "Getting some training in."

"Have a good time! See you later."

Ducking back inside, I find that Daisy managed to shoot the crayon out of her nose and now holds it up triumphantly. At least her mom won't be mad at me, even if I now have to confiscate a booger crayon.

"Alright, my little artists, let's get this place cleaned up!"

After the school day ends, I wander across the sun-drenched meadow toward my family's cabin. Even though I moved in with my grandmother a couple of years ago, I like to check back every so often. A household of three men can get messy quickly and my father is hopeless with housekeeping.

It's empty like I knew it would be. Dad is out patrolling, Cobalt is playing soccer in the clearing, and Indigo is finishing up his afternoon internship with my grandmother. She's the pack's healer, and Indie will take over for her someday.

The cabin smells like old leather and my father's aftershave, with an undercurrent of sweaty socks. The warm wood kitchen is fairly tidy, but I toss the breakfast plates into the creaky dishwasher and start it. Padding across the ancient brown carpet toward the bedrooms, I pause to transfer the laundry from the washer to the dryer before it gets musty. My siblings' shared bathroom needs a quick wipe down, and then I'm popping out the front door.

Sure, the boys could handle everything themselves, but my brothers are busy and my dad works so hard. My job ends early in the afternoon, so it makes sense for me to tackle a few chores and lighten the load on my dad's shoulders.

On the way to my grandmother's cottage, I dodge my students kicking a soccer ball back and forth. Despite my fatigue, I cheer them on. They love to play in the clearing between the diner, the school, and the supply shop.

Cedar's garden spans the north side, centered around an archway covered in snow pea vines. The delicate tendrils climb the frame but it's still too early for the soft pink flowers to bloom.

Cedar loves to talk about his garden, and I'm always happy to listen. With his smile in my mind, I veer toward the training building tucked into the edge of the trees. The garage doors are rolled up in the back, and two men grapple in a spray-painted circle.

A tall, tattooed figure leans against the steel siding beside Cedar. Slate serves as the pack's Beta or second-in-command. He's quiet like Cedar, but in more of a brooding artist way, instead of being lost in thought.

At the moment, their attention is fixed on the duo currently throwing punches and evading kicks. Onyx's swirling black tattoos curl over his biceps and across his chest. Opposite him, Slate's brother Jasper dodges Onyx's offense.

Jasper joined the pack last fall. He's all sharp lines and high contrast - startlingly bright teal irises and pale gold hair, against warm tanned skin. He defected from our rival pack and has been trying to earn his place here ever since.

Onyx ducks as Jasper swings high, but Jasper is clever and he jabs with his other fist, hitting Onyx in the shoulder. Onyx lurches back and attempts to turn his motion into a rotating kick, but Jasper darts in and sweeps his feet, tossing him onto the dirt.

With a dramatic groan, Onyx pushes up to sit. "I'm getting tired of that. Someone else needs to go next."

"Sorry, man," Jasper says with a laugh, offering his hand. Pulling Onyx to his feet, he turns my way, his bright eyes widening. "Marigold, do you want to join in?"

My nose wrinkles. "Not today, thanks."

"Too bad. I'd love to see what you can do," Jasper murmurs. A blush blooms over my cheeks. I avoid sparring with the boys, preferring to fight Hazel or even Cassia, one of the pack's Zetas, or warriors.

I settle against the wall beside Cedar. Slate stretches his arms and arches his back to loosen up before he faces his younger half-brother. Slate is leaner and taller, though Jasper has a few more pounds of muscle on him.

Jasper clenches and unclenches his fists. Swallowing, I avert my gaze from his glistening back and the way the muscles narrow to his waist.

"Did you have a good day with your students?" Cedar asks quietly.

My mouth curves into a smile. "Yeah, aside from a crayon incident with Daisy, it was a quiet day. Oh, and Starling brought a lizard in after lunch."

"Was it one of those geckos?" His head tips toward mine. He's a great listener.

"Yeah, I think?" I purse my lips, trying to remember. Once I saw the creature in her little hands, we hustled outside to release the poor reptile.

He nods thoughtfully. "Next time, let it go in the garden. I can always use more help with the grasshoppers."

"Sure thing."

My eyes are drawn back to the sparring brothers. Last fall, they fought in a formal challenge in this very ring over Hazel, Slate's mate. Jasper's birth pack attempted to steal her, but the end result was Jasper being disowned and joining our pack. He's proven himself loyal with how hard he works and how grateful he is for a life away from the militant pack his parents lead.

Like lightning, Slate steps closer and swings. Jasper's forearm knocks it away, but he's ready with a roundhouse kick. Slate's strike lands on Jasper's side and he grimaces. Stumbling back, Jasper sucks in a breath, as if he's in pain. I bite the inside of my cheek.

Regaining his footing, Jasper attacks, landing a succession of boxing-style hits before Slate hooks his leg around Jasper's ankle and shoves him backward. His back hits the dirt.

"You okay?" Slate asks, pulling Jasper up by the hand.

"Fine. I think I'm ready to call it a day. I gotta get cleaned up," Jasper says, wincing as he prods his ribs.

"Me too." Slate waves at us and walks into the training building to retrieve his belongings.

Still catching his breath, Jasper faces Cedar and me. Onyx laughs and shoves his shoulder, showing off the soil clinging to his sweaty skin.

Slate passes us, giving Jasper an apologetic shrug when he sees the dirt. "See you guys." I suspect his haste is an attempt to see Hazel before dinner.

Jasper steps closer to me, his typical cocky smirk in place. It softens his sharp features. "Did you enjoy seeing me get my ass kicked?"

"Always." I return the wink he gives me. Jasper wipes his bunched-up shirt over his forehead and neck. I take it from him and use it to gently brush his back off.

"Thanks," he says.

Cedar straightens. "See you at dinner," he says. Onyx follows after his twin, waving his goodbye.

Jasper strolls beside me, the evening light highlighting his blonde eyelashes. "We were talking about a campfire after dinner. Sound good to you?"

"Yeah, of course."

Looking pleased, Jasper waves before turning back to his cabin.

I finally resign myself to checking on my grandmother before dinner. The door jingles as I step into the stone structure Sable has lived in for decades. Her cottage sits just north of Cedar's garden, making harvesting herbs and medicinal plants convenient.

Grandmother hovers over the dining table, bundles of herbs spread around her hands as she sorts and stacks leaves of lemon balm. Her rolling pin thuds on the table, startling me. With gusto, she flattens the spikey leaves before tying twine around them and setting each in the pile. Lemon balm is good for insomnia, something that often bothers shifters with all of our wolf energy.

"Good afternoon!" I chime, slipping my sandals off and plopping onto the floral couch serving as my bed. The card table I use as my nightstand has been overrun by tiny bottles of pink liquid - rowanberry concentrate. It's not toxic like wolfsbane, but the bitter juice incapacitates our magic for a few hours and is helpful during a crisis. Superstition says rowan wood blocks enchantment, and I've always wondered if the berry's effect on our physiology may have played a role in that mythology. As fascinating as the compound is, I would prefer it if my space wasn't covered in individual doses of it.

"Hello, dear," my grandmother murmurs absently.

I draw a calming breath. "Grandmother, can I move these bottles somewhere for you?"

"Why would you do that?" She doesn't even look up.

"I'm trying to keep my area tidy."

"That's not necessary." Her eyes are stormy when she glances back at me. "Indigo will move them tomorrow when he finishes the task. You know better."

"I'm sorry, I wasn't thinking."

Her silver braid undulates like a snake as she shakes her head. "I'd think you'd understand by now - healing others comes first. Before personal space." She exaggerates those last two words, repeating phrases I've said in previous arguments.

I flinch, but she's only prioritizing her work over our comfort. It's understandable. Shame weighs me down, causing my shoulders to round.

"I'm sorry." My chest aches with resentment, but I won't upset her, not when everyone relies on her constantly. More than a few times, I've been woken by an injured packmate stumbling in at three in the morning.

Her frustration is clear in the way her fingers crawl across her plants. Sable is an incredible healer, but her compassion and gentleness seem reserved for her patients only. Her sharp words cut me.

I don't need personal space. I have a warm bed and a roof. The mantra repeats in my head as I change my shirt and wash up to my elbows. We don't get sick often, but I have no interest in being covered with children's fingerprints and whatever dirt or germs they carry on them.

My grandma forgot me in my two minutes at the sink, her face serene as she stacks the herb bundles into woven baskets. I should offer to help her or something useful, but it's easier to slip out the back door and enjoy the peaceful lull of the forest for an hour or so before dinner.

JASPER

My cabin is all knotty pine and classic plaids. It might be small and several decades out of date, but compared to the cold concrete houses of my birth pack, it's a haven. It's one of the older structures in the pack's community, serving as a guest cabin when needed.

I'm welcome to stay here as long as I need, but eventually, I'll get my own place. I've considered finding a roommate or maybe buying a trailer like some single wolves in our pack have done, but nothing seems like the right fit.

The front door squeaks as I push it open. I've learned no one locks their doors here. There's a sense of mutual trust and safety that feels like I've won the lottery.

I shed the remainder of my clothing and step into a steaming shower. The hot water eases the soreness in my muscles and the pain from my fresh bruises. For a few minutes, I tip my head back and let the water sluice down my body, feeling utterly content.

Scrubbed clean, I pull on black sweats and a fresh t-shirt before heading out. But as my hand lands on the doorknob, a knock echoes from the other side. Swinging the door open, I'm greeted by my mentor.

Hawthorne is the pack's Gamma, a mediator and ambassador, as well as our Alpha Heath's cousin. With his tall frame and dark hair, he's imposing, which serves him well in negotiations. When I first joined the pack, he questioned me about my father, and that became an ongoing discussion until I was helping him with gathering information on other packs as well. I'm endlessly grateful that Hawthorne took me under his wing.

Among our pack, he's patient and supportive. Watching him with his two daughters makes my chest ache. My father mostly ignored me during my childhood. So Hawthorne has become my role model for when I have my own family.

"Hey, what's up?" I dip my head in respect and hold the door open.

He waves his hand, indicating he doesn't need to come in. "I wanted to stop by and tell you the news. It looks like the Alpha Counsel is going to happen."

I want to pump my fist in the air and holler "Yes!" but I restrain myself. The Alpha Counsel is our most recent project. It used to be an annual meeting between all the local Alphas, but it hasn't happened in many years. Hawthorne feels that it's the most effective way to begin repairing the relationships between our neighboring packs and I agree.

"That's awesome," I say, unable to stop my giddy smile.

"They still haven't agreed to a location, but your dad finally confirmed, so that makes four of the five Alphas."

"Still no Nyx?" I ask, frowning. The sole leader of the Raven pack avoids gatherings when she can help it. I've never met her, but it still seems strange she would refuse to meet with all the other Alphas.

"We can't win them all." He quirks his mouth. "And Ironcrest wants to meet with us tomorrow. So that should be interesting."

"Really? What do they want?"

"I believe it'll be some sort of apology. Anyway, I'd like you to join in," Hawthorne rests his hand on my shoulder.

"Okay, I'd be honored."

"You did good, Jasper. You deserve the credit for making this happen. I know how many messages you had to send to finally convince them to participate."

"Thank you," I say, pride surging in me. It feels like I'm finally earning a place here - as long as the Alpha Counsel goes well.

"Let's head to dinner, I need to get the girls from Marigold," he says, pulling me from my mental celebration. Still smiling like an idiot, I follow him toward the diner.

Most of the pack is milling about waiting for Heath to arrive. Marigold stands chatting with Slate and Hazel, a toddler balanced on her hip. Her strawberry blonde hair tumbles from a claw clip and cascades down her back in gleaming waves. I love her hair.

"Dahlia," Hawthorne croons, lifting her from Marigold's arms. The toddler's brown hair is barely long enough to be pulled into two curly pigtails atop her head.

She excitedly squeals, "Daddy, dadda!"

"Ready to see what Mama made for dinner?" he says, his voice pitched higher. His mate, Crickett, serves as the pack's lead chef, and she makes most of the dinners we share together.

"She's so cute," I say to Marigold, watching Dahlia bob her little head. She hums in response, rubbing the spot on her arm Dahlia has been sitting against.

"I'm flipping-dipping starving," Hazel mutters.

Alpha Heath strides across the meadow. His pack members lower their heads in a sign of respect that ripples through the crowd, though conversations continue. He's an Alpha who is loved and respected, not feared. It's been enlightening to learn the difference.

True to shifter etiquette, Heath gets his food first. Slate and Hazel follow him through the line. Hawthorne goes next, taking food one-handed while holding Dahlia and coaching Daisy on how much food to put on her own plate.

After those senior leaders, it's open to anyone.

"Come on." I usher Marigold in and grab a plate.

Onyx bounds behind us, jostling Marigold. "Tamales!"

"Watch out," I warn, my hand going to the small of Marigold's back. She smiles prettily at me. But then Cedar walks in after his brother, and Marigold immediately diverts her attention from me to him. Sighing, I stack two tamales on my plate with a sizable scoop of rice and beans.

We eat at our usual table on the outskirts of the clearing where the trees cluster in as if to swallow us up entirely. Conversation is light, while Hazel reviews her training for the day and Marigold entertains us with her students' antics. I soak up every second, reveling in the connection and affection between everyone.

II
BONFIRES & BROTHERS

MARIGOLD

The campfire crackles as we settle on the split log benches and old Adirondack chairs weathered gray. The scent of woodsmoke mingles with the crisp pine air.

Cedar gathers an armful of kindling while Jasper snags the blankets we use during the winter months from the covered porch. Spring is solidly here, but the winter chill still creeps in once the sun sets.

"Feeling cold?" Jasper stands, a blanket draped over his shoulders with one side held out in an offer to share. When he first arrived, looking like a kicked puppy, I sat with him and shared a blanket, and since then it's been our tradition.

I let out a long sigh. It's been a day. I broke up two squabbles today and comforted crying children three times. When talking about school, I only share the cute moments, but the truth is most days, it's draining. As if sensing my tension, Jasper rubs his hand up and down my arm. I can't help melting into him.

Slate pulls Hazel into his lap in their favorite chair, tucking another blanket around them. She nestles her nose into his neck, placing a kiss across the ring of tiny scars that show they're a mated pair who have claimed each other.

"Do we have any s'mores tonight?" Slate asks. Hazel has a major sweet tooth, and he's always looking for ways to spoil her.

"I think the store is out of marshmallows," Cedar says apologetically. Onyx lets out a dramatic gasp.

"Are you serious?" Hazel pops up. "Do we have any at home, babe?"

Slate shakes his head.

"I think our mom made some brownies. Do you want some?" Onyx asks. Their mother is our resident baker and makes the most incredible desserts.

Hazel nods enthusiastically.

Happy, I tip my head against Jasper's shoulder. Onyx hands me a napkin with a thick chocolate confection, the top glossy and crisp.

"This is so mother-fudging delicious," Hazel moans through a mouthful of brownie, causing me to snort. She holds it out and Slate takes a bite. My heart squeezes at the gesture. It's what mates do, feeding each other. I hope someday I'll have that.

The first bite of brownie is gooey and chewy and intensely chocolatey. "Yeah, this is a foodgasm for sure," I murmur.

Jasper coughs on his own mouthful.

"Careful, don't choke," I warn. "You've had enough embarrassment today already."

Clearing his throat, he argues, "Hey, I landed Onyx on his ass. Just because Slate beat me, it doesn't mean anything. I was tired already."

Smirking at him, I lick a smudge of chocolate off my finger.

"Dude, I took it easy on you," Onyx says. "Hey, who do you think would win in a fight right now between me and Cedar? He hasn't agreed to fight me in ages!"

"You guys are pretty evenly matched. It's usually a toss-up," Slate says.

I have to agree with him. Neither twin seems to have the upper hand since they are the same build, trained by the same father, and neither one is particularly motivated to take their combat training seriously.

"I think I'd need to see you guys go at it again," I say, brows arching.

"It's a waste of time. Any real opponents will have a different fighting style," he says with a shrug.

Onyx scowls. "You sound like Dad."

"At least sparring keeps us in shape," Jasper adds, and I can't help but notice the corded muscle in his forearm as he crumples his napkin and tosses it into the fire.

"I have a better question," I interrupt. Time to lighten this conversation. Campfires are supposed to be fun! "My students were arguing about this yesterday. If you had to shift into any other animal, what would it be?"

"That's easy, I'd be a bear," Onyx declares, puffing up his chest.

Hazel gives him a knowing look. "No, I think you'd be a raccoon," she jokes, her lips twitching.

"How about a tiger?" Onyx asks, pouting.

Fighting down giggles, I add, "Maybe a possum!" Jasper lets out a laugh and I turn to him, raising an eyebrow in question. "What about you?"

Jasper bites his full bottom lip, his eyes drifting upwards to the stars peeking between the branches. "Maybe something that can fly, like a hawk."

"Oh, I love that idea," I murmur. My fingers press into the rough edge of the bench beneath us.

"I'd be a goat." Cedar states. Everyone stares for a moment.

Slate's brows draw together as he cocks his head. "A goat?"

"Yeah, they're helpful and they seem to always be having a good time."

Hazel wipes away a tear from laughing so hard. "Yeah, that checks out." She twists, cupping Slate's jaw. "What about you?"

"No idea. What would you pick for me?"

"Oh, let me think." She sucks her cheeks in. "How about a golden retriever?"

Onyx guffaws, nearly tumbling off the bench as he throws his head back.

"You don't think I'm more of a german shepherd?" Slate asks, his dark hair falling across his forehead as he leans back to narrow his eyes at his mate.

"How would you know? You guys don't have dogs," Hazel argues, her eyes sparkling.

"But we still know about them!" Onyx blurts, his words blending into laughter.

Jasper leans forward, arms resting on his knees. "What about something like a stag? Like those big elk. Very majestic. No one messes with them."

"Yeah, let's go with that," Slate agrees, gesturing toward his brother.

Watching Jasper's smirk, I have an idea. Bumping him with my shoulder, I say, "Actually, I think you'd be a fox."

"Why?" he asks, his voice dropping. I can feel his breath on my temple.

"You're clever and a smooth talker," I tease, fidgeting with the edge of the blanket. It's getting too warm under here.

"I'm not sure if I should be offended or flattered," he says, his smile far too charming. The brightness in his eyes reflects the dancing firelight, flames within seafoam.

"Better a fox than a golden retriever," Slate grumbles, though his voice is gentle.

Hazel traces the dark trees tattooed across his forearm. "I love you just the way you are." He leans in, catching her lips in a kiss.

Onyx lets out a cough that sounds remarkably like "Get a room."

"They have a room, several of them," Cedar answers automatically, his eyes on the flickering fire.

"What about you, Marigold?" Hazel asks, breaking away from her mate. Her amber eyes glow honey in the firelight.

Tugging my fingers through my hair, I debate. "A dolphin?"

"I love that idea," Jasper says quietly. My cheeks flush, his praise setting off a flurry of butterflies in my stomach.

He raises his voice for the group. "I've got one, what superheroes do you think could be wolves?"

"Wolverine," Cedar says.

"Obviously," I agree.

The fire snaps, a few sparks floating into the air and up into the purple sky.

Slate adjusts in his seat, his hands curling around Hazel's hips possessively. "What about Black Panther? He's all about family, community, and helping people, right?"

"That makes sense to me," Onyx says, producing a second brownie for himself and taking a huge bite.

The conversation lapses while we all try to come up with another answer. Hazel finally shrugs. "I have no clue, I'm not a comic girl."

"It's okay. You can't be perfect in every way," Slate teases, earning a pout from his mate. He murmurs apologies in her ear as she curls into him.

Onyx has that gleam in his eyes that means he's starting trouble. "Hazel, did we tell you about the time Slate peed his pants over seeing some raccoons?"

"No!" She shoots up. "I haven't heard about this."

Jasper chuckles. "This sounds good."

I press my lips between my teeth, trying to prevent my laughter from interrupting the story.

"It was nothing," Slate growls, "I was five, and we were having a sleepover, and Onyx dared me to run around the cabin in the middle of the night."

"In his boxers," Cedar adds, a reluctant smile brightening his features.

"He was such a chicken!" Onyx says, his grin showing all of his straight, white teeth.

"There were over a dozen raccoons on the porch and when I tried coming back in, they all hissed at me. Of course, I was scared," Slate explains.

I can't hold my giggles in any longer, laughing so hard that tears come to my eyes.

Cedar nods, "We accidentally left snacks outside. That's why there were so many."

"You peed yourself?" Hazel asks between fits of laughter.

Slate shakes his head. "I don't remember that part."

"I do!" Onyx says brightly.

Hazel softens, hooking her hands behind his head. "That sounds fun. I wish I had grown up with you guys."

My laughter dies away, seeing Jasper's expression dull. There's a stiffness in his posture that wasn't there a moment ago. Jasper and Hazel are the only ones who didn't grow up here. I know he doesn't like to think about the years he spent under his parent's rule.

Clearing her throat, Hazel changes the subject. "Hawthorne told me that almost everyone finally agreed to an Alpha Counsel! So it sounds like that'll finally happen."

"That's amazing," I yelp, grabbing his hand and squeezing it. He's spent hours over the last few months negotiating with our neighboring packs to arrange such a meeting, and it hasn't been easy.

The barest flush colors Jasper's cheeks. "It's a good step forward."

The moment is perfect until Onyx adds, "And your shit-head dad can't ignore you there."

"Onyx!" I grimace. At least he hadn't mentioned Sienna, the mother Jasper and Slate share. She's the one I'm frightened of between the two Alphas.

Jasper laughs bitterly, "I'm sure he'll do his best. But it doesn't matter. I won't be participating in the meeting, just assisting, if I'm there at all."

It has to be hard to face your parents after they publicly announced you were dead to them.

I give his hand another reassuring squeeze. At some point, his fingers have threaded with mine, and it feels too nice to break away.

Cedar stretches. "It's getting late and I have an early morning with Cheddar-belle and Cheesette." Hazel barks a laugh at the goat's names.

"Don't make fun of my baby girls," Onyx snaps, though his voice is playful. I burst into my own fit of giggles until we're both wiping away tears. Jasper smiles indulgently at me, his thumb stroking across my knuckles.

Cedar stands, smothering the flames and tidying up with practiced efficiency.

"You guys have been extra cozy tonight," Onyx observes lightly, raising an eyebrow at me. I drop Jasper's hand instantly.

What's his problem? We always sit together. And I'd share a blanket with Onyx if he offered.

A blush creeps up my neck. "It's cold, do you want me to freeze? I didn't exactly see you offering to sit with me."

"Don't be mad, I'm just saying," Onyx responds, lifting his hands in an offer of peace.

Hazel levels her gaze on me, her lips pursing. "Maybe you guys have been a little extra touchy tonight," she says hesitantly.

Jasper is silent beside me, and I can feel how uncomfortable he is as he wipes his palms along his sweatpants.

"So what?" I say, "he's *basically* my brother."

"He's not your brother," Cedar points out, straightening.

A growl escapes me. "I said basically." Swallowing, I plaster on my kindest smile. "Jasper is Slate's brother, and we grew up together. So he's like family, and if we were anything more, it would be kinda ick."

Jasper finally reacts, shrugging the blanket from his shoulders and letting it pool beside me. "You don't have to say it like I'm a toad," he mutters.

Oh, shit.

"I'm sorry! I didn't mean it like that." His frown deepens as I continue to babble. "Besides, if you were a toad, you'd be one of those adorable little tomato frogs."

"Toads and frogs aren't the same," Cedar says quietly, walking away.

Jasper raises an eyebrow, eyes sharp with skepticism. "A tomato frog?"

"They're my favorite reptile," I say, goading a smile out of him. "Amphibian?"

I study his face for a moment, begging him to ignore my stupidity. The last thing I want to do is hurt his feelings. Even after these last few months, he is still sensitive about fitting in. I know Jasper belongs here with us. He's a piece we didn't know we were missing until he arrived. But he doesn't see it that way.

"We okay?" I ask quietly.

"No harm, no foul," he says as his lips curve into a smirk. Jasper winks at me and my breath rushes out, relieved he isn't truly mad.

He stretches and steps away from our bench. "Night, everyone."

"Good night." I fold our blanket and hand it to Onyx.

Jasper gives me one last look, reassuring me that he isn't upset before I make my exit.

Hazel wraps her arm around mine as we both stroll home, our paths intersecting until we meet my grandmother's cottage.

Hazel and Slate's home stands a short distance northeast. It's a sprawling two-story cabin that sat unoccupied after Slate's father passed away. Over the last season, the couple has renovated it, keeping the original charm while modernizing fixtures and appliances. It's only been a few weeks since they moved in.

We walk in silence until my worry overcomes my good sense. "I feel like crap," I tell her in a hushed voice. "I can't believe I said that."

Hazel cocks her head, waiting for more context.

"About him being ick." Hearing the word again makes me cringe.

She raises her shoulders up and drops them with a sigh. "I shouldn't have said what I said. I wasn't thinking and I put you in an awkward position."

"It's fine," I say automatically.

Hazel's cheeks hollow as she weighs her words. "Honestly, I think it was on my mind because I've been concerned," she says.

My brows furrow as I look at her. "Why?"

"Like I said, you guys have been touchy-feely."

Scowling, I open my mouth to argue.

"I know shifters are more physically affectionate," she says, cutting me off. "And I get that he can't be physically close to me, so you're the only cuddly one available."

"That's all it is," I say, nails biting into my palms at the swirl of anger and embarrassment heating my cheeks.

"He really values your friendship. And it would suck if you accidentally led him on."

"That's not going to happen."

She's right though. I've enjoyed comforting and encouraging Jasper over the last few months, but maybe we've gotten a little too close. Holding hands was perhaps over the line.

"I'm probably worrying for nothing. And I don't think you'd ever do something like that intentionally. But he didn't grow up with close friends like you did, and frankly, you're always busy staring at Cedar, so I'm not sure you'd even notice if Jasper was staring at *you* that way."

I bite my tongue. I should listen to her. Hazel is shockingly insightful and usually correct in her assessments. The situation calls for more thought on my part.

Slate catches up to us as we reach the corner of Cedar's garden.

"Good night," she says as her mate takes her hand and pulls her against him.

"Thanks for watching out for us, Hazel," I say, even though she's thoroughly distracted by whatever Slate is whispering in her ear. The lovebirds walk into the darkness, stealing kisses as they go.

Jasper is a good friend. Someone I can rely on. But that's all it is. He's never given me any indication otherwise, and I've been hung up on someone else for most of my life. It's just a close friendship. Nothing to worry about. But maybe we should curb our physical affection, so people don't get the wrong idea.

Creeping into the cottage, I open and close the front door at a glacial pace to avoid making any noise. Slipping my shoes off, I tip-toe into the hall.

My grandmother's bedroom door is closed. I quietly visit the bathroom and change into an oversized t-shirt I stole from Cedar years ago. Recoiling at the rusty squeak, I ease the sofa bed out and crawl under the covers.

Fatigue presses down on every one of my muscles. But before my eyes can drift closed, I hear a door latch click and swing open. My grandmother emerges from her workroom, a tub full of glass jars clinking in her arms.

Sitting up, I rub my eyes. "Good evening, Grandmother."

"Oh, you're back. Good, you can help me," she announces, setting the tub on the table.

Laying back, I sigh. "Sorry, I'm really tired."

"Don't be selfish, we need to prep these," she says dismissively.

I bite back a groan and pull the covers off. There's no arguing with her when she's like this, though I'm too tired to deal with it.

Fifteen minutes later, I'm cautiously pouring rowanberry juice concentrate into the tiny jars. Even with a funnel, it's tricky. My hands slip several times.

"Watch it," Sable hisses. She sounds nothing like a grandmother. She's the pack's crabby healer and I've had enough.

"I'm too tired to be any help. Let me get some sleep and I'll work on it before school."

She whirls on me, careful to not slosh the pink liquid she's holding in a quart jar. "You're always staying up late with those friends, and now you can't be bothered to help your pack?"

Tears prick my eyes. This feels like the last straw. I should keep my mouth shut, but if I saw a friend or one of my students being spoken to like this, I would tell them to stand up for themselves. Time to take my own advice.

JASPER

It would be kinda ick. Apparently, I'm ick.

The heat of her, through two layers of fabric, went from a comforting warmth to a searing burn when compounded with my embarrassment.

Stripping off my shirt, I grab a glass of water and lean against my kitchen counter. Not that I need Marigold to think that I'm desirable, but surely I'm better than a tomato frog.

My glass makes a plink as I set it aside and pull out my phone. What the fuck is a tomato frog? Bulging gold eyes stare back at me. Its vivid orange-red skin has a black stripe down its pudgy sides. Damn, it is pretty cute.

I'm wound too tight to sleep yet, so I settle across my bed with an old detective novel I found on the shelves of the cabin when I moved in. The pages are yellowed and someone has written notes in the margins, which somehow make the book more enjoyable.

As the protagonist stumbles across a second victim's body, someone raps against the front door.

Apprehension prickles through me like frost, leaving a primal alertness in its wake. It's after midnight. Pulse racing, I pull open the door.

"Hey."

Marigold's doe eyes stare back at me. "I'm sorry to bother you."

A huge t-shirt drapes over her lean build, bunching around the waistband of her joggers. She's scrubbed her face free of any makeup, leaving her looking raw and somehow ethereal. Darkness smudges under her eyes, triggering a protectiveness that has me stepping closer to her.

"Are you okay?" My stomach clenches.

Her smile wavers for a split second. "Yeah, I'm good."

Placing a hand on the small of her back, I lead her inside, closing the door to block out the gloom and cold. Marigold looks around my cabin, her lips parted slightly.

Seeing her like this, my heart rate is not slowing. She's always making sure everyone else is comfortable and happy, but I can see sadness beneath her sunny smile.

"So what's up?" I ask, hooking a thumb into my pocket.

Her fingers curl around the strap of a backpack thrown over her shoulder. "I sort of got in an argument with my grandma."

"That sucks," I say cautiously.

"It's fine," she says, "It's just... There isn't room for me in her cottage. And she's so focused on her work, she doesn't give me any space. I'm tired enough after a day of teaching, I can't be her assistant when I get home. It's too much."

"That does sound like a lot." My hands travel to her upper arms, steadying her as her words spill out of her like a damn breaking.

"And today she called me selfish! It's not like I was sitting around doing nothing all day, but she expects me to jump to whatever task she thinks of at all hours of the night. There's been times lately when I can't even open up my sofa bed because she's packed the room with her projects. I don't think I can wait until I save up for my own place."

By the end of her rant, she's deflated, gaze on the ground, lashes wet.

"Marigold, I'm sorry. That's really unfair."

She sniffles. "Thanks."

"How can I help?"

Those blue-green eyes meet mine and her tongue swipes across her lips. "Well..."

"Anything." And I mean it.

"Can I stay with you tonight? Until I figure something else out?"

My stomach flips. "Really?"

I expect she'd have potential housemates fighting to have her. She's wonderful. The idea of sharing a space with her is unexpectedly exhilarating.

"Never mind, it's rude of me to just show up." Her face closes off.

"No!" I blurt, "I was only wondering why I'm the lucky person you asked."

"Oh," she answers, hesitating, "Well, my brothers like having their own rooms, so I don't want to take mine back. Not to mention I don't want to face my dad over this. And I first thought of staying with Hazel. But.."

"But she and Slate are all over each other," I finish for her. "I wouldn't want to stay with them either. Who knows what you'd see or hear?"

She giggles, pressing a hand over her mouth. "That's about right. So that left you."

Nodding, I cross my arms. "Sounds like I'm your last choice."

Her brows furrow. "I think my last choice would be the twins. I can't deal with that much Onyx."

She says nothing about Cedar, but I'm not an idiot.

"I can go, don't worry about it, Jasper." She shrugs, turning toward the door.

No way am I letting her go.

Taking a wide step, I place my palm against the door so she can't open it. "Why would you do that?" I ask, putting on an air of confidence I don't feel.

"Cause you don't want me here," she answers.

"Absolutely not true. I would love to have you. I have an extra bedroom and you're my best friend," I say, "one of my best friends, I mean. You should stay here as long as you need to."

She flings her arms around me in a hug, her face pressed into my chest. For a moment, I'm floating, a wonderful friend who smells like lemon and rosemary snug in my arms. The instinct to protect and provide surges in my chest.

Breathing through the rush, I finally say, "It's late, let's get your room set up. You'll probably want some extra blankets. That room gets cold."

She steps back, a teardrop sliding down her freckled cheek.

"Hey, none of that. This is a fun friend's sleepover, right?" I say.

"Sorry," she says, batting away her tears and smiling brightly.

"You don't have to apologize,"

The door to the spare room opens with a creak. A twin bed sits against a window framed in rounded wood trim. Marigold pads across the thick rug and slouches onto the coverlet, slinging her backpack onto the small desk beside her with a thud.

"Is this okay?" I grip the top of the door frame, leaning in without stepping across the threshold.

"It's great, thank you." Marigold pulls her feet up and wraps her arms around her knees. She looks so vulnerable, it takes all my self-control to not scoop her up. But that feels like crossing a boundary. Instead, I locate a thermal blanket and drape it over the foot of the bed.

"Okay, well, the bathroom is the middle door and my room is at the end. Come get me if you need anything."

Her breathing has slowed, her expression softening. She deserves a comfortable space and a roommate who appreciates and respects her. That's something I can provide.

Tapping the door frame, I wander to my bedroom and lay back on my bed. Eyes closed, I listen to the sounds of her closing the bathroom door, running the faucet, and then a few minutes later, closing her bedroom door.

This woman called me *ick*. But her luminous eyes don't say ick to me, they're full of the warmth and affection I'm starving for. But if I'm not careful, I could mess this up. I'll never forgive myself if I hurt or upset her.

She's one of the best people I know, the first one I look for at gatherings, and one I linger to talk with. And now she's in my home. At this rate, I'll never get to sleep.

III
SNUGGLES & SUSPICIONS

MARIGOLD

Sleeping in a real bed for the first time in almost two years is a revelation. I want to moan from how good my muscles feel as I stretch and pull the covers higher under my chin, sinking back into the warmth. Maybe I'll steal this mattress when I find my own place.

My phone beeps, warning me it's time to get moving or I'll be late.

Rolling out of bed, I stumble toward the bathroom, grateful I put away a few toiletries last night.

The bathroom door is closed. I stare for a moment, comprehension slowly creeping into my brain.

The door swings open and my new roommate faces me. A dark towel wraps his waist, and his platinum hair looks ashy as water drips down his neck. His bare chest gleams.

This isn't anything like watching him spar or strip before shifting from across the training room. He's so close I can smell his soap and see water droplets like pearls across his shoulders.

My inhale turns jagged and I step back carefully. Not an appropriate time to swoon.

"Good morning," he says, a cocky grin showing off his dimples.

My mouth opens and no sound comes out. His confidence wavers, his expression flickering. "Went for a run this morning."

"Sounds fun." I finally say, failing to keep my eyes from roving. Across his ribs blooms a green and yellow bruise.

For a bruise to still be visible overnight is surprising, meaning it's either very fresh or he was hit hard. "Jasper, what happened?" I motion to my side.

He blinks and looks down, huffing when he realizes what I mean. "It's nothing. Slate got me pretty good yesterday."

"Why didn't you go see my grandma? That looks nasty, she could have helped."

His clear aqua eyes meet mine. "It's fine. It'll be gone by lunch."

"Please take care of yourself," I say, holding his gaze. With a wink, he reaches over and lightly tugs on the fluffy braid I put my hair in at night.

"How'd you sleep?"

Pulling out the hair tie, my fingers unravel the braid into loose waves. "Honestly, really good. I didn't realize how poorly I was sleeping at my grandmother's."

"Good," he says. For once he doesn't seem quite so sure of himself. With an odd smile, he steps around me.

As Jasper disappears into his room, I shudder, trying to shake off all the tension from our encounter. I didn't realize having a male roommate would involve quite so much bare skin and bulging muscles.

Today feels like a day to look cute. A few swipes of makeup, and my favorite sweater with strawberries stitched down the sleeves paired with black leggings, and I'm ready to go.

Jasper's already left when I come out of my room. I'll have to learn more about his work schedule, now that we are roommates.

The cabin is further from the school building than my grandmother's cottage. I keep to the trees instead of cutting into the meadow. It'd be too easy for someone to spot me walking up from the south instead of my usual route.

Today will be busy. The children have a book report to finish and after lunch, we are taking a nature walk to look for insects. Science is a close second to my favorite subject after art.

I can't help but scan for my friends as I pause at the doorway. A few pack members walk in various directions, but no Jasper. Not that I'm looking for him specifically. I'm sure he's busy today too.

JASPER

The Alpha of Ironcrest arrives in a gray SUV. As he steps out and adjusts his jacket, the sunlight glints on his short silver hair. Zephyr has sharp features and dark eyes. Everything about him reminds me of a blade - polished, sharp, and as likely to help as harm depending on the situation.

His pack's Gamma trails behind him, dark hair falling over his eyes. He's noticeably shorter and wider but has laugh lines that suggest he's friendly.

Zephyr's Beta is conspicuously absent. But likely she was left at home as de facto leader.

Hawthorne greets them, walking across the gravel lot to shake the Alpha's hand. Apprehension skitters across my skin. Ironcrest's request to meet before the Counsel could be for any number of reasons, but I don't trust Zephyr.

Spying from the hallway window, I watch the trio walk around the side of the office, where a door leads straight into our largest meeting room.

Heath strides toward me, followed by Slate and Hazel. "Go ahead and wait in the room, Jasper. We'll be in after they're settled." Entering last is a power play.

My breathing is slow and even as I pull a calm mask over my anxiety. This is the first time I've seen anyone from another pack since defecting from Granite Ridge and joining Bracken Creek. An heir leaving their pack is unheard of, and I'm not sure what reactions to expect. Hopefully none. This meeting isn't about me.

A live-edge conference table stretches the length of the room, surrounded by heavy, cushioned chairs for a dozen people. Zephyr lounges in a seat toward the center, facing the door. His cold eyes flick over me and stop on my face. I hold his gaze for a moment before looking away. Long enough that he knows I am not afraid of him nor am I ashamed of myself. Any longer, and it would be a challenge.

Muscles coiled tight, I take my place against the wall, off to one side. Hawthorne sits across from Zephyr but down two seats.

"Alpha Zephyr, you remember Jasper. He is a Zeta in our pack now," Hawthorne says. Zeta, a guard. A respectable ranking, though it's not an accurate description of my position. But Zephyr doesn't need to know I was the one pulling the strings to arrange the Alpha Counsel.

"A Zeta? How ambitious of you," Zephyr says with a cruel smile. A flush crawls up my neck and my hands ache to clench into fists, but I don't give him another sign of my discomfort. His opinion doesn't matter. He doesn't need to respect me, as long as he respects our Alpha and Betas.

Finally, the door opens and Heath fills the entire frame, Hazel and Slate hidden behind him. He's taller than I am, and wider too, so he dwarfs everyone seated. The three wolves rise, and Zephyr reaches out to shake his hand.

"Good to see you again, Zephyr," Heath says.

"Likewise." Zephyr sits at the same moment as Heath. Hazel and Slate sit on either side of him, and Hawthorne is at Hazel's left hand. I take the seat beside my brother.

"Hello, Dell," Heath says.

"Alpha Heath," the Ironcrest Gamma tips his head respectfully.

"I hope your pack has been well," Zephyr says.

Heath folds his hands, resting his forearms on the table. "It's been a good winter for us. And yours?"

Zephyr picks lint off his sleeve. "Successful. We have two newly mated pairs and welcomed a set of twins."

I've only visited Ironcrest once, but I know it's one of the larger packs. Close to Bracken Creek's size, but smaller than Granite Ridge. But I don't remember many teenagers or young adults. Perhaps they have been recruiting. The idea prickles like pins and needles through my body.

"Congratulations," Heath says warmly.

Zephyr's smile is smug. "Thank you."

Heath pauses a beat, his eyes never leaving the other Alpha. The dominance struggle between them is suffocating, and the hair on my arms rises. But Heath's authority feels like loyalty and encouragement, and Zephyr's feels like arrogance.

"I'll admit, I'm curious to know what you'd like to discuss," Heath says expectantly.

Leaning back with his fingers steepled, Zephyr takes his time deciding what to say. His relaxed pose reeks of arrogance. "I felt we should clear up any misunderstandings about the unfortunate difficulties your heir faced last fall."

"Ah, misunderstandings." Heath echoes, his face betraying nothing.

We all knew Ironcrest aided Granite Ridge in taking Hazel hostage. So far, their denial has kept a shaky peace. If he admits to it now, it will have to come with apologies and reparations, otherwise Heath will be forced to take action.

Hazel's knuckles are white where she grips her chair arms, though her shoulders are relaxed and her face politely serene. Beside me, Slate is slowly leaning forward, lining his feet up under him to prepare for a fight. I take a slow audible breath, hoping he will join me on instinct. He ignores me.

"I'm eager to hear any new information. Last time we spoke, you were unaware of any involvement," Heath prompts.

Zephyr swallows, dipping his chin in a show of remorse that no one would believe. "Unfortunately, I did uncover something."

Dell drops his gaze to the table. Heath and Slate make quite the overbearing pair. Though Zephyr and Dell are not in our pack, and therefore felt none of our shared emotions, even a human could sense the rising tension.

"Granite Ridge took Hazel and held her for several days before she was returned to you, correct?" He knows damn well what happened, and that Hazel escaped with assistance from me. We poisoned the entire pack and I defended her while she raced for the border and Slate.

Heath plays along. "Yes, I believe Sienna wanted a foothold in claiming our pack by forcing Hazel to become mates with her heir."

I appreciate Heath leaving my name out of it. But Zephyr's gaze travels to me anyway. His neutral expression slips for a second, showing pure disdain. Hawthorne leans forward, a defensive barrier between our visitors and me.

"That always seemed like a foolish plan to me." Zephyr sighs. "She wasn't even a pack member, not really. What claim would she have even had? Your pack never would have accepted a rival's heir mated to an outsider who only shared a familial connection."

My hands clench under the table. Zephyr's jab at Hazel annoys me, more than his offense toward me. Down the pack bond, irritation ripples, and I can't tell if it's primarily Slate, or perhaps the entire room.

"What information did you have for us?" Heath asks, redirecting the conversation.

Unfortunately, Zephyr isn't finished. "It's a good thing your Beta took a liking to her. Keeps anything from getting," he says, pausing, "messy."

"My heir would be quite capable on her own. But paired with a powerful mate, my pack's future leadership is secure."

It's true. Slate is even stronger than I am. Not because he is about two years older and a few inches taller, but because of his natural drive.

"Yes, of course. You are blessed," Zephyr continues.

He is antagonizing us, purposefully drawing this out. Heath must have realized it sooner because his pose has relaxed to match Hawthorne's. Only Slate still looks murderous, and that would be the case regardless.

"Ferris approached me for help but never specified any plans. He must have known I wouldn't support him in something so-" He searches for the word. "Deplorable."

"Afterwards, I discovered some lower ranking wolves went behind my back." His repentant expression seems sincere, but Heath's mouth stays a flat line. He doesn't give any indication that we were already aware of their involvement.

"It's unfortunate those wolves forgot their place. I've banished those involved."

By banished, I have to assume they went straight to Granite Ridge.

"And I've made it clear to Ferris that if his alliance means standing against our other allies, then Ironcrest is not interested."

Silence stretches, Heath cocking his head as he regards Zephyr, reading little clues as to his truthfulness. Apprehension churns in my gut.

"I appreciate your apology and that you took their punishment so seriously," Heath finally answers. "I hope you're addressing any issues of loyalty. It must be difficult to manage such a large pack."

It's as close to an insult as Heath can get without outright disrespecting him. He's baiting him back, testing his intentions.

"We've been assessing to be sure our remaining members are obedient," Zephyr answers. Dell nods.

"Are loyalty and obedience the same thing?" Hazel says. Her voice is strong and steady. The corner of my mouth curves at her boldness.

"I guess not. But both are required, are they not?" Zephyr's smile is snake-like. Slate bristles at how Zephyr's eyes slide over Hazel.

"Perhaps," Heath says, pacifying.

"If there is anything we can do to assist your pack and rebuild our friendship, please let me know," Zephyr says.

"Your offense was against my heir so I will leave that up to her," Heath says, nodding toward Hazel.

Her eyes narrow at Zephyr and his smile fades. "You were our ally once, but that relationship had deteriorated even before Granite Ridge's actions, correct?"

"Unfortunately, yes. It's past time for us to correct the situation." Despite his respectful words, his lip curls for a split second before he regains his composure.

Hazel considers for a moment, causing Zephyr to grind his teeth.

"Alliances are built on communication. In addition to your participation in our upcoming Alpha Counsel, I think it would be wise for our Gammas to speak on a regular basis. I'm sure they can find ways we can collaborate." Her voice is soft but firm.

"A commendable idea."

Dell leans forward in his seat. "I look forward to hearing from you," he says to Hawthorne. "It will be good to stay in closer contact."

Hawthorne nods curtly.

"How has your contact been with Ferris in the last few months?" Slate asks.

"Minimal," Zephyr answers, "I have tried to keep the channel open, but his belief that Granite Ridge is superior to all other packs makes it difficult to find any common ground. I'm afraid we aren't the ally he was hoping for."

Interesting word choice. It's true that Ferris and Sienna believe they are above the other packs. But they wouldn't withdraw from negotiations.

"Hopefully we all can find a way to reconcile peacefully," Heath says.

"We will see," Zephyr says.

Neither leader seems to believe that reconciliation is likely between Granite Ridge and the surrounding packs. Knowing their misdeeds, I am not surprised.

"You've given us a lot to think about. Was there anything else we needed to discuss before the upcoming Alpha Counsel?"

"Nothing that needs to be addressed today."

Heath straightens, his hands falling to his knees. "Well, would you like to enjoy the lunch our chef prepared?"

My brows crease. Offering a meal to Zephyr is a way to offer alliance and friendship again. I know that's the goal, but warning bells are still ringing in my head.

Zephyr shakes his head, pushing his chair back and standing. His fingers adjust the sleeves of his coat while his eyes travel over each of us. "I'm afraid we must be heading back. Our work is never complete, is it?"

"Such is the role of a leader," Heath says, his tone a little colder than before.

Hawthorne steps forward to open the door for our visitors. "Another time."

"Of course."

Heath remains standing so I hover nearby, waiting. After our guests have driven away, Hawthorne returns, his expression unreadable. The two men exchange looks.

"Well, how do we feel that went?" Heath asks.

"Interesting," Slate says, "He seems sincere, but I'm not eager to trust him."

"I'm not sure I expected him to own up to the role they played," Heath says, his hand running over his short beard. "Perhaps Zephyr still has a sense of morality."

"If he was telling the truth," Hazel says.

"It's hard for me to believe that he had pack members acting outside of his command," I say.

Hawthorne crosses his arms. "Their pack has never been as close-knit as ours, but you have a point."

"Do you think he ordered their actions?" Heath asks, his dark eyes boring into mine.

"Honestly, yes, I do," I answer.

Hawthorne frowns. "No Alpha would lend out their wolves for hire."

Despite my nerves, I raise my chin. "I know our Alpha would never do that, but Zephyr has shown to be unpredictable. And it's not like Ferris to seek out individuals from another pack when he has plenty of his own."

"Did you know anything about the Ironcrest wolves?" Hazel asks, her amber eyes wide.

"No, I wasn't told any details. I wouldn't have known at all if I hadn't smelled them on you."

"Okay," Hazel says, bobbing her head. Her hands go to Slate's arm and he tugs her closer.

"It might be a good idea to increase surveillance," Slate suggests.

"We can look into it," Heath says.

"I also feel that we should consider more offensive training," I say.

Hazel nods. "I think so too. We've been training in how to defend our pack, but we might need to attack at some point."

Slate frowns, "Fisher would disagree with you."

"Fisher will train what I ask him to," Heath says. "I think we all need some time to process, and we can revisit the idea of offensive training tomorrow."

"Yes, Alpha," we echo.

MARIGOLD

As the school day ends, a certain gleefulness bubbles up inside of me. Rather than my grandmother's sofa, I'm going home to a cozy cabin and a good friend who is extremely nice to look at.

The smell of fresh cut pine, cinnamon, and wool wraps around me once my feet step onto the knotty pine wood floor. Under the homey scent of the cabin, I can detect Jasper - he's faintly spicy like cardamom, coffee, and something sweeter like vanilla.

But Jasper isn't in the living room or kitchen, and his bedroom door hangs open. Hesitantly, I peer in. A queen bed stands with the headboard against a wide window with a line of little plants on the sill. A shirt is tossed over a chair and his quilt is thrown back to show crimson sheets. Apparently, his meticulous personality doesn't extend to keeping his room perfectly tidy. It makes me smile even as my fingers itch to fold his laundry and make the bed.

I trudge to my own room, slip off my shoes, and flop onto my newly beloved bed. The house is so quiet, but it isn't a lonely sort of stillness, it's peaceful. As I relax, my exhaustion becomes harder to ignore. Maybe one solid night's sleep isn't enough to make up for the last two years. I can't help but slip into a late afternoon nap.

If I dream of anything, I can't remember when I wake. The cabin is tranquil, like when I drifted off, but the light from my window has faded. Hopefully, I haven't missed dinner.

Stretching, I take a few deep breaths and try to wake myself up. The scent of food filters in, telling me that either I've missed dinner or I'm very late.

Grabbing a hoodie, I rush out of my room toward dinner, but skid to a stop in the open living room when I spy an overflowing plate of barbequed meat and a loaded baked potato on the kitchen peninsula.

Jasper brought dinner back for me. My throat clogs and my eyes prick. No one has ever gotten me dinner when I was too busy to attend. I'm always the one making sure everyone else is fed. Not the other way around.

Grabbing my plate, I head toward the back door. It's propped open with a rock that's painted with a paw print, a relic of a previous tenant.

Jasper sits on the edge of the porch, one knee drawn up to steady his hand while he drags a small blade across a chunk of wood, shaving off thin curls.

"Is this for me?" I ask to be safe. Amusement flickers across his face in response to my silly question. "Thanks. I really appreciate it."

"I can't let my roommate go hungry," he says. His smirk twists my stomach.

"Did you tell anyone about our… situation?" My voice drops off.

He shakes his head, causing his pale hair to flop over his forehead. "I didn't think you'd want people knowing. I can see how it would look weird." With a sigh, he rakes his fingers through his hair and sweeps it away from his face.

"I've got a lot to thank you for," I mutter between mouthfuls of potato.

"How about you start by taking it easier on yourself?" He bumps his shoulder against mine. The familiarity is comforting, but I have no idea what to say to him.

We sit quietly, his knife scraping and cutting away slivers of wood, and my fork steadily clearing my plate. I finish the last bite and take my dish to the sink. On the way back, I snag a pair of beer bottles from the fridge.

A lone overhead light illuminates the porch, casting long shadows down the steps. Jasper's night vision is superior as a wolf shifter, and he's able to continue his whittling when a human would have had to stop.

I hand him a beer. "So what are you making there?"

Jasper holds up the rough shape, rotating it for me to admire. "You can't tell?"

"It's a bobcat." I guess the first thing that pops into my head.

He scowls. "Really?"

"Oh, an owl?"

"Not even close."

"A hedgehog?"

"Stop, they're getting worse," he says, laughter breaking through his serious demeanor. "It's gonna be a fox."

"Oh, it looks exactly like a fox. Really great job." My hand clamps over my mouth, stopping my giggles.

"You said I was like a fox, so I figured you might like a little fox," he says absently, digging the tip of his blade under the bulbous top, now carving out what might be the muzzle, though it's hard to be sure.

"This is cool, actually," I say, trying to encourage him, though it looks like a blob to me.

His exhale is audible like an amused huff. "Well, Marigold, I've seen you do all sorts of crafty things with your students, but what activities do you like to do just for you?"

"I can't remember the last time I had spare time to do anything creative," I say, giving in to the urge to rest my head against his shoulder. He's warm and steady, warding off the night's chill.

"Well, what would you do if you had time?" he presses.

"Nap." The glass bottle slowly twirls as I twist my fingers.

Jasper holds the wooden figure up, turning it side to side and measuring with his thumb. Satisfied, he returns to deepening grooves that might be the sides of the legs. It's looking foxlike already.

"Other than naps. I know you're hiding more talents from me," he says, his smirk sending my heart tumbling.

"I like macramé."

His blade pauses and he regards me for a moment. "Like the knots with the rope? Making hanging plant holders and stuff like that?"

"Yeah," I answer, "it's called cord, but you've got the idea. I haven't gotten to do it since I was a teenager."

"That's actually pretty cool," he says, now cutting into the wood to carve out what looks distinctively like two pointed ears.

"Did you think I'd be boring? Like my secret hobby is watching paint dry or organizing socks?" I try to sound indignant.

"Don't diss sock organizing. You have no idea what I do in my private time," he says dryly, turning the little statue over in his hand to inspect his progress.

"I knew it," I mutter. Jasper rolls his eyes but then pauses. My arms prickle with tiny bumps from the cold. He's staring at my skin.

"It's late. We should go inside." Standing, he tucks his knife away and holds out his hand for me. Despite the dropping temperatures, his palm is warm.

He leads me inside, the patio door clunking shut behind us. I'm not ready to call it a night, and neither is he because he leads me to his sofa. I have to admit it's far more comfortable than my grandmother's.

A faint smile brightens his features as he wraps me in a rust-colored plaid blanket before building up the fire in the old cast iron wood-burning stove. Warmth fills the small cabin and I breathe in the scent of woodsmoke and sweet barbeque.

As Jasper settles beside me, I drape the blanket over his shoulders like we always do, but it feels different. We aren't around a bonfire with our rowdy group of friends. It's just us. His skin warms my chilled arm. Awkwardly, I smooth the edge of the fabric.

"Tell me more about your students." His voice is velvety and soothing.

"What about them?"

"I don't know much. Tell me everything."

My fist bunches up the blanket against my chest as I think. "Well, I've got the older ones, like Willow and my brother Cobalt. They've started some online classes, but aren't totally independent yet."

Jasper nods along like this is the most fascinating topic ever.

"And then I've got my younger students, who are pretty much all handfuls. I mean, Daisy keeps shoving different things up her nose every time I turn around. Starling fights me on everything - it's making her mom crazy too. Even Elwood, who I would have considered my easiest student, is starting to get emotional over the smallest things."

A slow smile spreads across his face as I talk. It's not the cocky smirk he wears most of the time. It's warm and genuine, with actual happiness shining through instead of an expression for show.

"How old are they?" he asks.

"Six, seven, and eight."

"Haven't shifted yet?"

"Nope, and I know that's why Elwood is being so difficult. It'll be any day now. As long as it's not during class." I pinch the bridge of my nose.

Jasper chuckles silently. "Have you ever had a kid shift in your class?"

He had no idea. "The older ones do it all the freaking time, especially if I'm being hard on them. It's impossible to argue with a wolf, after all. But I've never had a kid experience their first shift while in class, thank the goddess."

"Then maybe Elwood will be your first."

"Shut your mouth, you'll jinx me." There's no venom in my words, but I knock on the wooden coffee table for luck.

"Sorry," he says ruefully. Exasperated, I use my forearm to shove him away. He retaliates by wrapping his arm across my shoulders and holding me tight.

Mouth pursed, he looks thoughtful. "After spending so much time with your students, do you think you'll want a lot of kids someday?"

That's a loaded question and a complicated one. "I don't know. I see how hard it is for the parents sometimes. How exhausted they can be. And I'm barely getting by some of these days. I can't imagine being responsible for a pup all the time, making sure it gets fed and sleeps enough and doesn't disappear into the forest."

"No kidding," Jasper says, "I'm terrified of the idea of being a parent."

"Why?"

His teeth press into that bottom lip as he thinks. "I don't think I'd have any clue how to do it."

"No one has any clue, you figure it out together with your partner and get lots of help from everyone around you."

A certain solemness tugs at the corners of his mouth. The air is heavy and I can feel turmoil emanating from him. The silence feels like a rift between us that I can't cross.

His mouth creases. "My parents were not exactly involved when I was a kid. We got shuffled around, stuck with different training groups and watched by random guards.

"And when they needed us to project the right image, we were dressed up and told to act a certain way." He pauses, as if unsure if he should continue. I meet his gaze and wait. "And if we misstepped, the consequences were usually pretty painful."

"Are you kidding me?" I blurt, anger heating my skin.

Jasper exhales in a rush, leaning back against the sofa and looking at the ceiling. "Yeah, they weren't afraid of punishing us like any other pack member. Beating, withholding food, whatever."

He's quiet like he's trying to think of anything else and not relive some of those memories.

I knew his parents were awful. They've committed numerous crimes, and it's easy to deduce that they weren't warm and caring parents either. But the idea of them hurting Jasper as a child has me seething. My nails cut into my palms. But this anger doesn't help him, so I let it burn through me and quickly cool.

Rotating to face him, I wrap my arms around him and squeeze. He encircles my ribs and pulls me closer. Suddenly, I'm in his lap, my ass over his legs. His arms band around me with comforting pressure.

My breathing stutters, but Jasper doesn't seem to notice. Or he doesn't care. I focus on comforting him, running my fingers through his silky hair.

"You didn't deserve that," I murmur.

He buries his face in my hair and stills, each breath slower than the one before. He's calming down. The moment could be ten minutes or ten seconds. My brain shorts out and I've lost all sense of time and place.

Slowly, Jasper loosens his hold and I'm able to slide onto the sofa beside him, though his arm stays across my shoulders.

"You're nothing like your family," I say softly.

"Thanks." Clearing his throat, he untangles himself and stands. "It's getting late, and I'm gonna take an early morning run again."

"Good night," I say hurriedly, folding the blanket and setting it aside neatly.

"Thanks, Marigold," he says, his smile smaller and slightly sad.

I look into his eyes, noticing they're slightly red. "Any time."

The solitude of my room seems so vast after being wrapped up in Jasper's hug, cocooned in a thick blanket. The smell of detergent, dust, and dirt I've tracked in is astringent compared to his comforting scent.

Pulling the covers up to my chin, I force myself to relax. If I'm being honest, the proximity of him alone in his personal space has every nerve in my body on overdrive. I can hardly think straight.

He's just a friend. But hell, I'm not immune to utter masculine perfection. The golden stubble across his jaw and the way it feels against my cheek. The size of his hands over my hips as he embraces me. The more of his heart that I see, the more I adore him. I might be in trouble.

IV
ROSEMARY & REJECTION

JASPER

My beautiful roommate dominates my thoughts all morning. She gets ready while I am running and then slips past me to grab breakfast at the diner before heading to her classroom.

Even after she leaves, I can smell her herbal scent all over my cabin. It's tempting to step into her room and bury my nose in her pillow, but that would be creepy - not to mention she might be able to tell, so I keep my feet firmly at the threshold.

Driven to distraction, my performance at training suffers. Fisher pairs me with Onyx, and normally I would have him on the ground in seconds. But he whirls around me and twists my arm, forcing me to my knees.

"See? I can absolutely whoop your ass!" he croons, turning to make sure there were witnesses.

"You're ridiculous," I say, brushing myself off.

Onyx grins. "Maybe, but I still won."

Fisher walks past and crosses his arms, scowling at me and his son. "Get your head in the game, kid."

"Yes, sir," I reply automatically.

"Want to go again?" Onyx bounces between the balls of his feet.

My wrist twinges as I rotate it. "Sure." I roll my shoulders before stepping back to the mat. "Hey, can we switch patrols? I'd like an earlier lunch today if that's okay."

"No problem."

Onyx doesn't win a second time, but I go easy on him when I pin him against the mat.

Across the gym, I spy Fisher grappling with Slate, the older man slowly losing ground.

Two and a half hours later, Onyx is taking my patrol with Cassia and Vale, and I'm headed toward the meadow.

Right on time, the wildlings pour out of the schoolhouse and tumble toward the diner to get their lunches. I wait for Marigold to follow them, but she doesn't.

Minutes tick by, and I begin to suspect that she is choosing to work through lunch, or is simply too distracted to remember to grab food.

Absolutely unacceptable.

Chewing my lip, I try to remember how Marigold prefers her hamburgers. Cheese, bacon, who doesn't love bacon, and maybe some veg? I take it easy on the sauce because I can't recall her eating mustard or ketchup in front of me. Surely she likes the secret sauce Crickett makes, but if not - I'll rush back to the lunch spread and make her a new one. She deserves to eat what she likes.

I push open the classroom door with my back while holding both lunch plates. Marigold putters around the tables, her long hair swaying as she moves, twisted into a thick braid. She's wearing a dress, a dark goldenrod color with tiny burgundy mushrooms scattered across the fabric. It hugs her trim waist and flares over those luscious hips.

With a cough, I force my gaze up to her head. I really shouldn't be looking at her hips. Or that ass. But the soft curls escaping her plaited reddish-gold hair are just as distracting.

She turns at the sound of my footsteps and smiles. It hits me like sunshine after a lifetime of shadow, warm and a little blinding.

"Did you forget to eat again?" I tease, holding up the food as an offering.

"You didn't have to do that," she protests, closing the distance between us. I have a sudden impulse to hug her, maybe lift her off the ground. Delicately, she takes the plate and hops onto the nearest table.

"Thank you." She stuffs three potato chips into her mouth at the same time.

Between bites of cheeseburger, I survey the classroom. I'm not sure I've actually been in here before.

"This is a really nice space. I love how much of the kids' art is on the walls. I'm sure they feel really special," I say, thinking out loud.

"Thanks," Marigold says, a rosy tint spreading across her nose and cheeks. Her ankles cross and uncross twice.

Wiping the salt off my fingers, I realize I should have brought drinks. Marigold must have the same thought because she takes a drink from her hydro flask and then holds it out to me. Sharing drinks, that's a new thing. I'm not about to turn her down though. With a slight hesitation, I close my lips around the built-in straw and take a long drink.

"Is this flavored water?"

Marigold shrugs with a guilty smile. "Yeah, I think today it's strawberry-watermelon, maybe? It helps me drink more water. Otherwise, I'm so busy chasing these kids around that I forget to drink anything and end up dehydrated."

"Smart." I take another sip, loving the way it reminds me of her. "So will you be home right after work or do you have plans?" Her lips curl into a smile at the word *home.*

Looking away, she shrugs. "I think I'll stop by my dad's cabin for a bit. Not sure I'll be back before dinner, but we can eat right away and then have some hangout time afterward."

Her dad's cabin... her father is a Zeta and happens to have the late afternoon patrol, so he won't be home. Indigo will be with her grandmother apprenticing, and her youngest brother, Cobalt, always plays soccer with the other kids his age until dinner. Unless she's babysitting Cobalt, it sounds like she's visiting an empty cabin.

"Why?" I ask tentatively, against my better judgment.

Marigold hesitates, taking a bite of her hamburger. I watch her chew and swallow, not ready to let it go. "I like to check in on them."

That's evasive.

My eyes narrow. "Aren't your dad and brothers all out of the house between school and dinner?"

"Oh, yeah," she answers, her voice a bit higher. "Sometimes I like to help out a bit. You know?"

I didn't know, but I nod along and toss the last bite of my lunch into my mouth. Mentally, I catalog each of her words so I can mull them over later because it sounds like she's going over to help out with housekeeping and that would be strange.

Before I can question her further, Willow, Elwood, and Daisy storm into the classroom, arguing loudly. I catch the words wolf, gray, and biggest.

"Shush, you won't know what your wolf looks like until it happens, so chill," Marigold scolds, clearly familiar with the argument.

She shoos them to the table where she's laid out various math worksheets with the kids' names written in bold sharpie across the top so they don't grab the wrong one. It must be tricky preparing so many different grades at the same time.

"I'll see you tonight." She's busy, and I'd better get ready for patrol. At least she turns and waves at me before more kids run through the door and steal her attention.

My hand grips the door frame as I look back. She's beaming even as she instructs her rowdy students, like sunshine that can't stop shining. My afternoon duties suddenly seem dull in comparison, but I won't shirk my responsibilities.

Striding across the meadow, I'm joined by packmates also assigned to afternoon scouting. In the training building, we strip and shift into our four-legged versions.

Taking a deep breath, the scents of the entire pack stream through my consciousness. I can pick out Hazel's honey scent mixed with Slate's woodsy smell.

Onyx, Marigold, Heath. And I can sense the general emotions of my packmates clearly, now that my human inhibitions are wiped away.

A gentle contentment simmers between all the members of the Bracken Creek Pack. I'll never get tired of these feelings, after twenty-plus years of jealousy, anger, pride, and greed from my birth pack. In lieu of avoiding my pack's bond, I sink into it, letting it fill me.

I lead our group northeast, toward Ironcrest. We circle the pack's boundaries, looking for any hint of invaders, rogue wolves or other packs. All is calm. Moving west, our group picks up speed.

Patrol isn't only about safety. It's about running together as much as enforcing our borders. The small groups are always varying, and today I run beside Slate and Aven, a reserved woman a few years older than us. She's talented enough to hold a higher role than her Theta title, but she isn't as dominant as other females like Cassia and Hazel. She's a steady presence as we venture deeper into our territory.

Pine needles churn under my paws, my nails gouging the soil. My ears swivel to pick up the sounds of little creatures and even larger prey. The sense of freedom that comes from running as a wolf is intoxicating. It's why I shift for my own short run every morning.

After a couple of hours, we head back toward our clearing, the day's work done. I slow near the school building, spotting a familiar strawberry blonde head of hair.

Marigold stands in the doorway, smiling and chatting with Cedar. She laughs, throwing her head back. My muscles coil and I have to suppress a growl as she reveals a length of creamy neck and chest to another male.

I've been so stupid. Every one of my thoughts has been taken up by this woman, and she's busy pining over someone else. I knew she had a crush on him, but it didn't seem real when she was touching me, curled up on my sofa, resting her head on my shoulder.

Feeling sick, I lope toward the training building to shift back. Even after dressing, I'm still fighting the jealousy I never expected to feel over my friend and roommate.

MARIGOLD

The afternoon goes quickly. After lunch, my older students work around the pack, assisting adults with various jobs to gain experience. The remaining younger students are eager to finish math and earn some art time, and I'm happy to let them get out paints and paper.

Sitting beside Daisy, I doodle little cartoon wolves across a page while I praise the children around me. Their concentration is impressive as they build their own masterpieces.

After releasing my students for the day, I linger out in the meadow watching them play for a while. Honestly, I'm hoping to see Jasper come back from patrol.

Cedar steps out of the diner and heads toward his garden. "Hey, Marigold," he says in passing.

"What are you up to?" I ask. His feet slow.

"My mom wants some rosemary and chives for dinner," he answers. He grows all sorts of herbs and I love joining him in the pack garden.

"I'll help you!"

"I don't need help," Cedar says, "but I'd enjoy the company."

Beaming, I fall into step beside him. "Perfect."

We pass through the archway and my hand brushes against the trailing vines. He heads down the central path without glancing back.

"I love this time of year," I share, swinging my arms and enjoying the warmer weather.

"I do too. The transplants are all doing nicely. We're starting to see more bugs."

The walkway circles around the barrels that contain most of the herbs Cedar grows. Rosemary and mint overflow their containers, always trying to take over the rest of the garden.

He pulls a tiny pair of shears out of his pocket, making me smile at his quirky habits, and snips several sprigs. I take them from his hands, trying to be useful in some small way.

A lower, long garden bed with a protective screen arching over the top holds the delicate herbs. With practiced expertise, he harvests chives from among the thyme, oregano, and marjoram.

"Marigold, you smell like Jasper," he states, standing to face me.

My fingers run along the collar of my dress uncomfortably. It's such an unexpected accusation and his impartial tone gives nothing of his interpretation away.

"He and I hung out yesterday evening," I answer, biting the inside of my cheek. It's technically true. Hopefully, he's satisfied and lets it go.

His dark eyes study me. "Are you dating him?"

A flush crawls up my neck. This is the exact assumption we wanted to avoid.

"Absolutely not. No." I throw my hands up, almost launching the rosemary into the next garden bed. Whoops! Clutching the sprigs together, I cross my arms.

"So why do you smell like him?" he asks.

My mouth gapes open as my heart races. He isn't buying my excuse. Repeating it will make me look like a liar. The best option is the truth.

"I'm temporarily staying in his second bedroom," I explain.

"Interesting." His face stays passive.

"Nothing is going on! I needed a space of my own and he has the room, and it's been fun." My hands wave to emphasize my point, and I have to gather the herbs together to avoid losing them.

"Cool," he says. Apparently, that's enough of an explanation for him because he heads back toward the diner without another word.

After delivering the herbs, we head toward the training building to meet up with the patrol that has returned.

"Are you guys busy?" Hazel asks. Cedar shrugs.

"Not really, what's up?" I say.

Hazel glances behind her. Slate strolls across the meadow toward us, Onyx and Jasper beside him. "We were thinking about a short hike before dinner. It's too nice out to waste. Do you want to join us?"

"Sure," Cedar says.

"Yeah, sounds great." I have to agree with her, it's too lovely out to stay indoors. The trees smell fresh and green with new growth. Wildflowers have started to bloom.

"How was your day?" Slate asks Hazel. She swings their clasped hands as they walk. Adorable.

"Great," she answers, smiling up at him like he is her moon and stars. I find myself sighing and looking toward Jasper. His clear turquoise eyes gaze ahead, framed in blonde lashes lit up with filtered sunlight.

We wander north-east toward an area with an incredible view. Slate loves this spot. The musty smell of decaying leaves and the crisp scent of pine resin sink into my lungs as we get further from our community and into the thicker forest.

Jasper slows to walk beside me

but stays silent. Our wrists brush and I lift my hands instinctively, clasping them together nervously.

"Did you have a good patrol?" I ask, making my voice cheery.

He nods, not looking at me. "Fine. How was the afternoon with your students?"

"Fine," I say slowly, drawing the word out.

"And you had a good time with Cedar?" he says, his tone cold.

My smile melts into a scowl and I study his expression for more information. He looks irritated, but I can't imagine why. "I guess. I helped him harvest some herbs for Clove. So we are getting her herb dinner rolls tonight if we're lucky."

He purses his lips, silent.

"Are you okay?" I ask.

"I'm good," he says, finally looking at me. I search for hints of anger or hurt in his bright eyes, but he's an enigma. I can tell he isn't happy, but whatever he's feeling is layered and he's keeping it contained.

Slate asks a question I don't catch, and Jasper speeds up to walk alongside his brother. Onyx takes his spot.

"Hey, Goldie," he says, "I'm sorry for giving you a hard time the other day."

"What are you talking about?" I ask. He's always pulling some prank or joke, there's no telling what he's referencing.

"About you and Jasper. At the bonfire," he says.

I shrug. "It's nothing. I owed him an apology after I put my foot in my mouth. But it's all good."

"Cool, yeah," Onyx says, his midnight blue eyes widening as he relaxes.

"Check out this view!" Hazel says, waving us forward. I stand beside her and Hazel drapes an arm around my shoulders. "I'll never get tired of this."

Being a new wolf, everything is still fresh for her. She reminds me why I love being in this pack. The sun is lowering on the horizon, but we still have an hour or two until it gets dark. The clouds skimming the distant peaks are tinted pink against the blue sky.

"Hazel, truth or dare?" Onyx asks. He settles on one of the boulders along the edge.

Hazel folds her arms, narrowing her eyes on him. "Truth."

"Does Slate use your skincare products?" Onyx asks.

Hazel bursts into laughter, looking apologetically at her mate. "I cannot confirm or deny that this handsome man likes to use the same moisturizer as me."

"It's got SPF in it," Slate says with a shrug.

"Knew it!" Onyx says, grinning.

"Okay, my turn," Hazel says, wrinkling her nose as she surveys potential victims. "Marigold, truth or dare?"

"Dare," I say, placing my hands on my hips.

"Alright, I'd like you to try yodeling. I've always wondered if we could get a good echo up here." Hazel grins wickedly.

Pressing my fingers to my eyelids, I shake my head. This is going to be so embarrassing, but a dare is a dare. Stepping closer to the edge, I suck in a deep breath and let out my best impression of a yodel. It's so off-key, I sound more like a goose than a Swiss cow herder.

When I finish, everyone is laughing. A blush colors my cheeks, but I'm pleased my friends are entertained.

"That was amazing," Hazel wheezes, squeezing my arm. It's worth it to see her laugh.

"Okay, Marigold, what's it going to be?" Onyx asks.

"Jasper," I say, smirking. "Truth or dare?"

"Truth." He stretches out his legs, a lazy confidence rolling off of him.

"What's an embarrassing childhood story of yours?" I ask.

Jasper taps his fingers against his mouth while he considers his answer. "When I was five, I shot an arrow through my foot."

"What?" Hazel asks, straightening.

Shrugging as if it's nothing, he explains, "I was messing around with a crossbow. I've got a nasty scar from it."

"Wow," I say, wincing as I picture one of my 5-year-old students with a crossbow. No one in our pack would let a child near the weapons we store in the training building.

228

"Satisfied?" he asks, something uncaring in his tone.

I wrap my arms around myself and nod.

"Cedar, truth or dare?" Jasper asks.

"Truth," Cedar says.

Jasper's jaw ticks, and his gaze lingers on my face in a way that sours my stomach. "Do you have romantic feelings for Marigold?"

"What?" I squeak, whirling on him. "What is the matter with you?"

Cedar quirks half in his mouth in an apologetic smile. "I adore her, she's like family. But nothing romantic."

I want to sink into the dirt. My skin is flaming. The whole group shifts their weight uncomfortably. Gaze on the ground, I can't bring myself to look at either Cedar or Jasper. His answer was casual enough, but everyone here knows what a loaded question that was. The back of my neck prickles.

"Cedar, it's your turn," Hazel prompts. I'm grateful we can move on, but my face is still burning.

Clearing his throat, Cedar says, "Slate, truth or dare?"

"Dare," Slate says with a bold grin.

"Jump into the creek," Cedar says.

"No problem." Slate's off, heading toward a less steep incline until he can reach the riverbed. I don't bother watching him strip and jump in. Onyx whoops and jogs after him. Hazel stands on the edge, shouting encouragement and Jasper joins her, though he keeps glancing back at me.

Cedar studies me, his dimple showing as he grimaces. "Did my answer bother you?"

"No!" I say way too brightly. "Of course not!"

"Alright," he says slowly, as if he doesn't believe me.

"It's fine," I say, holding his gaze to support my lie. The longer I stand here, the louder my blood rushes through my ears, until I'm in danger of swaying on my feet. "I'm not feeling great. I'm gonna head home. Can you let them know?" I ask with a wave toward Hazel.

"Bye, Marigold." Cedar dips his head, his eyes flicking away from me.

Sucking in a breath and slowly exhaling, I turn my feet south, trying to resist breaking into a sprint on my way to Jasper's cabin.

Jasper. Did he feel some measure of this embarrassment when I said essentially the same thing about him? It seemed like a good thing at the time.

But when Cedar said it, I felt so small, so disregarded. I guess being told you're like family is only good when the person wants to be close to you in that way.

Of course, Jasper didn't have a years-long infatuation with me, but if I caused him even a fraction of humiliation, I owe him an apology.

V
CONFESSIONS & COOKIES

JASPER

My feet skim the steps and only hit the porch once before I'm through the doorway of my cabin. Sensing her in her bedroom, I slow my breath and knock softly on the open door.

Marigold sits cross-legged on her neatly made bed, her fingers tugging at the braid in her hair, unraveling it. Her nails snag on a tangle and she lets out a growl. I ignore what that sound does to my body.

"Hey, hey, don't take it out on your poor hair," I tease, crossing the room. Her face lights up in that dazzling smile she wears like armor, though it's looking dull at this moment like she can't quite fake it.

Tentatively, I sit behind her and start to untangle the knot. "You don't have to," she protests, covering the snarl with her hand.

"Just sit and let me do this," I say. Her hands drop to her ankles and her shoulders tense, but she obeys. Her hair is lustrous and I revel in running my fingers through it. Gently, I tug apart the braid until it loosens.

"Thanks," she says hoarsely, almost a whisper.

"Did my question bother you?" I ask, my chest tight.

"It's not that. I'm being ridiculous."

"I love it when you're ridiculous, but you don't seem ridiculous right now, so what's upsetting you?"

Twisting, she peeks over her shoulder at me. "I'm really sorry I said you were ick the other day, that was so messed up, I was put on the spot and felt flustered, and it was such a dumb thing to say."

"So I'm not like a brother?" I ask, a sly smile creeping in.

She rolls those luminous eyes. The last few inches of the braid unravel and I reach for the hairbrush left on the desk.

"I can brush my own hair," she says, snagging it out from under my fingers.

I hold my hand out. "I want to. It's time someone took care of *you* for once." She blinks at me but lays the brush in my outstretched palm. "I see how hard you work for everyone else, all the time."

The first drag of the brush through her hair causes her to let out a soft hum of pleasure.

"Your hair is gorgeous," I murmur. She tightens her shoulders and then lets out a sigh. "You okay? Did I actually upset you?"

"I feel so stupid."

"You're not," I say.

"I've literally spent the last ten years crushing on Cedar and he feels nothing toward me. And everyone knows, and I'm so embarrassed. How could I be this idiotic?"

"I'm sorry, Marigold," I say. "It was horrible of me to ask that and put you guys on the spot in front of everyone."

"I think I'm glad you did. I'd rather know, and I'm not sure I would have listened otherwise. I'm not mad at you, just humiliated."

"Don't be. Everyone adores you, and you have nothing to be embarrassed about. I was a jackass. I was irritated."

"What was bugging you?"

Silence stretches between us. But after what she shared, she deserves an honest answer. "I was jealous." My ears burn and I can't look at her, but I take a deep breath and keep speaking the truth. "There're times when we're talking and he walks in and suddenly he has all of your interest."

Her lips part in surprise. "I'm sorry. I didn't realize."

"I know I don't have any sort of claim to your attention. But you're not second to anyone else for me. And I guess I wanted to be your first choice too."

She's quiet, her expression thoughtful.

Section by section, I brush out her hair into gleaming waves. Her nails dig into the fabric of her dress across her thighs, wrinkling it.

"Better?" I ask. She gives me a mhmm noise of approval.

"Jasper?" she asks. I set the brush aside and run my fingers through her hair, smoothing it back into a sheet of rose gold down her back. She tips her face upwards and closes her eyes. "I think you are my number one. I'd rather be here with you than with anyone else."

I can't resist grabbing her around the waist and hauling her closer in a tight hug. Her hair falls across my face like a silk curtain that tosses back as she squeals and laughs. Every noise is like music and my heart races.

Her shoulders rise and a flush turns her skin from freckled gold to pinkish bronze. We both sink down until we're settled comfortably across her twin bed, her head against the dip of my waist below my ribs.

"I don't know why I didn't flat out ask him years ago or simply get over it and move on," she muses. Reaching out, she tugs my foot closer, running her fingertips over the scar from the crossbow, though she doesn't say a word about it.

"I get it," I reassure her. "It's nice to have someone to fantasize about, and he's a decent guy." I should stop talking, but I can't help myself. "But he isn't what you need. You deserve someone who is crazy about you. Someone who sees you as a partner and cares about your goals."

She turns her face against my shirt. "Don't say I need Onyx."

My laughter bursts out of me and she joins in. "Onyx doesn't deserve you. You're perfect." The moment tightens around us, her doe eyes widening.

She turns on her side and it breaks the tension. "You never told me about that meeting yesterday."

I describe Zephyr's dramatic apology, and the way he evaded responsibility and subtly snubbed Heath. Marigold curls her lip at the worst parts. When I finish, she rolls to her stomach and props her head on her hands, elbows on the mattress.

"I agree. His wolves wouldn't randomly go off and work for another pack. He ordered them to do it, and he's trying to make us believe otherwise."

"Yeah, but what bothers me is how thoroughly he blamed my dad. If they are such good allies, he wouldn't do that, unless he had a really good reason."

Pausing, she frowns. "You're right. That's really suspicious."

My hand flops down, brushing across her upper back. "Maybe it'll be obvious at the Alpha Counsel. I'm sure Hawthorne and Heath will see right through any shit they try to pull."

"Are you worried about seeing him?" she asks quietly, and I know she doesn't mean Zephyr.

"No, it'll be fine. He can't do anything to me." I say, wishing I fully believed it. I know my pack will keep me safe, but that doesn't mean my parents won't find a way to attack me with their words and accusations.

Before she can ask another question about my problems, I shoot back. "Why do you do chores at your dad's? It seems strange. I mean, your brothers are older, Indigo is almost an adult..."

Her lips thin, but she doesn't try to spin it or lie to me. "My dad is busy and it's hard for him to take care of the cabin. My mom always did pretty much all the housekeeping."

Her mom. I knew nothing about her mom. "I didn't know, you've never told me," I say quietly, hoping she'll continue. She obliges.

"She died from complications from having Cobalt. So it's been about ten years. I was twelve."

"You tried to fill her shoes taking care of the boys?" I guess.

Her voice shakes a little. "Lots of moms helped take care of Cobie. It wasn't like I was caring for a newborn or anything."

"How did your dad handle everything?"

Marigold wets her lips and I follow the motion as she presses them together between her teeth. "Not great. He kinda shut down. Indie and Cobalt needed all of his attention, so I took care of myself and tried to help as much as I could."

My hand runs down her arm again and back up. "That sounds hard."

She raises her chin and meets my gaze. "Honestly, the hardest part was missing my mom, especially as a teenager."

"I'm so sorry." Gently, I tuck her hair behind her ear.

"I feel awful, because there are people like Slate who lost a parent within the last few years, and for me, it's been a decade. I don't feel like I have a right to grieve after all this time. But I do. Something reminds me of her, like when Crickett makes her favorite snickerdoodle cookies, or rainy days, those were her favorite, and it feels like it's fresh. Like I just lost her."

Her confession hangs between us. I've never lost a parent, so I have no idea how that feels. After how terrible my parents were, I can't imagine missing them with any intensity.

"What would you tell a friend who was grieving?" I ask.

She exhales slowly, her face relaxing as she thinks. "Um, that it's okay to feel sad. That it's going to last a long time and never really go away," she answers, her words starting slowly and picking up speed, "and that your sadness will start to mix with happy memories eventually, and it'll be nice to remember them, even if it still hurts at the same time."

I study her face as her emotion seeps out. "So isn't that what you should tell yourself?"

A smile flashes across her face and she reaches out and smacks my abdomen. "I get it, you goober."

"Hey!" I yelp, grabbing her upper arms and pulling her hands out from under her chin. She shrieks, trying to swat me again, her smile becoming a genuine grin.

MARIGOLD

"How are you doing?" Hazel asks, her amber eyes watchful as she sips her lemonade. It's hard to hide anything from her, and I don't want to, but there are a few things I'm not ready to share.

"Fine." My tone is light.

We're settled around a picnic table, kids running back and forth in a vigorous game of tag. Usually, our girls' lunch is the highlight of my week, but today I'm feeling a little wary.

"That was pretty awkward on the hike yesterday. I don't know why Jasper asked that. I wanted to smack him." She wastes no time getting to the source of my uneasiness. With a lopsided smile, Hazel sets her drink down and the ice clinks against the glass.

A blush creeps up my neck and I slowly exhale. "It's okay. We talked about it. He was being stupid, but I'm not mad." My fingers run over the worn grooves in the picnic table, smooth from years of daily use.

"I'll still smack him if you want," Hazel offers. Her nose scrunches up, making her look deceivingly unthreatening.

Chuckling, I go back to my cobb salad, loaded with smokey bacon, eggs, and sharp cheese. The only way a salad is acceptable. We are carnivores after all.

"So, are we not going to talk about your huge crush?" she asks pointedly. I choke on my bite and the lettuce sticks to my throat. It takes a few coughs to clear my airway.

"What do you mean?"

"Marigold," she says, "as long as I've known you, you've been hung up on Cedar. Hearing what he said yesterday must have sucked."

"Oh, yeah." I take a drink, needing time to think. "Honestly, I think I was kinda over it. I was more upset with Jasper being pushy than what Cedar said."

"Oh." Her eyebrows rise incredulously.

Shrugging, I set my fork down. "It was a teenage infatuation. I'm not sure when it faded. I didn't even really realize. But I guess I grew out of it."

"So it's nothing to do with the fact you keep going over to Jasper's cabin every night?"

I almost spit out my drink. How did she know? My impulse is to deny it, but Hazel is too perceptive for that to work. "I can explain."

"Oh, yeah?" she asks, a smug smile crossing her features. She loves having one-up on me, which is fair after all the times I teased her about Slate before they got together.

My fork scrapes my plate as I push a sliver of hard-boiled egg through the remaining lettuce.

"You know how I was frustrated staying with my grandma. It was getting worse." She nods sympathetically. "I finally reached my breaking point, so I asked if I could stay in the second bedroom in Jasper's cabin."

"Why didn't you come stay with us?" Hazel asks, not guilting me, but in a sweet way.

"You and Slate need your space. You're still newly mated."

"We would have loved to have you," she argues.

Rubbing my eyes, I finally admit, "You guys are all over each other all the time. I can't imagine how you are behind closed doors. I certainly don't want to be in your guest room for several weeks. I love you, but I have my limits."

Her cheeks flush and she bursts out laughing. "We're not that bad!"

My stare turns deadpan. "I'm pretty sure he was feeling you up the other night around the campfire."

"No!" she denies, though her blush tells me I'm not far from the truth. "You turned this around on me, but we were talking about you and Jasper." So much for the conversation moving on. "You're not over Cedar because Jasper is becoming a thing for you?"

"We're roommates. Totally platonic," I say, keeping my tone even.

Hazel scoffs. "I wonder if he sees it that way."

"He does." Scowling, I stab a huge piece of chicken and stuff it into my mouth to avoid answering whatever ridiculous question she comes up with next.

Her gaze connects with mine as she leans forward and drops her voice. "Marigold, remember, I know Jasper." She pauses, suddenly serious. "He's been denied the love he needs his entire life. And you are basically a fountain of encouragement and affection. If you're not interested in him like that, then you need to be careful."

Swallowing, I frown at her. "I've been keeping a normal distance. Not being touchy-feely, like we talked about."

"It's more than that. You guys are spending a lot of time alone together now. Even if you're not all over each other, having all that time to talk, I'm sure you guys are getting closer." She rakes her nails through her hair. "If you're not firm with your boundaries, I have no doubt he'll fall head over heels for you."

Shaking my head, I think about how comforting and sweet he's been. "He might be my best friend. But that's it." Hazel's mouth opens in mock horror. "Other than you! My other best friend. He's been so kind and supportive. And respectful."

"I know how great he is. But that doesn't change the situation. I'm not worried you guys are mistreating each other. I'm worried you're crossing lines you don't want to cross," she says.

"I think you're overthinking this. It's been months, and we're clearly only friends. A few extra hours together aren't going to change anything."

"So you're not going to rebound with him?" she asks.

"There's nothing to rebound over!" I say, annoyance creeping in. With a breath, I let it go. "Okay, well what should I do? Because I'm trying to be a good friend. But if you worry he's catching feelings, I'm not sure what to do. I'd rather not confront him about it. That would be mortifying, especially if you're wrong."

My stomach churns at the thought of confronting him. What would I say? *You're not allowed to fall in love with me?*

"I think you need to set clear boundaries with him then."

"Like what?"

She leans back, tapping her fingers on her arms as she thinks. "Avoiding being too physically close is a good start." If only she knew about the hours we spent curled up together in my bed last night talking about our feelings. "And not getting too deep with stuff. Baring your heart and all that." Too late for that one too.

Folding my hands, I cock my head and give her a relaxed smile. "No problem. Don't even worry about it."

That might be the biggest lie I've ever told my friend.

"Okay," she says, her eyes narrowing.

"So how are you guys? How's the new cabin? Did you finish organizing the kitchen drawers?" Thankfully, she lets me steer the conversation away.

"Yeah, but Slate already rearranged everything. Which I guess is okay. He's the one using it most of the time."

"You lucky girl," I say, laughing. Slate spent the holidays learning to bake her favorite chocolatey treats. "Hey, have you heard anything else from Heath about internship assignments for my students?"

The conversation wanders between lighter topics until we are out of time. Hazel heads off to lead a patrol and I dive into a research project with my class.

After school, I'm eager to head home. Jasper had today off work and I'm curious what he's been up to. A soft clink of ceramic drifts between the trees, audible over the crunch of pine needles under my feet.

The cabin smells like cinnamon and burnt sugar, cozy and slightly bitter. I'm stunned, pausing in the doorway. "Whatcha doing?"

"Good afternoon, Roomie," Jasper calls from the kitchen.

Stepping forward, I cock my head, trying to take in the scene. Jasper is standing in the kitchen, holding a spatula and a mixing bowl. "Are you… baking?"

His smirk is so smug, I want to wipe it off his face. "Maybe."

Walking around the counter, I can feel warmth emanating from the oven. Bags of flour and sugar line the counter. Leaning over his shoulder, I spy a bowl of cookie dough before he waves me off with a spatula.

"Before you get up in my business, I got you something." He plunges the spatula into the mixing bowl and sets it aside with a thunk.

Grabbing a shopping bag, he hands it to me, his mouth stretching into a wide grin. It's from the local hardware store. Inside sits a huge skein of woven cord, a couple of thick dowels, a pair of high-end scissors, a few s-hooks and metal rings, and a tape measure.

"Are you serious right now?"

"Did I get the supplies right? The internet wasn't exactly clear."

"Jasper, this is way too much," I say, clutching the bag to my chest instead of shoving it back at him like I should.

He shrugs like it's nothing. "I thought you could make something for our cabin."

Our cabin. That's a first.

"I'm serious, this is like sixty or seventy bucks worth of supplies," I argue, trying to remember exactly how expensive this stuff is. "Let me pay you back."

"You can, with a cool wall hanging." He raises an eyebrow, waiting for my argument. Sure, I'll bite.

"Hey, that's worth way more than sixty bucks," I tease, crossing my arms. "Don't push your luck."

"Even with the best friend discount?" His begging puppy-dog eyes melt my resolve.

"You are unbelievable."

"Believe it, baby," he murmurs, almost to himself, turning back to his baking.

Setting the bag aside, I follow him back to the mixing bowl. A darkly burned batch of cookies sits scattered across a wrinkled sheet of parchment paper by the sink. A fine dusting of flour lightens his black shirt into charcoal.

"Looks like your first attempt didn't go so well."

He scowls at me, though I know he isn't serious. "I've never baked cookies before. Give a guy a break."

"Hey, Jasper?" I ask and he turns to me. "Thank you for the craft supplies. It's really sweet." I hold open my arms, and he pulls me close. While he's savoring our hug, I dip my fingers into the bowl beside him - where a pyramid of flour sits mostly unincorporated over the creamed sugar and butter.

When Jasper releases me, I swipe my fingers across his face, leaving a streak of white powder across his tan skin.

"Did you?" he says, surprise dropping his jaw open.

"Yep!" I say, flouncing away with a gleeful cackle.

He grabs my wrist, pulling me back. "I don't think so. Come back here and help me, if you're so eager to get involved."

"No thank you!" I squeal, yanking my hand away and jumping back.

"Marigold! I really need your help," he whines, trying a different tactic.

Crossing my arms, I smirk at him. "Make me."

For a split second, our eyes lock, mine full of challenge and his full of shock melting into delight. But then he's lurching forward and I have to run.

Tearing out the front door, I dart around the side of the house and pull my shirt off in one smooth movement, leaping right out of my pants as my wolf form overtakes my skin.

That moment of transformation is exhilarating, my four legs stretching as I fall back toward the ground. The scents around me become high-definition, every rustling leaves loud to my wolf ears. The second my paws hit the earth, I'm off, dodging trees and leaping over the foliage.

Jasper pursues me, his huge white wolf faster. Glimpses of snowy fur flash in the edges of my vision as I listen to his steps. I wait for the moment he tackles me, but it doesn't come.

His shoulder pulls level with mine until we are running side by side. Our breathing syncs up, his stride shortening to match mine. Wanting to see what he's made of, I dart sideways and race north-east. Surprisingly agile, he keeps pace with me.

Bumping my side into his, I playfully snap at him. His teeth gleam as he bares them back at me. He can catch me, but can he keep me? I throw my weight into him, throwing him off course.

Finally, he takes the invitation to really play. Leaping forward, he throws his paws up, looping one over my back. I twist, pushing him back a step and trying to throw him to the ground. A growl rumbles out of him and I shiver at the rich sound.

On his second lunge, he allows me to take him to the ground. He rolls over onto his back, his paws framing my ruff. I snip at his muzzle, snapping my jaws closer to his nose.

For a moment we're suspended, me over him. His glowing teal eyes meet mine and I can see how much he loves being in his wolf form. Most shifters do. It's what we're made for. I've noticed his white fur streaking past my window in the mornings.

Gracefully, he rolls to his feet and bends into a classic play-bow. Why yes, I'll happily join you. As I lower my own front-half, he springs forward.

I chase him downhill toward the water, and then back up the slope across the north end of our territory. Faintly, we can hear the afternoon's patrol east of us.

Racing through the trees together is thrilling. As wolves, we can run for hours. But it occurs to me that he may have left the oven on, so after a wide loop, I lead us back home.

Jasper disappears around the corner, allowing me privacy to shift back and pull my clothes on. Rounding the edge of the cabin, I find a deliciously shirtless man standing on the patio waiting for me.

"Now will you help me bake?" he asks, looking far too pleased with himself as I avoid looking at his chest.

"Fine." Grabbing his hand, I drag him into the kitchen and start checking his recipe. It looks good so far. "I think you baked them too long."

"I baked them for twelve minutes like the recipe says." He's baffled and it's adorable.

I triple check the temperature. "Different ovens heat differently. This oven might run warmer or colder, but without an oven thermometer, I can't tell."

"Do I need one of those?" he asks.

"No, but it's a safe bet it does run ten degrees hotter, maybe fifteen. We can turn it down and see how they bake." The buttons chirp as he follows my instructions.

As he mixes the flour in, I tear off more parchment paper and lay the baking trays out. He sets the bowl of dough in front of me with a thud. "Look good?"

Nodding I scoop the first cookie and plop it onto the tray.

"Wait, you missed a step," he says, picking the dough up and dropping it into a smaller bowl and rolling it around. Cinnamon sugar.

"You're making snickerdoodles?" I say, spinning to face him.

He doesn't look up, finishing rolling the cookie dough in the sugar mixture and setting it back on the cookie sheet.

"Jasper?" I prompt.

Finally his cyan eyes flick upwards. "Yeah?"

"You're making snickerdoodle cookies after I told you about my mom." I speak slowly, wanting his confirmation. His smile turns guilty.

Shoulders tensing, he scoops another dough ball and tosses it into the sugar. "Maybe I'm craving them after you mentioned it."

"Asshole." He laughs as I swat his arm.

My assumptions about the oven temperature prove correct. The second tray of cookies come out golden and gorgeous. Some edges are a little too brown, telling me the dough wasn't mixed thoroughly. But I don't think he needs a critique, not when it's his first time baking cookies. Practice smooths out many mistakes.

His bright eyes watch my face as I chew my first bite. I nod, giving him a thumbs up. He visibly relaxes, taking a cookie for himself.

"Pretty good for a rookie, right?" he says, his cocky smirk back. As I turn back to scoop the rest of the dough out onto one last tray, I hear him say, "a cookie rookie," under his breath. Glancing back, I crinkle my nose with amusement so he knows I heard him. That earns an embarrassed laugh.

Jasper insists on doing the dishes and I settle on the sofa with another snickerdoodle cookie. He hums as he scrubs, the running water and clinks of bowls and measuring cups forming a dissonant accompaniment. I watch his profile, admiring the curve of his lips and cut of his jaw.

By the time the kitchen is clean, it's time to meet everyone for a community dinner. We don't bother arriving separately, though he stands a bit further away from me once we arrive in the clearing. I want to grab his arm, but I try to respect the silent boundary. Hazel is right, we should keep a little distance. Even if I don't really want to.

VI
CAMERAS & FIRST KISSES

JASPER

Storm clouds roll over the treetops along the north-east edge of our territory. Onyx carries a box of electronics as Slate picks out spots to install security cameras. They're rated for all-weather outdoor use, so a few raindrops aren't going to interrupt our work.

The increased monitoring along our shared border will allow me to breathe easier. Heath allowed Hawthorne and I to pick out the tech, and Onyx helped because he's good with electronics.

"Hazel told me Marigold is staying with you," Slate says, looking straight ahead.

Onyx swings around, his mouth gaping. Thankfully, he manages to control himself long enough to hear my answer.

"She had some issue with her grandma and asked to crash with me." Shrugging, I say, "The cabin has two bedrooms. It would be dumb to tell her no." That might be downplaying it, but I don't like how stiff Slate's posture is.

"Wait, how long have you guys been living together?" Onyx asks.

Sighing, I rake my fingers through my hair and push it out of my eyes. "About a week."

"She could've stayed with us. We have a second bedroom too," Slate says. I frown, really not wanting to have this conversation, but luckily Onyx jumps in.

He snorts. "Really, dude? You guys are so handsy, we're all glad your cabin is one of the farthest away. No one wants to stay with you."

My brother glares at Onyx with an expression that would stop me in my tracks, but Onyx just barks out a laugh.

"It's no big deal. I've got plenty of space and she's nice to have around," I say.

Slate halts, looking up at a gnarly oak tree. "How about this one?"

I breathe in, testing the scents. Our scent is starting to fade here, but the hint of Ironcrest is so faint, I almost can't smell it.

"Looks good to me." Grabbing a low branch, I haul myself up, anchoring my back against the trunk and wedging my feet against the largest lower branches.

"So she's baking in your kitchen, singing in your shower, walking around in her bunny slippers." Onyx hands up a little camera along with the hooks and a screwdriver.

"I don't think you have a clue what women behave like," I say dryly.

He doesn't need to know I was the one baking in our kitchen. Marigold does have a lovely singing voice in the shower - also something I don't want to share.

Onyx gives me a strange look, his typical grin absent. Whatever he sees must irritate him, because he scowls at the tree trunk.

Flicking the camera on, I hold it against the trunk where there's a split that will camouflage the tech.

"Angle it down a bit," Slate says, monitoring the live feed with his phone. I adjust per his instructions. "Perfect. This one gives a really clear view."

It only takes a moment to affix the security camera in place. I hand the tools back down to Onyx and then lower myself onto the nearest branch before letting myself drop. Leaves flurry around my feet as I land.

"How many more?" I ask.

"Three," Onyx answers sullenly.

"What's wrong?" I ask.

"Nothing," he says, refusing to look back at me.

A fine mist of rain filters down between the branches and coats my arms and face.

"Let's hurry this up, I don't want to get soaked," Slate says.

We walk in silence, but Onyx's mood continues to decline. After he makes an angry scoffing nose low in his throat, I finally speak up.

"Just tell me what's pissed you off."

For a moment, he glowers at me. "We all saw how upset she was the other day. You were being an asshole. And she's always had a thing for Cedar and you forced them to face that, and Cedar wasn't ready. So now that's ruined."

He's right, but I can't bring myself to feel remorse. Cedar's feelings aren't my priority, Marigold's are. I don't care if I ruined anything for him. Onyx is delusional if he thinks anything would have happened between Cedar and Marigold given more time.

Sure, I could have handled things better, but it was worth it. She's freed from that one-sided relationship. I'll take any shit I get for what I said, knowing that Marigold is happy.

Voice level, I speak to Onyx in the most reasonable tone I can muster. "I'm sorry about that. I already apologized to Marigold. If they're meant to be together,

I'm sure it'll still happen. But if your brother says he doesn't have feelings for her, maybe you should trust that."

Onyx's lip curls, some acidic remark brewing. But Slate decides to step in. "So nothing is happening between you two?" he verifies.

Huffing, I throw my hands up. "No. She's a friend who needed a place to stay. It's no different than if she stayed with you," I say with a pointed look at Onyx. If one more person asks if we are now dating, I'm going to shift into my wolf and eat them.

"Maybe she should," Onyx starts, but Slate has had enough.

"We need to get going. As much fun as this has been, I'm ready to be done for the day." Slate's tone leaves no room for arguing.

"Agreed," I say.

We secure the next camera, and I can see Onyx softening. He won't apologize, but he nods at me while handing over tools and is meeting my gaze again.

As soon as the last camera is in place, we head back. It's really raining now. My t-shirt clings to me, and Slate and Onyx's longer hair slicks to their necks. We stash the tools away before parting.

"So I'm the only one who doesn't have a beautiful girl to go home to," Onyx complains, back to his usual mildly irritating self. Slate rolls his eyes and laughs before taking off.

Marigold won't be off work for a while, but I don't see any movement through the classroom windows. Hopefully she's enjoying a quiet afternoon.

Knowing I shouldn't bother her at work, I go home.

Rain patters on the roof, filling the cabin with soft music. Perfect weather to curl up with a book and leftover cookies. The afternoon is quiet, at least until Marigold comes home.

Her scent reaches me right before her voice hollers, "I blame you!"

"What?" I call back, loving her sass.

"It finally happened." She leans around the doorway to my room and I set my book aside on the round table beside my armchair. Her hair is dark with water and her shirt and sweats cling to her.

"Elwood and Starling were fighting, and it was kinda bad, and then Elwood had his very first shift - while we were on a freaking nature walk! And he took off, and then it started raining so we couldn't even track him properly!"

"I'm so sorry," I say, jumping up and meeting her. "I wish I had known so I could have helped."

My hands go to her upper arms. She's chilled.

"It's fine. His brother was right there, we actually found him pretty quick." She shrugs with a cute half-smile. "Just not quick enough to keep me from getting totally stressed out and drenched."

She motions down her body as if I hadn't already been acutely aware of the way her clothes plaster to her figure. Her giggle is a bit manic and it leads to her entire body convulsing in an uncontrolled shiver.

242

"Geez, Marigold, you're freezing." The giggle redoubles followed by another shiver. "Stay here. You need to warm up."

Grabbing a blanket off my bed, I wrap her up and hand her one of the snickerdoodle cookies off the kitchen counter. While she nibbles on it, I crank the tub faucet all the way to the left. Once the water heats, I set the stopper of the vintage claw-foot tub.

Marigold follows me into the bathroom and stands by the sink.

"Since you had such a stressful day and you're cold, I thought a bath would be really good for you." The Epsom salts dissolve into the hot water easily and the air fills with the scent of lavender.

"A bath?" she echoes, like it isn't right in front of her.

"Yeah, it'll warm you up and the salt will help your muscles relax so you aren't sore tomorrow." Rubbing her arms, I slide past her in the narrow bathroom and pause at the doorway.

"You're spoiling me." Her smile makes it worth it.

"I'm not done. It's almost dinner, so I'm gonna grab us food. And after your bath, we can eat by the fire and I'll open a bottle of wine," I find myself saying.

"That seems excessive."

She might be right about that, but I can't help it.

"You don't need to do any of this," she protests.

Chuckling, I tug the blanket off of her and give her a little push toward the steaming tub. "I want to. You deserve it."

"I don't want to be a burden." Her vulnerability shows through.

My hands grasp her shoulders so I can look her square in the face. "You're always taking care of everyone else." She opens her mouth to argue. "Don't deny it, I've seen it. So now it's your turn."

She scowls at me. "That's not your job."

"Well, someone needs to do it."

She reaches up and tugs at my shirt. "Can I convince you to let *me* get food while *you* enjoy the bath?" She cocks her head. "You seem like a bath guy."

I know she doesn't mean to flirt, but my breathing slows as my heart rate increases. Deliberately, I step back. "Absolutely not."

"Oh come on." Even her whiny voice is adorable. Her lip pouts and I raise my hand to touch her on instinct. Catching myself, I twirl my finger, ordering her to turn around.

"Get in your bath now, or I'm going to put you in it myself."

"You wouldn't dare." She crosses her arms.

"Marigold, don't make me throw you over my shoulder." My thoughts fill with the image of her ass in the air, legs dangling, while I grip her thighs to keep her steady. Not helpful, but better than the image of climbing into the bath with her.

"Fine. But I'm washing dishes tonight." Rolling her eyes, she starts to lift the hem of her shirt.

Blood rushes in my ears as I shut the door and lean my back against it. Of course I knew she'd shower in my bathroom, but the idea of her soaking in that steaming bath is too enticing to dwell on.

This amazing woman bends herself into a pretzel caring for everyone else, encouraging them with her bright smiles and boundless energy. But after living with her, I see the exhaustion underneath. She deserves someone taking care of her. And until I'm forced to stop, that job is mine.

Dinner is a chicken stir-fry with snow peas and carrots over rice. I've had similar food in town, but my parent's pack would never have served anything so flavorful. I set the plates on my chunky wooden coffee table and locate one of the bottles of Sauvignon Blanc that the internet had said was sweet and mild.

Waiting for her, I attempt to read a few more pages, but all thoughts of reading fall out of my brain when she emerges wrapped in only a towel and tip-toes to her room. Freckles cover the expanse of skin across the top of her chest.

Make-up free, hair wet, but now flushed with heat from her bath, she's the most attractive woman I've ever seen. She comes out in the same oversized sleep shirt she arrived in the first night.

"Oh, I love stir-fry night," she says, grabbing the plate further from my seat and nestling down beside me.

"Yeah, it's great," I say, barely remembering to grab my own food.

She leans her cheek against my shoulder briefly. "Jasper, that really did make me feel a hundred times better. Thank you."

My eyes are on her shirt. There's something about the faded design that bothers me. It seems masculine, which is fine as long as it's hers. But what if it's not.

She dives into her food, stopping only to take a long sip of the wine.

"You like it?" I ask, smiling over my own glass.

It clinks as she sets it down on the table, and her hand drops to my thigh, squeezing. "It's delicious. I didn't know you're a wine connoisseur."

Shaking my head, I set my own glass down so I can wrap my arm around her waist. "I'm not, I have the internet on my phone."

"I've heard of that. Something the teenagers have," she jokes.

It's easy to laugh with Marigold. "Something like that."

"You are younger than me," she says, cooly, though a teasing smile begins to curl her lips.

"Not by much."

"Young hoodlum," she says, scrunching up her face into a scowl. She's adorable.

"At least I know how to use the internet."

Marigold snorts, covering her mouth with the back of her hand. "You're ridiculous."

We lapse into companionable silence, and I finish my meal before she does. Eating quickly was a survival technique growing up, and those habits are slow to unravel. But I'm happy to enjoy Marigold's warmth soaking into my side as she takes tiny bites and savors the last of her dinner.

When she stands, I stand too, but she pushes me back down. "I get the dishes, remember? You agreed." She refills my wine glass.

It's not a bad view. She sways to music in her head while she washes up the two plates and sets them on the counter. They belong to the diner, not the cabin.

Despite the fire, the chill of the rain seeps into the living room too. Once she's satisfied with the kitchen's cleanliness, Marigold ducks into her room.

A moment later, she lets out a little shriek.

I scramble around the coffee table and have her half in my arms before she lets out a laugh.

A slow drip falls from the ceiling right into the center of her bed. The leak has spread across her bedspread and surely soaked down into the sheets.

"Ah, shit."

"Yeah, not ideal," she agrees.

I strip the linens and place a huge bowl under the leak, but that's the best I can do for tonight.

"You should take my bed tonight. I'll sleep on the sofa," I say, grabbing a towel to clean up the spilled wine on the coffee table. Luckily the glass rolled and hadn't broken.

She scoffs. "It's a pretty big bed, I think we can share it."

The glass slips again, but I manage to catch it before it clatters down, giving away my surprise. "Are you sure that's a good idea?"

Shrugging, she leans against the kitchen counter. "We've cuddled up plenty of times. This time we'll be unconscious. That's less scandalous than laying in a bed awake."

It's weird reasoning, but I can't find any reason to disagree. Unfortunately, something is still bothering me.

"Is that your shirt?" I ask.

"Um, yeah? Well, I think it belonged to one of the twins originally, but I've had it for years."

It shouldn't bug me, but it does. She's in my house, and I don't like the idea of her wearing another guy's shirt.

Biting my lip, I stalk to my dresser and dig through the drawers for the softest faded shirt I can find. Marigold stands in the doorway, watching, bemused. Shoving it into her hand, I say, "Here, wear this one instead."

"Okay," she says, her eyes sparkling. Thankfully, she understands the possessiveness that drives shifters. She disappears for a moment, and I sink onto my bed, feeling like an idiot.

That sense of euphoria returns in full as she climbs into my bed and stretches out beside me on her stomach, crossing her arms and setting her chin on them.

My shirt drapes over her back and clings to her hips. It looks so much better on her than it ever did on me. I want to pull her to me, but I settle for admiring her.

The room is warm and the only light comes from the dim lamp on my bedside table. In sunlight, all of her colors are bright and dazzling, but in this low light, I notice the upturn of her nose and the curve of her cupid's bow, and she's somehow more lovely.

"You know, Hazel told me one time that your old pack has very few females," she says, surprising me. That was out of nowhere.

"Yeah, they like to recruit single guys. No distractions from work."

"That sounds awful. So are the guys absolutely feral over the girls they do have?"

I laugh, resting my head back against my pillow. "More like they compete that much harder for rank, since only the top positions get a mate."

"Wait, what?" She pops up, frowning at me.

"What?"

That bottom lip purses as she cocks her head at me. "Are you saying the Granite Ridge pack doesn't allow wolves to choose mates the normal way? It's assigned with rank?"

Shrugging, I roll onto my side to face her. "Yeah. Only the strongest should breed, or that's the idea."

"That's insane. And sounds miserable."

"They don't claim their mates. So if someone loses position or is killed, the other is still available. It's about duty, not love or even support." I try to explain the best way I can. Growing up, it was normal. It took becoming a teenager and seeing other packs and humans in town to realize it was odd.

"Definitely insane. Doesn't that seem terrible to you?"

I chew my lip. "Yeah, it is. But I was going to be the Alpha, so I always knew I would have my pick. Or more likely be paired with a political match."

Up this close, the interwoven tendrils of sapphire and malachite in her irises mesmerize me as her gaze holds me captive. She's studying me and I'm not sure I measure up.

"Are you disappointed you lost that opportunity?"

"No way, it's a relief. Now I can be with whoever I like and there's no pressure."

She hesitates for a beat, wetting her lips. "Did they ever try to pair you up with anyone?"

"Other than Hazel, not really. But they would have if I had stayed. There were lots of discussions about it, but most of them I wasn't involved in. Just informed later."

"Did you like Hazel at first?"

Oh, that's awkward.

I take a moment, thinking through my words. "I did, but she was the first person I had met who was sincere and kind. I barely knew her and I wanted to be around her. And then I discovered her entire pack was like that."

"Oh." She tilts her head slightly, her lips rounded.

"Honestly, she saved my life. I didn't know a pack could be like this."

"Jasper." Her voice is soft, empathetic. But I don't need her comfort, I need to express myself.

"And you are the kindest, brightest person in the pack. You made me feel so welcome and accepted."

"That's sweet, but anyone would have done the same."

"You're not anyone. You were the one I wanted to be around from the first day I arrived."

Tension thickens the air until I can't catch my breath.

She clears her throat, looking away. "What do you think you want in a mate? More of a housewife and mother like Crickett? Or a partner to go into battle with, like Cassia?"

"I don't care," I say, giving into the urge to run my fingers through her hair. When I brushed out her hair a couple of days ago, I learned how silky and soft those reddish gold waves were. Even slightly damp, it's divine to feel those glossy strands slip across my skin.

"Well what do you want in a partner then?" She's so serious, my chest tightens. I didn't expect her to care.

"Um, I guess someone who is loving. I want someone I can talk to and have fun with." A blush washes over my face, and we're so close, there's no way she misses it. "What about you?"

"I don't know." She presses her lips between her teeth, the way she does when she's nervous. "Someone who sees me."

The trust in her expression draws me in, making me feel wanted. I run my knuckles down her cheek, brushing her hair back. She leans into my touch, her eyes fluttering closed. My breath catches as she tilts her face toward me, and I can't resist, not when she's filled up my entire world in the last few days.

Impulsively, I lower my lips to hers, my nose brushing her cheek. She presses back, her mouth smooth and warm. The drag of her lips against mine is the single most earth shattering sensation I've ever experienced. My fingers tangle in her hair, trying to find an anchor as my world is destroyed and put back together in a single moment.

She draws back and stares at me, eyes half-lidded. "That was my first kiss," she says quietly.

What? The gravity of that truth crashes around me. I kissed my best friend and roommate. Fuck.

"I'm so sorry. That was so stupid of me. I wasn't thinking," I say in a rush.

She shrugs, her face still pink. "It's okay. It's no big deal, really."

"We can pretend it never happened." What if she's angry that I robbed her of that experience with someone she really loves? Dread sinks in my gut.

"Sure, never happened." Her voice is higher, emotional. Is she going to cry? Fuckity double fuck.

Is she going to move out? Did I just ruin the best thing in my life? "Please stay, I promise I won't be an idiot again."

"Jasper, chill," she says, reaching out and running her fingers through my hair. Her nails scratch down my scalp, cutting through my panic. I'm able to take a slow breath.

"I'll sleep on the couch. You can have my bed. I'll give you space." I start to get up.

"Really?" Her voice is sarcastic. I freeze, half-upright.

"Stay. I like this." She tugs at my arm, and I'm shocked and thrilled to be pulled down beside her again. She could do absolutely anything to me right now and I'd happily go along.

My heart thumps in my chest so hard I'm sure she can feel it. But she rolls on her side and places my arm over her waist, not releasing me until I've scooted forward and pressed my chest to her back.

"Much warmer," she hums, wiggling her ass back into me. Surely that wasn't intentional. I have no way to hide the reaction my body has to her, but if she notices, she doesn't say anything.

I keep my head back, away from her silky hair or the warm skin of her neck, even though I'd love nothing more than to press my nose against her skin and breathe in the scent of rosemary and sage.

"This is really nice," I say quietly. She murmurs a soft noise of agreement, but nothing else.

Sleep seems impossible with her soft body against mine. But eventually her breathing evens out, and ages later, so does mine. Sleep is peaceful, and when I wake up with her still in my arms, I'm filled with this feeling of tightness I can't shake.

I kissed my roommate and best friend. And if I'm being honest, she's been my secret crush for a long time, even if I was too dumb to recognize it. Nothing else can explain my private obsession with her smell, her hair, the way she smiles. Everything about her.

Could she feel the same way? The way she clings to me gives me hope. But most likely, she hasn't realized anything yet. Maybe I can help with that. What's a little flirting between roommates?

VII
SPARRING & SUBTERFUGE

MARIGOLD

"Good morning, Sunshine," Jasper murmurs into my hair before he climbs out of his bed. My muscles are liquid and I couldn't follow him if I wanted to. The sheets smell like him. Burying my nose into my pillow, I breathe in the soft spiced scent. It's so comforting, I start to drift off again.

After his morning run, I hear the shower crank on. I'd better get myself up. But it's so cozy, I don't move until he comes into his bedroom wrapped only in a towel, with an expanse of wet, golden skin that heats my blood.

Memories of his mouth against mine bombard me, urging me to leap at him, wrap myself around him like a deranged sloth. Suck on that full bottom lip.

Maybe I'm less okay than I said.

Scrambling out of bed, I head into my room to change, giving him privacy. And as I shimmy out of my clothes, I don't think of him taking that towel off. Not one bit.

Saturdays are for sparring. Every pack member takes either a position like Theta or Zeta, or a normal job, like mine. But regardless, everyone needs to train and be prepared to defend our territory at any time.

I meet Hazel in the training building. Her dark hair bobs in a perky ponytail. "Ready for some exercise?" she says, as if she doesn't work out every single day. Hazel's only been a wolf for a few months, and she trains harder than anyone else to make up the difference in experience. As the Alpha's heir, she has to be ready for challenges. Yet again, I'm glad to not have a leadership position within the pack.

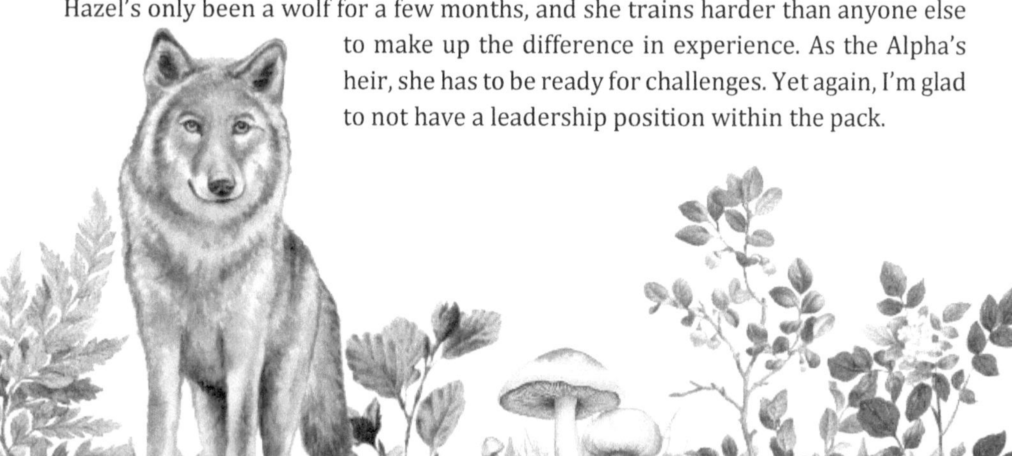

Teaching might also make me sweat, but it's way more fun than the endless training exercises that leave bruises across Jasper's ribs.

"Yup!" I twist at the waist, swinging my arms and giving her a bright smile.

Hazel's eyes wrinkle as she smiles back. "You look peppy today. More than normal, I mean."

"Hey, ladies!" Onyx yells through the open garage door. A few older wolves are setting out for a run, but otherwise it looks pretty quiet.

I toss my jacket down on a bench. "Hey Onyx, ready to get your ass handed to you?"

"You couldn't handle me," he shoots back with a grin.

Warmth presses against my arm as a hand slides across my lower back to grip my waist, igniting sparks under my skin. "Don't waste your time with him." Jasper's voice leaves goosebumps along my arms.

"Think you can do better?" I flirt back, leaning into his chest.

One eyebrow arches. "You'll see." Sliding past me, he greets everyone. Cedar is missing, and Onyx makes an excuse for him, something about the chicken coup.

"Marigold, you up for a match?" Hazel asks.

"I'll take on Jasper, actually," I announce.

"Are you sure you want to fight me?" he asks, warning in his eyes despite the fact it's clearly what he wants.

Shrugging, I hold my arm across my chest in a stretch. "Hazel can train with Slate today. I want to see what you've got."

This leaves Onyx, and he decides to practice with weaponry, throwing slim daggers into a target nailed to a tree. Slate is more than happy to grapple with his mate, and within minutes they're trading punches and kicks in the graceful way partners do when they know each other's movements as thoroughly as their own.

"Ready?" Jasper asks, ushering me onto the blue mats. "Want to up the stakes?"

"How?" I bounce between the balls of my feet, psyching myself up.

"Loser has to give the winner a massage," he murmurs.

"Sure, I'd love a massage."

Jasper watches me, utterly relaxed.

Edging forward, I take my first strike, my fist flying at his shoulder. His arm knocks it aside, but instead of simply blocking, he surges forward, forcing me to step sideways and wrapping his arm across my upper chest and hauling me toward him. He could easily put me in a headlock. Biting my cheeks, I resist the urge to melt into him. The corded muscles of his forearm stand out, begging for me to run my fingers along them.

"I think you're my favorite sparring partner, Sunshine."

"What's with the nickname?" I ask, waiting for him to release me, instead of struggling against a hold I know I can't break. That is, without kicking his shins or scratching his face, or some other move that would injure him. And I like my room-mate uninjured, to be honest.

250

"I think it suits you," he purrs, voice quiet enough it's private. The heat of his breath feathers against my ear. My body shivers and he releases me with a low laugh.

Frustrated at my reaction, I set my weight back and twist, aiming a hard kick to his ribs. Grinning, he grabs my ankle and uses my own momentum to throw me onto the mat. Walking past, he waits for me to scramble up.

That was humiliating. I thought I was a bit better than this. I've beat other opponents. But other opponents don't lean in and whisper distracting words.

"I'm going to get you back for that," I say, panting.

Taking my time, I look for an opening and feint a punch followed with a swift kick to his thigh, lower so he can't grab me. His smile returns, something akin to pride warming his face.

He likes when I successfully land a hit? Fantastic.

I step closer, ready to try the same trick again. But the scent of baking spices wraps about me, muddling my focus. He gets close, too close. I can't land a hit when his forearm shoves my chest, and his other hand grabs my shoulder, twisting me as I fall backwards. My torso hits the mat, arms pinned behind me in his grasp. His knees frame my hips as he kneels over me. "Had enough? I'm happy to throw you on your back a few more times if you're not done."

Growling in irritation at his teasing, I wrench my wrists free and roll to my feet, causing him to step back. His cocky grin usually amuses me, but right now I want to strangle him.

I throw another punch allowing him to block it, but then hook my other hand at the nape of his neck. Not a traditional move. He hesitates, trying to read my intentions. Putting my weight into it, I grab the arm he blocked with and tug, while pulling his entire body sideways. He goes down like a rock. My knee hits the ground beside him and I grin down triumphantly.

His blonde hair fans across his forehead and I like seeing his typical sleek composure ruffled. He smiles back, sweet and genuine. "Very good," he praises, his words lighting my whole body up.

Why is he so stunning? It's unfair to the rest of us.

After two more matches that include me landing on my back approximately five times each, Hazel suggests we shift and find the twins for a good run.

Jasper's hands find my hips as he leans in. "We can finish this later, if you like."

"Maybe, if you behave yourself," I flirt back, blushing at my own breathy tone.

That was interesting. Last night, he said it was stupid to kiss me and told me to pretend it never happened. But the way his hands grip my skin and pull me to him, I'm not sure what to think.

Onyx retrieves Cedar, and we all shift, stashing our clothing away in lockers. My reddish gold coat looks particularly bright against Jasper's snowy white as he rubs his shoulder along mine.

Slate leads us toward the doorway and into the trees. Energy floods me, excitement that is not only mine.

Jasper's white wolf dashes ahead, nipping at Slate's tail as the boys race. Hazel runs beside me. The forest chatters around us, swaying branches, scurrying chipmunks, and even the hurried chirruping of western tanagers.

The boys are out of sight when we hear the rustling and growling. Excitement seeps through our pack bond. We increase our speed until they come into view.

Onyx's dark wolf rolls on the ground with Slate, while Jasper bounces around them. As Slate pins Onyx, Jasper dives for him. They collide in a whirl of gray and white, snapping and shoving with paws.

Jasper subdues Slate for a moment, but the older brother squirms free and abruptly dives at him. With a bark, Jasper takes off running again. Onyx and Slate give chase.

Hazel watches them go, and I'm confident if she was in her human form, she'd be rolling her eyes. Stepping closer, I nudge her muzzle with my nose in a sign of affection. She tilts her head, ears swiveling. With a wag of her tail, she dashes after the boys, inviting me to give chase.

Our endurance as wolves is considerably better than as humans, and it's another hour before we are panting and finished with our play. I haven't won a single game of chase, but the attachment and loyalty between us is stronger than ever.

JASPER

Eight of us gather around the meeting table, the air heavy. Heath sits at the center, with his heirs beside him. Hawthorne rests across from him, with me at his right hand. Fisher, our Delta and trainer, sits on his other side.

To Hazel's right slouches Sable, Marigold's grandmother. The healer's long memory of the local packs has been helpful in preparations for the Alpha Counsel. And at the end perches Linden, our business manager. With mousy brown hair and a reserved demeanor, Linden often joins our meetings to take notes for logistics, budget, or supplies, but I don't know him well. Being a few years older, we've never socialized together.

"How large of a team do you think each pack will bring?" Slate asks. Hazel leans back in her chair, her fingers tapping against her chin.

Hawthorne exhales. "I would expect around ten. Their top three, and then half a dozen guards or so."

"We should set a maximum number," Hazel muses.

Sable purses her lips. "Setting a rule about how many wolves an Alpha can bring is a sure way to make them wary and trigger them breaking that rule." Hazel frowns at her.

"We already have some advantage as the hosts, though it's minimal. I don't think anyone will bring twenty wolves, it would make them look frightened," Heath says. "They'll want to appear confident and powerful in their own right."

Nodding, Hawthorne adds, "Ferris and Zephyr will likely display wealth in any way they can. And all of them are likely to bring not only their closest advisors, but also their most physically impressive."

"Displaying power without numbers," I conclude. Hawthorne's mouth quirks, his approval sending a satisfied warmth through my chest.

"So who do we want to bring?" Fisher asks.

"Everyone here, although I think I'd prefer you stayed behind with our pack as leader de facto in my absence." Fisher nods at Heath's edict.

"There is no reason for me to join you." Sable raises her chin. Heath nods in acknowledgment.

"So how many additional Zetas and Thetas should we bring?" Slate asks.

"Two," Heath says, "Lazuli and Cassia." The mated pair make an impressive team. Lazuli stands tall and intimidating with his athletic build. Cassia is smaller, but she is perhaps our strongest Zeta. She's quick, clever, and fairly ruthless, although only in a fight. It's quite the contrast to her calm temperament and role as a mother to Oliver, the youngest baby in our pack. He's six months younger than Dahlia and only recently started running.

"I'd like for us to have additional security measures," Hazel says.

"Yes?"

"Perhaps additional members standing by at a distance? Vale, Elm, and Aven?" Slate suggests, mentioning the last three of our warriors. Elm is Marigold's father and the oldest of our Zetas, and Vale is the youngest Theta at barely eighteen, though Vale's talents at scouting earned him the position as a teenager.

Several people nod at the suggestion. Taking a measured breath, I say, "Perhaps a hidden stash of additional weapons within easy reach?"

Fisher's lip curls. He knows I mean handguns, and he disdains them. Though we pack in shots of wolfsbane which disable our opponents instead of kill, he still sees it as dishonorable. That belief makes him a critic of me.

"Yes, please arrange that," Heath says. I fight to keep my face relaxed when I want to smirk. Hazel's gaze flicks to me and her mouth twitches in a subtle praise.

Heath sits up straighter. "What do we know about the objectives of each pack? We need to consider how their desires may conflict."

This is Hawthorne's area of expertise. He leans forward, speaking directly to his Alpha. "Zephyr seems intent on rebuilding an alliance with us, at the expense of his relationship with Ferris. So we are primed for a conflict between them in addition to Ferris's general dislike of us. But outside of them, I don't foresee any requests or complications from the Valley Pack. So it's whatever we bring to the table."

"What are we pushing for?" Hazel asks. Her wide brown eyes look up at her uncle.

"Peace and order," Heath says simply.

Slate frowns. "We need to publicly hold Granite Ridge accountable for their recent offenses toward us."

"Do we?" Sable asks. I scowl at her. Knowing the depths of her unkindness to Marigold has set the healer in a new light for me, and I see her compassion extends furthest for those she is healing, and least for her family.

"Everyone is already aware of their crimes," Hazel says, crossing her arms. As the chief victim, her word will weigh the most in this matter.

"Do you want a public apology or other repercussions?" Heath asks.

Hazel's face scrunches up as she thinks. "Only if it benefits the pack. My pride is not delicate." Her uncle nods approvingly.

Respect for Hazel rises up in me. Less than a year ago, she was living as a human in Los Angeles. But now she has blossomed into a generous and competent leader.

Smiling at her, I joke, "I mean, you already took their heir away from them, so there's that." She rolls her eyes at me. From the corner of my eye, I catch the slightest smirk on Hawthorne's face.

"We could focus on our requested agreements including a counterbalance for their slights," Linden suggests, surprising me.

"I like that idea," Hazel says. Slate's brows crease together. I suspect he'd prefer a public display of groveling and punishment.

Everyone pauses, the topic heavy. Finally Heath says, "We need to carefully consider what changes we may enact. And have variations prepared to adjust for the other pack's input.

"The goal is peace. So we must consider the actions that threaten our peace and what measures we can take to curb them."

"Granite Ridge's thirst for new recruits," Slate says automatically, and I have to agree.

Heath glances around, checking the faces of all of his subordinates. I give a small nod.

"They have outright stolen wolves from nearby packs," I say carefully, "but not from our neighboring packs, excluding their move against Hazel last year. So they have deniability. So whatever guidelines we push for agreement need to take that into account."

"What about using phrasing that better fits what they are claiming to do?" Hazel asks.

"They say the other wolves are *choosing* to join them," I say grimly.

"You could call it head hunting," Hazel says, earning confused frowns. "Or poaching. They're poaching wolves from other packs."

"How can that be monitored or enforced?" Fisher asks.

"They should be held accountable. If we push the point of their offenses toward us, we could ask for interventions such as inspections," Slate says.

Heath sighs. "Unfortunately, I think that's unlikely to work."

"It's more than fair," Slate says, his brow furrowing.

"That doesn't mean it's doable," Sable reprimands. Slate's mouth thins, his irritation a physical sensation through our pack bond. He's hot headed when it comes to his mate.

"There has to be solutions we haven't thought of yet," Hazel says, smoothing things over.

The debate trails off, eventually being set aside for a future discussion. As the last order of business, Hawthorne outlines the top leadership of each pack to remind everyone of names and positions.

My parents, Ferris and Sienna, of the Granite Ridge Pack, will likely bring whoever their current Beta is, though that role changes hands often so we have no assured name. And perhaps they will bring their heir, my younger sister Ember. I'm curious how her training has evolved in my absence, since she is now first in line and not a spare. Knowing her, she's probably ecstatic. I'm not doubtful she had been scheming to remove me at some future date, and I did it for her.

Zephyr leads Ironcrest, with a Beta named Beryl, and his Gamma, Dell. Beryl is effectively Zephyr's heir, for he has no mate or children that we are aware of.

Unfortunately, Nyx of the Raven Pack will not be joining us, therefore the only other pack participating will be the Valley Pack.

Cashel has led the Valley Pack nearly as long as Heath has led Bracken Creek. He's our closest ally. He's likely to come with his heir, Beta, and son, Malachite. Hawthorne reminds us that his Gamma is a cousin, Zinnia.

My head is swimming by the time we're done. But during the Counsel, my only role is to observe and interpret the actions of the leaders that I know. And to provide security. I won't even be at the table.

We've discussed and planned for this meeting for months, but now that it's concrete and fast approaching, anxiety gathers in my gut. Particularly with Zephyr's strange meeting a few days ago. I have no idea what to expect when I set eyes on my parents.

The tension in my shoulders uncoils as I approach my cabin and hear giggling from inside. Marigold is perched on the sofa with a stack of papers on her lap.

She looks up and her face brightens from relaxed amusement to affection.

"Whatcha up to?" I ask, settling beside her.

Holding up the pages, she says, "Just grading. Do you want to help?"

"How would I know what's correct?" I ask, spinning the pink felt marker from the table between my fingers.

"It's math from elementary school, I think you can manage," she says, giving me a lopsided grin.

"Sounds doable," I say, hand squeezing her leg pressed against mine. She extracts a paperclipped bundle from under the pages she's already marking up and sets it across my lap.

"Anything that's wrong, circle what's incorrect and they'll have to redo it in class. And if it's the word problems on the next page and they didn't show calculations, circle the empty space where calculations should have been."

It's easy enough. There's only six pages, and they're pretty close to perfect. Marigold leans over, throwing her head back in a laugh. "Check this out," she says, holding a page up.

"If you have eight apples," I read, "and eat five of them, how many do you have left?"

Marigold reads the scrawled answer, "An upset tummy." I snort, checking the name at the top - Daisy. "She is so sassy," Marigold says, giggles punctuating her words.

A few pages later, I hold out a paper toward her, it's from one of the younger students. "Triangle, square," I read, "hexagon, and..." pausing for dramatic effect, I point to the rhombus, "a squished square."

"Geez," she says, rolling her eyes.

I work through the rest of the pages fairly quickly, and help Marigold with a second bundle. Math finished, she pulls out a larger pile of multiple choice quizzes.

"These are super boring. I've been putting them off for ages. Do you want to watch a movie or something while I suck it up and finally grade these?"

"I don't have a T.V.," I say, frowning.

"My laptop has a bunch of movies loaded up. Pick whatever you like." An ancient, thick laptop sits closed on the coffee table, a charging cord snaking over to the wall.

Easing it open, I spot a folder labeled movies right on the desktop. Marigold's nose is in her tests, and she sticks her tongue out as she starts writing a note on one. I smirk, seeing her selection of cheesy early 90's slasher thrillers and chick-flicks.

"You've got some interesting taste in movies," I say.

She wrinkles her nose, pushing her knee into my hip. "Hey, these are classics."

"Any preference?"

"Pick something you haven't seen."

I'm familiar with most of them, but haven't actually watched most, save for a few horror movies. Trying to avoid overthinking it, I pick a particularly cheerful looking romantic comedy.

Marigold hums her approval, and I can't help reaching my arm around her shoulder so she nestles against my chest. I'd watch anything if it meant she was this close.

Eventually she completes her grading and she slides down until she's laying across my lap. My hands groove through her hair, marveling at how the reddish gold waves gleam in the low afternoon light.

"We need to get dinner," she realizes as the credits are rolling. I want to stay there with her, stroking her hair and enjoying her smiles, but she needs to eat.

We're late for dinner, and everyone else seems to be sitting with relatives. Many people are already finishing their meals and cleaning up.

Luckily, Crickett hasn't put the food away yet, and we're able to heap Chinese food onto plates.

Marigold picks a quiet table on the edge of the gathering. We sit across from each other, and I miss being close, but it's nice to watch her expressions as she tries the fried rice.

"So if you had a different job from teaching, what would you do?" I ask, curious.

She takes a big bite of sesame chicken and stares into the distance while she chews. Eventually, she says, "probably something where I get to help lots of people. Like being a hairdresser or handyman. What about you?"

"Environmental lawyer," I answer without thinking. I used to imagine life among humans, when I thought perhaps that would be my only escape. One I'm glad I was too cowardly to take. A wolf without a pack is cut off from a vital part of themselves.

"Why?"

"I'm not sure," I say. "I took a lot of classes on environmental sustainability in college. And it seems like something worth doing. If I wasn't involved in a pack, I guess."

"Interesting," she says, studying me. "Okay, new question. You win the lottery, what are you buying?"

I shrug. "I don't know."

"What about a fancy sports car?" she asks.

"I've got the car I want."

"What about something ridiculous like a lifetime supply of your favorite candy. Or a bathtub full of sprinkles."

"That sounds like *your* dream." And now I'm imagining her in a bathtub of sprinkles with whipped cream instead of bubble bath. Freaking fantastic.

"Maybe." Her giggle dances around me, infusing warmth into my skin. "But I think I'd prefer a swimming pool full of marshmallows.

"What would you buy?"

Marigold pauses, nibbling on the tines of her fork. "I would have said my own cabin. But I'm kind of enjoying staying in yours." She grins at me, and it draws out my own smile in response. "But a car would be nice. Something practical but also cute like a sunflower yellow jeep."

"I could see you in something like that," I say. It's tempting to make that vision happen, but a new car is not a gift you give to a friend. Maybe someday.

She asks more inane questions and we laugh over our answers. It's a luxury to eat together during a pack dinner. No one bothers us or even looks twice at us, or not that I notice. It feels normal, like we are a couple. For a few minutes, I can pretend.

VIII
METEORS & MAKEOVERS
MARIGOLD

Tuesday goes by in a blur of teaching and cleaning, but on Wednesday, I'm committed to babysitting Hawthorne and Crickett's brood so they have a date night - or date afternoon, since their children are so young. It's something I do every other Wednesday. Hawthorne is cool with my temporary home, so I'm left with the task of entertaining a toddler and young child in Jasper's cabin.

Oh, and I may have forgotten to tell Jasper about it.

"Ready to add the salt?" I ask Daisy, holding my breath as she wobbles the measuring cup on the edge of the bowl.

Jasper steps through the front door and stops short, blinking at the young guests we have. "Hey guys, what's going on?"

Daisy spills the cup of salt half in the bowl and half over my hand and across the counter.

Smiling maybe a little too wide, I say, "I'm babysitting. Want to help make some playdough?" Sighing, I sweep the salt into my palm and dump it into the bowl.

He recovers quickly, shucking off his hoodie and crouching beside Dahlia's blanket to ruffle her dark curls before joining us in the kitchen. "It's like making cookies?"

"Easier, because you don't have to bake them." Daisy holds onto the edge of the spoon while I begin to stir in the salt.

"Cool, what's in it?" He pokes at the lumpy dough.

"Flour, salt, cream of tartar, water, and whatever we use to make it smell good or add color," I quote from memory. It's not my first time making playdough.

To my horror, Jasper pinches a blob of dough from the bowl and pops it into his mouth. His eyes go wide and with a quick jolt, he spits the dough into the sink.

"It's pretty salty," I say apologetically.

Turning back with a strained smile, he says, "I know that now."

Daisy snorts between laughs. Once she's recovered, she narrows her eyes at Jasper. "You can add the flavor if you want, normally it's my job. You can borrow it if you really want."

"Really? What flavor are we making this delicious dough?" he says, playing along. My hands tighten on the bowl, resisting the urge to hug him. He doesn't have to help entertain her.

"Pumpkin spice!" Daisy blurts.

Frowning, I look between her and Jasper. "But it's spring time. Pumpkin spice is for fall."

"So?" Daisy says, little hands going to her hips.

Jasper smirks and our eyes meet, exasperation mingled with amusement. "What makes up pumpkin spice? Because I definitely don't have any pumpkin." He opens the spice cabinet. I'm concerned how old most of those seasonings are because they probably came with the cabin, but it won't matter for playdough.

Clicking my nails on the bowl, I try to recall. "Cinnamon for sure."

"Done," Jasper says, plunking the little glass jar down.

"Nutmeg and allspice?" I guess. He has nutmeg but not allspice. "Oh, and ginger, of course."

"And again, we have success. Three out of the four isn't too bad."

Daisy nods enthusiastically. She reaches for the ginger. Jasper takes the bowl while she sprinkles the pungent spice over the dough. They make a great team, so I go to Dahlia and lift her onto my hip so she can watch her sister pour an ungodly amount of cinnamon into the dough.

"Watch it with the cinnamon. That can bother your skin," I say. Jasper takes hold of the jar to temper Daisy's enthusiastic shaking.

I can't help but smile as Jasper struggles to mix in the spices.

"It's probably time to knead it by hand," I say.

Jasper hesitates only a second. Then he's plopping the lump onto sprinkled flour and folding it over with his palms. Watching his hands work is mesmerizing.

"Have you kneaded dough before?"

He shrugs. "I may have been watching sourdough videos online. Like where they decorate them all fancy."

"Impressive," I say, my eyes following his rhythmic folding and stretching.

Baby Dahlia tugs sharply on a lock of my hair, pulling me from my stupor. Wincing, I extract my hair and begin bouncing on the balls of my feet to keep her happy. She's getting too big for this.

"How does that look?" Jasper asks, his expression vulnerable.

"Great. Can you toss it in that plastic bag?" He complies and zips the edge closed. I grasp the bowl and take it to the sink with my free hand.

"Why don't you guys go play and I'll clean up," Jasper suggests. But Daisy growls her disagreement and seizes his hand.

"Go," I say. "I've got this, and you could do with some fun." He takes Dahlia from me and follows Daisy. She drags him toward the bathroom. While I wipe down the counter, Daisy brushes his pale hair and begins to wrap tiny rubber bands around tufts of it.

When Jasper walks out again, I can hardly breathe for the laughter shaking my entire body.

"Glad you're amused," he growls.

"You're so pretty," Daisy coos, her hands holding Dahlia's to help her sister bumble across the wood floor.

Jasper comes up behind me, hands hugging my waist. "Don't you think I'm pretty too?"

"Very much," I say, twisting to face him. Fingers linked behind his neck, I admire Daisy's styling. "And you smell amazing," I say, leaning closer to smell the sprinkle of nutmeg and ginger across his chest.

"Careful," he rumbles. My heart jumps into my throat at the sly smirk on his handsome face.

Feeling flustered, I turn back to the girls. "You guys want to paint? We've got to go outside, and we need to put on extra shirts." Daisy claps and Dahlia squeals. I can feel Jasper's eyes on me, but he stays quiet.

It doesn't take long to outfit the girls with smocks and fingerpaints. I lay a stretch of butcher paper across the ground. The girls happily draw rainbow lines and dots across the paper.

Exhausted, I drop into the closest hammock. I don't mean for my eyes to close, but I can monitor them with my inhuman hearing.

"Oh, this looks good," Jasper says. Sitting up, I look from him to the girls. My mouth falls open. The girls have moved from their canvas to the exterior wall of the cabin. So much for monitoring them.

"I'm so sorry," I stutter, rushing to grab their hands and peel them away from their defacement. "Daisy, you know better."

"I was serious, I think it looks great," Jasper says, chuckling.

Hawthorne and Crickett pick that moment to arrive as I'm still staring at the girls' artwork. Leaning in, I hiss, "I'll clean this up." We rush back to the porch to present the girls to their parents, tugging their smocks off as we go.

"We painted the house!" Daisy blurts, looking proud. Crickett's mouth tightens into a concerned frown.

"Don't worry about it. Just a little finger paint. It washes off easily," I assure her.

"I want my playdough!" Daisy whines.

Crouching, I look into her eyes. "We talked about how that playdough is for the classroom. You can play with it tomorrow with your friends. Remember?"

"Oh, right," she says. Hawthorne rolls his eyes at his daughter's antics and leads his little family away.

"Thank you, Marigold. You are the best!" Crickett hollers over her shoulder.

Once they're gone, I unfurl the hose and begin to spray the log siding. The paint runs down, making puddles swirling with pink and blue. As I'm stepping closer to concentrate on a particularly stubborn area, the snap of a branch startles me. Swinging toward the noise, the hose comes with me.

The water is still pressurized from my hold on the hose, and the spray soaks Jasper from chest to knees in a split second.

His surprised expression is so cute and my nerves so frayed, that I can't help but burst into a fit of giggles. For a moment, he blinks at me, mouth slightly open. The hose sprays into the dirt at my feet.

"I'm so sorry," I say, fighting back another fit of giggles. Spell broken, he stalks forward, reaching for the hose in my hands, but I twist away.

"Marigold, give that to me," he says, his low voice caressing my skin. He sounds far too calm for someone scrambling to take something out of my grasp.

"No way!" I say, backing up a few steps and grinning like a maniac. But Jasper is incredibly quick, and when he darts forward, I cannot react in time. His arms clamp around mine, and in the struggle, water shoots straight up and covers us like rain.

"Happy now?" he asks, water dripping off his nose and eyelashes.

"Yeah, I am," I snicker, trudging over to turn off the hose he's now pointing at the ground.

We stretch out on the wooden floor of the patio, letting ourselves dry before we traipse across the cabin's wood floors.

Stretching my neck to look at Jasper, I say, "I forgot to ask, how goes the Alpha Counsel prep?"

"Fine. We spent ages going over everyone we know from each pack that might be there. And I know a lot of them, but it's still a lot of new names to learn."

He looks up at the beams above us, the fading evening light haloing his profile. He's breathtaking.

"So your parents will be there," I say quietly, "And maybe your sister?"

"Maybe. I'm not sure how much they're training her, since she's their heir now and everything. They won't bring her if she isn't ready to make a good showing."

"Have you talked to her at all?"

He turns his head, aqua eyes meeting mine. "The two times I texted her, she sent back a picture of her middle finger."

"That gets the point across, I guess."

His lips curl in amusement.

"Would you try to talk to her if she comes?"

"If I can. But I doubt I'll get a chance."

"Are you okay with that?" I probe, my tone gentle.

He sighs, turning his head back and staring at the ceiling. "No, but it's her choice. It's a two way street. And to be realistic, she'd probably try to gut me given the chance."

"That serious?" I ask, my brows furrowing.

"That's just a Tuesday for Ember," he says, fondness in his voice.

"How did you turn out so normal?" I joke.

He sits up, one eyebrow raised in challenge. "Maybe I'm not that normal, after all."

"Normal is overrated," I mutter, climbing to my feet. The dripping has mostly stopped, and I'm ready for a fresh set of clothes.

JASPER

The week slips by, a blur of planning and training drills. Slate takes his anxiety out on all of us during training, and Fisher is ecstatic to let us sweat.

Friday is the worst. Setting up tables and chairs on a remote corner of our territory is not a pleasant task. But the entire team pulls together and we get the job done. Once it's finished, I'm covered in dirt and sweat. We hike back as humans. Everyone is getting hungry and hungry wolves are usually grumpy.

Brushing my hands together, I cross the clearing back toward home. If I hurry, I should have enough time to shower before dinner.

Marigold's voice filters around the training building, and I can't help but detour. Coming around the back of the building, my feet slow when I see her. Her glorious hair is pulled into a high ponytail and her hands grip a crossbow. She looks like a warrior goddess.

Cassia, Fern, and Hazel watch her, giving out tips and encouragement. Cassia and Fern are both accomplished fighters, and Hazel has taken to the training like she's been here her entire life. I couldn't have put together a better group for Marigold to train with.

With a vicious grin, Marigold levels the barrel of the crossbow at the plywood target. Narrowing her eyes, she fires. The arrow embeds dead center. Pride wells in my chest.

She resets and shoots again, another perfect shot. After the third time, I realize she's more than proficient, she's incredible with a crossbow. It's wildly sexy and terrifying at the same time.

Cassia, Fern, and Hazel all whoop and cheer her on, covering up the sounds of my approach.

Marigold hops on the balls of her feet, looking pleased with herself. As she turns toward her friends, she catches sight of me. The last thing I want is to interrupt her training, so I simply raise an eyebrow and smirk.

As I'm turning away, Fern spots me. "Jasper, come see if you can challenge Marigold. None of the rest of us can best her."

Marigold's smile is apologetic. "He spent the whole day setting up for the counsel tomorrow. I'm sure he doesn't want to."

"Are you scared to go up against me?" I dare.

"You're going to regret that," Hazel says with a dark laugh.

Marigold loads the crossbow and hands it over. "Are you familiar with this style?"

"Yeah, it looks about the same," I murmur, brushing her hand with mine before she steps back, looking expectant.

With a slow breath, I level the muzzle at the target, already a pincushion for her bolts. One more breath, focus on steadying my hands, and I shoot.

It hits the target on the outside edge. But at least it doesn't fly off into the trees.

"That was really good," Marigold says. If I didn't know her so well, I wouldn't catch the patronizing undertones.

"Thank you," I say, stepping closer than necessary to hand the weapon back. She reloads and with practiced motions, shoots a bolt within a millimeter of mine.

"Show off," I huff. She grins, warmth and sunshine flooding my blood, and the embarrassment is entirely worth it.

"Go relax. I'll stop by before it's time for dinner," she says quietly. The sudden urge to kiss her, maybe on the forehead, pushes me a half-step forward before I catch myself.

She's already passing the crossbow off to Hazel and giving her tips as I stiffly walk away.

After my shower, I come out of my bedroom in clean clothes with my hair still damp. Marigold sits on the sofa with her feet tucked up. It looks like she's waiting for me.

"You look kinda tired," she says sweetly.

Shrugging, I plop down next to her. "Thanks," I say with a sarcastic smirk. "Though I can't say the same about you. Beautiful as always."

Her smile turns shy. "Hazel invited us to hang out after dinner."

"Campfire?"

"No, apparently there's some meteor shower. I guess they usually watch it together, but she thought we might like to join them." Reading between the lines - no Cedar or Onyx. Just the two of us hanging out with another couple.

"I like the sound of that. But do you want to?" I ask cautiously.

"Yeah, it sounds fun. We should bring a couple of blankets though." She pops up and takes my hand, pulling me toward dinner.

I don't let go of her hand until the trees part to reveal the rest of our pack chattering away.

Plate full, I settle at our group's favorite table. Benches creak as friends join us, eating and laughing. The stories and jokes wash over me. I'm happy to soak up the warm familiarity. The light slowly fades and my thoughts center around the girl beside me and our plans for what sounds suspiciously like a double date.

MARIGOLD

"This is the Lyrid meteor shower. It'll be better the later it gets, heading toward morning. But I know tomorrow is a big day, so I didn't want to keep us up too late," Hazel says, squeezing Slate's hand.

We hike toward the cliffside, enjoying the sounds of the woods after dark. Bugs chirp and little nocturnal animals rustle as they start their days.

Jasper walks beside me, glancing over every few steps. My heart jolts as his hand brushes against mine. It must be a mistake. But when it happens again, like electricity zinging through me, I start to doubt.

Instead of making a fool of myself, I wrap my arm around his bicep. It allows me to touch him and eliminates the awkward brush of our hands. This is how friends walk together. Right?

From the smug look on his face, I'm not so sure.

The trees open up to a million stars. I've lived here my entire life, but it still fills me with a sense of wonder.

The sounds of the river below are louder in the night. Without speaking, the boys spread the blankets out a few feet away from each other and we all settle.

I should not feel this nervous, but my heart races as I unfold our second blanket and drape it over our legs. Already the air is turning icy, but that isn't what causes me to shiver. It's the heavy silence and the heat of the man next to me.

Jasper misreads my shiver and pulls me down against his side so his arm cushions my head. His other hand draws the blanket up to cover all of me. Luckily, Hazel and Slate are too wrapped up in each other to pay us any attention. It's still silent, but now the blood rushing in my ears drowns out even the sounds of the water.

"So we're looking for shooting stars coming from the south and we should get to see one every five minutes or so. But maybe less because the moon is fairly full." Hazel's voice cuts through my haze.

The moon drenches the sky around it, washing out the stars' lesser light. It's almost entirely full, and I know that phase means our instinctual urges are stronger. That must be what's happening, because the heat of Jasper's body is burning me, branding my soul.

"You need to relax," he whispers, turning so his lips brush the shell of my ear. Flinching, I stiffen further. "What's wrong?"

Deep breath, slow exhale. "I guess I'm feeling jumpy," I whisper back.

Jasper nods, a hardly perceptible motion. Instead of letting it go, he runs his free hand down my arm and takes my hand. His thumb digs into the pressure point between my thumb and index finger and it takes all my self-control to keep my gasp silent. Releasing, he massages my palm until I relax into him.

Limply, I offer my other hand to him, and he repeats the process. He'd probably start on my shoulders too, but we are distracted by the first shooting star streaking across the sky. It fades as quickly as it started. I can't help but let out an excited squeak.

Jasper's head turns again, his breath warm on my cheek. "You're adorable."

"Like in an annoying way?" I bat my eyelashes at him. He chuckles and turns back to the glittering sky.

His answer comes after a long delay, so quiet I almost miss it. "Like perfection."

He rests his hand across my stomach, right above my belly button. It's under the blanket, so our friends can't see how his fingers spread out to touch more of me over my cotton shirt.

Another light catches my attention, followed by another star close behind it. As more meteors cross the sky, the majesty of it captures me. I can't look away, although I am always painfully aware of Jasper beside me. My hands have moved to his bicep, gripping him like he's my emotional support childhood blankie. His muscles ripple as his thumb strokes down my midriff. The motions are lazy, as if he isn't aware of what he is doing.

It seems cheap to interrupt the majesty of stars streaking across the sky, and I can barely keep my breath even, so I don't even attempt speech. Slowly, I melt against him and forget everything but the stars above and his touch.

Jasper wakes me up with a soft touch to my cheek. "Marigold, we better get home. Tomorrow is a big day."

He tucks one of the blankets around me as we walk back, keeping his hands on my waist. Hazel and Slate say their goodbyes and head eastward.

In our cozy cabin, Jasper leads me to his bedroom, takes off my shoes, and trades my blanket for the comforter. I don't even remember him climbing in beside me. My sleep is dreamless.

IX
ALPHAS & ANXIETY

JASPER

The Alpha Counsel meets along our northern border which serves as a central point between Ironcrest and Granite Ridge. Only the Valley Pack will have to travel far, but Cashel and his team are always welcome in our territory.

The day is clear and the weather mild. The perfect setting for a meeting of the most powerful wolves in the region.

Cashel arrives early, greeting Heath with a hug. Heath's hand stays on his friend's shoulder as they part. "It's good to see you."

"You as well." Cashel is a stocky man with dark skin and curly hair. "How are you feeling about this meeting? What are we concerned about?"

Heath doesn't hesitate. "Zephyr met with us recently and blamed all of last fall's events on Ferris."

Cashel nods, rubbing his jaw. "Any theories on what's going on between Ironcrest and Granite Ridge?"

"We will see if they have any conflict today," Heath answers darkly.

The Valley Pack's Alpha looks to me. "Jasper, look at you in your new pack."

I shuffle my feet, forcing a polite smile.

"Jasper has settled in well. He orchestrated today's event, actually. I'm sure you won't be surprised to hear that the other packs took quite a few letters to convince them to participate," Heath says. The pride in his voice warms me. My weeks of effort did not go unnoticed.

"Let's see how it goes," Cashel says, his voice thick with apprehension I find mirrored in my grim smile. Determination and dread swirl in my chest.

Slate seizes the Alpha's attention and I relax, watching as Cashel takes Hazel's hand and introduces her to the Valley Pack Beta, Malachite. He looks like a younger version of his father.

Hawthorne wanders over after exchanging pleasantries with Zinnia, Cashel's third. She's a slim woman with her dark hair shaved into a pixie cut. His expression shifts from amused to concerned as he looks me up and down. "You doing okay?"

"Honestly?" I ask. He nods. "I feel like I'm going to throw up."

Clearing his throat, Hawthorne steps closer, his eyes commanding my attention. "It's going to be fine. We're prepared for this. You, more so than anyone else. Trust yourself."

"I'm not sure I see how a meeting with Ferris is going to go well."

"Ah." Hawthorne tips his chin down to meet my gaze. "Your father is outnumbered and outmatched. He'll be forced to play nice."

"That's what I'm afraid of," I admit. "He's not going to take kindly to the pressure." He squeezes my shoulder reassuringly.

Sounds of wolves drift through the trees, followed by rustling and then footsteps. My fists clench as the Granite Ridge Pack comes into view. It's a bigger group than I expected. My parents have brought more than a handful of guards, including Aries, a great brute with long black hair, and Flint, a wiry and pocked wolf who I've wanted to disembowel since childhood.

Ferris wears his favorite leather jacket over designer jeans. He'll take any chance to show status or wealth. Beside him, Sienna wears a lacy red camisole and black leather pants. For someone who ran through the woods and then shifted from wolf to human, she looks ridiculously glamorous. Her eyes flicker to me, though she shows no emotion. My father is stone with not a single twitch in my direction.

"Ferris." Heath greets him, noticeably cold in comparison to how he greeted Cashel.

"Heath," my father answers, a grim smile on his face. Heath doesn't greet Sienna, and she raises her nose in the air, clearly offended, but my dad does nothing to appease her. Theoretically, they should be equals, but he's never given her that respect in these types of official meetings.

Slate stands beside Heath, his arm tight around Hazel's waist. Her claim mark scars are highlighted by the wide-neck top she wears. Sienna's lip curls as she regards them.

To her credit, Hazel's political smile never wavers, but I can sense her anger through the pack bond. Slate's as well. It's understandable. Sienna isn't only my mother, she's Slate's mother too, though we have different fathers. She left when he was an infant, and if that wasn't enough reason for his disdain, she's had it out for Hazel since she arrived last year. Slate may not care about Sienna's lack of a role in his life, but any offense against his mate is unforgivable in his eyes.

Heath breaks the tension. "Ferris, you remember my heirs, my niece Hazel and her mate, Slate."

"So nice of you to bring them," Ferris replies cooly.

Sienna gives a cat-like smile. "Unfortunately, our Ember had to stay home, but I would like to introduce you to Hawk."

A slender young man steps forward. His reddish hair is brushed back into a bun and freckles cover his skin. "He joined us from the Alpine Pack, son of the Alpha. He is Ember's Intended."

Heath nods curtly. "Congratulations."

"Thank you," Hawk says, his voice rough, like he doesn't speak often. His posture squares off, like he is striking a practiced pose to hide discomfort. I can't help but study him. I've never met anyone from the large pack a day's drive north of us.

My sister has an Intended, a mate for someone not yet an adult. She won't turn eighteen for a few more months. Did she pick this wolf, or did our mother arrange it? Does she even like him? Nausea churns my stomach. It's not the kind of news I expected, and it shouldn't bother me as much as it does.

Cashel shakes Ferris's hand and Hawk's, sharing his own congratulations.

Finally, Ironcrest arrives. Zephyr strides forward, flanked by his Beta, a fierce woman named Beryl, and his Gamma, Dell. A collection of guards follows silently.

His cold gaze sweeping the group, Zephyr says, "No Nyx, I see."

Heath shakes his head. "No, she couldn't be persuaded."

"Typical." Zephyr shakes hands with each of the other Alphas.

The leaders settle around the table. Between Alphas, Heirs, and Betas, all seats are full. I stand beside Hawthorne, keeping my posture rigid and my eyes on our enemies.

Aries and Flint stand opposite us, glowering from the other side of the table. Despite six months apart, their hatred of me burns bright.

"I'd like to thank all of you for making the trip and contributing to the first Alpha Counsel in eight years." Heath starts, his deep voice commanding attention. "Preceding this counsel, Ironcrest met with us. Zephyr, would you like to share what we've discussed?"

I'm not the only one watching Ferris and Sienna for their reaction.

Zephyr threads his fingers behind his short hair and leans back. "Yes, I let the Bracken Creek Pack know that I recently expelled several wolves after discovering they contributed to the abduction of the Bracken Creek heir last fall."

The air crackles with tension. I suspect everyone is thinking the same thing. Beryl's eyes are on Ferris, making her thoughts perfectly clear.

"I don't think we have to address those dramatics again," Sienna says, her smile thinning.

"It wasn't discussed originally, so I'm not sure why you are saying 'again'," Slate says, his words like ice.

Cashel sits forward. "Considering it was a major conflict between two of the four packs represented here, I think it should be addressed."

Ferris's arrogance soaks into his every word. "Considering our valid claim on the female was challenged and you schemed to take one of my children from my pack, I think the matter is best left in the past."

My nails dig into my palms, but I give no other outward sign of my pounding heart or the blood rushing in my ears.

"Our challenge was more than you deserved when you had committed a crime against us," Hazel says. Zephyr smirks.

"Peace." Heath holds up a hand. "My pack is willing to move past the incident, as long as Granite Ridge upholds the peace measures we are working to pass here today. But we will not be forgiving again." Sienna scoffs. From Slate's tense posture, I can tell he is struggling to accept our Alpha's words. But Heath has made his decision. "Before we discuss them, does anyone else have any other grievances?"

"I do," Zephyr says, "Ironcrest has been having some issues with the Raven Pack crossing our borders."

Malachite leans his forearms on the table, mimicking his father's pose. "That's a serious accusation."

"Unfortunately, it's true. So far it seems to be just scouts. I believe they're testing our security for weaknesses. A condition of our participation is support in addressing this problem."

"Noted. What support are you requesting?" Heath says.

"I simply need to get in touch with Nyx. She's surprisingly difficult to reach."

"Not a problem." Heath turns to the other two Alphas.

"Granite Ridge has no grievances," Ferris says, his face lacking its typical intensity. It makes the hair on my arms stand up.

"Neither does the Valley Pack," Cashel confirms.

"Excellent," Heath says, though his tone is flat. "Then we can proceed to some of the measures we'd like to propose."

"Let's hear it," Zephyr says.

"I think it's time we renewed our commitment to not take wolves from each other's pack, particularly against their will."

"Agreed," Cashel says. Zephyr nods.

Ferris smirks - actually smirks. "Granite Ridge agrees." As if they hadn't actively been taking wolves captive. My teeth grind together hard enough my jaw clicks.

"Secondly, we feel it would be wise if all Alphas maintain a phone line where we can contact each other."

"I'm not going to carry around a cell phone so you can call me whenever you want," Zephyr drawls.

"I'm sure your Gamma could handle it," Cashel says, his smile not reaching his eyes.

"We will see about it," Ferris says.

"Fine." Zephyr rolls his eyes.

"Lastly, in addition to a regular Alpha Counsel, I recommend our representatives, such as our Gammas and their apprentices, begin to meet regularly with the goal of greater pack cooperation."

"How regularly are you thinking?" Cashel asks.

Ferris looks away as if the table isn't worthy of his attention, "Waste of time."

"Would you prefer we meet without you?" Zephyr says with a sneer. Ferris crosses his arms and sits back.

"How about bi-monthly? Or quarterly," Heath suggests.

"Quarterly sounds good to me," Zephyr says.

"Quarterly, it is." Cashel folds his hands.

"In the future, we should consider inter-pack gatherings," Heath suggests, "but for now, our Gammas can meet regularly and we can reconvene the Counsel in six months."

Ferris frowns. "The Counsel meets annually."

"In the past, the bonds between packs were stronger. Perhaps if we had maintained those relationships with regular meetings, we could have avoided some of the conflicts of recent years."

Cashel nods. If I remember my history, Zephyr became an Alpha only five years ago when he challenged for his position.

Nyx is younger as well, but the remaining three packs were led by the same Alphas for much longer. They know the history because much of it was caused by their hands.

"Anything else?" Ferris asks.

"Do *you* have anything else?" Cashel asks him. Ferris scowls at him.

"I'm sure you're all eager to get home. I have no more agenda items," Heath says.

They make small talk for a few more minutes, though it's obvious Ferris believes he is above such things. Zephyr's words feel insincere and make my skin prickle. Cashel and Heath make little effort to continue the conversation, and soon everyone is looking to their teams.

Ferris stands, Sienna rising gracefully after him. Without a word, they walk away, falling into a practiced formation.

Hawk walks behind Sienna, in the place I would have occupied. As their forms retreat, my lungs relax and I can draw a full breath again.

"I'll be off too," Zephyr announces, snapping his fingers to call his wolves forward.

Finally it was just our team and the Valley Pack's representatives. "Come sit down," orders Heath.

Hawthorne takes the empty seat on Heath's other side, and I join him. Dell sits across from me.

"Would you like to stay and debrief, my friend?" Heath asks Cashel with a genuine smile.

"As I said earlier, what is going on with those two?" Cashel says, gesturing toward the empty seats across from him.

Slate rests his forehead in his palm, elbow propped on the table. "The thing that concerns me the most is how quiet Sienna was."

Exhaling harshly, I look up to meet Slate's gaze. "And the fact Ferris was so calm. Aside from that outrageous version of events he spewed, he went along with everything peacefully."

Cashel's Gamma, Dell, tips his chair back. "What about Zephyr's accusations about Nyx?"

"That doesn't sound like Nyx. She doesn't like to leave her community. Why would she invade Ironcrest territory? She has more land than she needs already," Dell says.

Hawthorne nods. "We'll talk to her and see what's really going on."

"Sounds good. Keep me updated." Cashel stands. "Have a good afternoon, friends."

As we folded up chairs and prepare to leave, Slate finds me and says, "We agree that was suspicious as fuck right?"

"Yeah, but I have no idea what they're playing at."

He shakes his head, walking back to Hazel and kissing her cheek while she chats with Heath. Her warm smile seems to soothe him, reminding me that I have Marigold at home, and I'd like nothing more than to go wrap my arms around her and kiss her, if she'd let me.

X
BREAKFAST &
BORDER DISPUTES

MARIGOLD

All the knots came back to my fingers easily, and in the last two days I've made a handful of plant hangers. Jasper has a collection of little houseplants in his bedroom, but the light is much better in the living room.

Humming to myself, I screw hooks into the wood planked ceiling and link the loops up. Carefully, I nestle the pots into each, leaving a line of hanging plants along the sunniest window. They should grow much faster now.

I step back and smile. It looks great. What else can I do?

Digging around, I find a pair of sunflower-print throw pillows in the back of the linen closet. They look perfect on the sofa.

Dishes washed, my bed re-made (though I have no intention of returning to it), and books organized by color, I finally sprawl across the sofa and enjoy the late afternoon sunlight pouring in, filtered by the plants.

"That looks great," Jasper says, stepping in. He holds two dinner plates in his hands. "Hungry?"

I smile contentedly up at him, accepting my plate. His smile is warm, but the tightness around his eyes betrays his worry.

"I hope you don't mind, I installed the decor you requested as payment," I say. Jasper rotates one of the plants to inspect the macrame encircling the pot.

"You decided on plant hangers instead of a big wall piece?" he asks.

"You can't afford a big wall hanging from me," I say. Sitting up, I reach for his hand and pull him down beside me. His arm goes around my waist automatically and my stomach flips. There's something in his touch, the way his fingers dig into my skin, that is more possessive than normal. Either he's more upset than I realized, or we've taken our relationship to a new level.

"How was the counsel?" I ask, taking a bite of the lasagna. It's delicious.

He takes a few bites of his dinner before he shares, "Overall, it went well. But, I don't know, Ironcrest and Granite Ridge were acting strange."

I grip the top of his leg, a few inches above the knee. "What do you mean?"

He sighs, sinking back into the cushion and pulling me closer with the motion. Concern over the counsel isn't enough to keep me from losing myself in the comforting cocoon of his arms.

Eventually, Jasper pulls me out of my reverie. "Well, my parents were really quiet. Didn't argue at all when Heath brought up an agreement to not steal wolves from other packs."

"That's always been against our rules," I say.

"That hasn't exactly stopped them in the past." His grip around me tightens.

"They won't get away with it again."

I can feel the expansion of his chest as he takes a slow, deep breath. "And then Zephyr was saying that Nyx is invading their boundaries. Wants sanctions against her. So we agreed to attempt to arrange communications between them."

Pulling back, I frown. "Nyx wouldn't do something like that."

"That's what I thought."

"Why would they say that?" I twist to face him, pulling my legs up to sit crosslegged. Our dinner plates sit forgotten on the coffee table.

He rubs at his jaw, thinking. "What if something has changed with Nyx's leadership?"

"I can ask my dad," I say. From the blank look on Jasper's face, I realize he doesn't know, "My mom was from the Raven Pack. My grandparents live there."

His eyebrows shoot up. "Really. You're the connection Heath mentioned." My shoulders tense in a quick shrug.

"Yeah, we visit them maybe twice a year. The Raven Pack is tiny. They can't keep watch over all that land effectively. I've always wondered why Ironcrest or Granite Ridge don't try and buy some of that acreage."

He stares at me.

"What?"

"That's it," he says. I can see thoughts flying behind his eyes.

"What's it?" I prod when he falls silent.

"That's what Zephyr wants. If he says Nyx is the aggressor, he can set them up to take her territory without consequences. Or at least without full consequences. He has an excuse."

Winding a lock of hair through my fingers, I consider his theory. Logically, it makes sense. But the idea that a pack would attack another pack unprovoked is barbaric. Shifters don't go to war without a serious reason.

"Are you going to tell Heath about your idea?" I ask.

"Definitely." He chews his lip. "I'll see him in the morning. That'll give me time to think it through."

"Do you think Granite Ridge is in on it?"

"That's the thing, I can't tell. Ferris knows now that the other packs know what they did to Hazel. He should be defensive or at least angry. He was so calm, it felt unnatural to me. And Sienna hardly said a word." His voice begins to wobble. Sensing his need for support, I scoot closer.

"You'll figure it out."

"I can't shake this feeling they're after me. Or after Slate and Hazel. I'm not sure. It's like they're so carefully not looking our way, the absence of any snide remarks or threats feels wrong. Sneaky, I guess."

There's real fear in his eyes. Cautiously, I reach out and brush his mussed hair behind his ear. "They can't do anything. We won't let them. And we have allies to help if they really do throw everything they've got at us."

He has no answer and instead studies the floor, his worry a heavy thing clinging to him. The droop of his shoulders, the tightness around his mouth. I can't stand it.

"Hey!" I say, squeezing him tighter. "No more of this. We are a badass pack, and we have the most incredible leaders protecting us, including you. And I know you'll keep us safe."

Remembering our deal from a week prior, my hands find their way to his shoulders and I dig in, thumbs kneading his muscles. He lets out a long exhale and his eyes close. I urge him to turn away from me, giving me more access to his back

Working my way down, the heels of my hands press along the line of muscle on either side of his spine. His head falls forward. The tension starts to ease once I begin long strokes down the line of his shoulder blades.

"Better?" I ask.

He turns those soulful eyes on me and I can't breathe. I couldn't move if I wanted to. The depth of adoration mingling with sadness paralyzes me.

"I don't deserve you," he murmurs, twisting toward me. My hands glide from his shoulders up to hook around his neck. His blonde hair slips over my fingers.

Feeling dizzy, I suck in a ragged breath, trying to keep my head. But his hands are on my hips, pulling me into his lap.

Suddenly the only thing I want in the universe is to get as close to him as physically possible. Maybe that's always been what I wanted and my walls are too brittle to stop me any longer. Our faces are inches apart, hands gripping, abdomens pressing.

"I was thinking about last week," he says, his voice vibrating through me. "And if I had known that was your first kiss, I would have done things differently."

"I…" I have no idea how to respond to that.

He keeps one hand on the small of my back, but the other skims my jaw. His skin might be flames, the way it burns me, but it feels so good as his thumb strokes down the column of my throat. I can't look away. He's a cobra, toying with his prey, and I desperately want to feel his fangs.

"If you don't want me, please tell me or just walk away." His voice is hoarse, none of the soothing rich tones he usually has.

Swallowing, I press my hips forward, aligning more of our bodies together. That will have to be answer enough, because there's no way coherent words are coming out of my mouth right now.

He holds me in place, eyes searching for something. Is he deciding if *he* wants this? When I'm about to melt into a puddle in his lap, he tilts my jaw, fingers tightening around my jaw and throat. A thrill runs through me.

Pulling me to him, he uses his grip to hold me still as our lips collide.

While our first kiss was heavenly, this one feels different. It's intentional. Methodical. Sparks shimmer from every place we connect, pooling low in my core.

My lips part and his tongue tentatively teases me, coaxing my mouth open for him. It's a jolt in my gut, the lush feeling of his tongue against mine.

He overwhelms me, and I sink backwards on the sofa, his legs hemming me in. The weight of him presses me into the cushion, solid and reassuring.

We kiss over and over, firm, soft, sweet. I'm addicted and I don't want it to end. But when I slip my hands under his shirt and start to pull it upwards, he hesitates. I can feel his smile against my lips as he whispers, "This is your first kiss redo, so let's not go from zero to a hundred."

That makes me giggle, despite the fact I also want to lick him and bite him and drag him to bed. He kisses me once more, and then stands up and offers his hand.

We get ready for bed, and I step into his bedroom, feeling jittery. He pulls me against him, my head tucked under his chin.

"Better first kiss?" he asks, barely above a whisper.

Blushing, I nestle in closer. "No complaints about the first one. But I think that might have been the best kiss in the history of the universe."

"I can't disagree."

"So is that a one-time redo, or is this something we do now?" My attempt at casual fails, the lilt in my tone giving away my insecurity.

"If you like."

"So we're friends who kiss?" I ask, hoping he will demand more.

"Is that what we are?" he asks, the hesitation in his voice triggering a flash of panic that constricts my lungs.

"I think I'd like to do that again," I say carefully, looking for a reaction. "And I think it's safe to say you're basically my best friend, so at the very least…"

"If that's what you want," he says, pressing his face into my hair..

"It sounds good to me," I say. I'm too frightened he will pull away.

His heart beats through his skin against my cheek. He's anything but calm. The moment feels fragile.

Nervously, I say, "I think I like kissing you. And with how stressful everything has been, it's probably good for your stress, too." Maybe I mean it as a joke, but it just comes out breathy. All my emotions are layering and muddying my happiness. I need to shut up.

"Okay," he says, his thumb stroking my ribs.

Despite the unease churning in my gut, the shock of emotions has exhausted me, and I can't keep my eyes open. His warmth soaks into every fiber of my being, relaxing me. If this is all we have, it's enough for now. And with time, surely I can convince him he wants more.

JASPER

"Wake up! It's getting late and I miss your face," Marigold calls, breaking through my sleepy fog. Had I slept so late that I missed my morning run?

The bed is empty and a flash of disappointment needles me.

Best friends who kiss. Good for stress.

So this was an outlet for her. A safe way to explore what she likes. I'm a test dummy.

I should break this off, tell her it's real or it's nothing. But she's scared, flighty, unsure of herself. She'd choose nothing and I would lose her.

Damn it.

I drag myself out of bed and throw on fresh clothes. The house smells of butter and sugar, so I'm not surprised to find Marigold in the kitchen, polka dotted oven mitts on her hands and a tray of steaming blueberry muffins on the stovetop.

The real issue is Marigold's clothing or lack thereof. Under the vintage ruffled apron, she's wearing a pair of boxers that look like the ones I typically sleep in, slung low on her hips, along with the world's tiniest tank top. Where's the loose shirt she slept in? A mile of midriff stretches between her top and bottoms. If she takes the apron off, I may collapse where I stand.

She turns those blue-green eyes on me, and I jerk forward, trying to act passably normal despite my heart pounding.

"Good morning, Sunshine," I say, kissing her cheek. It's Sunday, a whole day to relax - once the leadership debrief is finished.

Reaching for plates in the cabinet, I startle as she swats at me. "Go sit down," she commands.

I prop my fists on my hips. "If you think you're going to serve me while I sit there and do nothing, you're damn wrong. You do everything for everyone else, but in this house, I get to take care of you." She blinks at my declaration while I grab two plates and select the biggest muffin for her. I can't help but smirk at her wide-eyed surprise as I cut open the muffins and slather them with butter.

The fridge is devoid of fruit, but at least we have milk, and I set two glasses of it on the table beside our plates, before settling in a chair and pulling her down into my lap.

"Really? I'm eating my breakfast from here?" she quips, slinging an arm around my neck.

"Yeah," I say, grinning up at her, far too pleased with myself for the little that I did. "I like you right where I can keep an eye on you."

Rolling her eyes, she takes her first bite. I'm captivated as her tongue swipes her lip to get the small crumbs.

With my free hand, I lift my breakfast and take a bite. But the hints of cleavage under that apron are wildly distracting. After my second bite nearly misses my mouth, I admit, "I think it would be easier for me to eat if you were wearing a bit more clothing."

She scowls at me. "That's ridiculous." And then, proving a point, she unties the apron and tosses it over the empty chair.

I try to keep my eyes on her face, but that lasts about half a second, before I'm hungrily surveying the way her breasts stretch the thin, black fabric, barely contained.

"Fuck," I mutter.

My fingers skim the waistband of the boxers on her hips. I can't help dipping a finger under the edge, biting back a groan when I feel nothing but smooth skin. Suddenly, I'm not hungry for breakfast. In fact, I might starve to death if I don't get my mouth on her skin..

Marigold tilts her head, her smile turning sly. "Sorry, I'd better go get dressed," she teases before popping to her feet and taking a step toward her bedroom. My hand shoots out and grabs her wrist, pulling her back into my lap. "Oh, did I get it wrong? Am I wearing too much?" She's too sassy for her own good.

The most beautiful flush stains her cheeks, spreading down her neck. I close my mouth over her inner wrist still constrained in my hand, biting the skin gently. The contented sigh slipping from her mouth is intoxicating.

She reaches for the hem of her shirt, and I band an arm across her stomach to stop her. "If you take anything off, I'll miss my meeting."

"We can't have that." She squirms against me. Rose gold hair cascades against my cheek.

"Not only the meeting. I probably wouldn't let you leave this cabin for days."

"Oh, no." She draws out the words, her voice dripping with honeyed sarcasm while her hand comes up and she slowly slides the spaghetti strap over the edge of her shoulder.

A low growl escapes me, my control slipping. "Marigold, I'm serious." I can't peel my eyes away from that stretch of bare skin from neck to shoulder and the way it dips above her clavicle.

"So am I," she whispers, temptation in her eyes.

That's all it takes.

Shoving our breakfast dishes back, I lift her onto the table. Her blue-green eyes glow from within, and those pillowy lips part in surprise. Her knees separate as I stand and press into her.

She lets out a giggle that sounds like pure light as I press a hand to the small of her back to keep her from falling back into our plates. Through the rush of need, I'm barely aware of her hands going to my neck and jaw, before she's kissing me and I'm devouring her.

Her tongue runs along my lips, urging them open. My heart stutters at the way she nips her teeth over my bottom lip for a second before delving into a deep kiss that leaves me starved for oxygen.

With a cute little snarl, her nails press into my skin, spurring me on. I break off from her mouth, kissing her jaw and then the hollow right under it.

I'd like to take my time, but it's too much of a frenzy as I'm kissing and licking along her neck, looking for a spot that will make her moan. Knowing that no one else has ever done this makes me illogically possessive.

As my tongue teases the skin right at the base of her throat, she lets out a little choked sound. I suck softly, loving the way her nails dig in and her thighs squeeze my hips. I could spend all day doing this.

"More," she whimpers.

Her hand closes over mine and drags it up to her breasts. She follows it by pulling at her tank top, but somehow I stop her. I'm not sure where the willpower comes from. "Keep your clothes on, woman," I say through clenched teeth. However, I can't help myself from running my thumb down the line of her breast, between them, and then over her nipple. The thin fabric does nothing to hide the shape of her.

She takes advantage of my fixation, pressing her own mouth to my neck. The feel of her tongue running along my throat makes me bend, pushing into her, my hand tightening over the softness of her breast. The minx responds by tipping her hips up, so I'm pushing against the warm center of her. I'm grateful in that moment for the thick black sweatpants between us, because those boxers are not enough of a barrier. She compounds it with a nibble of her teeth on my neck.

Too much.

I step back, gasping for air or anything that can calm the inferno burning me alive.

Marigold is flushed, her eyes glowing despite her pupils eating up the irises. Her chest heaves while she regains her breath, and then she throws back her head and laughs.

Dumbfounded, I stare at her. My brain struggles to restart rational thought. When she looks back at me, she says, "That was fucking amazing." All I can do is shake my head and gawk at her. "Do you really have to leave?" she asks, biting her lip as she stares boldly into my eyes.

The challenge of her tone gives me something to focus on other than the scent of her skin. Slowly, I lean in, letting my breath feather across her neck, keeping my lips a millimeter above hers. She arches, desperate to resume devouring each other, but I stay barely out of reach. "I really do."

Walking away, I have to adjust myself. Her disappointed growl follows me out of the house. Closing the door behind me, I lean back against it, heart beating frenetically.

What the hell was that? Friends that kiss, my ass. That was a full-blown seduction.

It takes all my self-control to not race back into the cabin. If that is her idea of friends with benefits, I cannot imagine her feelings about being mates. Shoving my hand through my hair, I tug at the roots aimlessly.

With great effort, I force myself away from the door. There will be time later to figure out what Marigold is thinking. I have a feeling that whatever she wants, she'll get. This woman will be my undoing.

Heath paces, making all of us terribly uncomfortable seated around the table while our Alpha stands. The emotions pulsing through the room are suffocating.

Slate rests his forehead in his hand, looking more than a little stressed. Leaning in, I ask, "Where's Hazel?"

"Running patrol," he answers quietly. "She wanted to check the Granite Ridge border this morning."

Hawthorne's hands are folded in his lap, his ankle propped up on the opposite knee. He's had a decade plus of experience over Slate and I, and it shows in how calmly he faces everything.

After what seems like hours, Heath speaks. "I've been thinking about Ferris and Zephyr's alliance. They were meeting regularly for a long time, and now Zephyr seems to have truly renounced him."

"Like he said, he could have realized it was better for his pack if he was aligned closer to us and the Valley Pack," Hawthorne offers, though he looks unconvinced.

Slate drags his hand through his long hair. "Do we think it's a farce?"

Heath sinks into a chair, opposite Slate. "That's my intuition, yes."

"That would explain Ferris's lack of reaction. Not protesting our statements, not trying to place blame on anyone else," I say.

"But why?" Slate asks. "What are they playing at?"

Gripping the edge of the table, I swallow and share my theory. "My mind keeps going to the Raven Pack. It seems unlikely that Nyx has been aggressive toward Ironcrest."

"I agree," Hawthorne says, "I asked Elm last night, and he feels the same. He is contacting his relatives there for us."

"Thank you," Heath says. "So what about the Raven Pack, Jasper?"

I exhale stiffly. "If Zephyr paints Nyx as the aggressor, he has grounds to retaliate. And who knows how far that retaliation could go."

The entire room goes still. Slate's dark forest eyes connect with mine, his gaze intense.

"He wants to take over the Raven Pack," Heath concludes.

Hawthorne curses. "Do we think Granite Ridge supports the plan? Maybe they are working together."

"That would explain their show of standing apart, so no one would suspect their alliance in the matter," Hawthorne muses.

"Diffusing suspicion," I conclude.

"We need to talk with Nyx," Heath says.

Slate sighs. "If she'll see us."

"We'll head up there if we have to," Heath answers.

Hawthorne pinches the bridge of his nose. "That will be an uphill battle."

"Hopefully Marigold's grandparent's come through for us, then," I mutter without thinking. Slate glances at me briefly as I say Marigold's name. Clearing my throat, I say, "We need to watch those cameras we installed, and I think we should consider drones."

"Drones?" Hawthorne echoes, his eyebrows rising. Heath's mouth turns downwards, but he looks to Slate.

"If we have any evidence to support our suspicions, it's more than warranted. But ideally, Nyx would agree and we could stay on her side of the border to block anything from happening," Slate says.

Hawthorne nods. "We really need to talk to her. I'll see what else I can do."

Heath looks to Slate. "Set up a special patrol to run the borders along Granite Ridge, Raven, and Ironcrest." The Beta nods. "Jasper, send me the information on drones. Cost, how long it'll take to get them up and running, all of that."

"Yes, Alpha."

"I'm going to call Cashel and see what he thinks. Let's check back in the morning, or come find me sooner if you have anything notable."

With that, we are dismissed. Slate trails after Heath, and Hawthorne claps me on the back as we head toward the door. "That's clever thinking. I hope you're wrong, but I suspect you aren't."

"Thank you, me too," I say grimly. We walk together toward the training building, but as he steps through the metal door, I turn south toward my cabin and the gorgeous girl waiting inside.

XI
PICKLES &
BRAKE PEDALS
MARIGOLD

I've barely finished cleaning the kitchen when Jasper arrives home from his meeting.

"What have you been doing?"

I spin and take a step back, pressing my back into the edge of the kitchen counter.

"Did you seriously clean while I was gone?"

I scowl at him. "What did you expect? That I'd be lying in bed pining after you the entire time you're gone?"

He's all tension and bright aqua eyes as he closes the distance between us, wasting no time as his mouth presses to the spot on my neck that makes me shiver.

"Is this supposed to be a reward or punishment?" I ask, breathy.

Jasper growls, scraping my skin with his teeth. "It's a hello. If I was rewarding or punishing you, you'd know it." I could melt into a puddle in the middle of the kitchen from the heat in his eyes.

"Did the meeting go well?" I ask, the words spread out as my brain turns to sludge.

He halts his work and leans back to look me in the eyes. The glow of them shows how turned on he is, and suddenly I'm doubting if we will do anything else besides ravage each other today. That would be absolutely fine with me.

"They agreed with my assessment. We're putting together a plan. Everything is going to be fine."

Relief washes through me, relaxing my muscles and giving way to a burning desire to touch every bit of him that I can. With the stress lifted, I can keep him all to myself without any guilt. At least for a few hours.

"So what do you want to do today?" I ask, hoping he says stay in bed.

"I'd like to take you on a date," he says.

"Wow," I say, my grin widening until my cheeks hurt. "What's the plan?"

"You'll find out. Nothing too crazy, but I think we'll have fun," he answers.

Resisting the urge to squeal, I kiss his cheek and head toward my bedroom to put on real clothes. "But we have to be back in time for dinner. I invited everyone over for a game night. I hope you don't mind," I say over my shoulder.

His eyes go wide. "You did?"

"Um, yeah. They all know about our living situation now, so why not? I can cancel if you like or ask Hazel to host."

A slow smile breaks out across his face. "No, it sounds great. Just unexpected."

After some deliberation, I pick a yellow sundress with tiny white daisies all over it. It might clash with my hair, but I don't care. The dress makes me happy, and Jasper must like it too because his lips part silently when I walk out of the bedroom.

He's wearing jeans for once, though they are black like most of his clothing, paired with a black Henley. It might be casual, but damn if he doesn't look scrumptious.

It's a quick walk to the parking lot, and we don't see any of our packmates.

Jasper's car is a sleek and sporty SUV. Black of course. It's shorter than the trucks the pack owns, and somehow much fancier. He opens the door for me and I slide onto the leather bucket seat.

"Wow, that's a lot of buttons," I mutter as Jasper settles into the driver's seat and pushes another button to start the car. The steering wheel has a little shield in the center with a tiny stallion. I have no idea what brand it signifies.

He grins at me, throwing the car into reverse and smoothly pulling onto the winding road to take us to town.

"This is a nice car," I say, peering at the central flat-screen display. Jasper hums, smiling as I continue, "Do you like it better than the one you had to leave behind?"

He shrugs. "It's a newer model of the same thing. I like what I like."

"Oh, cool," I say. He turns from the dirt road onto the highway and I admire the trees whipping by.

He glances at me. "Do you want to get your own car at some point?"

"Probably not," I admit. "I don't even drive." That gets his attention.

Frowning, he asks, "Do you know *how* to drive?"

I shrug. "Never learned. It didn't seem important." He shakes his head, and his hand goes to my leg, sliding higher until my entire body is tingling. He stops, fingers gripping high on my thigh, the hem of my dress pushed up. I have half a mind to grab his wrist and shove his hand higher, but that's a bad idea while he's driving.

His hand lifts as we exit the freeway for the tiny mountain town that sits about twenty-five miles from the pack. I've been in town a few times, but it's so small, there isn't much reason to visit.

Jasper parks on the curb in front of a brick building. I tug my dress back down before he opens my door and helps me out. Our fingers weave together and he leads me to a brick archway. The sign says "Birch & Brew".

"This is my favorite coffee shop. Well, the only coffee shop within a hundred miles, but it's still great. I finished my degree online right here," he rambles, pushing the heavy wooden door open. Is he nervous?

The smell of caramel, cream, and coffee swirl around us. The steam wand on the espresso machine hisses as a barista with green hair froths some milk. The sounds of country-folk music resonates softly.

"What would you like?" he asks, squeezing my hand gently.

"Tea, please."

"Something fruity or something creamy and spicy?"

"Spicy sounds lovely," I say, unable to resist breathing in his scent. It somehow fits in this coffee shop with the acidic coffee and sugary syrups.

Jasper orders a fancy cold-brew coffee for himself and a hot honey chai latte for me, before pulling me by the hand over to a couple of leather armchairs in the corner.

He strokes the inside of my palm with his thumb while we wait, making my whole arm prickle, until he has to release me to stand to get our drinks. I accept the warm cup and take a sip. The spices remind me of Jasper. Delicious. I should not be turned on by a chai latte.

"So I know the last school day was kinda rough. But tell me about good days," he asks, lounging back in his seat. If I had come into this coffee shop and seen him for the first time, I'd be too intimidated to speak with him. He's magnificent with early afternoon light hitting his pale hair and highlighting his straight nose and full lips. I'm convinced he is prettier than I am.

"Marigold?" he prompts, and I snap out of it.

"Okay, you want wholesome and cute, or funny?" I ask.

"Funny," he says, eyes gleaming.

"This happened before you came, so I don't think you've heard the story yet." Sitting forward in my seat, I drop my voice. "So this one is actually my brother's fault. Last year, when Cobalt was nine," I pause, my hand covering my mouth as I try to stay in control long enough to tell the story.

"Yeah?" he asks.

"Okay, when you were like ten or eleven, did you ever go through a phrase where you were drawing…" I choke back a laugh at his confused expression. "Male parts?'

Jasper snorts, shaking his head. "I don't think so, but I've seen kids do that."

Taking a deep breath, I nod. "So Cobalt was doodling peens on his notebook. Not the stuff he turned in, just the notes I wasn't supposed to see." Jasper shakes his head, his lips pressed together to suppress his grin. "Well, of course the other kids got in on it."

"So what happened?"

"Daisy turned a page in."

"Oh, no."

I nod. "I asked her what was drawn on the corner of her math quiz." I pause, enjoying his eyes going wide. "And she said it was a pickle."

Another rough laugh escapes him.

"So I had to go through everyone's notebooks."

"Of course."

"And I find a lot of these drawings. But everyone is claiming they're pickles with eyeballs"

"Naturally."

"So I sit them down, and ask why they think these are pickles. And Starling looks me dead in the face and says, 'Because Cobalt drew a stick figure eating one. So they must be pickles.'"

He drops his head, body shaking with laughter. "Seriously?"

"Yes. A stick figuring *eating a pickle*."

"Stick figure…" he says between laughs. I nod, reaching out and running my hand down his back as he calms down. "What did you do about your brother?"

Shaking my head, I cross my arms. "Let my dad deal with it. Honestly, it was probably Indie's fault as much as Cobalt's."

"He seems like a trouble-maker when he wants to be," he says, and I have to agree. I love my brothers, but they are a lot to handle.

"You're a great teacher. And you're funny," he praises, taking my hand, flipping it, and kissing my wrist. I can't help but be disappointed I'm in my own chair and not in his lap. Public space and all.

Back in his car, he pulls out of town, but then slows and parks on the side of the road.

"Whatcha doing?" I ask, fidgeting with the leather seam of my seat.

Jasper smirks. "I think you should drive."

Spluttering, I shake my head. "No thank you. This is a really nice car. I'd rather learn on a junker so if I screw something up, it's not a huge deal."

"It's fine," he insists, running his hands over the steering wheel.

"Bad idea."

He opens his door and slides one leg out. "I'll be right here. We can go slow."

"Seriously, what if I bust your car?" I say, reaching over to grab his sleeve and keep him from climbing out of the vehicle.

"Marigold, you can do this." The command in his voice silences me.

The driver's seat is overwhelming, with so many indicators and knobs. Jasper points out the speed and how to change from Park to Drive to Reverse. I know the basic mechanics, but I've never tried to use them.

"Foot on the brake, and take it from Park to Drive," he instructs. I hold down the brake so hard, I expect to snap the pedal.

"Now ease off the brake, and it'll start rolling forward, and you can steer us off the shoulder into the road."

Gritting my teeth, I lift my foot, only to slam it back down when the car lurches forward a few inches.

"Try again," he orders, his hand coming up under my hair to massage the nape of my neck.

On the second attempt, I manage to roll along the side of the road. Slowly, I pull the wheel to the left until we're drifting onto the pavement.

"Okay, you'll need to add a bit of gas before another car comes along and gets pissed we're going five miles per hour." I shoot him an alarmed look and he laughs, his hand squeezing the base of my neck, thumb rubbing circles. Tentatively, I press down on the gas pedal. The second we surge forward, I yank my foot back and he smiles at me. "It's okay, Sunshine, try again."

Soon enough we're hurtling down the road at an impressive twenty miles-per-hour. But once another car pulls up and swings around us with a honk, I lose my nerve.

"Can that be enough?" I ask, my knuckles white on the steering wheel.

"If that's what you want," he agrees and then jerks forward when I tap the break harder than I meant to. Somehow I manage to slow and pull off into the grassy shoulder. A bush scrapes along the side of his car and I cringe, but Jasper seems unbothered. I reach for the door handle to get out, but he grabs my forearm and pushes the button to turn the car off. "Where are you going?"

"Swapping back," I say, frowning at him.

"You can climb right across," he says with a cocky tilt of his head.

Rolling my eyes, a reach for the door. "Yeah, I don't think so. I'm too clumsy for that." The center console is fairly low and flush, but I still don't like my odds of not kneeing him in the groin.

His eyes spark. Oh, crap, I know what that look means.

Before I can open the glossy black door handle, hands grab my waist and I'm hauled over the center console into his lap. I want to be angry, but I'd spent our coffee date wishing I was here, so it seems hypocritical to put up a fuss.

For a moment, he holds me, his brassy grin softening while he inspects me. Unable to help myself, I reach up and drag my fingers through his hair. He leans into my touch, eyelids drooping as he enjoys my nails against his scalp.

I love him like this. He's still charming, but the polished edges are washed away to show something real and genuine underneath.

Leveraging against the door and the dash, I lift one leg across until I'm straddling him.

"You make me crazy," he murmurs, his hands falling to my hips and slowly stroking over the fabric of my dress.

"I think you were already crazy," I tease.

With a growl, his hands slide up to run across my ribs, causing me to jerk away. He pauses and his eyes flick up to study my face, understanding dawning. If he starts to tickle me, I really will knee him in the groin.

A few heartbeats pass as he decides what to do, but then he's pressing against my back and urging me closer. Heat and spice envelops me.

After last night, I'd like to think I'm an expert at kissing Jasper. It's been my new favorite hobby, so when he scatters light, tormenting kisses across my cheeks and the edges of my mouth, I want to grab him and shake him. He's being a tease.

Instead, I grip the sides of his face and cover his mouth with mine. He tastes like coffee and vanilla and I'm lost in the blissful sensation. His tongue, his teeth tugging my lip, his hands roving. It's everything.

My dress has ridden up, exposing the length of my thighs. His hands track upwards, teasing the hem of my dress. I let out a frustrated groan and can feel his mouth curve into a smile.

Softly, he uses his hand to tip my jaw up and give him easier access to my neck. I arch my back and throw my head back. It's a display of trust and vulnerability, and from the hitch in his breathing, one he finds appealing. He kisses down my neck, nipping the skin and then smoothing over the sting.

At the base of my throat, his sharper canine teeth scrape my skin, causing me to gasp. He repeats the action, momentarily taking up all space in my consciousness. All I can do is hold on to his shoulders. His lips close around the spot and he sucks, following with a lick that sends sparks down to my toes.

He leans back enough to look at the spot, a wicked smile forming. I don't need a mirror to know he left a hickey. The possessive curl of his fingers on my hips and the growl he lets out is pure wolf shifter.

His next kiss is demanding, aggressive, and I love it, from the way he forces my lips apart to the unyielding pressure. Tension builds in my body as he slides his palms up my legs again, pausing at the top with the barest brush before descending. I can't take it anymore.

Blood pounds through my veins, beating so hard I'm sure he can feel my pulse everywhere our skin touches.

"Jasper," I rasp, my words choppy, "if you don't start touching me, I'm going to have to do it myself, because otherwise I'm going to die."

His laugh is evil. "Not sure what you're talking about, Sunshine." My nails dig into the skin on his biceps. He knows exactly what I mean.

My forehead falls against his shoulder, my eyes squeezed shut. Releasing my hold on his arms, I reach down between us and under the hem of my dress. Before I can touch where I need, his hand grabs my wrist with a guttural "Mine."

I'd love to make some clever comeback to that, but the second he says mine, all rational thought drops out of my head. I'm burning, about to break.

"You need it that badly?" he teases, his whisper almost inaudible. "Let me hear you beg."

"I did," I whine, the shake in my voice betraying my failing composure. My free hand slides under the collar of his shirt, loving the heat of his skin.

His chuckle makes my stomach clench. "You didn't."

Scowling, I open my mouth to argue, but the feel of his lips against my skin short-circuits my brain. He kisses further down my chest, tugging the neckline of my dress down. His mouth across the sensitive skin on my breast is enough to break down my resolve entirely. "Jasper, please. I need you."

Grinning, he releases my wrist and runs his palms up my thighs. Tentatively, he brushes his fingers across my panties. Light, teasing. On the second pass, he's firmer, and my body squirms in reaction.

"Hold still," he says softly, authority in his voice causing me to stiffen.

His teeth close on my breast, marking me again, as his fingers hone in right where I need him, swirling and pressing. The sharp pain punctuates the pleasure. My vision goes spotty, touch overwhelming the rest of my senses. His voice sounds far away as he says, "Good girl." I come so hard I think I might actually die.

Jasper gathers me up in his lap with my head against his chest. "You okay?" His words are sweet, but his tone is wicked.

"I didn't realize," I say, gathering up my scattered thoughts. "When it's just me, it doesn't quite hit that hard."

"You're saying I'm the best you've ever had?" I can hear the pride in his voice. My laugh is dry.

The weight of his arms around me is comforting, like an anchor holding me together. Finally he breaks the silence. "What do you imagine when you touch yourself?"

Closing my eyes, I say, "You want to hear that I think about you?"

"I think about *you*. Even before you moved in," he confesses, his cocky tone replaced with vulnerability. Nuzzling his nose into my hair, right behind my ear, he sends a shiver through my body. "So what about you?"

"Really, before?" I ask, a flush rising up my neck. He nods and I feel it more than see it. "Okay fine, I think about you, but only recently."

"As long as I'm it from now on," he says possessively, "In fact, you don't even need to do anything. Come to me and I'll take care of you."

Rolling my eyes, I tip my chin up and place a soft kiss on the edge of his jaw. "Sure." No girl would turn down an orgasm like that one. Talk about some amazing benefits with this friendship.

"I feel like I should return the favor," I say, shifting on his lap so I can cup his erection through his jeans. That can't be comfortable.

He kisses my cheek and then opens the car door. "As nice as that sounds, we should get going. We don't want to miss dinner."

"I'm fine with missing dinner," I say, reaching for his belt buckle.

Scowling, he shakes his head. "No missing meals."

With that, he slides out from under me, and heads around to the driver's seat, leaving me to fumble with my seatbelt like I've forgotten how my limbs work.

XII
RENEGADES & RECKONING

JASPER

Marigold eats with her dad and brothers, and I eat with Slate and Hazel. If they notice that every inch of my skin smells like Marigold, they don't say anything. If she was at the table, they'd definitely notice her flushed skin and the glances she keeps giving me, even across the meadow. Being roommates doesn't excuse eyeing each other like that.

I head directly home, but Marigold lingers, walking with Hazel. The girls are giggling and my stomach flips. It's not that I don't want anyone to know we're involved, but they will all assume we are well on our way to being mates and Marigold isn't ready for that label, if she wants it at all.

"Okay, what are we playing?" Onyx hollers the moment he's through the door. Cedar follows him quietly.

"I've got a new game for us," Marigold chimes, following them in.

"Hey guys," I say from the kitchen, pulling a 12-pack of IPAs from the fridge.

"I nabbed a few snacks from Crickett," Marigold says. She holds out a plate to me, grinning. It's stacked with cheese and salami, beside an impressive array of pickle spears.

"You got pickles?" I ask incredulously.

Marigold shrugs. "Just in the mood, I guess," she says with a wink. Using two fingers, she raises a pickle to her mouth and takes a bite. At my grimace, she breaks into silent laughter.

Hazel joins me in the kitchen, her dark brown hair loose around her shoulders. She hands me a casserole dish while giving Marigold a strange look.

"What did you make?" I ask, peeling back the tin-foil.

"S'mores bars," she says.

Onyx leans over her shoulder. "Wow, those look fantastic." He swipes a bar before I can even set them down.

Hazel's eyes crinkle as she smiles at him. "I added caramel between the graham crackers and chocolate. You're welcome."

"I love you," Onyx says before taking a huge bite and groaning.

Slate shoves him away and grabs Hazel around the waist from behind, kissing behind her ear as she cackles.

My eyes go to Marigold to find she's already looking at me. She smiles, showing her teeth, and slowly runs her tongue over her top teeth. Fuck. This is going to be a long night not touching her if she keeps taunting me.

"What's the game?" Cedar asks, opening a beer with a crack and a hiss.

Marigold pulls a card game out of her bag and waves it back and forth. The brown and gold cover says, "Sheriffs and Outlaws," with a little sheriff's badge over an old fashioned pistol.

We load up plates and lay out the cards. Slate sits on the sofa and Hazel sits on the floor between his legs. Cedar grabs the armchair and Onyx stretches out on the floor, leaving one seat open. Marigold sits beside Slate, tucking her feet up under her, and motions for me to sit beside Hazel with my back against the sofa right below her shins.

The game isn't terribly complicated and Marigold explains the basics. Everyone draws a card to assign their roles, but keeps them secret. Only the Sheriff has to turn over his card to reveal his role - it's Slate. He flips the card over with a sigh.

I lift my card and peek. Outlaw. To win the game, my task is to eliminate the Sheriff. There are two Outlaws so I'll have some help, though I'll have to figure out who. Anyone who fires at the Sheriff is likely the other Outlaw. But the moment we do so, the people assigned as Deputies will attack us and defend Slate. They win if the game ends with the Sheriff alive.

The last person is assigned Renegade. "The Renegade wins if they're the last person alive in the game," Marigold explains. I turn that over in my mind, trying to predict how that may play out.

Marigold hands me a stack of cards, a mixture of actions for shooting others or blocking their shots, along with a few random bonus cards to give special abilities.

"Any questions?" Marigold asks.

"How are we supposed to know who is what and who to shoot?" Onyx asks, a whine in his voice. He shakes his dirty blonde hair out of his eyes and squints at the cards in his hand.

Marigold winks. "You'll have to figure it out based on what everyone does. Most likely a Deputy won't shoot at the Sheriff, right?"

"Great," Slate says sarcastically.

"Aw, you'll be a great Sheriff," Hazel coos, ending with a dark laugh.

Shaking his head, Slate lays down a horse card, making it harder for us to shoot him. Hazel goes next, and with a flourish, she tries to shoot Cedar.

"Do you even know who I am?" Cedar asks, tilting his head with a curious look.

Hazel scrunches up her nose. "If I'm the Deputy, then there's a seventy-five percent chance that you're an enemy, right?" I almost miss it, but Marigold reaches out and pinches Hazel on the back of her arm.

"Alright." Cedar frowns, moving his marker down one life. We each get five hits before we are eliminated. Hazel looks up at Marigold, an innocent flutter of her lashes the only sign of silent communication between the friends.

Marigold cranes her neck and smiles sweetly at me. "Sorry Jasper." And she lays down a card to shoot at me.

"What the hell?" I cry out, just dramatic enough she knows I'm teasing. "Well, guess what? Too bad!" I say, setting down a card to block her shot. All five lives still intact. She pouts, crossing her arms and leaning back into the cushion. She's adorable.

I lay down a gun card before me so I can shoot people further away. Onyx lays down his own gun and Cedar fires back at Hazel.

"Watch it," Slate says menacingly.

"She could be the Renegade, out to trick you." Cedar points out.

"I would never!" Hazel rests her chin on Slate's knee, wrapping her arm around his calf.

Back to the Sheriff, and Slate lays down a gun so he can shoot further. "You're strategic," I note. He shrugs.

Hazel takes another shot at Cedar, and then Marigold takes a shot at me. With a glare, I send one back at her and she gasps. We both move our markers down one life.

While everyone's eyes are on Onyx's hemming and hawing over his next move, Marigold bends down low, leaning over my shoulder with her hair curtaining her, and murmurs, "I'm going to get you back for that."

My hand moves to her calf and I squeeze it lightly. Her smile is devious.

Onyx decides to lay a specialty card that shoots at everyone including himself, and only Slate and Onyx come out unscathed with blocking cards. Down to three lives.

In the next round, Cedar is eliminated. He flips his card to reveal the role of Deputy.

"Whoops!" Hazel says. "Sorry, Cedar. Thought you were an Outlaw."

Marigold studies Onyx, her lip between her teeth. She decides he is the next target, and over the next two rounds, both she and Hazel work to eliminate him.

This gives me a chance to shoot at Slate. Unfortunately, it proves to be a mistake, because he still has plenty of blocking cards and all five of his lives. Sliding my marker down to zero lives, I groan and flip the card over to reveal Outlaw, a twin to Onyx's role card in front of him.

"I knew it!" Marigold says. She grins at Hazel who is looking far too pleased with herself. Slate who is looking suspicious of both women.

"One of them has to be the Renegade, and the other is your Deputy," Cedar explains the obvious, resting his chin on his fist and studying the pair. Slate lays down another bonus card which gives him an unnecessary ability to shoot further, effectively buying himself time to figure out which girl is which role.

"She's the Renegade," Hazel accuses. Marigold narrows her eyes at her. Hazel's next shot is at Marigold, and Marigold fires back.

"I'm the Deputy," Marigold says, pressing her lips together as Slate looks between them.

"Sorry," he says, shrugging and laying down a card to shoot Marigold.

"Thank you, honey," Hazel says, kissing his outstretched arm.

"How could you do that?" Marigold says. She slaps her hand over her role card and slowly slides her palm back to reveal her designation as Deputy.

Slate grimaces, looking at his mate. She laughs and thumps down a final card to shoot Slate and win the game.

"Sorry, babe, I'm the only winner this round!" She lets out a whoop, and Slate grabs her and hauls her up into his lap, scolding her while kissing whatever he can reach.

I flip Hazel's role card to confirm - Renegade.

Marigold's fingertips skim the nape of my neck before she stands to get a drink.

Cedar says his goodbyes and then heads out, mentioning something about a long day tomorrow transplanting something in his garden.

Marigold folds her legs under her, settling back on the sofa behind me. She holds a little plate with some chips and another pickle spear. It crunches as she takes a bite.

"Want some?" she offers, leaning forward.

"I don't actually like them," I say quietly, causing her to shake with silent laughter.

Onyx takes his seat and we all sit around the coffee table enjoying the remaining snacks and beer. It gets quiet, but it's the heavy quiet that makes my lungs constrict a bit. Slate and Hazel are both watching Marigold and me.

Hazel lets out a sigh. "Guys, we need to talk."

Nausea rolls in my gut. I'm not usually an anxious person, but nobody can hear "we need to talk" and not react.

"What's up?" Marigold says brightly, though the pitch is too high.

"It kinda seems like things have changed a bit. Did you guys start dating?" Slate asks.

Marigold startles in her seat, and I work to keep my face calm.

"We're roommates," I answer evenly. "And even if we did get involved, I would hope everyone would respect our privacy. I'm not sure why this keeps getting questioned." Hazel cocks her head and raises one eyebrow. She knows me too well.

"Hold on, what did I miss?" Onyx says, sitting back with a frown.

Marigold's mouth gapes, looking between Onyx and Hazel, her cheeks getting pinker by the second. "Okay, we kissed."

Slate bites back a smile, but Hazel narrows her eyes at me. "Just roommates?"

"Oh, no, it's not Jasper's fault. It just kinda happened. Like an accident," Marigold stutters. My muscles tense, a headache starting behind my eyes.

Onyx interrupts, "Are you fucking kidding me? Accident my ass. You become roommates and then decide to go at it? Easy access, I guess."

"How about you watch your mouth," I growl.

"How about you stop taking advantage of your roommate," Onyx says, venom in every syllable.

"You don't get a say-" I snap back, but Onyx stands, leaning into my space.

"Do you have feelings for her, or are you enjoying toying with her?" he asks, a deadly calm in every syllable that I've never heard from Onyx before.

"She's my friend," I say, standing to face him.

"Then knock it the fuck off." His eyes flash electric blue, and I know we are seconds from a fight. Wolf shifters losing control is dangerous for everybody.

I'm sure my own eyes are glowing a similar shade. I can feel my wolf answering his challenge. Because of my higher position in the pack, I'm driven to react to disrespect or challenges, like the bold stare Onyx is currently giving me.

Marigold's hands go to my arm, but Hazel tugs her back.

"Onyx, back off" Slate warns, the authority in his voice breaking through the tension.

Onyx turns and storms out, slamming the door behind him. Finally I can turn, and Slate's eyes are lit up green as he regards me. I take a deep breath and push down the instinct to fight and defend.

"He's really upset," Marigold squeaks, shell-shocked.

Hazel pinches the bridge of her nose. "I get the feeling friends with benefits isn't a thing for wolf shifters?" Slate nods, his shoulders sagging.

"Look, you guys know why we don't do this kind of thing. Your wolf instincts don't know the difference. You're going to start acting like mates and end up hurt because you don't mean it." Slate squeezes Hazel's shoulders.

"You'll ruin your friendship," she adds.

Nodding, Marigold wipes at her eyes and lets out a sniffle. I can't stand when she cries; it hits me like a punch to the chest.

"I appreciate your concern, but at the end of the day it's not your business and I think you've overstepped," I say firmly. Before Hazel can argue, I add, "You've upset Marigold, so let's circle back to this once we've all had time to calm down and think."

Slate takes Hazel's hand and leads her toward the door, giving me a sympathetic bro nod. Before the door shuts, Hazel calls out, "I love you Marigold. I'm here for you." I can't even be angry that she's already Team Marigold if this becomes a conflict.

"Well that went downhill fast," I grumble, walking back to the sofa. Marigold is curled up like a hedgehog, legs drawn up and cheek against her knees.

Taking a deep breath, I sink down onto my knees in front of her and slowly pry her hands apart. Once I get her to release her grip, her legs fall and she straightens into a seated position, though she's still hunched over. Her beautiful face is blotchy and her eyes are red.

"I didn't mean it like that," she whispers.

"I know," I say. That doesn't change that what they said was true.

She throws her arms around me, laying her head on my shoulder, so I loop my arms under her legs and lift her. She clings to me as I walk her back to our bedroom. We might be in trouble, but I can't sleep without her.

Gently, I lay her down on our bed and then walk around to the other side, pulling my shirt off as I go. She props herself up on her elbows, watching me. The tears on her cheeks are drying.

At the edge of the bed, I hesitate. What's best for her? To continue this physical relationship when she has no idea how to handle the emotional side? This is all becoming a mess faster than I realized, and we have to figure it out.

Sliding under the covers, I roll onto my side and prop my head up, mirroring her pose.

"I'm sorry," she says, reaching out to tentatively touch my chest, like she needs the contact. "I didn't know what to do with how upset he got."

"It's fine," I say, resting my hand on the hollow of her waist. "But I need to know what you want. We weren't clear before. Am I an experiment for you?"

Long, wet lashes frame those blue-green eyes. "No."

"So, what am I?" My voice betrays how desperate I am. I would give anything to hear that she loves me, because I am falling for her and I can't slow it down.

She takes a shuddering breath and sits up. "I don't know. It's still so new, and I feel... confused, I guess."

Confused is better than friends with benefits. A step forward she isn't ready to label.

"Do you want some space until you're not confused?"

Her strawberry-blonde waves sway over her bare arms as she shakes her head. "I don't want space, but are you okay with giving me time to figure it out?"

Without waiting for an answer, she slides her leg over me and pushes my shoulder so I land flat on my back. Leaning down, she lowers her voice. "Space is the last thing I want. I'm always thinking about you. I don't want to be apart. Is that bad?"

Her words are irresistible. She might not be ready to recognize her feelings toward me, but they're there. Clear in the shine of her eyes and the way her hands spread over my skin.

I answer by pulling her face down and covering her mouth with mine for a long, slow kiss.

Her breathing shudders. My thumbs wipe away the last of her tears as I frame her face with my hands. Unease shines in her eyes. This undefined connection between us weighs heavily across her and I want to take some pressure off of her.

Words tumble out before I can think better. "I'll be whatever you want me to be. I'm not going anywhere. Boyfriend, hook up, I'll take anything you give me. I just want you." I know how stupid it is, but it's the only way I know how to make things easier for her in this situation.

Marigold searches my face, as if she can sense the struggle raging in my heart and head. "Okay."

She gathers the fabric of her dress in both hands and pulls it over her head in one smooth motion. The world could have stopped spinning and I wouldn't have noticed.

My hands graze over her ribs and lightly skim the swell of her breasts. She leans forward, one hand on my chest, pushing herself into my hands.

"If you made me come that hard with your fingers, I'm a little scared of what you can do with your cock." Her voice is husky.

This girl is unbelievable.

My fingers dig into her skin. It takes two steadying breaths before I can speak. "That's the thing," I say, wincing at her parted lips and vulnerable expression. "I don't want to do *that* until I'm claiming my mate."

Swallowing, Marigold's face falls. "That makes sense." She rolls off me and stretches out, arms crossed over her bare breasts. A blush colors her cheeks.

"Where are you going?" I murmur, brushing her hair over her shoulder to expose that glorious bare skin. Her mouth curves into a hopeful smile.

She runs a hand down my side, thumb stroking my abs. Leaning in, I kiss her sweet mouth, putting all my longing and devotion into my slow, deliberate movements. We kiss and let our hands rove, until she lays her head down on my pillow and nestles under my chin. It feels incredible to wrap my arms around her and feel her breathing even out. She's addicting, and I have no guarantee she's mine.

XIII
CONFESSIONS & INVESTIGATIONS
Marigold

Slate knocks on our door the next morning. Jasper invites him in. "What's up? Do we have a change of plans for the day?"

Shaking his head, Slate turns toward me. "Actually, I was hoping Marigold would visit the Raven Pack with Elm today. Scope things out and get a feel for what's going on up there."

Jasper's words about the Raven Pack and Ironcrest echo in my thoughts. "Sure, sounds like a plan."

Slate leaves me with a nod. When I return to the table, Jasper tugs me into his lap and kisses me soundly.

"I need to go," I say.

"No," Jasper argues between kisses peppered down my throat.

Sighing, I sink into him. "A long run will give me time to think about us." He hums in response, his hold loosening so I can pull back. I give him one more lingering kiss and force myself to walk away.

My dad is waiting for me, sitting on a bench in the big steel training building. "Hey, Dad." He gives me a hug.

"Ready to see Heron and Breeze?" he asks, referring to my maternal grandparents.

"Let's go," I say, opening the door to my dad's faded green pickup truck. Once we're on the road, I ask, "So, what are we looking for exactly?"

"Mainly a temperature check. Is Nyx still the reclusive Alpha we all love, or is she possibly leading raids? Is there any sign of Granite Ridge or Ironcrest pushing in?" he says grimly.

"Alright, that sounds manageable."

"So what's new with you, kiddo?" he asks with a smile. Our last family dinner was dominated by Cobalt's stories of his recent adventures, and Indigo sharing about the new healing techniques he's learned during his apprenticeship with our grandmother, Sable.

"Had a fun game night with everyone last night. Oh and I went into town with Jasper and checked out the coffee shop there. It was cool."

"Just you and Jasper?" he says.

"Yeah," I say, trying to sound casual. My dad nods. Would he approve of me and Jasper? Silence stretches between us and I finally give in to the impulse to ask. "So, after working with him a while, what do you think of him?"

"Jasper?" His lips thin while he considers. "He's talented, that's for sure. Seems loyal, but it's only been a few months. Considering his parents, I don't think I'll trust him until it's been a few years."

That's not ideal.

"He's gotten really close with all my friends. I don't think he had friends or supportive leaders in Granite Ridge. He seems happy, so I don't think we need to worry about his loyalty," I argue.

"That makes sense." His tone ends the discussion.

Pulling down the Raven Pack's access road, I keep waiting for a guard to stop us, but no one greets us until we've reached their compound. While our buildings form a loose circle, the Raven Pack's buildings are huddled together in a tight block.

We approach the larger pack house and a pair of female Thetas stop us.

"I'm here to see my grandparents, Heron and Breeze," I say. "I'm Marigold, Ivy's daughter. And this is my father, Elm, her mate."

"We remember you," the taller woman says. Her black hair reaches to her waist in a glossy curtain. She's familiar, but not anyone I clearly recall from our last visit a few months ago. She nods to her partner, who disappears inside.

A few minutes later, the younger woman reappears and motions for us to follow her inside. The side entrance leads into a hallway, and our guide brings us past various meeting rooms and recreation rooms until we reach the foyer.

Breeze ambles from another hallway, a smile creasing her face. She holds her arms open, and I gladly hug her. It's been too long. "My sweet Marigold, you look so much like your mother," she coos. When she sees my father, her face chills. "Elm."

"Hello, Breeze. You look lovely," my dad says. She brushes him away and takes my hand to lead us down the hallway until we reach a door left open.

The studio apartment opens into a small sitting room with a bed tucked around a corner. Heron hugs me as well and then shakes my dad's hand. We sit in armchairs and sip bottled water.

"It's always good to see you. But this is unexpected," Breeze says. Her curly blonde hair is streaked with silver. Heron reaches over and takes her hand. They've been mates for fifty years.

"I wish this was simply a visit to see you. But there have been some recent events we need to discuss with you" my father says. "A few days ago, there was an Alpha Counsel. Your Alpha was the only one who refused to attend. But Ironcrest made some accusations against your pack."

Their faces become solemn. Asking them to speak about pack business without their Alpha is uncouth. But they know as well as we do that Nyx wouldn't speak with us.

I fiddle with my hands. "Zephyr claims that you are crossing his borders and testing their defenses. We know that's not possible, but we need to know what is happening. How have things been with Ironcrest and Granite Ridge in the last few months?"

"Oh, I see," Breeze says, looking to her mate. He rubs his thumb across her hand comfortingly.

Heron clears his throat. "What they're saying, the opposite is true. Ironcrest has been raiding our borders, testing our patrols, even taking supplies from our storage houses."

"Why haven't you guys brought this to the other packs?" I ask.

"You know how Nyx is. She feels we can handle it." Breeze says, giving me a pointed look. "So there's nothing you can do."

"We think Ironcrest means to fully invade, perhaps with Granite Ridge's assistance," my dad says, getting to the point.

"I can't see that happening. They're badgering us, not starting a war," Heron says mildly.

"Do you have defenses prepared if they do?"

"It doesn't matter. They're just causing trouble." Breeze turns her face away from us.

Grimacing, I lean forward, inserting myself into their argument. "But why would they make those accusations in the Alpha Counsel then?"

"To shift the blame, I suppose." Heron answers.

"Our leaders are concerned about a possible attack," my dad says.

"You don't need to worry. Your help will not be accepted anyway."

"Heron, you have to talk to Nyx," I beg, "Our help could mean the difference of victory or being wiped out."

"They wouldn't dare," Breeze sniffs.

"But what if they do?" I press.

Breeze stands, puttering into the kitchenette. "I don't want to talk about this any longer."

My dad focuses on Heron. "Would you let us inspect your borders?"

"Absolutely not," he snaps, "You won't find anything other than the disturbances I've mentioned."

"Can I speak with Nyx?" I ask.

"I don't think that's a good idea."

"I don't understand why you guys would reject someone wanting to help you," I say, frustration getting the better of me.

"We don't need anyone's help," Heron says, crossing his arms.

As sweetly as I can muster, I ask, "Can you at least tell us everything in more detail? In case Ironcrest starts to harass us as well? So we know what to watch for."

With some coaxing, my grandparents go over every detail they can think of, which, unfortunately, is not a lot. We leave disappointed and nervous.

JASPER

It's hard to focus on Hazel's report about patrols when my mind only wants to replay Marigold's words, *I'm always thinking about you. I don't want to be apart.*

It feels foolish to hope she'll decide she wants something permanent. Unfortunately, I'm so far gone, I don't think I could ever move on. This is my fault. I'm the one who decided to kiss her again.

"The strangest part is the lack of new markings along Granite Ridge," Hazel continues. "Ironcrest has maintained their borders, but it's not like Ferris to neglect his."

Heath leans back in his seat. "I think we can all agree they're acting strangely."

"Perhaps because they are also potentially preparing to invade the Raven Pack, they are focusing their forces along that border," Hazel says.

"It makes sense, if Ironcrest is accusing Nyx of aggression to justify their moves, Granite Ridge might choose a different tactic. In this case, keeping a low profile," Hawthorne suggests.

Heath nods, but my stomach is in knots. I can't tell if that edgy feeling is general anxiety about my parents' pack, or if there's something I'm missing.

A whiff of Marigold's scent drifts in, and I twist to see her approaching the meeting room, Elm behind her.

"How was it?" Hazel asks, standing to pull out chairs for them. Marigold sits next to her and squeezes her friend's hand.

Elm frowns. "Nyx refused to see us, but we were able to confirm that Ironcrest has been raiding the Raven Pack for the last six months."

"That's a long time," Slate says, brows drawing together in alarm.

"This isn't a reactionary plan. It's a long term strategy," Heath agrees.

"This proves Jasper's theory," Marigold declares. My heart jumps. "They're definitely manufacturing an excuse to take the Raven Pack over."

Hawthorne locks eyes with Elm and asks, "Are you totally sure about what they said?"

"Yes. Heron and Breeze might be prickly, but they are honest."

Hazel sighs. "So what do we do about it?" Slate grasps her hand, threading their fingers together, and she gives him a tired smile.

"They don't want our help," Elm says.

"So we do nothing?" Hazel protests.

Slate lifts her hand and presses a kiss to the back of it. "It definitely limits how much we can help."

"We may be jumping ahead," Heath says. "I should go up to see Nyx myself. She's not unreasonable."

"Thank you," Elm says quietly, looking down at the table.

"We can go tomorrow. Hawthorne, please leave messages so they have a chance of expecting us. I'd like to bring this whole team. Lazuli and Cassia can manage for a morning."

My heart rate picks up. It's unheard of to travel without leaving a Beta behind. Heath is more concerned about this threat than I realized.

"Alpha, may I come?" Marigold asks, her voice timid. Heath nods.

Protectiveness surges in me. If she's coming, I need her by my side. But only Slate and Hazel know about us, and Hazel isn't exactly supportive. As if feeling my tension, Marigold glances up and meets my gaze.

Once Heath dismisses us, I follow her out of the room. I'm done pretending to be indifferent to her when we are around the rest of our pack. Taking her arm, I lean in. "I missed you this morning. You looked stunning walking into that meeting and saying my name." At least I keep my voice low.

She runs her tongue over her lips but stays quiet.

Once inside our cabin, she halts, posture rigid. Her breath is shallow and her hands clench and unclench. I wrap my arms around her, waiting until she's ready to tell me.

Slowly she relaxes. "I didn't realize how serious this was. This could turn into a battle and people are going to get hurt. And I don't think Nyx will do what it takes to stop it." She spirals. "And I'm over here pretending you're some hookup. Like it means nothing to me. That's the furthest thing from the truth."

My muscles go taut, like I'm afraid to move and spook her.

She draws a slow breath. "Unless you're going to decide you're done with me, I don't see this ending. Because I don't want to live without you."

"I don't either. I'll never be done with you," I say, the words tumbling out before my brain catches up.

"What's wrong with me?" she says with a laugh. "We were supposed to be friends. Now I can't function without touching you. You're all I think about."

Every word is what I've been dreaming of.

Her back hits the door as I crowd into her space. I press a hand on either side of her head so she's trapped. "We could never have just been friends." Her mouth opens in surprise, but I can't stop. "I've been trying to resist you since I arrived. You're my sun. You're what I see when I close my eyes. You've worked your way into my soul."

Her eyes glow a glorious shade of warm blue and her expression is hungry. All the things I've been imagining doing to her flood my thoughts at once.

She's faster than I am. Hands grabbing my shoulders, she jumps on me and wraps her legs around my waist. I'm lost in her kisses. They're urgent and needy and everything I've always wanted. Fire burns across my skin, maybe coming from her touch, or maybe from inside of me. I'm consumed.

Every sense falls away except her skin on mine and the sound of her breathing, the little noises she makes. Her fingers tug at my hair and her thighs tighten as I push her back into the door. I can't get close enough.

My heart races and I can feel her's doing the same. Every inch of skin is soft and warm as my hands rove across the swell of her breasts and down her ribs. Finally I grip her ass and pull us away from the door. She clings to me, her mouth moving to the side of my neck, her tongue licking behind my ear and then her teeth nipping my ear lobe.

As I stride toward my bedroom, she whispers, "Just to be completely clear, I'm all in. I want to see where this can go."

Gently, I lay her down across my comforter and lean over her, my hands resting on either side of her head. "Good to know I'm not alone in this. That you feel the same."

Her eyes meet mine for a moment. The only movement is our chests rising and falling in a chaotic rhythm. Neither of us are willing to break the spell.

Slowly, her hand comes up and brushes the hair from my eyes. Gentle fingertips skim down my cheek and jaw. I turn to kiss her palm, and her eyes flutter closed. Taking her hand, my mouth closes over her pulse point, and then down the tender, pale skin of her inner arm. Her scent is warm and sweet, like sunshine and wildflowers.

"If you told me a month ago that we would be here, doing this, I would have never believed you," she murmurs.

"I would have," I say, grinning as her hands pull my shirt up to expose my torso. She licks her lips as her hands trail over the ridges of my abdomen muscles. I've never been so grateful for athletic shifter genetics. "Like what you see?"

Her teeth sink into her bottom lip. "You don't need *me* to tell you how gorgeous you are."

"It couldn't hurt."

She rolls her eyes. "You smug asshole."

"But I'm *your* smug asshole." My low laugh rumbles out of me as I lower over her. "For example, you are stunning."

She is. Her tan skin is flushed, her constellation of freckles standing out. Brightness sparkles in her lit eyes, her lips parted as a slow smile spreads across her heart-shaped face. That wavy reddish-blonde hair spreads around her in a halo. She looks like a goddess. And she's mine.

The quilt bunches under her hands as she squirms. I could stay here with her forever like this. Well, maybe not exactly like this. I want to touch and taste all of her. Right now.

Her hands ease my shirt up and I tug it over my head, tossing it away. She lets out an appreciative hum. I bury my smile in the smooth skin of her stomach, pressing kisses across her hips to below her belly button. Quiet giggles tighten her muscles under my lips. My hands move to her hips, loving her shiver as I hold her down.

Delicately, my teeth pull her waistband down, exposing more bare skin. Maybe I forget to breathe, because I'm dizzy. Spiraling. Or perhaps it's the sparks of electricity coming off her fingers cutting grooves through my hair. Nails scratching my scalp.

She tugs impatiently, the urgency returning to her motions. Her heels push against my lower back, pushing my hips down against her and my chest against her bust. She's lush and fits against me perfectly.

Our mouths crash together again. The difference between our first kiss and now is startling. Her tongue delves into my mouth. Bold. Demanding. I'll give her whatever she wants.

My hand slips under her shirt. Like most shifters, she doesn't wear a bra. There are no barriers to cup one breast and run my thumb over her nipple. She shutters and I do it again, her teeth closing down on my bottom lip in a quick bite.

"Don't start biting unless you want me to bite back," I warn. The words float between us like smoke. They represent everything we haven't discussed and what could come next. If this works and she wants to make this relationship permanent, I would gladly mark her as my mate. It chains my heart to hers, keeping us together forever. Not all couples take that step. It's shifters' version of marriage, without the option of divorce.

She doesn't respond. If she was nervous or scared, she'd say so. Marigold is never short on words. Her silence is confident, broken only by a moan as I draw her shirt higher and lower my mouth over her other breast.

With an insistent tug, she pulls my face back to hers. Our lips brush, press, drag, over and over until I've lost all sense of time. Her hands explore, but we don't take it any further. There's a seriousness underlying each touch. We are finally on the same page. This isn't for fun. It's devotion, and we both know what comes next isn't something done on a whim.

XIV
DRONES &
DEVIL'S SPAWN
MARIGOLD

Heath calls the team together in the morning. He drives the first truck with my dad and Hawthorne. Slate drives the second truck with Hazel, Jasper, and me. I'm grateful. In the back seat, I can distract myself by holding his hand and tracing the lines on his palm.

Thunder clouds approach from the south, their rolling gray matching my anxious heart.

Nyx's guard has tripled since yesterday, with six wolves standing around the pack house. My blood goes cold. Is this for us? Or have things escalated with Ironcrest?

Hawthorne climbs out and speaks with them. When it's clear he's being turned away, Heath joins the discussion. Two guards go inside, and after a long wait, they return and allow us entrance.

The meeting room is dusty. Heath sits and we all settle around him at the dated conference table. Hazel clicks her nails together anxiously.

"Nyx, " Heath says, rising as the Raven Pack Alpha joins us. She's younger than I expected, with olive skin and dark hair in a short bob.

"Sit down and tell me what you want," she says curtly. My hands grip the arms of my chair. Through our pack bond, I can feel a spike of irritation, but everyone's face stays calm and neutral. Heath begins, "Thank you for seeing us. I won't waste your time. We have reason to believe Ironcrest and Granite Ridge are planning a full-blown attack against your pack and we want to help you."

Nyx stays quiet for a long moment. "Why?"

"At the Alpha Counsel," Heath says, ignoring Nyx's snort, "Zephyr claimed your pack has been violating their borders and that you are the aggressors."

"So I've heard," Nyx replies dryly. "Not sure what his lies have to do with me."

Heath takes a slow breath, his hands loosening as he calms himself. If it was my father, he would have attacked Nyx for that tone.

"Ironcrest has the numbers, paired with Granite Ridge, they have close to one hundred wolves who can fight. I would prefer it if my ally was not wiped off the map."

Nyx's lip curls. "You don't need to worry about us. We've got things well in hand."

Heath's control starts to slip. "What is your plan if they invade? If one hundred wolves descend on your compound?"

She shrugs, and I don't expect an answer, but she finally says, "Lockdown."

"And all your packmates out of this building?"

"I'm sure they'll manage."

"Why are you refusing help?" he asks, anger seeping into his words.

"Because I don't need it," she says. "I think you should take your wolves and go. I don't want that devil's spawn in my house."

Jasper stiffens, and Slate leans forward menacingly. Even Hazel bristles. Heath's voice drops. "Jasper is a valued member of my team."

"Just get him out of here," Nyx says, looking down her nose at us.

Still reeling, I reach over to grasp his thigh, trying to give him whatever support I can. Heath pushes his chair back. "Thank you for your time, Nyx. We can see ourselves out."

Before she disappears, my dad abruptly stands. "Alpha Nyx, I would like to stay with my relatives. Let me see that my mate's parents are safe."

Her eyes narrow, but she says, "For Ivy's sake, I'll allow it. That one too, if she wishes." Her long black nails point at me, before she spins on her heel and walks out.

The idea of hateful, judgmental Nyx abandoning her pack and hunkering down is not something I can tolerate. If I have a chance to help, I have to take it. I look to my Alpha. "I would like to stay too."

Heath nods. "If that's your choice, please be safe. And we will figure out what else we can do to help."

My throat is thick, but I take deep breaths and stand with my father. I'll miss Jasper, but it's temporary. Heath leads us out and climbs in the truck with Hawthorne.

Jasper grabs my elbow and pulls me close. "I don't want you to stay. It's an unnecessary risk."

"I'm sorry about what she said. But I want to help."

"If this all goes sideways, you'll be trapped," he hisses, his platinum hair falling forward as he leans over me. "You can help from home."

"I'm sorry, I already decided. I'll be back soon."

"I need you," Jasper says, brows furrowing. The pain in his expression cuts away at my resolve.

Squeezing his hand, I remove it from my elbow and step back. "It'll be okay. I'll miss you." My eyes burn as I fight tears.

"What did he say?" he dad asks, frowning as he looks over at Jasper speaking with Slate.

"He doesn't want me to stay. He thinks it's too dangerous."

My dad crosses his arms. "That's not his business. He isn't your Alpha or your family." My heart twinges. "You're doing the right thing."

"I'm not sure, Dad."

He huffs and walks back inside the pack house. I'm going to follow, but I can't help but linger for one more goodbye with Jasper.

Instead, Slate goes from speaking to Heath to approaching me. "Marigold, we need you back at Bracken Creek with us."

I blink at him. "What? Heath said I could stay."

Slate's expression softens. "Jasper brought up some good points. We need your knowledge of the Raven Pack to advise us. And it'll be easier for Jasper to contribute if he isn't panicked about your safety."

Are you kidding me? The prickle of tears burns as anger fuels them. I could go to Heath and protest, but I already know he will back up his Beta. I hold no ranking, so I have no grounds to argue against him.

Numb, I climb into the truck. Jasper slides into the seat beside me, and Slate steers us back onto the road.

"I'm sorry," Jasper says quietly.

All my anger overflows, and I'm not even quite sure what I'm so upset about. Flashes of Nyx calling Jasper demon spawn, Jasper going behind my back, the idea of those Raven Pack members trapped outside the pack house and left for dead, it all swirls in my mind.

"I can't believe you did that," I mutter, feeling hollow.

Jasper reaches for my hand, but I pull away. "I'd rather you're angry with me and safe, than putting yourself in harm's way."

"That's not your call to make," I blurt, my heart rate accelerating. "I never thought you would be that controlling."

Slate looks over his shoulder. "Marigold-"

"Shut up, Slate, you're in trouble too," I snap. Hazel pats his knee and stays quiet.

"I don't want to control you, I want you alive," Jasper says, his voice dropping to a dangerous growl.

"That's not your job. You're not my mate, not my boyfriend," I say, my vision blurring slightly. It feels like stabbing myself with a knife, saying those things to him, but I'm so angry and scared, I want him to hurt the way I am. Even if I'll hate myself for it later.

Jasper looks straight ahead, his jaw tight. "Last night, you wanted to commit to me because of how serious everything was. And now you're pushing me away for the same reason."

Snarling, I hit the back of my head against the headrest. "I'm not scared, I'm angry that you're trying to make decisions for me that aren't yours to make, and you're going behind my back to manipulate the situation. If that's how you operate, I clearly don't know you well at all."

His chest rises in shallow breaths, but he has no response. The entire car stays silent, seeped in heavy emotion, until we reach the parking lot.

Heath calls Jasper and Slate away for a meeting to discuss our new tech surveillance, and I throw my arms around Hazel and cry into her shoulder until I am gasping for air.

Hazel rubs my back and holds me steady.

When I finally get ahold of myself, she squeezes my hands and says, "Okay babe, what do you want to do about the situation?"

My eyes feel gritty and my throat is thick, my chest aches. But under it, I feel so disrespected. He didn't trust me to make my own decisions. Is that how every major conflict is going to go? Because that's a deal breaker for me.

"I'm not sure," I say, tucking my forehead against her shoulder. Her hands run up and down my back, soothing me.

"You have any and all options. I'll beat his ass for you. We can trash his cabin or key his car. Anything you want."

Through the ache, I can't help but smile. She's loyal to the end and I've neglected our friendship during this whirlwind with Jasper. When she was falling for Slate, she never pushed me aside.

My hands tighten around her in a hug. "Thank you."

Her nails run through my hair, brushing it off my cheek. "You deserve to be treated the best. If that's Jasper, great. But if he is being a dick to you, I don't care if he is my brother-in-law. I'll neuter him without a second thought."

JASPER

Trudging after Heath, my heart thumps in my throat. Marigold was far more devastated than I expected, and now I'm walking away from her.

"Give her a little time, man," Slate says. "Hazel will help."

Will she, though? I love my brother's mate, but she is emotional.

"I've never seen her that upset." I scrub my face with my hands.

"Neither have I." I flinch at his words.

"I should have found another way. Or stayed with her."

"You know that's not reasonable. What you did was fucked up, but I would have done the same thing." He shakes his head.

"No, you would have dragged your woman off like a caveman."

Slate shrugs, a small smile lifting his mouth. "Maybe."

In his office, Heath pulls up the security feeds. We sit and watch the records on fast forward, slowing the feed whenever a group of wolves runs by. It's our patrols.

"Let's set a second patrol along that northern border," Heath says.

Slate nods. "I'll arrange it. Any specifics you had in mind?"

"Run it twenty-four seven. And I think it's time to use those drones," he says, leaning back in his office chair.

"Agreed." Slate looks at me expectantly.

Two drones arrived yesterday. "It might take a while to get them set up, and then I'll need to train a few people on using them."

Heath nods. "Maybe Vale, Aven, or Onyx."

"Onyx would be great at it," Slate says.

"Alright, I'd better get started. Can you send Onyx my way? I'll let you know when we are up and running."

The drones are fairly easy to set up, and within an hour, Onyx and I are flying them across our compound, trying to get the hang of it. Visibility would be better if it wasn't so cloudy, but overall I'm impressed with the little machines.

However, the light is fading and while they have night vision capabilities, I can already tell it will be tricky to fly them after dark. We are not experienced enough yet.

Heath observes us. "Looks good. Go ahead and run one in along the borders around the Raven Pack tomorrow, and see if we can spot anything."

"Anything else tonight?" I ask.

Already striding away, Heath shakes his head. "Go get some rest. I have a feeling tomorrow is going to be rough."

We stow the drones away and leave the offices. Darkness has fallen. Onyx grips my arm and nods resolutely before we part ways.

For once, I'm glad my cabin is close to the training building and offices. My jog slows on the porch, and as I step in, I breathe in her scent. It's faded like she isn't here. Frowning, I push open the door to my room, empty. The door to her room, empty.

My stomach clenches as I realize the bag she brought her things in is now missing from its spot hanging on the footboard. Striding across the room, I pull open the closet and reveal empty hangers.

No.

She's taken her belongings and left. My chest feels like I've been struck. I stumble and slump onto her bed. Where would she go? Back to the Raven Pack? No, she has no way to get there unless she runs, and she wouldn't disobey Slate. She's got to be with her brothers or maybe Hazel.

My gut roils and my shifter instincts surge. But I can't have this discussion in wolf form. Gritting my teeth, I head toward Slate and Hazel's cabin, trying to contain my pace to a fast walk when all I want to do is sprint.

Warm light glows from the windows, diffused by linen curtains I helped hang. Hazel picked a dark green paint for the front door, with brass hardware. I have to pause a moment before knocking. It won't help to start this conversation angry.

My knuckles rap on the glossy wood and my sensitive hearing picks up hushed female voices. Finally the hinges rasp as Hazel cracks the door.

Her body fills the opening, blocking my entrance and my view into their living room. "Jasper," she says.

"Is she here?" My voice is harsher than I intend.

"She doesn't want to see you." Hazel tucks her hair behind her ears, the only tell that she feels guilty.

My hand grips the door frame. "We need to work through this."

Hazel's brown eyes meet mine and I see resolution in her unwavering gaze. I won't be getting past her. "She'll come talk to you when she's ready. Not before."

"I want her to come home," I plea.

Slate steps onto the porch behind me and rests his hand on my shoulder. "It's okay. She needs some space."

Her safe space should be with me. She needs to be home. In our home. My mouth opens and closes but I have no response.

"I'll talk to her," Slate offers. Hazel's eyes narrow at him, but he shrugs. "Go home. We'll see you tomorrow."

My throat is thick. Slate takes one last look at me and steps past his mate. I can hear Marigold murmur a greeting to him, and it's like knives cutting into me.

"Good night, Jasper," Hazel says softly, closing the door in my face.

I can't seem to move my legs. Each breath is jagged. My wolf surges forward, overtaking my human form. My ripped shirt falls to the ground and I scramble out of my sweats, not caring if Hazel or Slate sees the evidence of my shift.

The anxiety buzzing under my skin slowly fades away. In this form, worries are dull, but the grief of potential loss still chokes me. My four paws stumble and regain balance as I lope into the forest.

Every step further from Marigold feels like a mistake. My path curves, bringing me back toward my brother's cabin. Snarling, I pick up speed and run past.

Needing to feel anything else, I increase my speed until there's nothing but the ache in my lungs and the burn in my muscles. Our endurance is for moderately paced runs, not full out sprints. Soon, I am spent.

I intend to return to my own home, but I finally slow outside of that same damn cabin. It's silent now, with all the lights dark. Panting, I stand outside of the window of their second bedroom. It's an art studio with a day bed pushed against the far wall.

Exhaustion strips away the remaining fear, until only sadness lingers. I curl up, white tail over my nose.

Those few hours of sleep do nothing to refresh me. Sunrise curls through the forest. With a shake, I force myself to trot away from Marigold so I can shower and change before getting to work protecting my pack. I'll be back as soon as I can.

The morning is filled with video surveillance. Additional volunteers need to be trained in using the monitors while our Thetas and Zetas are all busy preparing for the fight we all hope is not coming.

I miss lunch, and perhaps some part of me hopes that Marigold will notice and bring me food. But she doesn't. Why would she?

"Are you ready to use those drones?" Heath asks.

I glance over my shoulder. The lines of his face seem deeper, as if he hasn't slept either. "Yes, Alpha."

"Take Onyx and get going."

We drive around to the highway north of the Raven Pack. The drone's range is only about twenty miles, so we pull onto the pack's access road to stretch our reach. Not deep into their territory, still in the border region where we don't risk offending them.

The drone whirs as it lifts off the ground. I study the screen and navigate it higher as Onyx settles back into his seat and closes the car door. "I'm sorry about the other night," Onyx says after a stretch of silent concentration.

Shrugging, I say, "It's okay, no big deal."

"You guys get in a fight?"

I grind my teeth, trying to not imagine how upset Marigold is right now, while I'm miles away working to keep her safe. "I'd rather not talk about it right now."

Onyx looks out the window, respecting my request. "Do you think we'll find anything? I can't imagine Ironcrest actually making a move."

"Oh, they will. I hope I'm wrong, but I don't think I am. My dad wouldn't hesitate to invade another pack, and Zephyr is a narcissist."

We pilot the drones along the border between the two packs, following the coordinates Heath and Slate maintain. Just empty trees. Sweeping back north, we see a lone scout, but it's not clear which pack he is from. It's impossible to tell if the apprehension I feel is from the scout, the overall situation, or my fight with Marigold. Onyx seems unconcerned, so we continue our sweep.

The sun dips lower, but we still have at least an hour of light. I want to pack it up and leave, but Onyx has taken over piloting and he squints at the screen. "What's that?"

His mouth turns downwards as he slows the drone. "Shit."

A dozen wolves weave through the trees, headed directly west. I fumble my phone and type out a warning to Heath and Slate.

Onyx hands me the control and I circle around, trying to stay far enough away that they don't notice the drone. But as I push further into Ironcrest territory, I see another group of a dozen wolves, and then a third.

"Shit!" I say louder. "If they're making their move, they'll follow up with drivers. We need to get out of here."

Onyx's eyes widen. He knows as well as I do that if Ironcrest is attacking and they catch us on this access road, we are dead. Pebbles crunch under our tires as he turns the truck and hits the gas.

It's not until we lurch back onto the highway that either of us breathes. His knuckles are white on the steering wheel as we build up speed. Mile markers zip past.

As we pass the turn-off for Ironcrest's compound, we see a line of silver and white SUVs. We are safe, but it's a punch to the gut to know Ironcrest is fully moving against the Raven Pack.

Despite my best efforts, our drone can't keep up and we lose the connection. It drops into the trees somewhere along Ironcrest's southern border. Hopefully I can retrieve it in a few days with its tracker, if it's still in one piece.

Throwing the controller down, I type out messages to Heath, detailing everything we were seeing and answering his rapid questions.

In record time, we pull into Bracken Creek's dirt lot.

Pack members jog in and out of our training building. Heath stands in the middle, giving out directions.

"What's the plan?" I ask.

"We're going up there. Gear up for a full assault."

Onyx follows me to the storage lockers, and we pull on chest rigs and grab handguns and wolfsbane bullets.

The guns are a relatively new addition to Bracken Creek's defenses. After Heath learned of the weapons Granite Ridge keeps on hand, he agreed to upgrade our options as well. The wolfsbane bullets will knock a shifter out for half a day or longer, and a second bullet can be fatal.

"Are you ready for this?" I ask Onyx.

He narrows his eyes. "Those motherfuckers shot me last year. I'm about to get my revenge." He tugs the neckline of his shirt down to reveal a scar high on his chest.

"Sorry about that," I mutter, tightening the straps of my harness.

Onyx shakes his head. "It wasn't you."

It's kind of him, considering I was on the wrong side of the conflict when he was shot.

"Fifteen minutes and we roll out!" Heath shouts.

XV
BRAIDS & BATTLES

MARIGOLD

Hazel drags her nails along my scalp, combing out my hair down my back as I lounge on her couch. "I'm sorry," she murmurs. Her empathy does little to soothe the tension in every cell of my body. This waiting game is torture with my heart is cut from my chest.

The door bangs open and Slate walks in. "Ladies, it's time to fight."

"They're moving?" Hazel yelps. "Already?"

"Yeah." His apologetic frown is a thin line.

Hazel stands, offering her hand to me. "Okay, let's do this."

I roll to my feet, adrenaline flooding my system. Panic over Jasper's safety nearly overwhelms me, and my regret over leaving him doubles.

"Sure I can't convince you to stay back?" Slate asks Hazel, closing the distance between them and pinching her chin with his hand. When she scrunches up her nose at him, he leans in and kisses her.

The rolling thunder clouds loom darker than this morning, the ominous gray promising mud and an early nightfall.

With shaking hands, I pull on shoes and grab the tight athletic jackets we wear during winter training.

"Ready?" Hazel asks, her eyes blazing.

We jog across the meadow and into the training building. The pack is buzzing around us, both those who are going and those staying to defend suiting up and grabbing weapons.

Slate tosses a chest rig to Hazel, and I tighten down the nylon straps to fit her snugly. She loads her gear before turning to help others.

"Marigold?" Jasper's voice resounds, and I whip around to see him standing among the trees, staring at me like I am his salvation. It takes all my willpower to keep my feet planted and not race to him. As he approaches, I bite the inside of my cheek.

"Don't worry, I'm not going to the Raven Pack. Your meddling has me stuck on defense," I growl.

"Thank you," he says, relief stark in every sound.

"I'm not yours to worry about," I reply, bristling.

Jasper reaches out and touches my hair, braided in one thick braid down my back. It slips through his hand like rope. "Please tie this up."

"What?"

His expression hardens, lines forming near his mouth. "Pin your braid up. So no one can grab you by your hair."

The fight leaves me. "Okay."

"Be safe. We can talk when this is over," he says, walking away before I can gather my thoughts.

"Marigold," a low voice says. I turn toward Hawthorne. "Ready?"

The small group of adults staying behind gather around him. We are all that's guarding the rest of the pack while our fighters are busy rescuing our reluctant allies.

With a sigh, I join the circle and duck my head while Linden reads out assignments.

We watch the warriors of the pack load into vehicles to leave. Hazel jogs toward me, holding a pair of wicked looking daggers. "Jasper wants you to have these," she says. "Don't argue. He has good taste in daggers and I want you to have all the protection possible." She forces them in my hands and turns away before I can thank her.

My heart is in my throat as Slate's truck peels out, throwing up pebbles under the tires. Jasper rides shotgun. Hazel is right behind them with Onyx beside her. I have to hope they keep each other safe.

JASPER

The car wobbles over the uneven road as we exit our territory and pull onto the highway. With a crack, the clouds let loose and rain splatters across the windshield.

"What's the strategy you guys finalized while I was handling the drones?" I ask Slate. They were still debating when I had left for surveillance.

His eyes flick between the road and the mirrors, his knuckles white. We're going as fast as we dare with a wet road. "Hazel wants to lead your squad into the building to clear a path for evacuations. Heath's team will take care of them once they're outside."

"Sounds good," I say, hands gripping the car door as we pick up speed.

"My team will be going after Ironcrest leadership, and Fisher will be looking for stragglers," he rattles off, his voice surprisingly steady.

"Who are you taking with you?" I ask. Slate's team will be at risk as they seek out the most dangerous of our enemies.

"Onyx, Cassia, and Fern." It's a good team. Cassia is a vicious fighter, and Fern can match her. They will cut through the Ironcrest wolves without hesitation. Onyx worries me, but after everything he went through last year, I'm not surprised he sought out such a placement.

My stomach tenses up in knots while Slate parks the truck along the side of the main road. It means a longer trip on our way out, but prevents the vehicles from being bottlenecked or trapped in the trees.

Hazel leaps from the truck ahead, her eyes blazing like a war goddess. Beside me, Slate adjusts his weapons post-driving, his eyes on his mate. I can't quite tell if the heat in his gaze is protectiveness or reverence.

Our teams take up positions. There are around two dozen of us. Against an estimated fifty Ironcrest fighters and up to seventy Granite Ridge members- we won't know until we see them.

Hazel leads our group of four straight toward the pack house. Lazuli creeps long silently, his dishwater blonde hair looking like ash in the dimming light. Clove takes up the rear. She's the oldest in our group, but as Fisher's mate and the twin's mother, I don't question her capabilities.

Slate's squad stays close to us. Cassia and Fern stalk behind their leader while Onyx scans for danger at their back.

Through the trees, the last of the day's light illuminates chaos. The exterior doors stand wide open, the handles bent. Nearby windows are shattered, glass sparkling in the dirt. They've broken into the pack house. So much for Nyx's defensive plan.

Only a few Ironcrest Zetas stand guard, ready to assist their teammates as the Raven Pack wolves are pulled out of the building. Five younger men and women are led out. The frightened packmates cling together, Ironcrest warriors shoving them along.

A woman with dark hair stumbles and falls, landing on her hands and knees in the mud. Her captor yells, the words unintelligible in the havoc. She cringes as he pulls her upright by her arm, twisting it viciously. I see Hazel's hand go to her own arm. Cold fear settles in my gut.

Our team halts, allowing Slate's team to surge forward, guns drawn. Rapid shots announce our arrival, and the first of the Ironcrest wolves hit the dirt.

Heath's team bands around the Raven pack members, directing them toward the rendezvous location. Moving as one, Slate breaches the door and his team slips in. Hazel nods us forward and we follow the same path.

Inside the pack house, Ironcrest seems to be destroying as much property as possible while they take captives.

Shouts of enemies drown out my thoughts. Slate's team raises guns and opens fire. Shock paints every face. Ironcrest seems entirely unprepared for any sort of resistance.

Hazel motions us forward and draws her own weapon. Now it's our turn.

I level my gun at a large man running toward us and fire my first shot. His feet slip out from under him and he falls backwards. It's the first of many.

Slate's team disappears ahead of us, hunting for Zephyr. Hazel drives us forward, clearing a path through the central hallway while looking for Raven wolves.

Everything blurs. We clear the way and I make sure to stay at Hazel's shoulder, defending her back. The Ironcrest fighters are not armed like we are. Screams ring out down the hallways, and Ironcrest members shift into their four-legged bodies. Lazuli hands his two handguns over to Clove and shifts into his wolf form, leaping to meet the first enemy that sneaks past our gunfire.

My lungs ache and I drop at least a dozen bodies before we reach a larger communal space filled with frightened Raven pack members. The trail of bodies behind us makes my stomach sour, but they will recover in a few days. But this poison lingers so they'll be weak for months. We are crippling their pack in one night.

Hazel ushers the Raven wolves out, sending them down the hallway we arrived through, to where Heath works with Cedar, Vale, and Ewan to get them to safety.

Something heavy slams into me, sending me sprawling. Pain shoots up my hip and ribs. Clove leaps over me, swinging her fist toward a bulky Ironcrest man with black hair. Scrambling to get up, I draw my second gun, but I'm too slow. The man slashes at Clove and opens up a gash on her arm. She glares at the knife in his hand as he jerks backwards. Most shifters don't bother with blades when we have built-in claws and fangs, but I've always liked a good dagger.

Stepping past Clove, I aim and fire, watching his body collapse as the wolfsbane pollutes his veins. Clove snarls, gripping her forearms as blood streams between her fingers.

Hazel directs Clove toward Heath, and Lazuli goes with her, using his snapping jaws to attack any enemy we missed on the way in. As I step over the man who slashed Clove, I reach down and pluck the blade from his hand, tucking it into my tactical gear.

"Are you good?" Hazel yells, looking at me for a moment before she focuses back on our fight.

"Great," I shout. We move forward, seeking out victims and destroying their attackers as we go.

With a kick, Hazel snaps open a door to reveal a dozen Raven pack members surrounded by four Ironcrest wolves, two already shifted. Aiming, I drop the black wolf easily, but the gray wolf leaps at Hazel before I can react. Its jaws close around her arm, over her protective gear, as she's slammed to the ground.

A two-legged Ironcrest guard rushes me, yelling unimaginative profane threats as he collides into me. Pulling my third gun free, I shoot up into his gut. Wolfsbane splatters back at me, stinging the exposed skin on my hand.

Scrambling up, I witness Elm pulling the black wolf off of Hazel as she fires directly into its chest. The fourth Ironcrest man drags Elm back, hooking his arm around Elm's neck to choke him. Throwing myself forward, I twist as my shoulder hits the floor and fire directly into the enemy's back to avoid hitting Elm.

As his attacker falls sideways, Elm's knees hit the floor. We're all on the ground for a moment as the Raven wolves swarm around us, helping us up. Hazel directs the hostages toward Heath's team with hoarse instructions and hand movements.

Elm's eyes connect with mine. His expression is hard, but so is mine. A battle is no time for reconciliation, and frankly I don't care if he likes me or not. He's still pack, and I would defend him even if he wasn't the father of the woman I love.

The hallway quiets as we draw closer to the main gathering space. Elm leads the way and I cover Hazel's back. She stops suddenly as we enter the larger space.

Several enemies lay sprawled across the floor. Slate has Zephyr at gunpoint. Nyx sits primly with her hands zip-tied on a leather armchair, watching with a vicious curl of her lips.

Have we won?

There are still dozens of Ironcrest wolves unaccounted for, and when my thoughts are able to slow down long enough to process, I realize I have not seen a single Granite Ridge fighter.

Ice floods my chest, down my arms and swirling in my stomach. Granite Ridge is not here.

Hazel grabs my arm, frowning as she studies my face. "What's wrong?" I blink at her. "Jasper!" She gives me a shake.

"Granite Ridge," I manage to say, my voice breaking. "Not here."

Hazel's eyes go wide and she spins, striding toward Zephyr. Her hands draw her dagger from a back sheath - I recognize it as the one that I gave her. Despite Slate's shout, she storms up to the Alpha and shoves the blade against his throat.

"Where is Granite Ridge?" she snarls.

Zephyr looks away, his face a mimicry of boredom. The uneven flutter of his breathing and his blotchy face gives him away.

Hazel presses the blade into his skin with a snarl. Sneering, he finally answers her. "At home, I assume, since they couldn't be bothered to hold up their end of the deal."

Slate steps closer, demanding, "What deal?"

Zephyr stares defiantly into Slate's face. "They were going to split the Raven pack with us. They wanted the wolves. We were keeping most of the land."

"I need to get home," I say, almost doubling over as nausea rolls through me.

Slate's eyebrows shoot up, though his focus never wavers from his prisoner. Fluidly, Hazel withdraws, leaning close to her mate. "Granite Ridge may have used this as a distraction and decided to make a move on us."

"No," Slate says. "That's not.."

I don't want to hear his reasoning. There's nothing he could say that would stop me. It's everything I can do to keep my wolf from bursting through my skin as I sprint toward the exit.

As night air washes over me, I pull my gear over my head and toss it toward a wide-eyed Cedar. Clothes only half off, white fur bursts over my skin as my wolf instincts take over.

I barely register Hazel shouting to Heath as my powerful lupine form plunges forward, vaulting over bodies and foliage alike.

Racing downhill, I barely slow as I wade into the creek. It's not too deep here. Water slides across my back, but the chill is nothing compared to the fear slicing into me. My claws scrape on the rocks as I pull myself upward. I shake my fur instinctively, barely slowing as I cross the shallows and reach the shore. I'm back in our territory. Muscles coiling, I leap forward and up the slope.

It's miles back to our pack's commune and Hazel races behind me the entire distance. There's no time to thank her, but I'm fiercely grateful. When it comes down to it, she's my sister, more so than Ember ever was.

My ears strain to hear any hint of noise from our home, though there is still at least a mile to go. Wolves can run fast and far, but as a shifter, I am even faster. Pushing myself all-out, the distance goes by in a blur.

Adrenaline spikes as the scent of smoke reaches me. Past the outlying cabins, orange and gold light glows from the inner circle of buildings. Keeping out of sight, I stalk in a wide circle, creeping closer.

Flames lick around the diner, melting the linoleum and pulling the roof down over the ashes. Crickett will be devastated. I hope she is far from the fire with her two daughters. Hawthorne was tasked with protecting our home. If Granite Ridge has attacked, where is he?

Hazel creeps up beside me, a low whine echoing the feelings of shock and grief flooding our pack bond. Anger, too. So close to her, I can sense her emotions stronger than the others, but if I focus, I can feel a sense of grim resolution from others nearby. Aside from general proximity, it tells me nothing of their location, only that they aren't in too much pain.

The two of us circle around toward the south, past the burning building. Through the smoke, we watch unfamiliar wolves move in groups between buildings. The activity seems to center around our training building. I'm not surprised they've chosen it for their headquarters.

A dozen Granite Ridge pack members on two legs march in and out of the steel structure, removing some of our supplies and distributing our remaining weapons. My hackles rise.

Lined up along the edge of the picnic tables lay several bodies. None of them look familiar, and more than one has a crossbow bolt sticking up from their chests. I hope they are all enemies and none of our own packmates. There's no sign of Hawthorne, Marigold, Linden, or any others that stayed behind.

We move further south, trying to pick up any trail. With the shouts of our enemy and the crackle of flames, it's overwhelming. Smoke blots out my sense of smell. But Marigold is here somewhere. I have to find her.

MARIGOLD

Smoke blocks the moonlight and panic rises up, choking me. My students huddle in Cobalt's room - the one with the window facing the forest. As far away from the front door as possible without risking being trapped if the building gets torched.

I pace the living room, all the lights off, waiting to be found. Sending these children into the forest with enemy wolves circling would be a death sentence, but it's only a matter of time until we are discovered. Thank the goddess my family's cabin is one of the further buildings from the center clearing.

The sound of soft crying drifts down the hall. Peeking in, I see Briar holding Willow as she softly cries. Elwood is curled against her arm, with Cobalt beside him, doing his best to look brave. A fierce pride rears up. "It's going to be fine. Alpha Heath will be back for us any minute," I murmur.

I have to believe it. Heath will come charging back, leading all of our packmates in a rescue mission. Surely, Jasper is safe and sound.

My knuckles are white around two daggers. My gun is empty, drained during the first wave of Granite Ridge wolves. Hawthorne threw himself in their path so I could lead the children to safety. I have to hope Crickett and his daughters are still safe in their home's basement. Even worse, I have no idea where my brother Indigo is. He was with Linden when they attacked, and the older wolf would have gotten him to safety if possible. All I can do is trust and focus on the children in my care.

Taking a steadying breath, I pace back toward the door, around the sofa. The shouts of our enemies grow louder.

Blood rushing in my ears, I crouch and shuffle toward the front window. Dark figures block the moonlight momentarily, causing my heart to leap into my throat.

The door blows in with a bang. My teeth clench. I will not scream.

Three Granite Ridge wolves dart in, two humans and one shifted. No time to hesitate. Without waiting for them to spot me, I strike from my position beside the door. My dagger slices into the upper back of the taller man with all of my strength behind it. He drops with the blade embedded into his back, blood gushing in a way I've never seen before. His scream turns to a gurgle.

The second man grabs my arm, squeezing until I drop the second knife meant for him. My cry of pain is drowned out by his angry shout. His grip never lets up as he shoves me backwards and onto the sofa.

He looms over me. My nails dig into my palms, my panic bleeding into my muscles and weakening me. I will not give away the children's location - although the wolf will discover them in seconds anyway. With any luck, they'll be out the window already.

"What a pretty little thing," the man says, one hand grasping the back of the sofa beside my head while his grip moves from my wrist to my hair. With an ugly smile, he twists a chunk around his hand. I want to gag.

Gritting my teeth, I kick up, striking him between the legs. He grunts and doubles over, his breath on my face. The hold he has on my hair drags me sideways and tears spring into my eyes at the pain.

Wolf jaws close over his arm, causing him to drop his hold on my hair. A white wolf drags him backwards and to the ground. Shocked, I push myself up and scramble over the back of the sofa to gain some distance.

Another wolf snarls and stalks closer to me while the man across the sofa screams. Spit drips from his bared teeth.

Weapon. I need a weapon.

There's nothing. I'll have to shift. My hands grapple with the tactical gear. I have to get it off or I'll be tangled up.

The dark wolf growls, its hackles rising, making it look huge. Another step, and my vision narrows as my heart races so fast my chest aches. My hand slips on the buckle, fear numbing my fingers.

The wolf lowers, its haunches bunching, preparing to leap. This time I can't help the shriek that tears from my mouth.

With a dull thud, one of my daggers embeds into the wolf's ribcage, throwing him back against the wall. The body slides down to the wood floor, leaving a slick of blood on the old wallpaper.

"Don't fucking touch my mate," a voice growls. Slowly, I tear my eyes off the dying wolf and turn toward the gravelly voice.

Jasper stands on the other side of the sofa, naked with blood smeared across his mouth.

XVI
STRATEGIES & SCHEMES
MARIGOLD

Cashel meets us at the edge of his territory. His mouth is a grim line, but he doesn't hesitate to help us.

"I'm sorry to be coming to you like this," Hazel says, head high despite the child in her arms and the exhaustion weighing her down. "Until we can regather our forces to take back our home, we don't have many other choices."

"We have the resources and the space. Isn't this what allies are for?" Cashel reaches out to grip her shoulders. "They will regret every second they dared to spend in your territory."

Jasper's hand tightens over mine. Under his sweats and t-shirt, bruises cover his hip and ribs, causing him to limp. He's wiped his face the best he can, but blood spots his clothes and hair - and mine too.

The Valley Pack opens up a handful of cabins for us while their team puts together a second dinner that we share in a large meeting space. Like the Raven Pack, they have one central pack house, but with more individual cabins surrounding it.

Jasper eats with one hand, his other hand gripping my thigh possessively. Hazel eats across from us until our team from the Raven Pack returns. As the door opens to reveal more of our packmates, she launches herself across the room into Slate's arms with a cry.

Heath limps in, his arm over Cedar's shoulders. Fisher follows, his mouth a grim line.

They should be returning home victorious, but Granite Ridge swept that out from under us.

Jasper leans over and kisses my cheek before rising to follow Heath, Slate, and Hazel. Suddenly alone, I curl my arms around my knees.

A shadow blocks out the overhead light for a moment before my father sits beside me.

"You're okay!" I squeak, squeezing my arms around his shoulders. Tears prick in my eyes for the millionth time in the last few hours. "What happened up there?"

The gray streaks glint in his reddish hair as he shakes his head. "They surrounded the pack buildings and Nyx was so sure that all the security doors would hold. But in less than an hour, they broke windows and simply unlocked the doors from the inside."

"They weren't reinforced?"

"Most of them were."

"How could she be this stupid?"

Sighing, my dad picks up his bowl. "She's stayed so far away from everyone else, I don't think she had any idea what they were capable of. Maybe she believed they would never actually attack." He takes a bite of his dinner and I make no attempt to fill the gap in our conversation.

"How'd it go back home? I didn't get much information," he finally says. The tremor in his voice tells me how deeply he feels this, even if his words are casual.

Rubbing my hands over my face, I slowly exhale. "Within minutes of everyone's departure, Granite Ridge arrived. They were everywhere. I gathered the kids I was watching into your cabin. So it's a bit damaged, I'm sorry."

He cocks his head. "What do you mean a bit damaged?"

"I may have stabbed someone in the living room." His mouth twitches, prompting a grin to spread across my own face. "Three guys came in, so I stabbed one, and then Jasper took the other two out."

"Jasper," he says, more contemplative than questioning. "I saw him in Raven. He went back?"

Swallowing, I nod. "He's the reason most of us made it out. He realized Granite Ridge wasn't with Ironcrest in the attack and guessed what they were doing. He reached me just in time, and Hazel rescued a few others."

"Who was left behind?" His voice drops.

"I don't know for sure. I think Hazel was trying to account for everyone. They captured Hawthorne, and a few others. Crickett and the two girls are locked away, I think. Not sure who is with them. But they won't last long down there."

"We will get them back," he growls. I nod. "I'm so glad you're safe."

My head rests on his shoulder. "You too, Dad."

JASPER

"This is my fault. They wouldn't have come after us otherwise," I say, hanging my head.

Hazel's eyes blaze. "Absolutely not. If anything, it was revenge for what I did."

A low chuckle emits from Heath's reclined form. Marigold's grandmother Sable has cut away the pants below his knee and is wiping down the gash across his shin. "Unfortunately, this grudge extends far past your recent offenses."

"Worth burning buildings?" Hazel asks, her mouth downturned.

Heath nods. "As a child, Sienna thought she deserved to be the Alpha someday, but she was rejected over and over. She's wanted revenge since before you were born."

"The Granite Ridge Pack has always been in conflict with us, although it used to be friendlier. More rivals than enemies. But when Sienna went to Ferris, it got worse. And it's been twenty years of that festering."

Too many eyes watch me. Gritting my teeth, I slowly nod. "She's always been unpredictable and vengeful. I'm not sure why I ever thought this day wasn't coming. But you're right, when it comes down to it, I don't think this has to do with me or Hazel. It's always been her obsession."

"You more than most know what she's capable of," Sable says without looking at Hazel. Slate responds with a growl. It's a testament to Heath's poor condition that he does nothing to curb Slate.

"So what happened after we left?" I ask.

"We shot Zephyr to take him out for the day, and left him tied up in Nyx's care. A group of Ironcrest wolves retreated, but Nyx has plenty of prisoners to deal with. We got your call right around the time we were finishing off the stragglers that didn't retreat when they had the chance," Slate says, anger curling around every sound.

"Well, we were able to pull most of the pack out. From what I can gather, most of our elders are still there, along with Hawthorne's entire family, and Starling is with her grandmother. The rest of the kids aside from those three are all here safe."

"Glad to hear it," Heath says.

"My biggest concern is Hawthorne. And we don't know about Linden either, but we know for sure that Hawthorne took the brunt of their attack."

The room is solemn. Heath grips his chair arms with white knuckles, and it's impossible to tell if it's over his Gamma or the pain of the wound Sable is treating.

"So what are we going to do?" Slate asks.

"Get our home back," Hazel answers viciously, reaching over and threading her fingers through his. My lungs tighten. I don't want to be here in a meeting, I want to be with Marigold. But this is for her.

"Jasper, what do you think they'll do now? How will they fortify their position?" Fisher asks.

My teeth roll over my bottom lip as I try to force my thoughts in order. "They'll centralize. Hostages, leadership, resources, everything."

"What about defenses?" Heath wonders.

"Maybe cameras, but I think it's too early for them to have hacked into any of our tech so they're probably relying on patrols. And they like bigger patrol groups, so it's easier to hear them coming."

"We need a way to get inside and get our people out before it turns into an all-out fight and they can be used against us," Hazel says.

"Focusing our assault on wherever the hostages are held," Fisher begins. Slate holds up a hand, silencing him.

"The easiest way would be through the front door." Slate's voice drops, the determination bright in his mossy eyes. Something about his tone pushes away my conflicted thoughts. He's right.

And with that, we begin to brainstorm a plan to reclaim our home.

The cabin given to us is a two bedroom. Slate and Hazel take the other bedroom. When I stumble into the building after my brother and his mate, I find Marigold in the bathroom. She stands before the sink and scrubs her hands.

Closing the door behind me, I approach her cautiously. Her eyes are red but dry as if she's run out of tears.

"I have blood on me," she whispers. I see droplets drying to brown across her shirt and joggers. The skin on her hands is raw as she continues to scrub. I remember the enemy with my dagger sticking out of his back. It's the first time she had to kill someone.

"Hey, it's okay," I say. Leaning past her to the shower, I crank the handle over to red. "Nothing a hot shower can't fix."

Sniffling, she nods and allows me to pull her shirt over her head. "Thank you," she says. Her hands go to the hem of my shirt, and she gently peels it off me. My hands go to her waist, pulling her closer.

"You were amazing today," I praise her, "You saved them." It's true. Her students would likely be dead now without her bravery and quick thinking.

Her hands skim up my chest and stop at my neck as her thumbs stroke along my jaw.

"You took down two guys," she murmurs. "You threw that dagger right into that wolf before he could hurt me."

"I would do it again in a heartbeat to protect you."

Her alluring lips don't answer, instead, she presses a kiss to my mouth. There's more discussion to be had, but I won't rush her.

Hooking my thumbs into her waistband, I ease her pants down and then turn her toward the shower. Her grip on me tightens, pulling me with her. "You want company?" I ask, smiling wryly. She answers by tugging my hand under the water spray. "Anything for you."

Shedding my pants, I step into the tub and allow the shower spray to coat me. The tempered glass door slides closed with a dull thud. Water streaks down her stomach as she faces the stream and allows it to strike her face and front. My fingers work through her hair, untangling the remnants of her braid and massaging her scalp.

Finding some soap, I run my palms down her arms and then across her chest. She melts into me. The last of the soap rinses away and I'm drawing leisurely circles across the skin on her ribs.

"See? All better." I murmur into her neck. At the sound of my voice, she twists in my arms and resumes kissing me, this time fiercer and wilder. Her nails prick the skin on my back as she pulls me flush against her. Water drips from her closed eyelashes, hiding any tears she might shed.

She nips along my jaw, eliciting a shudder and causing my hands to clench in her hair. "Take me to bed." Blinking at me, she amends, "I need you to hold me and know we're okay."

"Alright, Sunshine."

We borrow towels and wrap ourselves up before creeping across the hall to our designated bedroom. Leaving her hair damp, she climbs under the blankets completely bare. Her wide blue-green eyes watch me, wide and vulnerable.

"So are we okay?" I ask cautiously, crawling across the bedspread toward her. Her tongue swipes her bottom lip and I'm tempted to forgo my questions so I can kiss her senseless. But we need to discuss us. I'm not going back into battle without knowing she's mine.

"Yes, I think so," she says.

Drawn to her warmth, I hover over her and nuzzle against her neck. She arches and presents her throat to me. I can't help the groan that rumbles from my chest. The wolf part of me loves when she's submissive.

"I'm sorry for going behind your back. I couldn't stand the thought of you being directly in the path of our enemies," I say before licking the skin in the hollow under her throat. She rewards me with a soft sigh.

"I should have talked with you first. I should have listened to you," she says, her hands sliding over my shoulders and pulling me down.

Breathing in her scent, I gather my courage. "So about what I said in your family's cabin?"

Her breathing halts and her eyes trail over my face while she gathers her thoughts.

"I'm sorry, you don't need to say anything." I murmur, "I just wanted you to know I'm ready to commit, whenever you are. And it's okay if you need time. Months or even years. I'm not going anywhere," I trail off.

"I want to," Marigold says. "There's no point in denying what we are." Her hand skims down my side. "This is forever."

Her words blaze across my skin, leaving a trail of heat and need. She wants me in that all-consuming and permanent way. The need to possess and mark surges in my chest.

"You are my mate." Her lips form the words that I'm desperate to hear. Everything I've wanted. My vision blurs for a moment and I have to suck in air to steady myself.

MARIGOLD

Jasper's eyes glow so brightly, I suspect they'll leave spots on my retina. His aqua eyes are incredible at all times, but when he's angry or aroused, they're spellbinding.

"Little mate, I want to make you mine," he says, that velvety voice deep and raw. My stomach swoops.

"Good. Make me yours." I nip his bottom lip, smiling back at him as his eyes widen. His surprised expression melts away to the cocky smirk I love so much.

He exhales, eyes narrowing. His lips skim over my skin again. "I want to claim you so badly. Are you ready for that?"

"Yes, mark me," I urge boldly.

His growl rolls into a groan. "I don't want to rush this because we're in this situation with tomorrow being dangerous."

"I don't care the situation, I want you," I argue, suddenly impatient.

"Are you sure?" he asks.

"Yes, please, baby," I beg, knowing how much he loves it. To emphasize my point, I hook my legs around his.

"I love you," he says, kissing me before I can answer. When he breaks away, I echo him. Reaching up, I thread my fingers through his damp hair.

His eyes are so dark, the aqua is a glowing rim. Hesitating, he bites that full bottom lip. "This might be uncomfortable for you."

"Worth it," I say, trying to reassure him even though I'm quite sure it'll be worse if we don't, considering the throbbing between my legs has me on the verge of humping him.

Keeping his gaze locked on mine, he slides his hand between us, teasing across my entrance and dipping one finger inside of me. My eyes flutter closed at his touch. Grazing upwards, he circles my clit, and my back arches against my will.

My nails dig into his side. "Jasper," I whimper. When I open my eyes, his focus is still on my face. "Next time I come, I want it to be on your cock."

He stiffens, the muscles along his back tensing under my hands. "You're making it hard to stay calm and be gentle," he says, his voice hoarse.

The joke is so easy, I can't resist. "Yeah, I make it real hard," I say with a grin. Snorting, his forehead falls to my chest.

"I can take it. I'm not made of glass."

"No, you're much more precious," he says, pressing a soft kiss to my sternum.

I'm out of patience. My heels dig into his ass as I whisper in his ear, "Then you better fuck me or I'm going to burst into flames."

His smile is wicked and my blood sings at the glint in his eyes. "If that's what my mate wants." Carefully, he lines himself up and nudges my entrance.

As he pushes in, my eyes squeeze shut. The stretch is blissful despite the discomfort, but as he reaches a certain spot, moderate pain jolts me. Gasping, I cling to him.

"Breathe, Sunshine," his soft voice commands. "Breathe." I obey. After a couple of breaths, my muscles relax.

"Doing okay?" he asks.

"Fucking fantastic," I reply, my words choppy.

He brushes his lips across mine and then begins to move.

"Oh," I blurt. "Oh!"

A growl rumbles from his chest. "You feel incredible."

I could say the same, but words won't form in my brain. Instead, I reach one arm above me and push against the headboard to hold my body steady.

"I love you," I murmur, saying it over again.

His smile is genuine. "I love you too." He slows and I let out a low whine in protest. "Patience," he whispers. Sliding a hand under my knee, he adjusts our angle. A little gasp escapes my mouth as he rolls his hips, the angle deeper.

My core clenches around him as I twist under him, trying desperately not to scream. But the feeling of his slow movements inside of me while I shatter is overpowering. He bends over me, stifling my cry with his mouth and tongue.

My pleasure comes in waves, flooding every cell in my body as he begins to move again. These aren't the smooth thrusts we started with, they're urgent. He drives into me and then he's slowing and pushing in harder. I watch his look of concentration as his composure splinters.

His breath is hot on my neck, and my instincts vibrate with the desire to bite and be bitten. He licks down my neck to the juncture of my shoulder. I want to beg, but I stay silent, knowing the instinct must be riding him hard as well. Sharp teeth press against my skin and I can't breathe. The cut into my skin is exquisite.

He moves back, his mouth slightly open and my blood on his lips. I push up, reaching for him, and he tips his head to offer himself to me. Reverently, I kiss and then bite into the muscle.

The tang of his blood barely registers as a swell of emotion washes over me. Warm affection, passion, the desire to protect, admiration. Everything he's feeling echoes in me, and for a moment I can't distinguish my emotions from his.

The bond between us settles and I return to myself. He is like a glowing presence and I suspect I will be able to sense when he walks into a room without needing sight nor scent.

"That's kind of a lot," I murmur. Jasper's answer is pressing his lips to mine, traces of our blood mixing as he presses me back down into the pillow.

The stroke of his tongue is now paired with a wave of his enjoyment along-side my own. I know he feels the same.

Finally he breaks away. "You've ruined me," he rasps.

"Good thing we can do that whenever we like," I purr into his ear. His answering growl makes my toes curl, as he withdraws and reaches for one of our discarded towels.

A blush heats my cheeks as he cleans me up. And somehow that leads to him touching me again until I'm whimpering his name into the pillow.

XVII
HOSTAGES & HEISTS

JASPER

"Good morning, Sunshine," I say, loving how her weight feels against me. Her head lays across my chest, an arm and leg thrown across me.

With a deep breath, she rolls off of me and rubs her eyes. "Where?" she starts to say before going quiet. I grip her waist and pull her against me, pressing a kiss to her temple. For a moment she stares at the ceiling.

"I think this is the happiest and saddest I've ever been at the same time," she says.

"What do you mean?" I ask carefully.

Marigold sighs and turns her face toward me. She tips her chin up to kiss me briefly before answering. "I've lost my home but I found my mate." She draws out the last word, testing it out with a tentative smile. It wavers, like she's unsure if it's okay to be happy when our friends and family are preparing to do battle.

"Tonight, after we've reclaimed our territory, you can just be happy," I murmur.

"Supremely happy." Her palm skims my chest, her lips touching my skin. She works her way down to the ring of pink scars from last night. A permanent marker of our commitment.

"Mate," I say, "As much as I would like to repeat last night right now, we have a lot of preparations to complete today. Are you feeling good?" Reaching up, I run my thumb over the matching circle of tiny pale scars that mark her as mine. Her happiness buzzes between us.

She nods. "Let's do it," I smirk and she rolls her eyes at me. "You know what I mean."

We dress in borrowed clothing. Coming out of our bedroom, we see Hazel and Slate eating granola bars and fruit in the kitchen. Marigold pads toward them without any hesitation. A flush creeps up my neck as I follow her.

"So what's the plan?" Marigold asks.

"We'll have a debrief on everyone's roles, and then it's time to kick some ass," Hazel says. Her eyes flick up to me for a moment.

"It's a good plan," I say, feeling uneasy with Hazel's full attention on me. Her eyes narrow. She doesn't like how much risk Slate and I are taking on ourselves.

"Alright, let's go," Slate says, pushing off from the counter. Marigold turns to follow him.

Glancing back at Hazel, I pause. One eyebrow is raised. Silently, she raises one hand to her own claim mark where it peeks out from her loose shirt. Unconsciously, I mirror her, adjusting the neckline of my shirt to make sure my mark is covered. The instant she sees my motion, her eyes widen.

Giving a slight shake of my head, I silently beg her to stay quiet. It's Marigold's news to share when she is ready, and this morning isn't exactly ideal timing for a celebration. Hazel's nod is subtle, and I let out my breath.

"Are you guys coming?" Marigold says, holding the front door open for us.

"Yeah, sorry," Hazel says, sliding past me and jogging to the door. I follow with deliberate steps, letting my mind turn over the details of our strategy as we walk to the debrief.

The sun has begun to dip below the tree line by the time Slate and I are trudging across Bracken Creek territory. Slate walks stiffly, his nerves showing in the clench of his jaw.

"How's Hazel feeling?" I ask.

He jerks as I shake him from his thoughts. "She's okay. Physically fine. Eager to take on Granite Ridge."

"Good."

"So," he says, hesitating, "you and Marigold?"

Pine needles crunch under my feet. "Fine."

"Sounded like you guys made up," he says lightly.

"We are not having this discussion," I reply with a dry laugh.

"Did you ask her to be your mate officially?" he asks.

There's no way I can lie to him. He would see through it instantly.

"You did, didn't you," he says, a wide smile spreading across his face. He chuckles, running his fingers through his dark hair to sweep it away from his forehead.

"I don't think she's ready to tell anyone," I say softly.

"So how'd you ask?

Shrugging, I rub at my arm. "Well, it wasn't so much asking, as it was calling her my mate as I killed a wolf who was about to attack her."

"Ah." Slate nods, as if this makes perfect sense.

"Last night she said she's all in," I finish my story.

After a few more steps, Slate asks, "Did you claim each other?"

My guilty smile is answer enough. Slate turns, his hand gripping my shoulder. "I'm really happy for you guys."

Coming from my older brother, it means a lot, and the emotion rising in my chest surprises me.

"Wolves ahead," I warn, tracking them by sound. Slate sighs. I know he'll hate this part. But it's necessary, and it was his idea. Even Hazel agrees that it's our best shot.

We continue to walk forward, unbothered as Granite Ridge wolves surround us. Snarls and barks echo through the trees.

"We're here to negotiate," Slate says, raising his hands in surrender. Our captors drive us forward, though Slate refuses to increase his speed despite the jaws snapping at our legs.

The circle of buildings surrounding the meadow looks mostly untouched, with the exception of the blackened diner. A few structural beams stand leaning against one another in the rubble. But at least it's the only destroyed building. I try to ignore the bodies, still uncovered a day later.

Sienna and Ferris have set up court in the training building. It's the largest space in our community and it's full of weapons. Two-legged guards take us from the patrol. Rough hands grip my biceps and tighten zip-ties around my wrists. I don't recognize many of them, and the ones that are familiar keep their eyes on the ground. Slate lets out a low growl as he's restrained and we are led forcibly toward the enemy's command center.

Inside is surprisingly quiet. Chairs have been brought in for the Alphas and benches dragged forward into a loose circle for subordinates to sit at during meetings.

"Isn't this a nice family reunion?" Sienna says, rising from her seat. She's in head-to-toe scarlet, standing out from the grays and blues around her. Her waist-length dark hair falls in dramatic waves and her eyeliner is sharp as a dagger.

"Hello, Mother," I say, the words painful as I force myself to meet her gaze.

She strokes my face. "It's so good to see you again. And both of you together! I never imagined this day would come."

Slate leans away from her touch when she tries the same motion with him. Clicking her tongue, she turns back toward Ferris.

"So what brings you back to me?" Her mate stands, resting a hand on her shoulder. Her lip curls at the contact but she covers it with a sly smile.

Clearing his throat, Slate says, "We are here to negotiate a surrender under terms that protect the lives of our packmates."

Ferris's cold eyes narrow as he stalks toward us. "I have everything I want, and we will get your wolves eventually. Why should I make any concessions?"

"When you negotiate with us, you'll find out," I say, meeting his stare boldly. I'm baiting him. He will make mistakes if he's angry. Maybe.

"Where are our wolves that you are holding hostage? I'd like to verify their safety," Slate demands.

"Don't worry, they're all settled in some cabin," Sienna says with a dismissive wave, her irritation sharpening her words.

My eyes flicker to the doorway, tracking the fading light. It's our only signal for when our teammates will move.

The red-headed wolf called Hawk stands at the doorway, gripping the frame as if he doesn't want to be forced any closer. His eyebrows arch at the sight of us with our hands shackled behind us. "Alphas, the Zetas have been unable to break into the supply shed. What would you like us to do?"

Behind Hawk, a slim girl with dark eyes and shoulder-length navy hair stalks forward. My sister. Unlike her Intended, she shows nothing but delight at my vulnerable position.

"Burn it," Ferris says without hesitation. Ember's mouth curves into a smile.

Sienna whirls, glaring at him. "Absolutely not. Use the captives. Surely one of them knows how to unlock it." She turns toward Hawk. "Use whatever force is necessary to persuade them."

Hawk looks between them, lines creasing his forehead.

"It's fine," Ferris says, dismissing him by turning his back.

Ember scoffs, crossing her arms petulantly. Still scowling, she moves away from her future mate to stand behind her mother. Those glittering dark eyes regard us as something vile yet interesting, like exotic roadkill.

With a smile that shows fangs, Sienna advances on us. "So what are you able to offer us?"

I raise my chin. "We need some assurances first. Like where is Hawthorne?"

"Oh the Gamma?" Sienna asks. "Somewhere around here." I wish I could read the thoughts behind her cold eyes, but she's as veiled as ever.

"Is he alive?" Slate asks.

"For now," Ferris growls.

Sienna sighs as if this is all tedious. I adjust my stance, trying to take the pressure off my injuries. Her eyes snap to the movement.

"What is this?" Her voice finally sounds surprised. She tugs my shirt aside, revealing the claim mark Marigold left last night. Even with two decades of experience dealing with her, I'm unable to read the expressions crossing her face.

"Well?" she demands.

"I guess that information can be a part of our bargain," Slate says. My hands clench into fists at the idea, but I trust him.

"Fine," Sienna huffs, turning back toward Ferris. "Why don't we sit down and have a talk."

Without looking at her, Ferris sinks back into his seat. "Whatever my mate desires." Sarcasm stretches his words. My mother does not appreciate being patronized. Her shoulders tighten as she sits delicately beside him.

Awkwardly, we perch on benches a few feet away from our mother, further from Ferris. Ember stands behind her father, her stance deceivingly relaxed. It's impossible to miss her hand drifting to the blade she wears concealed at her hip. If Ferris was to say the word, she would likely murder Slate without a second thought, and perhaps me as well.

"Now, tell us what you had in mind," Sienna says.

MARIGOLD

"They're in the training building like we expected," Onyx says, studying the battered drone controller in his hands. Muscles tense, he stands like a soldier and not the irreverent friend I grew up with.

"Can you see how many wolves are surrounding them?" Hazel asks in clipped tones, her eyes peering through the trees although we are too far to see our targets.

He shakes his head, his dirty blonde hair falling over his forehead. "No, I can't get any closer without tipping them off. Sorry."

"Thank you for being cautious," I say. Worry knots my gut. My mate is in the enemy's hands, and I have to trust they won't hurt him before we can free them.

"Let's go," Hazel commands. Down the line, our teammates shift into their wolf forms. Shucking off my shirt, I allow my light reddish-gold coat to ripple down my arms. The cloud of anxiety lifts as my instincts surge forward, loosening my chest so I can breathe.

The scent of damp wood, rotting pine needles, and lingering smoke envelops me. With a shake, my ruff shivers down my back, softening some of my excess energy.

Cassia brushes up against me, Fern beyond her. The pack bond is a light burning in my chest. I draw strength from the hopeful determination and the protectiveness that drives us forward.

No matter what, we will be successful and do whatever it takes to get my mate and our pack back safely. There is no alternative.

The group is quiet while a select few, including Vale and Ewan, move northwards. Hazel slinks forward, stepping carefully to stay silent. We follow.

Onyx stays back with Heath, eyes on the training facility as he flies the drone in cautious circles. I don't glance back at them, but their low voices are comforting.

A howl cuts through the twilight. A second voice lifts to join it. Low barks and shouts from our enemies respond, and within minutes, the Granite Ridge patrol turns north. They are noisy and it's easy to track their progress. With any luck, they'll be chasing our fastest runners far from the community, buying us precious minutes.

Hazel breaks into a run and I fall into step at her flank without thought. Our packmates follow, racing in groups of threes and fours. We weave through the trees as the sunset turns the pale green boughs into gold. This land is familiar. I could navigate with my eyes closed this close to the center of our territory.

The scent of the destroyed diner clouds my senses, the acrid melted plastic and charred metal burning my nose. The offensive smell of a rival pack thickens as we approach the largest cabins we believe hold hostages. Underneath, fresher scents of our family members and friends confirm our guess.

Swift and silent, we surround the first cabin. The moment the door opens with a creak, Fern leaps. Her paws hit a guard and throw him onto his back with a jarring thud. His hands flail, but he's unable to reach a weapon before Fern's teeth close over his neck. She dispatches him with little concern if he can recover or not. I can't fault her, not when her daughter and mother are held captive inside and this man would kill her given the chance.

Her black wolf disappears inside. I follow, pausing to grab the ankle of the downed guard and tug him away, shoulders heaving. We need a clear exit. Disgusted, I drop his limb and cross the porch to push through the ajar door.

The snarls of approaching enemies pull Hazel away, and most of our team follows her lead. They will face the larger threat while we retrieve our packmates.

Fern stands over another Granite Ridge guard, leaving a third one for me. The anger of the last day narrows my focus until I am a missile of fangs and fur. He attempts to draw a weapon, but my teeth sink into his arm before he can get his hand around the gun tucked into his belt. Claw, rip, tear. Blood pools across my tongue and I open my mouth to let it drip onto the floor.

Stepping off my victim, I look up as slim arms fling themselves around me. Fern stands in human form, supporting one of our elderly packmates while her daughter, Starling, squeezes my neck as her tears soak into my ruff.

"Well done, my dears," Starling's grandmother says.

"We're not close to done yet. Cedar and Clove have a rescue team ready to evacuate you. Let's go," Fern orders, her last words turning to a bark. She plants a kiss on her daughter's forehead and pushes her toward her grandmother before she shifts back.

Ears scanning for our enemies, I trail the rescued hostages until Cedar takes my place. He bumps my shoulder, a silent encouragement, while Clove takes Starling's hand.

The sounds of a battle filter through the trees. Fern and I break into a sprint toward the clearing. We race to reach our teammates as they leap toward the Granite Ridge wolves surrounding the training building.

Fisher wrestles with a brute of a wolf outside of the training building. As the larger black wolf pushes our trainer down, my father joins the fight, ripping it away. Working in tandem, they take down the wolf and move onto the next one together.

The training building's door is still shut, causing my heart rate to spike. Jasper and Slate are still in there with Sienna, Ferris, and an unknown number of cronies.

Before I can reach them, the Granite Ridge patrol pours into the clearing. A dozen more wolves throw themselves at us, jaws snapping.

With a vicious snarl, Hazel leaps at the wiry dark gray wolf leading the charge, knocking him into the dirt. As another silvery wolf rushes to his defense, my paws dig into the earth to launch myself forward.

The idea of someone hurting my loved ones turns my vision to a haze. My paws meet his unprotected ribs as I knock him to the ground beside the first. Hazel's jaws close over his neck, eliciting a whimper.

JASPER

Sienna's eyes go wide as howls filter through the metal roof.

"That's your pack here to surrender?" Ferris asks caustically, already pulling a knife from his belt. At his hand motions, the guards file to the door with guns raised. The first two open the door and step out.

Slate catches my gaze. I tip my chin down in the barest of nods. I'm ready.

"It's their whole bloody pack attacking," a guard shouts.

"Then we can take them all out at once," Ferris says. Sienna turns her focus from us to him, her lip curling.

"Subdue, not kill. Without spoils, there's no value left to be had," she says, her words too quick to sound confident. I frown at her. It sounds as if she doesn't want our pack entirely destroyed. There's no time to consider the implications as a bang sounds. The wall vibrates as if a body was thrown against the siding. It's followed by a trio of shots fired, a louder snarl, and a muffled scream.

"Get out there," Ferris growls. The remaining guards throw the door open and join the battle.

"Don't move," Sienna growls, taking out her favorite dagger. She looks between her sons and her mate, Ember hovering like a shadow at her shoulder. Ferris approaches the door, his blade raised defensively.

Slate nods, signaling that we cannot wait any longer. As we shift into our wolf forms, the zip-ties slip off.

Sienna lets out a furious shriek, backing away. She bumps into Ember, who looks gleeful at the change of events. She's always been bloodthirsty. Within seconds, she's shifted into her black wolf, her hackles raised to make her look larger than her petite form truly is.

Slate moves toward Ferris, his teeth bared. Sienna is mine, but Ember blocks my path. With a growl, I spring. Ember snaps at my shoulder, seeing if she can get me to back down or weaken my attack. Not a chance. We've been sparring since we were children. Her black wolf stands no chance against my larger white wolf, and I know how her mind works.

Ember crouches, using her smaller size to get below me. Her teeth close on my ruff, too close to my throat for comfort. My paws push back, propelling me away until I can lower my muzzle and force her to the ground.

Paws on her ribcage, I snarl, keeping my sister growling on her side. My message is clear - stay down.

Slate advances past us toward my father, belly low, lips pulled back to display his teeth. Ferris pulls a gun from a holster at his back. That's not a wolfsbane gun, it's real bullets. Fear splinters through me. Slate attempts to leap before Ferris can fire, but even he isn't faster than a bullet. Ferris brings the gun up to aim at him.

The shot gouges the concrete beside Slate's paws. He jolts away, stumbling in his attempt to regain his balance to strike.

Sienna's unintelligible yells echo in the large space, but Ferris pays her no heed. With a snarl, he adjusts his stance. He won't miss a second time.

With a sickening thud, a dagger embeds into his chest. His second shot goes wide and hits the back wall.

For a moment, everything is frozen. Seemingly in slow motion, Ferris tips forward, the gun clattering to the ground, before he covers it with his slumped body.

Ember ceases her struggle, letting out a piercing wine. She scrambles out from under my stunned paws, and shifts back, dropping to her knees beside his body. With frantic hands, she pulls out the blade and presses the heel of her palms against the puncture. Crimson seeps between her fingers.

My gaze searches for the aggressor. Slate is already backing Sienna against the benches along the back wall. Her empty hands are raised.

Tentatively, I step toward Ember and Ferris, toward the blade on the concrete floor. It's Sienna's. My thoughts are slow.

With the slam of metal door against metal siding, Onyx and Cassia scan the scene, weapons raised. Cassia grabs Sienna's wrist and twists her around, injecting her with Rowanberry from a syringe to prevent her from shifting before the woman has a chance to react. She lowers Sienna to the ground as the natural drug floods her veins.

Ember screams, her voice breaking. Under her hands, blood pools around our father. Ferris is terribly pale. Shifting back, I reach for the first aid kit that Fisher keeps on a shelf by the door.

Onyx grabs Ember, attempting to inject her as well. She snarls, yanking her arm away. He clenches his jaw, gripping both of her arms behind her. Like lightning, Ember twists and slashes, Sienna's discarded blade tight in her hand. The dagger swipes along Onyx's gut, slicing his shirt open at the side where his gear fails to protect him.

He lets out a pained noise but refuses to release her. Cassia catches Ember's wrist and knocks the knife away before she injects her. Ember thrashes and screams.

Onyx releases her with shaking hands, letting Cassia shove the girl to the ground to subdue her. Red stains his shirt.

I'm torn between helping my murderous father and my friend. Onyx makes the decision for me. "It's not deep. Don't worry about me." He grunts as he sits on the closest chair and hunches over.

Cassia has covered Ember's body with her discarded dress. With deft movements, she zip-ties the younger girl to a bench and Sienna to her seat before turning to Onyx.

I peel up my father's shirt to reveal the stab wound. It's weeping more blood than I've ever seen. With trembling hands, I press a bandage over it, hoping I can staunch the flow. His eyes are vacant and his breathing slows.

"Dad." My voice cracks and self-loathing surges in my stomach like nausea. I shouldn't care. He's an enemy, and he would have cut me down right after killing my brother.

Slate crouches beside me. "He's gone."

Slowly, I pry my fingers away. I've ripped out throats and sliced open enemies without hesitation, but something about seeing the light leave my father's eyes has shaken me.

"It's okay," Slate murmurs, his hands squeezing my shoulders as he steers me away. "There's nothing you could have done. It hit an artery."

Forcing a deeper breath into my lungs, I straighten. There are still people that need my help. I can't stand here and wallow in my shock.

Cassia pulls Onyx's gear over his head and wipes away the blood.

"Not cool, dude," Onyx mumbles at Ember, his face pallid.

"Don't be dramatic, you're going to be fine. It's barely a papercut," Cassia says. He laughs and then winces.

It's obvious the moment my sister realizes whose dagger sits abandoned and bloody on the floor. "What did you do?" Ember screeches at our mother, straining against the zip-ties.

"Choose my child over my mate?" Sienna asks quietly, her words a little slurred. Ember lets out an anguished scream in response. "You wouldn't be complaining if *you* were the child I saved," Sienna says before turning her face away.

Slate looks between them, his hand coming up to rub the back of his neck. He looks as confused as I feel. For someone who has spent her life attempting to destroy this pack, Sienna didn't hesitate to put her estranged son before her mate, jeopardizing her power in the process.

"You'd better get out there, boys. The fight's not quite over," Cassia growls, looking up from wrapping gauze around Onyx's torso and tightening the bandage in place.

Slate and I pull on our sweats and slip on the gear Cassia hands over. I try to ignore the blood along the side of Onyx's tactical gear as I pull it over my head.

"Ferris is dead, and Sienna is captive. You've lost," Slate shouts, slamming the door open.

The ground is strewn with unfamiliar figures. Our team has dispatched many of our enemies, but small pockets are still fighting.

Hazel whirls, daggers flashing. Fern leaps on a man staggering away from Hazel. A man I recognize as Flint ducks past Hazel's offense and grabs the strap of her harness, attempting to shove her to the ground.

Slate is already across the clearing, seizing the man by the back of his shirt and flinging him to the dirt. His weapon clatters away. He rolls but before he can stand, Slate is on him. Hazel watches her mate as he slams his fist into Flint's ugly face. Three strikes and Flint's lip and cheek are split, his form limp.

Slate staggers up, embracing Hazel as she smashes into him and kisses him roughly.

My eyes scan for my own mate.

The hulking form of Aries blocks my search. He bares his teeth, barreling toward me. Without hesitation, I draw the gun strapped to my chest, praying it still has ammo.

My hand is steady as I point the weapon at Aries. He slows, his grin bloody as if someone has already knocked his teeth loose. "You are too much of a coward to shoot me," he croaks.

"Try me," I say.

His growl is anything but human. I wait until he is a few feet away and shoot into his gut. It's not a fatal shot for a shifter, but enough to take him out of the fight.

Grunting, Aries stumbles, hand pressing to his wound. "I'm going to kill you."

Somehow, he trudges forward, raising a filthy knife. I dance back, readying another shot that never comes. I'm out of bullets. My hands pat over my gear, looking for more.

Aries closes the distance before I realize how fast he's moving. His boots kick my legs out from under me. My ass hits the grass. He looms over me and his face contorts. My lungs scream as if filled with glass as I suck in a rough breath. I need my head clear to survive this brute.

But Aries doesn't move. His eyes stare ahead, and he slowly sways and falls forward. I pull my legs back clear of him as he crumples. A crossbow bolt sticks out of his back.

Across the clearing, Marigold is already reloading and selecting her next target. I'm entranced by the elegant curve of her shoulders as she raises her weapon. She's magnificent.

"Your Alpha is dead, surrender!" Slate yells, firing his gun into the dirt beside a snarling enemy wolf.

There are few opponents still standing.

Marigold advances, her crossbow pointed at a tall figure. Hawk. He raises his hands, dropping his gun on the ground at her feet. Slowly, he kneels, allowing Fern to zip-tie his wrists.

Slate and Hazel similarly restrain the remaining Granite Ridge pack members.

Looking around, I can tell that some escaped. Less than a dozen still stand, and they are battered, heads hanging. Cassia walks Sienna and a sobbing Ember out of the training building, pushing them to the ground at Slate's feet.

Hazel glares at Sienna, advancing slowly with a dagger in her hand. My mother looks up at her, her face passive. It's strange to see her without either a cold sneer or a simpering smile.

A shout rises, a mix of victory and anger. While many are bloody, I see none of our own seriously injured.

A blur of reddish-gold hair and flushed skin streaks toward me. Marigold's weapon lies discarded in the grass. She launches herself, wrapping her legs around my waist as I lift her up. We cling to each other, reveling in the moment of victory. The emotion flowing between us is enough to steal my breath.

"We made it," I say against her neck.

She kisses me recklessly, not caring who sees. I wish the moment could stretch forever, but hesitantly I set my beautiful partner back on her feet and turn to face our pack.

Slate gives me a nod, holding Hazel tight to his side. Heath stands nearby, talking with Fisher. Fern and Cassia wrangle our prisoners into a row. No one seems to have noticed our intimate moment.

Marigold stills. I follow her gaze. Both my mother and sister watch us with haughty expressions. "Jasper, who is that?" Ember demands. She seems to be looking for a distraction. Surprisingly, Sienna stays silent, her expression unreadable.

My mate smiles wearily. "I'm Marigold." She slips out of my grasp and crouches a few feet from Ember. "I hope someday we can be friends, but that's up to you."

Ember glares at her, her mouth opening and closing before she snarls, "Don't count on it." Her sneer is hollow, her eyes haunted.

Marigold shrugs and rises. Pulling her to my side, I lean my temple against her hair. "She hurt Onyx," I say quietly.

"Really?" Marigold says sharply, turning to see our friend leaning against the building. "You doing okay, big guy?"

"Concerned for me, Goldie?" Onyx says flirtatiously.

She laughs. I'm too relieved to mind his tone. A teasing Onyx is fine. It's when he gets serious that we have to worry.

"Thanks, man," I say.

Onyx rolls his eyes. "That sister of yours, she's a piece of work." I have to agree with him.

Ember lets out an angry screeching noise, twisting to bare her teeth at Onyx. The last threads of her composure break away, and she's wild with grief and rage.

Onyx looks unimpressed, his eyes dull with pain. "Give it a rest, psycho."

Across the clearing, Cedar and Lazuli support a bruised and bloody Hawthorne limping toward us. Crickett runs toward him, clutching their toddler between them as she embraces him. Despite his condition, Hawthorne kisses her back and even wraps an arm around her shoulders. Dahlia squeals and clenches his dirty, torn shirt in her tiny fists.

On the ground with a bandage pressed to his shoulder sprawls a vaguely familiar boy with black hair. He's still a teenager. Kneeling, I eye his wounds.

"Get away from me," he growls. Blood mattes his shirt.

"You don't have to go back to Granite Ridge. Life doesn't have to be like that," I say, wishing someone had said the same to me much sooner.

"Piece of shit," he spits, gasping as his muscles seize.

"If you ever decide you want to be free, there are other packs that treat their wolves with respect."

The boy growls until I step away. Marigold runs her fingers up and down my inner forearm, the texture of her skin soothing me. "You can't help someone that doesn't want it."

I know she's right. But it still stings as I look over the injuries of my former packmates. Many of these people would have gladly killed me even when I was still heir of their pack.

My gaze sweeps to the unmoving bodies. It's a pity, but after exhausting our supply of wolfsbane, we were left with little other choice in our methods of attack.

XVIII
ANSWERS & AFTERMATH

MARIGOLD

It takes hours to gather the bodies into trucks and return them and the remaining Granite Ridge wolves to their territory. They'll have to handle their own burials. It's a relief to get them out of our land.

Sienna stands alone, her face ashen, as she directs her wolves.

"Do you want to stay and help her?" I whisper to Jasper. After everything that has happened, a feeling like pity wells in my stomach.

"Absolutely not. Our pack needs us," he answers immediately. Turning away from his former pack, he buries his face into my neck. The rise of his chest is comforting against my curves.

He's quiet on the drive home.

The moon peeks over the treetops. Heath stands in the middle of the gathering, leaning on a crutch. His left leg is bound up tight.

Hawthorne holds onto Crickett who is quietly weeping. Perhaps it's the shock of the day or the destruction of her beloved kitchen. My grandmother has already patched Hawthorne. Bandages wrap his torso, one bicep, and the opposite thigh. Despite leaning on his mate, he looks decent with color in his cheeks and a tired smile. Daisy keeps calling him a mummy.

Exhaustion permeates the entire pack. No one is injured worse than Hawthorne, and most only have shallow cuts and bruises. Through the pack bond, I can feel a sense of relief, multiplied by my bond with Jasper. Quiet discussions buzz around us.

My mate's arm wraps my shoulders, holding me against his side. It's comforting.

My hand rubs wide circles across his back, trying to offer as much comfort as I draw from him. He tightens his grip and presses a kiss to the top of my head. The air leaves my lungs in a contented sigh.

His pale hair is silver in the moonlight, a fine highlight outlining his straight nose and high cheekbones. Reaching up, I wipe a spot of blood off his jaw.

Hazel's brown eyes connect with mine. A wry smile curves her lips. It looks like she already knows about our decision.

"Did you tell?" I whisper, frowning at Hazel.

"Slate kinda figured it out." He shrugs, glancing up. "And he told Hazel, looks like."

"If she didn't already know." When I think about it, it's surprising she didn't see through us the moment we walked out of the bedroom this morning.

Our musings are cut short by Heath raising a hand. Silence falls across the clearing instantly Dozens of eager faces watch their leader.

"In all my years as your Alpha, we've never faced a threat this grievous. And despite our injuries, we are all still standing," Heath says, "more or less." He chuckles, motioning at himself.

"We have proven that loyalty and kindness are stronger than greed and revenge." The pride in his voice is unmistakable and it echoes through the emotions of our packmates like warmth spreading from person to person.

Slate takes Hazel's hand where they stand beside her uncle.

Heath glances over at them. "My heirs proved they can lead our pack without me. Their quick thinking and wise decisions saved many of our lives and homes."

Hazel's cheeks flush and her eyes go to the ground.

"That being said, it looks as though the damage to my leg will be permanently disabling. I believe it is best if Hazel and Slate take up the mantle of Alpha in my stead. They are capable and ready, and I know all of us will support them as they grow into the role."

Murmurs of approval echo around us.

Hazel's mouth falls open, but she allows Heath to pull her into a one-armed embrace. He converses quietly with Hazel and Slate.

Jasper's arm around me goes slack. His expression echoes Hazel's. But while Hazel recovers as Heath speaks to her, Jasper continues to blink dumbly at our leaders.

"Are you okay?" I ask. His mouth snaps shut. "What's wrong?"

Like breaking from a trance, he looks down at me. "He just stepped down."

"Yeah, pretty sure we all saw that happen." He frowns at me like I'm missing something. "Jasper, what's upsetting you?"

Clearing his throat, he explains, "My father always said I would never be Alpha until he was cold in the ground. He never would have handed his role over to anyone. The fact Heath would willingly retire and give up his authority."

"Oh," I say, understanding finally. Yet again, our pack has surprised him.

"It's unbelievable," he says, his voice scraping. His happiness for his brother is tinged with sadness, though I would have missed it if we weren't connected with a deeper bond. I know him well enough to be confident it isn't jealousy, but a mourning for a family other than his own. The differences between Heath and Ferris are vast, and I know sometimes those differences feel painfully unfair.

"You've always belonged here," I murmur, tugging him into a tight hug. "Not there. You've always deserved a family like this."

His hands grasp me like I'm his lifeline as he breathes in the smell of my hair until his breathing evens out. By the time we've broken apart, the gathering has dissolved. Hazel stands by Heath, accepting congratulations from various lingering pack members.

"Are you two done?" Slate asks, his fake irritation giving way to a smile.

Jasper smirks and I pinch the skin on his side in a silent warning. "Sorry, yes," Jasper says, "Alpha."

"We'd like to talk with you later. Can we stop by your cabin in a bit?"

"Of course," I say over my shoulder as Jasper pulls me away and spins me to face him.

"I don't think I want to share you once we get home," he whispers in my ear.

"This sounds important."

"So is checking on our cabin," he says. "I have a surprise for you."

"So impatient," I tease, anticipation prickling in my chest.

Before I can protest, he reaches under my knees and scoops me up in a bridal hold. "Hey!" I protest, kicking my legs. My fingers wrinkle his shirt. Striding through the trees, he peppers my forehead, my cheeks, and my nose with kisses.

"Hold on!" he says, tipping me up until I'm hanging over his shoulder, freeing up his other hand to open the door. My shriek turns to a giggle as he slides me back into my original position.

As we step over the threshold, he gives me that cocky grin. "Welcome home."

"Everything looks untouched. We got lucky," I say, surveying our living room.

"Do you like this cabin?" Jasper asks. He lets me slide down his body until my feet hit the ground.

"Yeah, it's great." I look around to see if he made any changes, wondering when he had time to arrange a surprise.

"Really?" he asks quietly.

"Yes, I love it." I laugh, quirking one eyebrow at him.

He takes a deep breath. "Good, because I bought it from the pack. It's not a guest cabin anymore, it's all ours."

The words take a moment to snap into place. "What?"

"We can get something else if you like," he quickly says.

"No, that's amazing." My feet leave the floor once more as he hugs me around the waist and lifts me up. My fingers curl into the back of his hair. "It's perfect, but when did you have time to buy it?"

"Last week."

We settle on the sofa and I grab his hand, my legs across his. Looking at his fingers instead of his eyes, I say, "I feel bad though. I don't have a lot of money, but I can help."

His deep laugh breaks my thoughts.

"What?" I demand, a blush coloring my cheeks.

"I've been putting away money from my family for years, in case I ever had to run. They have more money than sense. You don't even have to work if you don't want to. The cabin barely put a dent in it."

"Are you kidding me?"

It makes sense. I don't know much about cars, but his car seems expensive, and he never seems worried about how much things cost.

"I want to buy you a car too. Something yellow."

Shaking my head, I squeeze his fingers in warning. "No way."

"You can't stop me from getting you gifts." He pulls my hand against his chest so I can feel his heart.

"Yes, I can." My eyes narrow into a glare.

A soft knock interrupts our argument.

"Come in," I say, releasing him and swinging my feet to the floor..

"You deviants better be wearing clothes," Hazel grouches, pushing the door open.

"It would serve you right, after how you and Slate have been," I tease. Jasper buries his face in the crook of my neck and laughs silently.

"Why do I have a feeling you guys will be worse?" Slate sits in the armchair opposite us and pulls Hazel into his lap.

"So what's going on guys? I need to get my mate to bed," Jasper asks, a frown creasing his brows.

Hazel's eyebrows shoot up.

"For sleep," Jasper growls. "It's been a long night."

That's an understatement as the pale morning light begins to filter through the curtains of our cozy living room.

"Well, we are going to be Alphas," Hazel begins, pausing like she isn't sure how to continue.

"Pretty sure that's been the case for like six months," I mutter, trying to not giggle. Exhaustion strips away my filter, making my words goofy and thoughtless.

Slate rolls his eyes. "You know what we mean."

It's too easy to tease him. Hazel's grin mirrors my own in a moment of female solidarity.

"I'm really excited for you guys. You're going to be amazing," I say.

Hazel's blush is back, and Slate's hands tighten around her waist, probably sensing her discomfort. "Thank you. But we are going to need our own second-in-command."

"Yeah?" Jasper says.

"Of course," Slate says.

"We'd like you to be our Beta," Hazel blurts. Jasper freezes, his brows furrowing.

Squeezing his arms looped around me, I reassure him, "Who else would they want?"

He takes a slow breath. "I appreciate that. But I'm going to have to talk with my mate about it." My hand covers my grin.

"Marigold, you don't have to be Beta too if you don't want to. Don't get me wrong, we'd love to have you. But if you'd prefer not to, it's fine. I don't care that it's tradition for mated pairs to take the same position. This pack breaks with tradition all the time. I mean, Crickett isn't Gamma with Hawthorne," Hazel says. She's right. The tension in my shoulders unravels.

"So basically I don't have a choice?" Jasper asks, his smirk softening his words.

"Correct," Hazel teases back.

Jasper huffs. His voice drops, speaking only to me. "Sunshine, how do you feel about it? Should I accept? And we can get back to them about what you want to do."

I can tell he wants to. Despite his calm exterior, excitement bubbles through our bond. I'm excited too. He deserves the position after how hard he's worked to prove himself. Not to mention, his natural ability and dominance dictate that he should be second after Slate.

"Yeah, you should. You're the best man for the job," I say, kissing his cheek.

"Alright," he says.

"Wonderful!" Hazel's smile is genuine. I thought it was Slate's decision to pick Jasper, but seeing Hazel's expression, I realize it was her. I should have known. Slate defers to Hazel as often as possible.

"I'll be happy to talk details tomorrow, but it's extremely late," Jasper says, releasing me to stand. Hazel and Slate both hug him.

I throw my arms around Hazel. "Thank you for supporting him," I murmur in her ear.

"I should thank you for the same thing." Her arms squeeze my ribcage. "Good night," she says, waving as they head out the door. It closes with a click.

"Well, Sunshine?" he purrs, turning away from the front door.

"Honestly, I want to keep teaching. I'm not made for leadership, and I love my students" I say, my heart in my throat.

"Not a problem." He's unruffled.

"Are you okay doing it alone?" I ask.

Jasper chuckles. "It's fine. I want you to be happy, and I think I can handle things. I've got plenty of support. I mean, my brother was Beta for a few years before Hazel joined him."

"You're going to be amazing," I say, completely confident that he will be the best Beta possible.

"And if you change your mind, or get sick of those kids, you have a right to be Beta. The option doesn't go away because you decline right now."

"Thank you." I exhale, tension seeping away.

He stalks forward, closing the distance between us. I step away from the coffee table, toward our bedroom door.

"Marigold, where are you going?" he says, his voice dropping to a rasp that feels like velvet sliding across my ribs.

"Bed?" I ask.

"Come here." His command sends a shiver down my spine. His scent fills my lungs as he reaches me, hands going to my waist.

"No thanks," I say, sliding out of his grasp and pulling my shirt off in one fluid move. He reaches for me again and I shimmy out of range. My hands fold down my waistband, sucking in a breath at the cool air brushing my skin.

"You are really something." He darts forward, catching me around the waist. His body hems me in against the kitchen counter.

"And you are wearing entirely too much clothing." I giggle. To emphasize my point, I tug at his shirt, pleased when he allows me to strip it off. I stop when his shirt is over his biceps and elbows, blocking his face. He has to reach to pull it off the rest of the way.

I don't miss the opportunity to flit away again, luring him into chasing. A predatory smile lights up his face as his eyes begin to glow. I feint left but go right. He's quick on his feet and grabs my hips as I pass him. Hands moving to my waist, he backs me against our dining table.

"Still want to go to bed?" I ask in a breathy whisper.

He lifts me until I'm seated on the smooth wood. "I'm good right here."

"I think you'll need to clean the table after this," I tease.

"I think you need to shut up and kiss me," he quips back.

Leaning in, I tilt my head to kiss him, but instead nip his pouty bottom lip and lean back. "Make me," I purr.

His eyes glitter at my challenge. With deliberate movements, he pushes me back against the table and drags my sweats off, tossing them across the wood floor.

"Jasper," I gasp as he drags me forward until my ass almost tips off the tabletop.

Eyes glowing, he kneels. His hands lift my calf, fingers skimming over the floral tattoo that climbs the back of my leg. "I love this." He sets my leg over his shoulder and I swallow thickly.

Words fall away as his breath warms my sensitive inner thighs.

At the first swipe of his tongue, my back arches and a moan rips out of my throat. A blush warms my skin, but from the way his fingers dig into my legs, it's obvious he loves hearing my reaction.

"My mate," he says against my skin, his words claiming me all over again. It takes me a second to realize the overpowering possessiveness isn't mine. Feeling his emotions sends a thrill through me again. The connection goes both ways. His tongue swirling over me sets off stars behind my eyelids, and he groans at the shared pleasure. He's gentle but relentless, devouring me until I'm breathless and boneless.

"Come on, baby, I don't want to break the table if I get up there too," he says softly, lifting me easily. I sink into his arms, secure in the knowledge that he'll never let me go.

He lays me back across our bed, not breaking our connection for a second. His mouth is soft against mine. This tenderness intoxicates me in a new way.

"You are so perfect. I've never seen anything as magnificent as you with a weapon in your hand destroying our enemies," he says. Glowing aqua eyes pierce my soul.

"Don't ever risk yourself like that again," I say, "I can't lose you."

Jasper frowns. "If I have to, to keep you safe, I'll do it all again."

I open my mouth to argue.

"Sunshine, you would do the same for me. Trust me to not be reckless." The affection in his voice smoothers my spark of outrage. He further soothes me by kissing across my jaw and licking the skin below my ear.

"I trust you," I breathe.

His gaze flicks up to me, halting his progress for a moment. The emotion through our bond is a tangle of gratitude and relief. Didn't he already know I trusted him completely? But after his upbringing and then joining our pack where some wolves still view him with suspicion, I should have realized how much it would mean to him.

His mouth over my breast empties all thoughts from my mind. Nails scoring down his back, I urge his hips against my thighs.

The brilliant smile on his face makes my stomach flip. "Impatient?" he murmurs.

"For you? Yes," I flirt. My hand closes around his length, drawing him against me.

"Whatever my mate desires," he half-teases, half-swears, pushing forward to sink into me. Ecstasy buzzes under my skin.

The softness burns away as a frenzy builds between us. The night before, he was careful and controlled. That's not what I want now. The hard planes of his body press into my curves as we set a brutal pace.

Soft breathy noises escape me, and he answers by lifting my knee against his chest to tilt my hips. My eyes squeeze shut, my body trembling. The feel of his skin against mine is almost too much.

Beautiful tension builds in every fiber of my being until I'm crying out curses. He slows, grinding into me. His release hits me through our shared bond, enough to break me a second time.

Jasper barely separates from me, his arms banding around me like he can't tolerate the thought of not touching me. I listen to his heartbeat as we regain our composure.

I wipe my eyes, surprised to find wetness there.

"Are you okay, Sunshine?" he says, tightening his hold on me.

I nod, sniffling. "More than okay. I'm deliriously happy."

He kisses my hair. "Me too."

As the birds chirp outside our window in the morning light, I sleep deeply, safe at my mate's side.

XIX
EPILOGUE
JASPER

Spring has finally warmed and the morning air has lost its bite. The river's water flow increases as the snow at higher elevations melts. It's my favorite time of year, as the deer bear their calves and the deciduous trees sprout millions of new leaves.

Marigold stands beside me, her hair gleaming and her eyes bright. I smooth my fingers through my mate's hair, happy she left it loose today. Around us, star-shaped yellow wildflowers bloom - marsh marigolds. Their leaves are glossy green and heart-shaped.

Ahead of us, Hazel and Slate step toward the water's edge, hand in hand. Confidence ripples off them, reassuring the pack members gathered behind them.

Sienna stands on the opposite side of the creek, within her own territory. Beside her stands a towering wolf I recognize as Orion. His clenched jaw shows a measure of anger, but he stays silent. He was a Zeta when I left the pack, but the way he stands beside my mother gives me pause. Sienna prefers to surround herself with the most vicious wolves, but after losing Ferris, maybe she went for brute strength.

Behind Sienna, my sister Ember stands with her hands clasped behind her. Her smile is a poor imitation of our mothers, sly but also full of violent promises that Sienna hides better.

Ember's future mate, Hawk, has his arm around her waist, though there is space between their bodies. She's only six months away from becoming an adult and his claim still stands. I glare at his freckled face. My sister may be unpredictable and dangerous, but saddling her with a mate the moment she becomes an adult won't help anything.

"So what did you want to discuss?" Hazel demands, raising her chin. Slate's hands rest on her hips as he stands slightly behind her, a smug look on his face.

"Peace, of course," Sienna replies.

"That would be at odds with your prior actions, Alpha," Hazel says.

Slate dips his head and places a kiss on the stretch of her exposed shoulder, right over his claim mark. It's a reminder and a challenge.

"I hope you will believe me when I say that Ferris was the driving force behind our grievous assault on your territory," she says. We all know that's bullshit. "I would appreciate it if we could sit down and outline what restitution we can make. I want to move forward as allies."

"It takes time to build trust. And you have many years of deceit," Slate says, his voice low.

Hazel chews on her lip, glancing up at her mate. He nods, ending their silent conversation, and says, "But we will meet with you."

The tension lowers, though no one truly lets down their guard. Hazel leads Sienna toward the shallow end of this stretch of creek so they can stand ankle-deep and discuss matters privately. Sienna looks as if she's smelled something disgusting as she steps into the water and I want to laugh.

As the three Alphas speak quietly, I approach my sister. Stepping off a flat rock, I stop a few feet from her. Ember stands stiffly, her obsidian irises cold as she regards me.

"How are you doing?" I ask. She idolized both of our parents so Ferris's death must be difficult for her. It doesn't surprise me that she sees Sienna's actions as a betrayal, leaving her without a parent she can trust.

Her voice is hoarse and full of malice. "What do you care?"

"He was my father too," I reply, my tone a soft reminder.

Ember's nose wrinkles as she sneers. "I believe he said otherwise after you objectively failed the pack."

"Are you on speaking terms with mom?" I ask, nodding toward Sienna.

She decides not to answer. Instead, her hand goes to Hawk's wrist. "Someday I will be Alpha, and you will only be," she pauses, "what you are now." Her disdain is a physical weight, but I let it slide off of me.

"Happy?" I supply.

"Pathetic." She turns her nose up.

There's no sense in telling her that I'm now Beta. It wouldn't make a difference, and it's not the driving factor in my happiness or my sense of success.

"You are still my sister. If you need me, you can call, and I'll answer," I say, even though she pretends not to hear me.

Hawk regards me, the same indecision on his face as during our fight to reclaim our territory.

"Take care of her. If you hurt her, I will destroy you," I growl. He doesn't flinch, just regards me coolly. It still makes me uneasy to not know this male so close to my sister.

Ember's hand releases Hawk's as she turns away. Her nails are a sharp, black manicure against the white of her fingers as her fists clench.

I hope it's not the last time I see my sister. But just in case, I want to leave nothing unsaid. "Ember, I love you."

"Eat shit," she growls under her breath.

Exhaling sharply, I turn away. Marigold's blue-green eyes are full of concern as I make my way back to her, stepping from rock to rock. "That didn't sound good."

Sighing, I pull her close. "She's angry. She's always angry. But her world is upside down right now." She nods sympathetically. "Honestly, I'm worried what she'll do," I murmur against her ear.

"It'll be okay," she reassures me.

"I hope so. My father controlled her, and now with only my mother... I don't know."

Her hands tighten on my biceps. "You've done everything you can. Nothing that happens is on you." Her words help, but it's her sweet smile that breaks through my worry.

"Jasper," Hazel calls. She signals me to come over. I stride toward them, slowing as the shallow water ripples around my ankles. Sienna's smile thins as I approach. "You know our Beta," Hazel says with a vindictive smile. "Jasper, could you take some notes for us? I'd like your feedback."

"Of course," I say, pulling out my phone. She doesn't need notes from me, but she wants Sienna to see my new position. To show her that she was wrong. I busy myself typing into my notes app, resisting the urge to look up at my mother.

"Sienna, please continue," Hazel says.

She pauses for a moment before continuing to list her proposal. Every time Hazel interrupts her and asks my opinion on something, I can see her seething. After the second polite disagreement, Slate says, "I think we need to revisit this tomorrow. I'm not sure we will get much more accomplished today. It's getting late."

"If you insist," Sienna says, bristling. "I'll expect your call." She addresses only Slate, clearly done with Hazel and I.

"Thank you, have a good evening," Hazel says softly. Sienna tosses her hair and leads her wolves away.

"I think this calls for a celebration. Game night at our house?" Hazel says.

"After pack dinner," Slate adds, taking her hand as we cross back to our side of the boundary.

"Let me check with Marigold, but I'm sure she'll be happy," I say, going to my mate as we reach our companions.

"Alright, let's head home," Slate says, raising his voice for our entire team. With sure steps, he leads the way up the hill and into the trees.

Marigold squeezes my hand, her body brushing against mine as we walk. It'll take at least thirty or forty minutes to walk back, but the company is so pleasant, I wouldn't mind if it was longer. "How'd it go?" Marigold asks.

"Well, I think. It's hard to tell," I say, thinking. "Hazel and Slate kept Sienna off balance, so that was good."

She grins at me viciously. "I hope they knocked her on her ass."

Chuckling, I raise her arm and kiss her knuckles. "You're a violent little thing."

"I think you like it," she purrs.

"I like everything about you," I reply, my voice low. Her back muscles tense as she shivers lightly. Our steps have slowed, putting us at the back of the pack. Gently, I tug her to a halt.

"What?" She cocks her head, looking between me and our packmates disappearing between the trees.

"Nothing," I say. Marigold wrinkles her nose. "When we get back, it'll be dinner and then Hazel invited us over for a game night. If I have to wait hours to taste you, I'm going to lose my mind."

"Oh," she says, a faint blush staining her freckled cheeks.

She's eager for my mouth, slipping her hands around my neck and up into my hair. Our kisses are playful and heady. My blood tingles and sparks, like she's an electrical charge.

With little pushes, she walks me backwards until my back hits a tree. Her hands tug at my shoulders until I scoop her up under her thighs. With my arms busy lifting her, I'm at her mercy as she slips her cold fingers under the neckline of my shirt and trails her hot mouth down my throat.

She pauses on my circle of scars, the mark of her claim. I can feel her deep satisfaction through our bond.

"I want to take you home," I breathe. Holding her tight, I push my back off the tree and spin until she's pressed against it. Her eyes glow blue-green, her lush mouth open in surprise. I lean down, trailing my lips over her ear. "Or maybe I'll fuck you up against this tree."

"As appealing as that sounds, we should go, or we will miss dinner," she says breathlessly.

"We can eat at home," I reply, licking her throat. She shudders.

"But I want to go to game night," she manages to say, the words uneven.

"Alright," I say, ceasing my torture. Her feet lower to the leaves and I take a half-step back. Mild disappointment swirls between us, and I'm unclear if it's mine or hers. Hand in hand, we resume our walk. "You know what would make game night better?"

"What?"

"If we got some pickles."

She snorts, shoving me back. "You're ridiculous."

"What? They're a good snack," I jest. Her giggle is my favorite sound in the world.

SECRETS

AND

S'MORES

I

KISSING THE ENEMY

EMBER

String lights hang low, illuminating a sea of bobbing heads as the crowd of wolf shifters sways to the music. The barn wood is cold against my back as I watch, bitterness souring my stomach as I sip a stolen drink. Young adults from all five local wolf packs dance and drink.

Of all the "pack relations" schemes my brother has devised, this might be the only tolerable one. But as I'm newly single, my mood is too morose to allow for any sort of fun.

What would Hawk be doing if he was still here? I'm not naive enough to believe he would be dancing with me. He was loyal, but not really romantic. As my *Intended*, he should have claimed me as his mate on my eighteenth birthday. Instead, he returned to his family's pack several hours north of us.

Not that I blame him. The arrangement between our parents didn't account for sudden upheaval. Why would he want to join a pack where one Alpha murdered the other?

The blame lies with Slate, the Alpha of our rival pack and my half-brother. My father was fighting him and my mother took drastic action to protect her child. It's his fault I lost both a parent and later my future mate.

My eyes search the crowd for his dark head. Slate lifts a glass bottle and takes a long drink. His other arm wraps across the chest of his mate who leans against him while she laughs. They look ridiculously happy and it makes me want to claw out my eyes. Hawk never looked at me the way Hazel gazes up at him.

"You should come join us," Jasper says. His lean frame is clothed in black, making his pale hair and eyes stand out. He might be my full-blooded brother, but we are opposites in every way.

"Fuck off," I say, grateful for the darkness that hides the embarrassed flush crawling up my neck. I'd rather he didn't see me watching his friends like a despondent stalker.

"Someday, you'll get tired of being pissy all the time." Jasper's tone is resigned and it makes my skin prickle with irritation. Without a glance back, he crosses the clearing and rejoins his friends. His beautiful mate, Marigold, greets him with a sloppy kiss as he wraps his arms around her waist. She is sunshine, strawberry-blonde curls, and everything I could never be.

I can't fault Jasper for defecting from our pack and joining theirs. He seems happy against all odds. If I had someone looking at me the way Marigold stares at him, maybe I would be happy too. But since childhood, I was pitted against my brother, told I was second best. Being four years younger, I never stood a chance when we sparred.

Watching them only worsens my mood, but because I am full of self-loathing, I follow his path until I'm hovering awkwardly a few feet away from that golden circle of friends.

Another of Jasper and Slate's friends, the twin with dirty blonde hair named Onyx, observes me with narrowed eyes. I glare back. He's always watching me at these events, like he's hungry for revenge. His hand moves to his ribs and the scar I gave him the last time our packs went to war.

His navy eyes are heavy across my shoulders, so I straighten and raise my chin. The slightest curl to his lip gives away his disdain. Well, fuck him too.

"Ember!" Marigold cries, pulling free from Jasper and seizing my arm. She tugs me forward into their group.

"I swear, I saw Vale sneak off behind the gym with that girl from the Raven Pack," Hazel says, her words slightly slurred. Damn, how many drinks has she had? I suppose it doesn't matter. With a protective mate at her back, she's safe to indulge. I wouldn't dare to let my guard down by getting noticeably drunk like that. There's no one watching over me.

"Good for him!" Marigold giggles.

"Marigold," Jasper says, his brows furrowing.

"This is exactly what you wanted when you set these parties up," Hazel argues.

Slate's face is buried in her neck, his lips tracing lower over the circle of pale scars that mark her as claimed. His loose t-shirt neckline reveals the edge of his matching set.

The sight makes me squirm. It reminds me of everything I don't have. No mate. No true guarantee of my future ranking. Everything feels like it's teetering on the edge of a blade and if I slip, it'll be the end.

"I don't think he had random hookups in mind," Slate says, lifting his head to smile indulgently at her. Hazel scowls back at him.

"You don't know it's just a hookup. Maybe we will gain a lovely new packmate. Remember all the shit you guys gave us?" Marigold says, patronizingly.

"Yeah, well, you guys could have just jumped right to dating," Hazel says, crossing her arms and bumping the glass bottle in her hand against Slate's with a jarring clink.

My weight shifts from one foot to another. I shouldn't have come over here.

"Ember, where is your beau?" Marigold asks.

"Not here." I clear my throat. "Hawk went back to his family."

Hazel and Marigold let out sympathetic noises of understanding. Unfortunately, the boys are slower.

"So did you break up?" Jasper asks.

At the same moment, Onyx tilts his head and says, "When's he coming back? Shouldn't you be mates already?"

"Uh, yeah. It wasn't working as an alliance anymore," I say, embarrassment heating my cheeks again.

Onyx lets out a harsh laugh. "He finally realized what a raging bitch you are?"

I'm grateful for the anger that rises in my blood. It's better than the uncomfortable feeling of not belonging. I'd rather be pissed than lonely.

"Onyx, shut up," Jasper growls.

"Don't use that word," Marigold says at the same moment, glaring at Onyx.

A smirk flashes across his face. Those dark eyes, like starless skies, bore into mine as I bare my teeth at him.

"Maybe I'm the one who dumped him." I want to get in his face, draw a weapon to threaten him, do anything to retaliate. But I'm unarmed except for my hidden dagger and this hardly counts as a true emergency. So instead I give him a one-fingered salute and walk away before I make things worse.

His laughter taunts me, followed by a verbal lashing from Marigold.

Seething, I seek out the coolers of alcohol I know I shouldn't have. Grabbing two bottles between my fingers, I stride away to a dark corner where even Jasper won't bother me.

It'd be best if I went home. My mother's new Beta, Orion, is waiting to drive me back to our territory. But he's an asshole too, so he can wait.

I drink just past tipsy, still sober enough to fight, but perhaps not very well. It's stupid, but despite my rage, I remind myself to stay cautious. I can't trust allies to not take advantage of me. My pack was the enemy and I am no favorite.

A simpering girl from the Valley Pack pulls someone from the Ironcrest Pack past me and into the deepest shadows. I can hear a soft whine from one of them. If Hawk had wanted me like that, he would still be here. But if I'm honest, I didn't feel that way about him either.

"Look who's here lurking in the shadows," a low voice cuts through my reflective bitterness. Onyx moves through the darkness like he belongs here. Bathed in dim reflections, his hair is ashen and his skin bronze as he steps closer.

"Maybe I'm trying to be less of a bitch."

"What a noble cause," Onyx says, his eyes scanning me. "Look, I'm sorry. Marigold says I have to apologize.

"I don't want your apology."

"Alright, but I'm trying to do the right thing." His forearms rest against the wall as he leans into my personal space.

"I doubt that. Back off."

I try to ignore him, but his inhale is audible. "You smell good."

"Too bad you don't," I snap, even though it's a lie. I can smell his citrus soap mingling with sweat and something that reminds me of a bakery, like fresh baked bread.

The asshole smiles down at me. I hate that he's a head taller than me. I hate that he's pretty.

"Why are you still here?" My arms cross over my chest.

"Maybe I'm drunk and horny and I like it when women are mean to me," he purrs.

"You're pathetic. Find someone else to annoy." His eyes light up at my insult. I guess he was telling the truth about liking mean women. Then he's going to *love* me.

"Are you lonely since Hawk left you?"

He's cruel, cold and mocking, and I should not be attracted to him, but all the hairs stand up on my arms at his nearness.

"Like you always feel, since no one wants you?" My whisper is ragged, holding none of the malice I should feel. He should fear being this close to me. The last time we clashed, I made him bleed.

He's near enough I can feel the heat rolling off his skin. My hand presses to his chest, and I mean to push him away, but my intoxicated body reacts without my permission, brushing down the faded fabric and across his torso. Damn, he's a wall of stacked muscle.

"Ah, seems someone does want me." The bastard is delighted at my moment of weakness.

"Fuck off," I grumble.

His hand grabs my wrist, his thumb over my pulse. The contact of his skin scorches me. "Your heart is beating like a hummingbird."

"I'm considering all the ways I'd like to kill you," I bluff. "It's a very appealing idea."

He cocks his head, his eyes glittering with intelligence and mocking humor. "I don't think you are." His gaze drops down, to where my body has leaned into him. *Shit.*

He lowers his head toward mine and my lungs tighten. "I think you're thinking of *other* things you'd like to do to me."

"I'd settle for strangling, disemboweling, or a simple guillotine." I'm aiming to wipe the smile off his face, but instead it widens, pleased at my threats.

"We both know that isn't what you want."

His warmth is too tempting and it makes me dumb. He dips his head, lips near my ear. "I'm going to kiss you and you aren't going to stab me. Understood?" The touch of his breath triggers a shiver I try to hide.

I should shove him away. I should punch his handsome face. Unfortunately, my willpower is in tatters. A low moan of agreement escapes my throat. I mean it as a growl, but I'm too lost in the feel of him.

"Answer me," his command pulls a gasp out of me and my mouth opens. He reaches up and runs his thumb over my bottom lip.

"I won't stab you right now," I say, though it comes out as more of a whimper. My hands tighten against the fabric of his shirt and pull him against me, and at the same moment, he grabs my ribs possessively, pushing me against the wall hard enough my body jolts.

My vision glazes over. It's perhaps one of the stupidest things I've ever done, but damn if his mouth doesn't feel good against my neck. His tongue licks against my skin and his teeth graze, sending electricity zinging through me.

Something in the back of my mind yells to stop. He's the enemy, and he's made his opinion of me clear. Just because he's sexy as hell doesn't mean I should let him use me like this. But the way his hands run up my side and skims the underside of my breasts has me melting. My anger slips through my fingers, evaporating in the heat of him.

Sighing, I arch my neck as he presses forward. The shadow of a beard along his jaw scuffs my throat and my hands come up to reach for him, wanting more. Like lightning, one hand grabs both my wrists and pins them above my head.

"I still don't trust you," he says, his lips still against my skin.

Good. He shouldn't.

ONYX

Years ago, my brother, cousin, and I went cliff jumping at a river a few hours away. Over and over, we plunged off the rocks, aiming for deeper water, knowing that one slip could mean death. The rush was addictive.

That's what kissing Ember is like.

It's the last thing I should be doing, but I can't resist.

I can't keep my gaze away from the way her dark green hair highlights the emerald in her hazel eyes. Her heart-shaped face glows in the low lights.

My first mistake is getting too close, maybe because I feel guilty or maybe to feel the thrill of irritating someone who clearly would like to murder me.

But when her scent reaches me, all of those thoughts evaporate, and all I can think of is touching her. She's soft wildflowers and the sharp, metallic scent of lightning, so alluring I'm leaning in too close.

She wants me too. The glow of her eyes is a thin halo around her blown-out pupils.

My hand tightens around her wrists, stretching her out for me to taste. She's so pliant, melting against me - the opposite of her prickly personality. It's heady, the way she obeys my silent commands, opening her mouth for me. She kisses back fiercely. Her teeth nip at my tongue, sending a jolt straight to my hard cock pressing against her supple body.

I sweep my mouth to her jaw, wanting to taste more of her. A hushed noise from her throat sends my head spinning. It's walking the edge of a blade and getting away with it, and she feels so good.

"You kiss better than you fight," I whisper against her skin.

Her chest heaves as she struggles to get enough air to say, "Unfortunately, you don't."

Huffing a laugh at her insult, I use my free hand to tip her chin up so she's forced to look me in the eyes. "Don't lie to me. You've been enjoying this too much for that to be true."

"You're pathetic," she growls.

It's ice hitting my overheated skin. What the fuck am I doing?

My fingers are stiff as I release her and take a forcible step back. The cool air washes over me.

"Better pathetic than a psycho," I mutter defensively. Those startling eyes narrow and then she's moving, stalking off into the dwindling crowd.

Snarling, I adjust myself, gulping down the night air to try and calm the inferno raging through me.

That shouldn't have happened. I try to picture her months ago as she viciously slashed a knife against my side and cut into my skin. That's the woman I just kissed - someone who would gladly gut me.

But now all I can recall from that moment is the way her curves felt in my arms, still naked from shifting. Even then, it had been wildly distracting. That's how she managed to hurt me, or at least that's what I tell myself.

What's wrong with me? That was a fight, not a flirtation. Though I shouldn't be surprised. She's exactly my type - feisty, strong-willed, unpredictable.

Acidic disappointment eats away at me. If I had kept my mouth shut, it could still be on her body. I can feel the ghost of her up against me.

Shaking my head, I return to the dregs of the party to find Vale, the last member of our pack at the gathering. Pink lip gloss smudges his chin and I'm too irritated to tease him about it.

I'm not close with the younger wolf, but he's nice enough. Usually I'd stick with my friends or my twin, Cedar, but he had no interest in attending a party. The two couples headed home when they could no longer keep their PDA to a reasonable level, leaving me unsupervised to make poor decisions in the shadows.

"Have a good time?" Vale asks.

I grunt a non-answer, stalking toward the truck. "You good to drive, man?"

"Yeah, I was too busy to drink." His grin is irritating.

Normally, I wouldn't be angry with a packmate for finding happiness. But after I held a beautiful girl in my arms and then she insulted me and stormed off, I'm not in the mood to celebrate new relationships.

My foot kicks a discarded cup. With a scoff, I pause. The clearing is a mess, with bottles and cups piled by a nearby bin and a few scattered elsewhere.

"Do you know if they have a dumpster or something?" I ask.

Vale shrugs. "I can find out."

With jerky movements, I gather up the trash liner from the bin and shake it, making room for more cups. It only takes a few minutes to gather up the nearby trash. Vale returns to show me the small dumpster behind a nearby storage building.

It feels good to do something for our allied pack, though it does little to ebb my frustration with Ember.

The door to the truck slams shut behind me with a dull thud. My mood only worsens as Vale chatters about the girl from Raven pack.

As soon as the truck is parked, I leave him behind and head north. My family's cabin is one of the largest in the compound, rising two stories high with a wide porch. And right now, it's silent.

Laying in my bed and listening to my brother mumble in his sleep sounds like torture. My thoughts won't let me rest. I tug my shirt over my head and strip off my sweats, tossing them on the bench beside the front door.

Moonlight streams over my naked body for a split second before I sink into the wolf instincts and charcoal fur sweeps over my skin. Everything falls away, replaced with the animal urges to run, hunt, and protect. With a graceful leap, I land on the pine needles with all four paws.

The night is bright to my canine eyesight. The colors are faded, but every little movement catches my attention. Habit takes over as I lope in a lazy circle around the pack's collection of buildings and homes. Two of my packmates are on guard duty, but they're used to my midnight runs.

The wind ruffles my thick coat. Ember's voice echoes in my mind, breaking through my calm. Pulling back my lips to bare my teeth, I put on a burst of speed and break through the trees into the meadow. Moonlight highlights clumps of swaying wildflowers, with well-worn pathways between them. My paws glide between the newly rebuilt diner and my brother's garden to the north.

The air leaves my lungs in a defeated sigh. Maybe tomorrow will be better, or at least less dissatisfying. Returning to my human shape, I slip into my home and yank on loose shorts before flopping face down in my bed on the far side of the room from my brother. Cedar grunts and turns his head to blink at me, but he knows me too well to ask questions when I'm in a dark mood. Rolling onto my side facing away from him, I listen as he sighs and nestles back into his pillow.

Eyes squeezed shut, I beg my mind to rest. Memories of her warm skin and that floral scent force their way into my thoughts. As if punishing me, my brain replays her words and the way she glared at me.

I shouldn't have liked it so much. There were plenty of nice young women at the party. But none of them made my pulse race like Ember. It was like staring down a beautiful but lethal predator.

Unless I can get my head on straight, it would be best to avoid her. Maybe I'll stay home with Cedar during the next inter-pack gathering. The idea grates on me.

Despite my angst, sleep finally finds me.

II

HANGOVERS & HEIRS

EMBER

Eyeliner streaks down my face, turning me into a deranged raccoon. Half asleep, I turn on the shower and let steam fill my bathroom. It fogs the mirror, misty gray against the pristine white tile walls. My mother embraced the minimalistic aesthetic while decorating this house, and I hate it.

Twenty minutes of scrubbing later, I feel like myself again. With wet hair clinging to my neck, I yank on joggers and a sweatshirt before heading to the kitchen.

"Good morning, Ember," Sienna purrs. Others might mistake her tone for charm, but after eighteen years, I know it's a sign she's ready for a fight. She perches on the edge of her seat at the breakfast table, already in heels with her signature crimson lip. Her silk wrap dress hangs loose on her frame, the only sign she's grieved her spouse at all.

I'm surprised she hasn't taken a new mate already. There are a dozen dominant males in the pack who are more than eager, despite the risk, and it would help secure her position.

It's hard to stay Alpha when you murder your mate.

Whispers have circulated the ranks and many of the males are reluctant to follow a single female's leadership. But I suppose that's the consequence of building a pack made up almost exclusively of ruthless fighters, especially ones that aren't particularly bright.

My response is a grunt. I wait for her criticism, but the only sound is the cabinet hinge and the dry rustling of cereal hitting the bottom of my bowl, followed by the clink of a spoon.

Either she's playing at being a good mom this morning, or she's biding her time. *Fantastic.*

"So how was the gathering last night?" she asks after a delicate sip of coffee.

"Fine."

"I'd appreciate a more thorough answer." Her polite smile stays plastered in place.

With a deep sigh, I plop into my seat and shovel cereal into my mouth. The crunch echoes inside my head, drowning out the bleak thoughts that make up my mental playlist.

"Don't you have minions to report to you for these types of things?"

Her dark eyes study me for a moment. I hate that Jasper takes after our dad and I take after her. It's why I bleach and color my hair various shades of the rainbow every few weeks.

"Yes, I do. But no one else spoke with the Alphas of the Bracken Creek Pack." Her words are crisp, only a hint of her disdain toward her former pack shining through. If a stranger were listening, they'd never know that one of those Alphas is her oldest son from her first relationship, before she met my dad.

Leaning back in my chair, I cross my arms and tuck my leg under me. "Look, we barely spoke. Hazel was gossiping about her packmates and Slate was just drinking and groping her."

Sienna's eyebrows shoot up.

I almost regret my harsh assessment. "Not like he was drunk. He just didn't talk when I was there."

Her expression turns analytical and I resume eating my cereal to escape her assessment. "Anything else you'd like to share?"

"Nope." The answer is too quick. I force myself to meet her gaze for a moment, keeping the guilt churning in my gut from seeping into my expression.

No, *Mother dear*, nothing else happened. Only made out with the enemy. Yes, the same one I stabbed. No big deal. just let him suck on my neck while I ground against him like a shameless hussy. And now I'm ruined because every other man I've ever kissed had cold fish lips compared to him. Shit.

"I'm glad you had a good time because you're going to spend several days with them."

My breakfast catches in my throat and I splutter and cough.

"Why?" I choke out.

"I've requested your brother come home for a visit and bring his little mate."

"So?" My coffee does little to soothe me as I wait for her to explain.

"They suggested an exchange in order to ensure their safety, since, as their Beta, Jasper is technically also their Heir until those two have a child of their own."

My brain blanks for a minute. So much for holding my superior position as Heir over Jasper's head.

"An exchange," I repeat dumbly. "Who are you sending?"

"My own Heir, of course." Her manicured fingers press to her temple as if to ward off a headache.

"Can't you send Orion? Maybe I want to spend time with Jasper too." I know I sound like a whiny child, but spending time in enemy territory sounds unbearable, especially after last night.

"You can catch up with your brother on your own time."

Anger turns my mind sharp. "When would you have allowed that?"

"You had the gathering last night, didn't you?"

A frustrated growl builds in my throat, but acting like a petulant child won't change her decision. I have no autonomy here. Schooling my features to calm, I ask, "What is your goal for this visit? If I'm going to be shuttled off to our enemies, at least tell me what you're trying to accomplish."

Her lips thin, her features appearing predatory. "Daughter, you are going to visit your half-brother and his mate. You are going to be quiet and respectful. And if I require anything else from you, I'll tell you so. Until then, keep your eyes open and your mouth shut."

The icy command hangs between us. Sienna sips her coffee and returns her gaze to her phone. Finally, my emotions calm enough to speak.

"Am I going alone?"

She sets her phone on the table with a snap. "Do you need a babysitter?"

"Of course not." Masking my hurt with sarcasm, I force out a cold laugh. "Hopefully they won't murder me in my sleep. Pretty sure you don't have any other Heirs hidden around here to replace me."

She rolls her eyes and with a dismissive flick of her wrist, opens her phone again.

ONYX

My joints ache as I drag myself from bed. Each beat of my pulse feels like a blow to my temple, and my skin feels too tight. Feet clumsy, I head straight to the kitchen, the smell of my mother's cooking promising some relief.

Four people sit around our kitchen table, my parents and two guests. My mother pops up, grabbing a glass and filling it with water.

"How do you look so peppy?" I ask Hazel with a groan. She sits beside Slate with a tense expression like I interrupted an important conversation.

My father, Fisher, sits forward with his forearms flat on the table and his hands neatly folded. His salt and pepper hair sweeps back off his forehead. Feeling self-conscious, I rake my fingers through my hair and it out of my face.

"Well, we didn't drink like a dehydrated dolphin last night," Hazel answers with a patronizing quirk of her eyebrow.

The glass of water is forced into my hands. My mother's forehead wrinkles in concern as she discreetly hands me two pain pills. Do I really look that bad? "Thanks, Mom," I mutter before downing the medication and water.

"Come join us," she says, settling into a chair. Her cinnamon hair gleams bronze in the morning light. With a sigh, I slump into the seat between her and Slate.

"We were just discussing a proposal from the Granite Ridge pack," Hazel explains. My hand freezes halfway to the basket of warm pastries in the center of the table. "Not that kind, obviously. Sienna would like Jasper and Marigold to visit them for a few days, and in return, she will send Ember to stay with us."

"What?" I blurt, my mouth hanging open.

Her brows knit together. "Jasper and Marigold will go there, and Ember will stay with us. Like an exchange."

"Is that necessary?" I ask.

"Not really," Slate says. He lets out an audible exhale, his arms crossing. Hazel turns, her eyes narrowing at his reaction.

"You should get to know her. She's your sister." It sounds like an argument they've had before.

"Half-sister," Slate grumbles.

I focus on the pastry selection and grab a brioche bun filled with blackberries my brother grew. It's a cloud melting into sweet, sticky preserves. Being the son of the pack's baker has its perks.

"So?" Hazel says, her voice rising in pitch. Irritation trickles through the pack bond.

"She attempted to murder you when she first met you," Slate says dryly. His mouth pulls into a grimace.

"That's not exactly what happened," Hazel argues.

My body leans back from her, one of my eyebrows rising. "Let's not forget she stabbed me." My free hand motions to the exposed scar across the bottom of my ribs.

My mother clicks her tongue, crossing the room to grab a sweatshirt. I smile at her fussing and slip it on obediently.

"It makes sense, politically. She's their Heir, and Jasper is yours for now," my father says. Hazel crosses her arms with a pointed look at her mate.

Slate settles back in his seat, acquiescing to his mate's demands.

"Well, we can't have her stay with Hawthorne. Not with how young his kids are," Hazel says. "And Slate isn't comfortable keeping her with us."

"We aren't home enough to supervise her properly." His hand rests protectively on the back of her chair.

"So we're hoping you'll host her." Hazel says, turning to my father. "You're next in line, as our Delta. You have the space and there will be five of you to keep an eye on her."

My father has taken all of this in without visible reaction, but I can almost hear his brain calculating the risk. As the pack's trainer, he knows our people and our weaknesses better than anyone.

"Four of us," he amends. "We'll send Briar to stay with friends, and then Ember can stay in her room."

"Good idea," Hazel says, turning her sweetest smile on my mother. "Clove, I know this is a big imposition."

"No, it would be an honor."

"I really appreciate that," Hazel says, her eyes crinkling as she smiles.

Brioche eaten, I consider grabbing another pastry. There's a chocolate-studded scone calling my name and the sugar softens my surprise.

"Onyx," Slate says. His tone commands my attention and I fight the instinct to cringe. It's never good when he uses that voice on me.

"We'd like you to take the lead on guarding Ember during her stay with us. Vale can handle your tech duties for a few days, and we'll change up the patrol rotation to free you up."

Is he shitting me?

Thoughts of the scone dissolve as I rub my palm over my jaw. "Am I guarding her from our packmates? Or guarding them from her?"

"Both," Slate says. It's the diplomatic answer. We both know the latter is more likely to be necessary. "Are you up for it?"

"I'll think about it. We don't exactly get along."

"I'm sure you can handle her." Hazel squeezes my wrist and I already know I'll agree. When she turns those big amber eyes on me, I'm a goner. No wonder Slate never says no to her.

"Thanks," Slate says before smoothly transitioning the conversation to training topics. My father and my Alphas trade updates on recent developments and I tune out their voices.

My mind replays the feel of emerald hair brushing my cheek, her soft curves under my hands. It was supposed to be a thrill, just a bad decision in the dark. But now she's coming here and staying in my home. Heat prickles over my skin at the thought.

Something is truly wrong with me if I'm excited by an enemy sleeping in the room across from mine. One with a soft mouth and soulful eyes who would very much like to hurt me.

I'm fucked.

III

FRIED CHICKEN & FAILED FLIRTING

EMBER

Orion drives me to the parking lot, and I'm left to retrieve my duffel from the trunk before he peels out. He doesn't even bother to say goodbye or make sure I'm well received. The disrespect ruffles me, but there's nothing I can do.

Ahead, only the edge of the training building and the front of two office buildings are visible. Their community is sprawling compared to Granite Ridge's tight rows of houses and facilities.

A single guard watches me as he raises his phone to his ear. Not exactly the welcome I was expecting. Posture rigid, I fix my stare past him.

My brain whispers that I'm about to be ambushed and imprisoned. It's not logical, but last time I was here, our packs clashed and I was taken away with my hands zip-tied. It's not the kind of thing a girl forgets.

The training building has been refurbished. There are no signs of the destruction we wrought.

The image of Onyx leaning up against the training center's metal wall, making jokes while his hands cover the wound just below his ribs, blood seeping between his fingers, plays behind my eyes. He might be as crazy as I am.

"Ember!" Hazel hollers, striding toward me with Slate at her side. Her smile is welcoming as they reach me, and luckily she doesn't attempt to hug me.

"Alphas," I respond respectfully. My chin dips, though my eyes never leave their faces.

"I hope you have a nice stay with us. We are going to have you stay with our pack's Delta. His name is Fisher and his mate, Clove, is our pack's baker."

No faces come to mind at the names. "Sounds fine."

"Alright, let's head over there and get you settled." She leads us north, past the training building until I enter a meadow blooming with wildflowers. It's gorgeous.

Bracken Creek has been rebuilt. A new cafe sits in the same spot as the old diner we burned down.

Pack members wander around, going between their duties. A few curious gazes follow us, but I see none of the disgust I expect. Surely they know who I am.

My family was responsible for invading their home and severely injuring many of their packmates. Eventually, their hatred will come out, and then I'll know exactly where I stand.

With an even breath, I straighten my spine and stride forward with all the faux confidence I can muster.

The Delta's cabin stands two stories with large windows. Split-log steps lead up to the double front door.

A tall woman opens it. A few silver hairs streak her reddish brown hair, pulled into a no-nonsense bun. Lines crease around her eyes as she smiles at me.

Her partner looms behind her. His strong jaw and straight nose feel familiar. Before I can place him, another figure steps into view. Dirty, dark blonde hair swept back into a small ponytail, deep blue eyes that make my stomach clench, a mouth that curves in a mocking smirk.

Are you fucking kidding me?

"Ember, this is Clove and Fisher," Hazel says. "And you remember Onyx."

"Nice to meet you," I say, refusing to look at the man who had his hands all over me just days ago.

Clove's warm smile is genuine and I find myself drawn to her, but her mate's expression is colder, holding the suspicion I expect from this pack. Without wavering, I step forward. His judgment is fair and deserved and I won't let it get to me.

"We'll see you at dinner tonight." Slate says, stepping back and taking Hazel with him.

The Alpha female looks between her mate and me. "The pack eats together. Onyx can bring you down to the diner in time." Her shoulders rise and drop, her polite smile relaxing. "I think tonight includes some bread Clove baked?"

"Tonight is fried chicken, so Crickett requested buttermilk biscuits. I finished them about an hour ago," Onyx's mother explains. That explains the nutty flour scent Onyx has.

I draw in a slow breath before I realize I'm seeking out his smell. No way, not going to happen!

"Can't wait. See you all then," Hazel says, swinging her hand clasped in Slate's. He ducks his head in a goodbye nod.

"Here, Onyx, take her bag," Clove instructs.

Instinctively, I clutch the duffle tighter. "I can handle it."

"Just let me be a good host," Onyx argues. With a glare, I allow him to pry the bag from my grip. The brush of his fingers triggers a shiver and I tense my shoulders to stop it from traveling down my body.

Clove leads the way into their cabin. "We eat breakfast in the kitchen, and then bedrooms are down this hallway."

"You have a beautiful home," I say.

The kitchen is clad in blonde wood and pale marble countertops. Open shelving reveals jars of baking supplies. Tubs of chocolate chips and dried fruit. Powders I can't identify, ranging from dark brown to snowy white.

"This is our daughter's room. Briar is staying with friends for a few days, so you'll have privacy." Clove stops at a doorway. A smattering of pink stickers decorate the open door.

The Delta, Fisher, has disappeared, but Onyx still trails behind me. "Don't worry about anything you find in here. Bri's a weirdo."

"I won't snoop," I say, my hands clenching defensively.

"Thank you, dear," Clove says.

At the same moment, Onyx says, "Oh please, snoop away."

With a sigh, she ignores her son and continues, "Briar cleared out her top two drawers, so you can unpack into those if you'd like to."

It's so considerate, I stiffen. If the packs were reversed, I would be tossed into a basement and locked away for my entire stay. Instead, this pack has made an effort to make sure I am comfortable and welcome.

"It's only a few days," I say, my voice too high. "I can manage out of my suitcase. But tell her thank you for me."

"Of course. I'll leave you be. Onyx, keep an eye on the clock. It's only twenty minutes until dinner. I need to head back to help Crickett in the diner."

"Yes, ma'am," he says to her retreating back.

I blink at his respectful response. He's always been so rude or mocking to me, the gracious son routine startles me.

"You can just-" I start, holding my hand out for my duffle. Onyx sets it on the foot of the twin bed but doesn't back away.

"What do you want?" I ask, challenging him. His proximity flitters across my skin like electricity.

For a moment he is silent. Just when I doubt he will say anything, he murmurs, "Did you know?"

"Know what?"

He's lost his mind.

"That you were coming to stay here."

"Well, I obviously figured it out when they stuck me in a car and drove here," I say, obstinately refusing to answer his question.

"That's not what I meant. At the gathering. Did you already know about this visit?"

"I found out the next morning, dude."

He scoffs.

"What? Did you think I was setting up some sort of booty call before this *lovely* vacation?" I press, sarcasm heavy in my words.

"Well," he says with a shrug. His t-shirt rises with the motion to reveal the waistband of his gray sweatpants and a sliver of tan skin.

"You're the one who came on to me," I hiss.

"Are you serious? You grabbed me," he argues, his low voice a caress along my rib cage.

I've been here five minutes and I'm already fighting with this asshole.

"You're delusional," I shoot back.

"You practically pulled me on top of you," he continues, extending his vowels dramatically.

Forcing myself to step closer, I grab a handful of his t-shirt to demonstrate how absurd his claim is. "Yes, I grabbed you and suctioned your mouth on my neck. You had no choice." My biting words seem to weaken leaving my mouth. I'm distracted by the feel of his chest against my knuckles.

"That's pretty much how I remember it," he breathes. No longer angry, his words tease me, sending tingles from my chest to my toes.

"We were drunk," I say. Glaring into his endless eyes, I double down on my lie. "And you're a man-whore." I know it's a cheap shot and probably not true, but it's the only thing that comes to mind.

Onyx throws his head back and laughs, exposing his throat to me. Fuck, he's gorgeous. Unclenching my fingers, I step away, out of the haze of his citrus scent. Gulping down fresh air, I try desperately to clear my head.

The grin widening across his pretty face is a weapon in its own right. Most girls would swoon. I hold my ground, my teeth grinding together as I ignore the way my stomach flutters. Treacherous body.

"I'll see you in fifteen for dinner, Hummingbird," he says before closing the door behind him.

"You are such a dick," I whisper at the closed door. His low laughter echoes in the hallway, barely detectable even with my sensitive hearing.

Heart racketing in my ribs, I survey his sister's bedroom looking for a distraction from my heated skin.

Dried flowers splay in plastic frames along one wall. Christmas lights line the edge of the ceiling.

I would have given anything for a space like this. My sterile room back in Granite Ridge seems like a prison compared to this. Some sort of glossy green houseplant hangs from a hook by the window, the vines draping along the curtain rod.

The duvet is a creamy ruffled confection and I hesitate before sitting on it. The sheets and pillowcase are crisp and smell like detergent.

Curiosity wells up and I fold at the waist to peer under the bed. A low bin overflows with clothing, and beside it sit two soccer balls and a couple of wrinkled magazines. Reaching under, I extract a length of black ribbon, graying with age and dust. With two pinched fingers, I lay it across the dresser.

A stack of newer fashion magazines perches on the desk in the corner. These aren't teen versions, but luxury fashion, like Vogue and Harper's Bazaar. I've never read any of them. But from the creased corners, they look well-loved.

The desk holds gel pens, drawing pencils, and notepads. Under the school books, I find a sketchbook of fashion illustrations. Mostly dresses.

Who's heard of a wolf shifter who wants to design fashion? The thought makes me smile. It will be interesting to see what Onyx's little sister does as an adult.

A door past the desk opens to a tiny bathroom. Dainty white tiles cover the walls up to waist-height, where a wallpaper of teeny sea turtles rises to the ceiling.

Artwork above the toilet features a flamingo in a yoga pose with the words, "Let that Shit Go." Despite myself, I chuckle at it.

A girl could get spoiled in a room like this. Heading back to the bed, I tug open the gauzy curtains and take a deep breath. Maybe this won't be so bad. I can hide in here and avoid Onyx. Yes, that's a good plan.

Onyx

"Planning your escape already?" I ask, taking in Ember's tempting figure before the window. A patch of purple lupine flowers sway between tree trunks visible from Briar's room, their violet petals painted magenta from the fading sunset.

Ember spins, her eyes wide for a split second until her brain catches up and she settles into the wary glare I'm so familiar with.

"If I wanted to leave, I'd be gone already," Her hands go to her hips, eyes alight with a fire.

"I have no doubt." Playing polite host, I hold the door open. "Ready for dinner? You're about to be very impressed. I've been told we have the best food of any pack."

"Good to know," she says, breezing past me. Her sugary floral scent washes over me and I follow after her like a puppy begging for scraps. She's hostile and spiteful, but she smells amazing.

Inquisitive eyes jump to us when we enter the clearing. Most of the pack has gathered, though no one will eat until the Alphas do, per pack custom. We stroll toward my family, Ember doing her best to look unbothered, though I can feel anxiety rolling off of her.

Cedar and Briar stand beside our parents, Briar chattering away and Cedar listening stoically. He nods at me as we approach and Briar gives a little wave to Ember.

"Hi, I'm Bri," she says.

"Ember." She smiles, but it looks strained. "I think I'm staying in your room?"

"Yeah, hope you don't mind it." Briar scrunches her nose in a cute half-smile. "It's nice. Thanks."

If I didn't know better, I would think Ember was just another teenage friend of Briar's who is a little shy.

"Hey." A lanky boy with a tumble of reddish-brown hair joins us.

"This is Indie. He's Marigold's brother," Briar explains to Ember, her hand going to Indigo's arm. Ember looks between them and I wonder if she can see

Marigold's features in him. They have the same upturned nose and wide, friendly mouth.

"You're Jasper's sister, right?" Indigo asks.

"Yeah. Nice to meet you," she says, though her tone is flat.

My eyebrow shoots up at the way Indigo's hand comes up to cover Briar's. Big brother instincts kick in and I'm tempted to pull them apart. Only a sharp look from Briar keeps me in my place.

The pack stirs as Hazel and Slate enter the meadow. With a light touch on Ember's elbow, I lead her toward them. She jerks her arm away but thankfully follows my lead.

"Careful, you were almost nice there to my sister," I say, leaning closer to her.

She scowls up at me. "Yeah, I'm typically nice to decent people."

"What does that say about me?" I ask, slapping my hand over my heart with a dramatic sigh.

"I would think that is obvious."

That's a dangerously flirty response from someone who despises me. My pulse thuds faster. Before I can come up with a reply, we're interrupted.

"Ember, I hope you're hungry. Fried chicken is my favorite thing Crickett makes," Hazel says, waving her forward. I trail behind, playing the obedient bodyguard.

Slate reaches out and grips my shoulder, leaning in to talk. "Doing okay?"

"Great," I say, only slightly sarcastic.

Plates clink as we start down the buffet. Ember pinches her lush bottom lip between her teeth as she places fried chicken and roasted vegetables on her plate. I suspect she's hyper aware of the packmates lining up behind us from the way her gaze flickers around nervously.

"See, I told you we have the best food," I murmur as we exit the line. Her dark eyes travel from her plate to me and a hint of a smile curves her mouth before she turns away. Puffing up my chest, I follow Hazel and Slate to their favorite table on the edge of the trees.

Ember hesitantly takes the seat on the end, and I slide onto the bench beside her. Hazel and Slate settle across from us. Even once Cedar sits on Slate's other side, the table feels empty without Jasper and Marigold.

"You guys eat together like this every day? It's like some sort of celebration," Ember says with a curious tilt of her head.

Slate's brows furrow as he looks up at her. "Yes, of course. What does Granite Ridge do?"

"Um," Ember flounders, "It's not a social thing like this."

Hazel grimaces. "Think more prison cafeteria and less restaurant."

"That sounds appealing," I say dryly, not missing how Ember's mouth pinches.

"Ember, how are you liking our pack so far?" Slate asks.

She pauses, turning her fork over in her hand thoughtfully. "I've only seen this area and your Delta's house. But it's nice, I guess."

"Pretty different from Granite Ridge, right?" Hazel asks with a gentle smile.

Ember moves in her seat, her eyes on her plate. "The two packs are very different," she finally agrees.

"I mean, I didn't get to see that much of Granite Ridge either. I spent half my time there locked in a basement," Hazel says with a light laugh.

Slate's jaw clenches. Tension pours through our pack bond.

With a determined frown, Ember meet's Hazel's gaze. "You had dinner with the Alphas, saw most of our facilities, and even got to see the woods between our two territories."

"True," Hazel says, the friendly curve of her mouth looking forced. She expertly deflects the conversation. "So how have things been for your pack in the last year?"

We've gotten reports of how unstable the pack is, which added to Jasper's desire to investigate. Surely, Ember knows about those concerns, but she doesn't choose to be honest.

"We're fine. Rebuilding, just like you guys have done." She nods toward the diner with its fresh metal trim gleaming.

"We only had to reconstruct a building. You lost several of your packmates during the attack," Cedar interjects.

Her dark eyes narrow at my twin, her tone going ice cold. "Well, someone decided to fight with guns instead of tranqs and teeth like civilized packs do."

It seems my little hummingbird has reached the end of her patience. The air feels heavy between us, like everyone is waiting for a bomb to explode.

"Ember," Slate says slowly, "We didn't have much choice in the circumstances."

"How many wolves did you lose?" she snaps without missing a beat.

"We didn't start the fight." Slate is trying to be objective, but he lacks his mate's people skills. A tick in his jaw gives away how infuriated he really is.

"Neither did I, *big brother*," she says, tossing her fork down and stepping over the bench. Hands balled into fists, she stalks away.

"Well, that went well," Hazel growls at her mate. "You're certainly fighting like siblings already."

Slate scowls at Ember's retreating back.

Scrambling up, I'm several steps away from the table before I look back and gesture at our plates. "Can you?"

"I got it," Cedar cuts in. "Go."

"Thanks," I call over my shoulder, jogging to catch up with Ember. She strides into the trees, glossy hair whipping behind her as she shakes her head angrily.

"I don't need a fucking babysitter."

"Just making sure you don't go back and torch my home."

Before I can finish my joke, she's on me. Her index finger jabs my chest, the pointed black nail pricking my skin through my shirt. "I didn't ask for any of this. I didn't make our packs enemies, I didn't plan to take over your land, and I definitely didn't want to come here."

"I know."

My response must startle her, because she freezes, her eyes still on my chest.

"I don't think it means we have to be enemies just because our packs used to be," I say, offering a tentative peace.

Achingly slow, her hazel eyes trace up my neck, snagging on my mouth and finally reaching my eyes. "But doesn't it?"

"No."

"Everyone hates me. I can feel it. It doesn't matter. I don't need to make a bunch of friends here."

Considering how welcoming we've been, it irks me to hear that.

"I'm not talking about everyone else. I mean you and me."

A harsh laugh breaks out of her throat. "You've made your opinion of me very clear."

"Oh, really?" I say, waiting for her to clarify.

What opinion could that be? And was it before or after I kissed her and pinned her up against a building?

Her hand withdraws, her fingers threading together as she twists her hands absently. "Look, I don't want to spend this whole time being judged or blamed for everything my pack has done, or what I did under orders. I'd like it if we just started over."

"Fine by me. No judging or blaming. I can be civil if you can."

She studies me and I suddenly feel very exposed. Tugging at my neckline, I let out a slow exhale, trying to stay calm under her scrutiny.

"I can be civil," she says slowly, testing each word.

"Alright then, starting fresh as allies," I say, "So do you want to go back to dinner?"

Ember lets out a breathy laugh. "I really don't. But you should go back."

"That's okay. I'm good."

Her arms fold across her, hands gripping her upper arms. "Look, I'm sorry. I didn't mean to throw a tantrum. Slate just got to me."

My mouth falls open. Is she actually apologizing? There's a vulnerability in her eyes when she glances up at me shyly. This is a new side to her, a softness.

Hazel's scent reaches us seconds before she appears through the trees.

"Ember," she calls, her hurried steps closing the distance between us. "Are you okay? I'm so sorry. That was not how that conversation should have gone."

"You don't need to apologize for him," Ember says, her shoulders rising defensively.

"Slate didn't mean it like that. You guys really need to have a long talk and sort this out."

Ember wavers, clearly wanting to decline but respecting Hazel's rank.

"Look, we were thinking about a campfire tonight. I'd really like it if you joined us. It'll be a good time to hang out all together." Hazel tilts her head, brows bunched together in concern.

Ember's expression hardens. "No, thank you."

"I'd like to get to know you better, and I promise it'll be fun. There will be s'mores! Please come?"

She could order Ember to attend and she'd be hard pressed to disobey, but instead, she's asking kindly.

Ember's eyebrows rise. "Fine. Where do I go?"

"Everyone else is still finishing dinner, but then we'll head to Onyx's, actually. The twins have a great fire pit out back."

"Alright," she says begrudgingly.

"Awesome, I'll see you in a bit. Are you hungry? I can grab you more dinner," Hazel offers. I don't miss how Ember tenses, blinking in surprise.

"No, I'm good," she says, her tone softening.

With a hesitant smile and a nod, Hazel jogs back toward the clearing. She's broken through a layer of Ember's armor. Bit by bit, Ember is opening up, and I'm fascinated by the glimpses of what's under all of her anger.

IV
FLAMING MARSHMALLOWS
Ember

I was hoping the day was over and I could hide away from everyone, but instead, I'm stuck sitting around a campfire staring at my half-brother and his mate, and my one-time-makeout-partner enemy-turned-ally and his less personable twin. Not my idea of a fun evening, despite Hazel's promises.

She pops open the box of graham crackers in her lap and begins to distribute them in pairs. A square of dark chocolate joins the crackers, and then I'm being handed a wire rod with the biggest marshmallow I've ever seen stuck onto the end.

No one bothers to explain so I copy Onyx and thrust my marshmallow into the fire.

"So what do you think Jasper and Marigold are doing over with your mom?" Hazel asks. She rotates her marshmallow over the flames and I mimic the movement. The underside has turned a golden color on the edges.

"Who knows? His old house was given to someone else, so they're probably staying in the basement you enjoyed so much," I say. There's an edge to my words, but I can't seem to control myself. Anger and embarrassment are still fresh from our confrontation at dinner.

Shrugging, I continue, "So probably waiting around for Sienna to meet with them. And trying to not get beat up by the wolves who hate Jasper's guts for leaving."

Onyx's forehead falls into his open palm, like he's given up on the conversation. His hair sweeps over his hand and cheeks, shielding him from my stupidity.

"Hopefully it's going better than that," Hazel says. There's a coldness to her tone that I want to flinch away from, but I keep my shoulders back and my chin raised.

"We'll get a report soon enough," Slate reassures her. "I'm sure it's going fine."

Slate removes his marshmallow from the flames and pinches it between two graham crackers, sliding the stick out with a smooth movement. The marshmallow oozes out the side and he has to rotate it and take a bite to keep from making a mess.

Ah, so that's a s'more - a marshmallow sandwich. It's got to be overly sweet. I've only had marshmallows a handful of times in my life and never these giant ones. I stare as he takes another bite and chocolate peeks between the layers.

"Ember," Onyx says sharply, breaking my concentration.

"What?" I say, my attention snagging on a ball of flames at the end of the stick I'm holding. My marshmallow is on fire. Crap!

"What do I do?" I yelp, all dignity forgotten.

"Blow on it," Hazel coaches. Her words aren't absorbed. Waving my metal stick wildly, I attempt to extinguish the flaming marshmallow with zero success. The flames trail behind it like a burning ribbon.

"Woah, watch it," Onyx warns. He crouches beside me, grasping my wrist in one hand while the other extracts the marshmallow from my grip. His skin is hot against mine and he envelops my entire wrist.

My mind replays a flash of memory. His hand effortlessly holding both of my wrists above my head. My back against the cold, rough wall. His stubble against my throat. Sharp teeth against skin.

With a small shake, I clear my head in time to see Onyx bring the flaming confection toward his face. His lips part and he blows out the flames, leaving a blackened blob.

"Geez, Ember, were you trying to burn the shit out of it?" he murmurs. Maybe it's his deep voice, or the feel of his hand still holding my wrist, but my body is suddenly on alert. My skin feels overly sensitive as his body heat rolls across me. Even under the charred marshmallow and woodsmoke, I can smell his citrus and bakery scent.

"Maybe that's how I like my marshmallows," I say lamely.

With his lips quirked into a half-smile, he grabs my graham crackers and chocolate stack and assembles my s'more. The blackened outer layer cracks and the melted interior oozes through.

"Black like your soul," he teases, offering me the dessert I ruined.

My nose wrinkles as I scowl at him. "I've never cooked a marshmallow like this before," I admit quietly. Hazel and Slate are distracted with their own private murmurings, giving me a false sense of privacy.

"Don't tell me you make s'mores in the fucking microwave," Onyx quips.

"No microwave for me," I say, hoping he'll drop it. A beat of silence hangs between us, his navy eyes unwavering. A choking sensation tightens my throat as he raises a single eyebrow and smirks.

"You've never had s'mores before, have you?" Onyx finally asks.

"Don't be an idiot," I growl, my cheeks flushing under his stare.

Hands raised to pacify me, he backs away until he settles beside his brother.

Cedar still won't look at me, but I have a feeling he clinically analyzed my entire interaction with Onyx. More judgment. Fucking fantastic.

The burned s'mores sits in my palm. I ignore it, instead watching Hazel devour hers like it's a transcendental experience. Slate wipes a smudge of chocolate from her lip and licks it off his thumb. It would be cute with anyone else, but seeing my half-brother do that is gross.

"Perfect," Onyx says, lifting his own marshmallow from the flames. It's smoldering. His full mouth curves as he blows out the flames and assembles a s'more that rivals my own.

I can't help my wince as he lifts the s'more to his lips and takes a bite. His eyes close and he lets out a soft moan. When his eyes spring open, they connect with mine. "I like mine burned too," he says. I would assume he's mocking me, but he proceeds to eat the entire thing.

Frowning down at the cooling s'more in my hand, I weigh how embarrassing it would be to try it and then realize he was trying to trick me. But no one else watches either of us. With a sigh, I raise it to my mouth and take a small bite.

The charred flavor gives way to the sugary marshmallow. Bitter dark chocolate cuts the sweetness, tempered by the nutty graham cracker. It's divine.

I try to slow my bites to regain some of my dignity, but the dessert is delicious and I can't help but eat every crumb and then lick the sticky marshmallow off my fingers.

Onyx stares at the flames, but his smirk says, *I told you so.*

Hazel lets out a contented hum and snaps off a piece of chocolate to eat on its own. "That's better. I've needed a sugar fix all day."

"Was patrol really that bad?" Onyx teases.

Her amber eyes narrow. "Vale is still obsessed over his Raven girl. I swear, I've never heard the kid say so many words in the whole time I've known him as he did today."

Slate chuckles, his hands skimming down Hazel's thighs.

"Is he seeing her again?" Cedar asks.

"I guess she doesn't have a phone, so he wants to go there and make a big romantic gesture." Her head lolls back against Slate's shoulder. "I need Marigold to come back here and help. I don't know what to do with these teenagers."

"You should have seen Indigo and Briar tonight," Onyx mutters.

"Will you accept a new pack member or have him leave?" I ask, attempting to contribute to the conversation.

"I suppose that's up to them," Slate answers.

"Will Alpha Nyx cooperate in either instance?" My voice quiets.

"She should," Hazel answers patiently. "She's been opening up over the last year. She's even meeting with the Ironcrest Pack soon."

My eyes widen. Surely she misspoke. The Ironcrest Pack and the Raven Pack have been enemies for years.

"Are we okay with this information getting back to Granite Ridge?" Onyx asked softly, tipping his head in my direction.

My teeth click together, my jaw tight. So much for a friendly hangout. Anger rising in my chest, I wait for Hazel or Slate to reprimand him. Not that I expect anyone to defend me, but how dare he question them?

Spots dance in my vision from staring into the flames. I can't take any more teasing from Onyx, or worse, friendly sympathy. My teeth sink into the inside of my lower lip, a poor attempt to contain the chaotic energy battering around in my head.

"It's fine," Hazel says, her tone gentle.

"I suspect they already know. It's not being kept quiet," Slate explains. His calm energy starts to relax me, and I buck against the false sense of security.

Seemingly accepting his Alpha's answer, Onyx sits back. Beside him, Cedar leans forward with his forearms across his knees. "So Nyx is actually willing to meet with them?"

"Yep!" Hazel says.

"I guess she realized hiding in her den is no longer a viable option," I mutter before I can think better of opening my mouth again.

Hazel's head bobs. "Exactly!" Her agreement surprises me, and my lips part silently. "I think the power dynamic is different now with mediation and all the groveling Zephyr has done over the last year."

"Really? Like what?" I ask, feeling foolish for not knowing what was happening with our neighboring packs. It'll be something to correct as soon as I get home.

Slate answers, "He paid to repair all the damage from the fight."

Hazel giggles. "Zephyr seems quite taken with her, actually. He keeps sending gifts and she avoids him. This meeting is a big step for her."

"It'll be interesting to hear what they agree on," Slate says.

"Have you been meeting with Nyx yourself?" I ask.

Slate brushes Hazel's hair over her shoulder, answering without taking his eyes off his mate. "We've had a few calls. Not a lot. Ironcrest is always eager to talk, but both Raven Pack and Granite Ridge are still resistant to meeting regularly."

Hazel sighs. "I wish Sienna would agree to meet with us again, but having Jasper visit is a good step forward."

"So why the exchange? Do you really need me as a hostage to ensure his safe return?"

I wish I could suck the words back into my throat. Four sets of eyes regard me with varying emotions, from surprise to disdain.

"It's not about that," Hazel ventures. "We want to build relationships both ways, and besides, you've never spent time with your half-brother." Her hand tightens over Slate's.

"Right." As if Slate wanted to get to know me. With some effort, I keep sarcasm out of my voice.

"Speaking of," Hazel continues, "We'd really like to have you over for dinner. Just you and us, if that sounds good."

"When?"

"Tomorrow night. I'll make enchiladas."

"Okay." I've never had enchiladas either and I'm not even sure what they are. But considering how delectable dinner was tonight, I'm optimistic they will be delicious too.

"Want me to join you?" Onyx asks. Does he really think I need a guard to eat dinner with the Alphas, one of whom is my half-brother?

Hazel cocks her head, frowning at Onyx. "That's okay. Have some down time."

With a shrug, Onyx lifts another burned marshmallow to his mouth and takes a bite. I couldn't pull my gaze away from his mouth if I wanted to as he licks the sugar off his lips.

Hazel slips off Slate's lap and they rise. "We're calling it a night. See you guys tomorrow."

I return her little wave. Hand in hand, they disappear into the shadows.

"Alright, the lovebirds are off to their nest," Onyx jokes. "Anyone want more s'mores?"

"Um, no thank you," I say, voice rough. I can't meet his eyes after the way I drooled over him eating a marshmallow. "I think I'm ready to get some rest."

"Sure, totally."

The twins make quick work of extinguishing the fire and packing away the graham crackers and marshmallows. I notice the chocolate has disappeared entirely.

Onyx shadows me as I trail across the back patio and down the hall to Briar's room. Instead of going to his own door, he follows me to mine. I spin to face him.

"Can I help you?" I snap.

He leans against the door frame, invading my personal space. In place of the sass I expect, his expression is concerned. "Are you okay?"

"Fine. I mean, your brother is rude, but that doesn't bother me."

His chin dips, his night sky irises searching my face. "He's just like that. He isn't trying to be an asshole. He's just very honest and straightforward."

"Don't bother. You don't need to stick up for me. I can handle myself." My hands rest on the door frame, anchoring myself.

"You know, if you just talked to him, you guys would get along just fine."

"I seriously doubt that."

"But you and I get along just fine and he's much nicer than I am, I promise." He grins at my hesitation. "See? We aren't so bad."

"I didn't say you were bad. I said you were a dick."

"Not disagreeing," he says, that infuriating smirk back.

My pulse flutters in my skin, every sensation heightened as my body reacts to his nearness. Damn it!

Scowling at him, I say, "And you called me a bitch."

"I apologized."

"You said Marigold was making you apologize. You didn't actually do it. That doesn't count."

"What about the rest of what I did to you? Did that count as an apology?"

"Onyx," I warn. My thoughts have gone fuzzy.

"I like how you say my name," he purrs.

I know it's not genuine, but his silky words still affect me. Scoffing, I grip the doorknob at the small of my back and twist. Without breaking eye contact, I step back into his sister's room.

"Good night, Onyx." His tormenting grin is the last thing I see before I close the door between us.

My skin is tingly and hot. Does he enjoy making me uncomfortable? Though from what I can tell, he still hasn't told a soul about our encounter at the party.

Heart racing, I trade my clothes for a nightshirt and slip into the bed. The cool pillowcase soothes my heated cheeks. Eyes squeezed shut, I try to think of anything except the wolf sleeping across the hall.

V

LOOKING A LITTLE STABBY

ONYX

Feeling good, honey?" Mom asks, sliding a plate of banana French toast across the table toward me.

"Yeah." I take a deep breath. The soft floral scent of Ember lingers in the kitchen and the image of her tongue swiping her fingertips as she licks marshmallow from her skin flashes through my head. In one day, she's thoroughly under my skin.

I thought she was a dangerous flirtation, just a thrill. But the vulnerability she showed last night, all my protective instincts rose up, demanding that I care for her. Sometimes the wolf part of me can be such a simp.

With a rough sigh, I shove my fingers through my tangled hair. I need to pull myself together. She's not mine to protect. In fact, I'm quite sure she'd be furious if she knew what was going on inside my head.

"Good morning, Ember," my mother chimes, causing me to startle.

The girl stands on the edge of the hallway, the arch framing her curves. With emerald waves streaming down her back, face scrubbed clean of makeup, and oversized sweatshirt draping over one shoulder, she looks like a goddess.

"Good morning, Clove," she responds politely. Hips swaying, she drops into a chair as far away from me as possible. Could I move seats? No, that would be weird.

"French toast? I've got bananas and strawberries."

"Banana sounds good, thanks."

My mother catches my eye, a pleased curve to her mouth as she hands our guest a plate loaded with sliced bananas over brown sugar custard brioche.

We eat in silence, and my stomach clenches each time I catch her peeking at me through her lashes.

Finally, she breaks the silence. "So what's on the agenda today?"

Sipping my coffee, I regard her, enjoying the dimple in her cheek as she purses her lips impatiently.

"No plan."

Her lips pout as she frowns. In that moment, she looks so much like Slate, I have to cover my grin by taking another drink.

"I can't just sit here all day staring at you," she says with a scowl.

"Sounds like a fantastic day to me."

She huffs and slouches back. "You can't be serious."

"Well, what would you like to do?" I can feel my mother's eyes on us.

"I don't know, Onyx," she says with a roll of her eyes. "But I've gotta do something." She takes one look at my smirk. "Shut up."

"I wasn't saying anything."

Her cutting glare could have murdered me.

"Look, it's Saturday and normally we train on Saturdays. Want to head to the training building and check things out?" Hopefully my dad won't mind a guest.

"Yeah, that sounds interesting, actually."

We finish eating and my mother adamantly rejects her offer to wash dishes. It's another instance where Ember seems entirely normal, even kind, and my heart does a flip that I know will only end badly.

Ten minutes later she reappears in her version of training clothes. I'm used to women wearing loose t-shirts and sweats or maybe leggings to train. She wears a skin-tight black tank top and bike shorts that show a stripe of midriff.

Peeling my eyes off her skin, I take a slow breath. This would be easier if Ember wasn't so appealing. If she was just mean, I could ignore her, but she's complicated and every time she shows a different side, my defenses start to crumble.

"Ready?" I ask. That dimple reappears in her cheek as she nods.

As we cross the meadow, the three feet between us feels like a chasm, but she walks with her chin thrust upward and her shoulders back. She's trying her best to not look nervous and I respect that.

But there's no reason for her to be anxious. No one here would harm her. Mistrust her, give her suspicious looks, maybe, but no one would lay a hand on her. She's under Slate and Hazel's protection as their guest, not to mention our pack is generally peaceful - especially compared to the brutal way her pack operates.

She hesitates at the door to the training building. Last time she was here, we were battling and she was dragged out with her hands zip tied. Jaw set, she pushes the door open.

My father looks up. Most of the teenage wolves in our pack circle around him, including my sister. Indigo straightens beside her, puffing his chest out. With a wave of his hand, my father dismisses the students.

"Dad, we were hoping to join training." I keep my eyes on the ground in a sign of respect. As I walk closer, I'm pleased to see Ember falls a half-step behind me, allowing me to take the lead.

"I don't think that's entirely appropriate. Do you?" he says, clearing his throat.

"Sir, I can't just sit alone in a room the whole time I'm here," Ember argues, "Let me test myself. I'd like to see how I stack up against your wolves."

My father pauses, and I look up to see him studying Ember. She is stone, unwavering under his judicious stare.

"Alright, but no weapons. The Alphas led patrol out a few minutes ago, so you'll have the place to yourself. But I'll be out back with the pups."

"Thank you Dad," I say, shoulders dropping in relief.

"Can I use a small dagger or maybe a staff?"

Has she lost her mind? I didn't expect my dad to allow her to participate at all, and now she's asking to be armed?

"Hand to hand or go back to the cabin," my father says over his shoulder. With a few motions, he ushers Briar and her friends out of the building.

"Yes, sir," Ember grumbles to his back.

At the door, he twists and fixes me with a hard look. "Onyx, I'm expecting you to enforce my rules. I'll be right outside if there is any trouble."

"Not a problem." I hope it's true. Ember scowls as he props the door open, and I suddenly wish that all of our weapons were behind locked doors. At least the firearms are inaccessible. She looks ready to draw blood after what my father said.

Her voice drops as she draws closer to me. "Do we really have to obey him? He seems easy going."

"Don't let him hear you say that. He's been our pack trainer for twenty years and I can promise he isn't remotely easy going," I caution her.

Ember shrugs, hands flattening along her hips. "My pack's Delta is always yelling and hitting anyone who doesn't obey fast enough. Your dad isn't like that. I can't see him hurting anyone."

"You know there's other ways to gain respect other than violence."

"Ineffective ways."

"I don't think you've had very good trainers."

"Come fight me and find out."

"Do you have any weapons on your person?"

"No." The words are light, flippant. Somehow, they ring untrue.

Eyeing her figure, I can't see where she would have tucked a knife or other weapon, but after several battles and serious injuries, I know to trust my instincts. "Are you lying?"

Her face brightens into a true smile, although it's more a devious grin than something joyful. I'm still shocked by the difference. She's stunning. "Come find out."

It takes all my self-control to not launch myself at her. But the possibility of injury lingers in the back of my mind. "Ember, I don't want to get stabbed again. You're looking a little stabby right now."

That smile reappears, like a punch in the gut. It'll be impossible to fight her when I'm distracted by it. "Look, I promise I won't stab you."

I hold out my hand, the littlest finger extended in a childhood ritual.

"Really? A pinkie promise?" she asks, but she takes my finger with her own. With a light shake, we seal the vow.

The second my hand leaves hers, she attacks. Considering the girl comes up to my collarbone, she is shockingly aggressive.

Her hands grab my shoulder, jerking me forward while her knee comes up to hit the inside of my thigh. Too close to my balls for comfort. Between the pain and the instinct to curl up protectively, my body goes down hard. She shoves me to the floor at her feet, and I roll over to look up at her smug smile with that enticing dimple.

Struggling to draw in breath, I push myself into a seated position. "Damn, I did not expect that."

Ember gives a little shrug and offers her hand. The need for revenge pulses through me. Instead of allowing her to help me up, I yank her down, hooking my foot behind her ankle and drawing my knees up to pull her feet out from under her as she tries to compensate for the pull of my grip.

With a snarl, she lands on her ass, hands catching her before she falls entirely flat. "Dick," she growls.

"You didn't fight fair. Why should I?"

"How was that unfair?"

We sit facing each other, our glares more playful than malevolent. After a few deep breaths, I push up to my feet and offer my own hand. She swats it away and rises gracefully.

"You really think you can handle me?" she taunts, beginning to circle me. My feet move without thought. I may not have the discipline or skill that comes from daily effort, but I was raised by the pack's Delta, and the basics are built into my blood. When we were kids, I could best Slate easily, though he outpaced me somewhere around age twelve. In the last year, I've taken my training seriously now that I hold a pack ranking.

Ember darts in, swinging with a closed fist. My arms are longer than hers and I hold her back with a hand to her chest, right below her neck. Her wide eyes blink at me for a second, and I use the pause to slide my hand up to her throat with a soft grip.

Her mouth opens, eyes dilated. Her expression is distracting, and I run my thumb along her skin. In that instant, Ember leans back and kicks forward, the bottom of her foot connecting with my stomach. Stumbling back, I struggle to find my footing. She doesn't wait for me to recover.

Teeth bared, she leaps at me. Twirling out of my grasp, she slams a fist into my ribs. Instead of letting her get enough distance for another hard strike, I grab her waist and drop to the mat.

On the ground, I use my size to pin her, carefully restraining her wrists. She growls up at me. "That would never work in a real fight."

"Maybe," I reply. "What's this?"

Gingerly, I slide a small knife from her waistband.

"That's just for emergencies," she snaps. "Give it back!"

My brows pinch at the fear in her voice. "Ember, you don't need it here."

"I don't trust anyone here. Don't you dare," she snarls.

My grip on her weapon tightens. "After all this time we've spent together, you don't trust me?" I mean it as a joke, but some part of me is actually hurt.

"Why would I?" she spits.

"You said you didn't have a weapon."

"I told you to find out."

"Well, I did. And I think I'll hold on to this for now. You can have it back afterward. I wouldn't want you to slip and hurt yourself. Or me." Her eyes blaze as I set it to the side of the mat. Considering how angry she looks, it's not safe to let her keep it. I like my body without knives embedded in it, thank you very much.

Ember rolls to get her feet under her and I move with her to stay close, my head dipped toward her's. The second we are further apart, she will punch me in the face. I can sense that truth with every bit of my intuition. The result is that we stand chest to chest, her dark hazel eyes looking up at me in surprise.

"Is this how training is done in Granite Ridge?" I ask, casually drifting to the side so we can begin to circle one another.

She closes her teeth over her bottom lip and I don't expect an answer. Finally, she says, "Not really, we do more drills, and then when we spar, it's usually a competition."

"Do you guys do that a lot?"

"Yeah." Her tone is flat and cold.

"Are there prizes?" I ask with a forced grin.

"Usually whoever does well gets dinner, and those that do poorly get the shit beat out of them."

"Are you serious?" I ask, my feet halting.

Without warning, she surges forward. My shock costs me a fraction of a second, but it's enough. Throwing my weight onto my back foot, I grab her arms so I can push her aside, but I can't get a clean hold on her. We go down in a tangle of arms and legs.

Her nails dig into my forearm and she pins me with a defiant sneer. I could knock her off easily. She doesn't have the weight to hold me down. But the look of triumph in her eyes gives me pause.

It's not until I feel metal against my ribs, where my shirt has pulled up, that I realize what she's doing.

"Ember, don't." My words are more plea than warning.

Bold hazel eyes stare back and her hand trails up until she grips her knife tight to her breast. "Onyx, just let me have this. I never go without it. It's for emergencies and I promise not to use it unless my life is in danger."

Relief courses through me. She isn't about to disembowel me.

"I think we're done training." I try to keep my tone neutral, but disappointment tinges each word.

She pushes back as I sit up until she's hovering over my lap awkwardly. Already, her knife is tucked away, and she gathers her hair into a twist at the nape of her neck. I find the line of her jaw and the curve of her mouth fascinating as she glances away from me.

"So what about wolves who aren't ranked? In your pack's competitions," I ask, trying to bring back our conversation.

Ember shrugs and sits back on her heels. "Everyone holds a rank in Granite Ridge. If they can't fight, they don't have a place with us."

That doesn't make any sense. How does their pack operate? "What about seniors?"

"We don't really have any," she says, cocking her head at me, as if she's unsure why I'm questioning her.

"What about kids? What age do they have to start training?"

"Um, twelve-ish? I think I started at ten, actually. But we don't have a lot of kids. We occasionally take in strays, so there are a few teenagers."

"Your pack isn't exactly normal. You know that, right?" I blurt without thinking. Mentally kicking myself, I shove my hand through my hair and brush it away from my forehead.

"So I've been told." There's that lip curl again. I'm not sure if she's showing disgust at her own pack or defensiveness at my judgment.

"Do you ever want something different?" I ask, unsure of what I'm trying to gain in this conversation.

"Why is *this* considered normal?" She questions me, opening her hands in a sweeping gesture. "Just because you grew up with it?"

"Well, no," I argue.

With a haughty laugh, she tucks a leg under her and rises. Anger shines in her eyes and the tightness around her mouth. "It's amazing you guys ever stood up to us."

"Excuse me?"

Her eyes rove down my body as I stand to meet her. "Your pack is weak."

Hot anger floods my blood, drowning out the empathy I had for her. My tone is harsh and I can't help it. "We aren't weak. And we don't beat each other half to death and then starve our packmates as punishment."

"That's not how it goes," she says, her arms crossing. A beautiful flush rises up her neck.

"Tell me I'm wrong. You're always expecting a fight. Why is that?" I push forward, demanding an answer with my direct gaze.

"Of course I am," she hisses.

"Why?" I won't let this go. I need to know what drives her.

"Because I have to fight for everything I have. It makes me stronger." Her pose is regal, chin up, shoulders back.

"You shouldn't have to," I argue.

A flash of teeth almost pushes me back a step, but I hold my ground. The green glow to her eyes is threaded through with gold.

It wouldn't surprise me if my own eyes were that cool blue they turn when I'm upset or turned on.

"Not all of us have a fairytale childhood."

My hands go to her upper arms, keeping her from turning away from me. She doesn't seem to notice, her tongue darting out to wet her lips.

"My pack saw me as a punching bag. If I wasn't tough, I'd be dead." The cold resignation in her words makes my heart pound. No wonder she's so defensive.

Instinctively, I pull her into my chest. She stiffens and with a dry cough, she asks, "So, are we about to fight or fuck?"

My laugh is raw. "No, I'm comforting you."

"Well, it's weird," she protests while settling against me. I could rest my chin on the top of her head if I wanted to. She fits against me perfectly.

"Do you want me to stop?" I ask.

"In a minute," she murmurs. Slowly, her muscles relax.

Taking in a deep lungful of air, I lose myself in her scent. It's a walk in the meadow in the moments before it begins to storm. Electric, sweet, and heady.

The door bangs open and Ember leaps back, as if we were never touching.

Patrol pours in, chatting while they head for their lockers. Hawthorne nods at me in greeting, his eyebrows rising as he takes in Ember's flushed skin. Thankfully, he leaves us alone.

With a sigh, I uncap a water bottle and offer it to Ember. She hesitates before taking it, and doesn't drink until I've had half of the second bottle.

"I think I'm ready for a shower," she says, making a face, "You got your sweat on me."

The distance between us shrinks as we walk northward toward my home, our arms almost brushing.

The house is quiet. Before we go into our separate rooms, Ember pauses. "Look, I shouldn't have told you any of that about my pack. I was being kinda emotional and it wasn't very accurate."

The lie stings.

"Really? It seemed true when you said it. And I like hearing about your life," I say.

Her eyes narrow. "Don't worry. It won't happen again."

"Ember," I say, hoping to stop her from disappearing. It doesn't work.

She begins to close the bedroom door between us, but before it clicks shut, she says, "Just forget it, Onyx."

VI
SAUCY BURRITOS & HALF-BROTHERS

EMBER

I'm grateful to be having a private dinner tonight, even if it's with my half-brother who hates me. The suspicious stares of Onyx's packmates follows me all afternoon, making me sick to my stomach.

It was a relief to head northeast toward Hazel and Slate's cabin. Onyx walks with me, his careful glances monitoring my emotional state. Since when is he part-babysitter and part-therapist? I want to push him away, but the attentive concern is something I've never had before and it's oddly comforting. Ever since he held me after our fight, he's been quiet.

Onyx raps his knuckles on their door. A soft squeal and garbled voices inside tells me Hazel is way too excited about our dinner.

The door swings open with a soft creak. "Hi, Ember," Slate says. "Thanks, Onyx. See you later."

My guard hesitates, his eyes bouncing between me and my half-brother. "Bye," I say, hoping he gets the hint and leaves. All of these moments between us are getting confusing and muddying up my thoughts. I'm looking forward to clearing my head, even if it means spending time with a sibling who hates me.

Jaw clenched, Onyx finally turns away and steps off the porch.

"Thanks for coming," Slate says, stiff and polite.

My arms cross defensively. I don't want to be here and I hate pleasantries. It would be better if he would air his grievances and we could deal with it. Although that might lead to me being chased out of their territory. Not the worst thing that could happen.

"Ember, do you want some soda?" Hazel calls. Slate holds the door open as I step into their home. The cabin feels old with warm wood trim running along the floor and the ceiling. The front door leads into a cozy living room with a set of leather armchairs and matching sofa. Further in, Hazel buzzes around a small kitchen. The shiny appliances stand out against aged, worn cabinets. The cabin is decidedly a mix of vintage and masculine design styles. Framed sketches dot the walls throughout.

"I'm good with whatever," I answer, pausing in front of a drawing of a waterfall. The pencil is blended until the gradients are smooth, making the flow of the water in the foreground ethereal. It could pass for a photograph but somehow it portrays more emotion than a still photo ever could.

Hazel appears at my side, holding a chilled soda can in a koozie printed with a wolf wearing sunglasses. It's the most ridiculous thing I've ever seen.

"Slate is an amazing artist. It seems to run in the family." Her smile is sweet and genuine, and it feels unwarranted. I'm not deserving of her kindness, of anyone's kindness, least of all the girl I saw as an interloper needing to be disposed of when we first met.

Shrugging, I look back at the artwork. "Yeah, it's nice."

She watches me, waiting for me to volunteer personal information, but I have nothing to say to her. Her human upbringing is obvious at this moment.

"Ember, would you like to see the rest of the cabin?" Slate asks. Hazel sends him a look of gratitude as she heads back to the kitchen to finish some sort of salad.

Slate shows me the office through a door beside the kitchen. The room is set up with a drawing table and a computer desk. Tattoo equipment covers two shelves above the desk.

"What's with the tattoo gun?" The question slips out of me before I can reign it in. Slate's arms are covered in tattoos, down to his wrists, so clearly he likes them.

His mouth curves into the first real smile I've seen. It feels familiar, and I realize he has the same smile as Jasper. My heart tugs at me, reminding me that I miss my idiot brother. I'd trade Slate in for Jasper if I could.

"I did a tattoo apprenticeship a few years ago. I'll tattoo you if you want, some day." Slate offers. The stern Alpha persona is gone and he's putting out a calming charismatic energy. I feel drawn to him and I don't like it.

"No thanks," I say cooly, but then curiosity gets the better of me. "Did you do Onyx's tattoos?"

"Yeah," he answers. "I've done everyone's tattoos. Jasper even got his first one a few months ago.

"What?" My brother let Slate tattoo him? It feels a bit like a betrayal. Another sign that Jasper has fully integrated into this pack and left me behind.

Slate heads back to the door. "Yeah, Marigold's wolf with sunflowers. Ask him to show you when he gets back."

"Maybe."

Upstairs holds only their bedroom, with a wide king bed covered in an old quilt, and a line of bookshelves on the wall opposite the windows. I would guess Hazel is the reader, since Slate seems to be the artist out of the two of them.

"Dinner's ready!"

Back down the staircase, Hazel sets a casserole dish with a vibrant red sauce on the round table. I leave the empty seat to my right between Slate and myself. His arm goes to the back of Hazel's chair possessively.

In short order, my plate is loaded up with a sauced-up chicken burrito and a pile of salad sprinkled with tortilla strips and tomato. The enchiladas are delicious.

Swallowing her first bite, Hazel smiles sweetly at me. "So, Ember, are you artistic at all like your brothers?"

"No really. I don't draw or anything."

"What do you like to do?" Slate asks.

"Um, not much. I listen to music, I guess."

"Oh, like what kind of music?" Hazel's voice brightens.

"All kinds. Two thousands rock is good. Nineties rap. Anything with a good beat. I'm not picky."

"I love that," she says. "It would be fun to trade some music. Do you ever read? Marigold and I have a little book club."

"Not really."

"Okay, well if you want to join us, you don't even have to finish the book. We'd still like you to hang out with us."

"I don't think there will be time before I go home," I say with a tight shrug.

"Of course. But you could always drive over for the day," she suggests.

"My mom wouldn't like that."

After a minute of silence, Hazel runs her hand along Slate's forearms and squeezes his wrist. They exchange looks.

Slate clears his throat. "Look, Ember, I wanted to apologize for yesterday. I know the conflict between our packs was difficult for all of us, and I'm really sorry you lost your dad."

I could have choked on the bite of meat in my mouth. Swallowing forcibly, I dab my mouth with my napkin, desperately sorting through the conflicting emotions caused by his confession.

"It wasn't your fault," I settle on. It's tempting to blame him. I have for a long time. But after spending time here, I'm questioning the truth of it.

Slate's voice drops. "I honestly don't know what possessed her to do that."

It's painful to meet his gaze. "You're her child too."

His mouth curves into a grimace. "She picked him over me a long time ago."

It feels too close to bonding, having a vulnerable conversation, sibling to sibling. I don't want to be close with him. Some day we will be Alphas of separate territories and may have to face off.

"Well, I hope you feel special now." The words are ice daggers.

Hazel sighs, her mouth turning down at the corners. Good. I'm their political hostage, not a long lost sister to embrace. So why do I feel so wretched?

Hazel fills the rest of dinner with small anecdotes about Jasper's time with their pack over the eighteen months. It sounds like he's had a lovely time building a life with them and his new mate. Without me.

It's a relief when they wish me goodnight. Probably a relief for them too, since I wasn't contributing anything to our conversation. They even trust me enough to allow me to walk back to Onyx's cabin unsupervised after I assure them I know the way.

The moon illuminates the leaf-strewn pathway from their cabin to the central clearing, and it's not hard to find a smaller trail from the underbrush leading south toward the Delta's cabin.

It's cool and quiet, and I feel my tension unwinding. Drawing in a lung full of pine air, I let the stress of that dinner trickle away. Starlight illuminates the boughs of fir and maple trees as I wind my way toward my temporary home. The forest is lush south of the river, and my territory seems dry and devoid of life in comparison.

It's not far to the two-story cabin I'm staying in. The evening is so quiet and lovely, I sink into a chair at the fire pit to decompress.

A dark gray shape moves through the trees ahead. My hand goes to my blade, just in case. A wolf approaches, walking with his tail curled upward and his gait friendly. That citrus scent hits me.

"Onyx," I say. He rests his muzzle on my knee and my hand goes to his head without thought. The fur around his ears is silken and I can't help but dig my fingers in. A low rumble emanates from his chest.

Too soon, he pulls away and trots a few feet away into the forest. "Did you even go home? Or have you been hanging around this whole time?" I ask, even though he can't answer me right now.

His dark eyes watch me reproachfully over his shoulder.

"What are you waiting for? Go run. I'll head back to the cabin. I can make it on my own."

He chuffs, swinging back toward me and nudging my hand. Before I can pet him, he pulls away.

"Fine." Giving in, I tug my shirt over my head and drape it over the chair. "But you're coming back to get my clothes. I like this outfit."

He answers with another chuff. As I strip off my leggings, he watches me boldly. He's seen me naked before, but it feels different now.

As soon as my clothes are piled together, I shift. Black fur overtakes my pale skin and I drop down onto four paws. The forest lights up around me, bright as daylight. Onyx wears a charming smirk on his muzzle. He's a fine looking wolf, dark gray with black across his back. Lighter gray-brown peppers his chest and down his belly.

With a wag of his tail, he bolts. My wolf instincts surge, ready to chase him. It feels so good to give in to that urge. My paws dig into the soft earth and launch me forward, wind threading my fur like a caress.

Onyx weaves through the trees ahead, and I duck my head and increase my speed to catch up to him. He zips forward, just out of reach.

Trees whip past, and I spot a dark trailer to our right. Onyx turns, curving our path eastward. I cut the curve and playfully snap at his tail as I get closer.

Wolves are meant to run, and my body floods with feelings of contentment. My instincts whisper that this is right where I am meant to be.

He never lets me catch him, and being a smaller wolf, I can't close the distance. But utter satisfaction soaks into my being as we lope back toward his cabin. His granite wolf scales the porch steps and shifts back to human, grabbing a shirt off a stack of clothes set out.

I turn my eyes away from his body. "Ember," he murmurs, "shift back." Peeking, I realize he's holding up an oversized shirt for me instead of dressing himself.

It takes me a minute to focus enough to shift back. The naked man standing here waiting for me doesn't help my concentration. With one hand crossing my breasts, I accept the shirt from him. Like a gentleman, he focuses on dressing himself while I slide the soft cotton over my head. It drapes down to mid-thigh.

Onyx stands in sweatpants, chest bare. Endorphins linger in my blood, and I can't help but smile at him. He stares at me, a stupid grin spreading over his handsome face. We are a pair of idiots. Especially him, opening himself up to his enemy. But we don't feel like enemies right now, and I can't wipe the smile off my face.

Silently, he pulls the door open and we pad toward our bedrooms. His door hangs open and I can see Cedar sprawled across one of the two beds. Onyx follows my gaze and then rolls his eyes.

Instead of going to his own room, he follows me to my door. I twist toward him, wondering what he's thinking. He moves forward into my space until I'm leaning back against the closed bedroom door.

"Did you have a good time at dinner?" he whispers, his lips moving to my ear. The skin across my cheek and ear light up like he's touched me, though I can only feel his breath.

"Not really," I say honestly.

"I didn't like it either," he says. "I prefer when you eat dinner with me."

My hand flattens against his chest and I mean to push him away, but can't bring myself to do it. He takes it as an invitation to touch, and one hand goes to my hip. His thumb digs into my skin through the thin cotton shirt.

"Onyx," I say in warning.

"Ember," he answers. The rumble of his voice skitters goosebumps across my skin. "I like you in my shirt," he says. His mouth drops to my shoulder and he gently bites my shoulder through the cloth.

"You're running high off your shift," I choke out.

His navy eyes shoot to mine, his head coming up so fast his dirty blonde hair flops over his brow. He ignores it, all of his focus on my face. I want to shrink under the intensity.

"No," he starts, "I can't stay away from you." The draw of his brows and the downward curve of his mouth tell me he doesn't want to feel this pull toward me. I'm a guilty pleasure.

"You're attracted to angry women who hurt you." It's a statement.

His eyes narrow and my heartbeat picks up. "I'd rather fight with you than be with anyone else."

"Don't say things to me like that," I hiss, pleading. "You don't actually like me."

His brows furrow, mouth curving into a slight frown. I wait for whatever cutting barb is coming my way.

"I like you too much."

Pushing off the door frame, he walks away from me. Cold washes down my chest and stomach in his absence. He likes me?

His door clicks closed, and I numbly let myself into Briar's room. Adrenaline from his touch still rages, compounding the hormones already in my system. It's too much. Exhaustion seeps in, and I curl up in the bed. Before passing out, my fingers twine through the wide neckline of the shirt, bringing it up to my nose. His scent is faded after going through the wash, but it's still there. It seeps into my lungs and into my very being as I lose myself to sleep.

VII

CHEESETTE &
CHEDDARBELLE'S
FABULOUS DAY

ONYX

Soft laughter floats through the cabin, pulling me from sleep. My arm covers my eyes, and I lay there listening and trying to sort myself out.

Last night after dropping Ember off with Slate and Hazel, I shifted and circled their cabin. With my sensitive wolf ears, I heard flashes of their conversation and it didn't sound pleasant.

Slate has been my ride-or-die since we were kids, but he is failing to connect with Ember and it makes me heated. She deserves a brother who supports her. And besides, she's the future Alpha of an ally pack.

But last night, running with her, I knew I was in trouble. She's going to go home soon, maybe tomorrow, maybe today. And I'm addicted to her. Every wolfish instinct I have pushes me to get close to her. Those animal instincts don't understand that she's leaving.

When I make it to the kitchen, wearing only sweatpants low on my hips, Ember isn't sitting at the table where I expect her to be. Instead, she's at the kitchen counter with a round of bread dough in front of her. Flour dusts her palms and across her loose t-shirt.

My mother leans over her, murmuring encouragement and instruction as Ember folds the dough and presses it flat with the heel of her hand before turning it and repeating the process.

Her eyes are bright, a soft smile on her lips. This is not the same girl who I kissed at the party. The difference is staggering. I was hoping to draw her attention by showing up half-dressed, but instead she's got my jaw hanging down as I stare at her.

Scrambling for something to ground myself, I grip the kitchen table and drop into a chair, unable to take my eyes off of her.

"Morning," she says, glancing over her shoulder at me.

My voice doesn't catch the first try, but I manage to return the greeting. "How did you sleep?"

"Good," she says, already focused back on her kneading.

My mother hands her a small knife and draws lines in the dough showing her where to cut. Ember makes three slices up the dough, stopping just short of the top, and then braids it. With a flourish, my mother tucks it into a baking dish and sets it aside to rise.

"Fantastic. You are a natural at this."

Ember's eyes widen, as if this is the first praise she's ever received.

"What did you make?" I ask, dying for a scrap of her attention.

Ember dusts the flour off and slides into the seat across from me. "It's just a brioche. Hopefully it's good."

"It'll be delicious," my mom interjects. "You've got at least two hours before it needs to go into the oven. I can keep an eye on it for you." The microwave beeps as she reheats a leftover breakfast sandwich for me. She uses sourdough to make her English muffins, and I've loved them since I was a kid.

"Thanks, Mom." The sandwich is cheesy and greasy with bacon, and I immediately follow it with one of yesterday's scones, a banana, and a tall glass of milk.

Ember watches me, picking off little chunks of a scone and popping them into her mouth with an amused expression in her eyes. "So what are we doing today?"

"Since I don't have any patrol duties, I'm not sure." Rising, I tuck my dishes into the sink. "What do you want to do?"

"You can always help Cedar with chores," my mother calls from down the hallway.

"That sounds interesting," Ember says. Her arms fold over her chest and I'm not sure if she's being sarcastic or not. I know Cedar isn't her favorite person, but he's my twin and she's ... something I'm not ready to label.

"Let me show you his garden and we can see if there's anything fun we can help with."

She glances at the brioche rising on the counter with a damp kitchen towel draped over it. "I'll think about it." That small smirk is back. "Why don't you put some clothes on? Not everyone wants to see your abs."

Leaning back in my chair, I grin back, loving every second of this exchange. It would look like nothing at all to anyone else, but I see her opening up and enjoying herself. It's everything I hoped for.

"We both know that's not true, but I will anyway, just for you," I snark back. Striding to my room, I'm surprised her soft footfalls follow me. My heart speeds, but I keep my movements casual.

Stepping into my room, I leave the door ajar, and I can feel her lingering in the hall. "Hoping for a peep show?"

Ember rolls her eyes, stepping into my room. It's strange seeing her in my space.

"I'm happy to show you anything you want," I say, twisting and flexing as I reach for a shirt from my dresser.

"You're delusional," she says, the beautiful pink tint to her cheeks betraying her, "and messy." She's not wrong. There's a visual divide between my space and Cedar's. Gingerly, Ember steps over some clothing strewn across the floor.

"I had a feeling you liked video games," she mutters. While she examines my shelf of game discs, I tug my shirt over my head.

"Would you want to play some time?" I ask, coming up behind her to look over her shoulder.

She tugs a disc from the shelf. "What about this?" It's a car racing game.

"Really?" I ask.

She tucks the game back with one finger. "Maybe."

"What about this one?" I yank a zombie game from the shelf.

"No way," she says, wrinkling her nose and shaking her head so emerald hair cascades over her shoulders.

"Okay, what about…" Holding out Minecraft, I raise an eyebrow.

She tilts her head and stares at it.

"It's a building game. You really didn't have much fun growing up, did you?"

Her shoulders slump the slightest amount, but I'm so attuned to her body language by now, it's a meaningful change.

"I only got to play whatever games Jasper was given," she says, sighing as she steps back from the shelf.

"We can fix that! We could play today. I have a pair of cat ear headphones that would look great on you."

That earns a laugh. "Why do you have those?"

"I'll have you know, I look great with cat ears," I say with a grin. "With this game, you can make anything you want. There are different kinds of blocks and-"

"I think I'd rather play the racing game. Those were my favorites," she says, cutting me off.

"Sure. I'll get it set up," I say, reaching for my controllers.

"How about after we do our gardening?" she says, though I see a flash of a smile as she turns away.

Her fingers trail along my shelves as I finally pull on a black hoodie. "Alright," I say, "I'm all set. How do I look? Like the most handsome man you've ever seen?"

She exhales a laugh, shaking her head as she walks out of my room. I follow her back to the kitchen and we wash the breakfast dishes and wipe down the counter. It feels good to work side by side with her.

"Ready to garden?" I ask her.

"If you insist."

We find Cedar in the center of his vegetable garden, where the long beds are covered in a tunnel of mesh to protect the most delicate of his produce.

"Mom wanted us to come help you."

Cedar looks up from his work and scowls at us. "You can't help with this."

"What are you doing?"

With a dramatic sigh, he brushes the dirt off his hands and stands to face us. "I'm transferring seedlings into the garden. It's tricky. Their root systems are delicate."

"Fine, sorry we wanted to help."

"Would you guys feed the animals?" He eyes Ember curiously.

Her arms hug her waist defensively, but she nods and takes a measured breath. "I think we can handle that."

"Great, Onyx knows what to do. Let me know when you're done."

I could smack him on the back of his head for being rude, but he gave Ember a chance and she seems interested.

"Alright, let's start with the chickens," I say. Ember's hand flies to her mouth at my words. "Did you not know we had chickens?"

"Yeah, I did. I mean, I heard them. But I didn't think about visiting them." Her expression stays neutral but I can sense the excitement bubbling up behind her rambling words.

"The chicken coop is here," I point to the larger structure beside Cedar's storage shed. "Come on."

Her arm brushes mine as we walk the narrow path, and for a moment I almost reach for her hand. Before I can, she moves away.

"Wow, look at them," she says, peering through the chicken wire.

"Here, grab that bucket," I say, pointing at a feed tub. "We do two scoops of grain feed, a cup of vitamin powder, and a cup of their supplements." She holds the bucket while I fill it with scoops of chicken food.

"Now how do we give it to them?" she asks, peering down into the bucket in her arms.

"They have a feeder we have to refill. And we can't forget their treat." With a wink, I pull out a bag of dried mealworms.

Ember leans away, nose scrunched and mouth downturned. "Bugs?"

"Yeah, they love them!"

The hens cluck when we duck through the low door and close the wire gate behind us. With practiced movements, I unlatch and pull the lid off the feed silo. Ember bites her lip as she tips the bucket and pours in the hen's breakfast.

"What do we do with the worms?" she asks, warily eyeing the hens waddling to the feeder.

"Just scatter them," I say, offering her the bag.

With a grimace, she takes the bag and tips it down so a few mealworms scatter across the floor of the coop. Before she empties the bag, half a dozen hens zero in on the worms and rush toward her. Their wings slap her as they scramble for their favorite treat.

"Onyx, they're attacking me," she yelps. Despite her distress, she stays still, letting the feathered chaos batter her calves.

"You're okay. They aren't hurting you," I say in a low, soothing voice. Stepping closer, I plunk the lid back on the feeder and reach for her. My thumbs rub small circles into the curve of her waist while she watches the hens peck the ground around her feet.

"See? Friendly chickens," I say finally.

"Are they always like this?" she asks, her voice clear despite her eyes being wide.

I can't help the chuckle that escapes me. "You haven't been around animals that much, have you?"

"Why would I?" she snaps. "Can you get me out of here?"

"No." My grip tightens on her waist. "You can do this. They're just silly, fat birds. And you haven't finished giving them their dessert."

"Seriously?" Gritting her teeth, she rotates, emptying the bag out in a wide circle. The rest of the coop joins in on the madness, pecking and clucking excitedly.

It takes a few minutes for the girls to calm down. Ember's breathing evens out as she stares at the flock.

With one last squeeze, I let her go. "Picada," I call, looking for my favorite chicken. She sits in a nesting box and watches us, standing when I call her name. Gently, I scoop her up and turn back to Ember.

"This is Piacatta. Here, pet her. She's very sweet."

Tentatively, Ember strokes Picada's feathers.

"See? Nice chickens. They were just excited about breakfast."

"Do they all have names?" A smile tugs at her mouth and she looks down at the chickens bustling around their little coop.

"This one is Cutlet, and here's Cacciatore," I say, pointing out the chickens I've named. "Kiev, Curry, Satay, Fricassee, Alfredo, Teriyaki." Ember lets out a small laugh, but she smothers it with the back of her hand.

"Here, let's refill their water and go feed the goats."

She strokes Picada one last time. I set the hen back in her box, murmuring thanks to her for being such a good girl.

I use the hose to refill the girls' water before leading Ember over to the goats' pen. She stops at the fence and rests her elbows against the top.

"The smaller one is Cheesette and the bigger one is Cheddarbelle," I explain. Cheddarbelle trots over, her soft, brown ears swaying. "They're Nubian goats. Either Cedar or my dad has already milked them today, so we just need to refill their food and water."

"You milk them?"

"You haven't seen my dad's cheese kitchen have you?"

"His what?"

"Yeah, he makes goat cheese. You've eaten some already. But it's really messy, so Mom doesn't let him use the normal kitchen. He's got a whole set up. I can take you there later."

"You guys are so weird," she mutters, the slight curve to her mouth giving away her amusement.

After I refill their water, we load up on feed and treats and let ourselves into the goat pen. Cheesette walks out of their goat house and swings her head around to stare at Ember with her rectangular pupils.

"They're a little creepy," she says, her voice hushed as if the goats would be offended if they heard.

"Not my baby girls," I joke, holding my hands over Cheddarbelle's ears. They're so long and floppy, they swing below my hands. She shakes her head to knock me away.

"I'm sorry," Ember says to Cheddarbelle. Pure delight shoots through me that she's playing along.

"Here," I thrust an apple slice into her hand. "They'll love you forever if you give them treats."

I refill their food while Ember feeds carrots and apple slices to Cheddarbelle. Everything is fine until Cheesette joins in.

"Hi, pretty girl," Ember coos, petting the smaller goat. Cheesette tosses her head and lurches forward to ram into Ember. "Hey!"

There's no way I can reach her in time before her ass hits the dirt. Apple slices spill out of the container and both goats help themselves.

"Onyx!" she cries, waving at where Cheddarbelle's back hoof pins her shirt to the ground. "This is worse than the chickens!"

Shoving the goat aside, I pull Ember up. Half way, she lets out a shriek. "She's eating my hair!" I freeze, horrified as she wrestles a thick piece of hair out Cheesette's mouth.

"It's because you dyed it green. It probably looks like grass to her," Cedar calls from the fence. He watches our circus with a small smile.

"It doesn't look like grass," Ember protests. I can't help my guffaw at her outrage. She pushes Cheesette away. "No treats for you, you little shithead."

"Aw, she didn't mean that," I say, feeding a carrot to the smaller goat. Ember scowls at me.

"No accountability for being rude to guests? That tracks," she snaps.

"I'm *sorry*," I drawl.

Her hands shoot up. "Go back to babying your goats."

Cheesette shoves her nose into my palm, demanding more attention. I feed her my last carrot and give her a good ear rub.

Ember stands at the fence with a small and utterly smug smile on her face. Before I can question her, Cheddarbelle knocks into my back with her front hooves. I stumble forward and catch myself, but both girls are knocking into me with their hooves, trying to climb my back. Twisting, my ass hits the dirt.

"Hey!" I yelp, covering my head with my arms. But the goats both stick their noses in the scoop of my hoodie. Reaching in, I find a couple of apple slices. After the treats are removed and fed to the greedy goats, they leave me alone.

"Did you seriously put apples in my hoodie?" I ask, and Ember bursts into laughter. I vault the fence and grab her around the waist. "I can't believe you tried to get me mauled by goats."

"But they're so sweet, they would never maul anyone," she says, her voice high. As she laughs, her head tips back. I'm inches from her neck. Dark green waves tumble over her shoulders and down her back. She's so gorgeous it hurts.

Her hands go to my shoulders to steady herself, and then she's looking up at me with those eyes framed in dark lashes. She's stunning when she's angry or serious, but laughing - laughing Ember is something else entirely.

Despite the fact we are in the garden in the middle of the morning and anyone could see, I can't help myself. I'm pulled to her. She tips her face, a silent invitation, and our lips meet.

She's soft and warm, her mouth sliding over mine until her lips part. I love how she tastes like sugar and chocolate. Her fingers thread into my hair and I growl at the light tug as she pulls me closer. Her hips press into mine as I back her into the fence.

I'm lost to the feel of her. It's everything I remember from our first kiss and more. Pleasure and need mingle with affection. Her nails scrape my scalp as she clings to me, pressed between the fence post and my body.

One arm wraps around her waist to hold her up as her knees weaken. The other goes to the nape of her neck so I can angle her to kiss deeper. She lets out a breathy moan in her throat.

Her leg hikes up on my hip, like she's trying to climb me. Without thinking, I push my thigh between her legs. She squirms, grinding against me. My hand travels down to her ass, lifting her until she's half straddling me and my knee hits the fence post.

My mouth goes to her throat, nibbling as I lick and suck my way to the crook of her neck. "Onyx," she whimpers.

Her hands go to my shoulders, pushing me back. I release her, stumbling back a step as her feet hit the ground again. She grips the fence behind her to stay upright. Her glazed eyes find mine, her chest heaving as she pants.

What did I do wrong?

"We can't," she gasps. "Your brother is right over there," she gasps, tipping her head towards where Cedar is back to transplanting seedlings in the center of the garden. She steps closer again until her breasts brush my chest. "At least we can't do this here in the middle of your pack's garden."

Every thought is wiped from my mind. I want her so badly. This flirtation has built and built until she's all I can think about.

"Let's go back to the cabin," I say, breathless. She nods.

As we walk back to my family's cabin, I watch her. She glances at me, a small, sweet smile on her face. Her heart-shaped face is flushed and I want to kiss that blush from her nose down her chest.

I want her to stay. She can be happy here. I'll do everything I can to make sure of it. But she'll never want to stay when everyone is being cold and judgmental to her. If they can see her the way I do, that might change. She's already won over my mother. Hazel and Marigold won't be a problem. Mentally, I make a list of what I can do.

"I smell like farm animals. I'm going to go shower, but I'll see you after, okay?" she murmurs, slipping into Briar's room. I stare at the closed door dumbly.

I take the fastest shower of my life, and when I get out, Cedar is back. My mind races with everything I need to say. He sits at the kitchen table dipping vegetables in ranch.

Sitting across from him, I lean forward to get his attention.

"What's up?" he asks.

"I need you to be nicer to Ember," I say, trying to keep my cool.

"I am," he says, frowning at me.

"You've kinda been an asshole to her, questioning her every chance you get." Anger seeps into my tone.

"I'm not doing anything."

"Oh really? You've upset her at least twice, and you're definitely not being welcoming."

He watches me for a moment. "Why are you so upset about this?"

"She doesn't deserve it." My hands flatten on the table, trying to resist knocking the carrot out of his hand as he crunches another bite.

"She tried to kill you last year. She tried to kill Hazel the year before. She's been unkind to everyone since she got here," he says thoughtfully.

He doesn't see. He's taking everything at face value.

"She's trying. She's just reacting to how we are treating her. She's been really kind to our sister, to Mom. She's opening up to me."

Cedar gives me a long, critical stare. I raise my chin and narrow my eyes, daring him to say something stupid. It's been years since we actually fought and I'm itching to hit something.

"You're attracted to her. It's clouding your judgment."

The urge to smack him overwhelms me, but I know it's logic that will work with my brother. Slowly, I recount what's happened the last day. "The kind girl who baked with our mother this morning and then helped me with chores, that's the real her, and if everyone weren't so fucking judgy toward her, that's who she'd be all the time."

"I'm not sure about that."

He's impossible.

"Cedar, I swear, if you don't back me up on this," I leave the threat hanging. We both know I'd never actually hurt him, but I don't have a better way to express how important this is to me.

His arms cross and his brows furrow. "Alright. I'll do my best to be nicer."

It's not much, but Cedar always follows through on his promises. If he gives her a chance, he'll see what I see.

The shower noise from Briar's room cuts off.

"Thanks, man," I say to my twin.

"This is really important to you," he observes.

"Yeah."

Ember wanders in, wet hair against her neck and fresh clothes on her body. She winces as she slowly lifts the kitchen towel, and then smiles to find the brioche fully risen and ready to bake.

"What temperature?" she mutters, looking for the recipe card.

"Three-hundred and fifty, for forty minutes," Cedar says without looking up.

Ember swivels and blinks at him. "Thanks," she says hesitantly.

The oven beeps as she sets the bake temperature. While it preheats, she sits beside me.

Cedar crunches on a piece of celery. "Do you want some veggies?" he asks.

"Um, thanks," she says, accepting a carrot stick from him.

"Our mom makes the ranch too," I say, grabbing a celery stick for myself.

Crunching and chewing are the only sounds for a painfully awkward two minutes. I stare at Cedar, willing him to say something. Finally, he does.

"So, did you like the chickens and goats?" he asks.

Ember smiles weakly. "Yeah, they're cute."

"They're great for fresh eggs and milk," Cedar says, clearly unsure of how to hold a conversation with a girl.

"She met Picada," I say, proud of my favorite chicken who answers to her name.

"She was sweet," Ember agrees.

"I saw what you did with the apple slices," Cedar says, his mouth curving into a smile. "Pretty funny."

"Oh," Ember says, her cheeks tingeing pink again. I'm sure we are both having the same thought - was that all he saw? When did he go back to his garden?

We're saved by the oven chiming. Ember shoots up, peeking into the oven before she slides the brioche in. I can't help biting my lip as she bends at the waist to center the loaf pan on the oven rack.

Cedar crosses his arms, eyes narrowed at me when I look up.

"So what now? We've got thirty minutes," she says, dusting off her hands.

"Want to pick out a video game?" I suggest.

She props a fist on her hip and raises an eyebrow. "I believe I was promised a tour of a cheese kitchen?"

"If you want to."

It's not a quiet bedroom, but I can work with a cheese kitchen.

Ember follows me through the laundry room and into the addition my father built years ago.

"This is not what I expected," she mutters, the sunlight from the sky lights highlighting her cheekbones and the delicate tip of her nose.

We're squeezed into a narrow kitchen, standing on sealed concrete floors. Gleaming stainless steel lines the walls, including a commercial triple sink, a wide 8-burner range, and two refrigerators - one to store ingredients and one to age cheese.

Slipping my arm around her waist, I guide her forward, past the row of pots so large a small child could sit inside them.

"Honestly, I don't know anything about how cheese is made," she says, slowing her gait so she presses back into me.

I'm surprised at the euphoria that shoots through me at her nearness and the way she smiles at me. I'm thoroughly ensnared, and the danger of who she is and what she's done is fading away.

"It's pretty simple. We take the milk, it's stored in this fridge," I thump my palm against the closer fridge. "It gets cooked with rennet, which is actually a kind of mold, I think. Cedar can explain that better. Anyway, it forms curds, and we press out the whey which is like water until the curds are solid. It gets dried, aged, or whatever depending on the cheese."

Her lips part as she listens to me ramble. "That doesn't sound very simple."

With a rolling laugh, I herd her closer to the fridge to see what cheeses we can sample. She peers over my shoulder as I pilfer my father's current stock.

"Here, try this. It's fresh farmer's cheese, totally plain." Prying the lid off of a round plastic container, I grab a spoonful of the spreadable cheese.

Ember hesitates, pressing her lips into a line while she leans away.

"It's not bad, I promise."

With a little coaxing, she opens her mouth and takes a small nibble.

"So what do you think?"

"It tastes like milk." Her eyes open again, flitting from my chest to my face. "I can see how that could be good in a recipe."

"Yeah, it's not really a snack cheese," I agree.

"Got any others to try?"

We try a hard cheddar, a brie-style round, and some mozzarella.

"You can make all these different cheeses from goat's milk?" she asks, popping another pearl of fresh mozzarella in her mouth.

"Yeah. I mean, there's a flavor difference. But it all depends on what you add and how you treat the milk."

"Wow," she says, watching as I sprinkle salt flakes over the last bite of mozzarella and offer it to her. She eats it off the end of the toothpick and runs her tongue over her top lip to get the extra salt.

An alarm buzzes from the house, and Ember's eyes brighten. "Ready for some bread?"

"Go ahead, I'll be right behind you," I say, shoving containers back into the fridge before I can follow her. I'm just in time to watch her tug the oven mitts off of her hands.

Steam trails off the bread loaf, filling the room with the warm, nutty smell. My brother is nowhere to be found, and I'm grateful I don't have to share this moment with anyone else.

Her eyebrows are raised in a soft expression seeking my approval. Stepping closer, I make a show of inspecting the brioche before saying, "It looks perfect."

Closing her delicate hand over my bicep, she squeezes excitedly and my heart skips a beat. "Can we slice it right away?"

"It might deflate because it's really soft right out of the oven," I say. "Can you wait five minutes?"

She turns, her lip pouting as she frowns. "Fine."

With a chuckle, I gather up butter, the cutting board, and a bread knife while she watches her bread, hands clasped tightly behind her.

"Alright, it's probably been long enough," I concede after a few minutes.

Her teeth press into her lip in the most distracting way as she concentrates on flipping the tin over and dropping the bread onto the cutting board.

"Do you want some?" she asks, dragging the knife through the edge of the bread.

"Abso-fucking-lutely!"

Forget cheese - Ember holding out a slice of fresh bread slathered in butter is one of the most gorgeous things I've ever seen. My mouth waters.

Her eyes widen as she watches me take my first bite. Eyes closed, I tip my head back in ecstasy, exaggerating yummy noises so she never doubts how good it is.

She takes her own bite, her cheeks flushed and a shy smile on her face.

"This is the best thing anyone in the world has ever baked," I say, groaning as I take another bite.

"You're ridiculous," she says with a soft chuckle, wiping crumbs away from her mouth with the back of her hand.

"I'm serious. So good," I add with another groan.

"Yeah, but I'm so full now," she says, rubbing her belly. "I need a nap." A yawn proves her point.

I gaze longingly at the steam wafting off the hot bread.

"You can have more bread, Onyx," she says, smirking. "I know how much you enjoyed it. You could always take a second slice back to your room for some private time. I don't mind," she teases.

"Hey!" I scold, my laughter following down the hallway as she disappears.

I can't resist the second piece she offers, but I eat it over the sink and then wipe the crumbs from our first slices into the trash.

On the way to my room, I hesitate at her door. Her breathing sounds even, so now's not the time to bother her, no matter how badly I want to.

VIII
SECRETS & SIBLINGS

EMBER

The taste of bread still on my lips, I lay back on Briar's bed and replay this morning's kiss in my mind. The first time we kissed, we were tipsy and it was hot and angry. This time was light - stars bursting behind my eyes, electricity zinging over my skin. It was bright and scorching. It felt like he could burn away everything in my life and leave only him and that moment.

I want to let him. I want to forget the first eighteen years of my life and never leave this small window of time with him. I can even deal with the coldness from his packmates, if it means going back to his warmth.

But that is a daydream, and I know if I did something drastic like give up my ranking in my pack, I would resent him. I've worked for eighteen years to gain power, and I am one step away from being Alpha where I can control everything around me and no one will ever dare cross me again.

If I continue to get closer to him, it'll hurt worse when I leave. Or I could seize the opportunity and enjoy everything I can with him. Either way, I'll be heading home in the next day or two. If he gets me alone again, I don't think I'll have the willpower to resist him. The way he was devouring me with his eyes in the kitchen, I don't think I want to.

It might be worth it. I'm used to pain. I've got scars to prove it. So why not take advantage of this chance with Onyx? I can deal with the fallout when I leave. And if I'm insanely lucky, we can continue to meet up and spend time together even after I go home.

Mind made up, I lay there in a t-shirt and underwear and pray that he comes to check on me.

A light knock on the door sends a thrill down my spine. "Yeah?"

"Sweetheart, your brother is back. Do you want to come see him?" Clove's voice calls through the door.

All thoughts of Onyx shatter. Jasper and Marigold have returned, which means I am going home. It's over before we had a chance to start.

My throat burns as I pull on a pair of shorts and stuff the rest of my clothes back into my duffle. Onyx and Cedar meet me in the hallway, looking confused.

"What are you doing?" Onyx asks.

With a steadying exhale, I steel myself. "Jasper and Marigold are back, so I'm going home."

The look on his face guts me. His lips part and his brows rise. "Let's talk about this."

Cedar brushes past us, following their mom out the door.

"We knew I was only here for a couple of days. Since they're back, I'm going home."

"Wait," he says, reaching for me. I allow him to take my duffel and set it by the door. "What if you stayed?"

Frowning, I prop my hands on my hips. "I can't do that. It wouldn't be allowed."

"Fuck that," he hisses. "It's your choice. If you want to stay longer, I'll do whatever's needed to make it happen."

His low voice caresses my skin, and I feel my neck arching in submission. He shouldn't have this kind of power over me, but I love it. Closing my eyes, I focus on what I need to do. And it's not running away from my life because a hot guy flirts with me.

"Let's just go see what's going on, okay?" I say, my voice gentle while I take his hand. He threads our fingers together and it feels so natural that I'm momentarily stunned.

"Promise me you will think about it," he whispers. His pleading squeezes my chest and goosebumps break out over my arms. He doesn't know I've already been day dreaming of staying with him. That's how dangerous his influence over me is.

"Alright," I say simply. Stiffly, I pull my hand from his and he doesn't protest.

The silence is full of unspoken desires as we walk south, toward my brother and my way out of here.

My mother's red sports car stands out among the ivories and sage green trucks in the parking lot. Alarm bells go off in my head. Why would she drive them herself?

She's the first one I notice, with her dark hair in a classic chignon and her eyeliner so sharp she could cut someone. She stands beside Jasper and Marigold who speak with Hazel and Slate, but my mother's posture makes it clear she is not a part of their group.

Their hushed tones are impossible to hear over the birds chirping and the crunch of gravel under our feet. Onyx's father, Fisher, and the Gamma, Hawthorne, join the circle, and more hushed words are exchanged. Fisher's arms cross over his chest as he watches Jasper and Slate gesture while they speak.

Jasper looks up at me and I want to run to him. But the divide between us is too great. Dark circles smudge under his eyes and he looks paler than normal. Beside him, Marigold clutches his hand in both of hers tight against her stomach.

Sienna looks down her nose at Hazel, and the younger Alpha nods. Slate wraps his arms around his mate's waist, his eyes dark. My instincts whisper that something is wrong. The concerned curve of Hazel's eyebrows stand in contrast to the polite smile on her lips.

My mother gives a curt nod and turns on her stilettos. She's back in her car before I can reach them.

"What is she doing?" I snap.

Jasper cuts across my path, blocking me from her car. "Ember, wait!"

"Wait, what–?" My question breaks off as our mother reverses and peels out of the parking lot without me.

"It's fine," he says, "you're going to stay a few more days." His familiar voice soothes me and it's all too easy to submit to his will.

I bare my teeth at him, fighting against his influence. "Why?"

My brother stands his ground, facing my growing anger without visible re-action, though his gaze jumps to his mate. Marigold steps closer and takes his arm. "Your mom has a few things she wants to settle before you go home. And we wanted to spend some time with you."

"Why didn't she discuss it with me?" I growl, throwing my arm out to gesture toward her tail lights.

"You know how Mom is," Jasper says dismissively.

"I am her Heir, second ranked in my pack," I say, bolstering myself despite the bitter taste in my throat. It feels like a lie. "Not a child to be sent away whenever she gets tired of me."

"Let's just enjoy a couple days together and then you'll head home." Jasper sounds exhausted.

The rational part of my brain questions everything. Why does he look so bad? If he was a guest of the Alpha, it should have been a luxury vacation. But my feral instincts push those thoughts out of my head with the overwhelming sense that I'm being lied to.

"We are going to unpack and relax for a bit. But could we plan on spending tomorrow together?" Marigold asks with a sweet smile.

"Whatever." I spin, keeping my pace to a quick walk despite how badly I want to run.

As I pass Onyx, he turns to follow me, keeping pace at my side. Jasper's eyes burn into my back, but I ignore everyone.

My feet take me towards my temporary home without my guidance, which only serves to irritate me further. As we step into the quiet cabin, I hiss, "Are you happy now? You got what you wanted."

Onyx halts, his eyes dark when I finally look at him.

"Are you kidding? You're hurt. That's the last thing I wanted."

I ignore his words, unsure of how to take them. "Something is clearly wrong and I'm being treated like a child."

It only makes me feel more childish but I let him pull me into his arms. Cheek against his chest, he kisses the top of my head. I'm able to release some of the tension threatening to break me.

"I'm sure we will find out everything that's going on. And it'll be fine. I'll do whatever I can to help. And in the meanwhile, you get to stay a few more days with me."

His arms tighten around me. I know he's just trying to comfort me, but I can't help but take it as an invitation. Tipping my head back, I kiss his jaw. His stubble is rough against my skin.

"Ember," he rumbles. "We should be finding out what happened, not..." He trails off.

"Later," I whisper. I can't deal with my pack or my mother right now. Not when Onyx's body is pressed against mine. "Distract me. Please."

"You're going to be the death of me," he groans against my temple.

"Despite evidence to the contrary, no, I'm not," I tease, slipping my hand under his shirt to run the pads of my fingers across his scar. With a grin, he hoists me up so my legs wrap around his waist. He carries me through the kitchen and down the hallway to his room. Before I can protest, he tosses me down on his bed and turns back to click the lock.

"Are you sure you want to do this? I'm still leaving eventually," I ask, needing him to realize the situation.

"Even if you were leaving today, I would take every second you gave me." His words are punctuated by kisses up my neck as he crawls over me. "But do you? Because this isn't a distraction for me."

His expression is vulnerable, offering up a piece of himself to me. And I know I shouldn't, but I can't help myself. I want this and I want him.

With a nod, I tighten my legs around his waist again, reveling in the feel of him against me.

"You are stunning," he murmurs, sliding my shirt up to uncover my breasts. I gasp as his mouth closes over one. His hand goes to the other, softly stroking and running his thumb over my nipple. His tongue rolls across the other one, and I press my head back into his mattress.

Bunching his shirt up in my fists, I writhe under him. "Onyx," I moan. His response is a hum against my breast that nearly undoes me.

He moves to the other, his tongue licking over me. The arm not propping him up moves down, tugging at my waistband.

His head comes up, eyes silently requesting permission as his fingers trail under the edge of my waistband.

"Yes," is all I can manage. My hands tug at his shirt, and he shrugs it off so I can run my hands down his chest. His ab muscles tighten as he lowers down and slips out of reach. My hands skim up over his shoulders, feeling the cords of muscles flexing as he tugs my shorts down with his teeth.

Every molecule of my body is strung tight, feeling his breath against tender skin. Skin no one else has touched. He takes his time, slowly running his fingers and then his mouth lower.

"We are needed in a meeting," Cedar calls right before the door handle jiggles.

We freeze, his breath panting against my skin.

"Shit," I whisper. "What do we do?"

He slides my shorts back up my hips and rises up to a kneel between my thighs, looking disoriented. The door handle clicks as Cedar tries again.

"I'll go, deal with the meeting. You go back to your room after we're gone," Onyx says. The look he gives me is pure lust. His navy eyes glow dusty blue, like moonlight. His full lips are slightly parted, and I want them on my body, but we are out of time.

"Wait," I hiss, words clicking into place in my brain. "They're having a fucking meeting without me?"

"Maybe it's something totally unrelated," he reasons. "But I'll tell you whatever I learn, okay?

"Fine." I say.

"Onyx?" Cedar interrupts.

Onyx leaps up, yanking his shirt back on. As he unlocks the door, he blocks me from view, pushing his brother back. But Cedar's hand goes to the door to keep it from closing. The two males posture for a moment as Onyx tries to make Cedar back down, but the lighter-haired twin peers over his shoulder and it's too late. He sees me with bare shoulders, Onyx's quilt pulled over my breasts.

"Not a word," Onyx snarls at him.

A crease forms between Cedar's brows. "This is not a good idea. I warned you."

The door closes and I can barely hear Onyx's angry words as he leads Cedar away.

Heart racing, I slip my shirt on and peek into the hallway. There's no noise in the house, so I dart across to Briar's room and shut the door. Want and need rage through me, and I faceplant into the bed with a frustrated groan.

ONYX

Jasper looks like this is the last place he wants to be. He rests his forehead against the heel of his hand. Marigold leans against him, her cheek to his shoulder. Both look exhausted and decidedly grim.

Slate sits across from him, his mouth a thin line. Hazel runs her fingers over his wrist, drawing swirls with the tips of her fingers. To Hazel's left sits Hawthorne and then my father.

The pack bond resonates in the room with so many wolves gathered together. I can sense frustration and resignation rolling off my friends.

Cedar takes the chair past Jasper and I take the one beside Marigold. It makes me nervous to have my twin further away, knowing his inclination for sharing information without tact. Of anyone, he was the worst person to have caught up - except perhaps Slate or Jasper. They are going to be furious. Ravishing the Heir of another pack was definitely not in the job description when Hazel asked me to guard Ember.

Marigold sits up and squeezes my forearm. "Are you having an okay time?" she asks quietly.

Swallowing, I bob my head. She turns and smiles at me. I can tell the second she breathes in and catches Ember's scent on my skin. She goes still, her eyes flickering from my face down my body like she might find the girl tucked in my pocket. Her brows crease. Anyone else, I wouldn't worry. They'd assume it was because I was on guard duty. But Marigold snuck around with Jasper for weeks before they admitted their relationship to us. I'm screwed.

"Okay, let's deal with this," Slate says. His exhale is heavy.

Jasper sighs too, the half-brothers looking more alike in that moment. "So things aren't looking great in Granite Ridge," he begins. "Sienna has been ruling alone for the last year, and their pack is largely male."

"She hasn't taken a new mate and doesn't intend to," Marigold amends. "I think she really loved Ferris."

Jasper's jaw clenches. "Well, the talks among the pack members are starting to turn ugly. She's had to squash a few rebellious discussions already, but it's only a matter of time until someone challenges her."

Hawthorne's hand rubs his jaw thoughtfully. "And do we think she can win a challenge?"

"Against those fuckers they've got in that pack?" Slate says, his tone harsh.

"This is the consequence of building up a pack of brutish men, training them like a militia, and then telling them they are the superior pack. For years," Hazel says, emphasizing her words. "Sienna can't control them without Ferris."

"So what if she loses her pack? Who is likely to challenge her?" Hawthorne presses.

Jasper runs hand through his hair, already tousled from his anxious habit. "It'll probably be Orion or maybe Aries. And they're bloodthirsty. They won't hold our alliance. They'd probably attack Raven pack first, especially if they could get Zephyr to turn on Nyx. Then we would be next."

"We should prepare for a fight, then," my father says. Beside him, Hawthorne raises a pacifying hand.

"It would be best if Sienna wasn't ousted," Hazel says, shaking her head like she can't believe she is supporting her mate's mother who hates her.

"Well, what can we do?" Slate asks Jasper.

Jasper rubs his hand down his face. "I don't know."

"If we send any sort of support, it'll just make her look weaker. Short of going in and assassinating a third of her pack, I don't see anything we can do," Marigold says.

This is going from bad to worse, and I can't sit silently.

"What about Ember?" I blurt.

"She's staying here," Hazel says. "At least we can keep her out of whatever carnage is about to happen."

"Who is telling her what's happening?"

Slate's eyes bore into mine, his dominance pressing down until I drop my gaze. "We aren't going to tell her."

"Why?" I ask as respectfully as I can manage.

"What do you think she'd do if she knew?" Marigold asks softly.

Fear and anger swirl together, making me sick. "She'd want to go home and do something to help. But that's her decision to make. She's an adult and Heir of Granite Ridge."

"She's my sister, and I won't get her thrown back into that pack as it self-destructs." Jasper's words cut into me. "I know you don't care if she lives or dies, but I won't see her torn apart."

"Of course I want her safe," I snap. "But she has rights. I'm sure if we talk to her about the situation-"

"Have you ever talked with Ember?" Jasper interrupts me, his sky blue eyes blazing bright cyan. Marigold grips his arm, and I have no doubt she's feeding calming emotions through their mate bond. The rush of his anger lessens.

"I've talked with her a lot this week," I say, unable to stay quiet. "She's gotten a shit deal, but she's trying to do the right thing. And everyone is holding her pack's mistakes over her head."

"Onyx, I know this isn't fair to her. But we can't risk her running home and getting herself killed. If she's safe here, Sienna can focus on dealing with her pack. It's the only thing we can do to help. So you can't tell her anything." Hazel's dominance feels different than Slate's. Slate's is like a physical force pressing down on my shoulders. Hazel is like a warm blanket wrapping around me, drawing me toward what she wants and coaxing me to cooperate. I know if she wanted to, she could push harder, but she's gentle.

"Yes, Alpha," I say. The soft pressure releases me and the wolves around me relax in unison.

Ember is going to be furious when she finds out they kept this from her, but I'm powerless to help the situation.

"Please be extra vigilant. Whenever you aren't with her, make sure someone else is. Jasper and Marigold will take her whenever they can," Hazel says.

"Clove and I can take some of that responsibility on as well," my father adds. Hazel nods, looking between us.

"I'm staying in contact with my mother, so I'll provide whatever updates as soon as I have them." Jasper grips his mate's hand.

"Hopefully this resolves soon and she can go home," Marigold adds sweetly. Her words churn in my stomach. I want Ember to be safe and have everything she wants in this world, but I also want her with me. And staying here in Bracken Creek accomplishes several of those goals, though it denies her position as Heir.

Somehow I know she would trade her safety and happiness if it meant taking up the mantle of Alpha in her pack.

Slate dismisses us and I head back to my cabin, leaving my father and brother behind to talk with Jasper. Not caring about etiquette, I head straight to Briar's room.

Ember sits up on her bed, her expression open and vulnerable. It almost breaks me. I open my mouth and then close it, unsure of what I can say.

Gracefully, she rises and approaches me. Her hands rest against my stomach. I'd love to bypass our discussion and push her back onto the bed and kiss her until neither of us know which direction is up. But she is expecting an explanation.

"Jasper and Marigold were sharing about their visit, but they didn't say much." It's the truth.

Her brows furrow as she looks up at me, but she's patient for more of an answer.

"I guess your mom wants you to stay with us. Well, Jasper was the one who wanted it. Honestly, I don't know."

"Nothing else was discussed in the meeting?" she asks, gently requesting more information.

I drag my hand through my hair. "There were a few things the Alphas ordered us to keep quiet about. I'm sorry."

Understanding washes over her face. Her lips part for a moment, forming an "o" shape. I pull her to me, hands on the small of her back, but she leans away.

"I'd like some space. I thought I'd get some answers, but you can't, and it just confirms they're keeping something from me." Her tone is even, but it feels like the quiet before a storm.

My hold loosens and she pulls away. "Please don't push me away," I plead.

"It's been an emotional day," she says. "I think I need some actual rest. Can you close the door on your way out?"

"Ember," I say, wanting nothing more than to touch her. Her eyebrows shoot up, and I know she's made her decision. "Talk to Jasper or Hazel." It's the only thing I can say to help.

"I will." Her arms cross, and she watches me with a focused calm that scares me more than her anger ever has. Each step away from her feels like needles stabbing my skin, but I make it to the door and give her one last pleading look. Her gaze is distant, lost in thought.

Hating everything about the situation, I close the door, turn my back to it, and sink to the ground. My forehead rests on my forearm across my knees. She's hurting behind this door, so I sit outside and wait until she's ready to let me back in.

WHO DID THIS TO YOU?

EMBER

Dinner sounds unappealing, so I continue to lay in my borrowed bed and brood. Tears burn in my eyes but never fall. I want to fight, hurt someone, but not him.

Somehow in the last few days, Onyx became someone important to me. Someone I would protect, even refuse to hurt if we were on opposite sides of a conflict. He's more than a friend. The feel of his hands on my body sends goosebumps over my arms.

Even as disappointed as I am that he couldn't tell me what they said in the meeting I was excluded from, I can't be angry with him.

Tomorrow, I will confront my brother. But right now, there's someone else I can question. With a grimace, I pull out my phone to text my mother.

> And I'm your Heir, but you aren't treating me like your second.
> 9:10PM

> I will be sending you instructions tonight. I want you to gather some information while you are there. Be ready.
> MOM 9:11PM

I leave her text on read. Maybe she means asking questions, but I have a feeling she means spying. That's not going to happen. My position here is already precarious, but if I'm caught stealing information, they would imprison me truly.

Emotional drain melts into exhaustion, and I doze. A knock on my door wakes me.

"Go away, Onyx," I rasp, clearing sleep from my voice.

"I've got dinner for you, honey," Clove says.

Popping up, I rub a hand across my face and say, "Oh, thanks. Come in." The door handle starts to turn but stops.

"Mom, let me," Onyx mutters.

"Not a chance. Sit back down, or better yet, go clean yourself up," Clove scolds. Onyx's grumbles fade and once it's quiet, Clove opens the door fully.

"Thanks," I say, accepting the plate. An oversized croissant overflows with chicken salad studded with grapes. Another novelty for me. Taking a bite, I savor the creamy sauce and the bright crunch of celery.

"When did you have time to make croissants?" I ask between bites, smiling weakly at Onyx's mother.

Clove waves her hand. "Puff pastry is such a pain. I usually make huge batches and then freeze them. It's easier to make in the winter when the butter doesn't want to melt."

I nod, taking another bite. My stomach gurgles in appreciation.

"I appreciate you teaching me how to bake." The words get caught in my throat, but I force them out. "I'm going to miss you."

"You're welcome to come back any time."

"I don't think that's very likely. My mom is pretty controlling."

"Yes, I suppose she is."

"I need to find out what's going on. I can tell Jasper was lying to me. Do you know what they were meeting about?"

Clove's hand brushes over my hair, the way I always imagined a mother would do. My throat aches and my eyes sting.

"I'm sure Jasper will explain everything tomorrow. It'll be okay."

"If it wasn't a big deal, they wouldn't have kept anything from me," I mutter.

"Maybe," Clove answers. "But I have a feeling this is going to be a transformative time for you and your pack. They may need you, but you also need space and independence to grow. A little separation from your mother isn't a bad thing."

The truth of her words grips me. I would have given anything to be away from my mother's control and scrutiny. But it's the feeling of helplessness that turns my blood to ice. It's something I fight every day in Granite Ridge when wolves disrespect my ranking and my mother speaks down to me. If things go wrong, I don't have the power to stop it. Something deep inside of me knows that's why my mother didn't want me there. I'm too weak to be of any help.

"Ember," Clove says, pulling me from my spiraling anxiety. "Try to enjoy the time you have with us. Everyone here cares about you. You're safe. Make sure to rest and recharge."

"I will, after Jasper is honest with me." I'm not ready to let go of my anger, though Clove's kindness softens it.

"If that's what you need to do," she says, standing. I let her take my plate.

"Thanks, Clove."

"Good night, love." She opens the door and I hear Onyx scrambling out of the way. After she leaves, I listen to him settle back against the door. Ridiculous man.

My body itches to go open the door and let him in. I've already used him as a distraction before. But that wasn't wise. This time, I won't be opening the door and falling into his arms. I can't figure out how to deal with the situation when I'm distracted by his mouth.

I sleep fitfully, my heart aching. A deeper sleep takes me some time in the early hours and when I wake, it's late morning.

Scrubbing myself helps marginally, as does blow drying my hair smooth. A little extra eyeliner and I feel ready to face everyone.

When I open the door, Onyx falls back onto my shins. He smiles up at me sheepishly.

"Have you been here the whole time?"

He scrambles to his feet and shrugs. "I went to the bathroom once or twice."

I almost laugh, but remember the divide between us. He's just following his Alphas' orders. But being left in the dark is somehow worse when he's unable to help and clearly wants to.

"Where's my brother?"

"I'll take you to him after you eat some breakfast."

"Onyx," I warn, my nails digging into my palms.

"Breakfast," he answers in the same tone, the twinkle in his eyes the only sign he's teasing me.

With a scowl, I march to the kitchen and allow him to present me with some of the brioche spread with butter and jam. It's just as delicious cool, and despite my irritation, I eat the entire plate.

"We made this jam, you know." He scrapes the knife against the jar to capture a smudge of jam to spread across his last bite of bread.

I don't have the energy to respond. My cold anger gathers up inside of me as I mentally rehearse my discussion with Jasper, ready to unleash when my brother inevitably refuses to answer my questions.

"Everyone is at training. My dad and Slate ordered double training for the next few weeks, including weapons." My ears perk up at weapons.

The meadow is quiet. It's Monday, maybe the children of this pack are in school. A little spike of curiosity urges me toward the school to see if it's Marigold in the classroom, but I ignore it. My pack doesn't have a school. I did online classes, like my brother. But maybe someday, Marigold can help me set up a proper school for my pack when I'm the Alpha.

Onyx pushes open the door to the training building, and I'm surprised at how many wolves occupy the space. The garage door on the back side is open, and more wolves train in the dirt beyond.

A group of females grapple in a ring, while a few people lift weights along the wall. I hone in on Jasper, who stands in a line with a gun pointed at a target in the trees. He tenses and shoots, his shot landing off-center. He was always better with knives.

"Ember," Hazel says, using a towel to wipe her sweat off.

"I'd like to talk to my brother," I say, unwilling to look at the Alpha who is withholding information from me.

"He's finishing up some training. Can you wait a minute?" she asks. Her tone is casual, but there's an underlying command that prickles at me. With a jolt, I realize she's using dominance on me. From the soft brush of it, it's most likely unintentional. I wouldn't even notice if I was her pack. As soft as it is, it feels different than my mother's, and therefore alien.

Turning, I narrow my eyes at her. "Are you trying to start a fight?"

Hazel glances between me and Onyx, her cheek sucked in where she bites it. "No, but maybe it's a good idea to work off some of your aggression before you talk with Jasper? Just a bit of friendly sparring."

A minute later, we replace the sparring women in the ring. Onyx stands at the edge nervously. He's joined by a few pack members I don't recognize.

My focus narrows to Hazel. We've fought before, when she was human in the woods. She had a knife and I took it from her. Only Jasper's arrival saved her. But there are no knives here. Mine is tucked in my room, for once. And I have no reason to kill her. Regardless, I still want to win.

Hazel steps closer, hands up defensively. I'm a couple inches shorter than her, so I lower myself as I dart in, attempting to land a strike on her ribcage. She's incredibly fast, grabbing my wrist and twisting. I fall to a knee, snarling.

Hazel presses her advantage, trying to force me to the ground. Ignoring the pain, I grab her closer thigh and shove into her. She struggles to maintain her balance, throwing her weight onto me.

My wrist wrenches and my shoulder pops. We both fall sideways.

With a horrified expression, Hazel releases my arm. "Sorry!" she yelps, attempting to sit up. The pain in that arm is blinding, but I'm used to ignoring pain. Using my good arm, I slam into her collarbone, pressing her into the mat.

I press into her airway, observing the ways her eyes widen. She slams into my cheek with her fist, and I have to duck my head. Her weight shifts, her feet getting under me before I can drop lower, and then I'm flying over her to land on my back. All the air whooshes out of my body.

Hazel crouches over me, one hand rubbing at her neck. "Are you okay?" she asks, sounding distant.

Other faces join hers, but I can only focus on Jasper's glowing pale eyes. He hauls me up with rough hands, dragging me away from the crowd and into the trees.

Hazel's voice echoes, "Jasper, she's hurt!"

As I suck in air, my mind clears. My brother's face is twisted in fury.

"Is this what you've been doing here? Attempting to assassinate our brother's mate?" His words are barely above a growl.

"What?" I ask, holding my aching arm and trying to figure out how to pop it back into place.

"She tapped the mat. You could have strangled her!"

"I didn't see," I admit, my eyes dropping to the ground. "I didn't think an Alpha would ever tap out."

"She did it because you were hurt!" he hisses.

"I'm sorry! But she's the one who wanted to spar. If she couldn't handle it, she shouldn't have asked me!" Anger surges back into my body, turning up the pain in my arm until I'm choking on it.

"You should show her some respect. Hazel is the only one keeping you safe right now." I want to argue that I can take care of myself, but it hurts too much to form words.

"Stop it," Onyx growls, prying Jasper's hands off of me. He shoves my brother back. "She's hurt, you asshole."

Jasper looks me over and I bare my teeth at him.

"Dammit, Ember," Onyx mutters. He comes up beside me, using both hands to grip my shoulder and popping it back into place. I turn my face into his chest to muffle the small scream I can't contain.

"We need to talk about this," Jasper huffs when I look up.

"Yeah, there's a lot of things to talk about, since you're refusing to tell me what the hell is going on," I say. Neither of us moves so Onyx stays a weight against my good arm. His hand goes to the small of my back.

"You can't demand answers when you behave like that," Jasper yells. "You are so fucking lucky it was me there and not Slate."

It's too much. She's the one who wanted to spar. Yes, I lost control, but she beat me! Why is he acting like I tried to murder her?

Maybe because I did exactly that in the past.

I could tell him why. But I already seem weak. I'd rather have his anger than pity.

Memories assault me. Our mother glaring into my eyes, explaining we have to break Hazel. That she will either rise to the occasion or we have to kill her. Telling me to hurt her.

The sight of her blood across the floor.

My breathing accelerates and the world seems to blur. I have to get away. I tug my shirt over my head, and leap right out of my sweats as my black wolf takes over my body.

I lose myself in my canine instincts and let the chaos fall away. There's just the earth under my paws and the scent of little creatures in the woods. I'm in another pack's territory and I need to get away to be safe.

My sensitive hearing tracks another wolf following me, but I consider it with the detachment of a predator. They'll leave me alone once I'm out of their territory. I'm running as fast as I can. No reason to worry or change my path.

The land slopes downhill, and I thread through the trees expertly. My smaller wolf has the advantage, and my pursuer has to slow down. Finally I burst through the trees and leap into the creek. It's shallow here, but still wetting my belly as a wolf. But something tells me to stop. I shouldn't go into my pack's territory either.

The reality of my situation filters in, and I lose my wolf shape. Fur reveals skin, and I'm standing in knee-deep water, without any clothing.

A twig snaps, and I whip around to face Onyx. He raises his hands to show peace, but then lowers them to retrieve a clothing stash. I should walk to him and accept clothing and we can talk about this. But I'm so damn tired.

I sink down on a wide rock and hang my head. It's hot under my skin, but it doesn't matter. The water is icy as it swirls around my shins. The contrast grounds me.

"Hey," Onyx says, wading through the water. He's pulled on sweats and scrunched them up over his knees to keep them dry. It's worth raising my head to admire his bare chest. The spiky neo-tribal tattoos arc across his skin like black frost. I've never let myself stare at his tattoos before, only quick glances, but now I drink them in. The lines remind me of tiger stripes.

"Do you want clothes?" he asks.

What's the point? I drop my head again, the shock of my fight bleeding me out until I'm nothing but a husk.

"Ember," Onyx says. His voice is lower, darker. His shadow moves across me, and I don't realize until it's too late. His hand grips my shoulder as the other runs down my back over old scars from beatings. "What are these?"

I scowl at him, and even that seems to take too much effort. "I told you. When you do poorly at training, they beat you. Remember?"

He traces down to the scars on the sides of my thighs. "Can you tell me which wolves did this?"

Grimacing, I snag the shirt dropped over his shoulder and tug it over my head. "It doesn't matter. It's just how things are."

"It matters because I need to know who to kill," he says, the calm in his words scaring me more than any growl or snarl.

Shoving to my feet, I face him. "Oh, get over it. You're not going to save me. Just because I wanted you to fuck me doesn't mean you owe me anything, or that this is a relationship."

His stormy eyes only narrow. This isn't casual, fun Onyx. The intensity radiating off him takes my breath away.

"You know it's more than that. And I don't care if you say stuff like that to push me away. It's too late for that to work. I know you. And I'm going to do whatever I can to keep you safe." I gape at him. He lowers his head until his mouth nears mine. "And I'm going to do everything in my power to make you happy, because I think you've had very little of that in your life so far."

His grip is possessive, his fingers splayed over my skin under the shirt.

"I need to know the truth about what's happening with my mom and my pack," I say softly.

"Okay," he says. I freeze, staring at him. "If you promise to not leave until you've discussed things with Jasper and Hazel too."

"I don't want to talk with him," I argue.

"I'll make sure he's calm," Onyx promises, his eyebrows high as he waits for my response.

"Deal."

ONYX

Ember stands knee deep in the water with only one of my t-shirts on and she's so beautiful it hurts. She ran all the way to the boundary.

Jasper didn't follow us, but I can feel worry through the pack bond. I try to relay confidence to keep them at bay. I'm about to do something that will make him very angry.

If we aren't honest with her, she'll disappear and do exactly what they are trying to prevent. And now that I've seen the scars, I know her packmates have no problem hurting her. How could Sienna and Ferris let this happen?

When she becomes Alpha, it'll be harder for her to control those wolves since they've beaten her in the past. These wounds weren't from struggling and proving herself, they're punishment for being young and not yet strong enough to stop it.

I have to convince her to stay until things are safe. Until Sienna changes things in that pack and drives out all the people who would hurt Ember. I don't care if I have to go up there and take out those people myself.

"Some of the pack members are giving your mom a hard time and she wants to deal with them while you're here safe and can't get pulled into it."

She stands silently. If her mother is overthrown, she loses her ranking and potentially her membership in the pack. A dark part of me wants that to happen.

"I want to go home."

"I know," I say. "That's why I made you promise to talk it over with Jasper. He can tell you more. You going home right now might make the situation worse." I'm not convinced her mom cares about her safety, so it's likely true.

Her arms fold around her and she looks very fragile. "Alright."

"Alright," I echo her, running my arms over her shoulders and down her back. She melts into me. Moisture drips onto my chest, and I realize she's crying. "It's going to be fine."

When she looks up at me, the tip of her nose is red and her lashes clump together. "No, I fucked up. I showed how crazy I am and hurt Hazel. Slate will either lock me up or kick me out."

"Hey," I say, my hands rising until I cup her face and force to look at me. "Do you think maybe you fight like that because in your training, losing meant more than just a loss. It meant..." I trail off, one hand brushing over her shoulder blade.

She looks away, unable to meet my gaze. "If I can't control myself, I'm a danger to everyone."

"So you don't fight. You stay with me, bake bread, help with the garden, do whatever you want to do. Forget everything else."

For a moment, it feels like she'll agree.

Her hand tugs on the back of my neck and guides me down until our lips meet. The kiss is slow and soft, and I force my hands to stay still. She needs comfort, not a mauling.

She breaks away and whispers, "Thank you for telling me the truth." She pauses, and I can almost hear the thoughts in her head. "We should go back."

I pull her in for another kiss. "How about later. We're alone out here."

"They'll come looking for us soon, won't they?"

Groaning, I rest my forehead against hers. "When will we ever get some privacy?"

Ember's exhale is uneven, and I know she's thinking of all the reasons we shouldn't be together. But as far as I'm concerned, it's a done deal. I'm in this with her.

X
TEENY TINY CHICKENS
EMBER

Onyx holds my hand on the walk back. My mind spins with the implications of the situation. I want to go home and help my mother protect our position of leadership. But she doesn't want me there. I'm a liability in this situation - the young, female Heir in a pack of assholes. It's why she paired me with Hawk. A strong male as my mate fortifies my position.

But I can't help but wonder, what if that mate is Onyx?

The thought makes my stomach clench. It's too much to think about a future with him. I'm already indulging in this fling with him. It's all more than I deserve.

But what if?

When the woods thin and the fresh scent of his packmates reaches me, I squeeze Onyx's hand. "Hey, I don't want to talk with them about my pack yet. I need time to think. It's enough to just know."

His dark eyes study me and I feel like a bug under a microscope. "You'll still talk with them about it before you do anything?"

"Yeah. I promise."

His head bobs. "Okay, well, we still have to talk with Jasper and Hazel about today."

"I understand."

As we approach the training building, I keep waiting for Onyx to drop my hand. But he doesn't. My heart beat speeds up until my blood pounds in my ears. Memories of being zip-tied by these wolves and dragged away like a prisoner re-plays in my head until I'm squeezing Onyx's fingers so tight he stops walking.

"Hey, it's going to be fine. We can just explain, and I'll do all the talking if you need." Using our joined hands, he pulls me against him.

His citrus scent soaks in my lungs, calming and centering me.

"No, I need to own my shit."

He kisses my knuckles and we resume our walk.

Jasper meets us in the thinning trees on the edge of the pack's compound. He looks calmer, but his shoulders still tense at the sight of me. Dread weighs me down until each step feels like I'm knee deep in mud.

"This is interesting," he says, crossing his arms. His gaze is cold as he looks at Onyx and then our joined hands. Onyx squares his shoulders and faces my brother.

"We need to talk to you about what just happened."

"Meet me at my cabin in five minutes," he says before turning away and striding back toward the building. I watch his receding form, my dread turning to cold fear.

"I don't know where that is," I tell Onyx.

A hint of a smile softens his expression. "It's close. I've got you, don't worry."

I shouldn't need him, but I cling to his arm anyway. Jasper's threat that Slate would kill me seems all too likely. Hazel might want to dispose of me herself. It's only their code of ethics that keeps me from turning and running. They'd restrain me and return me to my pack, which is roughly the outcome part of me hopes for.

Marigold opens the door of the small log-style cabin. She's wearing a floral sundress with her strawberry blonde hair piled on top of her head. Her cabin smells like sugar and tropical plants. Golden oak lines the interior with warm plaids and accents of sunny yellow. A collection of houseplants grow across the large window in the living space.

"Hey, Goldie. There was an incident during training and Jasper asked us to come here to discuss it privately," Onyx explains.

"Oh, is everything okay?" she asks me. I have no idea how to answer. No. It's a wreck, just like it's been since the minute I arrived here. She must read my expression, because Marigold pulls me away from Onyx and wraps her arms around my shoulders in a tight hug.

Tears threaten again and I take measured breaths to keep them away. When she releases me, she looks me in the eyes and says, "It's going to be fine. You are family."

I have to look away. She leads me to the sofa and I settle beside Onyx while she gathers refreshments in her little kitchen.

By the time Jasper, Slate, and Hazel arrive, Marigold has set out a plate of cinnamon cookies. Jasper sits in the arm chair beside the sofa, and she perches on the arm. Hazel and Slate stand, and my hold on Onyx's hand tightens.

Slate's gaze narrows on our joined hands, and his frown deepens.

"Jasper told me what happened," Slate finally says. I note he says Jasper and not Hazel. She fidgets in her seat as he says it. "What is your side of the story?"

Swallowing, I take a deep breath. "I was really upset because I could tell something was wrong with my mother and my pack, and no one was telling me anything." Onyx runs his thumb over my knuckles, encouraging me.

"I went to find Jasper, and Hazel asked to spar. I don't know what happened. I got hurt and just snapped."

Despite my confession, Slate's expression doesn't change.

Hazel sighs. "I wasn't injured. Honestly, I could have pushed her away sooner but her arm was dislocated and I didn't want to hurt her worse."

Slate's grasps the back of the armchair as he frowns at her. "Jasper said she was out of control and choking you. Even when you tried to end the fight, she wouldn't stop. I'm scared of what would have happened if you hadn't gotten the drop on her."

"I wasn't in danger," Hazel argues. "I wouldn't have sparred with her if I wasn't confident I could protect myself. You guys are over reacting."

My gaze connects with Hazel and she gives me a small smile. For the first time, it really feels like she's on my side.

"I can't have you... snapping, like you said," Slate says, fixing me with a hard stare. "What's your plan for preventing that from happening again?"

"I will make sure I don't lose control," I say solemnly.

"Trying harder isn't the answer." Slate rubs his jaw, locking me in place with his emerald eyes. "You won't spar again"

"But-" I start to argue.

"With anyone." He cuts me off. "If you were a pack member, there would be a consequence."

"It's not her fault," Onyx blurts. My muscles tense as everyone turns their attention to the man beside me.

"She needs to take responsibility for what happened. And she is. What's the problem?" Slate asks.

"She reacted that way for a valid reason," Onyx argues. "She wasn't trained properly. I think with enough time with my dad, that can be fixed and she'll be fine."

"Granite Ridge's training methods are brutal," Jasper agrees. "But I was trained the same and I've never lost control like that."

"Funny you should say that," Onyx growls.

It's like my blood is turning to ice, my heartbeat fluttering out of control. I'm not sure why, but I don't want them to know. To know how weak I was.

"What do you mean?" Hazel asks, her eyebrows pinching in concern as she regards me.

"You need to tell him. I'm very interested to know if he was aware of what was happening," Onyx says, dropping his voice. Rage sharpens each syllable.

"No, I don't," I say, my voice barely catching as I tuck my legs up under me.

"Ember," Jasper says, his voice softening. "What's going on?"

All eyes are on me. My tight breaths aren't getting enough oxygen into my lungs, and they begin to sting and ache. The edges of my vision blur as I study the floor.

Silence stretches on. Fabric rustles and Jasper squats down beside me, getting low until his hands come into my view. Onyx's hand tightens around mine.

"What do I not know?" he asks. Something about his tone loosens my throat. There's no way to keep the tears from my voice, but perhaps I can speak.

"Onyx saw some scars from the trainers from when they'd hurt me as punishment after I lost fights." Hardly more than a harsh whisper, but the words are out there.

Every line of Jasper's body tightens and his jaw grinds. With clipped speech, he asks, "You were included in those?"

All I can do is nod. The movement causes a tear to escape. My movements are jerky as I wipe it away with the back of my hand.

I wait for him to call me a liar. When we were children, he always won. He was four years older than me, but that didn't seem to matter to the trainers forcing us to compete. And then he was safely at home with our parents while I faced the consequences.

Hazel slips out of her seat and returns with tissues.

"What are you guys talking about?" Slate asks.

Jasper stands, his hand brushing my shoulder as he steps back. "Granite Ridge likes to pit wolves against each other, and the loser will often get physical punishment as motivation. Some trainers take it too far."

"Yeah, far enough to scar," Onyx adds, his voice a physical rumble against me.

And there it is, out in the open for everyone to see. I don't think I can take their pity. I'd prefer their judgment.

"That's why you react so violently during a fight," Hazel fills in.

My panic swells again, and I rest my cheek against my knees, focusing on Onyx's stony face. Dark ocean eyes stare back at me, the residual glow of his emotions finally fading.

"I'm sorry," Jasper says, his voice rough. I can't look at him, but I can hear Marigold murmuring under her breath and running her hands down his back.

"Onyx is right. If you stay longer, Fisher can work with you to get control over your reactions. But absolutely no fighting any of my wolves."

"Okay."

"Thanks," Slate says, sounding more like a brother than the Alpha of a pack in that moment.

"That was a lot. We should all take a break and decompress." Marigold stands. Jasper follows her, his face full of tension.

"I think that's a good idea," Slate confirms.

Onyx doesn't release my hand as I stand, anchoring me as I sway on my feet.

"Hey," Hazel says, giving me pause. "What's going on with you guys?"

"You'll have to be more specific," Onyx says dryly.

"You're holding hands," Slate points out.

"Oh." My mouth parts, but I can't put words together. This wasn't something I had picked a label for yet. I didn't expect anyone else to know, but under the circumstances, I'm grateful he didn't let me go.

"We are seeing each other," Onyx says calmly.

My heart skips a beat before it begins to buzz against my ribs.

"You're dating my sister?" Jasper asks, eyes narrowed.

"Yes, when two adults are attracted to each other and enjoy spending time together-" Onyx says.

Slate cuts him off. "Are you sure this is a good idea? You are from different packs. Unless one of you wants to change that?"

Questioning my actions toward Hazel is one thing, but he has no right to interfere in my relationship with Onyx.

"It's none of your damn business. Look, I didn't ask him to be my mate. We are just figuring out how we feel. If it gets serious, I'm sure Onyx will consult you," I snap, though it's weak with exhaustion.

"Have you really thought this through?" Jasper questions, looking to Onyx.

"It's not up to you," he snarls.

Slate's jaw ticks, his eyes alight as he rises to meet Onyx's anger. But Hazel takes his arm, running her hand down it to claim his hand, soothing him. "Guys, this is great. Two people we care about are dating. It's not an international incident." The tension breaks, the entire room letting out a breath.

"Okay," Slate concedes.

"This reminds me of how you guys reacted to Jasper and me," Marigold says with a laugh. "Everyone needs to relax. One crisis at a time."

Everyone ambles toward the door, small looks exchanged between partners as we end our meeting. Footsteps slow as we reach the front door.

"How long am I staying here?" I ask, taking the opportunity to question the Alphas.

"I'm not sure. We are waiting to hear from your mother," Slate says. "We discussed maybe a week."

"Okay," I answer, something in the back of my mind reminding me that they are still keeping things from me. But after the emotional turmoil of the last hour, I can't find the energy to have that conversation.

"I'm glad you're staying longer," Hazel says. "I think we should do something fun to get your mind off things. Would you like to join us for a girls night?"

"I don't thi-," I start to say.

Marigold claps her hands. "No, it would be so fun! It's exactly what you need, and we need to spend more time getting to know you!"

"I can host," Hazel adds. "I promise we won't braid each other's hair or anything weird. Just hanging out and lots of snacks."

Usually I would decline, but something about Hazel's kindness eats away at me. Maybe I should try something new.

"When is this girls' night?" I ask.

"How about tonight?" Marigold asks.

"I'm down," Hazel says.

"Oh, wow. That's soon." I glance to Onyx, but he shrugs. "No reason to wait, I guess."

"Great! Come over after sunset." Hazel's nose wrinkles as she smiles, her head tilting towards her mate.

Onyx squeezes my hand as we follow them out of the cabin.

We grab a late lunch in Onyx's kitchen, and then I crash for a nap before my evening with Marigold and Hazel. Onyx seems to know that I need space to decompress. Today was humiliating, and I still have to face an evening with the two women mated to my grumpy brothers.

Time races by and I find myself standing on Hazel's patio. Onyx watches from the trees, though he's promised to go home and not patrol the cabin in his wolf form.

"Ember!" Hazel greets me, swinging open her door. "Come in, I've almost got drinks ready."

A small fire crackles in their fireplace, filling the cabin with warm light. Marigold gives me a little wave from the kitchen. She's emptying bags of chips into bowls.

I drift behind Hazel across the living space to the kitchen. "Here, let's take these to the coffee table," Marigold instructs, and I pick up two of the bowls - one of cheese puffs and one with BBQ chips. She adds a bowl of dip and a dish of chocolates.

The blender pulses as Hazel finishes our drinks. A bottle of non-alcoholic margarita mix sits by the sink. I take one of the armchairs, and Marigold sinks onto the sofa and tucks her feet under her. She tosses a cheese puff into her mouth with a grin.

"Here," Hazel says, handing me a wide goblet full of frozen pink margarita. She settles into the other armchair and helps herself to the glossy dark chocolates.

"This is so fun. Why don't we do this more often?" Marigold asks. Hazel just shrugs.

"Hazel, I'm really sorry about this morning," I say, feeling the weight of my mistakes still hanging over me.

She frowns. "You don't need to apologize. I get it. And it's going to get better." She states it as an inevitable fact, leaving me unsure of what to say.

"Hey, we are here to have fun and relax. No apologies needed." Marigold slides sideways to lounge across the sofa. "I really want to hear about you and Onyx."

"Oh, no," I say, burying my face in my hands.

"Oh, yes." She grins wickedly. "He was such a pain in the ass when Jasper and I got together. This is more than fair."

"Why? What was his problem?"

Marigold sighs dramatically. "For a long time, I had a crush on Cedar." She waves her hand in the air. "But he had zero interest in me. I think Onyx had always pictured us getting together some day, and he didn't take it well when he realized that wasn't going to happen."

"He has a big heart," Hazel says, her eyes crinkling as she smiles fondly. I squirm uncomfortably in my seat. "So what happened between you two? And when?"

"This is so embarrassing," I mutter.

Marigold giggles, taking a long drink of her margarita.

"Okay, I'll tell you about me and Jasper, would that be fair?" Marigold says.

"No, that's okay. I don't need to know about that."

"Then how about this? I'll spare you details about your brothers if you tell us about you and Onyx," Hazel teases. Scowling at her, I press my lips together.

"Please? I'm dying to know. I need details so I can tease him," Marigold whines.

Taking a fortifying sip of strawberry slush, I begin. "Remember the last pack party?"

"Um, yeah. It was last week," Hazel says.

"We kinda had a thing."

"A thing?" Marigold is almost bouncing in her seat.

"Yeah, he was annoying me, and next thing I knew, he kissed me." My cheeks burn against my palms as I attempt to hide my face.

"Holy kitty-titties, are you serious?" Hazel says, leaning forward in her chair. "So you guys make out, and then we ask him to watch over you while you stay with us." Her words tumble into laughter. "What are the chances?"

"Well done there," Marigold adds, grabbing another handful of cheese puffs. Tentatively, I reach for some chips. They're delicious, and they give me an excuse to pause my story.

"So what about after you arrived? How did you go from a random kiss to saying you're dating?" Hazel licks the sugar off the rim of her drink.

"I don't know. We were just spending time together. He's such a flirt," I whine.

Hazel laughs. "Yeah, he really is."

"Ew," Marigold says, pulling a face.

"When I was upset, he was sweet. He comforted me."

"I bet he was *comforting*," Marigold mutters.

"So yesterday we were feeding the chickens and goats, and I kinda pranked him," I say.

"Oh, we should prank the boys!" Marigold interrupts me, swinging her feet down to the floor as if she's about to jump up. "Sorry, continue, I want to hear everything, please."

Despite my embarrassment, I can't stop smiling. "I just stuck apple slices in his hoodie and the goats were all over him."

"Good one," Hazel says with an approving smirk.

"That still doesn't get you to dating. When did he make his move?" Marigold says.

"We kissed right after that."

"Ooh!" she squeals. "And he confessed his feelings?"

"Actually, Cedar caught us making out," I say, unable to meet their eyes.

Marigold sets her drink down and leans forward. "Dammit, I thought I was the first one to know!"

"What? You figured it out?"

"Honey, he came in smelling like you so strongly, I knew he had been all over you."

"Oh, no." I would melt into the cushion if I could.

"Jasper and Marigold did the same thing, don't worry," Hazel says, rolling her eyes at Marigold.

"Ew, that's my brother," I reply without thinking. Both girls dissolve into giggles.

"Your brother is a total Casanova," Marigold says with a grin.

"I'm really happy for you guys," Hazel says, turning the conversation back to me and Onyx. I cringe under the attention, but it's better than hearing about my brother's romantic escapades.

"There's just something about him I really like," I admit. "But I don't see how we can make it work. I don't want to hurt him, but I'm going back to my pack soon."

Both girls stare at me for a few seconds.

"Would you want to join our pack?" Hazel finally asks.

"I can't," I say. "I've got a responsibility as Heir, and Jasper already ran off. I'm all our pack has left."

"You can," Hazel says quietly, all her laughter gone. "Your pack isn't a healthy place to be. You deserve a safe and loving home. More than just Onyx. Jasper is here. We are here."

"But that's the thing, if I'm Alpha, I can change my pack," I say.

"What if Onyx went with you? We would hate to lose him, but it's not like it's far away." Hazel asks. I can't believe what I'm hearing.

"He has all his friends and family here. I couldn't do that to him. My pack is a miserable place to be right now, and it could be years before that changes." It hurts to say those thoughts out loud.

"So are you just going to be in a relationship even though you can't be together very often?" Hazel asks. Marigold grimaces.

"I don't know," I say.

"Okay, this is a fun girls night and we got all serious again. Everything is going to be fine. Love conquers all obstacles," Marigold says in a sing-song voice.

"Alright, it's your turn then," Hazel says with a wink.

"I don't think Ember cares," Marigold says.

Normally, I wouldn't want to hear any of it, but after what I just went through, it seems fair. Narrowing my eyes at her, I say, "Actually, I'd love to hear the story."

"Fine." Marigold cracks her knuckles and folds her hands over her knees. "I asked to be his roommate, and we got really close." Her tone is dreamy and I almost forget it's my brother she's talking about.

Hazel jumps in, "And you guys kept it all secret from us, sneaking around."

"We hadn't really figured it out," Marigold shoots back.

"When was this?" I ask.

"Last year, like three or four weeks before the whole invasion thing," Marigold says lightly. I tense at the mention of the pack conflict. It was the fight where I lost my father and then I hurt Onyx during the following struggle.

"He took me on a date out for coffee and let me drive his car and then we made out on the side of the road," she confesses with a manic giggle.

"You guys were ridiculous," Hazel says, rolling her eyes.

"Hey, your first kiss with Slate was right after he tattooed you, and you didn't even know he was a wolf," Marigold says.

"We don't have to talk about that," Hazel says, wrinkling her nose. "So, Ember, what kinda of stuff do you like?"

I blink at her sudden question. "Stuff I like?"

"What are your hobbies?" Marigold adds.

"Oh, I don't know." I shrug. "Listening to music, I guess. And I've been playing Jasper's video games that he left behind."

"Onyx loves video games." Hazel says.

"I know," I say with a smile I can't help. Her grin widens until she's beaming at me.

"I didn't see it coming, but I think you guys are good for each other. He can be kinda wild, but he's hilarious and really sweet and I think that's a good fit for you." Hazel concludes, looking satisfied.

"I appreciate that, but-" I start, but Marigold stops me.

"Hey, we are here for fun. No more worrying about problems. Everything will work out, and we are here for some girl bonding. So, I say we prank the boys."

"Slate was going to take them all out on a run," Hazel muses.

"I have just the thing. I thought they were so funny, I ordered them for an art project or something," Marigold says.

"What?"

Ten minutes later we're sneaking into Marigold and Jasper's cabin. It's empty and no sneaking is required, but the girl bonding energy has gotten ahold of me and I can't stop smiling.

Marigold comes out of their spare bedroom with a little baggy of tiny plastic chickens. She pops the bag open and pulls a few out to show us. They're about the size of my thumb nail, and absolutely adorable.

"I was going to make something with them for Cedar," she says quietly. "But this is better." We each take a handful and begin moving through the cabin, stashing them in partially hidden places. Marigold takes the bedroom and tucks them into Jasper's pockets. I tuck one behind the masculine looking bath products and then another behind the toothbrush that isn't bright pink.

"Alright, I'm all done here," Hazel whisper-yells.

"Me too," Marigold answers.

"Alright, who is next?" I say, feeling ridiculously excited.

Fisher and Clove look a little puzzled when we arrive, but Hazel is honest about the prank and Clove laughs for a while before she can nod her approval.

Hazel picks her way through the rest of the house to find anything specific to the twins, while Marigold and I take their bedroom. We tuck little chickens into the shirt pockets of the plaid work shirts Cedar prefers for gardening. She places one on top of his gaming console. I slide a couple into each boy's pillowcase and then tuck them up on the higher display shelves in between the various knickknacks from their childhood. One of them had a thing for painting pet rocks at some point, and they make the perfect platform for a chicken.

It's odd being in his room without him. I've been in here before, but last time it was heated. The sheets are wrinkled and I remember the feel of his mouth against my lower stomach. Despite all the reasons I shouldn't, I want him. More than just his touch. I'm quickly getting addicted to his thoughts, both the snarky ones and the kind ones.

"Okay, I think we're done here. There's only a few left to use on Slate," Marigold says, snapping me out of my thoughts.

We walk back to Hazel's cabin, and Marigold links her arm through mine. I stiffen, but then force myself to relax. It's strange having female friends, but they're sweet and seem supportive. As long as I don't make any mistakes, maybe I can keep these friendships.

Hazel laughs her head off while she tucks chickens in Slate's art supplies and then into his closet. Marigold drags me back to the sofa and we help ourselves to the snacks. I finally try a chocolate and it's divine. Just as I'm reaching for my second one, my phone buzzes.

> I need you to get some information from that pack without them knowing.
> MOM 9:06PM

What? Does she seriously want me to spy on them? They're our allies and they're trying to make good on that promise. Gritting my teeth, I type back.

> That's not a good idea. We need their alliance.
> 9:07PM

> That's why I said without them knowing.
> Mom 9:08PM

She sends a list of reports, like the locations of their security cameras and the schedule of patrols. Everything they'd need to raid the pack.

> Don't ask me to do this. It's not right.
> 9:10PM

> This is your duty and it's an order.
> Mom 9:11PM

> Why? How is this going to help the shit show you're dealing with?
> 9:12PM

> Do not question me. This is necessary, and you're going to do it.
> Mom 9:14PM

"Everything okay?" Marigold asks. I click my phone off and stow it away.

"Sorry, my mom is being annoying," I say, quickly picking up my half-melted margarita and sipping it.

"I know the situation with her sucks. But I'll second Onyx's offer for you to stay."

"Chickens are deployed and I'm starving!" Hazel announces, plopping down. She grabs the entire bowl of chips and starts to shove them into her mouth.

The conversation stays light, and Hazel laughs while telling us about Slate's initial flirtations and then about how they finally got together. It's sweet and makes me feel hopeful.

Footsteps on the porch announce Slate's arrival.

"It's late, let's head home," Marigold says to me.

Hazel wraps us in a tight hug before we slip out.

"Did you have fun tonight?" Marigold asks.

"Yeah."

"No, seriously," she says, giving me a hard look.

My arms cross over my chest. "I've never really had friends like this before, which sounds totally pathetic. But there aren't a lot of women in our pack and none of them are close to my age. So this was really nice."

"Again, this is why you should stay." She smiles, hoping I'll suddenly change my mind and agree.

"Thank you for everything," I say, waving at her as we split paths. She heads south toward her cabin with Jasper, and I climb the steps to the porch of Onyx's home.

Cedar greets me with a simple, "Hello."

The shower roars behind the hall bath's door, so I guess Onyx is occupied. Pushing the disappointment down, I close the door to my room. It's late and I really am tired. Despite the comfortable bed, my mind buzzes with everything from the last two days. The problems in my pack. My new friends. My mother's awful texts. But mainly, my new boyfriend.

My phone beeps with another message from my mother, demanding my attention. My stomach churns as I turn my phone to silent and place it face-down on the dresser, far from my bed. Tomorrow I'll have to face her demands. But not tonight.

XI

VIDEO GAMES & VIOLENCE

ONYX

Ember gets home from her girls' night late and goes straight to bed. I listen from the hallway as her breathing evens out. It might be desperate, but I can't help myself.

The next morning Ember bakes scones with my mother while I watch from the table. She listens to everything my mother says and asks intelligent questions. Her green hair shimmers as she laughs.

"What do you think?" she asks intently as I take a bite of the blackberry scone smeared with butter. It's still warm and the pastry is tender.

"You are an incredible baker. And don't tell my mom, but you might be even better than she is," I say. Mom smiles from the doorway before she heads out, giving us privacy.

"What should we do today? Since I have another free day being an unwanted and involuntary guest," she says.

A grin spreads across my face. "Want to play some video games?"

To my delight, she agrees.

She settles on the sofa in the family room while I run to grab a few video games. When my hand reaches for the case on my shelf, something small rolls under my fingers.

What the hell?

Pinching the item, I open my hand and frown down at a tiny translucent orange chicken. Frowning at it, I spot a second one sitting higher on the shelf, tucked behind a figurine. This one is green.

The chickens tumble in my palm as I wander back into the family room.

"Whatcha got there?" Ember asks. There's something more than casual curiosity in her voice, and I narrow my eyes at her.

"Do you know anything about tiny chickens?"

A beautiful flush rises up her neck as she buries her face in the cushion to stifle giggles.

"Seriously?" I ask.

Wiping at her eyes, she takes a deep breath to steady herself and says, "To be fair, it was Marigold's plan."

"Girls are weird," I grumble, tucking the chickens into my pocket.

Her amused smirk makes my stomach clench. She's stunning.

It takes a moment to focus with her so near, but soon I'm showing her the controls for a racing game.

She sits cuddled up against my chest. My arm is around her waist, so my controller sits against her hip and her head rests against the hollow of my neck. Having her soft figure pressed against me is distracting, and I crash my race car on the first round.

Before we can race again, Cedar clears his throat. He leans against the archway that leads to the hallway. "Hey, did anyone lose a tiny chicken?"

With a frown, he holds up a teeny purple bird between his thumb and index finger.

We dissolve into laughter and I drop my controller onto the rug.

"What?" he asks.

"I have no idea, dude," I wheeze. "But that's fucking hilarious."

Shaking his head, Cedar disappears back to his room.

"I hope he likes them," Ember whispers. Turning my head, we're nose to nose. "Cause there's a lot of them hidden in his stuff. Marigold primarily got them for him."

"So am I just a casualty and you guys mainly hit Cedar?" I ask, just as quietly.

When she shakes her head, her emerald hair shimmers. "Nope, all you boys got chickened."

Chuckling, I grab her chin and tip her mouth up to mine for a brief kiss.

With a wicked grin, she pulls away. "I think we were in the middle of a race."

It takes concentrated effort to take my hands off her and return to our game. But feeling her laugh vibrate through me as she plays the video game is another type of paradise.

Ember races recklessly, crashing her car and swerving off the road every few seconds. She scrunches her eyes closed and laughs. I could stay like this with her forever.

As my car races by with a first place banner, I pull her up until I can kiss against her neck, below her ear. She shivers against me.

"Have I ever told you that green is my favorite color?" I murmur, twining a lock of her hair around my finger.

"Hey, I'm trying to drive here," she says, rotating her shoulders.

"Is that what you were doing?" I ask, nipping at her skin. I've had enough video games with her intoxicating scent invading my senses.

She twists to face me and glares. "Maybe if you weren't so distracting."

"Game's over. Want to go again?" Her pupils dilate at my words and I smirk.

"Maybe in a minute," she says. She drops her controller onto the cushion beside us, and I set mine aside too. Achingly slow, her hand comes up to my neck and her fingertips slip below the neckline of my shirt. Why am I wearing a shirt again? More importantly, why is *she* wearing a shirt?

My eyes close at her touch, and I can feel her moving closer, her chest skimming mine. Kisses feather down my jaw, and I raise my chin to give her access. Her soft growl of approval nearly undoes me, but I let her control everything, my hands loosely around her hips.

Her other hand threads in my hair and she pulls, moving my face to where she wants me. One tentative kiss, and then a harder one. Her tongue licks across my mouth and I open. Her wildflower taste is the only thing I want in the world. Without breaking our kiss, she climbs over me until she's straddling me, her thighs over mine.

My hold on her hips tightens and I slide one hand up under her shirt and up her spine. The other goes to her ass. She's perfect.

Her phone in her back pocket buzzes. I pull it out and she jerks back, grabbing it from my hand. Biting her lip, she powers it down and tosses it aside. "Sorry, my mom is driving me crazy."

I don't question her. I'm too drunk on the feel of her against me. She grinds her hips down and my pulse speeds, blood pounding in my ears and my skin. The only cure for this fire is the cause of it.

Her delicate fingers brush hair out of my face and her glowing eyes lock with mine. A little eyeliner remains around her lashes, but the rest of her face is scrubbed clean so I can see the lightest spray of freckles across her cheeks and the bridge of her nose. She's stunning.

"Hey, I need to go see my brother," she says. Not exactly what I was expecting her to say. She eases off of me.

My pounding heart starts to calm. If she doesn't want to take things further right now, that's fine with me.

"Sure, let's go."

Her hand flattens against my chest. "It's something I need to do alone. Why don't you chill and enjoy your games. I bet you haven't gotten to play since I arrived."

Lifting her hand, I press a kiss to her fingers. "I've been occupied with better things." Before releasing her, I bite down on the meat of her palm, below her thumb. She jolts, her hips pressing forward against me. "Give me five more minutes," I say, skimming my hands up her thighs to her waist.

"Five minutes? Give yourself more credit than that," she says, kissing my cheek before she climbs off of me.

"Hey!" I say, flushing. "That's not-" She laughs. "When that happens, you won't be going anywhere for hours. Maybe days."

Grabbing her phone, she heads to the hall. "Seriously, just let me talk to my brother for a bit and then I'll meet you back here and we can pick up where we left off."

The promise leaves me adjusting my pants and taking deep breaths before I can get up.

Without her here, nothing holds my attention.

After getting a snack, I wander out of my cabin. Maybe I'll meet her in between the two cabins and we can go for a run and then have some quality time together out in the woods. The thought of her under me in soft grass is tempting.

I meander along the edge of the meadow, generally heading toward Jasper and Marigold's cabin, but as I near the south side, I catch movement through the tinted window of the tiny office I work out of. Maybe Vale is checking security camera feeds or something. I've been off duty for days now.

Jogging the distance, I pull the door open. Instead of Vale or Slate sitting at my desk, the chair is pushed aside and Ember hovers over the keyboard.

"Onyx!" she yips, spinning to face me. Her phone is clutched tightly against her breasts.

Confusion chokes me, anger burning it away. There are only a few reasons why she would be getting into one of our work computers, and none of them are good.

"Ember, what are you doing?"

Her mouth opens but no sound comes out. Fear oozes out of her and I hate that she feels any fear because of me, but it can't be helped. I wasn't the one who snuck into my office.

My approach slows, like she's a skittish animal. Making eye contact, I try to reason with her. "I was honest with you about everything. I need you to tell me exactly what's going on, and we can figure it out together."

Her breathing is ragged and she glances at the door. Gently, I take her elbow and lead her to the chair where I can pull her into my lap. She curls in on herself against my chest.

"I'll take care of it if you just tell me," I say, my anger replaced with worry as I feel how her pulse flutters.

With shaky hands, Ember unlocks her phone and shows me a string of texts from her mother - demands for all sorts of information about our security and resources.

My eyes catch on the last text.

Glancing at the computer, I can see she hasn't gotten past my password.

"I'm sorry," she whispers. "She's my Alpha too. I was ignoring her, but I have to do something to help my pack."

"You didn't do any damage," I say, my arms banding around her protectively. It's true, even if she intended to.

Her next breath shakes like she's fighting off tears. "What if something happens to her? I already lost my dad, and I know they're shitty parents but they're the only ones I have. What if someone challenges her and kills her, and I'm not there?" Her voice is raw, rasping until it's just a whisper

"I'm sorry. I wish I could do something to help with that. But I'm not going to lie. I'm glad you're here safe with me. If someone wants to take her out, they'll probably go for you too. I can't let that happen."

"It's not your responsibility," she whispers.

"I hate to break it to you," I say, nuzzling into her neck. "But I care about you."

Despite her despair, she smiles.

"I know my mom is awful and I don't want to be like her," she whispers. "I don't want to pick a mate because of his rank and treat my children like tools to be exploited. I don't want to rule by fear. It makes me sick that I believed her for so long."

"You won't be like her. You are so much better than that," I say, my voice scraping over each word.

She looks up at me through dark lashes, her expression vulnerable. But I'm not the only one standing behind her now. She's always had Jasper, and now she's won over Hazel and Marigold too. I know even Slate would stand behind her. We aren't going to let her get hurt if we can help it.

The harsh truth is that she's tangled up in her pack's troubles and she won't be safe until it's over. Even here, Sienna is sinking her claws into her. And one day of trust isn't enough to undo eighteen years of conditioning.

"Are you going to tell Slate or Jasper what I did?" she asks.

"You need to talk with them about all of this."

She snuggles in closer, her nose bumping against my neck and her breath ghosting across my skin. "I will," she says, and I feel the movement of her lips.

"Come on, let's go home," I say. I want to get her out of this stuffy office before someone finds us here and starts asking questions.

Besides, the way she's touching me brings up fantasies of laying her across my desk, and there really isn't room unless I shoved my computer off, and that's not a good idea.

XII

HEARTBREAK & HOOK UPS

EMBER

Fear ebbs as Onyx walks me back to his home, replaced with a self-loathing that I embrace. How could I let my mother derail the relationships that I'm building here? I bury the thought that it's all temporary anyway. It's getting easier to pretend that this is home.

The cabin is warm and bright with buttery afternoon light. Clove works in the kitchen, flour dusting her apron. Onyx's hand runs down my back reassuringly.

"Can you see when Jasper and the Alphas are free to talk?" I ask, my voice soft. Onyx nods and pulls out his phone.

Instead of fretting over the upcoming discussion, I ask Clove if I can help with her baking. After a few minutes, my shoulders ache with the repetitive motion of kneading the bread, but it's soothing.

Clove pulls the first batch of loaves out of the oven just as I set my second loaf into a pan to rise. The scent of nutty flour reminds me of Onyx, but also of his entire family. How would my life have been different if I had been raised in a supportive environment like this?

Onyx comes up behind me, putting his arms around me. I tense, glancing at Clove, but she wears a mild smile, her eyebrows rising as she focuses on her work.

"Everyone is heading over," he says into my ear.

"That was fast," I mutter.

"You are important, not just to me," Onyx whispers back.

"They've got to be sick of me taking up their time and energy."

Onyx's hands move to my hips, and I drop the loaf on the countertop as he spins me around to face him. He glares at me, and I swallow thickly.

"You are not a bother. You are worth it." His conviction makes me stammer, my skin flushing. Without hesitating, he leans forward and kisses my forehead before releasing me. Onyx settles into a kitchen chair, reclined with his feet out as he watches me.

Bemused, I turn back to my work.

"Here, I'll take over that," Clove says, taking my place in front of the dinner rolls I'm cutting and rolling. "Sounds like your brothers are here."

The door clicks open and familiar voices float through the house.

"Ready?" Onyx asks.

"No."

We take our discussion to the fire pit out back. Dappled sunshine highlights the rich, dark tones of Slate's hair, the same color as our mother's hair and what mine would be if I didn't change it constantly.

Jasper sits beside me on a bench, Onyx on my other side, while Hazel and Slate sit opposite in weathered Adirondack chairs.

Tension rises in my chest, choking me. I need answers, but this discussion is bound to be painful. It would be much nicer to play house with Onyx and ignore the reality outside our bubble.

"Ember, Onyx told us your mom has been texting you and pressuring you to send her private pack information?" Slate gets right to the point.

I glare at Onyx as he produces my phone and unlocks it before handing it to Slate. How the hell did he know the code?

Slate scrolls through the texts and holds it out to Hazel and then Jasper. Jasper lets out a low growl that somehow makes me feel better. Maybe he will be sympathetic.

"Sienna is going to turn on us if it keeps her in power," Hazel concludes.

"It won't," Jasper says, crossing his arms and scowling.

Slate runs his fingers through his wavy hair. "Look, I think we should send Ember back. It's becoming a risk to our pack."

My mouth drops open. I asked to go back, but I want it to be on my terms. Not exiled as a criminal. Beside me, Onyx is seething. I can feel his anger rolling off of him like heat.

"No, we just take precautions. Turn the phone off and take out the sim card. Let Sienna know we will keep her safe, but she isn't going to spy for her." Jasper says, frowning at Slate.

"How long until they take the fight here?" Slate demands.

"Will you guys just be honest and tell me everything?" I growl.

"She deserves to know," Hazel says softly, her hand squeezing Slate's forearm.

"If she decides she has to go home now, we'll have to lock her up." Jasper won't look at me.

I throw my hands up. "Fine, I'll just go now and find out for myself. Because I seriously doubt you guys will actually imprison me."

Onyx grabs my hand to keep me seated. When he finally speaks, it's cool and calm in a way that scares me. "See? If you don't tell her, it'll be the exact thing you were trying to avoid."

"Unfortunately, I think you're right." Slate says.

"What was that? I didn't hear you," Onyx says.

The Alpha curls his lip, staring Onyx down until the lower ranked wolf drops his gaze.

Jasper pinches the bridge of his nose and exhales slowly. "I got word this morning that someone challenged Sienna for Alpha. She killed him, but she's not in the best shape."

"What?" I yelp, starting to stand. Onyx tugs me back into my seat again. My instinct is to snap at him and to free myself, but I hold it in.

"If we send anyone to help her, it gives the pack a common enemy and puts her in a weaker position," Jasper says. His words sound like he's been debating this for a while.

"I need to go, at least," I argue.

"I'm sorry," Hazel adds, "but if you go back now, they'll use you against her. She needs to be able to fight without worrying about your safety."

"You don't believe I could help?" I ask flatly.

Jasper locks eyes with me, a hint of pale blue flickering in his eyes. "Do you honestly think you could take down someone like Flint or Orion?"

The sounds of the forest break the tense silence. He's right, I couldn't win in a fight against any of the huge males that make up the ranks of Granite Ridge. I'm powerless if they decide to no longer respect my claim as Heir.

"I know this isn't fair," Hazel says slowly. "But we will figure something out that doesn't include you getting hurt."

"What can you do if you can't send fighters?"

Slate and Hazel exchange a look before Slate answers. "We don't know yet. Hawthorne and Jasper have been talking to Sienna daily. They're working on a few ideas, but nothing has come together yet."

"Will you tell me when that happens?" I ask.

Jasper nods. "As long as you're being reasonable, yes."

"I'm not the unreasonable one at the moment," I snap. With a sigh, I try again. "Fine. Keep me updated. Am I free to just hang around like I've been doing? Or do you want to lock me up?" Sarcasm edges my words.

"Stick close and keep Onyx with you. Not too close to the road either. I don't want to take any chances." Slate rubs the back of his neck.

"And you'll stay?" Jasper asks.

"For now." It's the only answer I'm willing to give.

"Watch her," Slate instructs Onyx. I want to slap him, but then I remember that Hazel was snatched from their territory once. It's possible he's worried about my safety instead of thinking I'm a flight risk.

"I'm going to head back to keep working on this whole disaster," Jasper says, shaking his head as he stands and brushes off his pants. "Hopefully we will have some answers soon."

Hazel's concerned gaze lingers on me, and I'm grateful when Onyx drapes an arm over my shoulder.

"What are you guys gonna do tonight?" she asks.

"Dunno. Hang out," Onyx answers for us. Stomach in knots, I'm not interested in questioning him.

Hazel and Slate excuse themselves.

"What can I do to make you feel better?" Onyx asks, turning to bump his nose into my temple.

"I just want to get away from everyone," I answer honestly. He removes his arm. "No, from everyone else. Not you."

His pleased smile eases some of my turmoil.

"So what should we do?" His whispered question holds innuendo that brings a blush to my cheeks.

"Want to just take a walk?" I suggest. "I know we are supposed to stay close, but maybe we can head east, further from my pack?"

"Yeah, up the creek is really nice, near our border with Raven and Ironcrest packs," Onyx says thoughtfully.

"Two legs or four?"

His gaze turns hungry. Four legs means less clothing at the destination, but he reigns himself in. "Up to you."

"Let's just hike it. Slower sounds nice." I shrug. He puts up no argument, except to make sure I change into better shoes.

Five minutes later, we are walking along a faint trail I can hardly see, heading north-east. My legs aren't as long as Onyx's, but he slows his pace to match mine, and I stay close behind him until the trees thin.

The light through the branches takes on a pink tinge, but I don't fear sundown in these woods with Onyx beside me.

A squirrel scampers on an overhead branch, and a robin flits past, doubling back to check on us. Onyx smiles up at it.

"Your part of the forest feels different than ours," I murmur.

"Oh, yeah?"

"More alive." It hurts to admit, but I'm done holding back truths from Onyx. He's seen the worst of me.

"Strange," he says. "Do you guys have any forest management going on?"

"No." I frown at him. "What's that?"

"We have Ewan. He's a biologist and he focuses on managing our land and keeping it healthy. We've also got a retired gal who specializes in trees."

"Really? How interesting." His pack has so many jobs that our pack ignores. Someday I'll make sure we have something like that.

The trees part into a clearing. It's small, but the evening light streaming down paints the wildflowers in pinks and oranges. Grass bows under our feet as he leads me forward.

'This is one of my favorite spots," he says, hands going to my waist.

My neck cranes back as I take in the sheer magnitude of the trees surrounding us like a faerie circle. They must be ancient to be this huge.

"It's beautiful," I murmur.

"I've never brought anyone else here," he says, lowering his head to touch our cheeks together. My eyes drift closed at the feel of his skin brushing mine.

"I think I owe you five more minutes," I murmur.

"Five minutes," he echoes with a grin.

I lean back to look into his eyes. "You're the only person who has ever stood up for me like that. I've never felt like this with anyone else."

"I love the idea of you being only mine," he purrs suggestively, pressing a kiss to my cheekbone.

I give him a soft smack on his chest. "You know what I mean. Believing things can be better. Trying to help me."

His face goes from playful to intense, his gaze darkening. "I'm not going anywhere."

His mouth is hot on mine, insistent and rough. He nips at my bottom lip and I grab his shirt and tug it up. He slips it over his head and tosses it aside.

We fumble with our clothes, shedding items until just our undergarments remain. My limbs are clumsy as we sink down to the ground. With an arm hooked under the small of my back, he lowers me until my head rests on the soft grass.

Onyx sits back, his gaze exploring me. My skin flushes and I try to stay still, letting him look. It's difficult to not reach for him, but the satisfied smirk on his face makes it worth enduring the tension. And when he finally crawls toward me, I get a beautiful view of the muscles in his arms and chest moving under his skin. He is stunning. The curve of his cheekbones and the fullness of his lips are familiar to me now, and I find comfort in his dark eyes.

He breathes in against my collarbone and kisses up my neck until I can't stand it a second longer.

Cupping his jaw, I pull his mouth to mine. One kiss melds into another and my sense of time disintegrates. Pulse resonating in my skin, I press closer to him, feeling his heart pounding in response.

Breathing hard, he breaks away, looking down at me like I'm everything to him. No one has ever looked at me like that. Am I the only one for him? Maybe I'm just the newest in a string of girls for him. Once the thought hits me, I can't let it go.

"Onyx?" I ask. He pauses his work on my collarbone.

"Yeah?"

Nervousness rises in me, churning my stomach. I bite my lip, trying to sort through my thoughts. "Have you ever had another girlfriend?" I ask him.

With a thoughtful half-smile, he rolls onto his side, propping his head up in his hand like he's settling in for a good conversation. "No."

"Even a hookup?" I cross my arms over my bare breasts.

"Does what we did at that party count?" he asks. I shake my head. "Then nope."

"Are you serious?" I blurt out.

"I've never seen a girl I was that interested in until you." He states it like it's a plain fact, no big deal.

"Oh," I breathe out, shivering as his hand skims down my ribs and over my hips.

"What about you and Hawk?" he asks, nuzzling his nose against my jaw.

Exhaling sharply, I close my eyes and try to string words together. He's making coherent thought rather difficult.

"It was all arranged, and he was nice enough, but it wasn't like we were a real couple. I mean, he did the expected things like hold my hand and eat dinner with me, but I don't think either of us wanted more. He never touched me like you do."

When I open my eyes, he's staring into my soul. "I've hardly begun. I don't want a few kisses, I want all of you."

Every cell of my being tingles and I have to bite down on my lip.

He watches my mouth hungrily. "You're gorgeous," he rasps.

"You're a flirt," I say, the energy between us almost unbearable. It's a heavy pressure, and I feel like I'll burst out of my skin.

His brows furrow, his eyes boring into me. "I want you to be my mate."

My mind goes blank at his declaration. It's one thing to daydream about it, but another to hear him say he wants me in that all-consuming permanent way.

Without waiting for my answer, he kisses my jaw and leaves a trail down my throat to the crook of my neck. As he bites down lightly, I gasp, grabbing onto his arm. He doesn't break the skin and follows it with a lick that makes my toes curl.

"I'm not ready for that. Things are complicated." I manage to say, though my body screams yes.

He grins at me, his hair falling over his forehead. "That's not a no."

"It's a no for now. Ask me again when my life isn't falling apart around me."

"What about tomorrow?"

"Onyx!" I pinch the skin on his shoulder and he growls, snapping at my hand.

"Alright, I guess I can wait," he says, sighing dramatically.

I swat at him again, a laugh escaping me. He's so handsome with filtered light dancing across the bridge of his nose and the curve of his lips.

Threading my fingers through his hair, I admire him. On his brother, their square features look like an old movie star. On him, they're rougher with sharp edges. To me, he's perfect. And he wants me.

"So now that I have you alone, finally, what do you want to do?" he asks, a certain kindness in his voice. He's letting me take the lead and set the boundaries. That might be a mistake.

Looking boldly into his eyes, I say, "Everything."

He smirks. "Too bad you didn't agree to be my mate."

My lip curls into a snarl at the teasing.

"I suppose we can compromise. Call it a preview."

He's already moving, his hands gripping my ribs to keep me in place. I let out some sort of strangled whine at the words, and I can feel his dark laugh against my skin as he closes his mouth over the delicate skin at my waist.

"A preview?" I question with a hoarse laugh.

His hand slides between my legs, testing and teasing over the fabric. I let out another whine that destroys what's left of my dignity. It doesn't matter, all I need is him.

Slowly, his fingers slip up and down until I'm trembling and trying to press myself against him. His tongue licks below my belly button.

"Onyx, seriously," I beg in a desperate whisper.

His fingers thread under my panties and plunge into my core. The shock and pleasure overwhelm my senses and my back arches. He strokes inside me as he looks up to watch my reactions.

My thoughts scramble, unable to function under his onslaught. My hands close over his shoulder, my nails digging into his skin.

He pauses. "Do you want me to stop, or do you want more?"

"Don't," I gasp, "stop."

He chuckles and resumes, turning his hand and trying angles until he gets an embarrassing moan out of me. Eyes screwed shut, I only see stars, so I gasp when he flips me over and pulls at my hips until I lift up onto hands and knees.

"Can you stay like this?" he murmurs against my skin, his tongue dragging up my spine like my skin is sugar.

"Yeah." My back arches at the feel of him.

Bending over me, his hand curls under until he hones in on my clit. His soft but insistent touch threatens to shatter me, and I press my ass back into him.

It's overwhelming as he begins moving his hips, grinding his cock against my ass through his boxers. If we just removed the clothes between us… I can't get enough air, gasping as he ruts into me.

His movements slow as he focuses on what he's doing with his hands. Two fingers dip back into me, and I almost fall forward. Only his growled command keeps me from faceplanting.

With his other hand he slides his finger over my clit over and over, working me into a frenzy. Pleasure burns hotter through me, becoming an unbearable pressure. His fingers against me, inside me, the weight of him pressing into me. I'm so close to release.

I want to live in this moment forever, but I can barely tolerate it for these few seconds. His teeth clamp down on my juncture of neck and shoulder, holding there and barely pricking the skin, showing he could mark me as his mate - and I know in that moment if he broke the skin with his teeth, the magic would take and I would be his.

But he doesn't. Instead, he sucks the skin to leave a hickey. The hint of pain layered over the immense pleasure of his touch is the last thing I can take.

Cursing like a sailor, I break, shaking and tensing against the onslaught of pleasure. He groans as I squeeze his fingers and he presses into me.

He braces one hand on the ground, the other under my chest to keep me from collapsing. With whispered praises and peppered kisses, he stretches out on his side and tucks me against him.

"Goddess, I wanted to claim you so badly," he says. With a bashful grin, he scoots back and discards his boxers. I stare, realizing he came in his clothes. My cheeks prickle like I'm blushing, but my skin is already flushed. Tugging his sweats on, he cuddles up against me again.

The grassy earth shouldn't be this comfortable, but with his biceps under my head, I could easily fall asleep. Either Onyx feels the same, or he knows how tired I am.

"Get some rest," he instructs. "You need it. Especially with what I plan to do with you once you finally agree to be my mate."

"Dream on," I shoot back, barely able to string my words together.

He chuckles and presses a kiss to my ear. It's so tempting to drift off as he settles against me. His breathing soothes me and his touch makes me feel safe.

I'm lost in a haze, coming down from what he just did to me. I turn in his arms and kiss the tip of his nose. He smiles without opening his eyes.

"Rest," he rumbles, and I go still.

It's so peaceful, Onyx curled around me, his arm across my stomach. Time slips by and he dozes. Sunset melts into darkness, but the almost-full moon lights up our woodland haven. There are no predators around here except us, so it's safe for us to sleep if we wish.

Eventually someone will wonder where we are, but it's easier to pretend the rest of the world doesn't exist.

Onyx snuggles closer in his sleep, nuzzling into my chest. My hand goes to his head and I drag my nails through his hair. It's entirely possible I love this man.

I'd leave my pack for him.

The realization sends ice through my veins.

What would that even look like?

If I left, my mother would have to name another Heir, and by default it would be her new Beta, Orion. That would give him more power, and he already oversteps and stands against her every chance he gets.

Since things are already shaky, my mother will likely lose her position. She could be killed or maybe exiled.

If Orion or another of the males in the pack became Alpha, they would want revenge against Onyx's pack. My mother's lack of retaliation from our last battle is a sore spot for many of my packmates. Without her standing in the way, it's only a matter of time until they decide to move against the Bracken Creek pack.

I have to go back. The alternative is too risky.

Onyx moves in his sleep, his arms tugging me tighter against his chest. Heat radiates off of him.

But what if I went home and he came with me? I dismiss the thought as soon as it occurs to me. My pack would see him as the enemy. His life here is wonderful, and I can't force him into a new pack. He would be miserable and my pack would probably try to kill him.

How could I have been so stupid?

My heart hurts, pain stabbing through me worse than a physical wound. I can't have him. There's no way to make this work. At least, not right now. Once I am Alpha, I can repair my pack and change the culture until we can be together safely.

This bond between us grows stronger with every touch. The longer I wait, the more it will hurt to sever it.

If we will ever have a chance, I have to go back and demand the power I am due. The emotional hurt weighs me down, making planning difficult.

Watching him sleep, I can't bear the thought of telling him. He will insist on joining me. If I'm facing my treacherous pack, I need to know he is safe here.

Slowly, I move his arm across me until it lays between us. He barely twitches. Somehow, I know if he wakes up and asks me to be his mate again, I will accept, no matter the consequences to our packs.

As softly as I can manage I move away from him and rise. There's no need to gather my clothes, I'll just lose them when I shift.

Hand to my chest, pressing in as if I could reduce the pain of a broken heart, I look over Onyx one last time, memorizing the shape of his mouth and the way his lashes lay against his cheeks. His hair has lighter streaks from the time we've been out in the sun together this last week. His breathing stays slow and even.

There's no doubt about it. I am in love with him.

I can't stay here a minute longer. I'll lose my nerve.

With one last lingering glance, I sink into my wild instincts. My anger at the injustice of the situation drops away. Black fur covers my skin and in a split-second, I am a wolf.

In this form, I am graceful, weaving through the trees as I run downhill toward the border between Bracken Creek and Granite Ridge. In the back of my mind, every step leaves me screaming to go back to him, but it's effortless to ignore.

My animal side senses every little creature in the brush around me. The night is illuminated, making my journey easy. I'd never manage as a human, but in this shape, I leap from rock to rock and cross this deeper section of creek without hesitation.

It's time to go home and face this mess.

XIII
RECKLESS RESCUING

ONYX

Crickets chirp when I wake. From the warm moonlight, it's obviously still early evening. Ember and I should head back. But her warm shape is no longer curled against me.

My entire body goes stiff, tension through every muscle.

Where is she?

There are a dozen reasonable explanations, but somehow I know it's the worst one. She's gone. Her clothes litter the ground, so either she left naked or she shifted.

No.

This can't be happening.

The onslaught of violent emotions triggers my shift, and before I can think anything through, I'm in my gray wolf form leaping into the trees.

My wolf senses try to track her, following her scent northward. I lose it in the creek. Pain cuts through my panic. My paws stumble, and I throw my head back and let out a heartbroken howl.

Granite Ridge is on the other side of the creek. I cannot cross into that territory unprepared.

I don't know how I manage to get home. My paws shift to feet as I stumble up the steps to the front door. It's only by habit that I grab a pair of sweats and tug them on.

Cedar steps into the entry, his eyes wide with concern. I crash into him, pushing both of us against the wall. My twin grabs me, holding me up.

"She left," is all I can choke out. He muscles me toward the sofa, and I collapse, gulping down air to control my panic.

A few minutes later, Hazel bursts through the front door. She wraps me in a tight hug and I feel my head clearing. Slate enters behind her.

"Okay, what happened?" he asks.

Guilt eats away at me. I could have prevented this.

"We were out in the woods, and we dozed off. When I woke up, she was gone." My throat is raw, each word scratching. "I tracked her to the creek."

"Oh, Onyx," Hazel says, her hold tightening again.

Slate lets out a growl. "How could you have let this happen?"

"Slate," Hazel says softly. "That's not fair."

"It was his job to watch her. We shouldn't have let them leave the cabin."

Anger cuts through my haze of anxiety. It hones my mind and gives me something to focus on. Shrugging Hazel off, I stand to face my best friend. "You wanted her to leave so you should be happy."

"I wanted our pack safe and her to be safe too, and that would all be possible if you weren't too busy thinking with your dick."

I swing at him before my brain registers the decision. My fist connects with his jaw and he reels back. A split second later and he's on me, pressing me to the wood floor. The ringing pain in the back of my skull feels deserved. This is my fault.

His voice is dark and dominant. "Do not do that again, understood? You're not helping her right now."

My brain finally regains control and I stop struggling. The realization I just punched my Alpha horrifies me. I was thinking of him as my childhood friend, not my leader. He lets me sit up and I keep my gaze on the ground in submission.

"Understood."

"You two fighting really doesn't help the situation," Hazel says, crossing her arms. "We have to figure out what to do about this."

"I'm going to get her," I say without thinking.

"You can't do that." It's Hazel who stops me and I blink at her in surprise. "They'll treat you like an enemy, even if it's Sienna who catches you. She needs her pack to like her, and killing someone they see as an enemy would help her. I don't trust her to uphold our alliance right now."

"She's right," Slate adds. "We have to be smart about this."

"I can't-" I start to argue.

"I'll get Hawthorne and Jasper. We can get a hold of Sienna and sort this out." Slate heads to the door.

"Just hang tight. It'll be okay," Hazel says, smiling sadly.

Cedar watches from the hallway. I brush past him and head to the bathroom. It takes a while for him to go back to bed and fall asleep. It's just past two in the morning when I sneak out and head toward the parking lot.

While I'd prefer to shift and run, carrying clothing in my mouth is hard enough. I can't carry any weapons. For once, I'm grateful to be the son of the Delta, because I know the codes for all the locks in the training building.

I'm able to slip on a tactical vest and a couple of guns loaded with wolfsbane. To be safe, I also tuck in four small daggers. My black hoodie goes over the top so I can appear somewhat peaceful.

I grab the keys from the sun visor of my dad's beat up pickup truck and promise myself I'll save up and buy myself a decent vehicle soon. The gravel crunches on the drive out, but I timed my escape to when patrol is on the north side of our commune and shouldn't hear it. Even if they do, it'll be too late to stop me.

This is reckless, but I don't care. No one else is going to help. They'll put our pack first. But I can't live without her.

Pulling off the freeway, I park on the road that leads to Granite Ridge's pack buildings. I'm not sure how far it is to their buildings, so I stop closer to the freeway than I would have liked. It'll be a farther distance for our escape, but it's just as likely we will ditch the vehicle and run as wolves across the border.

I leave the truck unlocked with the keys ready, in case Ember is the one to reach it first.

The march toward Granite Ridge feels like miles and my heart races the entire time. There's no way to know what I'll find, except that Ember is there.

Cinder block buildings rise up in uniform lines. Two dozen identical houses line a street with a large and luxurious modern ranch at the end. The Alpha's house. Everything is quiet and I can't even hear a patrol. It's been at least three hours since Ember returned home, and it seems that everyone has gone to sleep.

The front porch of the Alpha's house is too exposed, so I creep around to the back. My footsteps are deafening with only the rustle of leaves to drown them out.

I pause at the back door, listening for any noise inside. A tense discussion, yelling, anything. It's silent.

The door comes open with a little work with a dagger. I step in, waiting for alarms to blare, but nothing happens. It's a kitchen, sterile and white with a double stainless steel fridge and eight burner stove my mother would love. But there is no warmth here. It looks like a catering kitchen, not a family's. But then again, Sienna doesn't seem like the type to cook.

Cautiously, I move through the kitchen into the hallway. It splits in two directions. The scent of Ember is faint and old, but I catch a stronger trail down the left hallway. I pass an office and finally reach a closed door that definitely smells like her.

The door is silent as I ease it open at a glacial pace. Ember sprawls across the bed, eyes on the ceiling. Her face is red and puffy like she's been crying.

When the door latch clicks behind me, she bolts up.

"Onyx!" she hisses, scrambling to stand and darting toward me. I open my arms, wanting to sweep her up romantically. But she grabs my wrist and drags me forward so she can reach the door behind me and lock it.

"What the fuck are you doing here?"

"You ran away," I say dumbly. "I came to get you."

For a moment, she flounders, her mouth working silently. Not exactly the reaction I was expecting.

"I left because I didn't want to be there with you," she says. "Clearly, I didn't want you following me."

"No, that can't be why," I argue. The adrenaline running through my body is the only thing keeping me going, and my thoughts swirl together into mud. "You don't want to be here. You want to be with me."

Her lips purse for a moment and her brows furrow, like she regrets what she's doing, but she shakes her head. "No, you need to leave. I don't know what they'll do if you're caught, but it won't be pretty."

"I'm not leaving without you," I say stubbornly.

"Argh, you guys have my phone so I can't even call Jasper to come get your dumb ass." She turns away, pacing the length of her room.

The walls are white, her bedding is ivory, and all of the furniture is pale wood. It doesn't feel like Ember. She belongs somewhere comfortable and cozy.

"I need to be here to help my mom. Once that's handled, we can revisit *us*." She motions between us, back and forth.

"Then I'll stay to help."

"You're going to ruin everything!" she says, her voice still hushed but rising.

Pounding on the door makes both of us leap. "Ember, open up. We have an intruder." A masculine voice sounds through the wood.

"Shit!" Her face pales, all of the blood draining out in panic. "You need to go out the window and run. Please, for me."

She shoves me toward the window and slides it open with one hand.

Before I can argue with her, she grabs my shoulder and forces me down and half out the window. I have to grab the sill to keep from tumbling out head first.

Her door blows open with a splintering crack, and I push off the window frame to get between her and the attacker.

"No, Onyx!" Ember yelps, clinging to my arm.

Hands shaking, I draw a gun and level it at the three men bursting into her room. They're taller than I am, filling the entire space. They close the distance between us before I can react.

"Back off, I don't want to shoot you," I say.

"What are you doing?" Ember screeches.

They don't stop. My finger tightens on the trigger and the gun fires, striking the first man. He staggers back and then drops as the wolfsbane hits his bloodstream. Before I can fire again, hands clamp around my upper arms.

Something strikes my head, and my vision swims, pain splintering me apart. Desperate to get back to Ember, I struggle against my captors. Their hold bruises as they jerk me back and down onto my knees.

My vision tunnels, black seeping in around the edges.

Another strike, and I lose consciousness.

XIV

TRESPASSING & TRAITORS

EMBER

"Get your fucking hands off of him," I snarl. A guard keeps his palm on my shoulder, pinching the muscle to let me know he will restrain me if needed. I'm being detained until Sienna and Orion can be roused.

Onyx lays across the ground, blood seeping from his hairline. I grit my teeth so hard it feels as if my jaw will crack. I won't show them weakness, because then I will be truly powerless to help him.

My mother fills the doorway, her hair twisted into a bun on the top of her head and a crimson robe billowing over her shoulders.

"You've been back for mere hours and already you're causing problems?" she drawls.

Her words sting, but I wonder if they're more for the benefit of the pack. Things are more complicated than I realized. She strides to Onyx and nudges him with her black satin slippers.

"Do you know who this is? He looks familiar." Her eyes barely glance my way.

"He's my friend. He was worried about me leaving in the middle of the night, so he came to make sure I was safe." My fists clench, aching to hit the men still holding me in place.

"I've been getting far too little sleep tonight. Someone one string him up and we can deal with this in the morning. Flint, you're in charge of his guard. Keep him in one piece. I want to know what he was doing in detail."

"Stop! He's my guest," I yell.

My mother pauses, looking me over. "Guests are announced and welcomed. They do not sneak into the Alpha's house."

My mother's men grab Onyx's upper arms and tug him out of the room, his legs dragging across the carpet. Jerking away, I slip from my captor's hold and follow them.

Out front of our cold concrete training building, they handcuff him to a steel pole. His head lolls as he sags to the ground.

Sienna has already disappeared back to bed. I clutch my arms around my middle, feeling vulnerable as the pack members dissipate.

Flint, a thin man with greasy dark hair, sits on a bench and watches me with beady eyes. I bare my teeth at him. I'm ranked far above him, so he should look away, but he leers at me.

Anger heats my blood, making me sick with the cold fear churning my stomach. Hours ago I was lost in my own world with Onyx. He was safe, and I was trying to keep it that way. Why didn't Slate and Hazel stop him?

My eyes burn, but crying will only make this worse. Glaring at Flint, I walk to where Onyx sags, his arms pulled back behind him. My knees sting as they hit the concrete and my fingers brush back his hair to see the wound underneath. Blood mattes his scalp and a single thin line of crimson runs down the side of his cheek to his jaw.

"Hey," I say softly. His breathing is ragged, so I can tell he's conscious, but his eyes are screwed shut in pain.

With a small groan, he opens his eyes and raises his face to mine. Pain flashes across his features.

"I'm sorry," I whisper. "This is exactly what I was trying to avoid."

His voice cracks. "You could have warned a guy."

I can't bring myself to berate him, even if he deserves it. "I thought if I left like that, you'd be angry with me. Not *follow* me. I didn't want anyone to stop me. I have to help my mom."

"I'd follow you anywhere," he rasps, his eyes closing and lines creasing his forehead and cheeks.

"I'm going to get you out of here. But I need you to swear you'll stay away until it's safe."

Running a hand down his stomach, I feel tactical gear under his hoodie. They didn't even bother to check him. Moving around to his side hidden from Flint, I lift the edge of his hoodie and slide out a small dagger. Keeping my back to our guard, I inch around to his hands and start picking at the handcuffs.

"Hey, what are you doing?" Flint says, leaning forward in his seat.

The blade slides into my waistband, the metal cold against my skin. "Checking his wrists. You guys were sloppy," I spit.

He sneers, crossing his arms and flexing, but doesn't take his eyes off me. There is no way I can get Onyx free with him here.

"Flint," I say, "what would it take for you to look away for a few minutes?"

His eyes narrow but he doesn't outright reject my offer. I can see the thoughts spinning in his slimy head. "It would take a lot to be worth it, but I think we could figure something out." His gaze drops lower, making his intentions clear.

Onyx snarls, pulling against his restraints. "If you touch her, I will gut you and feed you your own kidney!"

"Oh, did you find yourself a loyal puppy?" Flint says with a chuckle. "That's good to know."

I'm done negotiating and playing it cool. Rising, I focus my gaze on the older wolf. He's not much taller than I am and has always looked half-starved. I'm confident in a fight I could take him down.

Stepping closer, I draw the dagger out and touch the tip to my finger, rotating it.

"This wolf is mine," I say, my voice a threat, "and if you interfere in me getting my way, I will do far worse than he said. You will have wished someone would have killed you."

"I doubt you could do anything to me," he says, putting on bravado. But I can see the hesitation in his eyes. We've sparred before in training, but never with weapons.

"Will you keep your mouth shut?" I ask, drawing close enough to strike him.

"Why should I?"

Nervousness floods me, but I ignore it. I wish I could snap and go to a place where I have no control. This is so much harder with a clear head.

I let the dagger tip forward until it's pointed at his chest. He moves to take it, exactly what I was hoping for.

As he reaches up, I go low, slashing across his ribs as they turn toward me - shallow enough to draw blood but not cause serious harm. A warning.

He jerks back, his hand going to his side. The cut runs from the bottom of his ribs almost to his armpit. His shirt billows open and blood drips down his side. I smile at him.

"Will you keep your mouth shut?" I ask again, calm and cold.

He sits back down hard, baring his teeth at me. "You bitch, I can't wait until someone puts you in your place."

Why couldn't he just cooperate?

With my left hand, I swing and connect with his jaw, knocking him sideways across the bench. He wildly grabs at me, and I slice across his forearm, holding the knife sideways in my fist. He recoils, curling in on himself defensively as blood seeps between his fingers.

"Stay there or I will end you," I snarl before turning to free Onyx.

"The little wolf has bite," a deep voice says, making me jump. Onyx growls, unable to see past me as I spin to face Orion. He melts out of the shadows, moving too gracefully for a man that large.

"Beta," I address him coolly. Straightening, I block Onyx from him the best I can.

I'm never sure what Orion will do. He accompanied Hawk to join our pack, but stayed with us even when my ex returned to his family's pack up north. Standing a head above most of our packmates and with a vicious temperament, it didn't take him long to move up the ranks.

"Is there a reason you are attacking Flint and trying to free the trespasser?" he asks. He doesn't seem angry, just curious.

"I am taking charge of him. The handcuffs are unnecessary. He will do whatever I say."

Orion moves into my personal space and I refuse to step back, even though I have to crane my neck to keep eye contact. "Is he a lovesick moron you picked up during your little vacation?"

"No. And that's not your concern anyway." I hold my hand with the dagger up between us, an idle threat.

"I want to know if you have any attachments," he says, his voice low. "I'll walk you back to the Alpha's house. You shouldn't be out here."

Onyx lets out a snarl that sounds entirely animal. I half expect to see him shifted, but shifting with cuffs pulled tight and arms bound behind him would result in serious injuries.

Orion chuckles, placing a hand on my upper back. With a jerk of my shoulders, I shrug him off and move away.

"If this stray is a problem, I'm happy to eliminate him," he says quietly.

"If you touch him, I'll kill you," I say, rage in every syllable.

Orion shoves me forward, his hand brushing the back of my arm to let me know he'll grab me if necessary. "I'd love to see you try. Maybe I'll get my way tomorrow when we deal with him."

I allow myself to be herded back to the Alpha's house, and lock myself in my room with my heart pounding in my ears. With Onyx tied up outside, I can't possibly sleep.

Low voices in the hall tell me that Orion has posted a guard to keep me contained.

He's undermining me, but it's clear now that I've never been given any true authority. I'll have to seize it. But a fight against Orion won't end well. Strategy is my only strength against a brute like him.

It takes all my willpower to not scream and cry into my pillow. I feel so helpless, like every decision I've made has blown up in my face.

Eventually light filters in my window. I dress in all-black workout gear and pull my hair back into a bun. After some thought, I apply eyeliner and a red lip in the same style as my mother. It's time to take my birthright in full, and if all goes well, the man I love will walk out of here safe.

Sienna sits in the formal living room, holding court with her top ranked wolves. I ignore them and address my mother directly.

"I want the wolf from last night freed. He was my host during my visit and he was concerned for my safety. We are endangering our alliance by detaining him." With my shoulders back and my head high, I feel confident and my words come out strong.

She frowns, tapping a manicured nail against the glossy wooden table beside her chair. "Dear, he destroyed our alliance by breaking into the Alpha's home. He could have been assassinating you. He may have meant to for all we know."

"Absolutely not. I will vouch for him. It was the middle of the night when I left, and he was simply following me. The pack was asleep and he came straight to see me. You should be rewarding him for taking my safety so seriously."

"I'm afraid your word doesn't weigh enough in this situation," she says, her gaze flicking to the other wolves in her circle. "We are debating what to do with him. You are welcome to join the discussion, but you will not be overriding my counsel."

My nails dig into my palms hard enough to break the skin. In the past, I would have thought my mother was simply tormenting me. But now I see she's controlled by those around her. She's lost all her power in this pack, and she's clawing to keep her position.

With a huff, I sit in the nearest seat, leaving space between the other wolves and myself.

"As I was saying," Sienna continues, "I don't feel it's necessary to question him. There's no sign of any other trespassers, and if he was a scout, he wouldn't have come right in."

"I say we execute him. He threatened our Heir and he arrived with enough weapons to take out half our pack," Orion says, leaning back with his hands behind his head as if this was friendly small talk and not a deliberation over the life of another. His gaze goes to me and he smirks.

"You only want him dead because I want him alive and free," I growl, unable to help myself.

"So you prefer we just let him go?" the Gamma, Aster, a woman just older than my mother, questions.

"I've explained already, and the fact you can't accept my word is ridiculous and offensive," I say, my anger building.

"If we can somehow verify his intentions, hence the idea of questioning him, I am okay with sending him back to his pack," the Delta says. He's the oldest of the bunch, with gray threaded through his black ponytail.

Sienna crosses her arms and sighs. "Well, we have two strong opinions. I see the merit in what my daughter says, but also the wisdom in Orion's choice."

"I believe imprisonment until we can negotiate with his pack would be best," Aster says, rubbing the back of her head where her hair is buzzed short.

"No," I say, exuding every bit of dominance I possess. "You are going to release him into my custody, and he will stay with me. I am completely confident he means me no harm. He's been protecting me for the last week. He's showing loyalty by coming here, and we're treating him like a criminal. This ends now."

"He is a criminal, and now is not the time to be forgiving toward those that threaten our pack," Orion says, drawing out his words. His presence presses down on me, causing my anxiety to rise. "But if you feel so strongly about it, you're welcome to challenge me."

"I don't have to do that. You're the only one demanding blood here."

"I outrank them. Dearest Ember, you've been weakened by your time in that pack. This is for your own good." His smirk is ugly.

"I am Heir and hold power over you," I say, my hands clenching into fists.

"Prove it."

My mother's face pales, but if I reject his challenge, I've already lost. He'll kill Onyx. If my mother tries to stop him, he'll use it as a reason to depose her. I've made this so much worse.

"Fine."

ONYX

After Ember is taken away, two ugly fuckers give me a beating until the world goes dark.

When I come to, it's light and I've been stripped of my gear and weapons.

Shit.

No one speaks to me, but the entire pack has gathered. Far more wolves look at me with hatred than I would have expected. Things are worse between my pack and Granite Ridge than I realized.

The crowd's noise drops as Sienna approaches, followed by Ember and the huge man from last night. The Beta, Orion.

With great effort, I press my back against the pole and push myself to stand so I can follow their progress. They stop in the training ring which is just paint on concrete, without even mats for safety during sparring.

"Beta Orion would see the trespasser executed as a dangerous stray," a man with graying hair and beard says, "and Heir Ember wants him freed. A challenge has been issued."

No.

My heart drops. He is three times her size and twice her age. Without a weapon, I doubt I could take him. She's vicious, but this is insanity.

"Stop, let me fight," I yell, my voice giving out. "I challenge for myself!"

A nearby man thumps me in the stomach and I barely stay standing, sagging against my restraints. From the needle-like pain in my side, I suspect they broke a few of my ribs earlier. Shifter healing is fast, but not that fast. It will take a few days before I'm back to normal.

Shoulders close in, and despite my height, I can't see the ring. But I can guess when the fight starts. The crowd roars to life, crying for blood and yelling disgusting, suggestive taunts to my girlfriend.

A growl rumbles low in my chest as I listen for the sounds of strikes landing or pained gasps. Through a gap in the crowd, I see Ember darting out of Orion's reach, landing a kick against the side of his knee. He falls to one knee, but the crowd closes in before I see her next move.

She's holding her own, if the noises her packmates make is any indication. I want to cheer her on, but it hurts to breathe.

A deep masculine grunt echoes through the space, followed by a feminine yelp. It's killing me not being able to see. The distinct noise of a fist connecting with flesh sounds, once, twice. Two wolves snarl.

Legs part for a second and I see Ember on the ground, scrambling for a hold on Orion. He's gotten above her.

A whimper from her throat hurts me worse than the injuries I've received. I'll make his death slow for daring to hurt her. The crowd closes in and I pray she finds a way to knock him down and make him wish he was dead.

"Beta Orion is the victor!" A voice calls out.

No, no, no.

How is she? Black edges my vision as I strain to see her.

People part, and Sienna, Orion, and Ember stand in front of me. Ember's lip is split, and she holds her side. From the tension in her muscles to the way her posture covers that side, I have no doubt she's nursing broken bones. Her cheekbone is red and has started to swell.

Orion is leaning all his weight on one leg, but otherwise looks unharmed. He grins at Ember.

"Alpha, if I may?" he asks, bowing his head to Sienna.

"Yes, Beta?" She picks at her nails like this boring to her.

"Although I still believe he should be executed, I will offer his life to Ember as a gift. A mating present."

Who does this asshole think he is?

Ember clears her throat. "I'm flattered, and I will consider your proposal only if you set him free. I could never be mated to a man who kills someone I've asked to be spared."

"Fine," he says with a shrug, like it's nothing.

I should be relieved, but instead I can barely breathe. She can't possibly be considering him. The only upside is that I'll now live long enough to make good on the silent promises of pain and death running through my thoughts.

"Wonderful. He's been taught a lesson, and we can send him back to his pack with a warning," Sienna says as she saunters closer. With a cruel smile, she grabs my chin. Her spiked nails dig into skin, but I hardly feel it with all my other injuries. "Our alliance is broken, and any other interference from your pack will be considered an act of aggression."

Her pack cheers and howls around us, and I look into her eyes, like darker versions of Ember's. Instead of worry and warmth, I see ice and death.

I'm cut free and escorted to my truck by a handful of guards. Ember doesn't follow. Numbly, I allow them to push me into my truck and fumble with the keys. It takes all of my willpower to pull the vehicle onto the road.

Driving with one eye swollen shut is a bitch. The world swims around me and the truck keeps slowing as I lose focus. But somehow, I manage to get home.

The parking lot buzzes with activity. Hazel and Slate talk with packmates while Cedar and Jasper load equipment into a truck. At the sound of the engine, the group turns.

A dull sense of relief fills me, loosening my grip. Throwing the truck into park, I shove the door open and tumble out. Slate catches me, hoisting me up with help from my twin.

Hazel appears in my dimming vision, her eyebrows pinched and lips parted as she surveys my injuries. Everything sounds muffled, like I'm under a heavy blanket.

The rough hands grasping my body cause me to flinch, making me think I'm back at Granite Ridge enduring their punishments. My mumbled words do nothing to stop the blurring chaos around me.

"You idiot!" Hazel's voice breaks through, her words thick as if she is crying.

Cool wood presses into my back. The change triggers nausea, and I jerk sideways in time to throw up on the floor. It's darker in here, giving some relief to my pounding head.

An older voice speaks nearby, along with Hazel's worried tone. The words "Concussion," and "Broken Ribs," are repeated.

I must be in Sable's cottage. Good, the healer can patch me up so I can get back to Ember.

"Alright, you can sleep now. I'll keep an eye on you," Sable says, brushing my hair back and pressing something to my head. Instantly, the nausea subsides and the pain lessens. Relief soaks through me and my body finally relaxes. Sable fusses over me as I fade into a shallow sleep.

XV

IMPRISONMENT & UNLIKELY ALLIES

EMBER

The next couple of days go by quietly, and I spend most of my time resting in my room and letting my injuries heal. Dark thoughts overtake me, stripping away the hope and joy I had found in Onyx's pack.

My heartbreak seems trivial after Onyx almost lost his life. We are lucky Orion agreed to spare him, even if it was some kind of sick proposal to me. Joke's on him. I will never accept him as my mate.

After I tire of cold cereal and my ribs have healed enough I can breathe without pain, I walk to the cafeteria to get some hot food.

"Hey Ember, I'll sneak into your room if that's what you like," a man jeers at me. I ignore him and load my tray with meatloaf and powdery mashed potatoes.

A strangled yell startles me and a body thumps to the ground.

"Apologize," a deep voice commands. I spin to see Orion pressing his boot to the man's throat.

"S-s-s-sorry!" he says, choking on the word. Orion steps off his airway and raises an eyebrow at me before stalking off. He's waiting for his answer.

Feeling sick, I turn back to my food.

No one else bothers me while I eat the swill our pack serves. I would give anything for Clove's fresh bread right now. Although I'd give up bread for the rest of my life if it meant I could go back to Onyx.

There's no use in wishing.

I force myself to focus on the discussions at the tables around me. Orion's name comes up often and it seems he has the support of most of the pack, if the dozen wolves around me are an accurate sample.

He's the biggest threat to my mother, and he's asked me, the Heir, to be his mate. That is a clear path to becoming Alpha.

What will he do when I reject him?

Or should I set my pride aside, let my heart shatter, and agree to be his? It would keep me safe. He might refrain from challenging my mother and wait until she steps down. Either way, he would end up in power.

It's too much to handle. I hide away in my room for the rest of the day. My mother never visits me. Maybe, if she was honest with me, we could find a way out of this mess together. But that will never happen. Some rifts are too deep.

My best option is somehow eliminating Orion. And since my daydreams of being with Onyx are now intermixed with visions of murdering Orion, I have a head start in brainstorming solutions.

Unfortunately, I'm not fast enough.

That evening, as the sun lowers behind the trees, the roar of a crowd pulls me from my solitude. It starts as a hum that I almost ignore, but rises in intensity until shouts emanate through my windows and down the hallway.

With stiff legs, I scramble from my bed and push off the wall as I cover the distance. The pebbles prick my bare feet as I rush down the stairs and out onto the dirt.

The entire pack is gathered. What the hell?

With this level of uproar, I expect a formal challenge within the painted ring in the training building. Instead, the jostling pack circles around figures in the center of the main road.

Muscling my way in, I snarl as someone elbows my chest. Dust stings my eyes as dozens of feet shuffle around me. Throwing my weight forward, I push further into the mob.

"Ah, there she is," Orion says, his voice yelling over the din.

The wolves part, letting me through. I wish they hadn't.

Orion stands in the center with blood spattered across his shirt. He grins at me, his teeth red.

At his feet, my mother sprawls out. Her chest rises and falls, but her eyes are closed. Crimson streaks her face from a broken nose and her wrist bends at an unnatural angle.

"Mom!" I cry, dropping to the ground beside her. Reaching for her neck, I feel for her pulse. It's steady, and I exhale in cursory relief. Even with a shake, she doesn't wake.

Rising, I face him. "How could you do this?"

"The pack wants a strong leader," he says with a shrug.

"You're disloyal! Why would anyone follow you?" I growl, wishing I had a weapon.

"There's my feisty little wolf," he purrs. Without even glancing down, he steps over my mother. I flatten back until I bump into the wolves surrounding us. Still, he comes closer. "Are you ready to accept me as your mate?" he asks.

"Why would I do that?" I growl.

"I'm the Alpha now," Orion says. The wolves around us whoop and howl in approval. "You are mine now. I'm wondering if you'll give in, or if you'll fight. I love when females fight."

My heart races, in a way that makes me sick. Tingling spreads through my limbs, panic overcoming me.

"It's okay, you have time to change your mind," he says with a dark laugh. "Why don't you spend some quiet time thinking it over?"

He gestures to his cronies and hands seize my upper arms. There's no use in struggling as I'm led back into the house and roughly pushed through the door to our basement.

Stair treads cut into my ass and thigh as I slide down a few steps before grabbing the railing and halting myself. I deserve this. Without bothering to rise, I lay my head against the step and give up.

I can't even find the willpower to tell myself everything will be okay. Orion won't be a good Alpha. He won't be a tolerable mate. There's no silver living, because eventually war will come for Onyx and his pack.

Hopefully they can defeat us. But the bloodshed will be my fault. He will never accept me again, marked by another and responsible for even more death.

Eventually, I limp to the sofa and curl up, grim images of the future playing in my head.

When I wake, all is quiet so I suspect it's night. It's fully furnished like an apartment, but the lack of windows is disorienting. At least there are frozen meals in the kitchenette from when Hazel was locked down here two years ago.

It seems poetic that I'm now the one imprisoned down here.

I force myself to eat and clean myself up. There are a few spare clothing items, but even that doesn't make me feel any better. There's no way out. And what's the point?

ONYX

Two days later and every bit of me still hurts, but none of it matters when I had to leave Ember behind. My soul aches, distracting me from the work before me. Grabbing the arms of my chair, I force my focus to the screen in front of me, where Sienna looks down her nose at us.

Jasper shifts his weight, clearing his throat as he addresses his mother. "Please, I need to know everything you can remember. Any detail might help."

Sienna sits straight and proud, despite the purple bruise across her cheeks and the medical tape over her swollen nose. A small, vicious part of me is gratified to see her hurting like I am, but considering Ember is now in greater risk, my feelings toward Sienna are moreover apathetic.

"The details aren't important."

"Ember is still there," Jasper says patiently.

"Who knows what's happening to her right now," I snap, unable to stay silent.

"She's most likely preparing to become mates with the new Alpha," Sienna sniffs.

"You can't be serious." Jasper scowls at his mother.

She ignores him.

"I will do whatever it takes to get her back," I say, desperate to get her to care.

"You're not capable of what it would take," Sienna says, her cold, dark eyes meeting mine through the screen.

I growl, rising and slamming my hands down on the desk. "There is nothing I wouldn't do for her."

"Jasper," Sienna says, her voice light and unconcerned. "Tell me about this pup."

I bristle, but Jasper pats my hand. With a forceful exhale, I settle back into my seat.

"He's the son of the pack's Delta. He's ranked as a Zeta and is responsible for all of our digital security. Onyx is also the closest childhood friend of our Alpha and has his support."

Her gaze flicks back to me, contemplating my resume. It shouldn't matter. She's wasting time. What kind of mother wouldn't want to help her child?

Flexing my hands, I lock eyes with her. Time to lay everything on the table. "I am in love with her, and I believe she is with me too."

"It's easy enough to say that, but much harder to prove it," she quips. I want to throw the screen across the room.

"Give me a chance," I growl.

"What would you do?" Sienna asks.

"We'd like to remove Ember from the situation, just like you originally intended," Jasper explains.

"But what if she prefers to stay with Orion? That's the quickest and perhaps only route to power available to her."

"I was just informed she's currently locked up in your basement, so I doubt she's on board with Orion's proposal," Jasper says with clenched teeth.

My hands tighten on my chair so hard my knuckles pop. Jasper neglected to tell me that detail. No doubt feeling my anger through the pack bond, Jasper looks over at me with raised brows. With a slow exhale, I relax my posture, though my heart still pounds.

"Alright, what do you want to know?" Sienna finally says.

"What happened after Ember came home?" I ask.

"You came bursting in like a stalker and put everyone on the warpath," Sienna says, crossing her arms gingerly, avoiding her broken wrist.

"I was talking with her and we would have left together quietly," I say.

"Good job with that." The disdain in her voice raises my hackles. This mother-in-law relationship isn't off to a great start.

"You could have let us go. Those were your men."

"Unfortunately, it's not that simple," Sienna says.

"What do you mean?" I keep my tone civil, despite the venom I feel.

For a moment, Sienna purses her lips. I don't expect an answer, but she surprises me.

"Orion has been waiting for any excuse to challenge me. If I did anything outside of the pack's expectations, it was an opportunity for him."

"You were his Alpha," I say.

Sienna sniffs, picking at her manicure.

"After I left, what happened?"

"Ember hid in her room after Orion asked her to be his mate."

"So why did he challenge you?" Jasper asks, gentler than I can manage.

She sits back, her lips in a thin line. We both stare at her, waiting it out. After a moment, she huffs. "I told him he couldn't force her to be his mate."

"And he challenged you." Jasper fills in. "And now she's locked in a basement."

"We need to get her out of there," I say.

"Okay, let's talk strategy," Jasper says, smiling when his mother sits forward attentively. Somehow, we won her over. If we are lucky, she'll have the missing pieces we need to put together a rescue mission.

XVI
PROVIDE, PROTECT

EMBER

The day slips by and I spend it staring at the ceiling. Only the hope of violence against Orion drives me to eat a frozen meal and drink water from the sink.

When the door at the top of the stairs swings open, I expect Orion to come in and ask if I'm ready to become his mate. If I don't agree, the magic of the mate bond won't work and he can leave me to rot or perhaps try a little light torture.

I've resigned myself to my fate.

Aster stands there, clothing drapes across her arms. I watch her coldly as she makes her way down.

"What do you want?" I ask.

"I'm the only one coming to help you, so perhaps you could be polite." Her words are clipped, and there's an undercurrent of exhaustion.

"What's going on up there?"

"Orion has banished your mother, but he's not going to let you go."

"Is she okay?"

"She's alive."

Aster drapes a simple white dress over the banister and smoothes it with her weathered hands.

"The sooner you agree to be his mate, the easier this will be for you."

"I can't do that. He's a monster."

"You're the only one who has a chance to curb him. We need you." Her gray eyes stay on the ground. I've never felt much emotion through our pack bonds, but I can feel her regret.

"I'm being sacrificed, is that it?"

"You're doing your duty to your pack," she says simply. "He's going to come for you soon. I recommend you get ready."

"Thanks for the warning," I say, bitterness on my tongue. "I don't need a dress. I need a weapon."

"I'm sorry, Ember." She finally meets my eyes. I only see resignation in her gaze.

"If you can't help me, go away."

She does.

I pace anxiously, my nails digging into my palms. In a few hours, Orion will come for me. I'll have to accept to even have a chance at getting my hands on a weapon. Will that be enough for the magic to take? The idea of his claim mark on me makes me want to throw up.

Ignoring the dress, I tuck a fork into my waistband. It's the closest thing to a weapon I can find in this basement.

For too soon, the door at the top of the stairs creaks open.

"Ember, you're wanted," a guard calls.

Preferring to walk instead of being dragged, I march up the stairs and face my fate. Two younger men stand at the door, their heads bowed.

The front door stands open, and I pass through it, shoulders tense. Orion's broad frame is outlined against a lowering sun, the pack spread out before him.

"You summoned me?" I say, my eyes scanning for a weapon, an escape, anything.

Orion looks over his shoulder, beckoning me forward. Arms crossed, I step diagonally, forward but out of reach. Let everyone know how much I despise him. His lip curls and fear twists in my gut. Those eyes promise retaliation.

Engines rev in the distance, and dust plumes from a line of SUVs pulling level with our compound. Orion snags my wrist and tugs me against him.

The crowd turns, facing the newcomers.

The first door opens and Zephyr steps out. The Alpha of the Ironcrest pack smiles wide, his short, silver hair glinting as bright as his teeth.

"I heard we had a new Alpha to greet," he says.

Orion lets out a low growl, moving closer to me.

The older man strides forward, his guards falling into step behind him. The crowd parts as he approaches us.

An echoing boom sounds from our right, away from Zephyr's convoy.

Orion's hand seizes my wrist as dust sprays across us. The sounds of gunfire ricochets off the concrete block buildings.

Zephyr throws his arms out, steadying his people. "What the hell is going on?" he yells, just as Orion shouts, "Everyone down. Find them!"

Hands drag me back as the entire pack breaks into chaos. I'm pulled into the house, the noise dulling as the front door slams shut, closing me in. I scramble to get my feet under me.

"Who?" the guard yelps.

I don't care what the distraction is. This is my only chance. Jerking against his hold on my arm, I pluck the fork from my waistband and stab the tines into his side. He doubles over, releasing me.

Another set of hands catch me, and I thrash and struggle against the hold. "Hey, it's okay," a familiar voice says.

Twisting to see, I meet Cedar's soft blue eyes.

My panic clears, and I turn to see Onyx leveling a wolfsbane gun at the guard. Before the bleeding man can react, Onyx fires. The poisoned ammo takes seconds to render him unconscious. Cedar releases me now that I am steady on my feet.

"Hey, I heard you needed a rescue," Onyx says with a grin.

"Are you kidding me?" I cry, launching myself at him. He hoists me up, my legs hooking around his hips as I bury my face into the crook of his neck. The world falls away as I breathe in his scent. I thought I would never get to touch him again.

Far too soon, he lets me go. Standing back, I gaze at him in wonder. He looks perfect, all visible wounds healed. Terror grips me. I can't go through seeing him almost die again. "Why did you come back? What were you thinking?" I whisper.

"I was thinking I couldn't live without you," he says before he tugs me forward and captures my lips with his.

The dull darkness of the last few days falls away, my body coming to life again. Energy surges in every cell of my body. I kiss him like he's my oxygen and I'll die if we stop or even slow for a second.

"Now's not the time!" Cedar hisses.

He releases me. "As much as I love this, and love you, we need to go." Without wasting another second, he grabs my hand and leads me toward the kitchen.

"We need to hurry," Cedar says, taking up the rear and scanning behind us as we rush through my house.

"How did you manage this?" I hiss.

"A lot of wolfsbane and calling in favors," Cedar says.

"Zephyr was the distraction. We followed his group in," Onyx explains, pausing at the back door and peeking out. "Looks clear."

"And the explosion?"

"Drones and fireworks," he says with a grin.

Two guards lay unconscious between the house and the tree line. As we pass, Onyx kicks one in the leg and mutters, "Oops, motherfucker."

"Hurry, they're just up ahead," Cedar snaps, keeping pace behind us. Jasper's black car idles on the access road, just out of view of the main compound.

Marigold stands by the passenger side, a crossbow peeking over her shoulder. "Come on, you guys!"

Onyx wrenches the door open, pushing my head down as I leap in. The twins pile in behind me and Onyx pulls me up in his lap as he slides across the bench seat. I have no complaints. In fact, it's not close enough. I want to burrow into his skin.

Jasper sits in the driver's seat, another gun in his lap. "Hey!" he greets me, before turning the steering wheel and feeding gas to the engine.

The car spits pebbles with a sound like rain as he peels out and drives northward. Marigold's arm reaches across the center console to grip his thigh, her expression tense as she stares past us out the back window.

We hit the freeway and Jasper speeds, increasing the miles between us and the pack as quickly as possible. After twenty minutes or so, he eases off to the speed limit. We are all breathing easier and even smiling.

"Alright, I'd say that went pretty well," Marigold says, leaning her head back against the headrest.

"Much more successful than my first attempt," Onyx says, nuzzling against my temple.

"I can't believe you guys came for me."

"We weren't going to leave you there," Cedar says plainly, like it was the most obvious fact in the world.

"Why? I left on my own, and then..." I trail off, unable to verbalize what Onyx went through because of me.

"We heard shit hit the fan," Onyx says, kissing my shoulder.

"I suppose that's accurate," I say, my mind whirling through everything that has happened and what to tell him. Jerking upright, I glance at Jasper. "Do you know what happened to Mom?"

"She's recouping at Ironcrest," he says calmly. "But that's not where we are going."

"How is she?"

"She's doing pretty good, all things considered."

Marigold looks over her shoulder and gives me a supportive smile. "She's fine, just worried about you. She's the one who convinced Zephyr to play decoy actually. Turns out, he doesn't care for Orion or the northern pack."

"Neither do I," I said darkly.

Everyone is quiet for a moment. The road splits, and Jasper turns West, away from both his pack and mine.

"What happened after I left? Did he?" Onyx starts to ask, but can't seem to finish his question.

Looking up at him, I attempt to smile despite the choking feeling in my throat. "After he challenged my mom, he demanded that I become his mate and when I said no, he locked me up until right now."

I feel like I barely escaped a train crash.

"He'll never get near you again. And I'm going to make him wish he had never even looked at you," he promises. It's the best thing I've ever heard and I reward him with a soft kiss.

"So seriously, what's the plan? Where are we actually going?" I ask, feeling lighter than I have since leaving Onyx in the woods.

Jasper sighs, keeping his gaze on the road. "You guys are going to lay low for a while, and I am going to work with Slate and Hawthorne to put together a plan. Not totally sure yet what that'll be, but we need you out of the way. No more idiotic schemes to run home and challenge anyone."

His words sting. It felt like the right thing to do at the time. If I had known the consequences then, I would have made a very different choice.

"We'll drop you off at a vacation rental nearby. You'll hang out for a few days and then when everything is safe, you'll come home," Marigold says, looking pleased with herself.

"I'll be staying to give you back up, and keep you out of trouble," Cedar grumbles.

I reach over and squeeze his hand. "Thank you, Cedar."

Onyx kisses my forehead, and I fold my arms in until I am cocooned in his embrace. Everything has fallen apart, but somehow I'm more than alright. Alone, I had no chance of helping my pack and my mother. With Onyx and my friends, maybe there's a chance.

ONYX

The rental is a brick house at the end of a small neighborhood two towns over. Being ninety minutes away from everything makes me nervous, but it's worth it for the safety. Granite Ridge will never find her here.

Jasper's sleek, black vehicle pulls into the driveway and we climb out. Now I have her, all of the stress from the last few days dissolves, leaving me exhausted and a bit sore from wounds still healing. Sable said I had several fractures in addition to a nasty concussion, but shifters heal quickly and she helped it along with her salves and tonics. My bag in the trunk holds several of her concoctions. I wasn't sure Ember would be okay when we found her.

Jasper inputs the door code and we step into a silent house. I note the security camera at the door. What must the owner think, seeing five young adults arriving together, two of us limping in and clinging to each other like they just survived the apocalypse? At least we left our weapons in the car.

"We can't stay long, but I'm going to order some groceries and make sure you're all set for a while. Better to be safe than sorry." Marigold disappears into the kitchen.

Cedar and Jasper explore the other two bedrooms and hall bathroom. I open the interior door to the garage through the laundry room, revealing a ping pong table and a set of bicycles. Maybe our stay here won't be too bad. Frankly, it wouldn't matter if the house was completely devoid of entertainment. I have Ember back.

She brushes against me, peeking out. "Oh, don't tell me you love ping pong," she says, scowling at me playfully.

"It could be fun," I say, wrapping my arms over her shoulders in a hug. "We could try making it strip ping pong."

"Or not," Cedar yells from the hall.

Ember's nose wrinkles as she laughs silently.

"He's going to be a total cock-block isn't he?" I mutter, leaning down to kiss her.

"As much as I can't wait to test that theory, it's been a rough few days and I'm not feeling my best," Ember murmurs, allowing me to support her weight.

My instincts to protect roar to life, and I lift her up, one arm under her knees in a bridal hold.

"That's overkill. I just need a nap and some real food," she says against my shirt. But she nuzzles down against my chest and allows me to carry her to the master bedroom. Cedar will be fine in the kids room.

Gently, I lay her out across the bed and pull a coverlet over her.

"I'll rest here a bit, but I really am hungry," she says, a yawn breaking her words in half.

Food, provide, protect.

Marigold sits on the kitchen counter with her phone in her hand.

"I've almost got the grocery order done and it'll be here in an hour. I'm glad they have delivery. One of the benefits of a bigger town, I guess." She looks up and smiles at me. "You look happy," she notes.

"Yeah," I say. "Everything's going to be fine now."

They had to tolerate my incessant worries over the last few days as we put together a plan, negotiated with Zephyr to help, and I healed from the beating I took.

"Thank you, Goldie," I say quietly.

She slides off the counter and pats my arm fondly. "She's your mate, so she's family." My stomach swoops at hearing her called my mate. It's not official, not yet, but I love the sound of it. "Hazel is probably going crazy right now. We'd better text her."

The Alphas had to stay behind. They couldn't be involved in our smash and grab plan. And despite his grumpiness, Slate was supportive. Somewhere along the line, Ember won him over, or he knew Hazel would strangle him if he didn't help get her back.

"I even got you s'mores supplies," Marigold says with a wink before walking into the living room where Jasper sits perched on the edge of the sofa, texting on his phone.

"Oh, here," Jasper says, pulling Ember's phone from his pocket and tossing it to me.

"Thanks," I say, tucking it away for later. Right now, I need to secure sustenance for my girl.

There isn't much in the house, just a few basics the host was kind enough to stock, and a few random items previous guests had left. I find a box of crackers in the pantry that weren't expired and didn't seem too stale. It's better than nothing and I'm not about to leave her to go pick something up, not when food will show up on our doorstep in fifty minutes.

Clutching my box of crackers in front of me like I had gone out and hunted wild game for my beloved, I stride back into the bedroom.

Ember is sleeping peacefully. She's thinner than she was before. I hate the dark circles under her eyes and the hollowness of her cheeks. She's still beautiful and always will be, but the signs of her mistreatment make my stomach clench.

Setting the box on the side table, I stretch out beside her and tug the blanket over my own chest too. She lets out a tiny noise and turns in her sleep until she's tucked up against my chest.

A short nap won't hurt. Especially right now when Jasper and Marigold are here too. With her in my arms, it's all too easy to drift off.

"Dinner," Marigold calls, waking us. Ember startles in my arms, looking around wildly. I run my hand down her arm, soothing her until she locks eyes with me and relaxes.

"It's okay," I murmur. She lets out her breath slowly, her brows furrowing. "Come on, I know you're hungry."

"Yes, please," she says, climbing off the bed and rolling her shoulders.

Marigold, Jasper, and Cedar sit at the little kitchen table. Cedar is perched on a stool because there are only four chairs. Ember presses her lips into a thin line as she picks up a plate from the counter and slides into her seat.

She devours two grilled cheese sandwiches before she slows down. Marigold happily piles more tater tots and carrots onto everyone's plates. She must have used an entire loaf of bread to make enough sandwiches for five shifters.

"There's lots of easy-to-make frozen stuff in the fridge, like chicken tenders and lasagna. You guys should be fine," she says.

"Thank you," Ember says.

"Of course!" Marigold chirps, beaming at her.

Ember sets a tater tot back down. "So what did I miss while I was gone?" Her eyes meet mine, wide with guilt.

"I made it home and they patched me up," I say gently.

"He was yelling about going back for you pretty much the entire time," Cedar adds.

"We had to convince him a little strategy was needed," Jasper explains.

"Yes, because rushing in worked out so well the first time," Ember quips, her hand slapping over her mouth when she realizes what she said.

I chuckle. "No, you're right."

"I'm so sorry," she says, "I can't believe they hurt you like that."

"Not the worst beating I've had," I say with a shrug.

Cedar washes the dishes while Ember cuddles up to me on the sofa. Marigold and Jasper sit opposite us, hands linked over the side table. Jasper's thumb rubs circles over Marigold's wrist absently.

"Anything you can tell us would be helpful," Jasper says, pulling out his phone to take notes. "I don't think Sienna was being entirely honest with us and we don't know enough about Orion or the situation."

Ember pinches the bridge of her nose, gathering her resolve. Her bright hazel eyes move from me to Jasper. "It seems like most of the pack supports him. I don't know what he's been doing to win them over. Maybe they just respect his strength.

After everything with my father, Sienna definitely lost their favor. I didn't really pick up on it, but I've always-" She pauses.

"I know it's been hard," Jasper says softly. "Becoming Heir suddenly, trying to prove yourself especially when the pack is in so much turmoil."

"Guess what, I'm not Heir anymore," she says, her voice a little too high. My hand goes to her thigh. She's not in this alone.

"So everyone seems to like him?" Jasper asks.

Ember nods, sinking her teeth into her lush bottom lip. It takes her two tries to speak again, as if she's scared of what she's going to say.

"I don't think he desires me. He wants me as his mate to solidify his position as Alpha. So there has to be some dissent. But I honestly couldn't tell you who or how much."

My hold on her thigh tightens, and I have to flex my hand open before I hurt her. The reminder that he is demanding she become his mate heats my blood. I'm so ready to hurt this dipshit.

Sending my anger, she takes my hand and draws it to her mouth, pressing a sweet kiss to my knuckles. It feels so natural, like nothing at all, even though it's everything to me. I'm crazy about this woman.

"We can use that," Jasper says, leaning back in his seat. "I noticed a handful of wolves that seemed unhappy with him becoming second to Sienna. We might have a few allies."

"Why?" Ember asks. "Your pack won't want to interfere."

"You know just as well as I do that Orion's wolves will want war. Better to face them now than wait until they're stronger and prepared."

"Are you serious?" Ember says, her lips parted in surprise.

"Orion can't stay in power. We worked too hard to become allies with your pack again. Zephyr agrees, as Cashel. We just have to find the right way to do it," I say.

"I didn't realize." Ember breaks off her words with a yawn.

"It's getting late. We should head back, babe," Marigold says. "We can go back over our notes and make a list."

Jasper nods absently, still lost in his own head.

Jasper and Marigold both hug Ember and she squeezes them back. My heart is full.

Cedar retreats to the secondary bedroom until it's only Ember and I standing in the little living room.

"How are you doing there?" I ask softly.

She lets me wrap her in my arms, her chin tucking to her chest as she leans into me. "I can't believe I'm here. I thought it was over. Seriously, I had lost hope."

"No," I murmur, gathering her up.

"You almost died."

"Nah, it would take way more than that to take me out. Remember, you even tried to kill me and it didn't stick. They didn't stand a chance."

"Onyx," she says sharply, and I drop my playful smile. "I can't go through that again. Seeing you unconscious and bleeding. It was the worst moment of my life."

"Hey, hey, it's okay. It looked worse than it was." She probably knows I'm lying, but I don't know what else to say to make it better. It wasn't a great moment for me, and I definitely thought I wasn't going to make it out of there alive.

"Don't ever-" she starts to say.

"Come for you?" I interject. "Try to save you? Follow you?"

She scowls at me and pushes away, but I keep a hold of her waist so she can't move far.

"I'd go through all of it again for you." Her eyes widen and her mouth opens to argue. "It wouldn't be my first choice. If I could help you by taking a little vacation or maybe save you by getting a massage, that would be much nicer."

Gurgling laughter bursts out of her, and she wipes at her tears with the back of her hand.

"But don't think for a second I wouldn't do absolutely anything necessary to protect you." My voice drops, threatening all kinds of dark things.

"I'd do the same for you," she whispers. "In fact, I'm already planning several scenarios that involve torture for the men who hurt you."

"There's my beautiful, bloodthirsty girl," I say before lowering my head to kiss her. She tangles her fingers in my shirt, kissing back with the ferocity I love in her. We break apart just long enough for her to pull my shirt over my head.

She shoves me backward and we stumble toward the master bedroom. Finally, I have her alone in a proper bed, and this time she won't disappear in the night.

This isn't a distraction, it's devotion.

The door clicks shut and I press her back against it hard enough her emerald hair falls across her face. She lets out a low laugh. I tuck it behind her ear tenderly, running my fingers over the shell of her ear. She tips her head toward my touch.

"Be my mate," I say simply. No teasing, no speeches, just my heart laid out before her.

Her hand rests against my chest and her fingers tap while she picks her words. "I'm not a safe person to be with."

Grabbing her wrist, I move her hand to the scar across the bottom of my ribs. "I can take it. We already established that."

Her expression darkens. "I am going to reclaim my pack and be Alpha."

"Okay," I say immediately.

"Onyx," she says slowly, "it's what I have to do. And if you are my mate, you'd be Alpha too."

It's not a surprise. That's how it works for every pack. Yet, it hadn't crossed my mind that becoming Ember's mate would mean I became Alpha when she did. I've never wanted leadership or power.

Before, I thought she'd give up her position, but I know her better now. Looking into her determined gaze, I know she will make it happen. Nothing could stop her.

So do I want her still, if it means becoming an Alpha?

Yes.

Without a doubt.

"I'm sure Slate can give me a few pointers," I say, dipping my head to brush my lips against her cheek.

"Seriously, Onyx, I need you to be completely sure."

I fix her with an unflinching stare. "Yes. I will be your partner and mate, even if it means learning to be an Alpha."

Her eyebrows shoot up, her gaze softening and mouth parting. "Really?"

"I'll be your trophy mate," I say with a snicker. "Every strong Alpha needs someone pretty on their arm."

She slaps my chest, but her smile widens, her dimple visible. "I'm trusting that you are completely sure. Because I can't have you hold me back from my position."

"Ember, I would never hold you back."

"Okay," she says. When I don't react, she repeats, "Okay, I'll be your mate."

Her words don't sink in. Did she just accept? Is this happening?

"Onyx, did I break you?" she asks, tilting her head and pursing her lips.

"Wow," I say, "I thought I would have to beg for at least a week before you gave in."

"Are we going to make this official?" she asks, a nervous edge to her voice.

"I want to mark you and you mark me. But it can wait until you're ready," I say, my hands brushing down her ribs and waist before moving to her hands. Clasping both of her hands in mine, I pull them above her head, like when we first kissed.

"No, I don't want to wait. We should face this together, as mates in every way. And then my pack can't question you or treat you like that again."

"Like you'd let them get away with that," I murmur, admiring the way she's stretched out. Her back arches, her head tipping back against the door.

"Are you ready to become a Granite Ridge wolf?" she asks softly, as if that revelation would change my mind.

"I guess we will have dual citizenship, because it goes both ways, my little hummingbird." My words are nonsense, but I can't help but poke fun.

"Mmm, I like that idea. When I claim my position, I'll need help from your pack to clean house and rebuild the pack's structure. Make it healthy."

"Jasper will be thrilled," I say.

"Stop talking about my brother," she teases. "Stop talking about everything. I need to make you my mate like I need air."

"Yes, Alpha," I say a split second before our lips crash together.

XVII
SMOKING S'MORES
EMBER

There's no more talking. Everything that needed to be said was said. Every worry I had laid out, and Onyx soothed all of them. He's willing to give up his life for me. Together we will rebuild my pack until it's a wonderful place to live. But thoughts of planning and strategy will have to wait, because Onyx is undressing me.

He tosses my shirt over his shoulder and reclaims my wrists in his left hand, keeping me upright against the cool wood of the bedroom door.

I struggle against his hold, wanting to touch him, but he grins and resumes kissing me. The world falls away as he coaxes my mouth open. The feel of his tongue against mine sends heat flooding my body, flowing from my fingertips to my toes and gathering low in my stomach.

This man makes kissing an artform. The slow brush of our lips, the way his teeth nip at my skin as he moves down my throat and lowers his mouth to my breasts. No amount of twisting deters him. His hand only tightens and pushes my wrists up, until I'm desperate, drawn out and panting.

His head comes back up, a wicked grin on his face. "I'm going to bite you," he says, "Right here." He gives a demonstration, fangs pressing into the crook of my neck hard enough to sting but not break the skin. This time, I'm confident I want it, and I let out a whimper at the sting.

"I want to claim you, too," I say, my words breathy. I gasp as he bites a second time, this one harder, as if he is testing the limit. "Do it," I say.

He lets out a low laugh. "Not yet. You didn't think I'd go this easy on you?"

I'm not sure if I'm about to melt or burst into flames, but it's becoming unbearable. As if sensing my impending implosion, he finally releases my wrists.

It's all the urging I need. I launch myself at him and he grabs my waist, hoisting me up until I'm wrapped around him, my hands threading into his hair. Biting his bottom lip, I drag my nails along his scalp, earning a groan that makes my stomach flip.

He inches backward until we're falling onto the bed, his arms banded tight around me. My hair splays around us, enclosing his face, nose to nose with mine.

"I love you," I murmur.

"I've loved you for longer," he responds with a smirk.

"It's not a competition."

"No, 'cause I'd be winning."

I silence him by biting his neck, not low like a claiming, but high on his throat. He growls at the pain and pleasure as I suck at his skin. "I love when you're rough with me," he admits. A shiver runs down my spine.

Electricity buzzing under my skin, I push away until I have room to pull my leggings off. Onyx sheds his own pants and boxers and then helps me tug my leggings over my ankles. He nips at my ankle hard enough to leave a mark, and as I pull back, he hooks a finger into the edge of my panties and draws them down my hip, kissing the side of my thigh as he removes them entirely.

I watch his progress until my gaze strays to his naked body. My breathing goes ragged. He doesn't stop me or protest as I close my hand over his cock and slowly stroke down.

His eyes close, a look of ecstasy on his face. I stroke up and then back down harder, watching his reaction. He lets out a growl, his eyes opening, glowing a brilliant sapphire. "If you keep doing that, we'll miss out on other *more important* activities."

My hand withdraws, a flush burning from my cheeks to my neck.

"Fuck, that felt good," he rasps, crawling over me. I lay back, running my hands over the corded muscles in his arms, from his biceps down his forearms.

His mouth goes to my breasts for a short moment before he licks the curve of my stomach. I'm proud of my curves, but I still squirm under him. His fingers sink into the soft skin of my ass and hips, holding me still as he swirls his tongue over my clit. My vision goes white. He repeats the move until I can't remember my own name. Every muscle tenses, my back arching.

"Holy hell," I say, my voice trembling.

"You look magnificent," he whispered as he moves up my body and reaches between us. His cock nudges my entrance, ready for him. Slowly, gently, he pushes in with shallow thrusts, each one slightly deeper until he fills me entirely. My mouth falls open in a silent scream at the feeling of fullness.

"Even better than I imagined," he murmurs, the words almost inaudible, as if his thoughts are escaping without him realizing.

As he resumes moving, tenderly, attentively. My thighs close over his hips, pressing against him as my head turns sideways and my eyes squeeze shut to block out everything but the feel of him inside of me.

He picks up speed, growing confident at my soft moans as he strokes against my inner walls, sending sparks through my body. I'm so sensitive, and that burning pleasure intensifies.

My hands scramble for a grip on anything stable, my fingers curling around the bottom edge of the wooden headboard. He groans louder. "I'm not going to last long, you feel too good," he warns, the words broken and slurred.

Feeling my own orgasm looming again, I force my eyes open. His throat is bared to me as he moves against me. I want to kiss, bite, and mark him so bad it takes my breath away.

Releasing the headboard, I reach for him. His pace slows as he lets me pull him closer. Kissing down his neck, I find that juncture with his shoulder where the tendon is taut. It's tempting, and I lick across the skin. His inhale is audible, encouraging me.

He's mine, and I'm claiming him.

My sharp teeth close over his skin, tightening until the skin breaks in a dozen tiny wounds. His blood hits over my tongue and the magic hits me.

Adoration, arousal, and possessiveness fill every fiber of my being. I can't untangle his emotions from mine, and my nails dig into his shoulders as a whimper escapes me. Pleasure barrels over all of it, sweeping me up, and I don't know if it's mine or his.

His teeth cut into my skin, the pain nothing compared to the intense onslaught of feeling. It's as if every emotion is mirrored back, a reflection of a reflection until infinity.

I'm shaking, cursing, tears falling from the corners of my eyes into my hair. His forehead drops to my sternum as he sucks in deep lungfuls of air.

The emotion ebbs, until I can separate his feelings from mine. How does anyone adjust to this? He lifts his head and grins, and happiness soaks into me through our mate bond.

"This is crazy," I finally manage to say.

"Yeah," he replies, withdrawing and stretching out on the duvet cover beside me.

Reluctantly, I climb out of the bed and cross to the bathroom. After I clean up, he flips off the lights and tucks the covers around us.

"I can't believe we did that," I say with a laugh. "Everyone is going to freak when they find out."

Onyx brushes my hair back and nuzzles against the nape of my neck. He doesn't answer for a while, but then he says, "No one is going to be surprised."

"Will they be happy for you?" I ask tentatively.

Onyx chuckles. "They'll be thrilled for *us*." Affection bubbles up in my chest and this time it's mine. The hand draped across my waist tenses, and he drags me flush against him. He must have felt the warm fuzzy feelings reflected through our bond.

In the darkness with my mate holding me, I've never felt so safe. For once, I don't fight sleep but let it overtake me. It's short-lived, because my mate wakes me after a time, and we come together again before falling into a deeper sleep.

ONYX

A trail of smoke wafts from the oven when Ember cracks the door open. She lets out the cutest little squeak and scrambles for oven mitts.

"Everything going okay over there?" I ask, restraining myself from jumping up to help.

"Shush, it's fine."

Propping my chin on my fist, I suppress a smile. She insisted on making a surprise for us and wouldn't even let me see the ingredients. Teeth biting her bottom lip, she lifts a glass casserole dish out of the oven. The top is golden brown, not blackened, but smoke trails off of it anyway.

"Did you burn something?" Cedar asks, leaning against the doorway with his arms crossed. After three days stuck in a house with us, he is as grumpy as we predicted.

"Not you too!" Ember grumbles. Glass clinks as she dishes up her creation. She spins with a plate in each hand, a bashful smile lighting up her gorgeous features.

"What is it?" Cedar asks.

"S'mores!" she says.

Melted golden marshmallow flows over graham crackers on the dish I accept from my mate. She sinks down beside me and blows on her serving.

"I know you aren't super familiar with them, but that's not really how s'mores are supposed to be made," I tease.

She narrows her eyes in a playful glare. "Well, we don't exactly have a proper fire, and you said microwave s'mores aren't acceptable. So here we are."

Indulging my feisty mate, I pick up the graham cracker and take a bite. The top layer crunches beautifully and chocolate oozes out from under the marshmallow.

"Actually, this is great," I mumble between sticky bites.

"Are you just being nice?" she asks, eyeing her own s'more like it might poison her.

"No, seriously. Cedar, get one, you'll love it."

As Ember takes a tiny, testing bite, she lets out a little moan that has me thinking of carrying her out of the kitchen, but there's plenty of time for that later.

Cedar loads up two on his own plate and sits opposite us. "Any word from Jasper?" he asks.

"Nothing today," Ember answers glumly.

"What about from your mom?" he asks.

Ember licks sugar from her fingertips before answering. "She has been making all kinds of new friends over in Ironcrest. I'm a little afraid Zephyr will be my new step-dad." She looks slightly green at the idea, and I have to agree.

"I doubt it," my brother answers with a shrug.

"So what if they don't find a solution?" Ember asks, not for the first time. Through our mate bond, I feel her spike in anxiety. My hand brushes up her forearm. I love the way her emotions settle under my touch.

Instead of offering platitudes about trusting Slate and Jasper, Cedar fidgets with his fork. "I think we all know someone is going to have to challenge Orion for Alpha. I know you guys want to find another solution, but short of invading and taking over the pack, I don't see any other viable option."

I could punch him. Ember's heart starts to beat wildly and her emotions rollercoaster through fear, worry, and anger so quickly my head is spinning.

"Well, fuck," I mutter. "That's exactly what Jasper said not to do."

Ember grabs my hand, her nails pressing into my skin. "Onyx…" she says, seemingly unable to finish her sentence.

'It's okay," I say quietly, wishing my brother would leave. Or at least shut his mouth.

"We know he's right," she finally says, tipping her chin up as she regains her composure. I'm so proud of her. Despite being terrified, she's ready to face the wolf who beat her in a challenge just a few days ago.

I won't let that happen again.

"We don't know that," I argue.

"How long do we wait for another solution, then?" Ember says, barely above a whisper.

"Realistically, you have time. Things can't get that much worse in Granite Ridge in the next week or two," Cedar interjects with another shrug.

"See, we can give it time," I say, threading my fingers through hers and flipping her hand over.

She sighs. "If there was another solution, they would have found it by now."

"Fine. I'll challenge him for Alpha. I'm the mate of the pack's rightful Heir. He can't deny me."

"No!" Ember blurts. "I can't let you do that. What if he hurts you worse?"

I scowl at her. "I resent that. It took three of them and a set of handcuffs to take me down last time."

Cedar's mouth presses into a line, but he doesn't say anything.

"I'll do it," she says.

"No," I say, fisting my hand on the table.

"It's our only option," she argues.

"I can take him."

My brother lets out a dramatic sigh. "I'm not sure either of you can take him on your own, unless you find some advantage over him."

Ember taps her index finger on the table, her nail making a hollow clicking noise. Her lips purse to the side, looking adorable while she contemplates taking over a pack.

"Let's say we can find a way to defeat him in a challenge," Ember turns to me, reluctance written all over her face. "But would they respect us? Even if we beat him - what if they all just followed him anyways?"

"They'll follow you. Especially if Jasper supports your claim."

That's one thing I'm sure of. She is Ferris's daughter, so even if the pack has turned on Sienna, they have to bow to Ember if she claims her birthright.

"Not everyone will," Ember says.

"And those are the ones we have to get rid of. We already knew we had to clean house if we wanted to build a healthy pack. This way, we can cut out the worst of them right from the start."

Cedar stands and clears his throat. "I suggest you call Jasper."

Ember's gaze is distant as she turns over scenarios in her head, but her emotions remain calm with a touch of something warm swirling in our bond. Hope?

"I love when you're plotting," I say, pulling her hand to my mouth. Gingerly, I place a kiss over her wrist.

She bites her lip again. "I still don't like the idea of you fighting Orion."

My jovial mood falls away. "He dared to put his hands on you. And he tried to take you from me. I'm going to kill him."

She smiles as if I didn't just threaten murder. Challenges aren't supposed to be to the death, but it seems deserved in this case.

"As much as I'd like to see that, I think it needs to be me. I want to prove myself. And the pack won't respect me if you just swoop in and save the day."

"Don't let him land a hit on you or I'll go fucking crazy," I threaten, my voice lowering dangerously.

Her eyes are lit with a faint glow, her smile feral.

I love when she is sweet and nurturing, but I also love when she's feisty and demanding. I love every side of my beautiful mate.

"Are we really going to do this?" she asks, her cheeks flushing.

"We don't exactly have any other ideas. And I think it could work. But Cedar's right, we don't stand a chance unless we have some sort of strategy."

"Then we better figure it out." she murmurs, her eyes dropping to my mouth.

We can figure it out right after I take her back to our bedroom.

"You two are gross," Cedar mutters, dropping his plate in the sink. Shaking his head, he strides out.

"Poor guy," I say, leaning forward until I can kiss her cheek.

"He'll be fine." She wrinkles her nose as I nibble at her ear.

"But we better go back to our room instead of defiling the kitchen." Her giggles soothe my worries as I brush her hair off her shoulder to kiss over the pale scars that mark her as mine.

XVIII

BUBBLE BATHS & EX-BOYFRIENDS

EMBER

"Mom?" I ask, crossing my legs under me as I sit on the bed.

Her voice sounds distant, maybe irritated. "Ember, what do you need?" she says sharply.

"Um, how are you doing?"

"I'm fine." She sighs audibly, bringing a flush of embarrassment to my skin.

My hands curl into fists. "Last time I saw you, you were unconscious and looking half-dead."

"I'm sorry you had to see that. You don't need to worry about me." Her words are clipped. I can almost picture her picking at her nails in this moment, as if I am the least interesting part of her day.

"Okay," I say, trying to keep the sarcasm from my tone.

"Jasper tells me you're staying away... with that boy," she says, her casual tone anything but kind.

"Onyx," I snap. "His name is Onyx."

"What are you thinking, running around with him?" We've moved from dismissive to reprimanding, and things are about to get so much worse.

My shoulders tense, the anxiety spiraling through my body. "He's my mate."

"Please tell me you didn't."

"I love him and it's done," I blurt, recklessly adding, "I don't need your approval."

"And you don't have it." She's not angry. I'm not worth her anger, just her half-hearted disdain. But after everything I went through trying to help her and my pack, I'm not accepting it.

"Orion locked me up after I refused to be his mate," I hiss, a cold sweat prickling across my skin. I'd give anything to be less emotional - it's like I'm fighting my own reactions as much as I'm fighting her.

Her next words cut deep. "That would have been wiser than that boy."

How can she say that? "He almost killed you," I say dumbly. "Onyx has done nothing but protect and support me."

She huffs. Clearly that's not good enough in her eyes.

"Orion would have *used* me, and he's way old. He would have treated me horribly."

"Possibly," she admits, like it's an interesting possibility.

"How are you not concerned about that?" My question slips out, and to my surprise, she answers it.

"You are safest when you have power, Ember. And if I can't protect you, you need to find someone who can. Since you've chosen a mate who has no notable ranking, you've given away any future position you could have had. So I suppose it's best you stay away and not come back."

"I can stay with his pack and Jasper," I point out, the idea tempting me.

"If you like," she murmurs, distracted again.

"Actually, that's why I'm calling." I clear my throat, needing to recapture her attention.

"Yes?" she asks wearily.

"I'm going to retake the pack."

There. It's out there.

Silence rings through the line. Finally, she asks, "How on earth do you intend to do that?"

"I'm going to challenge Orion."

"You can't do that." She sounds horrified, her pitch jumping.

"I'm pretty sure I can," I say, taking a slow breath to steady myself. We don't need her approval.

"Ember, you will not win. You and your little mate will be slaughtered." She finally sounds worried.

"Geez, thanks for the confidence, Mom."

"I know you don't think I love you, but I have only ever wanted you safe," she says, acting like the concerned mother she isn't. It's too much. I want to scream at her.

"You didn't give a shit about me until Jasper left and you were stuck with me as your Heir." My words shake.

"That's not true."

"Look, I didn't need to tell you any of this." I say, the sting of her rejection turning my words bitter. "I don't know why I thought you'd support me."

"I support you making wise decisions," she argues. I cut her off.

"You support me doing what you want me to do. Regardless of how it hurts me. Consider this a courtesy warning of what I'm going to do. If you want to help, like actually help me, you can talk to Jasper about it."

"There's nothing to discuss!" she says, her voice growing louder. I've finally cut through her facade. But now that I have her full attention, I want nothing more than to end this wretched call.

"Mom, I need to go."

"You aren't going anywhere," she snaps back.

I ignore her. "Be safe. I'll talk to you when it's over and we have our pack back."

"Ember!"

I hold the phone away from my ear as she says my name again, louder. My fingers tremble from the confrontation, but I press down the red button to hang up and let out a long, slow breath.

"That sounds like it went well," Onyx says from the doorway, a half-smile on his face. He's so damn handsome, even with sympathy in his eyes.

"Come here. I need a pick-me-up after all that."

It's too much to handle, and his hands on me transport me to a higher plane, where my mother's bullshit doesn't exist.

He leaps on the bed, an eager puppy. I welcome his arm across my chest, pushing me down into the mattress. My legs unfold and my hair fans out around my head.

"You're so beautiful," he murmurs, lowering his face and trailing his lips across my forehead and down my nose.

"I don't know what I expected, but she just wants to control me." My fingers curl into his shirt in my frustration.

I love that he doesn't try to justify Sienna's behavior or argue with me. Sighing, I turn my head so he can nibble down my neck and run his tongue over my claim mark. He happily scrapes his teeth over the spot, forcing a soft groan out of me.

He pops up, a grin on his face. "It doesn't matter. You don't need her. She's not the Alpha anymore. You're about to be."

Before I can protest, he brushes his lips against mine and then presses firmly, encouraging my mouth to open. All my worries fall away as he kisses me, as fervently as the first time.

A contentedness settles over me, and I happily scratch my nails down his chest, hoping to leave red lines under his thin shirt. He grumbles, nipping down on my bottom lip.

I want nothing more than to slip out of our clothes and ravage each other until he's whispering my name like a prayer, but there's too much to be done and I'll be brainless for an hour afterward if we do that.

"As nice as this is," I say, hating every word, "I have one more call to make, unfortunately."

His hands knead over my shoulders, squeezing down my arm. "Want me to leave?

"Fuck, no," I say, closing my eyes and straining my neck at the pinching pleasure he's inflicting on my tendons. With one more kiss his hands drop away, leaving me desperate for more.

"Let's get it over with. I have a list of things I want to try with you, and it'll be really hard for you to make any calls while I do them," he whispers against my skin.

"You're not going to like this one."

"Why?"

Hawk picks up the phone after the fifth ring, when I'm about to give up and end the call. My stomach jumps into my throat and I lean harder into Onyx. The warmth of his chest feels good against my side, banishing the shivers of anxiety.

"Ember? Is everything okay?" His voice sounds odd, unfamiliar. It's been months since I spoke with him, but he feels like a stranger.

"Hi, Hawk." My voice falters, and I feel Onyx's hand tighten on my waist. "Well, not really. That's why I'm calling."

I should have called him months ago, to try and reconcile politically, even if we would never be mates. We could use his support right about now, but I doubt his family will give it.

"What's wrong?" His voice is sharp.

"Orion."

"What?" His voice lowers, sounding angry, as if he already knows what's wrong with that one word.

"He challenged my mom and took over the pack," I admit, praying he will help and that I'm right in trusting him.

"Oh, shit."

"Yeah."

"Sweetheart, I'm so sorry," he says. I prickle at his pet name for me. There was never any affection behind it and I know that now.

"Hi, Hawk." Onyx butts in, unable to help himself. He leans his cheek against my fingers gripping the phone, making sure his voice is heard. I press my lips together to keep from laughing at him.

"Uh, hi? Who is that?" Hawk sounds baffled. With a sigh, I press the button for speaker phone.

"It's Onyx, remember me?" My mate puts on a friendly tone, like he's reconnecting with an old friend.

"Sorry, no."

"I'm the one Ember stabbed during the battle at Bracken Creek."

Hawk coughs. "Oh, I don't think I saw that."

"Whatever, it doesn't matter. But I'm Ember's mate," Onyx continues, the words tumbling out. My mouth falls open and he gives me a wink.

Hawk takes a beat to process and when he speaks again, his tone is formal, as if he knows more distance is needed. I'm not his to protect.

"Congratulations. I hope you two are really happy."

"Thank you, I hope you're happy too," I say sincerely. " But I was hoping you could help me with the Orion problem. I need to challenge him and get my pack back."

"Ember, are you sure about that?" I can picture Hawk's face and the way he would raise a single eyebrow. No doubt he is making the same expression now.

"Yes."

"How can I help?"

"Tell me anything you can about Orion. We don't know much about his weaknesses. Anything that could help. Please."

"Of course. Let me think," he says, trailing off.

"I really appreciate it," I say, closing my eyes as Onyx trails his hand down my hip and thigh.

"He always liked it if he could manipulate people into doing what he wants, and honestly, he's always been cruel," Hawk says.

"That tracks with how he's behaving now," Onyx replies.

"But he's charming when he wants to be."

"We've seen that. Thanks." Onyx's words are edged with sarcasm. "Why the fuck did you bring this guy along with you?"

"Sorry, I know this doesn't help, but I do know my Dad sent Orion with money to buy gifts to win people over. I guess he's used that to his own advantage."

The idea of this powerful Alpha miles and miles north of our territory who may or may not support our enemy layers more fear on top of my undercurrent of anxiety. But we have to focus on the enemy in front of us, so I push it out of my mind.

"What are his weaknesses?" Onyx cuts in.

"His ego," Hawk says without hesitation.

"Can you think of anything else?" I ask.

"Let me talk to my sister and I'll get back to you."

"Thank you," I say, feeling less optimistic than before.

"I'm glad you've got someone who loves you," he says quickly. My eyes flick to Onyx, and he's already watching me with an intensity that sets my body aflame.

"Yeah, he's pretty great," I say with a smile.

"Good. Take care of her, man."

"I am," Onyx says, hanging up without looking at the phone. Gently, he rolls me onto my back. "That went better than the first call, right?"

"Yeah," I have to agree.

"See? Things are already looking up." I need his optimism right now. My mother's negativity rattled me more than I'd like to admit.

My mate's hair tickles my jaw as he kisses down my throat. When this situation becomes too much to handle, he's the perfect escape. It's easy to lose myself in his touch while his citrus scene fills my lungs.

With scattered kisses, he pulls my shirt off. I return the favor, forcing him to stop kissing me long enough to pull it over his head. The second it hits the floor, he jumps up to lock the door before leaping back on the bed with a playful grin.

"Everything is going to work out," he says, framing me in with his arms as he hovers over me. Instead of answering, I pull him down and nuzzle into the crook of his neck.

"Think about the future when we have our own house, all to ourselves," he whispers. The picture is beautiful, and my heart jumps. His teeth nip over my claim mark. "I can't wait to show off this to everyone."

My fingers skim over the place I know his mark is, even if I can't see it while he overwhelms my senses. "You're so tense," he says. I don't feel that, not when he's turning me boneless.

With a sharp exhale, Onyx sits up. The cold air washing over my chest makes me scowl at him. "What?"

"You are too stressed," he says, his eyes roaming over me hungrily.

"Yeah, but we were..." I reach for him, but he holds up a hand to silence me.

"Wait, I've got it."

My breath comes out harsh as he climbs off the bed and walks away. What the hell? My irritation keeps me from following him, and instead I open my phone back up to see if anyone has texted me an update. There's nothing.

The sound of a faucet sounds from the bathroom. Cabinet doors clang as he does whatever he's doing. Exhaling slowly, I lay back and close my eyes.

"Okay, my love, it's time to relax," Onyx says. I jerk up and my phone drops my chest and bounces across the duvet. Ignoring it, he takes my hand and ushers me to the bathroom.

The garden tub is steaming with bubbles piled on top. "You made me a bath?" I ask stupidly.

"I found bubble bath under the sink," Onyx says, his grin crooked. "Do you like baths?"

"I don't really do them." My arms cross over my breasts, my shoulders hunching.

"You'll like this one, I promise." He could convince me of anything when he smirks like that. My annoyance falls away as his clever fingers pull my shorts off and then his own sweats. With a steady hand, he guides me into the tub and then steps after me.

"Oh, it's a two person bath?" I ask with a laugh.

"Yes, strict quality control. How else would I know you're enjoying yourself and destressing properly?"

"Good to know my mate is a bath connoisseur."

"I'm a lot of things."

"A man of mystery," I tease as my toes dip into the hot water. "Oh, that's nice." Pausing, I look up at him. "Do we need to get a hot tub?"

"Only if it's private," he says, his dark eyes promising pleasure as his hands guide me into the tub.

We settle into the water and the steam caresses me. My back rests against his chest, my head leaning back until my temple rests against his jaw.

It's a little strange, but as his hands brush over my skin under the water, I find myself calming. The lavender of the bubbles obscures his scent, so I turn my face against his neck and breathe him in. He lets out a rumbling chuckle, and impulsively my tongue darts out to taste his skin. His laugh turns to a groan.

"Oh, sorry, am I interrupting your special bath?" I ask, leaning back and giving him an innocent smile. "I better control myself."

Water sloshes as he dives for me, crashing our mouths together. Bubbles splatter on my face and neck, his wet hands digging into my hair to keep me where he wants me.

Feeling victorious, I drag my nails down his soapy back. "So much for a relaxing bath," I hum.

"Damn, you're so…" he pauses, his teeth closing over my lip. My hips buck, pressing against him. "Slippery." It's my turn to tip my head back and laugh.

"I don't think we can do what we want in here," I say, breathless. "Maybe we relocate?"

"Not yet." Onyx's answer is a growl as he slides me back against his chest. I open my mouth to argue, but he silences me with fingers reaching between my thighs.

"Is this normal procedure for a bath?" I ask him, my teasing sounding desperate as he starts to explore my body.

He bites my shoulder firmly for a few seconds and says, "Time to stop talking." As if he knows I'll argue again, his other hand goes to my breast while he continues to rub soft circles against my clit.

There's no way I could speak again if I wanted to. An embarrassing moan escapes me. My body burns, the hot water intensifying it until I'm gasping and gripping the edge of the tub.

I want to reach for him and give him some of the attention he's lavishing on me, but I can hardly control my limbs. My knees fall open, giving him as much access as possible.

His free hand moves from my breasts up to my throat. My breathing hitches as he collars my neck, gripping softly without squeezing.

Whimpering pathetically, I surrender to his control. His thumb swipes down the column of my throat while he gently strokes my core. I'm lost in each movement, the waves of pleasure of his touch rising until I'm gasping and shivering. My back arches and I press my head back against him, my vision dancing with stars. My mate's soft voice murmurs against my ear. "You're so perfect. I fucking love you."

I've barely come down when he scoops me up and sets me on the edge of the tub. My mate dries me off and then dries himself with rough drags of the towel. I bite my lip as I watch his muscles flex while he contorts to dry his back.

"Enjoying the show?" he asks.

"It's okay, I guess," I quip back. With a playful snarl, he hauls me against his chest and walks us back to the bed.

Still blissed out from his ministrations in the tub, I stretch out and grin at him. "I believe I was promised an entire list of things done to me."

Onyx's wolfish grin rekindles my lust. "You sure you're up for that?"

I've barely nodded when he lifts my hips and lines us up. Our bodies fit together so perfectly, and I find myself murmuring how much I love him while he's buried inside of me. Murmurs turn to gasps and moans as we try new positions and angles. I'd like nothing more than to hide away with him for the next month. But after we're both spent, I know we have to face all the unspoken worries.

But for a moment, we rest quietly. Onyx brushes my hair back so he can press kisses along the curve of my ear. His arm loops over my waist, his chest against my back, our legs folded together.

"Is there any chance I can convince you to let me be the one to fight Orion?" he asks softly.

I wish I could say yes. It would be so nice to let him face this for me. There's plenty of good reasons to agree. But I just can't.

"Sorry, I've got to do this myself."

His breath ghosts over my neck. "Alright," he says with a sigh. I can sense how worried he is through our bond, and I love him for respecting my choice.

Turning in his arms, I face him. His stormy eyes are full of conflict, and I can't help but brush his hair back and run my hand down his striking face.

"I've got this. With you backing me up, I know we can win."

Perhaps he can tell I'm lying, but regardless, he kisses the tip of my nose and nuzzles down into his pillow.

"I don't think we have time for a nap before dinner," I say with a chuckle.

His answer is a rough tug on my hips to drag my closer. I almost miss his response, mumbled into his pillow. "Just let me hold you, for a while." Feeling treasured, I comply.

ONYX

Jasper and Marigold fetch us the next day.

Cedar answers the door, and Marigold greets him loud enough we can hear her clearly in our bedroom. Ember tucks the last few items we have into a backpack.

"Ready?"

She eyes my extended hand. I wiggle my fingers, trying to make her smile. With a deep breath, she squares her shoulders and threads her fingers through mine.

Jasper and Marigold stand in the living room, talking quietly with Cedar about pack updates. The second we come into view, Marigold lets out a gasp.

"Hey, guys," Ember says, her iron grip on my hand betraying her nervousness.

"You're mated!" she squeals, flinging her arms around Ember in a violent hug that pulls her away from me.

Ember's eyes widen and anxiety bleeds through our bond. "Careful, Goldie," I say with a chuckle, prying Marigold off my mate. She transfers to me, nonsensical words of happiness tumbling out of her as she squeezes me.

Jasper hugs his sister next and congratulates her softly while I work on extracting myself from Marigold's hold. She spins toward my twin.

"How could you not tell us?" Marigold swats at Cedar and he raises his hands defensively.

"It was bad enough being here at the time. They're not the most quiet pair," Cedar grumbles, his ears turning a red that matches the blush spreading across Ember's cheeks.

Her embarrassment burns through our mate bond, butting up against my own pride at showing off my beautiful mate. "It's okay," I whisper, landing a kiss on her cheek.

"Yeah, I know," she murmurs.

Clearing my throat, I regain the room's attention. "As much fun as this is, we need to get the show on the road."

We only have a few bags with us, so it's easy to load up Jasper's trunk and pile into the sporty vehicle. A moment later, we're pulling onto the road.

Ember leans against me in the back seat, anxiously swirling her thumb in circles around my knuckles. Cedar sits on the other side, staring out the window.

"So before we get into our plan," Ember says, taking the lead, "do you guys have any updates to share? Any new ideas?"

Jasper's pale hair shakes. "Sorry, no. Slate and Hazel haven't been able to find any common ground with Sienna or Zephyr."

"I don't think there's much they can do to help," she says. "We are going to have to handle this ourselves."

Marigold twists around, a line between her brows as she frowns at us. "What are you thinking?"

"I'm going to challenge Orion."

"Ember!" Marigold snaps, eyes going wide. "Do you think that's a good idea?" Jasper's knuckles are white across the steering wheel.

"I'm not going in unprepared. We need something to even the playing field, which is why I asked to come back to Bracken Creek."

That's my feisty girl, standing up for herself while being mysterious and irresistible. I hide my smirk in her hair by nuzzling against her neck.

"Oh, and Jasper?" she asks. "Can we borrow your car? I want to make a good impression when we go back. You can sit in the back seat and let Onyx drive, if you don't mind."

She's incredible. I don't even attempt to hide my grin as I peek at Jasper's reaction. His mouth thins and his jaw ticks. After a moment, he answers. "If it'll help, that's fine."

A small smile curves Ember's mouth and she meets my gaze in the rear view mirror.

Pulling into the gravel lot, we are greeted by several pack members. Cedar unfolds himself and heads straight to our parents. Ember moves to follow him out of the back seat, but I hold tight.

"What?" she whispers.

Reaching up, I tug the neckline of her shirt slightly askew, revealing the circle of tiny, pale scars. "I want everyone to see that you're mine."

"You're ridiculous," she says, rolling her eyes, but I can feel through our bond that she likes it.

Once I've retrieved our bags, I hold them both with one hand, keeping the other free to hold Ember's hand. No one will doubt our relationship. I don't want anyone to question or disrespect her.

My mother hugs Ember tightly, and tears glitter in her eyes as she steps back, holding Ember's shoulders firmly. "I'm so glad you are back. I missed you, dear. And now I get to keep you."

"Mom, I'm sorry, but it's just a quick visit. We have a situation to handle in Ember's pack." She pales at my words.

"Can we go see the healer?" Ember asks quietly.

Slate and Hazel stand in our path. "Am I seeing correctly?" Slate says.

"What are you seeing?" I tug Ember closer, squeezing her hand.

"You've claimed each other?" Hazel asks. A hopeful smile curves her mouth, though concern furrows her brows.

"Looks like it," I say with a smirk.

Slate opens and closes his mouth, emotions warring in his eyes.

It's Hazel who reaches out to embrace Ember. "Congratulations."

"Thank you," Ember murmurs, smiling at her brother's mate.

Slate relents, his face relaxing. "I'm happy for you guys, but maybe we should focus on the issue at hand."

"Stop being an ass," Hazel says. "After things are settled, we should have a party to celebrate."

"So what's this plan you mentioned?" Slate asks me.

"We are going back to Granite Ridge. I'm going to challenge Orion," Ember answers, raising her chin.

Hazel's intake of breath is audible, but Ember isn't done. She inches closer to Slate. "And let me be clear. If you even think about stopping me, I will consider the alliance between our packs to be null. I'm taking my pack back with or without your help."

Facing each other, the similarities are obvious - the same straight nose and intense gaze, the way they clench their hands when they're nervous and determined.

Slate's shoulders slump minutely and his head ducks. "I'm sorry you'd even worry that I would do that. Tell me what I can do to help."

"Thank you," she says softly, giving him a grim smile. "Can I see your healer?"

"Are you hurt?" Hazel asks.

"No, I just need her help with our plan," Ember explains.

"Alright, let's go to Sable's cottage." Hazel waves us forward. Jasper and Marigold trail behind, and the six of us make our way across the meadow to secure that advantage that my brilliant mate came up with.

XIX
FANGS, FIGHTS, & FEAR

EMBER

Onyx drove Jasper's fancy car into Granite Ridge territory, just the three of us. Marigold, Hazel, and Slate all wanted to come, but I can't risk accusations of Bracken Creek manipulating the situation. Jasper is family and the former Heir, so his presence cannot be disputed.

We drive straight into the compound and park in the dirt between the Alpha's house and the cafeteria. Dozens of people pour out of the buildings and surround us.

While the small gathering that we met in Bracken Creek was friendly and curious, the group that circles us in Granite Ridge is decidedly hostile.

Onyx and Jasper climb out of the car, boldly meeting their accusatory gazes. I wait until Onyx comes around to open my door. It's another calculated move and a way to show respect.

A few of the wolves drift closer, testing our boundaries.

"Back the fuck off," Jasper snarls, pulling his favorite dagger out. The lazy charm is gone, replaced with the promise of violence our parents modeled for us from our births. It's oddly validating to see him revert back, even if it's for show.

Onyx's expression is stony and his hand rests on the handle of his gun tucked in his waistband.

"So nice of my little wolf to come back willingly," a tall figure croons. The crowd parts for their new Alpha.

"Orion," I say, raising my chin and pretending I'm not two heads shorter than he is. "I challenge you for the position of Alpha, as is my birthright as the daughter of the late Alpha Ferris."

He lets out a booming laugh. My jaw snaps shut so hard it hurts, every muscle tensing.

"Why should I accept your challenge? You're not strong enough to force it. I could just let my pack have their way with you."

Onyx's hand tightens on his weapon and Jasper turns to face away from us defensively.

"I thought you were demanding I become your mate, just a few days ago. You wanted my claim to the position then. Defeat me, and you'll prove yourself."

He sneers. "Maybe I just wanted the youngest, prettiest thing in this pack. But I'm confident better options will present themselves."

"Funny, I'd rather be claimed by a guard from another pack than let you touch me." To make my point clear, I tug my neckline to show off my mark. Onyx smirks, not minding in the least that I downplayed his ranking.

Orion's sneer melts into a snarl as he bares his teeth at us. "You're nothing. I could kill him and take you if I wanted to."

"See? You're a fraud. An Alpha would never do that," I declare, my voice rising. "The pack cannot trust a leader who has no respect for our laws and traditions."

He growls, stalking back toward us. Gritting my teeth, I hold my ground, biding my time until the right moment.

"I challenge you, Orion, for the position of Alpha of Granite Ridge."

He stops a few feet away, glaring at us. "If you need to learn this lesson a second time, I'm happy to help. When do we fight?"

"Sorry, did you need time for a pep talk? Because I'm ready now," I drawl, my heart leaping as I hear a few snickers from pack members around us.

"Fine." He storms away, a few wolves stumbling back in their hurry to get away from his anger.

The entire pack has gathered, and they move loosely with us. Expressions range from disgust to curiosity, but it's the tinge of hope through the weakened pack bond that causes me to straighten as we walk toward the center of the street.

Orion stands ready, shaking out his hands like I'm not his first fight of the day. As I stop a few feet away from him, he looks up with a chilling smile.

"I can't say I'm disappointed. This way you'll still be begging me."

A savage growl rolls out from my mate. With glowing eyes, he paces on one side, keeping my packmates back. Jasper stands behind me, his intelligent gaze trained on Orion.

"Ready?" I ask. Fear flashes through my mate bond, my terror mixing with Onyx's frustration as the challenge begins. He'd give anything to stand in my place, but I'm not powerless.

Flexing my own hands, I prepare to cut this wretch down to size.

Orion moves first, like I expected. He's fast for someone that large. He barrels toward me, reaching to grab me, and I easily slip aside.

With a wide swipe, I scratch my nails into his forearm, drawing blood. The dried wolfsbane and rowanberry powder under my fingernails won't incapacitate him, but it should slow him down if it gets into his bloodstream and prevent him from accessing his shift. Hopefully it's enough to give us a chance.

Jasper shouts a warning and I spin back toward my opponent. His fist flies toward my face and I duck. Shifting my weight, I land a swift kick against his knee.

Orion's breathing quickens and he lets out a small grunt with each step. It's working.

He comes for me again and I can't dodge in time. The strike glances off my shoulder and pain explodes down the nerves in my arm and across my shoulders into my neck.

I stumble but regain my balance quickly. Orion faces me, his stance low and ready, but he doesn't attack again.

"Are you going to dodge me and hope for the best? Or are you going to try and take my rank from me?"

His words make me flinch. I can't afford to look weak, but if he gets hold of me, he could kill me in seconds.

"It's not my fault you're so slow," I shoot back, darting forward and swiping at his face with my other hand. His reaction is slower than it should be, thanks to the poison in his system.

Angry red cuts streak down his cheek and across his jaw. His roar shakes my bones. Before I can retreat, he grabs my wrist.

No!

With a twist, he forces me to the ground. My knees splinter, sending pain up to my hips until my entire body is stabbing needles. Tears blur my vision.

Orion's huge knuckles connect with my cheek, and the world turns white. I gasp for air on the ground. Dirt and rocks embed into my hip and arm, and my hair has slipped its bun, falling around me in a tangle.

Instinctively, I curl over my wrist. Crimson liquid drips onto the dirt, and I numbly realize it's coming from my nose.

A shadow covers me and I tense, waiting for the kick.

ONYX

Blood sprays from Orion's hit, and I cannot stand back and watch. Ember lays in the dirt, her eyes squeezed shut. The brute laughs as he stands over her petite form.

With an inhuman snarl, I leap at him. His eyes gleam as he takes me in.

My strike lands on his chin, sending him back into the edge of the crowd. He straightens, working his jaw. "Do you want to die? That would free up the girl for me." Blood shines on his teeth as he grins at me.

"You accept my challenge." It's not a question, but Orion grunts in acceptance. There's a hunger in his eyes, a desire for violence that makes my hands shake. I clench my fists to keep the tremble from showing.

He's slowing, stopping. If she got enough into him, he won't be able to shift. It's unlikely I can defeat him in my human form, even in his current state, but as a wolf, I stand a chance.

The panic and turmoil drops away as I fall to four legs. My tail swishes behind me as I gather my haunches under me and prepare to leap.

Orion's face scrunches, his eyes glowing with rage. He just figured out he can't shift. I won't waste this chance. All the tension in my body uncoils at once, launching me toward his chest.

Orion's defensive pose cannot withstand a huge wolf landing on his chest. He goes down, wildly attempting to block me. My jaws close around his arm and I snap the bone down by his wrist. The scream from his throat is sweet to hear.

Sharp and sudden pain blasts through my body, overwhelming me. Jumping back, I realize there is a blade embedded low in my chest by the joint of my front left leg. Clamping my teeth over the handle, I pull the knife free and toss it aside.

Orion laughs, spitting blood on the ground beside him. He still cradles his arm, but clearly he thinks he's won already. Blood flows through my fur and down my leg from the wound I can't even see.

My growl warns him to stay down, but the stubborn bastard kneels, struggling to pull himself in a standing position. Crimson coats his collar and seeps across his chest.

Gathering my strength, I leap again. But this time he's ready for me. His fist connects with the wound he already gave me, and the pain blacks out my vision for a second.

An undignified yelp escapes me, and I bite wildly as my legs give out. Orion grabs my front leg and pulls me sideways, squeezing and twisting. Memories of the beating they gave me last time I was here fill my mind, overwhelming my control. Snarling, I thrash and snap my jaws, connecting with his unbroken hand. Blood hits my tongue, but I can't see the damage.

The pain of my leg wrenching and stretching the stab wound is too much. Fear of what is coming next overpowers my wolf, and humanity comes rushing in. My body shifts back without my permission.

Orion's low laugh sends icy terror through me as he breaks my arm. I struggle to suck in air and stay conscious. If I don't protect myself, I'll be abandoning Ember.

His grip on me is too strong. My strength is fading as blood flows from my wound.

Something hits Orion, a blur of black fur, sending him sprawling. Blinking to clear my vision, I watch my beautiful little mate close her jaws over his neck and shake her head. Orion screams, yanking at her fur and trying to get a grip on her body.

With a vicious growl deep in her chest, Ember stays locked on him, her jaws clamped down with ruby liquid gushing between her fangs until Orion stills.

Ember's shift flows over her as she turns and moves toward me, landing on her knees on the dirt as I try to push up to sit. Pain screams through my chest and arm and I land back on the dirt with a strained noise.

Red coats her face, her bare chest, her hands. We're a matching set, bathed in blood. Her eyes shine wild, glowing like the wolf she is.

Reaching up with my uninjured hand, I brush her hair back. "You're incredible," I say, my mind swirling. But somehow I know it's important to tell her how beautiful and amazing she is.

Her smile is everything. I could die in this moment, seeing her happy. Black crowds the edges of my vision and I push it away. I've got plans with my girl.

"Onyx!" her voice says, sounding far too worried. I try to answer, but my throat isn't cooperating anymore.

XX
VICTORY &
VENGEANCE

EMBER

"Onyx!" I yelp, seeing his eyes unfocus and his muscles slacken. A new terror grabs me by my throat, strangling me. I can't lose him. He's been through worse; he needs to hold on long enough for his natural healing to kick in.

Jasper crouches beside me. "You just won back your pack. You need to address them. I'll take care of him." He forces a shirt into my hand.

"Are you fucking kidding me?" I snarl. His eyebrows rise, imploring me. "Fine!"

Standing, I yank the shirt over my head and then I look across the faces of my pack. Respect, shock, and anger reflect back, but I don't give a shit. "Get him into the Alpha's house," I growl, motioning to Onyx. "And get first aid supplies."

People shuffle where they stand. How dare they hesitate. My anger spurs my natural dominance, and I press down on all of them with my will, demanding their obedience with every part of my being.

Two men to my left step forward and reach for Onyx, lifting him up between them. Jasper steadies him, holding his seeping wound, as they walk toward the house.

Pointing to a female wolf I know wasn't fond of Orion, I demand, "Go get all the healing supplies we have." Of another, I say, "You, gather up anyone with medical experience. He is your Alpha and we will do everything to make him well and comfortable." They bow their heads and rush to obey.

Taking a breath, I look over the rest of the crowd. "Anyone who doesn't want to follow my rule, I suggest you leave now because I will not be merciful of any disloyalty. The pack will be changing. We are no longer at war with those around us. They are our allies. I will build a healthy pack where you can be happy. No more assigned mates. No more beatings during training. But I will not tolerate any disrespect to me or my mate."

Jasper returns, his hand going to the small of my back. "Sister," he rumbles, "tell me which trainers you remember punishing you like we discussed."

Do I want to hand those wolves over to him? They're older, and I know they won't respect me, not after how they treated me growing up. They enjoyed causing pain. Not wolves I want to build a pack with. With a shrug, I point to a couple of the trainers who were always bloodthirsty and ready to take consequences too far.

Jasper confirms their names, and I nod. With a smile that almost scares me, he grips his dagger and stalks toward them. I don't care what he does with them, as long as they're gone.

Addressing my pack again, I say, "I'm going to attend to my mate. If you don't want to support my leadership, pack up and leave now. Anyone still here by sunset, we will begin building a new pack together. Understood?"

The group lets out a mix of agreement and grumbles.

I leave them to make their decisions. Onyx needs me. Gritting my teeth, I jog toward my childhood home, bracing my aching wrist against my stomach.

Onyx lays across the sofa, and three packmates tend to him. His wound is clean and one man carefully sews up the wound. Jasper's bag sits on the ground at my feet, and I tear it open, hunting for the jars we retrieved from Bracken Creek's healer. As soon as the stitching is done, I apply a thick layer of salve.

My strong mate hardly makes a sound as we align his broken arm and wrap it loosely, leaving room for the swelling that is just beginning.

They offer to wrap my own wrist, but it's already feeling better. Just a sprain.

Jasper crouches in front of me and wipes the blood from my face with a damp cloth. "You did great."

"Thank you," I say with a weak smile, ignoring the fresh blood splatter across his shirt. "Will you stay and help me evaluate the wolves we have left once the disloyal have cleared out?"

"I'll stay for a day or two. And then I'm going to go home and come back with reinforcements. We aren't taking any risks while you establish yourself as Alpha."

My impulse is to argue that I can do it all on my own and his help is unnecessary. But after everything my brother and Onyx's friends went through to help me already, I find myself agreeing. "Alright."

Onyx's head turns, his eyes clearing as he focuses on me.

"Hey, you." I say softly.

Jasper stands and motions those around us to leave.

"You were magnificent," he says.

"You liked all that violence?" I ask, scrunching my nose when I smile.

He reaches up with his good hand and cradles my cheek. "I like everything you do. Didn't I tell you?"

"You might have mentioned it." I press a kiss to his fingers, despite the dirt coating them still.

"So we won," he says, sounding in awe of what we accomplished.

"Yup." Brushing his hair back, I sigh. Relief mingles across our bond. "How's it feel to be Alpha?"

He huffs a laugh and then winces. "At the moment, rather painful."

"It'll get better, I think. These wolves are so lucky to have you. I'm lucky to have you."

He shushes me. "Go see your pack. I'm going to lay here and focus on healing myself so I can help you."

"Promise you're feeling good?" I implore him to be honest. I need him healthy and whole.

"Great." Color is returning to his face already and his voice is clear. We're going to be alright.

Standing, I clench and unclench my hands. It's time to get to work cleaning this pack out.

EPILOGUE

ONYX

My fists clench as I stare at the security system's back end controls. It's almost perfect, but a couple of components aren't doing what I want. Considering I am updating three outdated systems and merging all the controls, it's a miracle that most of it's working.

Pushing my chair back, I stalk out of the cold office. I don't mind Ferris's taste in dark marble, so we haven't made any updates to this room yet.

I can hear Ember singing along to alt rock that is older than she is as she works on the family room. My feet slow in the doorway, admiring the sight. Hair now a vivid purple and tied up in a messy bun, Ember's hips sway as she drags a paintbrush down the built-in bookcases that span one side of the room. The bright white is covered by a sweep of dark emerald. Previously, the shelves were lined with expensive but soulless decor items. Soon it'll be actual books and a rather impressive record collection, all currently stacked across the two sofas while she paints.

Piece by piece, she's transforming this house into her own style - dark, rich, and colorful. I love it. It's cozy and feels like home.

Hands going to her waist, I lean down and kiss below her ear. She leans into my touch. "Hey, ready for a break?" I ask.

My hopes of luring her back to bed are dashed when she turns and says, "Yeah, I'm almost done here. Then we should go check on how everyone's doing today." Sighing, I make myself useful, cleaning up her painting supplies as she touches up the edges.

Ten minutes later, she's picking dots of paint off her wrists and forearms while we step off the porch and survey our pack. The cafeteria boasts a bakery case of treats, along with an updated kitchen in the back. Bracken Creek's chef, Crickett, has been training the two cooks to prepare food with seasonings and flavor. Meals have been steadily improving.

In the training building opposite, my father stands with his arms crossed, surveying the wolves sparring. He's teaching them to disable instead of harm, preparing the pack for any future conflicts we hope never come. A younger man and woman follow Fisher as he works - our replacement trainers. As a mated pair, they will both be Deltas, once Fisher is satisfied with their abilities.

496

Other wolves bustle around, completing various projects. Marigold stands in the center, giving out instructions and directing movements. One of the houses is being converted to a school. There's no teacher yet. There also aren't any children, but we want to be ready. A nearby empty house is being gutted so it can become a health clinic. We also need to acquire a healer, but perhaps Marigold's brother Indigo could take the position someday.

I hug Ember around the shoulders and give her a squeeze. "Look at everything you've accomplished."

"It'll be good when it's all done," she mutters, her gaze tracking the work going on around us.

As we wander forward, she points out two houses now sport wreaths on their front doors, and someone has even painted their front door a cheery yellow. The renovations at the house have inspired pack members to start personalizing their homes.

"Hey, I had an idea," she says, scuffing her feet along the dirt. "What if we took that empty house on the end and turned it into a rec center?"

"Yeah?"

"We could put in pool tables," she continues, "maybe some arcade games. One room could be a movie theater."

"That's brilliant," I say, kissing her temple. "Everyone already loves you, but imagine how much they'll love their Alpha after you give them a whole game *house*."

She laughs softly, a soft blush coloring her cheeks. "So are we going to the inter-pack gathering tonight?" she asks, a vulnerable look in her eyes.

"Yeah, I think we should. It'll be a chance to see your other brother," I say, pulling her closer. Her shoulders rise and drop in a sigh.

"I guess I need to change out of these painting clothes," she says. "Should I dress up for this party?"

"I love you in anything and nothing at all," I growl, hesitant to release my hold on her. But if we are going to the event, I've got work to get finished.

EMBER

I cling to Onyx's hand as we arrive at the party in an old pack car. Eventually I'll buy him a nice vehicle worthy of an Alpha. Maybe a sports car. Jasper can help. I'd like to see the two of them car shopping together.

Wolves from every pack mingle in the Valley Pack's central lawn. Onyx leads us toward the circle of Bracken Creek wolves. Marigold sits on Jasper's lap, and Hazel stands behind Slate with her arms draped over his shoulders, one hand playing with his dark curls.

Cedar stands and thumps his twin on the back. "How's it going?"

Onyx's smile is proud. "Great. I think everyone is taking to our changes faster than we hoped."

"That's wonderful," Hazel says, darting around Slate and throwing her arms around me. I'm getting used to hugs, and I even hug her back. As she pulls away, I see her wiping at her eyes before she plops into Slate's lap. His arms band around her waist, pulling her tight against him.

"I can't believe you guys are Alphas," Marigold says dreamily, cocking her head. "Seems surreal."

"You're telling me," I mutter. Onyx sits and pulls me down across his thighs. My breathing slows to match his, soothing me.

"Well, now that we're all here, there was something we wanted to share," Hazel says, clapping her hands together.

My eyes narrow at the nervousness in her voice. Slate's expression is smug. What on earth? Onyx and Cedar seem as puzzled as I am, but Marigold's hands cover her mouth, her eyes going wide.

"Are you serious?" Marigold squeaks. I'm definitely missing something.

Hazel's lip quivers, her mouth curving into a watery smile, but she nods. Marigold launches herself off Jasper's lap and squeezes her best friend around the shoulders.

"Okay, what the hell, guys?" Onyx asks.

Jasper's expression shifts from confusion to surprise. "Are you pregnant?"

My mouth falls open.

"Yeah, we are having a pup. Maybe two," Slate announces. My hands come up to keep my mouth falling open, mimicking Marigold's reaction.

My little nephew or niece. And a new Heir for the Bracken Creek Pack.

"Congratulations," Cedar says, looking happier than I've ever seen him.

"You guys! A little Hazel, or a little Slate if we're unlucky!" Onyx says, teasing his best friend. Slate shoves him half-heartedly.

"Wow, that's amazing," I say quietly. Hazel turns, taking my hand in hers.

"Thank you. They're coming into a safer world because of you. I know you're going to be an auntie, but I'd like it if you and Onyx were also godparents."

"Godparents?" I ask, blinking.

Hazel nods. "It's something my family does. Someone else to care for them and help guide them."

"We'd be honored," I manage to say, feeling tears burn in my own eyes.

"You too, Marigold," Hazel says. Her best friend squeals and bounces on the balls of her feet. I step back, tucking myself into Onyx's side, safe from flailing arms and being wrangled into group hugs.

Word of Hazel's pregnancy spreads outside of our group in minutes, with dozens of shifters around with excellent hearing. A line of well-wishers forms, and Onyx suggests we get a drink.

Wandering around the outskirts of the gathering, I notice my mate has a shit-eating grin forming on his face.

"Oh, no," I say, scowling at him. "What are you thinking about doing?"

"Nothing," he says.

A moment later, he's tugging me behind the nearest building. It's the darkest corner of the party, and thankfully devoid of horny couples making out. For the moment, at least.

"Wow, you take me to such nice places," I say.

"Maybe I just like it when girls are mean to me," he says, his voice caressing me. He leans against the wall with a devilish grin. The chill in the air nips at my feverish skin, and I step closer.

"You're such an idiot," I murmur, smothering my laugh by closing my lips over his neck.

"Yet you love me," he says, tipping his head to the side with a dramatic sigh.

"Why is that again?" I tease.

With a smirk, Onyx scoops me up, hands against my ass, and turns us until I'm pressed against the rough wood. His chest is solid, his grip stable.

He kisses me until I've forgotten where we are and what my own name is. The party continues on without us, and I don't care. I've got everything I need right here.

Finally Onyx pauses, sucking in air. "Let's go home," he says. Without waiting for my agreement, he grabs my hand and leads me toward our vehicle.

Digging in my heels, I pull him to a stop. "Hey, it's a nice night out. Do you want to run instead?" His eyes light up.

Stowing our clothing in the truck, we turn toward the forest. Black fur sweeps down my arms as I shift, and suddenly the forest is brighter. Night creatures scurry away as our paws grip the earth, propelling us into the trees.

The moonlight filters through branches as Onyx chases me northward, toward our home. Through our mate bond, I can feel adoration, desire, and playfulness as he snaps at my tail. As we cross the border, I slow. The trees are denser here in this corner of our territory, and I know patrol has the night off.

Halting, I glance over my shoulder at the dark gray wolf a few steps behind me. He cocks his head in a silent question. Closing my eyes, I reach for my human side, and let the shift change me back. When I open my eyes, Onyx stands just a few inches away, his hair mussed.

With a sweet smile, I reach up and run my fingers through his hair to untangle it. The intensity in his gaze takes my breath away.

"I've been thinking about getting you alone in the forest again," he rasps, lifting a hand to brush along my neck and push my hair over my shoulder. My whole body shivers.

"I had a feeling," I say, excitement rising as he closes the distance between us. His desire warms me through our mating bond, meeting my own.

"Did I mention purple is my new favorite color?" he murmurs before his mouth closes over my skin. My laugh is cut off by the feel of his teeth nipping the sensitive spot under my jaw.

The night's chill prickles along my back and his body heats my front, his handing rove down my ribs to my bare ass. We're wild things in the night, a tangle of limbs and unending kisses flowing into each other. Promises whispered against heated skin and soft moans mingle in the air. He is mine and I am his, and when we're done, we can return to the home we claimed together.

WOLVES
AND
WATERCOLORS

I
WILDFLOWERS IN CONCRETE

AURORA

Giant paper mâché dragonflies swing above my head as the buyer in front of me tries to haggle over a statue of a screaming possum. Jarrod, the gallery manager, isn't having it. "Sir, the artists set their prices. I can't lower it for you."

My highlighter yellow nails scrape paint splatter off my hands as I wait not-so-patiently. Finally, the collector buys "Existential Crisis" for full price and gets out of my way.

"Aurora, how are you, love?" Jarrod's braids gleam with pink threaded through them. Letters covered in rainbow feathers spell out "THE BUZZ" behind his head.

"Great, I got your message about picking up my pieces, but I did finish a few new projects I wanted to show you," I say, pulling my cracked phone from my back pocket and flicking open the photos app.

Jarrod makes a noncommittal but supportive noise in his throat while he steps through the arch to the storage room and collects my paintings. I tug my bottom lip with my teeth as he sets a stack of unsold paintings on the mosaic countertop between us. The sweet man even replaced my dilapidated cardboard with fresh sheets to protect my artwork.

"I heard a lot of compliments on this collection, and the woman who purchased the daisies was thrilled," he says.

"I'm so glad," I say brightly, despite knowing he is placating me. Only selling one work won't cut it. Smiling, I hold the phone up. "Want to see the new stuff?"

Jarrod swipes, squinting at my still-life paintings of wildflowers growing in concrete cracks. "Interesting imagery," he murmurs. "Oh, who's this?"

He swipes to a photograph of a young woman, dark hair spilling over her shoulders and light brown eyes identical to mine, her hands resting on a very pregnant belly. Her partner wraps his tattooed arms around her waist from behind, his dark curls shading his eyes. I've never met my sister's boyfriend, but he seems intense.

"Oh, that's Hazel, my older sister. She lives in the middle of nowhere up in the mountains."

"Did she have the baby yet?"

"I don't think so. But it'll be any day now," I say with a cheerful smile that feels strained. I need him to focus on my artwork, not my sister, if I have any chance of getting into next month's show.

"Boy or girl?" He's still beaming at the picture.

Shrugging, I run my thumb over the rough edge of the countertop. "It's going to be a surprise."

"I love that," he says, hearts in his eyes. "So I'm guessing you'll be off to visit her soon?"

"I can't take off," I say. "What do you think of the new collection? They'd be perfect for next month's show."

Jarrod's demeanor shifts. "Love, I'm not sure I've got the wall space. You know how competitive it is right now."

I don't, but I nod along. "Of course, I get it. You've been so generous in featuring me at the last few shows. But do you think my audience will miss me if I'm not there?"

"I'll keep a stack of your business cards on the counter for anyone who asks," he says. It's hard to be angry with Jarrod. He's the nicest guy in the industry, at least in my limited experience. But when I was a fresh, untested art school drop-out, he was the only one who would give me a chance.

"Okay, well, I've got some interesting new projects so I'll be back in a few weeks." I say with a shrug, sliding my phone back into my pocket.

"You can just email them, hon." He raises a pierced eyebrow. "Most artists email me and ship stuff. But it's always nice to see your beautiful face."

"I live so close and I'd miss you otherwise!" I say, scrunching my nose as I give him my most charming smile.

"Have a good spring break." He picks up his tablet and resumes his work. I guess I'm dismissed.

Hefting my stack of artwork onto my hip, I pass a line of paintings of blue heeler dogs dressed for different careers and push my hip against the door. It swings open and the chaos of the city street washes over me.

It's only two blocks to my apartment, past honking cars, clouds of smog and weed, and a shady Italian restaurant that I'm pretty sure is a mafia establishment. That's why I only get takeout from them and never dine in.

My feet ache from my morning slinging mimosas and margaritas poolside at the trendy hotel another block north. The tourists were rabid over our newest guava kombucha mimosa and I walked away with a couple hundred in tips. Thank goodness, rent is due soon.

With a scraping sound, my key gets me in the back door of the apartment building and out of the afternoon frenzy of downtown Los Angeles. Thankfully the elevator is repaired, because the last thing I want to do is climb five flights of stairs.

Shuffling down the checkered floor, I finally reach my tiny apartment and let myself in, trying to keep my paintings tight under my arm.

"Au-roo-roo!" Jordan croons from the kitchen. "I'm making scrambled eggs, want some?"

It must be nice to sleep in. She's chipper, bouncing from the stove to the sink and back, her glossy black hair shimmering like a curtain.

"Thanks, that'd be awesome." Passing her, I head straight for my closet where all my unsold paintings live. These join the stack. Some day they won't fit in the space, and that is when I will give up on my dreams. But not today.

The eggs are covered in furikake and piled on the thick milk bread her mom sends over every week from their home in Irvine. I eat my portion with a grateful smile. Jordan puts on a ridiculous reality show and we watch feckless D-list celebrities flirt on a beach while we eat our breakfast-dinner. Dinner for me, breakfast for her.

As she's leaving to get dressed for her evening acting gig, our third roommate arrives home. Devon brings her boyfriend with her, and Tyler winks at me while I scroll through my phone and pretend they aren't groping each other on our sofa.

Jordan is less tolerant when she emerges, pulling a loose coat over her sparkly jumpsuit. Glitter swirls over her high cheekbones, catching the light as she glares at Tyler. Within seconds, Devon and Jordan are shouting at each other. Tyler wanders into the kitchen for a beer, and I make a run for it before they ask me to weigh in.

Devon and Jordan share the master bedroom and I get the tiny secondary bedroom so I'm able to close my door and put on my ancient headphones. Cranking up my feminine rage soundtrack, I attempt some sketching, but my hand keeps drifting to my phone.

With a sigh, I give up and pull up my sister's phone number. As much as I deny it, I miss her. Hazel was the responsible one growing up, especially after our father passed. I was the free spirit she had to chase after.

"Hello?" Hazel says, sounding groggy. Oh shit, what time is it there? Only an hour later - it's barely past dinner time.

"I'm so sorry, did I wake you up?" I rush to say, my eyes roaming over the sketches pinned to the wall my bed is pushed against. Since Hazel moved to the mountains, more of my work focuses on pine trees and forest themes.

"Oh, Rory, no. Well, I guess I fell asleep. But it's all good."

"Are you getting enough rest? The baby isn't here yet, right?" Flipping over to lie on my stomach, I turn the page on the sketchbook and start drawing hash marks along the edge of the page.

Hazel's light laughter floats through the line. "Not yet. But I swear this last month is approximately one hundred and ninety-two days long. Simply existing is uncomfortable!"

"Sorry," I say, unsure how to comfort a pregnant lady. "So... Can I get your address? I want to send something for the baby."

"That would be so sweet!" Hazel yawns, and I find myself triggered to yawn too. "I heard that," she teases with a tired chuckle.

"I'm sure you did," I mutter. "So did you guys pick out names?"

"Maybe. Well, we are still debating, but we need to decide quickly. Slate has a lot of family names we were considering honoring."

"Yeah?"

"I'm not sharing any of them. You'll have to wait just like everyone else pestering me." A masculine laugh sounds through the phone line.

"Slate?" I ask.

Hazel hums her confirmation.

"Well, since he has a nature name, and so does everyone there you've mentioned, I guess you have to pick something similar? Might I recommend Pebble. Or maybe Rock."

Her snort makes me smile. "You're ridiculous. I'm not naming my baby Rock." Her partner's mumbled argument echoes behind her words. "No, babe, she's joking."

"You better go talk to your baby daddy," I say dryly.

"You'd love him. He's creative, like you," Hazel replies wistfully.

"Maybe you guys should come visit me."

"We'll have to come see Mom eventually," Hazel says darkly. It's my turn to hum in agreement. Our mother is not the most functional adult and she threw a huge fit when Hazel moved to that tiny town. The fact it was our dad's hometown somehow made her more upset. Uncle Heath was able to calm her down, but not before I received seventeen hysterical voicemails and somewhere north of forty text messages.

"Whenever that is, I'll look forward to it." Rolling over, I stare at my ceiling fan. She's probably looking out a window at the beautiful forest, and here I am in an urban prison. The walls coated in chipped paint seem to close in around me. My body cries out for some nature therapy.

"Bye, Rory, I love you!" Hazel smooches the phone and hangs up.

The noises of angry roommates press in on me, and I'd give anything to transport myself through the phone to my sister. She's the smart one.

A text vibrates and her address pops up in a bubble on my splintered screen. Curiosity prickles under my skin, and I hold down on the text until it copies. Two seconds later, google map pulls up satellite images for her home. Zooming in on the forest, there are a few trailers, a couple of larger buildings, and a smattering of cabins. The map won't load much detail, but I count at least nine cabins. One of them must be Hazel's.

Picturing my sister among those trees, my sense of longing intensifies until I have to press a hand to my chest. Geez, what's wrong with me? I've loved living in Los Angeles since I was eighteen and starting art school. But something has been whispering in the back of my head for a while. I'm not thriving. Exhaustion drags me down and my art is dry and stiff. I need a vacation.

Instead of sending art, maybe I should visit her. It'll have to be soon or I'll miss the baby being born. I can hold my niece or nephew, catch up with my sister, get a break from these crazy roommates, and spend time painting in nature. My new collection will be a hit, full of life and that special je ne sais quoi lacking in my recent work. Plus a few hugs from my sister would go a long way toward recharging my soul.

Decision made, I text the manager at the hotel asking for time off. They've been over-staffed and everyone is fighting for hours, so it's not a problem. Next, I map out the route and find a cheap motel at the halfway point. No reason I can't leave tomorrow!

Feeling hopeful for the first time in a long time, I change my music to nature sounds and curl up in my bed. My dreams are full of pine trees and dramatic possums dressed like firemen and construction workers.

II
UNEXPECTED
ARRIVALS
AURORA

The address Hazel gave me leads far up into the mountains. My junker car barely makes it. The entire second day, I'm driving with my fingers crossed while I belt out Defying Gravity until my voice is hoarse. It feels like bringing a piece of Los Angeles with me into this lush landscape, bolstering my courage.

The road hitches back and forth as I climb, late afternoon sunlight spilling warm and golden over the road in stark contrast to the black shadows of swaying treetops. Light reflects off the branches, casting a green tinge along the jagged edges of the shade.

From the rough grays, browns, and blacks of tree trunks, to the range of foliage of every size and shape in a million shades of green, it's stunningly beautiful. I'd pull over and paint on the side of the road if I could. But that would be dumb. First, get there, second, see my sister, and then I can go into art mode.

The sharp smell of pine resin radiates through my car's AC. It fills my lungs, imparting a buzz, a sense of excitement and adventure. Aurora's Awesome Adventure.

The GPS on my phone flashes with instructions to turn. It's a gas station. A dilapidated gas station that looks like it might be haunted. Ignoring the creepy building, I navigate around it to a dirt road.

The tree trunks close in, and I have to slow to avoid denting my car - though it wouldn't be a notable difference if I did. Sighing, I add a little more gas and speed up.

A squirrel leaps from one tree to another up ahead. Its fur flashes a brilliant rust tone. A smile breaks over my face. Letting my car slow again, I peek through the trees on either side, hoping to see more wildlife.

A flash of silver streaks between trees, too quick for me to get a good look. It doesn't reappear. Oh well. At least a tiny bluebird flits past my window and flutters up into the canopy. Beautiful!

The road ends in a dirt parking lot with two trailers. I recognize the configuration from the satellite map. The lot holds a dozen trucks and various SUVs. A sleek Jaguar sits on the end, the black metallic paint reflecting the trees around it. Someone here has some money.

After parking, I throw my door open and step out, drawing a deep breath of sharp mountain air. A woman dressed in head-to-toe gray strides toward me from the direction of the portable buildings. She's shorter than I am with rich, tan skin and chocolate curls.

Motion catches my attention. A tall, muscular man leans his back against the building. I get the distinct feeling he is providing back-up from the way he watches her progress with a frown on his face.

I face the woman with my hands up. "Hey! I'm here to see Hazel. She's my sister. I'm Aurora."

Surprise widens her eyes before she smiles politely. "Nice to meet you. I'm Cassia and this is Lazuli. If you give us a minute, he can find Hazel for you."

"That'd be great, thanks," I say, the words coming slowly as I observe the communicative glances between the two strangers. What have I stumbled across? They seem too official to be random neighbors. I'm getting major cult vibes.

With a nod, the man, Lazuli, jogs into the trees and out of view. Cassia stands a few feet away from me, her cool gaze steady and patient.

"It's really lovely out here. Very refreshing," I say awkwardly. Ah, the classic standby, the weather.

Cassia's mouth quirks up. "It's been unseasonably warm recently." Our shallow exchange visibly relaxes her and my stress lessens. Good to know she isn't an assassin waiting for permission to take me out for trespassing.

"Really? We had a cold snap in L.A." I say, threading my fingers through my hair and twisting it back off my neck. She's not wrong about the warmth. It would be perfect for jeans and a long-sleeve shirt, but in my fleece-lined hoodie, I'm sweating.

Lazuli strides out from behind the building, followed by Hazel and a tall figure I'm ninety-five percent sure is her partner, Slate.

"Aurora?" Hazel says, her brows furrowing. "What's going on?"

She doesn't seem excited to see me. I've made a mistake.

"I wanted to surprise you! I know you don't need a houseguest when you're about to have a baby, so I borrowed some camping gear. I can stay out of your way."

Her familiar amber eyes blink at me.

"It's so nice to finally meet you," Slate says, extending his hand. It envelops mine, warm and secure. He smiles and I almost fall over. No wonder Hazel decided to stay here. He's stunning with high cheekbones, a full mouth, and green eyes so bright I'm itching to paint them. Their baby is going to be gorgeous. Damn.

"You don't need to camp out. But, Rory, I really wish you had told me you were coming." My sister chews the inside of her cheeks, a nervous habit. The guilt piles on. How could I be so thoughtless?

"Where's the fun in that?" I ask with a weak smile, my shoulders pulling up towards my ears. Hazel pinches the bridge of her nose, looking away. I scramble to appease her. "But look at you! You're adorable!"

Hazel's nose scrunches up, uncomfortable with compliments. "I'm sure you've had a long drive and I need to get back to work. Can we take you to Uncle Heath's cabin? Our downstairs bedroom is a nursery now, so it makes sense for you to stay with him. He won't mind."

Slate looks to Lazuli and tips his chin down, signaling the other man. He jogs back into the trees and out of sight. Poor guy.

"I don't care where I stay. I told you, I can just set up my tent. Well, it's Jordan's tent, but it'll work just fine. I don't want to impose."

She sighs, falling into big sister mode easily. "Please don't argue. You're not staying in a tent when Heath has a spare bedroom." I tense under her admonishment, and she notices. Her tone softens. "It's where I stayed when I first visited. He'll be thrilled to have you, and you'll be really close to our cabin."

"Whatever you say, Mama," I chirp with a grin, hoping to lighten the mood. The dark circles under Hazel's eyes and the pinch of her mouth worry me. The last thing I want to do is add stress on her shoulders if she's already struggling. Maybe I can help.

She rolls her eyes. "It's weird hearing that," she says with a laugh.

"Better get used to it!" I say, relieved to see her relaxing.

"I haven't seen you in ages." She opens her arms wide. "Come here!"

I'm not a hugger, but my sister is the exception. It's cumbersome with her huge belly between us, but she smells like a warm autumn night. A sense of homesickness hits me - not missing Los Angeles, but missing a childhood following my big sister around. I tighten my hold on her upper back and tuck my cheek against her shoulder, soaking in the feeling. I should have come sooner.

"You'll have to show me what's so special about this place," I murmur. "Other than your boy toy."

Scowling, she releases me. "You can call him Slate." The man in question turns back toward us from his quiet discussion with Cassia.

"Or maybe brother?" I tease. "But I think I like referring to him as your baby daddy best."

"You're going to drive me crazy, aren't you?" she asks, her exhale audible. "So how long will we be enjoying your presence?"

"I've got a whole month off work, but I'll need to go back sooner if I want to pay my bills next month. But I couldn't miss the arrival of my first niece or nephew!" Dropping my voice, I step closer to my sister. "And honestly, I need to work on some new paintings for an upcoming art show and I figured painting the woods here would be good, and it'll keep me busy and out of your hair."

Her smile is indulgent. "As long as you paint something for the nursery, I'm on board with that plan."

"Did you bring art supplies with you?" Slate asks.

Nodding, I jerk my thumb back at my car. "Yeah, I've got everything I need."

"I've got a pretty decent collection, so if you end up needing anything, let me know."

Hazel gazes up at her partner like he hung the moon for her. There's a contented glow I've never seen in her before. Pregnancy and life out in the middle of nowhere agree with her.

"Is that my Aurora Borealis?" Our uncle strides towards me. More silver threads his golden surfer hair since I last saw him and his gait is broken with a subtle limp.

"Uncle Heathie!" I grin, throwing my arms around his middle. "I missed you! I can't believe you and Hazel are neighbors and I'm left out in the cold."

"Don't kid me. You love L.A. and the weather is gorgeous," he teases, his tan skin marred with deep smile lines as he grins. "I wouldn't consider that out in the cold."

"You should see how freezing it is here in February," Hazel says, rubbing her hands over her upper arms.

"So are you going to be my houseguest?" Heath asks.

"If you don't mind."

"Not at all. It'll be good to catch up. Let's get you settled and we can let Hazel get back to work. I think she's got a few projects that need her attention today."

Hazel works for Heath, or so I thought. But something about the way he dips his head to her feels off, like she's the one who is in charge. Surely not. And Slate is his assistant, or that's what Hazel told me when she first visited.

Heath looks at me expectantly.

Nodding, I fumble with my keys to unlock the trunk. "Sure! Lead the way."

Hazel wiggles her fingers in a little wave. "I'll see you in a bit. We'll have dinner together."

"Great, thanks. Here, I'll just get my stuff."

Heath lifts my battered suitcase from the trunk and marches off through the trees. It takes two of my steps for each one of his, and I'm half-jogging to keep up.

The forest glows green, new growth springing up all around me. The gradient of purples and blues from lupine flowers just budding takes my breath away and makes my fingers twitch for my brushes and paint.

Our grandparent's cabin sits nestled among the trees, so picturesque it makes my heart ache that I haven't been here before. We should have spent summers here growing up. Something about it feels so right, and I no longer have to wonder why Hazel decided to stay. It feels more like home than anywhere we rented throughout our childhoods.

Heath pushes the door open and we step into a cheery yellow kitchen, anchored by a well-loved vintage table with mismatched chairs.

"The guest room is right through here," he says, opening a door to my right. "There's a bathroom here," he says, moving into a masculine but comfortable living room, all brown leather and warm plaids. A vintage cast-iron stove sits on a sizable slab of rock in the corner. I can imagine how cozy this space is when a fire crackles in the stove.

"I really appreciate this. I didn't want to cause any issues, but I felt like I needed to see Hazel," I ramble, shaking out my hands nervously.

Health sets my bag on the table and places his huge hands over my shoulders. The warmth and weight relaxes me. "I'm glad you came to visit. We should have arranged this months ago. It's not a problem."

"Or years ago," I say with a wry smile. "It's been too long. But I'm here now and we can make up for lost time. But I really don't want to be in Hazel's way. I get the feeling she's pretty busy."

"Depends on the day, but I'm sure she'll make time for you. Just be patient while she works out the logistics."

"Aren't you her boss?"

Heath pauses, a thoughtful look on his face as he offers me a bottle of water from his fridge. As I take a few sips, he sighs. "Not anymore. I'm retired. Slate and Hazel have taken over all of my duties."

"Seriously?"

"Slate was my right–hand-man and Hazel has a knack for the work, so it made sense to let them take over. And now I've got time for some traveling and hobbies. It's been good."

"No wonder she's so busy," I mutter, not meaning to be unkind. It merely seems like a lot of work for her to handle, even with her partner's help. Heath was the team leader for as long as I can remember.

"I should go check on everything, but it'll be dinner soon. Why don't you relax for a while and either Hazel or I will come grab you for dinner?"

"Sure. I can entertain myself." Turning away, I scan the living space again, noting the lumpy pillows on the window seat, a tall bookcase in the corner, and worn-down hardwood floors. The space begs for me to cuddle up and rest, but my chest buzzes with the need to explore and get back outside. Patience.

"See you soon." Heath pats my arm and strides past me and out of the cabin.

The door clicks shut, leaving me in absolute silence. Rolling my shoulders, I grab my bag and head into the secondary bedroom.

Heirloom quilts cover the matching set of twin beds. A few paintings are hung over the knotty pine walls. Stepping closer, I greedily examine them. They're not mass produced prints, but probably painted by someone local. That makes me smile.

After shedding my sweatshirt, I lay back on the bed and exhale slowly. I can't wipe the smile off my face. Seeing my sister again filled a need I didn't know I had, and some uneasy, anxious part of me is soothed for the first time in years. This trip is exactly what I needed.

CEDAR

Hazel slumps into the chair across from me, the shadows under her eyes darker today. I've been supplying her with red raspberry leaves for tea, but she's clearly not sleeping well. Maybe some chamomile and more leafy greens would help. As soon as it was warm enough, I transplanted my spinach and kale seedlings, and the spinach is almost ready for harvest. I'll have to talk with Sable and Crickett.

"Cedar?" Slate asks, and I feel as if my mind is transported from my garden back to this meeting room in a rush of noise, everyone's voices flooding back in. From his downturned mouth, my Alpha knows I wasn't listening.

"Sorry," I mumble.

Hawthorne leans over, elbow on the table. "I know you don't enjoy handling your father's duties, but it's only another day or two." My father is the pack's Delta, or Trainer, and fourth in command. Hawthorne is third in command, so even though I'm acting-Delta while my parents are visiting my twin, Onyx, and his mate, Ember, in their new pack, I still answer to him.

"It's fine, I'm listening now. Just thinking about things," I say, raising my chin and meeting Slate's intense gaze.

"So what's the emergency?" Hawthorne asks Hazel, his tone gentle as if he was soothing his toddler.

Hazel doesn't appreciate being treated delicately. Her eyes narrow in irritation and the emotion rolls off her through the pack bond. With her hormones so strong, her influence and dominance are at an all-time high. My wolfish instincts whisper in the back of my mind to bow to her, but that would piss her off even more.

"My sister showed up twenty minutes ago," she says flatly.

The human sister from California? That's unexpected.

"She wanted to be here for the baby arriving," Slate explains. "We put her in Heath's cabin."

The door opens again and the former Alpha strides in, a wide smile on his face. "Sorry, it took longer than expected to get her settled, but she seems content for now."

"*Great*," Hazel says, sarcasm edging her words.

"I know you didn't plan on a visitor, but it'll be fine," Heath says, taking the spot beside her.

"When I first showed up, it caused a lot of problems," Hazel quips. "This isn't the best time to be playing at being a forest ranger and hiding our wolves. What if she sees something?"

Heath shrugs. "Then she finds out. We've negotiated for human family members of wolves to have immunity, so she's in no danger."

"Except it'll freak her out and she's a lot to handle on a good day."

"We won't let her," I say. I've got to do something to ease Hazel's discomfort. Even if it wasn't for the pack bond pulsing in my chest, she's still my friend. "We can keep things quiet, make sure everyone knows to shift far into the woods and to watch their conversations."

"That's what we did when you arrived," Slate says, smiling in the way he only reserves for his mate. Hazel relaxes against him, their connection dulling her agitation.

"You're right," Hazel says. "But I'd prefer she didn't find out her sister is a shifter. It's a risk we don't have to take and I have no idea how she'd react."

Hawthorne pulls out his phone. "I'll communicate with the other packs and make sure no one shows up unexpectedly."

"I'll make sure the rest of our pack knows what to do," I add, knowing it's what my father would do in this situation.

"Lazuli and Cassia are already talking to the patrol, so you just need to handle the unranked wolves," Hazel says, her mouth a grim line.

"Everything will be fine. You can enjoy a nice visit with your sister and relax until the baby comes," Slate says, turning Hazel's hand over in his own and massaging it.

"Relax," she repeats, eyebrows shooting up.

"Yes, relax," Slate reiterates, waves of calm emanating from him.

"Fine," Hazel says, exhaling loudly. "Someone text Jasper, please. My phone keeps giving me a headache."

"No problem," Hawthorne says. Jasper, Slate's brother and Beta, spends part of his week in Onyx and Ember's pack, helping them to rebuild alongside my parents. But if our pack is playing host to a human, he needs to know sooner rather than later.

"She's going to want to hike and see nature. We'll need to make sure someone is with her, obviously," Hazel says.

"We've got it," Heath answers, his low voice soothing. "We've got plenty of people who can keep an eye on her. You don't need to do anything but enjoy seeing her."

Slate gives a grateful smile to his mentor. "See? Everyone can handle this. We've done it before, remember?"

"Yeah, and how did that turn out?" Hazel says, rolling her eyes. "It took less than a week for me to discover what you were and then get myself kidnapped."

"It worked out pretty well in the end." Slate kisses his mate's wrist, drawing a tired smile from her.

"Should we be concerned she is going to turn out to be a shifter too?" I ask, concerned no one has considered this possibility.

Everyone looks to Heath. As the retired Alpha, he is the most qualified to answer. He scrubs at his chin. "I don't think so. Hazel was triggered by trauma and being claimed by her mate. Even if Aurora is latent, which I think is unlikely, it shouldn't manifest from a proximity alone."

Hazel nods, her hand rubbing at her stomach in wide circles. "I need to go talk to Sable about my birth plan to see if we can anticipate any problems Aurora's presence might cause."

Slate rises, helping her when her belly upsets her balance. She swats him away, and he smiles indulgently at her scowl as they make their way out of the room.

Hawthorne leans forward, eyeing Heath. "Do we know how long she's staying?"

"Until the baby is born, at least."

"Anything else we should know about her?"

Heath clears his throat, folding his hands on the table. "She's two years younger than Hazel and she's a painter. Hazel was always the easy-going responsible one, and Aurora was the free-spirited one. She makes friends easily, so she should get along with the pack just fine. My biggest concern is the fact she's fearless and sees most things as a challenge. We will need to be careful."

"Does she have a mate?" I ask, straightening at the look Heath gives me. "I mean boyfriend. Should we be concerned a boyfriend might show up?"

"She isn't one for serious relationships. Hazel would know for sure, but I don't think we need to be concerned about anyone else joining us." His brows crease and I drop my gaze.

"Alright, I'm going to go make the rounds. Cedar, can you go talk to Marigold at the school so she can get the students coached?" Hawthorne dips his head in respect to Heath before he strides out of the room.

"Good day, Alpha," I say, addressing Heath by his old title. He nods, permitting me to leave.

The meadow is quiet as I jog northward to the school building. Double doors stand wide open, allowing me to slip in silently. Sunlight swirls through the huge windows and highlights the rainbow walls, covered with a wallpaper of children's artwork.

Marigold perches on the countertop, surveying her students while they scrawl away at lined paper. The older students have already left for their work studies, so it's just the younger ones spaced throughout the room with their noses to their assignments.

Her strawberry blonde cascade of curls ripples as she leaps down and crosses the room. "Hey, Cedar!" Twisting, she narrows her eyes at her students. "You've still got eight minutes of silent writing. We'll have to redo the time instead of playing soccer if anyone interrupts." Satisfied her students are cowed, she pushes against my biceps, herding me outside. "So what's up?"

"We had a visitor show up," I say.

"Oh, really?" Her face brightens, eyes sparkling with interest.

"Hazel's sister."

"Aurora?" she squeals, hands clapping together. I suspected she would be excited, and it brings a smile to my face.

"She wanted to be here for the birth. They set her up in Heath's cabin."

"Oh, this is fantastic!" She paces, her smile widening until she's beaming sunshine.

"They wanted you to prep your students and make sure they know what they shouldn't say or do."

"Ah, of course. No problem." She nods sagely. "I'd better get to it."

"Thanks," I say.

Marigold spins on her heel, crossing the threshold before pausing and glancing over her shoulder at me. "Hazel once mentioned that Aurora likes plants. I guess she used to have a lot of potted plants before she moved into her tiny apartment with roommates."

Unsure of what she's getting at, I just nod.

"See you at dinner!" She winks, disappearing into the school. My sensitive ears pick up her instructions to the students. She will handle the kids.

Mentally, I review my list of packmates that need to be informed of our visitor. The supply center is closest, and Fern should be working there, so that's where I'll go next. It'll take a while to reach everyone, especially the seniors who could be in any number of places this time of day.

There are only a few hours until the pack gathers for dinner and everyone needs to know before then. When Hazel visited a couple of years ago, we had several weeks to prepare. Aurora is a surprise.

Admittedly, I am looking forward to meeting Hazel's sister. The way everyone describes her, she seems intriguing.

III
DIMPLES & DINNER

AURORA

Heath asked me to hang out in the cabin until he came and fetched me for dinner. But screw that. As cute as his vintage cabin is, I need to be outdoors. The clear air caresses my skin, soothing my lungs with sharp juniper and the musty scent of pine needles decomposing underfoot.

Slipping back out the kitchen door, I take a proper look around. Rough tree trunks rise around me, reaching toward the sky. Unable to resist, I run my fingers down the bark, savoring the texture.

Wildflowers and trailing scrub cover most of the ground, with worn paths through the underbrush snaking out in several directions. Everything feels so fresh and green and my soul soaks it up greedily, as if I had been starving for life until this moment.

With my sketchbook under my arm, I settle cross-legged on the edge of the porch. Delicate white flowers burst from dark greenery around the closest tree. My eyes follow the winding footpath as it darkens in shade and then brightens in sharp relief when the boughs part and sunlight streams down.

My pencil skates over the paper, the shape of the landscape forming with soft lines curving and crossing. The scale of this viewpoint is interesting. Close enough for details while still maintaining the towering scale of the aged trees.

A twig cracks and my pencil jolts from my hand.

Taking a steadying breath, I turn to search for the source. A man stands a few feet away with a sheepish expression on his face. The dappled sunlight gilds his

short, messy hair and highlights a square jaw. He doesn't have the refined features of my sister's partner, but there's something classic about him.

He moves with a grace I don't expect from anyone that muscled, his triceps flexing as he scoops up my pencil from the dirt and presents it to me. Not that I was looking.

"Sorry I startled you," he says, soft and low.

"No, it's fine," I stammer, forgetting all of my social skills in that moment. Sliding the pencil into the spirals of my sketchbook, I set it aside and wipe my palms along my torn jeans.

"You must be Aurora," he says, his gaze meeting mine. Gray-blue eyes like a brewing storm hold me captive. His pupils widen, swallowing up the blue.

"Yeah," I say, my mouth finally remembering how to speak. "I figured I'd get a head start with being a good Auntie and be here for the little one's arrival. Plus I haven't seen Hazel in like two years. A girl needs her sister sometimes, you know?"

This man listens to my babbling without moving or even changing his expression. Anyone else would have shifted their weight to signal that I'm making them uncomfortable. He stands still with those stormy eyes fixed on me like I'm sharing secrets of the universe. When he speaks, it's tentative and thoughtful. "I get that. I miss my brother when we go too long between visits."

"Yeah," I say, thrusting my hand toward him. "It's nice to meet you..." I trail off, hoping he takes the hint.

A calloused and warm hand envelops mine. "I'm Cedar. I'm cousins with Slate, your sister's m- partner." His mouth twitches into a frown for a fraction of a second.

I narrow my eyes, looking for the resemblance. His hand releases mine and cool air washes over my warmed skin, leaving a trail of tingles.

"I'd better get back to work," he says, ducking his head as he turns away. The back of his hair is just as messy as the front, short caramel waves going in different directions, streaked with platinum. My fingers ache to touch, but he's a stranger and I will definitely not be touching his hair.

On instinct, my eyes flick to his swinging left hand, looking for a flash of metal. Nothing. He seems older than me but not by much. Maybe he's Hazel's age.

"See you later!" I yelp, nerves rising up and tightening my throat.

Looking over his shoulder, he smiles at me. Full lips curve, hollowing dimples in his cheeks. Freaking dimples. My stomach clenches and I forget how to smile back until it's too late and he's already striding through the trees down a path I can't see.

Maybe it's all the exposure to nature, but he looked so vibrant and healthy. Hazel did too with her glowing skin and gleaming hair. If I stayed longer, would I start to look that lovely?

Exhaling slowly, I tip my face up and savor the sunshine across my skin. The soft rustle of leaves relaxes me as a breeze brushes against my cheek. Already, I feel better, like the nature around me is soaking into my soul.

"Hey, you," Hazel greets me. She moves slowly, somehow graceful even when her walk has become a bit of a waddle.

"Are you mad I came?" I ask, setting aside my sketchbook and pushing off the porch steps.

Hazel scoffs, her nose scrunching as she shakes her head. "Of course not. Sure, more notice would have been nice, but I could never be angry when I get to see you."

She supports her belly with a hand while the other rests on her hip. Instinctively, I reach a hand out, withdrawing before I touch her.

"Here, come feel. Baby is kicking a ton today."

My palms go to her belly. It feels hard, not squishy at all like I imagined. Hazel raises an eyebrow and then guides my hand to her side. The skin ripples under my fingers. I jerk back with a yelp.

"Was that the baby?" I cautiously reach for her again.

She laughs at my surprise. "Yeah, it's pretty weird, right?"

"So weird." I don't pull away the second time I feel it.

"They must like you," Hazel murmurs.

"How are you feeling?" I ask, dropping my hands.

She continues to rub her belly. "Pretty good, considering. I mean, this is getting rather uncomfortable, but I know it won't last that much longer."

"When exactly are you due?"

"Next week." She shrugs, unconcerned. "But first-time mothers usually go late, from what I've been told."

"Are you going to a hospital?" I ask, biting down on my lip as I realize that healthcare access might be a problem out here.

Hazel shakes her head. "I don't have any complications and we've got a nurse here who is more than qualified for a delivery. Actually, she's delivered most of the kids around here."

"That makes it sound more like a cult," I tease.

"That's what I said when I first got here."

"But, to be clear, it's not a cult. No weird rituals I'll need to watch out for?"

Hazel's smile is uneven, giving me the distinct feeling she's holding something back - not the reaction you want to get when you're worried your sister is a cult leader.

"Of course not. Just people working and hanging out. I think you'll like it around here. I did."

"Yeah," I say, my brows furrowing as I watch her for other clues.

"So, are you hungry? It's about time for dinner."

"Cool, where are we eating? Your cabin?" I ask, stepping back onto the porch to retrieve my belongings.

"Oh, actually everyone eats together most days. We have a chef and a baker, and it's just easier for them to make big meals for everyone," she says.

"Sounding a bit cult-ish again," I mutter, laughing dryly when she rolls her eyes at me.

"You'll want to grab your sweatshirt, Ror. It'll get cold once the sun goes down."

"Alright, *Mom*." Popping inside, I toss my sketchbook onto the dresser of the guest room and grab my sweatshirt off the bed.

Hazel waits at the steps, her arms crossed over her belly. "Come on," she says, seizing my hand and tugging me forward.

When she said everyone, she meant the entire community. Thirty or forty people meander around a clearing. The trees are sparser here and buildings form a wide loop. A vintage-style diner sits on the opposite side, where most people gather.

Dozens of eyes follow me. "How often do people visit? I'm getting weird vibes," I whisper to my sister.

Hazel sighs, her elbow jostling me as she unlinks our arms. "It's not that common, but I think most people know you're my sister so they're just interested because of that."

"What have you been telling them?" I ask, wrinkling my nose.

She leads us toward the door where Slate waits, talking with Uncle Heath. "Come on, it's a buffet," she says, allowing Slate to open the door for her.

"Wow," is all I can say as the smell of garlic and cheese hits me. A gleaming countertop stretches the length of the building, stacked high with platters of pasta, meat, salad, and bread.

Hazel grabs a plate and begins to load it with breaded chicken, pesto pasta, and fluffy slices of garlic bread. I follow her example and even take a serving of salad.

Slate and Heath trail behind us. It's as if everyone is waiting for Hazel to go first before they get their own food. As we step out of the far door, I spy a line forming out the door.

Picnic tables surround the diner, stretching into the forest. Hazel heads to a table on the south end and plops her plate down before sliding onto the bench with a soft grunt. Suppressing my smile, I take the seat beside her. Slate is right behind us and claims the spot on her other side.

"This all smells amazing," I mutter, drooling over the parsley-speckled garlic bread oozing with butter. I'm so enthralled with my food that I hardly notice as others join us.

"Hey there," a young woman says. She sits across from Hazel, wearing a vivid emerald sweater and a dainty daisy headband threaded into her reddish-gold hair.

"Hi," I say automatically.

"I'm Marigold. I'm sure Hazel has mentioned me, but I'm her best friend," she says with a confident wink. Positive energy radiates off of her, and I instantly like her.

"Oh, good to know she's got you and it's not a total testosterone fest over here," I say, tipping my head toward Slate.

Marigold lets out a giggle. "I'm so excited to finally meet you." She glances around the table. "Normally, my boyfriend, Jasper, would be here too. He's Slate's brother, but he's visiting their sister."

Nodding, I pick up my fork and pop a spiral of pasta into my mouth to have something to do.

Another person walks toward us, and I recognize the boy from earlier. Slate's cousin? Cedar? He walks with his head down, eyes on the ground. As he settles onto the bench beside Marigold, I clear my throat.

"Hey, nice to see you again."

"Again?" Marigold asks, looking between us with a smirk on her pink lips.

Cedar is unbothered. "Yeah, I walked past the cabin and she was outside."

"I was sitting on the patio drawing. It's gorgeous outside, I couldn't stay indoors," I explain, feeling a blush creeping up my neck even though I did nothing wrong.

"Oh, that's right, you're an artist!" Marigold chimes. "What's your medium?"

"Watercolor, but I like to switch it up sometimes. Pencils, pastels, gouache, but watercolor is my favorite."

"She paints landscapes," Hazel says.

"Oh! Are you going to paint while you're here?" Marigold asks.

"That's the plan," I say, reaching for the phone in my pocket for the question that always comes next.

"I'd love to see some of your work," Marigold says. With a shy smile, I hand over my phone with the photos app queued up.

Marigold swipes through, her face growing more animated. "These are freaking gorgeous!"

"Thanks."

"Slate, I think she's better than you are!"

"I don't doubt it," he rumbles, his eyes not leaving my sister.

"It's not the same thing," I mutter. "You know, I'd love any advice on finding good views for painting. Anything scenic or interesting is great."

"I'd love that, but I'm usually busy during the day. I'm the local teacher and those kids keep me busy." She shrugs and gives me an apologetic half-smile.

"I can take you," Cedar interjects. Those gray-blue eyes rise to mine. "I manage our garden, so my schedule is flexible."

"If you don't mind," I say, my whole body tensing. "But I'm sure you're busy. I'll be fine on my own, or you can just point me in the right direction."

"I'm ahead of schedule because of how warm it is. The spring planting is almost done, so I've got plenty of free time." He doesn't pressure me, just states the facts in that calm way of his.

"You definitely shouldn't go alone. I'd take you myself, but now's not a great time for hiking for me," Hazel says with a light laugh.

Heat creeps up my neck as I hold Cedar's gaze until he glances down. "If you are going to help me with finding locations to paint, I can help you in the garden. It's only fair, and I really like gardening."

The edge of his mouth quirks, like a smile is breaking through. Warmth stirs in my stomach. I'd love to see those dimples again. "Do you do a lot of gardening at home?"

"No, I wish."

"I've got everything handled, but you're welcome to come see it."

"I'd like that." I tear my eyes away from his and feel my blush redouble when I see how high Marigold's eyebrows are arching. A small smirk twists her lips. What did I do? I wasn't flirting. Maybe things are just so boring around here, anyone new is entertaining for them.

Scowling to myself, I stab another bite of pasta and look away into the trees as I chew. I must be reading the table wrong. This isn't a group of starving artists and actors in Los Angeles.

Hazel and Marigold discuss baby things while I disassociate. When Hazel stands, I blink in surprise. Our plates are mostly empty.

"I'd better get her home," Slate says, his hand on Hazel's lower back.

She lets out a yawn and then nods. "Yeah, I'm wiped. Rory, I'll see you tomorrow, okay?"

"Goodnight, Mama," I say, giving in to the urge to pat her belly.

Marigold rises and stacks our plates. "I'll drop these in the kitchen. Cedar, are you on dish duty tonight?" He shakes his head. "Good, you can walk Aurora back to Heath's cabin."

"Um, that's okay. I remember the way."

Cedar's open mouth closes.

"It's getting dark quickly and the forest looks different after dark. There aren't city lights out here. It's pitch black. You need someone to help you, sorry." Marigold leaves no room for arguing as she walks away, balancing the stack of plates in front of her.

"Sorry," Cedar says.

"I really think I'll be fine on my own," I protest.

He huffs, shaking his head. "She's right about it being dark. My family's cabin is near Heath's, so let's walk together. Just to be safe."

My lips press together, keeping my arguments contained. I pride myself in being capable, so the entire situation irritates me. But this gorgeous man wants to walk through the trees with me, and that's hard to say no to. I feel my resolve slipping. "Okay, fine."

Cedar allows me to take the lead as we cross the clearing. I may think I have a general idea of where Heath's cabin is, but as soon as we reach the shadow of the trees, I am entirely lost. But Cedar doesn't tease me or point out my failure. Instead, he walks beside me, subtly directing my steps with his own. My ego purrs. When was the last time I met a man who doesn't jump at the chance to say *I told you so?*

That appreciation is replaced with an unnerving sense of disorientation as the trees swallow up all available light around us. The starlight through the branches can't reach us and taunts me as it paints the highest branches in silver.

Grinding my molars, I slow and step carefully, trying desperately to keep track of the man a few inches away from me. Surely he won't let me walk into a tree. Does he know the forest so well he can walk in the pitch black? Haven't they heard of a flashlight?

My foot catches, my body jolting forward as my momentum turns to falling. There is no time to cry out, my body tensing for impact. Before I hit the ground, hands close around my upper arms, halting my nose-dive so suddenly, I let out an embarrassing "Umph."

"You okay?" Cedar asks as he levers me back to standing.

"Yeah, totally," I say, doing my best to sound cool and collected. Never mind that my heart is hammering in my throat so hard, I'm sure he can hear it.

He sighs, clearly not fooled by my bravado. It's probably the shake to my voice that gives me away. "Aurora, why don't you hold on to my arm. We are almost there, but I know it's too dark for you to see."

Gently, his hand finds mine, guiding it to his arm. Holy biceps. My breath stalls as I wrap my other hand around his arm, feeling the muscles shifting under my fingertips.

"Thanks for catching me," I murmur, internally berating myself for feeling up his arm, even if he placed my hand there.

He doesn't seem to mind or he's too polite to react. I can't see his face, but his voice is casual as he says, "No problem. This is exactly why I wanted to walk you back. It wouldn't be a good vacation if you broke your arm on our uneven trails."

"I appreciate that. I don't want to be a burden for Hazel. I'm worried I'm adding to her stress," I admit, though I'm not sure why I'm opening up to this almost stranger.

Cedar doesn't answer for a long minute, but his free hand covers mine. "Step up, there's a rock here," he says.

I ignore how his voice turns my stomach all gooey. He's my sister's new family, not someone in the city. She would have to live with the consequences if I hit it and quit it, and something tells me Cedar isn't a playboy on hookup apps.

His hand falls away from mine once we are over the offending rock, though I still cling to his upper arm. He's going to have to pry me off at this rate.

"I can tell she's excited you're here. I think she missed you."

My eyebrows furrow as the sentiment sinks in. "I missed her too. I should have visited a year ago."

Cedar's pace slows as Heath's cabin appears between the dark columns of tree trunks. "It seems to me that right now is the right time."

I'd like to question him, but there's something about his tone that feels sage, like he is an oracle passing down wisdom to mere mortals.

"Yeah, I suppose so. Well, good night!" I say, reluctantly releasing him before he tries to shake me off. Stepping onto the porch, I glance over my shoulder to see his striking profile illuminated by the cabin's golden glow. My assessment of him as an oracle feels fitting because in this moment he could pass as a Greek god.

"Good night," he echoes, shoving his hands in his pockets as he ambles into the darkness. I watch him until he disappears, and then shut the door and click the lock out of habit.

"Hey, Rory. You can leave that unlocked." Heath greets me from the leather sofa. He cradles a faded paperback with curling edges in his hands. "Have a good evening hanging out with Hazel and everyone?"

"Yeah, I can see why she likes it here so much."

He nods his head absently. "Yeah, it's not too shabby."

"I'm exhausted. I'll see you tomorrow."

Without looking up, he says, "I'll be out tomorrow all day, so don't worry about me. You can enjoy the cabin and the meadow, but don't go hiking without someone with you. It's too easy to get lost. We don't have marked trails."

"No problem." I don't have any plans for tomorrow aside from breaking out my sketchbook, so it's easy to agree.

A faint buzz vibrates under my skin as I wash up and curl up under the vintage quilt in the guest room. The day feels like it was endless, with my drive, settling into this cabin, and making new friends over dinner. They were all so nice, it makes me smile into my pillow. Not too shabby, indeed.

IV
SEEDLINGS &
SANDWICHES

CEDAR

Skipping my morning run has my skin crawling, but it would require a hike to get a safe distance away from our visitor's eyes, and I don't want to lose my entire morning. I should have gone. Whenever I go a few days without shifting, it feels like fur and claws might burst out of me without my permission. I'm on edge.

So I sink my hands into the dirt and close my eyes, letting the rich soil soothe my nerves. It's as familiar to me as my own tattoos. I've churned this earth, added compost and mulch, poured in vitamins. No one else understands the pride I take in this soil, but they all enjoy the harvest. That's enough for me.

My breath slows, my muscles relaxing as I let the handful of dirt fall from my fingers. Everything is fine.

A whiff of something unusual washes over me. It's slightly sweet, with a hint of resin and chalk, mingled with something smokey and earthy. My eyes pop open, my head swinging around until I spot her.

Hazel's sister wanders along the edge of my garden, trailing her hand through a patch of overgrown mint. The rest of my herbs grow in the center of my garden where I can keep an eye on them, but mint is such an upstart, I banished it to the border where metal garden bins can contain it.

Morning light draws a luminous line down her nose and over the cupid's bow of her lips. Her silhouette is clear through the light cotton dress fluttering around her knees. It's one of those bohemian styles with rough edges. Brown eyes, lightened to honey in the morning's glow, rise to meet mine.

My mind goes blank. What is she doing here? What do I say to her?

It takes her a few minutes to wind through the gravel pathways and reach me. Brushing the dirt from my hands, I gather up my tools and straighten.

"Hey," she says, quieter than yesterday. Shy, almost.

"Aurora."

"Is it okay that I'm here?"

"Yeah, you're welcome to explore," I say thickly. Of the entire compound, she chose my garden. Hazel and Marigold warned me, but I didn't think…

"This is amazing," she says, turning to survey the expansive space, taking in the tidy rows of wooden raised beds teeming with various greenery. "When they said garden, I didn't think they meant an entire mini farm." Her charming laugh caresses me and I sway forward.

"Yeah." I have to clear the grit from my throat. "We've got a lot of people to provide food for."

"I bet it's great quality compared to the grocery store, right?"

I nod. There's more to it than that, but I sense she understands.

"We have a chicken coop and two milking goats in the back," I say, gesturing to the sloped buildings on their side of my storage shed. A few larger fruit trees block most of them from view.

"Seriously?"

"Yeah." I rub the back of my neck, feeling awkward. "Do you want to see them?"

"No," she says quickly. "Um, not today, that's okay." Her posture curves inwards, her confidence wavering. Interesting.

"So what are you working on this morning?" she asks, changing the subject smoothly.

"I'm prepping to plant some seeds."

"Do you mostly plant from seed?" Those honey eyes study mine, and I turn my trowel over in my hand nervously.

"Mostly seedlings, but some things are better from seed."

She steps closer and I smell something floral under the scent of paint. Her eyes alight, mouth quirking into a smile. "Okay, let's get to work!"

"You don't need to."

"Just let me. When I get bored, I'll go paint."

Hands propped on her hips and her bottom lip jutted out, she looks so much like Hazel and yet so different. Hazel is rarely obstinate and never enjoys arguing. I have a feeling Aurora would love some verbal sparring.

"Alright."

"So what are we planting?" she asks, her hands sweeping out.

Picking up my tote, I sigh. "This part of the bed is going to be radishes, and the rest will be carrots."

"Great!"

"Here, I'll dig a small trench, and you drop the seeds in. Space them out about an inch apart, and we can thin them later." I place the jar of radish seeds into her waiting hand.

"Cool, let's do it."

She grins at me while I crouch and drag my trowel through the dirt. Three rows fit across the open space before I move over and start on the next patch. I can't help but peek at Aurora. With her tongue against her upper lip, she delicately sprinkles seeds along the lines I left behind.

"Does that look good?" she asks, meeting my gaze again.

My eyes drop to the dirt in front of me. "Oh, yeah. Perfect."

A low laugh tumbles out of her. "Glad I can manage dropping seeds in a hole." I'm not a fan of the sarcasm edging her words. It's a little too self-deprecating.

Standing, I shake the hair off my forehead. "I." My voice catches, and I have to clear my throat. "I'm getting my hoe for the next bed. It's a lot bigger."

Aurora pops up, one eyebrow raised. My words echo back to me, and I could burrow into the soil and die. "You know, a garden hoe, like a little shovel." My face is flaming.

Aurora grabs my shoulder as her head dips and she struggles to breathe through her silent laughter. Her nails prick my skin through my shirt, making my back straighten.

She comes up, her face a beautiful pink. "Did you seriously just say you're getting your hoe for the bigger bed?"

Scoffing, I fold my arms over my chest. "Yes, because I'm not thirteen years old."

Caramel highlights shimmer in her hair as she shakes her head. "You better go get that hoe," she chokes, not releasing my shoulder. It would be rude if I pulled away or removed her hand, right?

"Okay," I manage to say.

Aurora jerks her hand back, pressing her fingertips to the bridge of her nose. "Sorry," she says, the word breaking into a broken giggle.

"Okay," I repeat, stilted. My attempt at a polite smile feels like a cringe, so I turn and march toward my storage building.

When I return, clutching the red handle of my favorite hoe, Aurora is examining the jars of seeds in my tote.

"Did you collect these yourself?"

"Yeah." Pride warms my chest, allowing the tension through my shoulders to relax. I guess we are past the hoe debacle.

She stands, glossy hair brushing over her shoulder with the movement. "So can I see your hoe?" Apparently not. Her smirk tells me she's joking.

Exhaling audibly, I reach for my tote. Aurora snatches it up first. "I've got it," she says, fluttering her eyelashes at me. "Since you won't let me touch your hoe."

"Blooming bollocks," I mutter, marching past her and deeper into the garden to the open planter. Embarrassment prickling at me, I roughly yank the last vestiges of last year's growth and toss them into the path. I'll get them into the composter later.

"Sorry, too much teasing? I don't always know when to stop," Aurora says softly. That hand rests on my upper back. She is a touchy thing, isn't she?

"It's fine," I say gruffly, standing. That hand slides down my back before she pulls away. Ignoring the zing down my spine, I focus on dragging my hoe across the earth to even out a few spots.

"Okay," she says lightly. "So what are we planting here?"

"Beets and spinach. Mostly spinach."

We work in silence, and my mood slowly improves. Every time I glance up at Aurora, she has some look of concentration, usually involving her tongue against her top or bottom lip.

I don't want to admit it, but she's adorable. Her teasing might be torturous, but I could have asked her to leave and I didn't. She's pleasant to be around.

"That should do it," I say, stepping back.

She continues her work, inching behind me as she adds seeds to the last few feet. Finished, she brushes her hands on the skirt of her dress and straightens.

"Thanks for your help," I say.

"We both know you didn't need any help, but I appreciate you entertaining me. It feels good to get some dirt on my hands."

I blink at her. No one else has told me that before and it resonates with every cell of my being. She continues on as if nothing is amiss.

"I miss being around nature. I love my home, but the concrete jungle can't compare to an actual forest. Even suburbia with lawns was better than the city. Sometimes I don't think I can handle another year there." She rambles, setting jars into my tote and straightening everything absently. Finished, she looks up at me with a vulnerable smile.

"Could you be a painter somewhere else?" I ask, no other thoughts in my head. That smile burned them all away.

She shrugs. "I guess. I've never tried. But hey, this is like a painting vacation. Aside from seeing my sister. Obviously her and the baby come first." That beautiful pink tinge is back on her cheeks.

"You can do both," I say. "I'm going to do a little weeding and cleaning up. You should go paint."

With a lopsided smile, she hands me the tote of tools and today's seeds. Swallowing, I accept it from her, our hands brushing. With a rustle of fabric, she slips past me.

It takes all my concentration to focus on thinning the carrots from two weeks prior. Bees buzz through the early blooms, birds singing in the distance, but the only sound my ears catch is Aurora's pencil scratching across her paper. She's settled against the base of a tree in the corner of my garden.

Wild strawberry hugs the ground and crawls over the fence on either side of the tree. It must be my imagination, but it looks like every single white blossom is turned toward Aurora, like she is the sun. I can't blame the blooms. There's something about her that draws you in. She's a force of nature all her own.

AURORA

There are so many options for painting, I'm overwhelmed. First priority is something for Hazel. They don't know the sex yet, but paintings of plants are gender-neutral, right?

The world drops away as I sketch, starting with a series of rabbits and vegetables, inspired by the garden. It feels very Peter Rabbit. Next, I outline a little mouse reaching for a strawberry. Cute.

Movement catches my eye and draws me from my fixation. Cedar's back flexes as he reaches across a garden bed a few yards away from me. Somehow he's worked his way over here. I can't help the small smile curving my lips.

Once, he looks up, his gray-blue eyes intense under the messy mop of golden hair. My eyes dart down to my paper, pretending I wasn't ogling him, but he's such a commanding presence, I can't help but look back. His head dips as he focuses on his work. I can still feel his biceps under my hands, solid and reassuring. I really should stop touching him.

A grumble interrupts my thoughts. My stomach growls again. Cedar's head shoots up, his eyes locking on me. No way he heard my stomach from that far away.

"I'm ready for lunch. What about you?" he asks, raising his voice so I can hear him clearly. I make a thumbs-up and raise it into the air.

Adding a few flourishes to my artwork, I call it complete and stow my supplies away into my messenger bag. A shadow falls across me, and I look up to see Cedar offering his hand. He's steady and sturdy as he pulls me to my feet.

"Thanks."

He just nods in response and strides toward the archway on the southern end of the garden. I scramble to keep up with him, but after a moment, he slows. Pressing my lips together to hide a smile, I fall into step beside him.

"So is there a plan for lunch?" I ask.

"Crickett's diner has some sandwiches. Is that okay for you?"

"Great."

We scale the steps and pop into the diner. The windows leave rectangles of warm afternoon light splashed across the black and white tile floor. The counter is noticeably empty and I admire the expanse of polished chrome.

Cedar crosses to a deli case at the end. "Turkey or ham?"

"Either," I say.

He returns with one of each, a couple of bags of potato chips, and two bottles of water. With a tilt of his head, he ushers me outside. On instinct, I go to the same picnic table as last night. Cedar says nothing but settles across from me.

"What do you want?" he asks, cracking open a bottle of water and taking a drink.

"I'm not picky, but I'd probably like the barbeque chips more than cheddar."

"Sure, and how about I take the ham?" He claims the cheddar chips for himself.

"Works out perfectly," I murmur, picking up the turkey sandwich and unwrapping it. The bread is thick and the aioli inside smells like pesto. "Oh, this is good."

Cedar nods while chewing his own bite. Once he swallows, he gives me another of those rare smiles. It knocks every thought out of my head and I freeze with my food halfway to my mouth.

"My mom bakes all of our bread. And my dad made that cheese."

"No way."

His smile widens into something that could be considered a grin. "And I grew the lettuce, tomatoes, and cucumber."

"No wonder it's so good," I say, enjoying the flush warming his neck. I want to kiss the pink shell of ears when he blushes like this. As soon as the thought forms in my brain, I push it away. Ridiculous. He isn't remotely my type, he just has a nice smile.

"When did you start painting?" he asks.

The question surprises me. It shouldn't, but with my Los Angeles friends, no one would bother to ask. They'd be busy sharing their latest accomplishments. The past didn't matter, just what you had right now. But I'm not in the city anymore.

Cedar looks at me expectantly, unaware of my racing thoughts.

"I don't even remember. Forever. Remember those yellow watercolor palettes we got for school? I remember scraping the last of the paint out of those and layering it over construction paper obsessively."

"That's impressive," he said, and he sounds like he genuinely means it.

"What about you? Did you always want to grow food for people?"

He lets out an exhale, his shoulders rising and falling. Dark lashes frame his eyes as he looks into the distance. "No, but I didn't have any other plans. When I was a teenager, the gardener at the time, Tansy, needed help and I was looking for a job." He pauses, the shadow of a smile on his face. "I loved it. It's predictable, but then it's not because you're partnering with nature. Like this year it's been so warm, I finished all my seedling transplanting last week. Almost a month earlier than last year."

"Oh, yeah?"

"And there's a puzzle aspect to it. I can test the soil and add whatever the plants need, but sometimes it's not that obvious. I get to diagnose problems and figure out solutions. Nothing is rushed and I like the slower pace."

"That sounds really nice right about now," I murmur, imagining my life slowing down. Looking more like today and less like my typical frantic race between jobs and galleries, staying up late at night to paint in terrible lighting.

"Why?" His question is so blunt, it takes me a moment to string my thoughts into a coherent answer.

Setting my sandwich down, I wipe my mouth with my napkin. "Things aren't like this at home. It's always a mad rush. It's exhausting."

His mouth thins, those dimples reappearing though it isn't from a smile. Disappointment, maybe.

"It'll be worth it someday. If I keep hustling and getting my paintings out there, eventually they'll earn enough that I don't have to bartend or have a dozen roommates."

"You have a dozen roommates?" he asks, his hands gripping the table.

I can't help but laugh at him, but he doesn't seem offended. "No, just making a point. I only have two right now, well three."

His brow furrows like he's really trying to understand me. "And you have a house out there?"

"Just an apartment. Right now I have the second bedroom to myself, though I doubt that'll be the case very long."

"Why?"

This is getting into uncomfortable territory. Squirming, I pick at my chips and pop a couple of shards into my mouth. But when I finish chewing and swallowing, he is still trained on me and waiting for an answer.

"We can't make rent without adding another roommate."

Now it's my turn to be embarrassed, for a much more legitimate reason than saying an awkward sentence about gardening tools.

"That sounds difficult," he says, releasing me from my churning thoughts.

"It's not fun."

Cedar looks at me for a long moment. His dimples appear and disappear as his jaw grinds. In the end, he decides to say nothing. My breath rushes out of me when he stands and gathers up our paper plates.

"I'm heading back to work. I might use the blower to help with some leaves, so you might want to avoid the garden this afternoon." His dismissal isn't harsh, just practical. Still, it stings.

"Sure, totally. I'll see you around."

Hours later, I sprawl across the porch, staring up at the swaying branches around the cabin's roof line. I'm simultaneously out of creative drive for the day, but also exploding with inspiration. I was so right about this visit being good for my work.

Hazel leans over me, her sudden appearance startling me. I sit up fast enough to send a wave of dizziness through me. Hands anchored on the porch, I rotate to face her.

"Have a good day?" she asks, easing down beside me.

"Actually, it was very nice! I spent the morning in the garden."

"Oh." Her cheeks hollow as she chews them.

"Cedar was nice enough to let me plant some beets and spinach. We've got to grow lots of healthy vegetables for Mama and Baby." With a grin, I place my palm over her belly.

Her head tips back, eyes closed. The dark shadows under her eyes look worse.

"Are you getting enough sleep, sis?"

Hazel's dry laugh confirms my suspicions. "I'm too uncomfortable to sleep. I can't wait for this baby to get here so I'm not hurting constantly." She rubs at where her belly meets her hip.

"Only a while longer," I say. "What can I do to help?"

Her eyes open and she smiles at me. "I was thinking we could have a family dinner tonight. And Marigold planned a baby shower for the day after tomorrow. Ask her if she needs anything. I'm good. Slate won't let me work very much at this point. Not now that I'm officially a boat."

"Hazel," I draw her name out, chastising her.

She raises a hand and laughs. "I'm so over this, just let me joke. I didn't mind the rest of pregnancy but these last couple of weeks suck."

"Sorry." I wrap my arms around hers and lean my head against her shoulder.

"I'm glad you're here," she says, so quietly I almost miss it.

"Me too. So when is this family dinner?"

"An hour. At my cabin."

"Ooh, I can't wait to see it!"

"Great. I'd better get going."

I resist the urge to try and help her as she maneuvers to standing. Her smile is edged with discomfort as she waves at me and sets off through the trees. It worries me, but I'm not sure there's anything I can do.

Fifty minutes later, I'm dressed in something that doesn't have paint all over it, my hair brushed, and my nails scrubbed. It's my version of dressing up.

Standing on the edge of the porch, I wonder how I'm going to find my way to Hazel's cabin, when a couple walks around the edge of the building.

"Hey!" Marigold chimes, waving her free hand at me. The other is secured in the grasp of a man I don't recognize. The boyfriend. "This is Jasper," she says with hearts dancing in her eyes.

"Hi, I'm Aurora." Descending the steps, I shake his offered hand.

Jasper reminds me of Slate, but where Slate is dark, Jasper is pale. Even his hair is a platinum blonde that glows in the sunlight and makes Marigold's strawberry-blonde curls appear copper.

"Nice to meet you," Jasper says. "You really do look a lot like Hazel."

"Doesn't she?"

"I've heard that before," I say with an awkward laugh.

"You're so pretty!" Marigold reaches out to gently touch my arm. "We are here to get you for family dinner! Heath's cabin is on our way to Hazel's, we volunteered!"

"Lead the way!"

It's still light out, thank goodness, so I can walk beside Marigold until the trees and shrubs force us into a single file. Jasper's hand twists behind his back, keeping a hold of his girl. It's sweet.

We pass a smaller cabin, but that must not be the one, because we keep going until we find a cabin with a skillion-style roof. Voices drift out of the dark forest green door that is wide open, welcoming us inside.

Jasper pauses at the door until Marigold and I pass him. The cabin is full of warm wood, comfortable leather furniture, and homey plaid throw blankets. Framed charcoal drawings dot the planked walls. It's bigger than Heath's cabin, though it shares the same homey aesthetic.

Hazel stands in the kitchen, fussing over some sort of egg rolls. Slate hovers nearby, watching her and ready to help. She waves him off and turns toward us with a huge smile, holding up the platter in her hand. "Come in!"

She's prepared an entire spread of finger foods, mostly fried. Everyone fills a plate before settling around the living room. Even after we start to eat, Slate won't remove his hand from the small of Hazel's back. He rubs small circles as she leans into him.

"How was your first day?" Marigold asks brightly.

I swallow my bite. "Um, great. Nice. I went to the garden and did some sketching."

"The garden?" she asks. The front door swishes open. "Oh, speaking of!" Marigold's grin turns devious and I tense.

Cedar steps through the door. But no, the hair is wrong. It's longer and a bit darker. Not Cedar. Then Cedar steps in behind the man who must be his brother, Onyx.

Seeing them side by side is unsettling - there is no way they aren't twins. Copy and paste. And yet they look so different. Cedar is cleaner cut, brighter. Onyx looks like he probably used guyliner in high school.

"Hello, miss me?" The brother says, smirking as Marigold jumps up and throws her arms around him. When she releases him, he focuses on Hazel. "Stay there, sweetheart." He walks over and stoops to hug her.

"Missed you! Where is your beautiful girlfriend?"

Onyx shrugs. "Ember didn't want to leave things unattended. She'll be here for the baby shower though."

Cedar steps closer to my seat, and I tip my chin up to see his face. "Aurora, this is my brother, Onyx."

"The sister," he says. I set my plate aside and rise in time to get swept up in a tight hug. When Onyx releases me, I catch a scowl on Cedar's face. He's practically glaring at his brother.

"Nice to meet you," I say, sinking back into my seat.

The twins get plates, and Onyx sits on the floor against Hazel's chair, while Cedar sits beside me on the sofa.

"Cedar was saying you moved. How far away is it?" I ask Onyx.

"About a forty-minute drive north of here. Well, you have to go east, then north, then west. There isn't a very direct route. Not for cars, anyway."

"Will you go back home tonight?"

"Definitely. I don't like to be away from Ember overnight. These two would kill me if I didn't take good care of her, though she's usually the one saving my ass." He jerks his chin toward Slate and Jasper.

From the expressions on their faces, I suspect that is true. A few pieces start to click into place. "So your girlfriend," I start.

"Ember," Onyx supplies.

"Is Jasper and Slate's sister?"

"Yeah." Onyx says, sounding amused.

"But you and Cedar are Slate's cousins?" I speak my thoughts out loud without filtering them. At least I stop myself before I accuse him of dating someone he is related to.

Marigold lets out a laugh. "She just put it together." She presses her hand over her eyes. "You guys better explain." With a snort of laughter, her head falls onto Jasper's shoulder.

Slate rolls his eyes but sits forward and wets his lips. "Ember and Jasper are my half-siblings. We share a mom. Different dads. But on my *dad's* side, I have an aunt, who is the twins' mom. So they aren't related to Jasper or Ember, just me."

"Thank fuck," Onyx mutters.

It's my turn to laugh uncomfortably. "Okay, that makes sense, I guess."

"I know it's confusing," Hazel says, a wry smile overtaking her face. "No one exactly expected Ember and Onyx to hook up, but she was here to visit us and that's exactly what they did."

"Hey! Not a random hook up. Marigold, tell them." Onyx looks between them, scowling.

Marigold shrugs. "I'm not the one to talk about hook ups versus relationships. It took me ages to realize I was in love with Jasper and not just hot for him."

"It's okay," Jasper says softly, placing a kiss below her ear. I swallow, something inside of me twinging. I can't imagine having a boyfriend treat me that sweetly, or be that passionate in such a small way.

"Did you all grow up together?" I ask, curiosity getting the better of me. Could I make this any weirder?

"Well, Slate, the twins, and I did," Marigold says. "Jasper grew up a few miles north, but he moved here a couple of years ago. Luckily." She beams at her partner.

"And you know Hazel joined us a couple of years ago," Marigold continues. The best friend vibes are strong between them as Marigold winks at my sister.

My blood goes cold as I realize they're all in serious relationships, and then there's Cedar and me. It's like a quadruple partially-blind date. A triple date with two extra wheels. What does Cedar think about this? He tolerated me just fine in his garden this morning, but I know I can be annoying.

"You okay?" he whispers, leaning until his upper arm brushes mine. His body heat radiates through the thin shirt he wears. It's different than the white shirt he wore in the garden. I take the opportunity to look at him properly. He must have showered, because his messy hair lies smoother and darker, like it's still damp.

Instinctively, I take a deep breath. He smells like herbs - earthy basil, rosemary, and mint. I need another hit of that. I lean into him to take another lungful. Los Angeles would smell a lot nicer if they could turn that into a vape flavor. Cedar goes tense against me. Ah, crap. He asked me a question and I'm almost falling tits first into his lap.

"Sorry, yeah, I'm great. You smell good," I whisper back, embarrassed the last part slipped out.

Every nerve in my body goes haywire when he lowers his face toward mine and breathes in my hair. It's a good thing I'm already seated because my knees would have given out. He leans back, the smallest hint of a smile on his lips as he says, "You do too."

My mouth opens but no words make it out. Did he think I was flirting with him? Was I? Did he mean to flirt back? Or is he just returning a compliment so I don't feel stupid? My pulse races.

The conversation carries on around us, but Cedar's eyes stay on me. I snap my jaw shut, but then lick my lips to try and prepare something to say. It's no use. Those stormy eyes go to my mouth when my tongue darts out. Oh, that was the wrong thing to do.

"Aurora?" someone asks.

The trance is broken and Cedar looks away. I'm a muddled mess, stomach clenched, heart hammering, skin tingling.

"Rory?" Hazel asks, sounding concerned.

"Yeah, sorry, what?"

"Any last minute name suggestions for the parents?" Onyx asks. "They're gonna announce the baby name at the party."

"Shower," Marigold corrects.

"But you don't know if it's a boy or a girl." I cock my head, my brows furrowing.

Hazel's smile is secretive. "Yeah, we wanted a name that works for both." Slate leans forward and kisses her temple.

"Nature names, right?" I ask.

"I said Storm," Onyx says.

"I still think Jade would be good," Jasper says.

Onyx throws his hand into the air. "I second that!"

Marigold shushes him. "You just want a name like yours."

Shrugging, I give Hazel my best charming smile. "You know I already recommended Rock."

"Rock," Marigold repeats, squeezing her eyes shut as she smothers a giggle against Jasper's shoulder.

"Otherwise, Fox has become a pretty normal name. Or Lynx," I suggest.

Hazel exhales, shaking her head. "You guys are all ridiculous. I swear, we have this handled."

"Sure, but if you don't have all your options you can't know if you picked the best one," Onyx says with a patronizing smile. Hazel reaches down and flicks the top of his head.

"What about River or Skye?" I add.

"Rowan, Sage, Sorrel, Juniper, Clover," Cedar says.

"Those are good!" Marigold raises her eyebrows, twisting to see Hazel and Slate's reactions.

Hazel's head falls back against Slate's shoulder. "You guys can save those for your own kids. We're good!"

"I do like Sage," Marigold says, running her nails down Jasper's ribs. He leans in, whispering into her ear. She shivers.

"Geez," I mutter, pointedly looking away from the display.

Cedar chuckles, tipping his head close again. "They're always like that. You'll get used to it." His breath ghosts over my cheek.

"I'm surprised they're not the pregnant ones," I whisper back. His huff of laughter is gratifying.

"Give it a few months. I don't think Marigold will be able to wait once Hazel's baby arrives."

"That's sweet," I murmur.

Cedar's eyes flick over my face, analyzing in a way that makes me feel seen.

"Do you want to go hiking tomorrow? I can show you some spots that might be good to paint." His offer catches me off guard, and my heart swells.

"I would love that."

My cheek brushes his and he moves away. The flash of excitement fades away with distance, though I'm still painfully aware of where his legs have spread enough that my knee touches his thigh. Any other man, I would be pissed he was invading my space, but with Cedar, I don't mind. More than not minding, I like the contact.

"I need some chocolate," Hazel declares, and half the room jumps to accommodate her. I raise one eyebrow and she shrugs in response. She's got it pretty good here, and I have no doubt her baby will be spoiled to the max with so many uncles and aunties around. It's obvious I'm not needed, but nonetheless, I'm grateful to be here.

The rest of the evening races by, full of laughter and warm affection. The two couples can't keep their hands off each other, and even Onyx has his phone out to text Ember. I see a flash of some rather suggestive emojis when he fumbles his screen.

Cedar stays by my side, murmuring a quiet commentary into my ear whenever the others discuss something I know nothing about. My heart races each time, leaving me exhausted by the time everyone is ready to call it a night.

Marigold and Jasper offer to walk me home, and it might be my imagination, but Cedar seems disappointed. Maybe his scowl is unrelated, but it doesn't feel that way.

Everyone says their goodbyes, including everyone saying goodbye to Hazel's belly separately. She just laughs and rubs at that sore spot at her hip.

Onyx grabs me for a hug, leaving me feeling too awkward to initiate a hug with Cedar. I'll see him tomorrow anyway.

The night is solid darkness. Hazel is thoughtful enough to hand me a flashlight so I can watch my own feet and ignore the way Marigold's hand slips under Jasper's shirt. I have no doubt the moment they drop me off at Heath's cabin, their hands will be wandering to even more inappropriate places.

I'd like to be annoyed, but it just leaves me feeling lonely. Hugging my sketchbook to my chest, I flop down on my temporary bed and try to quiet my thoughts. In that silence, a muffled animal noise reaches me. Curiosity gets the better of me and I crack the window open a sliver.

The second howl is much clearer. It's haunting and beautiful, leaving me aching to paint the forest and moon in shades of black and silver. It's probably a coyote, but it sounds like a wolf. That must be why they don't want me hiking alone.

The idea of such a majestic creature running through the woods is inspiring, and I tug the quilt around my shoulders and nestle down, visions of dark trees and silver fur swirling in my mind.

V
PAINTERS &
ASS-PRINTS
CEDAR

It makes sense. Hazel wanted me to take Aurora hiking. I'm the one with the time. She already knows me. I'm the logical choice, and I almost have myself convinced that my reasons are completely selfless by the time I reach my garden.

Dew sparkles on shivering leaves, turning the garden into a glittering tapestry. I love early mornings like this. The rise of emotion leaves my muscles aching. Another day without shifting. I'll have to handle this tonight or I'm risking slipping out of control. It's never been something I've had to worry about. I'm the composed one, and while Onyx accidentally shifted more than a few times as a volatile teenager, I never did. Even Slate had a few outbursts over the years.

Yet I don't feel composed when Aurora appears in the garden entrance. Tendrils of baby peas sway around her as they work to climb the arched trellis. They reach for her as she passes through. She's in baggy jeans with her hair tied up in a ponytail, revealing the slope of her neck.

"Good morning!" She adjusts the messenger bag over her shoulder.

Moving without thought, I meet her in the middle. Her smile brightens and I take in the effect as my heart rate picks up. Even my stomach churns nervously. This isn't like me. With a quick exhale to steady myself, I focus on speaking. "Ready to go already? It's pretty early."

"Sorry," she says, those honey eyes turning regretful.

"Oh, no, that's not what I meant." I scramble to repair the situation. "I'm used to being the only morning person around here. You surprised me. A good surprise."

The smile that warms her face also seizes up my lungs. She's stunning, painfully beautiful with gold flecks in her irises and freckles dusting her tawny skin.

"Well, not anymore! I've always loved mornings. I'm a wreck late at night, not sure if you noticed last night." Her nose crinkles with her self-deprecating smile and her chin dips and she peers up at me through dark lashes.

"You didn't seem like a wreck to me," I murmur, drawing closer than I should. The air holds a chill and her sweater looks thin.

"Glad I hid it well," she says with a laugh. Her hands rub together as she glances around. "How's the garden?"

"Good."

She wanders past me, close enough I can feel her body heat. I turn to follow her, unable to help myself. She pauses by the two garden beds of freshly planted seedlings - the ones I planted the day before she arrived. They've rooted nicely and a new set of leaves unfurls on many of their stems.

"What are these?"

"Broccoli."

"It doesn't look like broccoli," she says sweetly, stooping to examine the plants.

"Seedlings often look the same. It'll be obvious it's broccoli as they get bigger," I reassure her. My hand rests on her lower back. When did I put it there? "And these are cabbage, cauliflower, and that whole bed is kale."

She twists to stare at me, her mouth playfully curved downward and one eyebrow raised. "Ew! Kale?"

"Not a fan of kale?"

"No! It's gross."

"Maybe Los Angeles kale is gross," I say, unable to help the smirk forming on my face.

"It's like the kale capital of the world," she says, letting out a laugh. It's husky and I feel it in my skin. The shake of her head flips her ponytail over her shoulders. "People drink it in green smoothies all the time."

"Well, my kale is better. Not as a smoothie. That's questionable. But cooked up with butter, it's delicious."

She straightens and I force my hand to drop away. As soon as the contact is lost, she sways closer. From her way her eyes look anywhere but at me, I conclude it's for warmth.

"Are you cold?"

Aurora shakes her head but then reconsiders. "I guess so, but don't worry, it'll warm up soon. I don't..."

Before she can finish her sentence, I tug my sweatshirt over my head and offer it to her. She scowls up at me. "I'm fine! Besides, I have a sweater already and now *you'll* be cold."

"Don't worry about me. I grew up here. I don't get cold until it's snowing." It's a lie, but I can't tolerate her discomfort. "Besides, I'm warm-blooded."

"Warm-blooded," she repeats, tentatively taking the sweatshirt and inspecting it. What possessed me to say that? Aurora doesn't seem to mind, because she slips my sweatshirt over her head. It falls to her hips and flops past her hands.

"Here," I say, taking one arm and rolling the sleeve up to reveal her delicate hand. Longer fingers end in a charmingly chipped manicure. They're an artist's hands. Repeating the move, I free her other hand, and when I look up, she's smiling again. "Better?"

"Much. Thank you. But do you want to run home and get another jacket? I don't mind waiting. "

"I really am fine. So how far do you feel like hiking today? We have a few options."

She cocks her head, her lips pursing. "I don't mind something longer. I've got my good shoes on and we are getting a nice early start."

"Okay, but we need to get water." I look around as if it might appear from the air. This girl disorients me.

Aurora holds up her bag. "I've got us covered. I grabbed extra sandwiches yesterday and two bottles of water each. Will that be enough, do you think?"

"You're amazing," I say, speaking before thinking again. But from the rosy flush filling her cheeks, she likes it. Pink blooms over her cheekbones and jaw, and I'm tempted to reach out and touch it. Would it feel warmer than the rest of her skin? She shifts the strap on her shoulder as if it's uncomfortable.

"You should let me carry the bag." I frown down at the canvas bag as if it has injured and insulted me.

"But it's mostly *my* art supplies," she argues, clutching the strap.

Sighing, I step back to give her space. "Fine, we can take turns. Deal?"

"Deal," she agrees immediately.

My eyes fall on the garden bed from yesterday. Neat rows of sprouts run the length of the planter. Carrot seeds take two weeks to sprout. Even the radishes take at least five days, usually longer. But there they are, little leaves reaching upward to worship the sun.

"Cedar?" Aurora asks, moving to my side.

"Is that the garden bed we planted yesterday?" I mumble, not taking my eyes off the sprouts.

"Maybe? I don't know. It's your garden." Her nervous laugh wraps around me, begging my attention to refocus on her.

"Yeah, I'm pretty sure it's the carrots and radishes we planted," I confirm, even while I doubt myself. "But that doesn't make sense."

"I've always heard radishes sprout fast, but damn."

Maybe I lost track of the days. I get lost in my own world, and with Aurora visiting, I've been distracted. It can't have been yesterday.

"Ready to go?" Aurora asks, looking over her shoulder at me.

"Yeah, sorry."

"You better lead the way!"

Nodding, I force my legs into motion until I'm passing the quiet chicken coop and exiting the north end of the garden. Aurora marches along a step behind me, flanking me just like she would if we were wolves running together. I steal glances at her when I can. Her ponytail sways as she walks. Leaves crunch under our feet cheerfully.

"Did you bring paints or just your sketchbook?" I ask, casting around for anything to discuss. Any safe topic.

"The whole shebang," she replies, that smile back. I focus on the path.

Silence stretches between us. We pass Slate and Hazel's cabin on the edge of the compound. If we went west, the ground would slope down until we hit the creek. But Bracken Creek slopes northward and carves out the landscape, leaving scenic overviews scattered along its length. As long as we don't go too far east and run into that waterfall and pond that Slate has claimed. Even knowing the Alpha couple are back home and not using it, I still have no desire to go near their private spot.

My calves start to burn as the elevation increases. I'm used to running this on four paws. Not that I can tell Aurora that. Grinding my teeth, I forge ahead.

"Okay, I need a break," she says, finding the closest rock to plop down on. "I'm not *that* out of shape, but I'm pretty sure there is less oxygen up here. That's a thing, right?"

"Are you okay?" I crouch in front of her, evaluating the flush in her cheeks. When she raises her head, her pupils dilate.

"I'm fine." It's barely more than a whisper. "Just need to get some air back into me, and you being so close isn't helping," she says with a dry laugh.

I step back so quickly, my heel snags on a plant, and I can't regain my balance. Windmilling my arms, I go down in slow motion. My ass hits the dirt with an embarrassing thud.

"Cedar!" Aurora launches herself at me, knees hitting the dirt beside me. "Are you okay?" Her hand cradles the back of my head, checking for injury.

It hurts to suck air back into my lungs. "I'm fine. Not hurt." My voice rasps.

"Thank goodness. There's no way I could haul you back to the cabin." I can't help but roll my eyes at her teasing.

With a grunt, I push myself up and stand. My tailbone and hip protest, but I ignore them. "Do you need more of a rest, or can we keep going?

"I'm good," she says. "Are you?"

"Yeah, of course."

Her gaze flicks down my body and back up, a small line between her brows. "If you're sure."

Feeling humbled, I trudge past her and resume our hike. Aurora follows, humming a soft tune I don't recognize. The trees thin as we near our destination. It won't be long now.

Aurora lets out a snort of laughter. I twist to frown at her and her nose scrunches up. "Cedar, I hate to tell you this, but you have a dirt print on your ass. It's impressive, really."

"Well, don't look," I suggest dryly.

"I can't help it! It's very distracting."

Swallowing thickly, I brush my hands over my rear, trying to rid myself of the dirt.

"Oh, it's not going anywhere." Her voice holds barely suppressed giggles.

A frustrated growl escapes me. For a second I freeze, reigning myself in. This is not the time to suddenly become emotional. Not here with her. Exhaling, I reach for her. Grabbing her shoulders, I pull her in front of me. "You can walk up here. Then you won't be distracted."

She twists at the waist, peering at me. "Your eyes look amazing in this light. Super blue."

Jerking away, I try to calm myself. Were my eyes glowing? Surely that frustration wasn't enough to trigger it.

"What? I just complimented your eyes. I didn't mean to be weird," she says, scuffing her heel through the dirt.

"I just got dust in my eyes," I say, rubbing at my lashes.

"Oh, I'm sorry. I'm probably making it so much worse," she says, folding her hands at her waist and slowing to walk beside me.

When my pulse settles, I risk a glance at her. She stares ahead, humming to herself. It's almost noon and the harsh sunlight reflects off her hair, turning it bronze. As if sensing my attention, she looks over and smiles at me. Lungs catching on my inhale, I look ahead.

The ground hardens from pine needles to rocks as we crest the hill. Aurora reaches out and grabs my forearm. "Oh, wow!"

"Is this good for painting?" I ask tentatively.

She moves ahead, her eyes wide as she takes in the sweeping view of the forest below us. Looking directly down, we can see the twisting creek. It's not a gaping distance down, but enough I wouldn't want her to fall. Trees rise up from the other side of the creek, forming an evergreen blanket rippling northward.

"It's beautiful. You know, I didn't need something quite this grand, but I love it." She stares at the view and I'm content to watch her appreciate the landscape that I call home.

"Are you hungry?" she asks, blinking back at me.

"I'm okay."

"I should eat before I start painting, or I'll forget to and I'm a monster when I'm hangry." She produces the two sandwiches from her bag and hands me one.

"We wouldn't want you to be hangry," I mutter, peeling the plastic off my food.

Aurora tears into her sandwich, chewing a huge bite. It takes me a moment to remember to start eating too. She devours every crumb and wipes her mouth. "I should have brought more. I didn't think hiking would make me so hungry."

"Take mine," I say, holding out the other half of my sandwich.

"No way," she says, frowning at me. "You probably need more food than I do." It's true, but I can survive a missed lunch. It won't help my control, however. Being in nature has soothed my wolfish instincts, but under no circumstances can I miss running tonight.

As I finish my sandwich, Aurora sets up her painting supplies. What looks like a handful of dowels turns into an easel, and she sets a thin canvas atop it. She clicks open a rectangular palette of glossy watercolors and pours some water into a cup. Wetting her largest brush, she swirls across an orange color and moves to the canvas.

I'm enthralled, watching her sweep thin washes of color over the surface. It looks like nothing at all, until suddenly I'm seeing the rough shape of the landscape - the deepest shadows and the brightest treetops. She switches from orange to blue with a smaller brush and begins to shape blurry trees along the horizon.

As she works, her tongue sticks out slightly, her brows furrowed in concentration. She's adorable. Dark lashes flutter as her gaze flickers between the view and her artwork. Hours could have passed, and I would have no idea. The sway of her hips as she works along with the fluid movements of her paintbrush are mesmerizing.

"Cedar!" she yelps, and I jolt forward, already reaching for her. "Look down there!" She points at the creek, her words squeaking with excitement.

Three wolves trail along the creek, the largest a dark gray, followed by a solid white wolf, and finally a smaller silvery wolf with bulging sides. Their forms are as familiar as my own.

"Oh, are those wolves? That one looks pregnant! That's amazing," Aurora says, creeping closer to the edge to get a better look.

"Woah, be careful," I say, grabbing her hand. Her fingers squeeze back, but she continues to lean forward to peer down at the creek.

The white wolf bounds across the water and disappears into the trees. The darkest one turns to the little silver wolf and licks her muzzle. Together, they turn south and pad out of view.

"That was incredible," she breathes. "I didn't know there were wolves around here."

"Only a few," I say. "They're pretty elusive."

"So we aren't worried about coming across them while hiking?" she asks with an elated grin. I shake my head.

Still beaming, she returns to her painting. I watch, feeling unsettled. No one would get caught by us walking through the woods, but it had never occurred to me that she might spot someone if we were standing at an overlook. It was careless of me.

For over an hour, Aurora shapes the landscape on her canvas, and once she has the basics down, she washes her brushes and sets them down. "What do you think?"

"I'm not an art expert," I say, "but it looks beautiful."

"Thank you!" Aurora packs up her palette and wraps her brushes up. Her movements are slow and methodical. She's gotten her energy and creativity down on paper, leaving her visibly drained but blissful.

Sighing, she lifts the strap of her back to sling it across her chest. I reach out and snag it from her. "My turn to carry it."

"If you insist," she says, watching me closely as I loop it over my shoulder and adjust the strap. Satisfied, she looks over the landscape one more time. "I wish we could stay until sunset."

"I don't think we want to navigate back in the dark. It would be really hard to do on foot."

"On foot?" she asks, and I tense. "Do guys have ATVs or something?"

"Um, a couple, but we rarely use them." I force my muscles to relax. No harm done, though I have to remember to be mindful with my words.

"Cool," she says, breezing past me and down the trail.

I walk behind her until the trail fades and I have to take the lead. Hopefully she isn't checking out the dirt print on my ass. In baggy sweatpants, it's not my first choice of body parts for her to admire.

The ground levels, and I know we are nearing the compound. Aurora must sense it too. "Cedar, I really appreciate you taking me to paint."

"Of course. Even if Hazel didn't tell me to, I still would have. You're nice to be around."

Aurora stops. My words run back through my brain, and I realize how they must sound. The frown she gives me holds more hurt than anger.

"I didn't mean it like that. She just suggested it."

"My sister ordered you to hang out with me?" Her voice is way too calm.

"I was asking her what you might enjoy. You said you wanted to find pretty places to paint."

Her lips press into a thin line. "Cedar, it feels like you're lying to me."

She can sense that? I'm screwed.

"Aurora, I'm sorry, it wasn't my intention."

Her brown eyes have turned cold as she studies me. Creases form around her mouth as her frown deepens. "Why not be honest? Now I feel like you were just doing your job and I'm a burden."

"No, I wanted to go with you."

"I don't need a babysitter to entertain me." The way her brows furrows pierces me. I've ruined it. "Can we just go back?"

Hanging my head, I obey. As soon as the cabins are in view, she strides past me. Without looking back, she says, "Sorry to take up your whole day. I won't do it again."

I'm an idiot. At least it wasn't pack information that slipped past me. I'd better stay away from her before I mess up even worse.

Feeling terrible, I shoot a text off to Slate and then let myself into my family's cabin. My room feels empty without my brother, and both of my parents are at dinner already. Good, I'd like to wallow alone. It's what I deserve after being so careless with my words to Aurora.

VI
BABY SHOWER SHENANIGANS
AURORA

It's baby shower day! During breakfast with Heath, I buzz with excitement. He smiles at me over his pastry and coffee.

"Are you coming to the baby shower?" I ask.

He takes a sip from his mug and sets it down. "I think I'll leave it for the young people."

"You aren't exactly old."

"Sometimes I feel it." He chuckles. "I already gave her several gifts, so I'll leave the partying to you guys. Besides, I've got something I've got to handle today."

"I'll come back with a full report for you on all the baby shower shenanigans."

"I look forward to it." He leans back and crosses his ankle over his knee, looking utterly relaxed.

Perhaps someone would stop to retrieve me, but I don't wait to find out. My pride couldn't handle it if it was Cedar *assigned* to me again. It's a bright morning outside, so I pick my way along the familiar trail to Hazel's house like a capable adult, clutching my trio of paintings to my chest.

Marigold buzzes around inside, adding individual cut flowers to bud vases scattered across the dining table, tucked between plates of food.

"Wow, this looks great!"

Her head pops up. "Aurora!" She squeezes me in a tight hug, rocking me back and forth enthusiastically. I'm not really a hugger, but today, it makes me feel better and I hug her back with one arm.

"What can I do to help?"

"Oh, I think everything is pretty much set. The games are prepped, food is out, and I think all the decorations are up." She props her hands on her hips and rotates to survey the room. Two gift bags perch on a side table so I add my offering to the collection.

Hazel descends the steps, gripping the railing for balance. Her belly has visibly dropped, slinging low on her hips. Marigold and I spin, both opening our mouths, but she raises a hand. "I know and I don't want to hear about it. At least I don't have heartburn anymore and I can breathe again."

"See? It's a good thing!" Marigold claps her hands together.

Hazel scowls but heads straight for the snacks. She piles chocolate covered strawberries on her plate with abandon and then heads to the armchair.

"Ready for us?" Vibrant pink hair grabs my attention as a petite woman slips through the front door. Cedar's twin walks behind her, his hand straying to her waist as they pause just inside.

"Ember!" Hazel says, pushing herself out of the chair awkwardly. Ember closes the distance between them and pulls her into a gentle hug. Pulling away, she runs her hands over Hazel's belly, murmuring a greeting to the baby.

Marigold frowns at Onyx. "I thought you couldn't make it."

"Heath and Hawthorne took my place."

"Very thoughtful of them."

"Something about a game I didn't want to miss?"

"Oh, you'll see." Marigold's grin is devious.

Slate and Jasper follow Ember and Onyx into the cabin, some friendly argument fading away as they survey the room. Slate moves to my sister, planting a kiss on her forehead and wrapping an arm around her. Jasper moves to Marigold and performs a similar ritual. I find my eyes straying to the door.

The couple I met the first day arrive next. Cassia and Lazuli. Cassia balances a baby on her hip. As everyone eats, I inch closer. Maybe it's my upcoming status as an aunt, but I'm drawn to her.

"Hello, Aurora, how's your visit?" Cassia says with a polite smile.

"Good! Your baby is so cute!" I offer my finger and she grasps it eagerly. Her fist is wet with drool.

"Sorry, she's teething. This is Poppy. Our son, Oliver, is with the babysitter."

"Two kids?" I cover my mouth with my free hand while Poppy yanks my finger back and forth.

"So far." Lazuli says, kissing his wife's cheek.

"That's plenty!" She laughs and swats at him.

Poppy releases me and I wipe my hand across my skirt. Lazuli whispers something to his wife, so I leave the lovebirds to their banter and wander back to Marigold. She stands by the table, her gaze sweeping the crowd and her mouth in an analytical frown.

"It's going great," I reassure her.

"Yeah, I think so too. Just trying to decide if it's time for a game."

"Maybe let people clear their plates first?"

"Good idea." She shakes off her serious expression. "So are you ready to be an auntie? You'll have to make these visits a regular thing."

"Hopefully," I say sincerely. It's gorgeous here and I feel incredible after a few nights of uninterrupted sleep and quiet days in the fresh air.

"Okay, I can't wait any longer! It's game time." The last sentence is shouted, and the room quiets. Marigold grins, addressing the group. "We have two games, and the first is a competition. I need five volunteers."

Among the familiar faces, I spot a few strangers, but no Cedar. Disappointment sinks in my chest.

"Slate, you have to compete," Marigold demands, before picking four others from the raised hands. Jasper and Onyx play along, along with Cassia and a gorgeous woman with long, dark braids named Fern.

Marigold produces five babydolls and a pile of diapers from a bin behind the table. She gives Slate and Hazel a guilty smile. "I know you're cloth diapering most of the time, but I figured you'd need a few disposables just in case. And I thought we could test them out! Let's see who can diaper their baby the most times in sixty seconds."

Fern lets out a throaty laugh and winks at the boys. "You guys are screwed. We're the only ones with experience."

Slate shrugs. "Might as well start now."

"Get your babies ready!" Marigold distributes materials gleefully.

The competitors sit in a row on the living room rug and pull their babydolls closer. Each has a stack of diapers within reach.

"Set, and Go!" Marigold yelps, jumping in place.

Disposable diapers fly as the boys struggle to place a diaper under their baby's butt and line up the tabs. Cassia and Fern move like professionals, unfastening their first diapers and slipping a second around their babies.

Onyx tears the tabs off his first diaper but keeps trying to fasten it anyway. Finally he tugs off the diaper and tosses it behind him. Ember and Marigold double over in laughter, and I can't help but join in. Even Onyx throws his head back and laughs wildly while he reaches for a new diaper.

Slate tugs a diaper off his babydolls too forcefully, causing his baby to somersault and land on its head. He stays focused, centering his baby and slipping another diaper under its butt, only to hit it with the heel of his hand and send it skidding toward Jasper.

"Watch it!" Jasper growls, picking his babydoll up by the ankle to avoid Slate's flying baby. His half-fastened diaper sags and flops down to its knees.

"And time!" Marigold squeals, bouncing in place as she claps.

Fern and Cassia hold up their babydolls with triumphant smiles. Slate sets his reclaimed baby down with a thunk, his face the definition of resigned. Onyx exhales dramatically and flings another torn diaper over his shoulder, but it curls around his hand and slings sideways to hit Jasper in the head.

"Let's see how many diapers you did!" Marigold manages to say between giggles. "Come on guys, it can't be that bad."

Slate glares at her, only for Jasper to shove his shoulder and knock him sideways into Onyx. Marigold shakes her head, counting their piles.

"Alright, in last place is Onyx with two diapers. At least you got two!"

Onyx pumps his fist in the air.

"And in fourth place is Jasper, with four diapers. Slate is third with five diapers! And then Fern takes second with twelve diapers and Cassia wins with thirteen!"

"Thirteen?" Onyx says, holding up his hand to high-five Cassia.

She smiles at him ruefully. "It's okay, you'll get better someday, when you have your own kid."

"No, no way, nope," Ember says, standing and stepping away from Onyx. He grins and scrambles up to pursue her. She shrieks laughter and darts out the front door with her boyfriend on her heels.

That's when I spot Cedar leaning against the wall. He looks like a kicked puppy. One look in those apologetic eyes and I'm rethinking our disagreement. What if I was being unreasonable? I should make things right. It wouldn't be right to risk making things awkward for Hazel. Though if I'm honest, I'm more interested in repairing the relationship so I can continue to enjoy his company.

"Cedar! Come here, I need you for the second game!" Marigold calls. Our eye contact breaks as he pushes off the wall and stalks toward the gamemaster. "Someone go get Onyx!"

Sighing, I reach for my plate to refill my snacks. It's time for some chocolate. Reaching for a strawberry, I pause. A tendril from the closest flower curls over the plate of strawberries. Why didn't Marigold trim this? I unfurl the tiny vine and wrap it around the bud vase until it's safely away from the food.

"Ready for Pregnant Twister!" I can't help but laugh at her second game. As Marigold lays out the floor mat covered in rainbow spots, I sidle up to my sister and sit on the sofa nearest her chair.

"How are you doing, Haze?"

"Good! Ready to heckle the shit out of these boys." We watch the line of four men walk out with balloons under their shirts. Hazel lets out a "Whoop!" and Slate gives her a flat look.

"Alright guys, normal rules, but you gotta protect your baby belly or you're out!" Marigold cackles and presents the spinner to Hazel.

"Slate, you're first!" Hazel flicks the arrow. "Get your right leg on Blue!"

A disgruntled Slate steps onto the mat and plants his right foot on a cyan circle.

"Jasper, right leg on Yellow, please," Hazel calls. He complies. "Cedar, right leg on green!"

It's not until she starts calling out hands that things get interesting. Slate crouches first, reaching one arm across the mat. Seconds later, Onyx folds over him so his balloon belly presses into the back of Slate's bowed head.

"Having fun, darling?" Hazel calls out. He lets out a grunt of indignation.

A few more spins and Cedar's butt hovers inches from Jasper's face. I almost choke on my strawberry thinking of yesterday's hike. At least his pants are clean now.

Onyx is the first to fall. He wiggles his ass in Slate's face and Slate gives him a shove. "Foul!" he hollers, crab walking off the mat.

"Sorry, babe," Ember says from her spot beside Marigold.

"Don't be so annoying next time," Slate mutters.

Jasper is next when he tries to reach between his own legs for his assigned color and tips forward. He flings his arm out but can't prevent himself from face planting across the rainbow dots and ramming into Cedar's shin. Cedar balances precariously with one leg crossing the other, and when Jasper bumps him, he topples over too.

Both boys laugh and I'm entranced. Hazel cheers for Slate, her face flushed and excited. He straightens and one of those heart-melting smiles crosses his face. Marigold holds up his hand in victory before he marches straight to Hazel and kisses her soundly. I have to look away and my gaze strays to Cedar. He stands in the kitchen, eyes already on me. His face is that unreadable calm that drives me crazy.

With a mental groan, I head his way. I hate apologizing, but it feels worse not to. For someone who picks fights constantly, I don't handle conflict well.

"I wanted to spend time with you," Cedar blurts before I can apologize. The ball of anxiety in my chest starts to unfurl.

As I draw closer, I reach for him to pat his arm reassuringly. "I know. I'm sorry, I'm a little touchy about being a burden. I shouldn't have gotten upset like that."

"It's okay," he says. My hand rests on his forearm and it feels too heavy to lift, or maybe he has more gravity than he should. His throat works as he swallows and my eyes follow the file of his throat and across his shoulders. Finally, I tear myself away and turn back to the party where Hazel holds court with the rest of her guests.

"Have fun with the game?" I ask, peeking over my shoulder at him.

"Oh, it was a blast. I think I want to play every future game with a balloon stuffed under my shirt," he says. I giggle at his dry sarcasm. A warm hand rests on the small of my back, sending tingles up and down my spine.

"I'd like to see that. You could even garden with a balloon baby."

He laughs. The sound is rough, like it doesn't get a lot of use. I love cracking that serious outer shell.

"Thank you everyone for coming," Hazel says, standing. "We have one more activity."

Marigold's eyes widen. It seems Hazel has kept at least one secret from her bubbly best friend.

"I've prepared a scavenger hunt and the winning team will learn the baby name we picked. And they can keep that information to themselves or share it."

I tense, competition gripping me. I have to be the first to know.

"Form three teams of four people each and then come get the first clue." She waves a trio of small cards above her head.

"Can we pick team names?" Onyx hollers.

Hazel's look is so derisive I almost cringe, but Onyx just grins at her. She rolls her eyes before answering. "Sure, pick a team name."

Onyx's eyes light up, and I turn to see Cedar shaking his head.

Grasping my hands together, I bat my eyelashes at him and pout my lip. "Will you be on my team?"

He stares at me, mouth slightly open.

"Well, will you?"

He coughs. "Yeah, of course. Anything you want." The words tumble over themselves.

"Cool." I feel the blush climbing up my neck. Making him flustered was accidental, but greatly enjoyable. "Who else do you think we can get on our team?"

"Onyx and Ember." He states it like a fact, no hesitation or second thoughts. When I raise an eyebrow at him, he shrugs. "Twin thing."

"Twin thing," I repeat to myself with a small laugh. People used to think Hazel and I were twins, but we were never that in sync. I'm interested to see Cedar and Onyx in action together. They're noticeably different yet matched like a set.

Without being summoned, Onyx tugs Ember behind him as they circle around the counter and join us in the kitchen. Twin thing indeed. "So what's our team name going to be?"

Ember rolls her eyes behind his back, her smile fond.

"Do we *need* a team name?" Cedar asks.

"You heard Hazel! How about the Super-powered Siblings?"

"Only two of us are siblings," I point out, propping a hand on my fist.

Onyx tilts his head. "Well, you are Hazel's sibling. And Ember is Slate's sibling. And we are, obviously." His eyes are darker than Cedar's. Like a night sky instead of a rainy day.

"Fine, whatever." I raise my hands in surrender. "Why don't you go get our first clue?"

He practically bounds away, and I survey his girlfriend. Ember exudes confidence. She's likely the shortest person here, aside from the baby on Cassia's hip, but she holds herself like a queen. A queen with vivid pink hair.

"Nice to finally meet you," she says. "Onyx said you've been hanging out with Cedar?"

"Um, not hanging out. Well, yeah, I guess so, actually." Now I'm the flustered one. Ember's eyes jump to Cedar's face above my shoulder. "We went hiking. I'm an artist and I wanted to paint some cool scenery. He was nice enough to take me to this gorgeous overlook."

"He is very nice, isn't he?" she says with an enigmatic smile. "He's done a lot for me and Onyx. Helped me out of some tight spots."

"You'll have to tell me more sometime, but right now we have a scavenger hunt to win. I'm dying to know the baby name!"

"Agreed." The glint in her eyes tells me she's just as competitive as I am.

Onyx throws his arm over her chest and tugs her against him while he holds up the first clue.

"What took so long?" Ember asks, tipping her chin up to peer at him.

"The other two teams couldn't decide on appropriate names. I had to help them out."

"Of course you did," she replies.

"Well, let's hear the clue!" I say, my eagerness getting the better of me.

Ember plucks the card from Onyx's hand and flicks it open. "*Where milk turns to treat, your next riddle you'll meet.*"

"Would it mean the diner?" Onyx asks.

"What about the girls?" Cedar rubs at his jaw.

Ember shakes her head. "No, I don't think so."

Onyx snaps his fingers. "It's gotta be dad's."

"Yeah!" Cedar nods.

"Okay, I believe the whole twin thing now. Please stop using shorthand and explain," I grouse.

"Did I tell you our dad makes cheese?" Cedar asks.

"Yeah." I cross my arms, waiting for an explanation. Onyx and Ember are already moving toward the front door.

"He has a whole kitchen built in the back of our house for it. Like with a fridge for aging the cheese and a commercial stove and one of those triple sinks."

"That definitely fits the clue." I feel Cedar's hand at my back again, urging me forward. We slip past the other groups, following his twin onto the patio.

Onyx takes off in a run, and I take a deep breath and push myself into a jog. I'm not athletic on a good day and definitely not in this thin mountain air. Cedar stays beside me, guiding me to their cabin.

We slip through a door on the side of the cabin and into the sterile workspace. The stainless steel countertops reflect the industrial style lights swinging above us. Two fridges stand against the far wall, and another door shows a cozy kitchen beyond - this is where Cedar grew up with Onyx and their parents. Any other time, I'd want to explore, but not when we have a task to complete.

Ember and Onyx search through the shelves for the clue. I circle, trying to spot anything that looks out of place.

"This is really cool," I murmur, surveying the ingredients displayed on open shelving. It's mostly spices. "Did you grow some of these?"

Cedar's voice is closer than expected and it sends goosebumps over my arms. "Yeah, all of the herbs. Not the spices."

"Oh, what's this?" I draw another card from between jars. Turning it over in my hand, I recognize Hazel's loopy handwriting. "We've got it!"

"Awesome!" Onyx spins, his mouth curving into a grin.

The door squeaks as Marigold pushes her way into the space. Jasper and two people I don't recognize follow her in.

"Let's take this somewhere else," Cedar says, ushering me toward the interior door.

"Did you guys find a clue?' Marigold asks.

"Nope, nothing here! Total bust!" Onyx says, his voice jumping in pitch. Marigold narrows her eyes and crosses her arms, but he just shrugs as we escape into the main house.

Ember closes the door behind us and spins. "Alright, let's hear it!"

Gingerly, I split open the sticker sealing the card shut and reveal the clue. "*Where feathered ladies play, your next clue is on display.*"

"Well that seems pretty obvious," Ember says.

Biting my lip, I glance up at Cedar. "The chicken coop?"

"Yeah." He leans forward, into my personal space. "Are you okay with that?"

"Sure, totally." I swallow the jittery feeling and paste on a smile. He studies me for a moment, but Onyx and Ember are already moving through the house, so he has to drop it.

It's a short jog from the cabin to the garden. The familiar space settles my nerves, but they spike again when we get close enough to the little building to see the chicken wire and plump birds ranging around inside.

"Hi, pretty girls. Did you miss me?" Onyx croons as he unlatches the cage door. Ember follows him in.

Cedar presses against my back, but my feet are heavy. "Are you okay with chickens?" His voice is soft in my ear.

"They're not exactly my favorite."

"You can stay out here." His hand runs up my back and rubs circles between my shoulder blades.

"I want to help. It's fine. I'm good."

"Okay," he says, frowning at me. When I don't move, he holds out his hand, palm up.

With an awkward laugh, I give him a high five and force myself through the coop door before I have to witness his reaction. I'm going to die of shame. But I don't want him to see my hands shaking or realize I'm sweating.

Onyx stands in the center of the small space, cuddling a white chicken to his chest. Behind him, Ember goes from cubby to cubby, looking for the clue.

The chickens ignore me. As I step forward, they move away, and I exhale in relief. This is fine. No chickens are going to attack me.

Gritting my teeth, I peek into the first cubby. A pair of beady eyes stare back. With a squawk, the hen lurches forward. I echo with my own screech and throw myself backwards. Arms close around my waist and catch me before I fall and crush a few of these mother cluckers.

Cedar's reassuring herbal scent envelops me, his hands warm against my ribs. He doesn't say a word, just sets me back on my feet and releases me. My blood rushes in my ears and I scramble to grab his arms and steady myself further. My fingers close over his, and he shifts our hands until our fingers lace.

"What happened?" Cedar asks, his voice low.

"That freaking chicken attacked me!" I hiss, scowling at him. From the corner of my eye, I see Onyx grinning at me. Relieved to have an outlet for my emotions, I turn and glare at him.

"I got it!" Ember says, waving a card.

"Good job, babe," Onyx praises.

She opens the card and scans it, before clearing her throat and reading. "*In a house among the trees, find your next clue with ease.*"

"What?" I say. "All the houses around here are in the trees."

"It's the treehouse," Cedar says.

Ember frowns at him.

"Hawthorne and Crickett have a treehouse behind their cabin," Onyx explains. Ember's mouth opens into an O, her hand drifting to the chicken in her boyfriend's arms. She strokes down its back, and I suppress a shiver.

"That makes sense with the clue," I say, eyeing the gate longingly.

"Alright, let's go. You'll have to put Piccata down," Ember says, laughing. With a dramatic pout, Onyx sets his chicken down.

Unable to wait a second longer, I unlatch the gate and push through. My hand feels cold without Cedar's fingers wrapped around mine. I shouldn't need his support. I'm being ridiculous.

Ember and Onyx pass me, breaking into a jog. But Cedar stops beside me. His brows furrow.

"Are you ready to go?" I ask.

"You're afraid of chickens and you didn't tell me."

"No, why do you say that?" My faux-confidence is broken when another shiver washes over me.

"You should have told me." His tone is soft, like a request instead of a reprimand.

"I'm sorry. Do you want me to confess all of my phobias to you?"

"Maybe just the ones we are possibly facing." He crosses his arms, and I can't help myself.

"Well, I don't like clowns either."

He ignores my snark and looks down my body like he is evaluating me. "Are you really okay?"

Jasper and Marigold's group enters the garden and sprints past us.

"I'm fine. Don't worry about it. Let's go get the next clue."

Brushing past him, I navigate out of the garden and break into a jog to catch up with Onyx and Ember. They lead us across the meadow and past the diner to another two story cabin. A towering maple tree hides a small treehouse in its thick branches.

Onyx scales the ladder and we crane our necks back to watch him search the tree house. It doesn't take long for him to find it, and then he climbs back down. A few feet from the ground, he holds out the card to Ember. His shirt has slipped sideways, revealing an oval scar in the crook of his neck. It looks like a series of dots painted in white ink or pale pink. What on earth would have caused that? His collar covers the marks again when he jumps to the ground.

Ember clears her throat and reads, "Find a crib, take a peek, and find the prize you seek."

"Back to the baby shower?" I ask.

"Yup!" Onyx gives me a thumbs up, and then takes off.

I can't keep up with them. My lungs tighten painfully and my muscles protest. Cedar slows his pace to stay with me. I wave him on, but he stubbornly stays by my side. Affection for his loyalty bubbles up in me, and I suck in deep breaths and force myself to keep moving. Finally, we make it back to Hazel's cabin.

Ember leads the way to the secondary bedroom they've converted into a nursery.

Hazel sits in a rocker, her hand resting on her belly. She lights up when we crowd into the room. "Have a good time?"

I double over, resting my hands on my knees. "Wish there wasn't quite so much running."

"But we won!" Onyx says, squeezing Ember and lifting her feet off the ground.

"Are you ready to hear our baby name?" Hazel beams. Slate slips past us to stand beside my sister, and she reaches up to take his hand.

"So what is it?" I say, straightening.

"We decided no matter if it's a girl or a boy, we are naming the baby Timber," Hazel declares. Slate's face breaks into one of his rare smiles as they look at each other.

"Timber," I say, testing it out. "I love it! It's so cute!"

"It really is a great name," Ember says. She leans over Hazel and hugs her.

"Thanks," Hazel says. "It was Slate's idea."

"Good job, Baby Daddy," I tease. He ignores me.

"Are we first?" Marigold says from the main room. The door swings open, and her expression shifts into a scowl. "One of you better tell me!"

"Sorry, I don't know what you're talking about," Onyx says.

"Onyx!" Marigold says.

"Goldie," he replies with a grin.

"You should just tell her. Otherwise she will pester us until the baby comes," Cedar says. I find myself drifting closer to him. In a room full of couples, it's nice to have someone to pair with.

Marigold and Onyx argue like siblings, while Ember and Jasper watch with identical smirks. Eventually, Hazel shoos them out. I'm disappointed when Cedar leaves too. Unfortunately, I'm getting rather attached to him.

The third group returns eventually. We've already cleaned up the remaining snacks, so they wish Hazel and Slate the best and leave. Even Marigold goes home with Jasper after she's satisfied with the clean up.

Once it's just me and my sister, I transport her gifts back to the nursery. Hazel settles in the center of the rug and unpacks all of the baby items. I carry things to wherever she tells me while she tucks items into the dresser in front of her.

"Happy with your baby shower?" I ask. She hums in affirmation, continuing to fold the tiny onesies into the pine drawer. "So, I was wondering about something."

She hums again, swaying slightly as she folds a baby blanket.

"So it's no big deal." Chewing my lip, I take the empty gift bags and fold them, laying them in a neat pile. With a deep breath, I force the words out. "I like hanging out with Cedar. He seems really nice. Does he have a girlfriend or anything?"

Hazel's eyes snap to mine while her mouth opens, closes, and then opens. "Rory," she begins.

"I wasn't thinking anything, just curious. I wouldn't want to accidentally flirt with a taken man."

"No." She sighs and smooths her hands over her belly. "Look, there's something you need to understand. The men here aren't like the ones in Los Angeles."

"No kidding," I mutter.

"That's not exactly what I meant." She hesitates again, and my heart does a flip. What is so difficult to say? With another exhale, she runs her fingers through her hair. "It's just that they're very serious. They don't mess around. Slate wasn't with anyone else before me, didn't date, nothing. And as soon as we got involved, he was completely sure I was the one."

"Aww, that's sweet," I say, ignoring the blush creeping up my throat.

"Cedar's twin, Onyx, is with his first girlfriend too. He ignored all women until her, and then he was all in."

"But they're just dating," I say, unsure of what she means.

"They live together. It's as permanent as any marriage. Shared finances, the whole deal. Just like Slate and me."

"Okay, so I'm hearing they don't do casual."

"That's probably the best way to put it. They don't date until they've met the girl they want to commit to," she rephrases, her cheeks hollowing as she thinks.

It's clear Cedar is off limits to me. Message received loud and clear. But if she can make me this uncomfortable, I can do the same to her.

"So, are you guys going to put a ring on it, considering you have a kid now?"

Hazel lets out a dry laugh. "We might."

"He's an idiot for not doing that already."

She shrugs, focusing back on her gifts. "It's not a priority for his family. Once they're serious, that's it. No ring required."

"Mom would be happy if you did, though."

"Mom can deal with it."

I can't help the bark of laughter bursting out of me. I like this new Hazel. Her take-no-shit attitude is way better than the people-pleasing habits she used to have.

"I'm really happy for you, you know that right?"

Her brows furrow for a split second as she regards me. "I appreciate that. I've got it pretty good, but I do miss you. We need to see each other more often."

"Yeah."

It's easy to agree. But it took me years to come visit her here, and she doesn't seem inclined to leave even for a short while. At this point, I can't imagine her back in the city. I'm the one who needs to change, not for her, but for myself.

CEDAR

The feel of Aurora's hand grabbing mine while she pretended she wasn't frightened of the chickens clouds my thoughts even after a night of broken sleep. She's all I thought about as I ran as a wolf through the woods. Even sitting at the kitchen table eating french toast, I'm thinking about the way her body relaxed when I touched her. This girl has her claws in me, and instead of concern, I feel some sort of giddy excitement.

"How was the baby shower, sweetheart?" My mother sits across from me and blows away the steam wafting off her mug. From the creamy, dark color, I suspect it's half coffee, half hot cocoa, her favorite.

"Nice," I answer without thinking. Angling my fork, I cut another bite and stack up strawberry and then french toast followed by another strawberry.

"Yeah?" She takes a sip, her eyebrows rising as she peers at me over her drink.

"They had some games. Onyx was last place in a diapering race. And Marigold made me play twister with a balloon under my shirt like a pregnant belly."

"I'm sorry I missed that." She laughs, the light sound filling the kitchen. "How is Hazel doing?"

I was so distracted by Aurora, I almost forgot to check on Hazel. Luckily, I remembered my duties. "Good, I think. She looked better yesterday."

"That reminds me, I need to start making lactation cookies for her," she says nonchalantly.

My ears perk up. "What goes into those?"

"The herb fenugreek."

I've heard of it, but I know I don't have any in the garden. That prickles at me. "Why didn't you have me grow any?"

"It uses the seeds. They wouldn't have been ready in time. You can't grow absolutely everything we ever need." She means to comfort me, but it just makes me feel inadequate.

"I grow a lot of medicinal herbs for Sable," I argue. "I can start some fenugreek now and you can switch from purchased seeds to our harvest as soon as they are ready."

Mom places her hand over my wrist and squeezes. "Love, you can't do everything for everyone. I'm sure Sable has a supply on hand already, otherwise it's easy to order."

"Let me know if I can help," I murmur, trying to shake off the sting.

"You're always helping. You're the most selfless person I know. But I really think you should consider what you want. Maybe it's time to move out and have some space for yourself." She searches my eyes, and I frown at her.

It's not the first time she's suggested I move out since Onyx left last year. But since she and my father are often gone, it seems impractical. I don't need my own cabin.

"Do you really want me out of the house?"

Tilting her head thoughtfully, she smiles at me. "I want you to have your own space where you can relax."

That doesn't sit well with me. "But what if you need me?"

"We got along just fine before we had you, and the same will be true when you leave someday. Besides, you'll still be nearby. You'll just have more privacy and peace and quiet."

Her words soothe my building anxiety. All of my friends have left their family's homes by now. But they all have mates. I'm happy waiting for that to happen before I leave home, but maybe I should reconsider.

"I'll think about it."

"Good. Have a good day, sweetheart," she says, standing and heading to the hall.

"Bye, Mom."

As I prepare to leave for my garden, I can't help but think - where would I go? Slate's old trailer stands empty, or I could get my own. I have plenty of savings, since my salary goes entirely into a savings account. The pack has grown and housing is scarce these days, but there are a few options.

Warm sunshine washes over me as I cross the patio and jog east to my garden. My heart settles as I pass through my archway and walk along the neat and tidy rows of happy plants. The earliest of the spring vegetables gleam on their stalks and herbs sprawl out of their pots. Companion flowers wink at me between the vegetables.

My heart jumps as a familiar figure materializes in the corner of the garden. Aurora sits cross legged against the same tree. The strawberry plants have overtaken the fence, little vines reaching for her. Her pink tongue sticks out slightly as she sketches.

My feet move toward her. I can't help it. Something about her draws me in.

"Good morning, Cedar," Aurora says, her smile small and shy, before she looks back down at her art.

I stand there, gawking like an idiot, until my brain starts processing again. There's something I have to do today, and maybe it's the perfect opportunity to help her adjust to the chickens.

"So there was something I wanted to show you."

"That's never a good thing when a guy in L.A. says it," she says without looking up from her notepad.

Frowning, I blink at her. "Um, okay. So you're not interested?"

"No, I am. Just joking." She spins the pencil over her fingers as she smiles up at me again. A beautiful pink flush stains her cheeks.

"Cool. Well, I've got to go get something. I'll be right back."

"Sure."

She goes back to her sketch, and I jog back the way I came, turning south toward the supply store. A special package should have been delivered in the early hours this morning. Sure enough, Fern types away on her laptop, a box with circular air holes covered in mesh sitting beside her elbow.

"Thanks!" I snag my package and walk back to my garden and Aurora. Soft cheeps emanate from the box. I pause in front of her and wait for her to look up. "Whenever you're ready, would you follow me?"

Her eyes narrow suspiciously. "Wait, are we going to the chicken coop?"

"Maybe."

"I'm not sure about this." Her voice jumps in pitch. She tucks her pencil into the spine of her sketchbook, freeing up her hands. She wrings them anxiously.

"You don't have to go in, just stand outside. I think you'll like my surprise." My reassurances seem to work, because she sighs and scrambles up.

Having Aurora trusting me makes my chest puff with pride. We stop a few yards from the coop and I ease open the lid to reward that trust.

Inside, nine yellow balls of fluff teeter back and forth.

"Oh my gosh! They're so cute!" Aurora bounces on the balls of her feet and covers her mouth with her hands. The excitement glittering in her eyes is all the reward I need. "Why do you have these?"

"We need to add a few hens to have enough eggs for everyone. Especially with baby Poppy getting old enough to eat solids and now baby Timber on the way."

"And these little fuzzy nuggets are going to provide them?"

I snort at her phrasing. "That's the idea. Do you want to hold one?"

"I'm just going to keep this one. It'll live in my pocket, okay?"

She croons over the little chick, and I can't help but smile. My plan is working and her fear over the birds is fading. "So chickens aren't so bad?"

"Hey, I didn't say that. That one almost attacked me." Aurora pulls back and lifts her chin defiantly. A little chick peeps from within her hands. She lowers her face and whispers reassurances to the little bird.

"You did stick your face in her nesting box, and she's broody," I say.

"Broody?" She cocks her head, waiting for an explanation.

"She wants to hatch her eggs."

"But you don't have a rooster," she says, her brows furrowing as she reluctantly lowers her chosen chicken back into the box with her siblings.

"Yeah, so she's sitting on dummy eggs right now. Normally, when they get like this, we have to break it by separating the hen. Especially in the summer when she could get dehydrated. But since we are getting these little guys, I figured she would be the perfect mom."

"You're giving her the chicks?" She puts it together and I'm impressed.

"That's the plan."

"That's so sweet. Can I help?"

"Yeah, they are a little over a day old already, so we need to get them under her right away."

"Let's do it!" She presses her lips together, the skin around her eyes crinkling as she smiles sheepishly.

We stare at each other for a moment, before I snap into action. Cautiously, I reach for the lid that reveals the nesting box the hen in question has been occupying all week.

"What's her name?" Aurora bites her lip, eyeing the coop.

"Coq au Vin. We call her Coco."

"Coco?" She echoes, looking relieved, as if a silly name makes the chicken less unnerving. The soft cheeps of the chicks seem to be relaxing her, bit by bit.

Slowly, I lift the outer lid to her box. Her dark head whips around, tilting to stare one eye at me. Taking a breath, I gently lift the first chick and show it to her. She blinks and lets out a soft trill.

Success!

With a slow and smooth movement, I tuck the chick under her belly and swipe an egg in a quick exchange. I tuck the sphere under my palm as I withdraw my hand so she won't see it.

Coco flattens her wings and fluffs her belly to accommodate her new chick. Perfect. It's exactly what I hoped to see. Dropping the dummy egg into the pouch tied to my belt, I hold out my hand. Aurora places another squirming chick into my palm.

We repeat the process eight more times until Coco has all of the babies tucked under her wings. When one little chick wiggles out, she pushes it back to safety.

"That should do it." I straighten and brush my hands off.

Aurora's expression is astounded. She moves to the side of the coop where she can peer through the chicken wire at the nesting boxes.

"How do you feel about chickens now?" I can't keep the hope out of my voice.

"I'm not sure. Better, I think? I still don't want to go in there, but maybe another day." She eyes the girls through the wire.

"So what caused you to not like them?"

She hesitates, glancing between me and the chicken coop. I can see the moment she decides to share, because her breath exhales and her shoulders relax. "Let's just say a field trip to a farm went terribly wrong."

My fingers tighten on the empty box in my hands. "How so?"

"I got left in the chicken coop and one jumped on my head. By the time the teacher got back, it had pooped in my hair and scratched me up." Her embarrassed laughter is husky.

"I'm sorry. That's shit luck." She raises an eyebrow at me, and I bury my face in my hand when I realize my accidental pun. "That's not, well, you know what I mean."

"You're funny." Her genuine smile hits me in the chest, taking my breath away. I thought she looked just like Hazel, but standing in my garden with morning light forming a halo around her, she looks uniquely her. I could never mistake her for anyone else. She's burned into my retinas.

"So what now?" She spins, taking my breath with her.

"What?"

"What are you doing the rest of the morning?"

I stare at her dumbly. "What do you want to do?"

"I'm not the one in charge of the garden, Cedar."

My name out of her mouth is so distracting, it delays her words from sinking in. Finally my brain processes her meaning.

"Oh, actually I need to make some cheese."

"You do that too? I thought that was your dad's thing."

"He's been busy working on a special project." I stumble over the words, unsure of what to say. I can't very well explain how he's handling retraining our neighboring pack that my twin is the new Alpha of. "But we're running low on cheese, and the girls' milk is adding up, so I was going to make a few batches of cheese to get aging. So we don't run out."

"That sounds like a lot of work."

"It can be, but it's worth it," I say with a shrug.

"Do you want some help?"

I study her. Is she offering just to be polite? "You've got your painting to do and this is supposed to be a vacation for you." Her mouth curves into a small frown. "But if you want to, I'm happy to have the extra hands," I backtrack.

She brightens. "Yes, I really would like to. I've never seen cheese being made, and it seems cleaner than farm chores?"

"You'd be surprised," I say with a chuckle. There's a reason the cheese kitchen is all stainless steel and is outfitted with a commercial triple sink.

The sound of stomping feet grabs my attention. Sable marches across the garden's north end, moving away from her cottage.

"Everything okay?" I yell, shading my eyes with my hand so I can see her reaction.

"Who is that?" Aurora asks, dropping her voice.

"Our nurse."

Sable throws her hands up, looking irritated. Her sharp voice reaches us clearly. "Just checking on Hazel. Everything's fine." From the speed she's walking, it doesn't seem fine.

Aurora tenses beside me. "I think I'd like to go check on my sister. Can I join you for some cheese making in a little bit?"

"Of course. It can wait until you're ready."

"Thanks." She strides after Sable. I watch her progress with an unsettled feeling in my chest.

VII
CONTRACTIONS &
CHEESE MAKING

ONYX

Hazel's living room is empty. Voices drift down the stairs. After a short debate, I scale the steps. Hazel sits up in bed with Sable stooping over her as she takes her vitals. Slate hovers beside her, his hands clenching and unclenching anxiously.

"Rory," Hazel greets me. Her face is placid like nothing is the matter. Slate's startlingly green eyes shoot up to mine, but he dismisses me and refocuses on his partner.

"Hey sis, how's it going?" Cautiously, I approach the bed, choosing to stand on the far side out of the way.

Hazel sighs dramatically. "It seems like I might be in early labor, maybe?"

"Are you kidding me?" I brace myself on the bed and look her over.

"Yeah, I think? They might be practice contractions, but they hurt more than they used to." Her words halt abruptly. She sucks in a breath and holds it. Her nose scrunches up.

Sable moves her hands over her belly and murmurs indistinctly.

"I think it's most likely early labor," the older woman declares.

"Holy crap," I say, sitting down to steady myself.

Sable steps back and folds her hands. "It'll be a while until you're in active labor. You've got at minimum a few hours, possibly a whole day. You should relax and get a good meal in."

"Can you get me some chocolate, baby?" Hazel asks, and Slate nods. Without a word, he brushes past Sable and heads out of the room.

"He's taking good care of you, it seems," Sable says.

Hazel's face breaks into a bright smile. "Yeah, he is. I can't wait for him to be a dad."

"I'll be back to check on you in an hour. I think rest is best right now, considering how active you've been. If your labor moves slowly, we can consider walking."

Hazel nods. Satisfied, Sable picks up her bag and heads for the door.

"So it's baby time?" I ask, crawling across the bed to sit beside my sister.

"I guess so." Her grin is elated. "You ready to be an auntie?"

"Definitely. And you're ready to be a mom, so it's perfect." I rub circles across her belly. The muscles contract under my hand and Hazel inhales sharply again. I can't help but hold my breath too.

She relaxes. "It's not bad, really. Mildly uncomfortable."

"Are you getting pain meds? Can they do that out here?" I ask, alarm raising my voice.

Hazel shakes her head. "No, and it's fine. Sable has some options for emergencies, but I can handle this. I'm in the best shape of my life. It'll be fine."

I want to argue with her. There's no reason for her to go through that pain. But she looks confident, and it's her choice.

"You should go enjoy your day. You can come back when things are getting serious, okay?" She pats my knee. "I just want to relax and read for a bit."

"Gotta squeeze one more book in before baby?" I tease.

"What are you up to today?" she asks.

"Oh, Cedar got new chicks for the coop and I helped him place them with a mama hen. She accepted them right away. It was really cool."

"Sounds cool." Her cheeks indent and her eyebrows raise an almost imperceptible amount. "Still enjoying spending time with Cedar?"

I bristle at the not-so-casual question. "He's my friend."

"Yeah?"

"Yes, we can be friends. I'm not flirting." I refuse to cross my arms like I want to. She must buy it, because she nods and leans back against her pillows.

"And goodness knows, he doesn't know how to flirt," Hazel says with a giggle.

He doesn't need to flirt. I bite back the thought. "So he was going to make some cheese and I think I'm going to go help."

"Jealous. I've never done that. It seems complicated."

"Want me to bring you some of the cheese?"

She smooths her hands over her belly and presses against her hip in the spot I know is hurting her. "It probably won't be ready for a while. They age it, right?"

"I have no idea. I guess I'll find out. I'll bring you some if I can." Reluctantly, I climb off the bed. "Don't have the baby without me, Mama."

"No promises. You better get back here in time. But seriously, give me some peace and quiet. This will be my last chance to be alone for who knows how long."

"Yes, ma'am."

I hesitate at the door, soaking in the sight of my wonderful big sister. She's glowing, a halo of radiance around her warm skin and dark hair. A contented smile curves her mouth, and I'm reminded how much she loves her life now. She's happier than I've ever seen her. It's everything I've ever wanted for her. But under that, jealousy twinges under my breastbone. Maybe someday I will feel the same sense of belonging and confidence in my skin.

Trotting down the stairs, I look around to see if there is anything I can help with. Dishes to wash, laundry to fold. I want to be useful. But everything is tidy. Slate has even hung up my paintings in the nursery already. Baby Daddy has it covered. Some of the tension relaxes from my shoulders, and I head toward the door.

She wants me to go have a good day while she relaxes and lets her body do its thing? Sure. I'll go make some cheese.

Cedar is still in the garden. He sits on the end of the garden bed that I helped him plant and picks out some of the baby plants.

"What are you doing?" I ask cheerfully.

He looks up, sweeping over me in an analytical way. "Thinning. Everything good with Hazel?"

"Yeah, she's started labor. But she said to not come back until tonight. She wants to relax during these early stages."

"So the baby is coming?" He stands, letting a pile of greenery tumble to the gravel path.

"Sometime tomorrow or maybe late tonight I expect."

His gray-blue eyes connect with mine and widen with excitement. I want to squeal and jump up and down, though anxiety over my sister giving birth weighs me down. Cedar seems to see all of this. "It's going to be fine. She'll do great. Sable has helped with dozens of babies. She knows what she's doing."

I let his strong arms pull me into a hug. The feel of his chest against my cheek calms the buzzing under my skin. The warmth radiates out to my fingers and toes.

"Thanks," I murmur. "I'm so excited, but also…"

"I know." His hand strokes over my hair and I sigh. The feel is exquisite and I wish he would bury his fingers into my hair, but his hand stops at my upper back like a gentleman. Mentally shaking myself, I step back and tuck my hands into my pockets. "So should we make some cheese? Sounds like a good distraction."

"If you want to."

"I do. Teach me, oh cheese maker!" My nose scrunches as I grin at him.

Cedar offers his arm and we walk out of the garden and past the school building to his family's cabin. At the front door, he pulls off his boots and I take off my tennis shoes before we cross the house in our socks.

"This is where you grew up?" I ask. It's so quiet, I suspect the house is empty.

"Yeah. This is my sister's room," he says, pointing at a door decorated with stickers. "And this is mine." He pushes the door open partially and I see a tidy space with navy bedding neatly made up. The far side of the room is empty.

"You shared it with Onyx?"

"Yeah." He scratches at the back of his head. "I haven't really done anything with the space since he moved out."

"How long ago was that?"

"Almost a year." His eyes stay on the floor.

Biting my lip, I ask, "Do you want to move out too?"

"Maybe. It's not really a priority, honestly."

"Waiting for a girlfriend to move in with?" I tease, my brain forgetting to filter my words.

He pauses, those distracting eyes slowly moving to meet mine. "I hadn't really thought about it."

It's not the words he says, but the slow way he says it that has my stomach clenching. There's nothing between us. A few hugs and friendly touches. Totally platonic. And yet it doesn't feel platonic.

Goosebumps prickle over my arms and I desperately try to recall Hazel's words. They don't do casual. He doesn't date around. He would expect this to mean more than it does. I'm going back to Los Angeles. The thought feels less and less real the longer I spend with him.

He looks away, breaking the tension before he ducks out of the hallway and leads us to the kitchen. We step through the side door, and finally we are standing in the cheese kitchen. It's as clean and bright as the day of the baby shower.

"Grab a few gallons from the fridge," Cedar instructs as he reaches for a huge pot.

Pulling the closer fridge open, I freeze. Massive clear buckets of milk line the three massive shelves. How many gallons are in each of these? How am I supposed to lift them? "Um, Cedar, I'm not sure..."

He appears at my back. "They're three gallons each. We need two of them. Here, I've got you."

Cedar reaches for a bucket and lifts it effortlessly. Not to be outdone, I grab the second one and heave it up. It's manageable, though I let out an embarrassing grunt.

"Got it?" he asks.

"Yes, I can manage to lift three gallons of milk," I say, scowling at him.

He raises his hands to pacify me. "I didn't doubt you."

My teeth grind together as I move the heavy bucket toward the counter and my arms protest as I attempt to lift it higher. Thankfully, Cedar is attentive and his hands close over the handle on either side of mine before I lose my grip. He lifts it onto the counter without a word.

"Now what?" I ask, shaking my hands to numb the ache of the handle digging into my fingers.

"We need to heat them up to eight-six degrees Fahrenheit. There are thermometers in the drawers in the island. Can you grab one?"

While I shuffle through the drawers, Cedar pours all six gallons into the pot. Nothing looks like a thermometer. Finally, he comes over and tugs out what looks like a kitchen timer with a probe attached.

"Seriously? That's not a thermometer, I swear," I say.

"But it is." He smiles at me and winks. My mouth falls open. Oblivious to my reaction, he pulls a spoon off the wall and begins stirring. "We have to heat this slowly and stir continually, otherwise it won't heat evenly and parts can overheat."

"So we have some time to kill?" I say, leaning against the counter beside him with my elbow against the cold steel.

Cedar's attention snags on the way my chest sticks out, and I bite my lip to keep from smiling. He clears his throat. "Can you stir? I need to get more... um, stuff." I want to gloat over how his cheeks tinge pink and his eyes glue to the ground. I'm flirting with danger, but I can't resist. His lingering looks and soft touches are driving me crazy.

We're alone here. The garden is open to anyone walking by, but in this small space, no one can see us. It's quiet. Private.

He sets two jars down beside the pot, and tries to take over the stirring again, but I don't release the spoon. His fingers curl over mine, and I peek over my shoulder. He swallows visibly but doesn't move his hand.

The thermometer beeps, and he uses his hold over my hand to tug the spoon out. Warm milk drips on the counter. "We need to add the culture."

"Okay," I say, breathless. He opens a jar and measures out a spoonful of powder. "Just sprinkle it over the top."

Gingerly, I take the spoon and do my best to obey his instructions. It peppers the top and floats there. "Do we stir it in?"

"Not yet. It needs a minute to bloom." We both watch the clock. "It's been long enough."

Grabbing the spoon, I stir the powder into the milk. "Now what?"

"It has to cook for a long while." His chest rises and falls. "It's converting the lactose to lactic acid."

"You like the science part, don't you?" I ask, pleased when he doesn't move away from me. The stove warms my back, and I can feel the heat of his body at my front.

Cedar's eyes flicker between mine, occasionally dropping down to my mouth. "It's interesting."

It's clear he's interested, but I suspect he won't do anything about it. I want to drag him closer and kiss him, but that last shred of caution holds me back. Taking a slow, unsteady breath, I speak my thoughts.

"Hazel said you don't date."

"You asked about me?" he says, his mouth curving into a smirk.

My fist props on my hip. "Well? Do you?"

"I haven't." His voice is hoarse, making my toes curl.

"That's not quite the same," I murmur. "If you haven't dated, have you kissed anyone?"

The pause almost kills me. He could get irritated with me or embarrassed. The pink flush is back in his cheeks but he clears his throat and says, "No."

Anxiety and excitement bubble up, stronger, buzzing in my chest. "Have you ever wanted to?"

Hopefully I'm being clear enough. He stills, tension through his shoulders as he holds our eye contact. "It hadn't crossed my mind."

"Not at all?"

"Not until recently," he admits, and my fingers itch to touch him, but I want him to make the first move. It's worth the infuriating amount of self-control I'm currently exerting.

His eyes lower to my mouth. I've almost got him. "You know," I say, wetting my lips, "we have over an hour with nothing to do."

He hums in agreement. The sound vibrates through my bones.

"If you wanted to kiss me, I think I'd really like that." A flush paints my own cheeks, turning my neck and ears cherry red. The moment waiting for his reaction makes me want to curl up in embarrassment. But he hasn't rejected me yet. It's a struggle to breathe.

"I'm not sure that's a good idea," he says, but his hand moves to my waist. His fingers squeeze and knead my skin and I know I have him. It's a fight to keep my eyes open with how good it feels.

"It's just us," I whisper.

CEDAR

My lungs seize up, and it's a struggle to keep air moving. I'm light-headed. *I think I'd really like that.* This gorgeous woman looks up at me with spellbinding golden-brown eyes and licks her lips. Damn it.

I shouldn't touch her. She's not an option as a mate. She's human and she has a whole life in Los Angeles. This can't end well.

My other hand goes to her waist too. The feel of her soft curves crumbles my resolve. I'm going to regret this.

She tips her chin up, her lips parting slightly. I shouldn't find her this alluring. It's not just how beautiful she is, it's the spark of life she carries with her. She's vibrant, unpredictable, and passionate.

Her delicate fingers brush across my chest. Sparks radiate out from the spot of contact. I'm pulled down like she's a magnet. The part of my brain warning me to stay away from her is fading, overwhelmed by a desire to please her. To taste her.

"It's okay," she whispers. I'm not sure what she means. It's okay if I don't kiss her? It's okay if I do? Would I be okay if I didn't? No. My decision solidifies and it unlocks something inside of me.

One hand grips her waist firmly, and the other moves to her jaw, hooking a finger under her chin to tip her face upward. Her eyes widen and her pupils devour her honey irises.

"Aurora?"

"Yes?" Her voice scrapes over me.

"You really want me to kiss you, don't you?" I ask, daring to tease her.

She nods, her chin bumping against my hand.

"How long have you been thinking about it?"

"A while," she says, swallowing and taking a ragged breath.

"And cheese making is what does it for you?" My tone is so serious, it takes a moment for her to catch my joke. Those beautiful eyes narrow and she pulls back, her mouth curving into a scowl.

"You know, you don't have to make fun of-"

I don't let her finish the thought. My arm scoops under her ass, lifting her and twirling us in one sweeping movement, away from the hot stove until I can set her down on the center work table.

Her mouth opens in a surprised gasp. She's level with me and her knees part to allow me nearer. I grab her hips and drag her closer to the edge, and her hands scramble to grab my shoulders. Her knees squeeze against my hips.

Breathing fast, she blinks at me with her lips slightly parted, waiting for my next move. My fingers tangle in her hair as I finally kiss her.

All rational thought leaves my brain. Her nose bumps my cheek and I tilt my head to better reach her. Her lips are soft and she brushes them against mine and then presses firmly. Fireworks go off behind my eyes. I press against the nape of her neck and kiss her harder. Her lips part and her tongue tentatively dips into my mouth. She's sweet, gentle, and I want to devour her.

Her fingers thread into my hair and a low guttural sound rolls out of my throat. She must like it, because her hold on me tightens. The feel of her against me, her mouth on mine, is bright sunshine and rich pleasure.

Time loses all meaning, and it's just her thighs against my hips, my fingers squeezing the curve of her waist, her lips moving with mine, my tongue against hers. With a little hiccup, she breaks off and leans back, letting out a giddy little laugh.

My chin falls to my chest, and I stare at the ground, awkwardly adjusting myself. If I look up, now she'll see my eyes glowing dusty blue. But then her head tips back, revealing an expanse of throat.

With a shuddering breath, I turn back to the stove and check that the temperature is holding steady.

My reflection in the polished backsplash reveals that my eyes have returned to normal, so I turn to face her.

"You okay?" A goofy smile curves her beautiful mouth, but her brows pinch as concern wars with her happiness. I don't want her worried, but all of this is a lot. Kissing her was an all-consuming experience, far more than I anticipated.

"I'm fine. That was…" I pause, studying her reaction. "Overwhelming. In a good way."

"We've still got more than an hour, I think." She grips the edge of the countertop and leans forward, revealing more of her cleavage.

"Is that a request?" I ask.

She nods. I should redirect her. It's madness to continue. But apparently, I've lost all common sense.

All the times I warned my brother he was being foolish by growing close to Ember echo back to me. Now I understand how little choice he had. She's a supernovae sucking me in. Despite knowing the potential and likely consequences, I'm happy to go along.

Aurora smiles as she grasps my shirt and tugs me back. My thumb strokes down her neck and across her collarbone. The way she shivers stirs an unexpected possessiveness in me. I want to be the only one who gets this reaction from her. Her teeth sink into her bottom lip.

Her floral scent fills me as my nose skims along her jaw. I place a kiss on her ear lobe and then trail down. She exhales a soft groan and tilts her head in an invitation.

I work my way down, kissing, tasting, nipping. Her nails dig into my ribs, encouraging me. "I like when you use your teeth," she purrs. "Go ahead and leave a mark. I want something to look at later."

Every muscle in my body freezes. Her words spark warring emotions so intense, I almost leap backward. She has no idea what she just said. Grabbing the counter, I focus on slowing my breathing and calming down.

"Cedar?" She slides off the counter and closes the distance between us. "Did I do something wrong?"

"No." I try to keep my eyes averted, but she won't let me. "This isn't a good idea. You're going home soon. And I like you, I really do, but this can't go anywhere."

"Yeah, of course." She smooths her hands over her hair, untangling it. "Sorry."

"It's time to add the rennet," I say, turning back to the milk and flipping the stove off. Without waiting for her to help, I measure out the liquid and add it. After stirring it in, I set the spoon aside. "We need to leave it undisturbed for a while."

"And I'm guessing you don't want to make out during that time," she says dryly.

"We shouldn't." The disappointment is heavy in my voice. She gives me an odd look with one eyebrow raised. Guilt churns my stomach. Maybe she will walk away and that will be the end of our friendship. The thought hurts. I'm desperate for more, more talking, more kissing, anything. "Would you tell me about your life in Los Angeles?"

Aurora sighs and settles against me. It feels right to wrap my arm across her stomach and let her lean into me. She chatters about her tiny apartment, her job bartending, and her roommates' crazy behavior. She makes it sound like an adventure but there's an undercurrent of regret.

She talks until the cheese is ready. I keep listening even while selecting a long knife and cutting the curds into chunks. Using a flat ladle, I slice horizontally. I stir gently to separate them and then let it sit for a few minutes.

Aurora talks about the galleries she's gotten shows in and how difficult they have been. I can hear her frustration even as she phrases everything optimistically.

Picking up the spoon again, I stir the curds slowly, trying to prevent them from breaking up while I turn the heat back on.

"So what are you doing now?" Aurora asks, peering in the pot with the cutest frown on her pouty lips.

"We need to slowly heat the curds up to one hundred and two degrees. They're really soft right now, but with heat, they'll start to firm up."

"This really is a lot of steps," she says, looking between the curds and me.

"I think they're just about done. We need to test them." Scooping a few curds out, I squish them together in my hand and then prod them. They fall back into individual curds easily. "If they stick together, they aren't ready, but if they separate again, we are good to go. Now we remove the whey."

"This is what whey is?" she asks.

Now that we're focused on the cheese, I've relaxed. My body hasn't gotten the message though, because my free hand runs down her ribs and across her stomach.

"Yeah, it's the water part of milk essentially. We can use it in place of milk or water in a lot of recipes and it adds protein," I explain, scooping out whey with a massive ladle until a minimal amount remains.

The door bangs open, framing Marigold. Her mouth is wide open, but she freezes, looking us over. Her expression melts into a smirk. "Oh, you guys look cozy."

My arm drops and Aurora steps to the side, creating space between us.

"Sorry, I didn't mean to interrupt, but it's baby time." Her mouth curves into a frown, like she really is sorry for breaking up this time we had together. It doesn't matter, I already ruined it.

"I'm going to go," Aurora says, pointing at the door with her thumb.

"I need to salt this and get it into the press, but I'll be around if you guys need me," I say lamely. There is no reason they'd need me.

Aurora leans forward and plants a kiss on my cheek. It takes all my control to not grab her chin and kiss her properly. With a regretful look, she disappears into the house to follow Marigold.

AURORA

The quiet of Hazel's cabin has transformed. Hazel's voice drifts down from the second story. Cassia and Marigold hover in the kitchen, talking quietly and glancing toward the stairs. Jasper sits on the couch, forearms resting on his knees, wringing his hands.

"Can I go upstairs?" I ask no one in particular.

Marigold nods and I jog up the steps. Hazel stands at the foot of her bed, bent over with her hands gripping the footboard. Her sweaty hair clings to her neck as she groans. Slate rubs her lower back.

"Honey, I think it's time for a shower. The hot water will help, I promise."

"Will it?" Hazel asks, though it's more a whimper. "Okay."

Sable looks to me. "Go start the water so it's hot for her." I jump to obey. When I emerge from the bathroom, Hazel is swaying in place, growling through another contraction.

"How are we doing?" I ask gently.

Hazel rounds on me. "If you ask about my progress or how long this will take, I will end you."

"Yes, ma'am." Tucking my hands behind me, I back up until I hit the far wall.

"Here, let's get under some hot water," Slate says, easing her toward the bathroom. Once the door closes behind them, Sable lets out a sharp exhale.

"Is everything okay?" I ask cautiously.

She studies the closed door. "Yes, it's going very well. She's reaching the hard part."

"How can I help?"

Sable's silver braid swings as she turns to face me. "You can let her hold your hand and break a few of your fingers. Or listen to her and offer a distraction if you can. Otherwise, stay out of the way and let her body do its job."

"Okay," I say meekly.

Uncle Heath fills the doorway. "It's baby time?"

"Yes and you can wait downstairs with everyone else. Except Marigold, send her up, please," Sable snaps at him.

"Any issues?"

"No, but there will be if you bother a mother in labor."

Heath nods and pushes off the door frame. A few moments later, he's replaced by Marigold. Her reddish gold curls are twisted into a bun and her normally wide smile is pinched nervously.

"Alright ladies, it's time to prep the bed. Take off the sheets and put down this." She pats what looks like a plastic shower curtain on the dresser, beside a plain white fitted sheet. "And the new sheet on top.

Marigold goes to one side of the bed, and I move to the other, and we make quick work of changing the bedding.

"Good, and she'll be close to pushing when she comes out. I already left her gown in the bathroom, but Slate might need help getting her dressed. We will see."

While we wait, I wander to the window. A row of houseplants line the ledge. I run my fingers over the glossy heart-shaped philodendron leaves and the round pilea leaves. Walking past the window, I trail my fingers over the spines of books on the impressive bookshelves covering the wall.

The door swings open and Hazel waddles out, now wearing a loose dress with her wet hair clinging to her neck.

"Looking good, Sis," I say.

She sits on the fresh bed and lets out a dry laugh. "Yep, I'm the height of fashion. Holy shit, that hurts!" She leans forward, bearing down as another contraction hits.

Marigold moves to her other side and Hazel grips her hand as well as Slate's. Their fingers turn white in her grasp.

"We're getting there. You're doing very good," Sable says, her tone even and calm.

Hazel lays back against the pillows and pushes wisps of wet hair off her forehead. Her eyes meet mine and the irises glow a molten gold.

"Um, your eyes," I stutter.

Another contraction starts, and Hazel bares her teeth, letting out a growl that raises the hair on my arms.

Marigold comes around the side of the bed and grabs my arm. "I think it's time we go wait with everyone else." She pushes me toward the door, but I plant my feet.

Through her lashes, I can see Hazel's eyes clearly glowing. As she grits her teeth, they look sharper. There's an animalistic glint to her that triggers fear deep within me. But she's my sister, and clearly I'm hallucinating.

"Get her out of here," Sable instructs.

Marigold pulls me toward the door when a crash startles both of us. One of the ceramic pots from the window lies shattered on the wood floor. The vine sprawls out of the shards, reaching up the wall and across the floor.

"What the?" Marigold asks, frowning at the pot.

"Now," Sable snaps, the authority in her tone finally getting my feet to move.

With Marigold at my elbow, we trail down the stairs. She clears her throat. "Hazel needs some privacy now but I'm going to go clean up that plant really quickly." She jogs back up the stairs, leaving me facing Jasper and Heath.

"How is she doing?" Jasper asks.

Heath rises and rubs a hand between my shoulder blades. The shock of Hazel's eyes has started to numb. I must have imagined it or the lighting in that room was stranger than I realized.

"I think it's going well, but she's definitely in a lot of pain. It's got to be getting close." Numbly, I plop onto the sofa beside Jasper. Heath sits in the chair beside us.

No one speaks. Marigold comes down with a trash bag tied up and takes it out back. Then she settles on Jasper's other side and holds his hand.

The light through the window fades and Heath walks around, turning on a handful of lights so we aren't sitting in the dark. After what feels like an age, Sable appears at the top of the stairs. "Baby is here, but she isn't up for a lot of visitors. One or two at a time and keep it brief."

Marigold catches my eye and smiles. "Aurora, why don't you head up first. And no spoilers."

"Thanks," I say, moving toward the stairs. My legs protest each step after resting on the sofa for so long. A gurgling cry comes from the master bedroom, but it's shushed quickly.

A pile of dirty linens sits right outside the door. Stepping past, I take in the dark room with Hazel curled in the bed. A tiny baby lays against her chest and Slate frames her with his arms. Sable bustles around, tidying up.

"Hey, ready to meet your niece?" Hazel asks, sounding exhausted but unbelievably happy.

I stop by her side and peer down at the little bundle. "It's a girl?"

"Yeah. Meet Timber Sage."

"Hi, baby," I squeak, my voice barely catching.

"Wash your hands before you touch the baby," Sable interjects.

Sighing, I peel myself away and head into the bathroom to scrub at my hands until they feel raw. I'm not taking any chances with my new niece.

Hazel readjusts her hold and Timber lets out a small cry. My stomach clenches. "Hey, sweet baby girl," I croon, running my knuckles over the dark downy hair covering her head. She follows my touch, her mouth opening and tongue sticking out. "She's so cute."

"It's time to try feeding again," Sable says.

"I'll give you your privacy," I murmur, moving toward the door.

"Thanks for being here, Rory." Hazel's puffy eyes are full of contentment.

"Congratulations." I've never been so proud of my sister. She's a mom. There's no doubt in my mind she's going to be amazing at it.

Marigold and Jasper stand when I reach the bottom of the stairs.

"She's breastfeeding right now. You might want to wait a few minutes," I warn. "But I'm going to head home. I'll see you guys tomorrow."

Heath frowns at me. "It's dark. Wait a few minutes for me to meet the baby and then we can walk home together."

"I can manage. I've got my phone with the flashlight app and I've walked the path between here and your cabin a bunch of times. I promise I won't get lost."

Heath opens his mouth to argue, but Jasper intercedes for me. "There's nothing out there that could hurt her. She'll be fine."

I don't mention the wolves I saw the other day because that won't help my case. I'm not wandering through the forest, just walking between two cabins. It's not far.

"Good night, everyone," I say, pushing my way out the front door before Heath stops me.

The flashlight on my phone illuminates dirt beyond their porch and I step carefully. Once my feet are planted, I hold the light up and look back and forth. The trees are thinner to the left and I know I have to go straight forward and slightly to the left.

As I pick my way through the brush, the sounds of the forest at night surround me. Bugs hum and chirp, and a clicking sound makes me look up. Dark forms like small birds swoop past above the treetops, and I watch their journeys through the gaps in the branches. Bats. The clicking stalls as an owl hoot echoes around me.

With a smile, I pick my feet up and continue walking home. To my credit, I only stumble once, but when my palm braces against a tree trunk, my hand stings.

A sense of accomplishment fills me when I reach Heath's cabin. I'm tempted to stay outside on the porch and enjoy the night, but exhaustion pulls me down. To compromise, I crack my window open an inch before washing up and curling up in bed. A red line crosses the inside of my thumb, but it's not actively bleeding. I'm tired enough, the dull pain doesn't bother me as I drift off to sleep.

VIII
POTHOS PAROXYSM
CEDAR

Slate summons me to their cabin in the early morning hours. I was planning on a run to work more of that heavy feeling out of my chest, but when my Alpha calls, I come. Hazel curls up on the sofa with baby Timber sleeping in her arms. Heath sits in the arm chair and Sable stands in the kitchen.

"How are you doing?" I ask, dipping my head respectfully.

Hazel's smile is tired, but she shifts her hold on her baby to show me the sweet girl's squashed-looking face. "We're great."

"She's adorable."

Heath clears his throat. "So there was an incident with Aurora."

My knees lock and I sway where I stand. "What do you mean?"

Slate motions for me to take the far armchair and settles beside Hazel. "She was in the room while Hazel was in labor."

"She definitely saw my eyes glowing," Hazel fills in. "We shouldn't have let her in. I don't know why I didn't realize what would happen."

"All of us can bear that blame," Slate says, placing a kiss on her shoulder. "But more importantly, something else happened."

I land in the chair roughly, my hands gripping the arms. I should have been here. I kissed her and sent her off without thinking twice.

"One of my house plants fell off the window after it started to grow. It almost quadrupled in size. All the plants on the window at least doubled and that was enough to knock one of them off."

It's the last thing I expect. "What?"

"Something affected the plants," Sable summarizes. Her mouth thins, irritated at my slow response. "Something supernatural."

"And we think it's Aurora? What about Timber?"

"We thought about that," Heath says. "But the timing makes sense to be Aurora. You've spent the most time with her. Have you noticed anything strange?"

Leaning forward in my seat, I prop my elbows on my knees and rest my forehead against my palms. What have I noticed about Aurora? My exhale is slow and uneven. "She helped me plant some carrots and radishes on her first full day here. That was two or three days ago? And they're almost ready to harvest."

"Those are fast growers," Hazel replies without looking up from her baby.

"Not that fast. They shouldn't be sprouting until tomorrow or the next day at the earliest. I've already thinned them. It's like they're three or four weeks old and not three days."

"So plants are growing like crazy around her," Slate says, looking to Sable. "What does that mean?"

"It might be a coincidence. But perhaps we have a green witch on our hands."

The words echo in my head, sending my heart racing. The girl I kissed in the kitchen isn't a normal human? She's got her own magic? That can't be possible.

"That's not a thing. Is that a thing?" Hazel's head swings back and forth, confusion knitting her brows.

Heath taps a finger on his leg. "My grandmother once told me we had witches in our family line. I thought she was trying to scare me into listening. Maybe not."

"That's not possible," Hazel argues, tipping her head sideways as she frowns at her uncle.

Slate lifts her hand and kisses the back of her knuckles. "You just learned you were a shifter two years ago. Is it so hard to believe Aurora might be a witch?"

"Wouldn't we have seen evidence growing up?"

"She hasn't been around a lot of nature until now," Heath replies.

Rubbing at the back of my neck, I consider the implications. "So what are we going to do?"

"Watch her." Hazel sighs and tips her head until her temple rests against Slate's shoulder. "Let's just see what happens. Once we can confirm the situation, we will have to talk to her."

"Talk to her?" I echo. "About her possible magic, or everything?"

"Hopefully just her magic. But we will see. I'm not ruling anything out. She's family."

Heath nods. "Let us know what else happens around her."

"And this is my assignment?" I clarify.

"She seems to want to spend time with you more than anyone else," Slate says.

"Her first priority has been her sister," I correct. "But she's trying to be respectful with her time."

Hazel sighs. "Yes, I know. She's been great. But she's very keen on you and now that can help us."

"Yes, Alpha." My stomach churns. Now it's truly my assignment to stay close to Aurora. Should I tell them what happened? Cautiously, I say, "She's been flirting a bit."

My body tenses as Hazel pinches the bridge of her nose. "I'm sorry. I thought she might. She thinks you're nice and cute. I told her guys around here don't casually date. Just tell her you're not interested next time she does something flirty."

Swallowing, I nod. My mouth is dry, my pulse pounding in my ears. I really needed that run.

"Good luck and let us know," Hazel says. Timber lets out a small cry and her attention refocuses immediately.

With another respectful nod, I back out of their home and close the door behind me. Being outside helps a little, but I'm still on edge. I should go for a run right now, but my curiosity about Aurora wins out. There's some driving need to make sure she's okay.

The sun warms the treetops, casting a dim glow across the forest floor. It's still very early, but Aurora is a morning person like I am. My feet lead me to Heath's cabin.

On the way, I pass my family's cabin. The wildflowers along the blue siding have grown up to a ridiculous height, especially along the addition. Maybe they have been overgrown for a while and I failed to notice. The copious blooms are unusual this early in the spring.

Heath's cabin is similarly surrounded by flowers. Lupine stems grow past my knees and overtake the pathway as I approach. The sound of a shower drifts from a bathroom window left open a few inches. My feet slow.

From the bathroom window unfurls a glossy pothos vine. It trails down the wall and tangles with the shrubbery below. Even as I watch, the vine sends out tendrils and grasps stems and leaves of the plants below the window.

I jerk to a halt, staring. I've never seen a plant move like that. There's nothing normal about the way it vibrates and two new leaves burst from the stem, uncurling and turning toward the early morning light.

Green witch, indeed.

Any doubt I had about her potential magical status is quelled. My mind whirls as I stand there, watching steam drift from the window and the pothos vine as it climbs across the bushes.

The water turns off. A startled yelp resounds, along with a bang. A string of curses follow, but I'm already in motion. I sprint around the cabin and through the kitchen door. Aurora lets out a louder screech, and I can hear her hyperventilating.

Knocking my fist against the door, I ask, "Aurora, are you okay?"

Perhaps she doesn't hear me. Her words are garbled and rising in pitch, as if she is panicking. I have no idea what could be in the bathroom with her, but I'm not waiting any longer.

With a deep breath, I ram my shoulder into the door and break the lock. The door shoots open but catches before it can move more than a few inches. Vines crisscross over the space, making the entire bathroom look like a jungle. The steam is scented with Aurora's floral smell mixed with the scent of leaves and new growth.

"Aurora?"

"Cedar?" Her answer is tentative and shaky.

"Are you okay?" I shove the door forward another inch and the vines push it back.

"I'm okay, but I think I'm trapped."

"Just the plants?" I confirm.

"What the hell is happening?"

Raising my foot, I stomp on the lowest of the vines restraining the door, but only one breaks. "Hold on, I'm going to get you out of there." Looking back into the kitchen, I spot a chef's knife on a magnetic bar along the backsplash. That will do.

Armed with a blade, I begin to saw through the vines keeping the door closed. For every inch I gain, the vines reform and begin to curl around my feet. I'm going to be trapped too.

"Aurora, I need you to calm down. You're making this worse."

"Excuse me, but I can't imagine you would handle it any better if your houseplants suddenly decided to hold you hostage!" A dull thud tells me she's smacked something, maybe the wall.

"Hey, take slow breaths. I need you to calm down."

Her ragged breathing slows as she attempts to follow my instructions. The rapid growth around my ankles slows, and I'm able to cut myself free. My progress forward is slow, and every so often, Aurora lets out a low whine.

It's only a few feet to the shower, and when enough vines are cleared, I can see her huddled with the shower curtain wrapped around her. Wet hair clings to her neck and shoulders.

"Hey there," I say, giving her my best winning smile.

Her wild eyes fix on me. "What is happening?" she repeats.

"It's going to be fine. I'm getting you out of here and then we will figure it out." My words come out confident and steady, which is not even close to how I feel.

The knife is coated in green sap from slicing into the vines. When I've made a clear path, I begin tugging away the vines that have wrapped around Aurora. It makes me nervous to have the knife so close to her skin, so I pull the vines away before cutting them off entirely.

Aurora shakes where she's standing. Her white fingers grip the tan shower curtain, even once she's free of the vines.

"I can go get you some clothes or a towel," I offer. We both look at the towels on the hooks that are so wrapped up with leaves and vines that they look like they've been in the forest for generations.

When I turn back to find something else for her, she lets out a protesting whine. "Don't leave me. Just get me out of here."

"Okay, come here," I say, reaching for her. It's impossible to look away. She drops the dripping shower curtain and allows me to scoop her up. Her arms curl over my shoulder blades and her legs straddle my hips as she clings to me. My arm curls under her bare ass. Water runs down her hair and soaks into my shirt.

Slowly, I trudge back across the bathroom. Her fingers dig into my back as she shivers. "It's okay," I murmur. "You're good. Everything is fine."

I carry her to her bedroom, and then set her on the bed as carefully as I can manage. Her arms cross her chest, her cheeks blazing red. Looking anywhere but that bare expanse of skin, I back out of the room and shut it.

Heart pounding, I rest my back against the door.

"Cedar?" she calls.

"Yeah?"

"I don't really want to be alone in here."

Resting my forehead against the door, I exhale slowly. It occurs to me in that moment, I would do anything she asked. With one more breath to steady myself, I turn the handle and slip back into her room.

Aurora stands by the dresser with her hand holding onto the drawer. An oversized shirt drapes over her frame, and she's holding a pair of bike shorts. I look at the wall while she pulls them on. The bed creaks when she sits back down.

"So, um, that was weird," she says, her voice sounding hoarse.

"Yeah." I scratch the back of my head, ignoring how the room seems to sway.

"Did I just hallucinate, or did the house plants attack me during my shower?"

"Yeah, that about sums it up."

"I don't know what to do with that information." She laughs dryly and presses her fingertips to the bridge of her nose.

Swallowing, I approach her bed and sit on the end, leaving a couple of feet between us.

"I think you should go talk to Hazel and Slate about it," I offer.

When her amber eyes meet mine, they're glittering with unshed tears. "What's wrong with me?"

"Nothing is wrong with you," I say, louder than I intended.

"Seriously?" She waves her hand toward the door.

Her chest shakes as she fights tears. Wiping at her face, she sniffs and looks up at me. "She's going to think I'm nuts."

"Come on, I promise she will be understanding."

Aurora takes my hand. She pauses to shove her feet into sandals, but allows me to guide her out of the cabin and down the steps. Her steps are shaky, and my vision narrows to her bright eyes and the feel of her hand in mine.

"So nothing is wrong with me, but you have to take me to see my big sister?" she asks with a sarcastic edge. The fingers curled around mine tighten. "That sure sounds like a problem to me."

There's no convincing her without offering some truth. I can't share the pack's secrets, but I can point out her truths.

"Do you remember the first day you helped me in the garden? Those radishes and carrots are almost ready to harvest. They look like they are several weeks old, not several days."

"That can't be right," she mutters, shaking her head. Her eyes cast around the ground as if the plants near us might spring up to capture her at any moment.

"And did you see that a plant fell off the window ledge in Hazel's room when she was having the baby?"

"Yeah, that was freaky."

"The plant grew, like tripled in size, and that's what pushed it off. All the plants in that room at least doubled."

The quiet, "No," she gives in protest sounds less confident.

"I noticed the wildflowers growing around my dad's cheese kitchen and around Heath's house have gotten massive in the last few days."

She spins and looks over the cabin. "Looks the same to me."

"After Hazel had the baby, she asked Sable about the house plant falling. She thinks you are a witch."

Even her breathing stops. Aurora is a statue. Her hand pulls me to a stop so I turn and put an arm around her. Her eyes stare straight ahead. I take a loud, slow breath, trying to encourage her to breathe. Finally she does, sucking in air to say, "Are you kidding me?"

I can feel her pulse in her fingers and where our wrists touch. Shaking my head to clear my focus, I try to explain. "No. Apparently there are some green witches in your family line way back generations ago."

Aurora shudders as she lets out a hysterical laugh. "I'm, what, flinging around plant magic? I'm sorry, I'm not that delusional."

"Vines just trapped you in the shower and I had to cut you out with a butcher's knife."

"That was a chef's knife," she corrects, her voice going up an octave.

"I'm not sure what other proof you need." Frustration overwhelms me.

"Are you saying this was my fault?" she snaps, getting louder. It feels like a physical blow.

"It wasn't saying you intentionally grew them," I say, trying to deescalate her. My head is pounding. The squeeze of her fingers starts to sting.

"So these inexplicable things keep happening and it's all because of me because I'm some kind of monster."

"No!" I don't mean to yell.

Aurora rips her hand from mine and takes a step back. Her eyes narrow in accusation. "I don't even know what you want me to believe!"

"Just wait and listen," I say, my voice growling.

"Your eyes..." Aurora stares, her lips parting in shock. I drop my gaze to the dirt and duck my head, but she isn't deterred. "No, I knew I saw Hazel's eyes glowing and your eyes are doing it too right now!"

"Listen!" I say, my hands clenching into fists.

"You want me to think I'm sort of witch, but then you're acting all freaky! I know you're lying to me. I can feel it." She's yelling, throwing her hands out dramatically.

I can't handle it. My pulse thrums in my ears and my skin prickles. I drag my nails down my arms, trying to quell the irritating hum increasing throughout my muscles, aching my bones. Anger flickers in the corners of my mind, the wolfish side of me bringing out baser emotions. Stress narrows my vision until she is all I can see.

When I try to step forward, my ankle catches on plants that have grown up and twisted around me. Their hold is so tight, I pitch forward and throw my hands out to catch myself.

My shifter instincts win out over the yelling in my head. One instant I'm a clumsy human falling, and the next second I'm a reddish-blonde wolf landing on four paws with the shreds of clothes drifting around me.

Aurora lets out a scream so intense, my ears pop. Her hands clench into fists before she turns and starts sprinting through the trees.

I should run to get Hazel or Heath. What I really shouldn't do is chase her. So of course that's exactly what I do.

Predator instincts kick in and I'm racing after her before I can stop myself. The floral scent mingling with the chemicals of paint, something so uniquely Aurora, overwhelms my senses. I'm going to catch her.

My tail whips behind me. I catch every movement, the way branches bend as if they're reaching for her even after she's passed, the churn of dirt under her bare feet. Her flip flops flew off as soon as she took off running. She's fast, but I'm faster. I close the distance in seconds.

My ears swivel, taking in the sound of her footfalls. My pace slows, allowing me to approach without spooking her. The clever girl must know she can't outrun me, so she tries hiding, but with her scent imprinted in my brain, there is no escape for her.

Muzzle to the ground, I creep toward the tree she's tucked herself again. It's a towering cedar tree, though my wolf brain doesn't see the irony in that. She huddles against the massive trunk. The honeysuckle vines covering the tree's roots have grown up to blanket her. Hundreds of white blooms open as I watch.

The sound of soft crying shakes me from my animalistic mind. With mental effort, I shift back to human. Now I'm the one embarrassingly naked, but there is no way I'm leaving her here alone.

"Aurora," I call, crouching down to peer between the branches. The sniffling stops. "Hey, it's okay. I'm not going to hurt you."

Tentatively, I reach out and tug some of the plant aside. It curls back, revealing her head and shoulders. She's curled in on herself. Her wet hair is mussed from her wild sprint.

"Can you come out? I promise I'll answer anything you want to know. No more secrets."

"Really?" Her voice is shaky, but I can tell I've got her hooked.

"Yup. Come on," I say, slowly extending my arm to trace my fingertips over her shoulder.

"Okay."

The plant loosens and she's able to shrug it off. When she reaches out, I grab her hand and help her crawl up and out of her hiding place. As soon as she's standing, her eyes flick down my body and back up. "So... you're naked. Like really naked."

A snort in expected laughter. "Yeah, that happens when you turn into a wolf."

"You're like a werewolf." Her mouth parts, her lips forming a small circle.

"We prefer the term shifter," I say, a growl under my words.

Her eyes meet mine and she looks in control for the first time since her shower. "I have so many questions."

I bite my lip, thinking. I don't want to make a bad situation even worse. "Are you okay knowing more? It's a lot of dump on top of the witch thing."

"Hey," she says, holding up a hand. "Thinking about your freaky werewolf stuff is way easier to handle than the idea that I'm a witch, so let me have this."

"If you insist. But are we going to have this entire conversation while I'm naked?"

"I'm good with that." Her mouth curves in a devious smirk that I like far more than I should.

"Of course you are."

"Is it bad I want to kiss you even after I saw you turn into a dog?" She whispers, like it's a shared conspiracy.

"Hey, not a dog. Don't say that."

"Sorry, werewolf, shit, shifter!"

When she smiles sweetly and meets my eyes, I know we're going to be okay. "Come on, I need to get some pants."

"But look at that ass," she teases.

"You really have a thing for asses, don't you?"

"Just yours."

When I glance back, her smirk wavers, her expression tense.

"I'm flattered. Come on, I've got some clothes on the porch."

"Why do you have clothes on the porch? Oh, turning into a wolf, of course. I got you." She follows me, muttering to herself. We thread our way through the underbrush and I find the path oddly clear. It only takes a few minutes to reach my family's cabin.

While I tug a pair of sweats on, Aurora crosses to the swing. It's a hanging daybed my dad made for my mom years ago and it's loaded with pillows and a cozy blanket. Aurora wraps it around herself and sits with her legs tucked under her. When I sit beside her and push off the ground to send us swinging, she wraps an arm around my bicep and cuddles close, setting her chin on my shoulder.

It's so nice sitting together, her warmth soaking into my bare skin, but I know we have concerns to address. "So what do you want to know?"

"Hazel's eyes glowed." She gets right to the point.

"That's not a question," I say, flinching when she glares at me. "Okay, yes, Hazel is a wolf shifter too. Your dad was too, and Heath is, obviously."

"How many people here are shifters?"

"Everyone."

"Are you freaking kidding me?" Her eyes widen, her mouth opening and closing for a moment as she processes.

"Nope."

My steady demeanor seems to calm her, and she takes a few slow breaths. "Are you telling me I've been the only human here this whole time?"

"Yes, that would be accurate."

"That's crazy." Her tone is quieter now.

I extract my arm from her grip so I can wrap it around her shoulders. Together, we sink backwards until she can rest her cheek against my chest. The skin-to-skin contact is comforting.

"Except I'm some sort of witch?" Her voice wobbles.

I throw my other arm across her, caging her against my chest. "That doesn't mean you aren't human. You're just an extra special human."

"Enough of that. Okay, so how often do you turn into a wolf?"

I can't help the smile forming on my face. The matter of fact way she states it is so charming. Closing my eyes, I try to focus on my words and not the warmth of her body stretched out along my side.

"Whenever I want to. But honestly, I need to shift and go running every few days or I start to feel antsy. Pair that with some major stress and accidents are possible, like what just happened."

"I'm sorry about that." Her voice is quiet. "I was freaking out. I didn't mean to upset you so much."

Shaking my head, I squeeze her briefly. "No, I should have been fine. It's my fault for skipping so many runs and not managing my emotions. That shouldn't have happened."

"I'm really glad it did. I could sense there was something you guys were all hiding from me. It was driving me crazy."

"You're very intuitive."

"Or you guys aren't as discrete as you think."

"Do you know how often I had to hide my eyes from you? Especially when we kissed." The words tumble out without much thought.

Aurora pushes up, turning her head to stare at me. One eyebrow slowly rises as she studies my face. "Really?"

Despite the nagging suspicion that I will regret it, I nod.

Her eyes search my face, and slowly she lowers her mouth to mine. I have plenty of time to stop her or protest, but I'm hungry for it. She knows who I am now. There's honesty between us.

Her warm mouth brushes mine, and she comes back for a second soft kiss. It's tentative, and I can't help grabbing her jaw and holding her still so I can kiss her harder and deeper. Her lips part with a small gasp. I take the opportunity to nip at her bottom lip and she makes another of those beautiful noises.

She pulls back, blinking until her eyes focus on mine. "Wow," she says, admiring the glow of my eyes. I can see the brighter blue reflect back in her honey irises. "That's pretty cool."

The pads of my fingertips feel rough as I drag them down her cheek and over her jaw. "Glad you like it, because you get that reaction out of me pretty easily."

"Is that your way of saying you like me?" she teases.

When I don't reply, she quiets. The teasing and kisses are just a distraction when there is so much unsaid between us. Like the fact she's ignoring her newly discovered status as a green witch. But she can take her time. No need to come to terms with that many supernatural revelations in the same afternoon.

Her tone darkens. "Can we wait to talk to my sister? I don't think I can face her right now."

"Sure." I shouldn't agree, but I'd probably do almost anything for Aurora at this point.

"Soon. I just want some time to process."

Somehow time to process turns into soft kisses and whispered reassurances. She licks the corner of my jaw and right under my earlobe, making my eyes roll back in my head.

Leaning back, she smiles smugly.

"You know when we were making cheese?" The need to explain sits heavy like a weight on my chest. "I stopped us kissing because you said something, and you didn't mean it like this, but I was startled."

"What did I say?"

"You asked me to mark you," I say somberly.

Her nose wrinkles as she frowns at me. "I meant a hickey."

"For wolf shifters, when we commit to someone as our partner, we bite them to leave a mark. That's why I reacted to what you said."

She's quiet for a moment, thinking. "Is that the marks I saw on your brother during the scavenger hunt?"

"What did you see?"

"A circle of scars. I'm thinking it was a bite mark? Did Ember do that to him?" She tilts her head, a wisp of curly brown hair falling over her face.

'Yes. They exchanged marks."

Her next question comes hesitantly. "What about my sister?"

"She wears Slate's mark and he has hers."

She nods slowly, running her teeth over her bottom lip. "That's why they don't care about getting married."

"There's some magic behind it. They can feel each other's emotions somewhat. I'm not sure how much, since I've never experienced it, obviously," I explain.

"That must make things *interesting*."

"We call them mates." It's important to me that she understands these relationships. "It's just as serious as marriage, but with different consequences if you break up. The emotional bond can't be severed as far as I know."

"Then does anyone ever break up?"

"We aren't built that way. It almost never happens. The only case I know of is when Slate's mom left his dad, which is why he has two half-siblings."

"What happened to his dad?" she asks, her brows furrowing.

"He died."

"What?" she yelps, twisting in my arms.

My hand brushes down her back, soothing her. "Not from that, but the long-term stress of the betrayed bond didn't help. We're not meant to be separated from our mates."

"It sounds serious," she says, her voice trailing off.

"Yeah," I say, tightening my hold and urging her to settle against me again. The soft sway of the swing lulls us into a quiet peace and I savor the feel of her melting against me. She lets out a small, contented noise. For a moment, I can pretend that she's mine.

Aurora

"Oh, you guys look cozy." Hazel's voice jerks me awake. Cedar's arms tighten around me, keeping me from tumbling off the swing. I'm grateful but simultaneously horrified.

In the past, I never would have cared if my sister found me with a boy. But this is different. Cedar is different.

With a sigh, I push myself up to sit. Cedar follows until we sit side by side and face Hazel. I feel like a guilty teenager. My sister props her hands on her hips and purses her lips.

Slate stands behind her, a smirk on his face and a baby carrier strapped to his front. The top of baby Timber's head pokes out, wisps of dark hair curling in patches.

Cedar ducks his head and rakes his fingers through his messy hair.

"How are you feeling?" I ask Hazel, the disapproval in her expression keeping me from jumping up and hugging her.

"I'm fine," she says curtly.

"Haze, you had a baby like twenty-four hours ago. Are you sure you should be walking around like this?"

Hazel ignores my concern. "I think we need to talk."

She probably means about me and Cedar becoming some sort of item, but her tone irritates me. She's the one who disappeared into the woods and became a wolf shifter and kept it secret. If she wants to discuss uncomfortable truths, fine. "Apparently I'm some sort of plant witch."

Her eyes widen, but I'm not done.

"Not to mention, you turned into a werewolf and didn't bother telling me." Crossing my arms, I tip my chin up defiantly. Cedar tenses beside me.

Hazel gawks at me. Slate steps up beside her and wraps an arm around her waist. "Why don't we go inside? She's not wrong. You should still be resting."

She lets out a huff and crosses her arms. Part of me feels viciously gratified, but moreover, guilt settles in my gut. I don't want to be fighting with my sister.

Cedar holds open the door and ushers us into a quiet living room. Hazel settles on the squishy sectional, and I sit on the other side, not quite ready to let go of my annoyance. Slate and Cedar sit between us.

Biting my lip, I refuse to talk until Hazel breaks the silence.

She lets out a long sigh. "I'm relieved you know the truth, honestly. It's hard keeping anything from you."

It's the best thing she could have said. I think the fact my sister kept such a huge truth from me bothers me more than finding out I might have some sort of magic myself.

Timber lets out a little whimper, so Slate unclips the carrier so he can cradle their baby and gently rock her. Hazel watches for a moment before returning her attention to me.

"We have rules about not telling people. It was dangerous when I discovered the truth. But things have changed, so it should be okay that you know. Even so, we should keep it quiet for now. And obviously you can't say anything to anyone. Mom doesn't know."

"Of course!" I rush to assure her.

"How did you find out?" Slate asks.

Cedar stiffens beside me. I wet my lips, glancing his way, wondering if he would prefer to answer. He meets Slate's gaze reluctantly. "She had some issues with the house plants in Heath's house and I was helping her."

"I got really scared and I was kinda screaming at him and freaking out." I jump in.

"I lost control and shifted." He rests his forearms on his knees, fingers laced together as he hangs his head, the image of a repentant man.

A cold silence stretches and I get the feeling this is a punishable offense.

"Maybe my magic did something to him," I suggest. "It's my fault."

Hazel's hand goes to Slate's knee, as a silent exchange happens between them. He nods. "Perhaps we should have told you sooner. Maybe that difficult situation could have been avoided."

Swallowing the lump in my throat, I gather my courage to ask the question simmering in the back of my head. "So if Dad was a shifter and you are, does that mean I am too?"

Lines form around Hazel's mouth as she studies me. "No, we don't think so. It's really unlikely."

"Wait, how can we know for sure?" Even the possibility sends ice through my veins. It's terrifying and yet alluring.

"You'd start showing signs. Fast healing, hair and nails growing quickly, improved senses."

Frowning, I lift my hand to study the small cut below my thumb. The scab has barely formed. No super healing here.

"This is a good thing," Hazel says warmly. "It means you aren't stuck here. If you were a shifter, you'd need to stay with us or join another pack."

"Pack?" I raise an eyebrow at her.

"Oh, that's what this is. Why we all live together." She sweeps her hands out.

"Like a wolf pack?"

"Kinda. It's a little different, but that's the idea. We're built to live in community. Shifters don't do well in isolation."

"How does it work here? Is it basically a really close-knit neighborhood that gets furry together every so often?"

Hazel rolls her eyes. "No, there's more to it than that. Everyone has different roles and jobs, and we all work together. Some people are protectors, like Lazuli and Cassia who you met." The image of them watching me as I arrived flashes through my head. "And other people handle things our community needs, like how Cedar cares for our garden. His mom is a baker. Marigold is a teacher."

"What's your job?"

Hazel clears her throat, her eyes flicking to Slate. "We're the Alphas."

"Excuse me?"

Slate smiles, admiring my sister as she purses her lips, thinking before answering. "We're the leaders."

"You've only been here for like two years. How can you be in charge?" Heath's words replay in my head, taking on a new meaning.

"Heath was Alpha for a long time. As his closest family member, I became his heir. And Slate was his Beta, or second-in-command. When Heath got injured, he decided to officially step down, but he still helps us a lot."

"So it's like a monarchy?

Hazel scrunches up her nose and shakes her head. "Not like that. It's skill based, mainly. If I wasn't capable of doing the job, he wouldn't have made me Heir." She tilts her head, thinking. "Not just skills though. A lot of it is personality. Almost power levels. How do I explain this?"

At some point, Slate gave Cedar the baby, because Timber's chubby cheek rests against Cedar's bare chest. He leans back against the back of the sofa, letting his steady breaths lull the baby back to sleep.

Something about his hands enveloping Timber's tiny, sloped back and the way her little fists curl up against his skin, it makes my stomach flip. The thoughts in my head float away.

"Oh, Rory, look!" Hazel says, jumping to her feet. She snatches a houseplant off a table by the window and holds it up. The vines unfurl and lengthen.

My mouth falls open. As we watch, the sudden burst of growth fades and the plant stills. Only the tendrils reaching for the floor gently sway as Hazel holds the plant at eye level and stares at it.

"I think that resolves any lingering questions." The pot makes a ceramic clink as she sets it back on the glass table. "Did you feel anything when that happened?"

"Um, no." I look between my sister and the plant by the window, now still. "I didn't feel anything and I definitely wasn't trying to do that. Are we sure it's me?"

"The seeds you planted, remember?" Cedar says quietly.

Pressing my lips together, I lean back against the sofa, mimicking his pose.

"Okay, so we have a couple of things to consider," Hazel says. As she slides back into her seat, Slate wraps an arm around her waist and pulls her tight against him. The touch reminds me of how Cedar held me on the porch. My toes curl and my breathing goes ragged. That will be something to consider later.

"I don't understand why I would suddenly start affecting plants out of nowhere."

"You've never been in a place like this before," she says, sweeping her hand out. "And being around all of us might have had something to do with it. That's just a guess. I would have to ask Sable."

"Right. So do you think it'll go away when I go home?"

Slate shakes his head. "We can't count on that."

"It's going to be a problem when I start making all the plants go crazy during a gallery show," I say with an awkward laugh, pressing the heel of my hand into my eyes.

"You'll need to figure out how to control it," Cedar says softly.

"I have no idea how to do that!"

My outburst startles Timber. Her baby blue-gray eyes pop open and she lets out a cry. Cedar pats her butt, but she starts to flail her little fists.

"Here," Slate says, taking his child back. He murmurs comforting words to Timber, but her little face screws up and she starts to wail.

Hazel reaches for her. "I bet she's hungry again. Get ready for diaper duty, Daddy." My heart warms at the way he gazes at her in adoration as she positions their baby and tugs her shirt up. As soon as she offers Timber her breast, the baby latches and the room falls quiet.

"Hungry girl," I say, utterly distracted from the problems at hand.

"Alright, so, getting control," Hazel says without looking up from her baby, "I'm not entirely sure, but we can ask Sable and Heath."

"I suppose trying to get things to happen on command would be the first step so I can figure out what I'm doing to cause this," I say.

Cedar nods. He turns in his seat, his thigh pressing against mine. "I'll help you. You should come to the garden and practice. You've already worked some magic there, so maybe it'll be an easier place to trigger more."

"Thank you."

"That sounds like a plan to me," Hazel says. "Keep me updated on how it's going."

"Aurora," Slate says, catching my attention. "We know this probably means staying longer. Let us know how much income you're missing out on and we can help with your bills."

"No, that's not necessary," I argue.

His vivid green eyes narrow and I stiffen. "It's not a problem, and it's best if you don't go back home and have to work triple shifts to get caught up. The stress won't help your situation."

"Okay." I can't help but agree when he turns that intense scrutiny on me.

Hazel looks up from her baby and smiles at me, a little sadly. When she looks back down, her chocolate hair falls like a wavy curtain over her face.

"We should go," Cedar says, his hand going to my thigh, just above the knee.

"But it's your house," I say, my brows furrowing.

"You guys are fine, you can stay and hang out or go," Hazel says without looking up. "We'll be out of here as soon as Timber is done with second breakfast."

As much as I'd like to stay and watch baby Timber, the weight of new magic presses down on my shoulders. It's been a day, and it's only early afternoon. With that thought, my stomach lets out a growl.

"Let's go get some lunch," Cedar says, crossing to the door. He holds it open for me, and I move forward automatically. The way his hand goes to the small of my back feels natural, but I don't doubt that Hazel and Slate noticed. Hopefully she isn't too unhappy with me.

Cedar's arm wraps around my waist, keeping me close as we head toward the diner.

"I'm okay," I say. "Really."

"I know." He leans closer, speaking quietly. "I'm not under any delusion that you need me. You're very capable. Maybe I just want to be near you."

His words shiver across my skin, drawing me closer. It would be too easy to forget my magical problems and get lost in him. For just a moment, I lean into his warmth and let all my worries fade.

IX
CINNAMON ROLLS
& CONTROL
CEDAR

Aurora's first day attempting to use plant magic on command results in exactly zero progress. She gets more irritable as time drags on and she stares at the garden beds and curses under her breath. Eventually, she calls it a day and goes home.

It bothers me that I can't do anything to help. Once she leaves the garden, I head to Sable's cottage and rap my knuckles on the door.

The silver-haired healer yells, "Come in."

Pushing the door open, I duck my head to step into the small work room. Bottles line one wall on imperfect handmade shelves. Bouquets of dried plants cover the ceiling, many of which I placed there for her.

"Cedar, is everything okay?" Sable says, her small figure framed in the stone arch that leads to the living space of her home.

"Yes, I'm fine."

"So what brings you over to visit me today?" Without waiting for an answer, she disappears. Looking around awkwardly, I decide to perch on a spare stool. When Sable reappears, she hands me a mug of tea.

"What did you put in here?" I ask.

"Nothing you should worry about," she says with a wry smile.

Closing my eyes, I breathe in the steam wafting off my mug. A lemon scent hits me first. Tentatively, I take a sip. When I look up, Sable is watching me expectantly. It takes two more sips to identify the flavors. "Lemon balm, lavender, and is that passionflower?"

"Very good." She takes a long drink of her own tea.

"Do you think I look anxious?" I ask, feeling curious.

She clears her throat. "Most males would be in your position."

"Excuse me?"

"With a supposedly human mate suddenly displaying magic."

The tea gets caught in my throat and I almost spew some of it out as I cough. "She's not, what? We aren't even dating," I splutter.

"Drink your tea, son."

I blink at her. Why would she say that? She can't know that I kissed Aurora. Besides, it can't go anywhere. Clearly there is no real relationship between us.

Sable ignores me, setting her tea aside and tidying up some of the supplies on her work table.

"I was hoping you would have some guidance on helping Aurora develop some control over using her magic so she can go home." I emphasize the last words.

Sable snorts and turns to face me with her hands on her hips. "What was happening when she used her magic?"

"Nothing."

"That's not true." Her eyes narrow, cutting into me.

A rub the back of my neck, trying to think. "She grew plants when Hazel was in labor. And when she was scared and upset. So those are high emotion times. But she also planted seeds when she was calm and those later grew. And the other time, she was in the shower."

"Interesting."

"I don't see any connection."

"Interesting," she repeats.

Blowing out my breath, I stand. "Do you have any other advice?"

"Talk to her."

"I have been," I say, trying to keep the frustration out of my tone.

Sable is unbothered. "Unless you want to help me with making more salve, go away. There won't be room for you in here once my nephew arrives anyways."

"Yes, ma'am." I may be one of Sable's favorites because of the ingredients I grow for her, but I know better than to get on her bad side. She ignores me as I move to the door and close it behind me carefully.

On the walk home, I run over the incidents in my mind.

First, the seeds we planted together. She was calm, maybe happy. It certainly wasn't a high emotion moment. Perhaps she was excited about being in a new place and seeing her sister, but that can't compare to the out of control emotions that spurred later magic.

My cabin is empty. I flop down on my bed, feeling dissatisfied. The empty room bothers me. Maybe my mother is right and I should get my own place.

Aurora's face fills my mind. The way she shook as she ran through the forest after I lost control. That plant growth was from fear. But what happened right before, when she was in the shower? Why was it different from the other showers she's taken since arriving?

With a sigh, I roll over and bury my face in my pillow. I'll have to talk with her tomorrow, and maybe together we can untangle this.

I'm up with the sun. It's my routine, though I would be lying if thoughts of seeing Aurora didn't motivate me to move faster.

Standing in front of the mirror, I stretch my arm across me and twist, feeling my sore muscles protest. With a measured exhale, I brush my fingers through my unruly hair. What does Aurora see that made her want to kiss me? She's beautiful and surely had her pick of men wherever she goes.

I've never considered myself handsome. I don't have Onyx's confidence or charm. Turning my head, I consider the way my olive skin has turned bronze in the sun. It's nice, I guess. But now isn't the time to turn vain. With a shrug, I head to the kitchen.

Cinnamon wafts through the air, along with butter and caramelized sugar. "Good morning, sweetheart." My mother holds up her mug of coffee in greeting. A tray of cinnamon rolls sit on the stovetop.

"Morning. Can I take a couple of these to go?"

"Of course." She goes back to solving her crossword puzzle while I dig in the cabinet for a to-go container.

Cinnamon rolls clutched in hand, I head toward my garden. When it stands empty, I backtrack to Heath's cabin. Aurora is my priority today and I see no reason to pretend otherwise.

The front door clicks open and Heath steps out.

"Good morning, Alpha," I say, dipping my head.

"Cedar, do you need something?"

Keeping my eyes on the ground, I shake my head. "I'm here to see Aurora. I'm helping her with the plant magic situation."

"Ah, of course. She's in the kitchen. Go ahead." He strides past me, leaving me alone in front of his cabin.

With a purposeful deep breath, I scale the steps and knock on the door. It swings open and Aurora stands there. She's in a baggy shirt that reveals an expanse of collarbone. Bike shorts cover her lean legs leading down to bare feet.

"Cedar!" She tucks her poofy hair behind her ear with an unguarded, sleepy smile and steps back to let me inside.

"I brought you breakfast," I say, setting the container on the kitchen counter.

Her eyes light up. "What is it?" Without waiting for my answer, she pulls the lid off and lets out a little squeal of delight. I can't help my smile as she grabs a fork and pulls the cinnamon rolls toward her. When she sits, one knee is propped up, like she's ready to leap up at any moment.

A soft moan escapes as she takes her first bite. Her eyes close, dark lashes against her cheeks. I stare, unable to help myself.

"Your mom made these, didn't she? They're still warm!" She uses the side of her fork to cut another bite. "Is the second one for you or am I super lucky?"

It takes a moment for her words to click in my brain, so she's staring at me when I finally nod. Her amused smile is worth my mild embarrassment. She leans out of her seat, tugging a drawer open and fishing around until she produces a second fork. "Here."

"Thanks." My movements are sluggish as I cut my own bite of the second pastry. I'm utterly distracted by the sleep-mussed Aurora perched beside me. Her smile is lazy, face bare and glowing, icing smudged on her lip.

Without thinking, I reach out and swipe my thumb over her top lip. She freezes, her lips slightly parted. I freeze too, unsure of what to do with the icing on the pad of my thumb. Her gaze heats, her eyes lowering to my mouth and her tongue wetting her lip.

Feeling bold, I bring my thumb to my mouth and suck the icing off. Aurora watches me with blown out pupils, her irises a thin ring of amber. She looks like she might launch out of her seat onto me, and I think I would let her.

The moment stretches, hot and brittle. Finally, I clear my throat and cut myself another bite of our breakfast.

Aurora finishes her cinnamon roll and stands. "I'll just go get dressed." She hesitates, watching me. Unsure what to do, I nod.

Aurora chews on the insider of her lip, puckering it, before she makes up her mind and walks past my chair. The soft breeze is full of her scent and I turn my head to follow it.

Her door shuts and I can hear drawers opening and light footsteps as she gets herself ready for the day. When she reappears, she's in jeans and a cream sweater that offsets her tawny skin and dark hair.

"Want to head to the garden?" I ask, standing.

"What's the plan?" she asks nervously, her mouth turning down.

I give her my best reassuring smile. "I'm going to help you figure out the magic stuff."

"Okay." Her vivacious energy is subdued under the weight of her unpredictable abilities.

As I hold the door open for her, I place my hand on the small of her back. The sweater is soft under my fingers. She leans into my touch. The connection means our walk to the garden is slower. I admire the way the dappled morning light paints her face, highlighting her eyelashes and the curve of her cupid's bow.

She hesitates at the edge of my garden. "So what's your grand plan exactly?"

Light pressure on her waist guides her through the archway. This time, I know I'm not imagining the way the plants reach for her.

"It seems to me the first step is to try and trigger your magic, so we can determine what causes it to happen. Then you can work backward to isolate and control that factor."

She turns, hands on her hips. A bit of her fire has returned in her eyes. "Now why didn't I think of that?"

A shrug. "So what were you feeling when it happened last time?"

"In the shower?" she asks, her voice going high.

"Yeah, that seems like the largest amount of magic you've created, don't you think?"

"Nothing happened," she snaps, her cheeks flushing.

I tilt my head, studying her. "You're being evasive. If it really was nothing, you wouldn't act like this."

Dark hair ripples over her shoulders as she shakes her head adamantly. I should let it go, but something keeps me pushing. "Aurora, you can tell me."

She drags her hand down her face and goes to sit on the wide edge of a garden bed. "I was *thinking* about stuff, and I guess I was…" she looks away, her ears turning pink. "Excited."

"Excited."

"Oh my gosh, can we just move on?" She presses her lips in a thin line.

"I still think it's our best example, and it's worth figuring out," I mutter, sitting beside her and resting my forearms on my knees, hands loosely folded.

"Cedar!" she scolds. "I was fantasizing. Okay? Happy now?" Hands going to her face, she hides behind her fingers as her cheeks darken further.

"Fantasizing? About what?"

A growling noise of frustration rips out of her. Hands clenched, she turns to me, face flaming. "Someone."

My brain splutters for a moment. That's fine. She's allowed to fantasize about anyone she wants. Taking a slow breath, I try to push away the jealousy unfurling in my gut, but it's not enough to keep my questions back.

"Who?"

"You! I was thinking about you, you gorgeous idiot." Delicate hands come up to her face again, hiding her blush as she falls sideways into me. Her shoulder hits my chest, and my arms come up to steady her on instinct.

Me?

"What?"

Aurora

Cedar stares back at me, and I start praying that the ground eats me whole. But considering the weird stuff happening around me, that's probably unwise. Maybe I should make a run for it. Surely this level of embarrassment will kill me if I stay here and let it.

Before I can decide what to do, Cedar's hands grab my waist and pull me over. I slide off the bench and onto his lap until I straddle him. One of my hands grips his shoulder and the other tangles in the collar of his shirt.

His stormy eyes meet mine for a second that feels like an eternity. I can't breathe, can't think. There's only the overwhelming draw to him.

Tentatively, he brushes his nose against my cheek until our mouths touch briefly. I seek him, angling my head until I can kiss him properly. His hold on me tightens.

Why were we talking when we could have been doing this?

The rough way he pulled me onto his lap contrasts with the soft, gentle way he kisses me. I melt into him, pressing my hips forward and dragging my hand down his chest.

There's a solidness to his form that I've never experienced before. The boys in Los Angeles build muscle in the gym and they're meant to look good. Cedar's body is earned through hard work and wild runs through the woods.

I can taste cinnamon and sugar as he strokes his tongue against mine. It's intoxicating. His thumbs brush the bottom of my breasts and I let out an embarrassing whimper. It's all I can do to grab his hand, slide it under my shirt, and hope he gets the message. He does.

We break apart, and I gasp for air to calm my racing heart while he whispers praise against my skin. My back arches at the reverent feel of his hands, his lips tracing my jaw and working down my throat. Only my grip on his shoulders keeps me from floating away.

Every caress sends tingles racing through my veins, burning pleasure warming my core, stars behind my eyes.

Cedar lets out a startled yelp and something brushes my hand. Blinking past the sunlight, I spy stems of greenery wrapping around his elbows and waist, moving across my hands, curling around us.

Getting upset will only make it worse. He must realize that too, because he whispers, "It's okay. Not a big deal." A soft kiss to my cheek softens my shock.

Realizing what I have to do, I plaster on a cheerful smile and wink at him. "Totally. Let me just chill out and figure out how to undo this. Or you can use those big muscles to bust out of it."

"I don't want to hurt my plants," he says with a pouty frown.

"Of course you don't." I exhale in a dry laugh and rest my forehead against his, closing my eyes. "Hold on, let me chill."

Calming down is no easy task. Cedar's hands are still under my shirt, and he moves to cup my breast and run his calloused thumbs over my nipple. It makes me squirm.

"This would be easier if you weren't touching me."

"Then maybe get off my lap," he says with a chuckle. "Or we can stay right here and get pulled into the garden bed."

Rolling my eyes, I push off his lap and stand. Anxiety surges at the loss of his touch, especially when I see the greenery threading around his waist and up his chest. It's getting worse.

With a deep breath, I turn away and start pacing back and forth, trying to work out my nervous energy. As I chew my bottom lip, I think about what I want the plant to do - recede, go back into its designated space, release my boyfriend.

Boyfriend? That was an odd thought. The vines grow visibly, and I have to shake out my hands and slow my breathing.

Focus.

The vines are going to return to their original state. Or at least release Cedar. They can grow all over their garden bed if they just let him go. My feet halt in front of him, and I reach out and grab his shoulder to brace myself as I lean over him and concentrate.

His hand comes up to cover mine. A calmness soaks into me, soothing my churning thoughts.

When my eyes open, the plant is unfurling and loosening. With a smile that shows off his dimples, Cedar gently moves the plant off his body and into its assigned space.

"I did it!" I can't help squeaking and jumping on the balls of my feet.

He stands and scoops me up, spinning me in a circle. A joyous laugh escapes my throat, and I throw my head back and let my hair ruffle in the breeze.

When we stop, he sets my feet on the ground and cups my jaw. "You did amazing." The brief but firm kiss he plants on my mouth makes my toes curl.

"I think I can control what it does, but I'm not sure about how to… I don't know, activate it?"

"Hmm, I have a few ideas." Cedar takes my hand and threads our fingers together. "Here, I've got some grape vines that have been pretty sickly and slow growing the last couple of seasons. Do you want to see if you can do anything with them?"

"I'm like your secret weapon or something, aren't I?" I say, grinning at him.

Cedar raises an eyebrow. "You aren't a secret or a weapon."

"It's sweet when you put it like that," I say, wrapping my other hand around his bicep and pressing my face into his shoulder.

"Come on, my little green witch," he says, tugging me forward. The moniker doesn't make me cringe like I expect. It feels good. Affectionate.

We pass the chicken coop with the hens clucking ominously. Berry bushes and a fence of grape vines line the back section of the garden.

"Here, these ones." He stops us beside some scraggly looking vines. "It's still early, but they should be budding. Especially with how warm it's been. They shouldn't still be dormant."

"Maybe they just need a little encouragement!" I walk the length of the fence, inspecting the sad looking vines. Compared with the rest of the garden, they look ancient and dry.

"Okay, let's do some growing," I say, trying to call on the feeling from earlier.

Nothing happens.

Cedar comes up behind me and wraps his arms around my waist until my back is pressed to his front. "Try again."

My eyes flutter closed and I focus, trying to feel any sort of life force in the vines. Still nothing. I narrow my eyes, trying to see any signs of new growth. "I'm sorry, I don't know if I can."

Instead of reassuring me, Cedar lowers his head and nibbles on my earlobe. I can't help but tip my head and groan at the sensation. His hold around my middle tightens and I lean my weight against him.

The grape vines quiver and small buds break out over the length of the vines. Cedar releases me and I sag momentarily without his support. The growth on the vines halts.

"I'm sorry, I have to de-bud them real quick," he says with an apologetic half-smile. Before I can question him, he squats and begins cutting those new shoots off the lower part of the vines. It only takes a few minutes. I watch, fascinated. "It's so we can train the new growth," he finally explains while moving to the next vines.

"Resume?" I ask when he straightens. He nods and steps closer. I grab his collar and yank him to me. Our mouths crash, lips sliding together, his tongue in my mouth. He squeezes my waist, walking me backward until I hit the wall of his storage shed. With a firm hold, he presses me against it and one of my legs come up, hiking over his hip. His hand goes to my ass, grabbing in a way that makes my eyes roll back in my head. The growl rolling from his chest is decidedly not human, and my eyes shoot open.

Glowing dusty blue eyes stare into mine with such intensity, I forget to breathe. He pants, revealing slightly elongated canines. Have mercy on me.

Self-consciousness shutters his expression and his eyes flick away. Unwilling to miss a second of him, I grab for his jaw, pulling his face back toward mine. "I want to see you," I say, breathy.

His expression relaxes, a smile revealing those dimples. I give into the impulse and lean forward to kiss the edge of his mouth and then lick a dimple. He lets out a throaty laugh.

"I wasn't hiding my eyes. I was checking on the grape vines. And I think we should probably stop." He eases back and my leg falls. I want to protest, but he leans in and murmurs, "For now." Goosebumps break out over my arms.

The grape vines are massive, curling over the fence and draping down the other side. The new leaves are the size of my open hand.

"You did amazing."

"But there isn't any fruit!"

"We shouldn't have a harvest until July at the earliest. You've already made them look like it's June or even early July. We can wait for the fruit. I'm sure it won't take that long." He squeezes my hand. "Look at the other berry bushes."

"Oh!" My mouth hangs open as I walk between the various sprawling berry bushes. They've doubled in size and are covered with blueberries and blackberries.

"Don't worry about the raspberries, they aren't in season yet, But we can harvest some blueberries now if you like." Cedar's hand brushing down my back sends shivers through me.

"You'd better be careful or we will make this entire garden grow out of control," I joke.

He frowns and withdraws his hand. "I suppose you'd better get a handle on this quickly then. Otherwise, I'm not sure we can continue."

If that isn't good motivation, I don't know what is. I press my lips together to suppress a laugh. It doesn't work. A ridiculous cackle escapes me, until I'm doubled over laughing. Cedar's hand rubs up and down my back, even as he laughs too. Trying to regain my composure, I reach for him and use him for support as another round of laughter captures me.

"I appreciate the extra growth, but it really will cause problems if you don't figure out how to stop it from happening," Cedar finally says.

"I know, babe." Going on my tip-toes, I kiss his cheek and then walk away. I'll need a little distance before I can keep working on my magic.

Cedar harvests blueberries while I sit against the storage shed and admire the way his triceps flex as he reaches for the berries. He's wearing gloves, but I still have a wonderful view of those arms.

Taking those feelings, I hold my hand over the patch of grass beside me and urge it to grow. After a few seconds of concentrating, it sprouts up. When I release my mental hold, it stops.

"Cedar!" I jump up, waving my hands. "I got it to start and stop!"

He sets his basket aside and jogs over. I close my eyes to concentrate and produce the same results again.

"Well done! What were you doing to trigger it?"

"Admiring you," I say. "So I'm thinking it's arousal?"

Cedar shakes his head, his caramel hair flopping over his forehead. "I don't think so. What about when Hazel was having Timber? Or the other day in my house?"

"Oh, you're right." I click my nails together, thinking.

With a sharp inhale, Cedar turns to me. "It's not arousal. It's affection. Any strong emotion would do it, I think. But affection is the common thread in those situations."

"It happened when I was scared too. So yeah, any emotion. But those positive feelings like watching you hold Timber, that must have done it earlier."

"Me holding Timber?" he asks, tilting his head in that adorable way he does.

I can't stop my smile. "I liked seeing you holding a baby. It was pretty attractive."

"Really?" he asks, his tone going dark. With a sheepish smile, he lurches forward to crawl over me. My eyes close as he nuzzles into my neck and kisses down my throat.

"Remember, I don't have good control yet. We might make the entire garden overgrow so badly you'll be pruning for the rest of the month," I say, pausing to moan as his teeth scrape over delicate skin.

"Fine," he grumbles, backing up until he sits beside me and leans his head back against the wall. My gaze tracks the bob of his Adam's apple as he swallows.

"I think I'll have control soon," I say, trying to encourage him.

He sighs. "And then you can go home." The thought pierces me like a physical pain and I flinch. Home, not here. Back to the city.

"Oh, yeah." I turn away from him and rest my head back too, mirroring his post. "Would you come visit me in Los Angeles?"

His answer is slow. "No." My heart sinks. "I don't think I could come see you and then leave you there."

My throat burns and I have to take a few measured breaths to relax. "I guess I can understand that."

"I'm sorry," he says, reaching over until our fingers thread together, palms still pressed to the lush patch of grass that I grew using magic born of my affection for him.

"Before I go home, could you do me a favor?" I ask, so quiet my voice barely catches.

There's no hesitation this time. "Yes."

"Can I paint you as a wolf?"

X
CAPTURING THE WOLF

CEDAR

The night air cuts against my skin, finding its way through my thick coat. Our warm weather broke, leaving me wishing for a jacket. The cold discomfort suits my mood, though.

Aurora made it very clear she is going home to California and there's nothing I can do about it. It wouldn't be fair to beg her to stay. She barely knows me. She shouldn't uproot her life on a whim after a few kisses and compliments.

I plunge into the creek, letting water soak into the soft fur at my belly. I could have found a shallow area to cross, but this is the most direct path. I'll dry soon enough. Muscles burning, I charge up the hill into Granite Ridge territory.

If the patrols notice me, they don't interfere. All of the wolves in Granite Creek know me. The Alpha's twin brother.

The land flattens and I'm able to increase my speed, crossing the last mile easily. I start on the south end of the compound, heading for the recreation center Onyx and Ember created. Before entering, I stop and focus on the human part of my brain, allowing my body to shift back to two legs. A storage bench tucked beside the door offers a selection of clothing. I grab a pair of charcoal sweatpants and tug them on, followed by a maroon shirt.

Pack members play pool and foosball inside, and a few watch a movie in another room, but Onyx and Ember are absent. No one pays me any attention aside from a few nods of greeting.

Heading out of the recreation space, I jog north. The cafeteria is empty, as is the training facility. They must be home.

If it was our family home, I would just enter, but considering how Onyx and Ember can be, it's safer to knock and wait. It's only a moment until my brother pulls the door open.

"Hey!" he greets, throwing his arms around me. Since taking up residence in another pack, he's been more demonstrative of affection, so I hug him back and follow him inside.

A video game fills the television screen, paused. Ember looks up from her seat on the sofa, a book draped across her lap. "Cedar, what's up?"

"Felt like a good, long run and some time with family," I say, my voice hoarse after breathing in the frigid night air.

"Sit down. Are you hungry?" Onyx asks. I wave him off.

"You seem serious," Ember says, twisting in her seat until she's sitting up properly and can look me over. "More than normal, I mean."

Onyx barks a laugh and falls onto the cushion beside her, draping an arm around her middle until she leans into him.

Unsure of where to begin, or what to even share, I rest my forehead against my palm, elbow on my knee, and study the carpet. If I don't explain everything, my brother won't understand; he will probably mock me instead of helping. But he knows what it's like to fall for someone who can't stay. Except in his case, it worked out. I know I won't be that lucky.

"How's Aurora's visit?" Ember asks, her tone hushed.

That's as good a place as any. "She's a green witch."

Ember nods. "Hazel told me her concerns when we visited the baby."

"She made the houseplants in Heath's cabin go crazy and I had to cut her out with a chef's knife," I say, smiling at the memory. It was terrifying, but it ended with her in my arms, the truth laid out between us.

"That sounds nuts," Onyx says. "So she knows, it's for sure?"

"Yeah. She's been practicing her magic in the garden. She did about four months' worth of growth on the berry bushes in about five minutes."

"Really?" Ember cocks her head. "How strange. I've never heard of this type of thing."

"Sable and Heath said there was some witch magic in his family line. I'd never heard of it either."

"And she's doing well with it?" she asks.

I nod. "She figured out how to stop it when she wants, and how to trigger it. It's not perfect yet, but it's amazing progress."

"So why do you look like she burned your garden down?" My brother furrows his eyebrows, giving me an inscrutable look that reminds me of our father.

This is hard to admit. I swallow, my jaw ticking.

"You like her, don't you?" Ember asks softly.

Exhaling, I nod. My throat is thick and it's hard to form any words. "We were hanging out and she kissed me." I can feel my face flushing.

"Oh man, my baby brother got his first girlfriend!" Onyx teases, followed by a yelp of pain when Ember pinches him for being a jerk. "I don't see the problem. You like her, she likes you, this is great."

Ember glares at him. "She doesn't live here, not to mention she's not a shifter."

"So convince her to stay. Make her fall in love with you, make her your mate, she'll be happy, you'll be happy." Ember pinches him again. "Hey, don't do that."

"You deserve it. Stop being an idiot."

"I'm going to make you regret that later," he purrs, quiet enough I can pretend to not hear him. Ember rolls her eyes, but I don't miss the way her hand caresses his ribs. Ugh. I've seen enough of these two touching each other to last a lifetime.

"Look, she has a whole life in L.A.: a job she likes, galleries that display her paintings, friends, roommates, an apartment. I can't ask her to walk away from all of that when I can't offer her anything except myself."

"That's worth more than a shitty job and tiny shared apartment," Ember says. "But you're right. She has a life there, and if she decides to move, it needs to be because she wants to, not solely because of you."

A sense of defeat hits me, and I drop my head back onto my hand.

"All you can do is make your feelings clear, and make sure knows her options. If Hazel and Slate don't want a human joining their pack, we can make room for you guys here." Onyx presses a kiss to Ember's temple while she speaks.

"I appreciate that."

"I'm really sorry, man," my brother says. "It hurts to be in love and have them leave." His arms tighten around Ember, no doubt remembering their time apart.

"I'm in love with her," I argue. "We just kissed a few times."

"Sure." Onyx says, allowing the conversation to move on. "So, a plant witch. That's crazy. What sorts of stuff has she been able to do?"

The pressure falls away and I launch into stories of the house plants knocking off window sills, vines grabbing my ankles, honeysuckle shielding her. My brother and sister-in-law laugh, but in between, their expressions grow more concerned. It must be obvious how I feel about her now, and we all know she's leaving. Maybe afterward, I'll come stay here for a while until the memory of her fades and the worst of the heartbreak is over.

Sometime after midnight, Ember and Onyx say goodnight and go to their room. I stretch out on the sofa and doze. When morning light breaks through the windows, I leave the borrowed clothes on top of the clothes washer and shift into my wolf form.

The morning run is invigorating. After hours of ruminating on the subject, it's clear that the pain is unavoidable, even if I avoid her from now on. I can't do that. I'll make the most of the time we have together and then deal with the conse-quences later.

AURORA

"Are you sure you're okay doing this?" I ask for the tenth time. Standing in the garden, I clutch my paint bag and my collapsible easel, a canvas tucked under my arm.

Cedar laughs, running a hand through his gilded hair. The early morning light hits his sun kissed skin, lighting up the line of his jaw and cheekbones. This man is so handsome.

"I said yes. It's fine."

"But it feels kinda private," I whisper, stepping closer. "I've only seen you as a wolf once, and that was accidental. It seems, I don't know, intimate."

He lowers his mouth to graze below my ear, catching my earlobe with his teeth for a second before he pulls back. "It's not. The whole pack goes running together all the time. I promise, we have done much more intimate things already."

The seduction in his voice makes me shiver. Forget painting, I want to jump him.

As if reading my mind, Cedar steps back and pulls his shirt over his head. My eyes widen and I glance around us to see if anyone else is around.

He laughs at my expression. "I can't shift if I'm dressed."

"Oh."

Shirt tossed over the side of a garden bed, he takes a step forward and shifts right out of his pants. Apparently there are no boxers to worry about. I stow that information away.

A wolf I can only describe as reddish-gold stands before me. The tapered line of his muzzle is beautiful, as is the white fluff under his ears. He looks so soft.

I expected to feel fear, but it's gone. My brain knows it's Cedar and my heart feels so much for him, I know I'm safe. With a smile, I sink down to my knees and reach for him. He lets me thread my fingers into the silky fur around his neck.

On instinct, I dig my nails in and scratch like he's a dog. His nose goes up in the air and he leans forward, a goofy pull to his lips. It's almost like he's smiling. I continue scratching, and then switch to petting down his scruff and over his shoulders. His fur gets rougher on his back.

"You are really beautiful," I murmur. "Like a big golden retriever."

He chuffs in response and stands. A white tail brushes against me as he turns and trots a few feet away. I can't help but laugh.

"I'm just saying, I think you'd be a great snuggle buddy in his form. You're very fluffy," I say over my shoulder as I set up my easel.

My brain slides into painting mode, and I survey the scenery to map out the basic shapes, areas of light and dark, and any details in the foreground I can use for framing. Cedar's tail lashes, and he lowers his head while watching me.

"What?"

His sleek body turns, pacing back and forth, before sitting, standing again, and then laying down. His head moves back and forth.

"Are you wondering how to pose for me?" I ask with a grin. He stops moving and watches me with eerily familiar blue eyes. "Can you just sit? Face this way a bit, so the light hits your profile." He obeys my hand motions. "There, that's perfect."

Once in place, he goes still as marble. I grab my phone and snap a picture of the entire scene to reference later when the light changes. Then I select my favorite sketching pencil and get to work laying out the proportions.

My tongue sticks out against my top lip as I detail out Cedar's form. It takes several attempts to capture him, but I'm happy with my work. Radiating out from him I begin adding the little flowers and stems that stand out from the garden beds. In slow layers, I add more and more detail while keeping the center focus on his canine shape.

Sketch finished, I step back and compare my work to real life. It's almost perfect. With a soft eraser, I fix a few details down at the bottom edge and redraw them. Now it's perfect.

Cedar hasn't moved an inch, even though at least thirty or forty minutes have passed. Once I rough in the shadows, I won't need him to stay there. With practiced movements, I lay out the warm browns I've selected for the underpainting and a selection of brushes for the work.

My gaze flickers between the garden and my canvas as I layer shadows, creating highlights by what I leave untouched. Time ceases to have meaning and I'm lost in my work. When the underpainting is finished, I set my brush down and step back. The vision for the painting to clear on the canvas and the reference is no longer necessary.

"Cedar, I'm done for now. Do you want to see?"

His coat shimmers in the brightening sunlight as he trots over to me. Between one step and the next, he transforms, until a very naked Cedar stands a few feet away from me.

I keep my eyes on my painting as he dresses.

"That's incredible," he says, his hands going to my waist as he steps up behind me.

"Thanks. I was feeling inspired."

It's so easy to reach behind me and cup my fingers at the back of his neck. As I turn my head and tip my face, he lowers to meet me and our mouths connect. His chest is heated by the sun and it scorches my bare arm.

He kisses my mouth and then my nose and forehead. A happy sigh escapes me, and I turn back to admire my work while leaning into his hold.

"It'll take way longer to add all the color, but the bones are there."

"Do you need me back out there?"

He's so sweet, I squeeze his wrist affectionately. "No, I don't need a reference anymore, and I have a picture as back-up. But I appreciate your willingness to strip down and get furry for me."

I feel his laugh more than hear it. It vibrates through me, warming me from my chest to my toes.

"Can I do anything to help?"

"Just keep me company."

Cedar proves an excellent assistant as I lay out all the colors. He fetches me water, washes my first set of brushes, and identifies the names of several flowers when I ask.

"You're spoiling me," I murmur.

His response is a kiss to the edge of my jaw. Ignoring him, I dip my favorite round brush into cadmium yellow and transfer it to an empty rectangle. Adding a scoop of phthalo green, I swirl and blend until I have the perfect leaf color. I build up the plants around Cedar's wolf with short dabs of my brush.

"I could watch you paint all day," Cedar whispers.

"You're welcome to," I quip back, smiling to myself as I dilute my olive green and wash it over the garden beds surrounding wolf Cedar's golden shape.

"Why did you want to do this in the garden?" he asks over my shoulder.

My sigh is contented. "Seems like the place for you. Don't you think?"

Another kiss on my neck elicits my own version of a growl. "I'm trying to paint here. You're making it very difficult. Here, help me move into the shade. I'm going to get sunburned otherwise."

Cedar chuckles at my scowl as we carry everything to the corner of the garden. I settle with my canvas across my thighs and leaning on my knees, my back against the trunk. Cedar's arm slings over my shoulders as he watches me work.

He is endlessly patient as I work deeper desaturated shadows into the edges of the artwork. Finally it's time for my favorite part and the most time consuming - details.

Mixing more green into my olive tone, I roll my thin brush into it and lazily drag it up from the garden beds to add natural looking stems. Feeling particularly pleased with myself, I sweep my hand over and nick Cedar, leaving a streak of green across the side of his hand. He rotates his wrist, looking at the color.

"I thought you wanted to work," he purrs.

"Maybe I'm ready for a break."

He's careful as he grasps my painting by the back frame and sets it across the closest garden bed. I shove my palette aside with clumsy movements. A streak of gold wipes across my wrist. Before I can clean it off, calloused hands frame my face and seize my attention.

I'll never grow tired of his intense expression when he looks like he wants to devour me. My heart picks up and my thighs squeeze together. Slowly, savoring the moment, he draws me toward him. I can feel green paint transfer from his hand to my jaw, but I don't care.

As if his wolf is waiting under the surface, his eyes light from within until they flare with supernatural magic. His breathing is shallow as his fingers lace into my hair.

My legs uncurl as I move to my knees, hands braced on his thighs. I want to kiss him, but this suspended moment is delicious tension and desire. Reaching up, I touch the pad of my finger to his bottom lip. He nips me, and I gasp at the sharp edge to his teeth. It should be scary, but heat thrums through me. I'm vibrating, desperate to move.

Just before I combust, he closes the distance and kisses me. These aren't the languorous kisses from the day we worked on controlling my magic. It's more than enjoying each other, more than his desire to please me.

There is something claiming to the way he dominates my mouth, kissing me deeply and controlling my movements with a light grip across my throat. I may be above him, but in this moment, he owns me.

My hips wiggle, seeking pressure and friction. One of his hands runs down my back and over the curve of my ass.

In one swift movement, he rolls me over and cradles my head as my back hits the grass. My breathing stutters, every piece of me quaking as he braces an arm over me and looks down. Messy golden hair frames his rapturous expression.

Trying to anchor myself, I took my fingers over the back of his neck, scratching my nails against his scalp. His eyes close, and he turns his head to kiss my inner arm. With slow kisses and soft bites, he works lower. I shiver at the sensation, ending in a giggle as gold paint wipes across his cheek.

His devious grin sends sparks through me and my stomach clenches. He pauses, wiping at the paint and touching some to the tip of my nose. It's silly, but somehow I've never felt so treasured.

The sweetness melts into heat as I pull his mouth to mine, unable to help myself. I need him. He lowers himself until our bodies press together. The weight of him is a wonderful torture. My knees part on either side of his hips, lining us up in a way that makes me crazy.

I'm burning up, and he is my only relief. His hand sweeps under my shirt, leaving gold fingerprints as he squeezes my waist and brushes over my ribs. Desperate for more, I mimic his movements, sliding my hand under his shirt. Fingers run over distinctly masculine abdomen muscles, finding the side of his ribs where I've spied botanical tattoos in those moments he is shirtless. I want to study them, learning every line, but not right now. Right now, I'll die if we stop kissing.

"I want you, alone and with less clothes," I murmur, turning my head until my lips brush over his jaw and then the side of his neck. He rocks into me and I gasp. As he repeats the movement, I close my teeth over his skin, biting down hard enough I know I'll leave a mark. His fingers dig into my skin, the pain a beautiful contrast that sharpens to the pleasure of his sweatpants-clad body rubbing against the thin fabric of my loose pants.

"Seriously, we're out where anyone could see us, and I want to do things to you that shouldn't be done in public," I growl, leaning my head back until I can see his glowing gaze.

This seems to pull him back to earth. He blinks, his eyes scanning my heaving chest, shirt pulled up to reveal the edge of my bra, and the way his hips are slotted between mine.

With a deep breath, he backs off me until he sits on my knees. Disappointment pierces me as I push myself up to sit facing him.

His fingers rake through his hair as his eyes drop to my knees.

"I didn't want to stop," I protest gently.

His eyes meet mine, and the blue light has faded until his typical stormy gaze stares back at me. "You're right, we're out where anyone could see."

"So let's go somewhere else."

He sighs. "I don't think that's a good idea."

The sting of rejection is sharp and my instinct is to hide the pain. Forcing a cheerful smile, I turn back to my painting supplies. "Alright."

"Can I still watch you paint?" he asks, sounding remorseful. His hand runs up my arm like a tender apology.

Nodding, I gather up the items that were scattered as I flung them aside in my hurry to reach him. He places my canvas back in front of me. As my heart returns to normal, I add water to my palette and resume detailing my painting.

Cedar stays close, his hands on my body. Every so often, he presses a kiss to my shoulder or neck, as if he can't help himself. It's not what I want, but it's still a lovely way to spend the day.

Hours slip by and the painting gains realism. Adding highlights always sparks excitement, and I squeeze Cedar's hand. He only leaves my side to fetch us lunch. After eating, I go back to work. It will take several days of work to finish the painting, but I want to capture as much of the magic in this moment as I can before it fades.

As afternoon shadows crawl toward us, Cedar squeezes my thigh to get my attention. "It's going to be dinner time soon. I think we were going to have a campfire tonight. Do you want to go?"

"Yes!" I set my brush down, grinning at him. "That sounds great."

"Okay." His returning smile makes my stomach flip. He could ask me to scrub toilets and I would gladly agree when he looks at me like this. Luckily, a campfire sounds fun. I picture cuddling up with him in front of a fire as everyone chats and laughs. Hazel mentioned campfires being her favorite, but with the baby's arrival, they haven't happened.

"I can't wait."

He kisses my cheek in response.

XI
CAMPFIRES
& KISSES

AURORA

The fire is already lit by the time we arrive. My hands rub at my arms to fight off the chill. Cedar steps closer and presses his chest to my back, replacing my hands with his own. His warm palms send tingles up into my shoulders and down my back.

The fit pit behind his cabin has a trio of half-logs surrounding it with a pair of weathered Adirondack chairs tucked between them. Onyx sits perched on one of the logs and pokes at the fire, building it up.

He looks up and grins. "You can come sit by me!"

Cedar's hand curls around my waist protectively, pulling me tighter against him. A growl rumbles from his throat, warning his brother away.

I'm so surprised, a laugh bursts from me.

"Sorry," he mutters softly against my hair.

Onyx raises his hands to pacify Cedar, though his small smirk is telling. Before Cedar can react, I pull his hand off my waist and twine our fingers together. With purposeful steps, I lead him past his brother and settle onto the other log. Cedar sits beside me, placing himself between me and Onyx.

"You guys have a good day?" Onyx asks, one eyebrow quirking up.

"Actually, yeah. Did some painting," I say.

"I can see that?" he says, his smirk no longer small.

I turn to Cedar, my brows furrowing. Then I spot it - a streak of gold across his neck, dipping under his shirt near his collar bone.

"Crap," I mutter. Reaching up, I rub at it and the dried paint peels away easily. "There, I got it."

"Too bad, I like having a reminder," he whispers. Before I can respond, footsteps interrupt us.

Hazel lets out a huge yawn and drops into an Adirondack chair beside me.

"No Slate or Timber?" I ask.

She shakes her head. "I don't think she can be around the smoke yet. Besides, it's way past her bedtime. Slate's pretty tired too. He's been taking the nighttime wake-ups."

"That's sweet of him."

She smiles and tips her head toward me conspiratorially. "It's really nice having someone there to just pop the baby on my boob. I hardly have to wake up and he deals with the dirty diaper after."

My nose scrunches up as I laugh with her. Motherhood suits her. There's a confidence about her that she never had before she came here.

"What are you guys whispering about?" Onyx says, his forearms resting on his knees as he leans forward.

"Baby stuff," I answer.

Onyx sticks his tongue out and Cedar bristles beside me.

"Hello my darlings!" Marigold arrives in a flurry of reddish-gold curls and huge smiles. Her positive energy shimmers around her and I'm suddenly curious if I could tap into it for magic.

She throws her arms around Hazel and sways while squeezing her tightly. Jasper appears at her side, and once she releases my sister, the two drop into the open Adirondack chair. Marigold perches across his lap and his hand settles at her hip possessively.

I glance at Cedar. His eyes flicker from his brother to me, and the small, private smile he gives me makes my stomach flip. Those dimples are irresistible.

He tugs at my hand and leans closer. "Stop looking at me like that."

My teeth have sunk into my bottom lip suggestively and entirely unintentionally. Oops. I relax my face, adopting a demure smile in place of my former flirtatious expression.

"I want to hear everything about Timber!" Marigold says, clapping her hands together before lacing her fingers over her knee.

Hazel sighs. "You just saw her a few hours ago when you babysat for my meeting."

"I know, but you didn't tell me much about how the last twenty-four hours have been!"

"The same," Hazel says, rolling her eyes. "She's not that exciting yet. She makes cute poopy faces, loves feeding, and she sleeps a lot. No smiles yet, but it's really early."

"I can't *wait*! If you don't take a picture of her first smile and I'm not there, I'm going to freak out." Jasper jostles his partner, pulling her against his chest and distracting her.

Hazel laughs lightly, looking into the flames. Her eyes squint, and then she breaks into another lengthy yawn, her hand coming up to cover her mouth.

"Anyone ready for some sugar?" Onyx asks, pulling a woven tote bag from behind his seat.

"Yes, please!" Hazel makes grabby hands, and Onyx obliges by popping open a glass container and removing something rectangular wrapped in wax paper.

"They're salted caramel blondies. Ember put a layer of Oreo crust on the bottom, I'm not sure why but it's killer."

He passes two over to Marigold and then offers them to us. Hazel has already ripped hers open and takes a huge bite. She groans dramatically.

"I think she knew I needed at least a little chocolate," she mumbles through her full mouth.

Onyx winks, taking one for himself.

"Tell her thank you so much!" Marigold says before taking a bite of hers.

A sense of warmth fills me. Everyone is so kind, but also clever and funny. Hazel's decision to stay makes even more sense. I feel the temptation. A bite of the chewy blondie makes it even more appealing. Who needs Los Angeles when you have nights like this?

I could trade in the bustle of the city and the endless parade of tourists making demands and galleries turning me down - living here in the quiet forest with a wonderful adopted family sounds so much better.

"So how's the green witch magic?" Marigold asks me.

"Well, I think I've gotten it mostly figured out. At least enough to not cause any miniature natural disasters anytime soon."

"Really?" Marigold's eyes widen in surprise.

Nibbling at my bottom lip, I look around for something I can demonstrate with. The closest plant is a patch of beautiful blue-purple lupine flowers. That'll work.

Cedar squeezes my hand, feeding me the warm affection needed. Eyes fluttering closed, I feel out the living pulse of the plant beside us. It's becoming second nature to slowly feed those bubbly emotions fizzing in my veins into the peaceful life, feeling it spark and quiver in response. My eyes flutter open to see new leaves sprouting and blooms opening fully. That should be enough. Relaxing, I withdraw my connection. The plant settles.

Marigold and Hazel's mouths hang open. Jasper's eyebrows have disappeared under his flop of pale hair, and Onyx's eyes wrinkle as he grins at me.

Cedar's thumb swipes across my knuckles in silent praise and a surge of emotion fills me. It takes conscious effort to reign it in and not direct any magic at the growth around us.

"I'm really proud of you. That's really impressive," Hazel says.

"Yeah, that's wicked cool." Onyx slow claps his hands.

Shrugging, I glance up at Cedar through my lashes. "Cedar is the one who figured it out."

"Figured what out?"

Swallowing, I sort out how to explain without embarrassing either of us. "The trigger was strong emotions. Hence the house plant growing when Hazel was having her baby. Once we figured that out, it didn't take much work to isolate the feeling of channeling it, my magic I guess it is, and then feeding it into the plants."

"Good job! So you can go home now, whenever you want to." Marigold's tone drops, as if she's sad at the thought.

"Yeah, I guess." It's hard to feel excited about going home. That's a problem for tomorrow.

"I'm sure it'll be nice to get back to the city, but we will miss you." Hazel reaches over and places a hand on my knee. "Promise to visit regularly?"

"You know I will."

Silence stretches for a beat, every individual lost in their own thoughts. Hazel removes her hand and wraps it around her arms. I curl into Cedar's side and savor the feeling of his hands tracing patterns over my skin.

"I still can't get over the plant growth thing. What else do you think you could use your magic for?" Marigold asks, her blue-green eyes bright in the firelight.

"Oh, I have no idea. You mean aside from getting plants to grow?"

She nods. Everyone else's eyes watch me curiously, and I feel myself tensing. Cedar's hold on me tightens as he senses my anxiety.

"I'm not sure I'll get the chance to find out."

Marigold tilts her head, her smile smaller. "Maybe next visit."

Onyx breaks the melancholy and frees me from everyone's attention as he leans forward and asks Jasper a work question. I try to follow, but there are so many unfamiliar terms, I'm lost. Something about security feeds and patrols. Cedar adds a few comments and even Hazel jumps in, leaving me to stare into the flames and contemplate the heavy weight of managing my new magic without this supportive circle.

Hazel lets out a huge yawn and stretches her arms above her head. "Look, this is fun and all, but I'm freaking tired. I'll see you all tomorrow." Hazel shoves herself out of her chair.

Before she can leave, I rise and reach for my sister. She hums softly as we hug. There are only so many hugs left before I leave, and the thought hurts. I can't help my small frown as I sink back down into my seat.

Hazel gives me a wave before she wanders into the trees.

"Is she okay without a flashlight? It's totally pitch black out there." I ask Cedar, eyeing the heavy night.

He nods, his smile wry. "We can see in the dark, remember?"

"As wolves, yeah, but…"

His golden hair flashes in the flickering firelight as he shakes his head. "All the time."

"Are you serious? That's not fair. All I can do is grow some plants," I grumble playfully while I nestle into his side.

"Sorry," he says, shrugging with a smile that says he isn't remotely sorry.

"I guess this means you'll have to walk me home." I revel in the heat in his gaze and the way his hand tightens on my thigh. "You know, I'm feeling kind of tired too. Want to call it a night?"

"Sure." He doesn't argue, just takes my hand and gives everyone an excuse and leads us into the darkness.

CEDAR

Aurora doesn't seem tired as we walk away from the campfire. Her eyes are dark in the starlight, and she's back to biting her lip and looking at me like she wants to devour me. Heat rises in my chest, unfurling into a flush crawling up my neck.

Fingers laced together, we wander toward her cabin. She sighs dramatically. "You know, I didn't really want to go to bed. Not exactly."

I slow and raise an eyebrow at her, though she can't see it in the darkness. She smirks and continues, knowing she has my full attention. "At least I was hoping you'd come with me."

"I am," I say hesitantly, glancing up at the lights of Heath's cabin through the trees.

"No, I want you to stay over," she says, her voice dropping as she moves into my personal space and slides her hand under the edge of my shirt. Her fingers are cold, and electricity radiates out from her touch. "Do you want to?"

Thoughts swirl through my head, analyzing and overthinking her words before I reign them in. Her face tips up expectantly, those soft, brown doe eyes blinking at me. Trusting, wanting. She's so gorgeous it takes my breath away.

I have to clear my throat to talk and even then, the words stick and rasp on the way out. "I'd like that, but honestly, I'm scared of what Heath would think."

"Seriously? I'm twenty-three. He can't make a fuss." Her pout is adorable, and I just want to kiss it off her face, but I hold myself back. That would be a sure way to end up out of control.

"I'm sorry, I don't want to risk disrespecting him by inviting myself into his home." Her pout transforms into a disappointed frown. "But my parents are staying over with Ember and Onyx. So my home is empty." I trail off.

The change in her expression is instantaneous. Her eyes brighten, eyebrows rising as her mouth pulls into a stunning smile.

"Do you want to?" I ask, my mouth curving its own smile.

"Do you want me to?" She cocks her head, squinting through the darkness to ready anything she can from my form.

There's only one answer I can give her. "Yes."

My fingers tangle in her hair, angling her face so I can kiss her soundly. Her hand under my shirt skims lower, briefly dipping under the edge of my waistband and muffling all the thoughts in my head instantly.

Moving on instinct, I tug at her hair and expose the side of her neck. She moans as I drag my tongue across the soft skin under her ear and under her jaw. Her exquisite moan turns to a gasp as I nip at her throat.

"Are we going?" she asks, breathless and eager.

"Yeah, but I think Onyx, Marigold, and Jasper are still there." I've never been in this situation before, and my heart pounds.

"Around the front?" she asks, almost incoherent as her nails press into the skin at my side.

"Good idea." My thoughts are jumbled, but going around to the front door seems like a good solution.

She releases me and instead grabs my hand, pulling back the way we came. I can't help but smile at her eagerness, though she's heading off the path unknowingly.

"Slow down there. Here, let's go this way." With gentle pressure, I guide her around wide enough that we won't be noticed. We move quickly, my heart leaping as she trusts me to steer her.

Coming around the front of the cabin, I push the door open and she brushes past me. As soon as the door shuts, she spins and loops her arms around me. I hoist her up, squeezing her ass as she wraps her legs around my waist.

Somehow we make it down the hallway to my bedroom as she licks and sucks the skin at my neck. The distraction makes it a challenge to not run into the wall, but I'd rather die than have her stop.

We tumble onto the bed, and I twist so I land under her and she's sitting in my lap. She doesn't stop, clinging to me and peppering my skin with kisses. Her hips grind against me, rotating in a fluid movement that coils tension in every particle of my muscles. There's no way she can't feel my hard cock under the two thin layers of fabric separating us.

This beautiful girl digs her nails into my shoulder blades, her breasts pressing into my chest and the heat of her scorching my skin. It's overwhelming. If I don't take control in this situation, I'll embarrass myself.

Pushing her gently, I guide her down onto her back. She looks up at me, adoration in her eyes. I'm unworthy, but the fierce affection I feel for her keeps me from pulling back.

"I want to make you mine, but you're going home in a few days," I admit, my voice rough with emotion.

She holds up a finger to my lips, her eyes bright. "I don't want to think about that. It sucks and I don't want to waste the time I have here being sad. Let's have fun together and make the most of it, okay?"

It's too tempting. Something in the back of my head rings warning bells, and for most of my life, that would have been enough to stop me. But not with her. She's made it clear how much she wants me, and even if it's temporary, I want her too. It's an all-consuming, driving force that I'm done resisting.

"Can I?" I ask, trailing my hand across her waistband and tucking my fingers under. She squirms, nodding emphatically with a breathless moan. As if she senses my inexperience, she settles with her knees open, giving me full access.

Her back arches when I slide my hand under her soft shorts. A string of garbled words pours out of her mouth when my fingers slip lower, exploring.

"Yes, there," she gasps. Her nails dig into my shoulders, and I dip my head to claim her mouth, quieting her next moan.

She's untethered, face flushed and breathing uneven. It's my new favorite way she looks. When I slide a finger inside of her, her eyes flutter closed and her hips roll. Her whispered words finally come together. "So good, don't stop."

Unable to help my grin, I add a second finger and admire the way she shudders. Curling them, I experiment until I find an angle that causes her writhe.

Bringing her to this point gives me so much pleasure, I would think she had her hands on me, but she grasps the sheets and pants into my pillow.

Leaning forward, I trail kisses down her neck, adding tender bites that earn me soft whimpers. Her hips buck again when I drag my fingers up and circle her clit. The wetness on my fingers glides over her most sensitive part. The way her mouth parts as she grinds against my hand is enough to leave me starving for more.

Her bright brown eyes pop open. "Can I touch you?" she manages, chest still heaving.

I nod, watching her as she fumbles and reaches for my hips. She eases my sweats down my hips and frees my cock. The way she licks her lips almost has me coming right then before she's touched me.

Her hips roll and I focus on resuming my ministrations. She wraps her hand around my cock and strokes up and down. My head falls forward until my forehead rests against her collarbone.

She tenses, and I look up to study her face. Her back arches, her breath coming in quick, shallow gasps as she curses into the pillow. After a moment she relaxes. Her eyes open and she grabs my wrist with one hand. "Stop, fuck, I'm going to die if you keep touching me, that was too good."

Her hand resumes working my cock as I brace my forearms on either side of her head. "Come for me, all over my stomach," she whispers, grinning at my reaction to her filthy words.

She knows exactly what she's doing, and I can't help but thrust into her hand. A moment later, I'm spilling over her bare skin, blinded with the pleasure of her touch. Her grin is triumphant when I still. "Good boy."

I'm too blissed out to react to her teasing. Plus, I kind of like it.

Feeling disoriented and a little high, I find a towel and wipe it across her hips. She sits up, her smile still wide.

"Come here and hold me," she says, reaching for me. I'm happy to oblige.

There isn't much room in my narrow bed, but she snuggles up to my chest and folds her arms against her perfect breasts. I can't help trailing my fingers over one, and she shivers.

The way she presses into me worries me. I grab the blanket draped across the foot of my bed and cover us.

"That's nice," she murmurs, eyes closed.

"You need anything?"

She resumes snuggling against my chest and mutters, "Just you."

XII
GOODBYES
AURORA

Laying in Cedar's arms, I've never felt so safe in my entire life. He's seen me vulnerable and raw. He watched me pour out my soul onto the canvas - I've never painted in front of someone like that before. And now, he nuzzles in my hair and makes me feel absolutely cherished.

"I wish I could stay like this forever," I say, my thoughts escaping without filter.

Cedar kisses the shell of my ear. "Then stay."

"I can't." Turning in his arms, reach up and I brush his hair off his forehead. "I'm not a shifter. This isn't my home. I don't belong here."

"Your sister and niece are here," he says, a solemn hope in his expression that hurts my heart.

"She's a shifter like you, and I'm not." *I don't belong anywhere now.* I swallow down my melancholy thoughts and place a kiss on the tip of his nose.

Cedar clears his throat, his focus never wavering. "How much longer are you going to stay?"

The answer feels heavy. "Unless I want to start begging for money, I'll need to leave in the next day or two."

"I'll pay your bills," he says.

"I can't let you do that," I say, frowning. "Besides, you have no idea how much an apartment in Hollywood costs."

"Enough you have to have a bunch of roommates," he says softly, not condescending but concerned.

"I need to go back," The words sound hollow to me now. Absently, I twirl my fingers through the caramel curls behind his ears.

"Not right now."

Cedar tightens his hold, drawing me flush against his chest. It's all too easy to sink into his warmth and pretend this is my life. Slowly, drowsiness creeps in, and the rhythmic rise and fall of his chest and the steady beat of his heart lull me into a deep sleep.

Cedar is still sleeping when my internal clock wakes me. Pale sunlight filters through the blinds on his window. My small movements wake him. The sleepy smile on his face melts me. Knowing this is the only time I'll ever wake in his arms feels like a knife in my heart. It's entirely unfair that our lives are so far away. I'd give anything to keep him.

"Morning," he murmurs, kissing my forehead.

Sighing, I snuggle closer. "No, it's the middle of the night and we should go back to sleep."

"Unfortunately, I've got a lot of work to do today. For some reason, my garden is growing out of control. I need to cut some plants back before they take over their neighbor's spaces." His dimples show when he grimaces, laughter dancing in his eyes.

After kissing me soundly, he crawls out of bed and begins to dress. A heaviness settles over me. It's time. If I stay any longer, I'll never recover from the heartbreak. Already, my heart is fracturing.

Clutching his blanket over my chest, I clear my throat. "I'm going home today."

Cedar goes still, and a beat passes before he turns to face me with his brow creased. "I thought you had a few more days."

A sense of wrongness washes over me. "Well, I've got control of the magic now, and if I wait too long, I won't have time to earn enough money for rent."

Standing in just sweats, he's imposing. His arms cross and he frowns down at me.

"I know, I know, you can help, but I can't accept that," I say, crossing my own arms defiantly.

"Do you *want* to leave?" he asks finally.

My heart and mind both scream *No!* But that won't help either of us. Taking a slow breath, I nod. "It's time. I'm ready."

Unconvinced, Cedar watches me for a moment but holds his tongue. When I keep my expression blank and say nothing, he goes back to dressing. My stomach sinks as he pulls a shirt down to cover those beautiful tattoos.

It takes too much effort to drag myself out of his bed and pull my clothes on so I can leave when he does.

The morning is brisk and I cross my arms again for warmth. Birds chatter and squirrels fuss in the branches above us. My emotions are a cacophony of sadness, regret, and frustration all competing for my focus alongside nature's morning choir.

When Heath's cabin comes into view, Cedar pauses. "I'll be in the garden," he says simply, raising my hand to kiss across the knuckles. "Will I see you later?"

"I'll try." It feels untrue.

The soft lines around his eyes almost shatter me. He draws me closer and kisses my lips softly. My body wants to cling to him and my heart aches. He is everything I don't deserve.

"I'd like more time to say goodbye," he murmurs into my hair. "But just in case, please know the last few days with you were everything to me."

There is no response that would be adequate after that declaration. My heart flutters in my chest and my eyes sting. I turn, seeking him, and our lips meet in another slow kiss. The kind of kiss that bleeds emotion. It's the only way I can tell him how I feel about him.

Too soon, the sounds of a community waking around us destroys our peaceful moment. I unclench my fingers and release the collar of his shirt. His fingers slip out of my hair.

"Goodbye, Cedar," I whisper.

Those stormy eyes search mine, before he kisses my forehead and walks away. Part of me wants to race after him, fling myself into his arms, and hold tight like a baby monkey. But I can't.

My steps are stiff as I follow the familiar path back to Heath's cabin. The door squeaks as I push it open and step into the cheery kitchen.

"Good morning," my uncle says, looking up from his phone. A half-eaten plate of eggs sits on the table along with a mug of black coffee.

"Morning," I say, cringing as I wait for his questions about where I've been. They never come.

After a few moments of silence, Heath looks up again and raises one brow. "Is everything okay?"

Exhaling, I straighten and force the words out. "I think it's time I go home."

"What makes you say that?" Setting his phone down, Heath takes a drink from his mug, his eyes never leaving me. He's calm and collected, but there's an intensity about him that churns my stomach.

"I've got the whole plant magic thing under control, and I can't take more time off work. Not if I want to pay my bills."

"I understand." There is none of the resistance that I secretly hope for. "I'll miss you, but you'll come back to visit soon, right?"

"Of course. Maybe in the fall before the holidays hit."

"Sounds like a plan. Let me know possible dates and we will be ready for you." He leans forward, hands draped casually across the table. "I'm happy to help, Aurora. It would be my privilege, and well worth the cost if you can come visit more often. Maybe you could take the whole winter off from the hotel and stay longer."

"I really appreciate that. I'll think about it."

He releases me from his attention and my body relaxes. "Well, I'm going to go get my stuff together."

"Need help?"

"I'm good." With an awkward wave, I slip out of the kitchen and into the small secondary bedroom.

My paintings are carefully stacked against the far wall and the newest one stares back at me. Cedar's beautiful wolf surrounded by his beloved garden. There's a vibrancy in the painting I can't take credit for. Even without the details finished, it's bursting with life. It would be an excellent centerpiece for my next show, but I feel guilty taking it with me. Something so authentic deserves to stay here.

With reluctant hands, I wrap it and set it aside to give to Cedar. A parting gift so he remembers me. Maybe it's cruel to leave him with a reminder of the girl who fell for him and then ran away, but I can't help myself.

Possessions packed, I look around the cozy little room. A sense of finality sinks into my bones. Even though I have every intention of returning to visit, it won't be the same as this first time.

Leaving hurts, and my instinct is to grit my teeth and speed through it with my head down. The sooner I return to my normal life, the sooner this will fade away and be a happy, warm memory. The thought stings.

Bag slung over my shoulder, I detour to Cedar's cabin and lean the painting against the door frame. He'll find it later and I can avoid his sad puppy dog eyes.

My sister is my last stop. She's lounging on the patio enjoying the morning sunlight as Slate paces back and forth with a fussing Timber.

"Everything okay?" I ask, sinking down beside her.

She throws a hand over her mouth to stifle a yawn before answering. "Yeah, just had a long night. What's up?"

"I'm going home."

"I figured from the bag," she says, tipping her head toward me. "I wish you'd stay, but I understand. I'm so sleep deprived, I don't blame you for not wanting to stay longer."

"No, that's not it. I've loved seeing you. And it's okay you're busy. You had a baby, Haze." Guilt pangs in my chest. "I'm sure it's a lot to handle. Can I do anything to help?"

She smiles. "Nah. Marigold won't stop coming and cleaning, Clove and Crickett have filled our fridge with food, and Timber is only happy when she's attached to my boob or outside walking with Slate. Hence," she says, waving an arm in her partner's direction as she trails off.

"I'm sorry I wasn't more useful."

"I didn't expect anything from you." She reaches up and smooths my hair behind my ear. "But it was lovely to see you. And I'm so glad you met Timber." Another yawn punctuates her words. "When you come next time, maybe she'll be sitting up and laughing or whatever. It'll be more exciting."

"I love you," I say roughly, throwing my arms around my big sister. "You're the best big sister and an amazing mom."

Pulling me tighter, Hazel murmurs into my hair. "Love you too. I'll miss you. Stay longer next time."

Timber lets out a squall and Slate steps up on the porch. "I think it's time for another feeding."

"Alrighty. Is this what they meant by cluster feeding?" Hazel askes, accepting Timber from her partner. With practiced movements, she settles her baby in the crook of her arm and tugs her shirt down. It takes a few attempts to get Timber to latch, but then Timber drinks happily.

"I'll want daily updates, Mama," I say. Gingerly, I take Timber's waving hand and give it a little squeeze. "Bye, my little niece. I love you! I'll see you soon."

A sadness that has nothing to do with Cedar sweeps over me as I untuck my legs and force myself to walk away. Leaving shouldn't feel like something is being ripped away from me. Maybe it's proximity to my hormonal sister.

Hazel blows me a kiss and waves before turning her attention back to her baby. It felt so right being near her again.

The walk south to the parking lot is quiet, though several people wave in greeting. No one is that friendly in Los Angeles. Carefully, I lift my paintings into the trunk, and then tuck my bag in the back seat.

The car grinds to life, the sound feeling unnatural after so many days without it. Chewing my lip, I roll the wheel and slip it into reverse. The car lurches a few inches and stops abruptly. The momentum jerks me forward.

Frowning, I throw it into park and fling the door open. What the hell is stopping my car from moving? As I step out, a stalk of greenery sprouts at my feet and curls over my shoe.

A veritable patch of bushes has grown up around my car, stems twining into the wheels.

Suppressing curses, I clench my hands into fists. The bite of nails into my palms triggers another surge of growth, forcing me to step back.

So much for having control.

With a deep sigh, I reach out and brace myself against my car. I have to get this under control. After several deep breaths, I sense the power I am putting out without meaning to. It takes a few attempts to bend it to my will, but eventually the plants withdraw.

Why is it so difficult to leave?

Climbing back in my car, I keep a tight lock on my ability while I reverse out of the spot and roll toward the road. As I wind through the trees on the access road, my tension eases. The tug to stay lessens, though it leaves behind a gaping emptiness that grows with every mile.

I have to force myself to pull onto the freeway. It's several hours to reach the motel I've picked as my half-way point. Tomorrow, I'll travel the rest of the way back to the city and resume my life. Nothing to do but go through the motions and wait for the emotions to clear. If they ever do.

CEDAR

The garden feels empty and somehow lifeless. My favorite place in the world isn't the same now that I know what it's like with Aurora in it. I need to harvest the spinach she planted and thin the beets, harvest the blackberries, and a million other tasks. But instead, I sit under the tree where she painted me and stare into nothingness.

When I took a break for lunch, I found the painting wrapped in brown paper outside my front door. It's now safely tucked in my room. She captured my wolf perfectly, sunlight streaming across my fur and the garden looking wild around me. That's what I want in this space now, and it's not possible. Not without her.

Exhaling slowly, I rest my forehead against the arm slung across my knees. Closing my eyes doesn't alleviate the deep ache of loss. I feel like I've lost a limb. A chunk of my soul is cut out.

"You doing okay there?" a deep voice says.

Swallowing, I look up to see Heath. He walks forward, his gait uneven, and lowers himself onto the ground to sit beside me.

"Sir," I say, all the greeting I can muster.

"Aurora went home," he says.

"Yeah."

"I'm concerned about you." He folds his hands and studies me over.

"Why are you concerned about me?" I say, though it sounds silly when I'm this moody.

Heath sighs. "Did I ever tell you about my brother, Reed?"

I shake my head but stay silent. Heath never speaks about Reed. My father told me the basic story, but I've never even heard his name spoken by anyone else.

"My brother wanted to apprentice to be a healer. He even studied medicine." He pauses, thinking. "He was older, but I don't think he ever wanted to be Alpha, but our father wouldn't hear of it. Anyways, Reed decided to do pre-med in California, and this was before online classes of course. And then he met Sheila."

"Hazel and Aurora's mom," I say, acknowledging what I already know.

"He fell hard before he even realized what was happening. I've seen it over and over. Hazel and Slate fought it. Even your parents were oblivious for months. That bond falls into place long before our brains catch up."

My brain hurts with the implications of what he's saying so I lean my forehead down again and close my eyes to listen.

"Anyway, Reed came home and tried to pick up where he left off. He only made it about two weeks before he couldn't sleep, barely ate. He was useless without her. So he left to be with her."

"Did he ever tell her he was a shifter?" I've always wondered.

"I don't think so. He would have if their kids had been born shifters. He would have had to. But that never happened." Heath scrubs at his face. "I don't think it will do anyone good if you pretend you're fine. I know how close you became with Rory."

There's no use in arguing. "How did you find out?"

Heath exhales in a dry laugh. "You guys were kissing all over the garden. She smelled like you for most of her visit. Oh, and Marigold saw her going home with you last night."

"She told you?" I ask, raking my fingers through my hair.

"Jasper told Hawthorne," he says with a chuckle. Of course. I don't know why I was expecting any sort of privacy in this pack.

"I asked her to stay and she said no. I tried to tell her how I felt, but I didn't want to make her feel worse. And now she's gone."

Heath nods along to my confession.

"So what should I do?"

"I can't give you the same advice I would have for anyone else in this situation, because I know you. You will stubbornly refuse to do something you see as selfish. You'll let yourself be miserable instead of inconveniencing anyone else."

"No," I argue. He raises an eyebrow and silences me.

"Go to her. Work together to find a solution that allows you to be together. Maybe you could split your time between the city and here. That's the kind of compromise that relationships require. Aurora has a good heart, and if she loves you too, she'll be willing to work something out."

Each word sinks into me. It feels true and right.

"I don't want to abandon my job here."

"Tansy can train someone new. Your position here is not more important than your happiness. The garden will be fine without you." He shakes his head. "But if you want to catch up with her, you need to get going. I'll text you the motel address."

"Yes, Alpha."

Something primal drives me, and I'm moving out of the garden before a decision is made. When I glance back, Heath is leaning his head back against the tree trunk with his eyes closed and a contented smile hinting on his face. It bolsters my resolve, knowing the man who I consider an uncle supports me.

It takes only minutes to reach my family's cabin and gather a few belongings. My mother works in the kitchen, layering pastry while she hums along to classic rock.

"Mom." I step closer. "I'm going after Aurora."

She turns, lines forming around her warm eyes as she smiles at me. "My sweet boy, I'm very glad to hear that." Despite the flour on her hands, she pulls me into a tight hug. "Go get her."

"I'm not sure when I'll be back. If she wants to go home, I'm going with her."

"Alright, sweetheart." She squeezes my arm, leaving another flour-print. "I'm proud of you."

Frowning, I reiterate, "I'm probably moving away."

"I had a feeling this would happen," she says with a wry smile, finally reaching for a kitchen towel. "It'll all work out. Don't worry. Just go get her."

I'll have to call my dad later because he's helping my brother today. Aurora has a head start of several hours and I can't wait any longer.

The thought that it might not work out terrifies me. But the idea of losing her is worse. Everything in me craves her presence, yearns for her laugh and her touch. It'll have to work out - I'll do whatever is necessary.

Clutching my backpack, I head toward the parking lot and jog to my family's spare truck. The keys wait on the sun visor, and then I'm pulling onto the dirt road that will take me away from the only home I've ever known and toward the home I'm choosing.

XIII
MOTELS, MAGIC, & MATES

AURORA

After a drive-thru dinner, I pull into the motel parking lot. The sun has barely set, but the atmosphere feels heavy. When I step out of my car, I spot a handful of men standing by the fenced-in pool, smoking. They look like thugs with dirty wife-beater tank tops, baggy jeans, and chains. Dangerous people in the city look nothing like them, but it doesn't change the warning I feel when I study their body language. Their eyes follow me up to the motel room.

Heart in my throat, I click the safety lock and wedge the chair under the door handle along with a rolled-up towel. The security measures help me to relax. Flopping on the bed, I pull out my cell phone. I've barely touched it the last week or so. The idea of scrolling social media makes my head hurt, but I do have a few messages from Jarrod.

Anxiety fizzing in my chest, I hit the call button. After four rings, he picks up. Voices blur together in the background.

"The Buzz Gallery."

"Hi, Jarrod. It's Aurora. I saw you had something you wanted to discuss?"

"Yes, love! I reviewed the pictures you emailed over." His voice is high and bright. "I've got to say, your work has never looked this good. Whatever you did is working! I can feel the atmosphere through the pixels. I'm dying to get my hands on the real thing."

"Well, I'm on my way back. I can get them to you tomorrow night or the next morning. I'm on my way back already."

"Alright. So, what was it that inspired you?"

"Oh, just being out here in nature, I think. I also met someone. But he lives here, so that's over."

"Aurora, love," he says, suddenly stern. "If you come back here to Los Angeles and go back to painting sad little flowers, I will never forgive you. If you found a muse, you'd better turn your ass around to go back to them."

"I can't. I've got responsibilities. And maybe I like living in the city." The excuse sounds weak and my voice loses conviction before I can finish speaking.

"No one likes living here. And you wouldn't need a second job, I bet. I'm sure the cost to live there is lower. And I can sell these paintings, love. I'll make sure you have a wait-list of buyers. We can triple your prices, I swear."

"You haven't even seen them in person yet!"

"Ship them! Don't you dare show up back in this concrete butthole."

My laugh is manic. "Jarrod, are you freaking kidding me?"

"I never kid about art, love. Oh, I've got customers. See you soon, or not! Bye, now." The line goes dead.

My phone tips out of my hand and I roll over, burying my face into the comforter as I let out a muffled scream.

What if I went home to drop off the paintings and waited to see if Jarrod really could sell them for triple price. And then I'd have time to pack up her things and arrange a move with Hazel. That would be the smartest move.

Maybe, with some luck, I could change my life.

Even the thought of moving to be with Cedar and Hazel has my heart racing. It's too good to be true.

It's unlikely to work out. Jarrod was probably wrong. I shouldn't get my hopes up.

I want to sketch. It's the only way to get this nervous energy out. Unfortunately, my art supplies are in my bag in the car. I shouldn't have left them out there.

Scrunching my nose in frustration, I pull my shoes on and head for the door with my car keys in my fist.

The motel's dim lights barely illuminate the dark parking lot. At least it's quiet. The stale smell of smoke and gasoline makes me gag after a week of breathing crisp pine air.

"Hey, pretty girl," a nasally voice croons.

I twirl, looking for the cat-caller. In the city, I would have ignored it and kept walking, but out here I feel isolated. Vulnerable. There are no bystanders to protect me or shops to duck into.

A man pushes off the block wall. His clothes hang off his gaunt figure. "I can't believe you're out here alone."

There's no use in ignoring him. "I'm not alone. My boyfriend is in our room."

"Little liar," a second man says, coming from the other side of me. True fear spikes like ice in my chest. As I scan the parking lot, I see no one.

Turning, I stride back in the direction of my room. The taller man steps in my path. "Rude too. Maybe we need to teach you some manners."

626

My hand goes to my back pocket, but I left my phone in my room. How could I be so stupid.

"You don't want to do that," I say, keeping my voice low to hide my fear. "You need to leave me alone."

"Why?" he says, stepping closer.

I'll only get one chance to run, and I know better than to glance the direction I plan to go and give away my move. My muscles tense and I keep my eyes on the immediate threat.

As he takes another step, I launch myself sideways. Darting around him, I race for my room. I'll only have seconds to get the door open and locked behind me, or risk them following me into the private space.

Hitting the door, I slide the keycard and watch it blink red. Hand shaking, I try again.

"Where do you think you're going?" Nasal voice says with a laugh that sounds like a farm animal.

"Get away from her."

The men look up and my heart jumps into my throat. Spinning, I take in Cedar. He holds no weapon, but the promise of violence in his voice is enough to make the men take a step back.

The taller one regains his arrogance and makes a poor choice. "You weren't with her earlier. She isn't anything to you. Go away and mind your own business."

Cedar bristles and takes a step closer. "She is mine, and if you touch her, you'll wish you were dead." I shiver at his dark tone.

"You think you're a hero?" the thinner man says, throwing his hands up and advancing on Cedar.

Everything happens so fast. Cedar grabs the man's shoulder and yanks him forward, winding back and slamming a fist into the guy's face. He drops, blood gushing from his nose.

The taller man abandons me and rushes toward Cedar. Metal flashes and I shriek a wordless warning before he shoves a knife into Cedar's gut. Eyes flaring bright blue, he grips his opponent by the shoulder and throws him into the block wall. He scrambles up and hobbles away.

Cedar sways on his feet and reaches down, tugging the blade from his stomach. My words are incoherent babbling, trying to stop him, but it's too late. Blood seeps into his shirt, spreading rapidly.

"We need to call 911." I feel for my phone in my pocket again, and then search for his. It's on the ground with a shattered screen.

Tears pooling in my eyes and hands shaking, I press my key card to the door. Finally it turns green. The moment it unlocks, I shove the door open and dart in, grabbing for my phone. It's dead.

Cedar stumbles in and sits on the bed. Hands shaking, I plug my charger cord into the wall outlet and connect my phone. It drops from my hands when Cedar falls back on the bed.

"Cedar!" my cry echoes in the small, cold room.

He mumbles something about being okay.

"You most certainly are not!"

Sinking on to the bed beside him, I press my hands over his wound. Terror races through me until my entire body trembles. His hand drapes over mine, gently squeezing my wrist.

I love him. I can't lose him.

That love mingles with my fear, heightening both until I'm bursting with that buzz I now recognize is magic.

There are no plants to absorb it. I can't contain it. It pours out of me, through my hands into Cedar's chest. Instinct guides me, and somehow my fear ebbs as my affection for him swells.

Cedar gasps, his eyes going wide. He pushes up, sitting and twisting to face me. I let my grasp on the magic slip away, pulling it back into myself.

For a moment he stares at me, and then he pulls his shirt up, wiping at the blood to uncover perfectly smooth skin. No wound.

I poke at the spot, jerking back when he squirms.

"I'm fine. You healed it," he says, taking my bloody hand in his own.

My thoughts are jumbled. "I can't, what?"

"Shifter healing is fast, but not that fast. It had to be your magic."

"No way." I gawk at him. Wiping my wrist across my cheeks, my skin comes away wet. I was crying. Still am.

He grins at me, wiping at his stomach again.

"You almost died!" Choking on a sob, I smack his chest with my palm.

Catching my wrist, he brings it to his mouth and places a kiss on my pulse point. "I'm sorry, Little Witch."

"It's not your fault!" Launching forward, I fall into him. His blood soaks into my shirt, ruining it, but I don't care. The healed skin it reveals soothes something inside of me.

He wraps his arms around me and laughs softly into my hair as more tears drip down my cheeks.

"I was so scared," I confess. Craning my neck back, I fix him with a glare. "You aren't allowed to ever get hurt like that again."

"I'll do my best."

As I scowl up at him, he lowers his head and brushes his lips over my forehead, trailing kisses over my cheekbones. Greedy for his touch, I turn in his arms until I can kiss him properly.

With my arms wrapped around his neck, his hands pressing the small of my back to urge me closer, we kiss until the room is spinning.

"Seeing you like that was the worst moment of my life," I gasp. "I don't think I can live without you."

He pauses, lifting up from where we've sprawled, tousled hair framing his handsome face. "Good, because I feel the same."

As if that was all that is needed to be said, he lowers his mouth to my neck and nibbles at the skin. Curling against him, I hook a leg over his hips and run my hand down the bare skin of his back, enjoying how the muscles flex under my fingers as he moves, curling around me protectively.

"I love you," he murmurs without taking his lips off my throat. Vibrations zip through my skin and blood like the love he promises. Warmth fills me up from my chest, radiating out to my hands and feet until I'm desperate to shed our clothing lest I burst into an inferno.

"Me too," is all I can say, flames licking under my skin. The words are barely audible, but he knows. This man can read me, attentive to every expression and half-spoken word. He cares about all of it, and I know I am safe with him. He's proven over and over he will protect me and take my side.

Days ago, I would be thrilled to take him back to Los Angeles with me, but now, I only want him. Everything else fades away.

My shirt peels over my head and I'm not even sure whose hands did it. His teeth nip at my bottom lip, urging me to open for him. As he kisses me deep, his tongue delving in, my hands drag down his sweats and remove his last piece of clothing. He's already pulling my shorts off.

Rolling again, I kneel over him. He pushes up to sit, lowering his lips to my chest as I unhook the clasp of my bra. As the straps fall over my shoulders, he cups my breast gently. Tentatively, he lowers his mouth to it, and I tighten my grip on his shoulders, grinding my hips down on him.

That delicious tension builds until I want to climb into his very skin.

We tumble over, his mouth trailing down my stomach as he pushes me to my back. Featherlight kisses mingle with small bites, until I'm grasping at the sheets and opening my mouth in a silent scream with my eyes screwed shut.

The lace of my panties drags across my thighs as he removes them. A second later, his mouth ghosts over the sensitive skin on my inner thigh. There's no time to prepare before he's licking and touching the most intimate part of me. The moan I let out is embarrassing, but there's no time for shame.

With days of unresolved need between us, I'm ready to explode at his first touch. Words jumble in my mind and I'm reduced to a nonsensical mess of gasps and whimpers. It takes two attempts to speak, but finally I string words together. "Cedar, I need you inside of me, right now."

He stills, looking up at me. Those glowing eyes make my heart leap and stomach swoop. Slowly, he moves up my body, kissing my stomach, breasts, and lips before resting his forehead against mine. "I want to, but I don't have-"

"I'm on the pill, so we can just, please, I'm going to lose my mind." My words pour out, thoughts half completed. I'm still trying to speak when he nods and kisses me again.

Heart racing, I reach down between us and grip his cock. My body hums at the chance to touch. His harsh exhale raises the hair on my arms as I stroke him. Eagerly, I pull him into me. Time seems to slow as my focus narrows down to the places our bodies touch. His movements are slow, controlled, as he eases into me part of the way. Head bowed, his brow furrows as he bites his lip.

"Okay?" I say, gripping his face so I can see his eyes and the hint of fang pressing into his full bottom lip.

"I'm trying to make sure I'm gentle with you," he says.

The situation crashes over me and I let out a laugh. "You could slam me into this headboard until I can't see straight and I would still say thank you and ask you to do it again."

His eyes widen and I turn to kiss the inside of his forearm braced beside me. "Come on, my wolf," I urge, tightening my thighs on his hips. "I'm not delicate."

With a look of devotion, he pushes into me, filling me until our bodies are flush. His eyes rove over me, reassuring himself that I'm pleased. Weaving my fingers into his hair, I angle my head to kiss him, only releasing him when he rolls his hips. Luscious pleasure fills me, washing over me, filling me.

There's no shady motel room, no world around us at all as he sets a pace that makes my toes curl and my mouth spill out words of praise that might be gibberish. The feel of his body pressing into mine overwhelms everything else I know.

"I want to claim you so badly," he rasps, his breath warm on the shell of my ear. I shiver at the words, remembering what it means. Commitment.

"Then do it." Leveling my gaze to stare directly into his eyes, I speak my truth. "I want to belong to you in every way possible."

It's all the permission he needs. With a swift movement, he turns his head and sinks his teeth into the crook of my neck. The sharp pain of sharp fangs cutting into skin and muscle wrings a muffled scream from me, but the sting mingles with the intense pleasure ripping through my body.

My hands scramble for purchase, wrapping around his neck to hold me steady as he slowly withdraws his teeth and licks the tender spot. Buzzing magic rips out of me, magic I didn't even realize I was holding back. The wound seals over, the pain vanishing until I am shaking with a sense of ecstasy. Magic flows into Cedar too. His head drops, his cheek brushing my temple as he slows and shudders with a guttural growl.

He breathes in the scent of my hair, and everything is still for a moment before his head pops up and he inspects the bite mark. Even without touching it, I can tell the skin is healed.

"Are you good?" he asks quietly, leveraging off of me, he drops onto his side. I turn to face him until we're settled chest to chest, just like last time. But now, everything is different.

"Never better. How does it look?" I tilt my jaw to give him clear access.

"Perfect." He traces the spot. As he relaxes into his pillow, the dim light hits his neck and chest. My eyes focus on the place where his shoulder meets his neck - the same location as my new mark. A pale line swirls over his skin like a scar. Leaning forward, I narrow my eyes as I study it. A silvery vine swirls across his skin, complete with leaves and tendrils.

"Hey, babe, I think I did something." I can't look away from the mark that must have come from my magic.

"What?"

"I may have accidentally claimed you too."

Frowning, Cedar crawls out of bed and strides to the sink along the back wall, beside the door to the toilet and shower. My teeth sink into my bottom lip as I watch his naked body unabashedly. The harsh light flicks on, illuminating his golden skin. He stares, completely silent as he tilts his head to examine the spot. In the light, it can't be missed.

"Are you okay with that? I can try to remove it."

Slowly, a grin spreads across his face. When he turns, I'm stunned by the intensity of his joy. In two steps, he's dropping onto the bed and crashing his mouth down on mine.

His insistent kiss steals all thought. For long minutes, I'm lost in the feel of his lips on mine and the way his hand brushes over my new claim mark and then winds down my chest.

When he finally releases me, I smile back. "So you like it?"

He hesitates, and I can see thoughts churning in his head. "I thought this would be one sided and you would wear my bite but have nothing to mark me as yours. But I should have known better. You are extraordinary."

My mouth falls open.

"Can you feel our bond?" he prompts.

Closing my eyes, I breathe out and open myself to feel everything around me. The pulse of life and magic is strong around me, but it's the touch of something unfamiliar that I focus on. Drawing it forward, I sense a delirious happiness mingled with surprise.

"Yeah, I think so." The happiness surges, leaving no doubt I'm sensing his emotions.

"We can test what it does for you, but you should be able to generally track me and feel my emotions and some physical feelings."

"Oh." The intense ecstasy that left me shaking from right after he marked me comes to mind. Maybe I was feeling more than my own pleasure. From the pride swelling in my chest, I suspect all of his emotions are reflected back to me. It'll take work to learn to distinguish his feelings from mine, but I'm confident I can manage it.

"So now that we've committed our lives together," I say, trailing off.

He kisses the tip of my nose before answering. "I'll come to Los Angeles with you. Or anywhere else you want to go."

"What if, and just hear me out, because I know this is a crazy idea," I say, "What if we moved back to your home?"

His hand stroking over my arm stills. "You don't have to do that."

"I want to."

"My only priority is your happiness. Where we live doesn't matter." He is deadly serious.

"That's the thing," I say, picking my words carefully. "I've never been as happy anywhere as I was there. Even before we got together. My sister is there. It's so full of life. I've never had friends like that before. I don't want to be anywhere else."

The other reasons won't help convince him. Making my partner happy is important to me and he will be happiest at home with his family and friends. And the same goes for me. I want to be with Hazel and Heath, and especially baby Timber.

"You really want to live with us?" he asks, a smile breaking over his face.

"I love you." It bursts out of me, uncontrollable. "I'm happy anywhere you are, but if that's with your family and mine, that's even better."

"I love you." He echoes, his voice rough. The glow is back to his eyes and I eye his full lips and the hint of fangs I know they hide.

XIV
HEALING & HOME

CEDAR

The pine needles crunch under my truck's tires as I pull back into the pack's lot. Aurora's car creaks in behind me, and I promise myself that I'll replace it with something newer. Maybe something with room for large canvases and as much paint as she could ever want.

Vale walks around the corner of the office and stops abruptly. As we park and climb out, he smirks before turning on his heel and jogging back the way he came. No doubt he's notifying Slate and Hazel of our return.

Aurora is buzzing with nervous energy. Circling my family's truck, I pop open her door and rest my forearm on the top edge.

"It'll be fine. Everyone will be happy to have you," I say, stooping down to kiss her forehead.

"Hopefully." After a moment of chewing her lip, she nods and pushes herself out of the car. The door makes a dull thud as I close it behind her.

Her hand slips into mine as we walk toward her sister's cabin. Her belongings can wait in the car until we've sorted out where she's staying. Hopefully with me, but since I'm still living with my parents, that may not be her first choice.

Aurora's hands shake as she knocks on Hazel and Slate's door. She clasps them together and wrings them. My fingers squeeze the small of her waist, pulling her out of her spiraling thoughts. She smiles up at me and some of her tension eases.

"I don't know why I'm nervous. This should be fine. And if they make a fuss, I can just remind them I've got magical abilities that apparently can heal people. Who would turn that down?"

The door swings open and Hazel stands there, baby Timber asleep in a sling. Her left arm hooks under the baby while her right hand grips the door.

"Rory," she says, looking between us with her brows pinched.

"Hazel, I don't mean to spring something else on you, but I want to stay." Aurora rushes to get all of her words out. "I love it here, and my gallery manager said the paintings I just sent are way better than anything I painted before, so it makes sense for my career.

"And I don't really want to be away from you and Timber. And I kinda love Cedar, yeah I definitely love him, and I want to stay with him. Plus I have this magic that I can use to help, so I'll pull my weight. I can help Cedar with the garden or whatever else..."

Hazel's eyes widen as her sister continues to spew out convincing arguments. Just as Aurora's pitch rises to songbird levels, Hazel turns on her heel as disappears into the cabin.

Aurora stutters to a stop and turns to me, her lips parted in shock.

Slate's muffled voice drifts through the open door and then Hazel, sans baby, launches herself at Aurora. She flings her arms around her neck and hugs her aggressively as they tangle in a mess of limbs and wavy brown hair.

"I'm so glad," Hazel cries while Aurora mumbles something about making room and helping. Their hug devolves into swaying and gripping each other's upper arms. Tears well in Aurora's eyes and Hazel sniffles.

"You're not mad?" Aurora asks, her voice thick.

"Why would I be mad? This is amazing. I didn't think you'd like it here, but you seemed so happy, I started to hope." Hazel's words tumble over each other.

"It doesn't feel real, but Cedar and I made the decision." Aurora trails off, covering the claim mark I gave her last night. Reluctantly, she removes her hand.

"No way." Hazel's mouth falls open again. Aurora gives her a sheepish smile, and I step closer to reassure her. As she leans forward, Hazel narrows her eyes. "That looks like it's a few weeks old."

"It's from last night." Aurora pinches her bottom lip with her teeth. "So, as it turns out, I can heal people too. Or at least myself and Cedar."

"Why did Cedar need healing?" Slate asks, filling the doorway. Timber sleeps in his arms, oblivious to the emotional reunion happening on their porch.

Aurora's attention refocuses on the baby. Gingerly, she lifts her out of Slate's hold and rests her against her chest.

"What happened?" Hazel asks quietly.

Sighing, I admit, "A few low life idiots were harassing Aurora at her motel when I arrived. One of them had a switchblade and used it on me. But I'm fine. You can't even tell he cut me." As proof I lift my borrowed shirt to reveal unmarked skin.

Slate's frown tells me I'll be drilling self-defense with him for the foreseeable future to make sure no one gets the drop on me again.

Aurora's eyebrow quirks as she looks between us. Maybe she senses my emotions or simply reads the silent communication between me and my cousin. She bounces on her heels and pats Timber's back softly.

"Hi, sweetheart. Guess what, I'm going to stay here with you," she coos. Timber sleeps on.

The sight of her holding a baby squeezes my chest into a pleasant ache. It's so easy to imagine us with our own little ones. Like Slate grew up with me and Onyx, Timber can grow up with her cousins.

"So if you're staying, where are you going to live?" Hazel asks, sinking into a patio chair.

Aurora should talk with her sister. I brush my hand along her upper arm, and she hands over the baby. Timber barely whines and quiets as soon as I begin swaying.

"Well, I'm thinking I'll stay with Cedar. I mean, he asked me to." She curls up on the chair closest to Hazel.

"We'll figure something out," I say.

"You could always use Slate's old trailer. It's empty and pretty nice. That'll work until you're ready for your own cabin. I think we need to build a few new ones."

"That's a good idea." Slate praises his mate and she reaches up to take his hand.

"That would be perfect. Thank you," I say.

Aurora is watching me with her bottom lip caught between her teeth, but it's not anxiety seeping through our bond. Apparently she likes seeing me hold a baby too. Later, when we are alone, I'll ask her all about what she's thinking in this moment.

Hazel reclaims her sister's attention, and the girls chat about the trailer and plans for getting Aurora settled. Timber stirs and I begin pacing. Slate falls into step beside me, his dark green eyes thoughtful.

"So magical healing ability?"

"Yup."

He rakes his fingers through his dark hair. "Anything else?"

Swallowing, I tilt my head to give him a better look at my magical mark. His eyebrows rise. "Well that's unusual."

"She's from a line of shifters. I'm guessing her magic is particularly compatible with us. Not that we can test it, but I'd guess she can't do nearly as much to help a normal human. It felt like she tapped into my shifter healing and accelerated it. My wolf instincts reacted to it in a way I haven't felt before."

"Interesting."

The women rise and Aurora slips down the steps to stand beside me. Her hand skims up my arm and settles on Timber's back.

"Here, let me find the key. We tried to close it up so you'll need to turn the water back on too. Slate can help if you need." Hazel hurries inside, returning a minute later with a key hanging from a leather loop.

She gives Aurora the key and takes her baby from my arms.

"Thank you," Aurora says, smiling sweetly at her sister.

My hands go to her waist, drawing her to me until her back rests against my chest. "Want to grab your stuff and see about moving in?" She nods.

Our walk back to the car is slower. Aurora has relaxed now that her situation is settled. She breaks the silence with her musing. "I'm surprised how easy that was. I figured I'd be stuck at Heath's for a while until we figured things out. Didn't expect a new place to live offered up like that." Her lashes flutter as she glances between my face and the ground.

I reach up and brush my fingers over her claim mark. "You're pack now. We take care of each other. Food, housing, money. We have our own, but everyone is generous, and Slate and Hazel do a great job managing everything."

"I'm not used to anyone taking care of me. Not since Hazel went to college." Her hand takes mine, lacing our fingers. I tug her to a stop and wrap my other arm around her shoulders, pulling her into a hug.

"You're mine and I'm yours. Regardless of the pack, we have each other and you'll never be alone again."

Her eyes shine when she looks up at me. Instead of answering, she tips her chin up and kisses me. Affection and gratitude pours through our bond, catching my breath in my chest.

We stand there for a long time, kisses replaced with soft words and affectionate touches. Eventually, I remind her of our plan and we resume our walk to the parking lot.

An hour later, her bags are stowed in the trailer, and we've gathered a few of my belongings as well. Luckily most of Slate's furniture remains, though we will need to pick up a few items. A bed with a bare mattress sits in the single bedroom and the leather sofa still occupies the living space. The television is missing, but that doesn't matter to me. I've never been a gamer like Slate and Onyx. If Aurora wants one, I'll happily fulfill that desire, otherwise we have each other and our garden.

Aurora tucks clothing into dresser drawers as I put toiletries away in the bathroom adjoining the bedroom.

A knock sounds at the trailer door. Aurora crowds behind me as I open it. My mother bustles in with a pile of linens in her arms.

"Hello, loves! Thought you'd need some sheets!"

"You don't need to do that," Aurora says, accepting them. "But thank you."

"We have so many extras. You guys can get something you like better in the future when you have time to do a little decorating." She pats Aurora's arm affectionately.

"Thanks, Mom." I duck my head, a touch of guilt at moving out prickling at me.

"We're so happy for you both," she says, smiling indulgently at Aurora. "I've got two beautiful daughters-in-law. How did we get so lucky?"

Aurora sets the sheets on the bed before coming back to give my mom a hug.

"Alright, I'd better be off. You guys make a list of everything you need. I don't know how much kitchen stuff Slate left behind, but it all came from Crickett's originally, I'm sure." She laughs as she heads out the door.

Aurora clicks the door shut and spins. "I love her."

Hearing she likes my family warms my heart. "She adores you," I say, pulling her to me.

"No, like she is amazing. I think I like her more than you," Aurora jokes.

My attempt to scowl at her makes her laugh as she tugs me down for a kiss. It's sweet and innocent, but heat sparks between us. She gasps for air and grabs my shirt, clinging to me.

Scooping under her thighs, I lift her up to sit on the kitchen counter. After another deep kiss, I break off. "Are you really happy here?"

"Stop asking me that. I'm so happy I feel like I'll wake up and it was all just a fantasy." She tucks her calves behind my thighs and pulls me closer until my hips bump the edge of the countertop. "Now let's break in this trailer."

My eyebrows shoot up, and she throws her head back with a soft laugh that causes my stomach to lurch. She's gorgeous, light painting her dark hair into shades of burnt caramel. I'm busy admiring the line of her jaw and the way her lips part when she straightens and slides off the counter with a shrug, pushing me back.

"If you're not interested, that's fine." Her teasing tone invites argument, so I give it to her.

"There's no time I'm not interested in you," I murmur, threading my fingers into her hair. Lowering my head, I let my breath ghost over the shell of her ear before I nip at her earlobe.

"Yeah? I think I need a demonstration. You know, for science." Her smirk taunts me.

She meets my kisses hungrily, tugging my shirt up until she can run her hands over the tattoos across my ribs. We break apart long enough to shed clothing, and then I walk her back to the mattress.

I'll never get enough of this woman. She groans when I drag my teeth over the claim mark and her hips buck. Soon, I'm lost to her, unable to tell which direction is up or what my own name is if it wasn't for the reverent way she repeats it as I sink into her.

Later, she lays across my chest and nuzzles against my skin as my breathing slows. "You really liked seeing me holding a baby," I say, the thought escaping me unfiltered.

She grins. "Yeah, it's kinda hot. I love the idea of you with a baby."

"So you want kids?" I ask, clarifying.

Her fingers trail over my stomach. "Yeah, I always imagined having a whole bunch of kids. Please tell me you want kids too."

"Yeah." My smile is indulgent. I want to give this woman anything and everything she desires. If she wants a pack of kids, I am on board. "I liked having a brother and sister growing up, and Slate and Marigold were always there too. It was like a big family."

"I love that. And not to put any pressure on us, but it would be cool if our kids had cousins close to their age to play with. I'm thinking Hazel and Slate will have more kids eventually, so maybe we will be ready by then." Her smile is sunshine and warmth.

"I'm ready when you are."

A beautiful flush paints her cheeks. "Maybe a couple of years? We'll see."

"Sounds good," I say, lifting her hand to my mouth so I can kiss her fingers and bite the meat of her palm. Her nose scrunches up as she grins at me.

"We should finish unpacking," she says, her eyes drifting closed. "At some point."

"We have all the time we want," I say, brushing my hand down her back. There's nowhere else I want to be. Everything is perfect. Aurora's contentment purrs through our mate bond, reassuring me that she's happy. Peace settles on me, and my eyes drift closed too.

EPILOGUE

CEDAR

Panic filters through our mate bond. I drop my tools, and sprint out of my garden, moving north until I reach the trailer that has been our home for the last few weeks. Hazel and Slate granted us land to build a cabin on, close to my garden, but it will take months to build.

Aurora isn't in the living room or kitchen when I enter. "Love?" I call out.

A startled little noise comes from the bedroom. I waste no time striding across our small home and pulling the bedroom door open. Aurora sits cross legged on our bed, holding one hand behind her back.

"What's wrong?" I ask, squatting in front of her and looking up into her eyes. Moisture wells in the corners, piercing my heart. Gently, I wipe the tears away. "I'll fix whatever it is."

She lets out a shaky laugh. "I don't think this is something that needs fixing. Or I hope not." Her chin wobbles.

"What is it?" My voice drops low.

"Please don't be mad."

Frowning, I go to my knees and lean against the bed, placing my hands on the side of her thighs. "Never."

"Okay." With a shaky breath, she moves the hand behind her back and holds out a white, plastic stick. It takes a moment for my brain to process what I'm looking at.

"We're pregnant?" I ask, finally looking up at her face.

Hope shines there in her small smile and the way her eyes crinkle. She nods and sniffles.

"That's amazing!" I say, rising and framing her face with my hands while I kiss her. She answers with passion, parting her lips and swiping her tongue into my mouth. The test falls to the floor, forgotten, as I show her how excited I am.

She breaks off our kiss and peers at me. "Are you sure it isn't too soon? I mean, it's been like no time at all."

Chuckling, I lean forward to kiss her shoulder. "We get a few months to adjust before it's born, you know."

"I just don't know how this could have happened," she says suddenly.

"Really?" I say, raising an eyebrow.

"Not that," she says, slapping my bicep. "But I'm on the pill."

"You also have magic that makes plants grow, heals wounds, and makes fruit grow. And you used magic on yourself, remember? We should have seen this coming."

"Oh," she says, eyes wide as she thinks it through. "We're gonna have to figure out some other birth control then, because I don't want to pop *that* many babies out. Three or four is probably more than enough."

"Sure. We'll figure it out. In eight months," I promise, lowering my mouth back to her skin.

"How are we going to tell everyone?" she says, clearly distracted. Sighing, I flop onto the bed beside her. She turns onto her side, the wheels turning behind her eyes. "What about the cabin? Will it be ready in time?"

"I'll make sure it is," I say, rubbing my hand down her arm to soothe her.

"There's so much to figure out," she says. "Baby names, birth plans, and how do you feel about having a gender reveal party? Or do you want to keep it a surprise?"

Smiling, I fall back onto my back and fold my hands behind my head as she spirals into endless baby thoughts and plans. I'll be happy with whatever she decides.

AURORA

"Almost ready to go?" Cedar asks, placing a kiss on the top of my head. "You'll be late if we don't leave soon."

"I'm ready!" I stand, resting a hand on my belly. Some shirts don't quite reach the top of my pants now, but at least I can still fit into those pants. Hazel already gave me a stack of maternity clothes, so I'm ready for when I get too big for my current wardrobe.

Cedar is overly attentive as we walk down the steps and out of the little trailer. "I can stay home if you want," he offers.

"Go see your brother. Otherwise Ember won't come to girls' night."

"Okay." He insists on walking me to Hazel's cabin, and I don't mind. The plants may move out of my way, but my eyesight is still terrible.

He waits at the steps as I knock on Hazel's door. Marigold throws it open and flings her arms around me, bumping against my belly as we hug. When she releases me, I look back and blow a kiss at my mate. Only then does Cedar shed his clothes and shift into his wolf. I watch from the doorway, enjoying the sight of his reddish-gold form trotting into the trees.

"Come on," Marigold says, grabbing my hand and tugging me inside.

Baby Timber is on the rug, sitting up and chewing on a little rubber wolf teether. "Did you like your half-birthday present from your auntie?" I ask, squatting down to greet my little niece.

I almost lose my balance when I rise, grabbing the arm of the sofa to balance. Hazel watches from the kitchen and laughs.

"Enjoy seeing me struggle?"

"It's only fair," she says with a cheeky smile. "Besides, it's just beginning. Get ready for all kinds of awkward, unbalanced, uncomfortable…"

Holding up a hand, I stop her. "I know. I'm ready."

Marigold slouches on the sofa, her hand going to her own smaller bump. "Aren't we just a bucket of fun?" She giggles. "Hazel, when are you having another one?"

"Ugh, hopefully not anytime soon." She scoops up Timber and bounces the chubby baby on her hip. "We can only handle so many babies at once. Especially with Miss Fertile over here." She jerks her thumb at me.

"Not my fault I've got magic," I say, wiggling my fingers at Timber. She rewards me with a sloppy, wet smile.

"Did you get ultrasound pictures?" Marigold asks, leaning toward me excitedly.

Sinking down beside her, I dig them out of my pocket. She snatches them and the row of black and white photos unravels, hitting her knee.

"Okay, I don't know what I'm looking at. Mine don't look like this. Our last set looked like a jelly bean."

"Well, you only have one baby, don't you," I grumble, pointing as I count out all three little blobs and point out where you can see arms and legs.

"You poor thing," she says, rolling her lips inwards to stop her smile.

Taking my ultrasound scans back from her, I look over the images fondly. A few more months, and I will have my hands full.

"We'll help you, don't worry." Marigold says, rubbing her hand over my thigh and knee.

Rolling my eyes, I shake my head. "Cedar is so excited for daddy duty, I don't think any of us will get a chance to do anything. He'll make Slate look like a slouch."

Hazel huffs a laugh. We all know Slate's attempts to handle every single diaper change and baby task possible, though Timber only wants Hazel right now.

Marigold sighs. "Jasper too. He found those baby dolls from the shower and was practicing diapering and swaddling." She covers her mouth, eyes crinkling as giggles escape her.

"He's ridiculous," I say.

"But so hot," Marigold says dreamily.

Ember sinks onto the last spot on the sofa, between Marigold and Hazel's spot in her armchair. "Ugh, you guys are so mushy."

"Get used to it," Hazel teases.

"I'm happy being an aunt. Thank you very much." Ember reiterates, eyeing Timber from where she sprawls across Hazel's lap. She grabs her mother's shirt and lets out a whine.

"You just ate!" Hazel says, frowning. Timber reaches again, pinching Hazel's breast. "Oh fine." She settles Timber against her to feed.

"So how was the Alpha Counsel yesterday?" I ask, looking between Hazel and Ember. My understanding is limited, and Cedar doesn't care for politics, but the annual meeting of all the local packs' Alphas seems to be a serious event.

"It was fine until Zephyr started simping over my mom in front of everyone." Ember sticks her tongue out and pretends to gag.

Hazel barks out a laugh. "I'm sorry you have to deal with her, but you have to admit she's far more tame than before."

Cedar has told me about Ember fighting to become Alpha after her mother was deposed in a mutiny. It sounded like a bloody affair.

"I can't believe her," Ember says, crossing her arms and slouching back into the sofa cushion.

"Alright, that's enough politics for girls' night!" The room relaxes as the stressful topic is dismissed.

"So what kind of trouble should we get into tonight?" I ask, grinning.

"I have a few ideas," Marigold says, her own smile widening.

An hour later, we're breaking into Crickett's kitchen to steal snacks. Well, we use Hazel's key, so it's not exactly breaking and entering. Marigold keeps laughing uncontrollably, but Hazel wears Timber in a carrier over her chest so her hands are free to grab Marigold and cover her mouth.

Ember pushes the door open and slips inside. I'm right behind her, leveraging the door wider to fit my curves. Hazel and Marigold follow, but we all stop right inside the door.

The front of the diner might be dark, but we failed to notice the kitchen light on.

"What the hell are you guys doing?" Crickett asks. She stands with her hands on her hips, her apron smudged with red.

"What are you doing?" Hazel asks. Marigold breaks into a round of giggles.

"Making my red sauce," she says, scowling as she turns back into the kitchen.

"Sorry, can we help?" Marigold chokes out.

Crickett turns back and narrows her eyes. "Alright, get in here."

She puts us to work chopping tomatoes, mincing garlic, and washing fresh herbs. Hazel stands in the corner and sways to keep Timber sleeping.

We're still cooking when the boys find us. Jasper comes in first, a charming smile softening his features when he sees his partner with tomato guts on the apron that hangs over her belly. Slate is next, and he goes to Hazel silently, kissing her soundly before peering down at his daughter.

"We're going to bed. Good night!" Hazel calls, following her mate out.

"Good, clear out my kitchen," Crickett says, shooing us out.

"Can I stay?" Ember asks, crossing her arms defiantly.

Crickett softens. "Of course. Here, check on the caramelizing onions, will you?"

We leave them to cook, following Jasper and Marigold out of the diner's kitchen and down the metal steps.

"How did you guys end up cooking in the diner during girls' night?" Cedar asks quietly.

Shrugging, I wrap my hand around his arm. "No clue. We were trying to pilfer snacks. You know how I get without enough snacks."

He looks down at me, his expression analytical. Without warning, he scoops me up.

"I can walk!"

"But I like holding you," he says.

We pass the skeletal structure of our new cabin and head into the trailer we still occupy. "Did you check the art show?" he asks, setting me on our bed.

My mouth falls open. How could I overlook my show tonight? It's my third one since moving, and each one was bigger than the last. Nerves churn in my stomach until I'm nauseous. "I can't believe I forgot."

He hands me our shared laptop and I log into the online bidding system. Scrolling through, I pause when we reach my pieces. "Holy shit!"

Cedar peers over my shoulder. "Your work is the best thing in that gallery. I bet the price gets even higher."

"Either way, this is incredible." I blink at the screen. Jarrod wasn't kidding when he said he could sell my work for triple, but this is way more than triple.

"You deserve it," Cedar says, his hand lingering on the top of the laptop screen. Taking my hands off the keyboard, I allow him to close it. He sets it aside before leaning over me and placing a kiss on my cheek, and then one on the corner of my mouth. I turn, seeking his lips with my own.

"My beautiful mate," he growls, moving his mouth to my throat and licking over the claim mark. My hand goes to his jaw, tilting his head so I can get a good look at the magical tattoo I accidentally manifested across his skin. It's grown over the last few months, the vine dripping down over his collarbone. I don't mean to push any magic into him, but it tends to happen when we are intimate.

Hungry to see more, I tug his shirt off. My fingers trail over the mark, and then down over his newest tattoos. Splashes of watercolor cover his pec, swirling down to connect with the botanicals inked across his ribs.

His hand goes to my hip, his thumb rubbing over the tattoo of his paw print that Slate applied a week after we moved in together.

"I love you," I say, smiling at his glowing dusty blue eyes.

"Me too," he says, lifting the edge of my shirt. I raise my arms, allowing him to strip it off.

"Show me."

His touch ignites a burning low in my stomach, stoking the buzz of my magic. The forest around the trailer is growing out of control, but I can't help it. As he lays me back and strips me bare, I release some of it through the trailer and into the grass and brush around us, spreading it as wide as I can to temper the results.

"That feels good," he murmurs, reacting to the sensation of my magic through our bond. The last of the excess magic drains out of me, leaving gaping desire. Feeling my need through our bond as strongly as my magic, Cedar's movements become frenzied as we come together. His utter devotion leaves me breathless.

When we both are satiated and exhausted, he curls his arm around my belly protectively. Sleep tugs at me, but his profile is beautiful bathed in moonlight, I can't help but sit up and grab the little sketchbook I keep in my bedside table.

Portraits have never been my thing, but drawing Cedar is different. The line of his jaw, the slope of his nose, the curve of his lips are as fascinating to me as any landscape.

He stirs, those beautiful gray-blue eyes opening and focusing on me. "You need sleep too," he murmurs, slipping his arm around my hips and pulling me down the bed and against him.

"Fine. But you're sitting for another painting soon."

His laugh is hoarse. "Sure."

Satisfied, I tuck the sketchbook and pencil back into my drawer and cuddle up against him. His heat soaks into me, relaxing my body and mind. The soft sounds of nature mingle with his steady breaths until I'm lulled into deep sleep.

SNOWDRIFTS
AND
SOUL MATES

PROLOGUE

VALE

Scouting doesn't typically end in bloodshed, but you never know. It was my fault, I was rushing in my excitement for the inter-pack gathering tonight. My dark wolf blends into the shadows, so I'm often assigned patrols at night. Thankfully, not tonight. It's my first chance to attend one of these parties, and I'm curious about the wolf shifters from our neighboring packs.

Our pack's healer, Sable, stands with her hands on her hips, clicking her tongue as her apprentice, Indigo, applies butterfly bandages to the nasty cut running down the inside of my forearm. One clumsy moment and I lost my footing, paws slipping on damp rocks. I hadn't realized how bad the injury was until I shifted back.

Indigo presses a third bandage down on the bottom edge of the cut, holding the skin tight with his other hand. Auburn hair falls over his eyes and he shakes his head to clear his vision. "That should do it," he says. Releasing me, he turns to Sable with a hopeful expression. She scrutinizes the work and then nods curtly.

"Thanks, man," I say, twisting my wrist and flexing my hand. The salve he applied took away almost all of the pain and stopped the bleeding, so I am good to go.

"You need to watch your paws," Sable lectures. "I'm tired of seeing you in here." Lines crease her stern face as she scowls at me.

"I wouldn't want you to miss me," I say, trying to make my smile charming as I push off the exam table and stand.

The door swings open and a younger packmate breezes in, bringing the scent of strawberries in her wake - Briar, the youngest daughter of our Delta, or Trainer. Her dark blonde hair is twisted into a messy knot high on her head, tendrils framing her face as she regards me. "Get in a fight with a grizzly bear?"

"Nope, just clumsy," I say, shaking my head. She shrugs.

Indigo looks over his shoulder from where he scrubs his hands. "I'm done for the day. Are you ready to go, Bri?"

"Are you going to the pack gathering?" I ask, frowning.

"Yup, Indie managed to convince Marigold to bring us, since apparently some of the other packs are bringing some teens," Briar says, grinning. It must be nice to have a sister who is mated to the Beta and best friends with the Alphas. Not for the first time, I'm reminded of my stark lack of family in this pack, or anywhere. But in the years since I showed up as a scrawny teenager, the Bracken Creek Pack has been nothing but kind and caring.

"Are you coming?" Indigo asks as he puts away the box of bandages and the jars of salve he used on my injury.

"Yeah."

"We should drive together!" Briar says. "I don't want to show up with my grumpy brothers." Indigo chuckles, and she scrunches her nose at him. "Or your sister either. Marigold and Jasper still can't keep their hands off each other."

Sighing, I scratch the back of my head. "Sure. I'll meet you at the trucks in twenty minutes. I need to change."

"Sure!" Briar bounces out, tugging Indigo along with her and chattering about her day helping his sister with the class of young wolf shifters. I watch them ahead of me as I walk through the garden. They're both on the cusp of adulthood, figuring out what role they'll play in the pack they were born into. In a few years, they'll be mated, probably to each other, and have their own homes, maybe have a few pups. I pretend I don't want that, but I do. Unfortunately, there is a lack of options for me in this pack. If I'm honest, it's why I want to attend the inter-pack gathering.

My little trailer cabin sits past Crickett's Diner on the southeastern edge of the pack's compound. After cleaning myself up and changing into a nicer outfit, I'm ready to go. Anxiety bubbles up in my stomach as I cross the meadow to the little dirt lot by the Alpha's offices. Briar and Indigo stand by my truck, jostling each other and laughing over some private joke.

"Get in," I say, sliding into the drivers seat and grabbing the key from atop the visor. Valley Pack is hosting, and they're the closest of our neighbors, so five minutes later we park along the road and pile out. Some shifters run and shift there, but most drive so they can bring coolers - and so they don't have to limit their clothing options.

Music pours from speakers sitting on the porch of the Alpha's house, and a crowd of young shifters mingle and dance. A few faces are familiar. Alphas Hazel and Slate stand to one side, Slate's arms around her middle protectively. Beside them, Slate's brother Jasper, their Beta, has his hands on Marigold, Indigo's older sister. Blonde curls spill over her shoulders as she laughs at whatever's being said. Briar's twin brothers round out their group, one telling the jokes and the other quietly observing.

Briar pulls Indigo away through the crowd, and soon the two friends are dancing awkwardly, Briar hopping on her feet while Indigo watches her with hearts in his eyes. I scan for anyone else I know, but there's no one.

Sliding a hand into my pocket in an attempt to look casual, I head over to the drinks. No one would stop me from grabbing something alcoholic, but I'm too much of a ruler follower for that. As I reach for a bottle of cola, a girl reaches for the same one. Delicate fingers end in black polish. Long, dark hair falls around a pale face with delicate features and huge, expressive eyes.

"Sorry, go ahead," I say, gesturing to her.

She pulls back, pressing her hand to her chest. "No, sorry, it's all yours. I'm good." She's so adorable, I can't help but smile. Instead of taking the bottle, I dig through the ice until I find a second one, and then pick both up and offer her one.

"Oh, thanks," she says, flustered. I wait for her to walk away, but she doesn't. We stare at each other for a moment. "I'm Azalea," she says, "but I go by Lea."

"Lea," I repeat. "I'm Vale." I hold out my hand without thinking, and she giggles as she takes it. The awkwardness of the moment falls away as her skin brushes mine. I need to know this girl. "What pack are you from?"

"Oh, Raven Pack." She tucks hair behind her ears and I admire a tiny, gold ear cuff. "You're Bracken Creek Pack?"

"Yeah," I say.

We wander together, chatting about our packs and our lives. She's an only child to a single mom, niece of Alpha Nyx. She likes computers and is apprenticing in the Alpha's office. I tell her about being a scout, joining the pack a few years ago. She's easy to talk to, and I'm fascinated by everything she tells me. She's stunning, and I'm a goner.

SIX YEARS LATER

I
SCANDAL AND
A SAFE HOUSE

LEA

Ironcrest Pack is larger than Raven Pack. As my mother pulls her car into their sprawling parking lot, she sings its praises, which is odd considering a few years ago, Ironcrest tried to invade our pack. And my mother is the queen of holding grudges.

A group of Ironcrest wolves meet us and greet my mother respectfully. I am ignored, but that's for the best. My mother, Gamma of the Raven Pack, visits other packs regularly, but she doesn't typically drag me along. Arms crossed, I follow the group into a nearby meeting room.

More Ironcrest pack members wait inside and I tune out the conversation as my mother graciously greets them. I can feel their eyes crawling over me, so I turn away to stare out the window.

"Azalea," my mother says. Her tone is sugary sweet and it sets off warning bells.

"It's Lea," I correct automatically.

She ignores me. "I'm delighted to introduce your mate. Negotiations are done, and as the niece of the Alpha..." she keeps talking, but I'm stuck on the first sentence. My mate? Did I just have an auditory hallucination?

A stranger steps forward. He's older than me and handsome, but it doesn't matter. I'm not looking for a mate, especially not an arranged relationship.

"What?" I say, interrupting my mother. She gives me a sharp look.

"We are so glad to welcome the niece of the Alpha," another woman says. "Relations between the Raven Pack and Ironcrest Pack will be strengthened by this union."

"I don't think so," I say, frowning.

"Azalea," my mother says, warning in her voice. "It is agreed. Show your gratitude at this wonderful opportunity to serve your pack and receive a strong mate."

My mouth hangs open. She is trading me for political gain. Blinking, I expect the image to change. There is no way this is happening.

The man steps closer. "Azalea," he says, and my name sounds wrong from his lips.

"Give me a moment," I say, heading for the door. It slams behind me, the sound jolting me. Storm clouds roll across the sky, matching the turmoil in my head.

My mother follows me out, hissing, "Get back in there. You have a responsibility., and at twenty-five, you should be grateful they were still willing to take you."

"Do I have a choice?" I ask, my arms falling to my side.

"No." She raises her nose, looking down at me. The prideful smirk turns my stomach. "I packed some things for you. You are staying here with your new mate."

The door opens again and a few of the Ironcrest wolves step out, watching me warily.

"You'll apologize, greet him properly, and smile, Azalea."

"Lea," I argue. My nails dig into my palms as I look between those present, the pain anchoring me. This is why she refused to tell me why we were visiting Ironcrest. She knew I wouldn't agree, but if she's counting on my cooperation now because of the audience, she is seriously mistaken.

"Now," she presses.

"I can't." This is insane. Turning away, I march toward the car. But I don't have the key. Crap.

"Azalea," a man calls after me. "Lea!" My intended? Absolutely-fucking-not. "Stop!" That sounds like a good reason to not stop.

Breaking into a run, I look wildly for some escape. More voices call my name and I have to get out of here. My hands grapple with my shirt, tugging it over my head and tossing it to the ground. Shoving my pants down, I leap forward and land on four paws, my silvery gray fur ruffling as I burst into a run.

It's freezing, but my thick coat protects me. I turn west, heading to my pack, but as I hear other wolves take up chase, I know there is no sanctuary there. I need more time to think. Heading for the dense forest, I turn south and dart forward, speeding as fast as I can and hoping they lose my trail. Snow flurries around me, covering my tracks, and if I'm lucky, that will be enough.

My paws churn up the fresh powder, my tail whipping behind me as the ground slopes gradually downward. The animal brain has taken over, racing forward with one objective: escape. My life was already suffocating me, but this new demand is intolerable - my breaking point. I can't remember the last time I felt happy, but as I crest a hill and the earth falls away in a sharp descent, a sense of elation explodes in my chest. My paws stumble and it's all I can do to stay upright as I hurdle down the slope. I'm finally doing something selfish and it feels so good, even as my muscles burn.

Ahead, the stream stretches wide and shallow. Slowing, I leap to the closest rock. Balancing carefully, I leap to the next one, but it's slick with moss and water, and I teeter for a few seconds. Instead of falling, I push off and attempt to leap for the next one. My paws slip, denying me traction, and I fall short.

My legs and chest hit the water, icy cold flooding my veins. The shock has me gasping and twisting my head back to keep from submerging entirely, smacking a rock in the process. I scramble to get my paws under me, but the motion wrenches my back leg. Whimpering, I twist to see it's wedged between rocks. The pain sucks the air from my lungs.

I shift back to human, icy water running over my bare legs as I push to my knees and reach back, trying to shove the rock aside and free my ankle. My hands are numb and shaking, and pain screams through me, whiting out my vision. Gritting my teeth, I tug myself free.

Vision blurring, I curl over my leg. Blood washes away in the stream as my ankle begins to swell. I know it's bad, but I can't stop. Snarling, I push myself up and limp toward the shore. If I'm going to be captured, at least it won't be in Ironcrest territory.

As the cold water numbs my ankle, the pain in my head flares. Flinching, I raise a hand to touch at the side of my head. A tender spot screams in pain when I touch it, causing me to double over. The move sends sharp pain shooting through my ankle, as I lean weight on it to try and stay standing.

Trying to straighten, my head throbs and I fall to my hands and knees, a low whimper coming from my throat. This is the worst pain I've ever experienced - my ankle feels like someone took a hammer to it, and the headache is compounding it, making it impossible to think clearly. Exhaling, I push back up, only to fall again. I'm only halfway across the stream. It's so cold, I'm shaking, shivers wracking my entire body, sending stabs of headache through my skull and down my neck. My numb hands slip over the rocks as I try to pull myself up. Everything goes black, but I fight to stay conscious. I am not going to die here in the snow in the middle of a stream less than a foot deep. I should call for help from my pursuers, but I can't. I won't.

BRI

Snow crunches under my paws. Ugh. We should have finished our patrol already, but Indie heard something to the north, so we circled back. One more pass along the border and we could go home and cozy up for the impending snowstorm.

My sensitive nose catches a whiff of someone from Raven Pack. It's familiar, but I can't place it. Indie glances back and cocks his head, the tan fur along his ruff shaking as he slows his pace.

Following my nose, we trot along the treeline. The scent of damp leaves and mud overwhelms the scent, but I know we're close. A shock of pale skin and dark hair comes into view, and I dart forward.

Lea, a friend from Raven Pack, is stretched out in the water. Eyes closed, her head and shoulders lay across the muddy bank, her hips and legs in the rushing water. Her ankle looks like someone blew up a balloon inside of it, blood weeping from the scrapes as purple bruises bloom across every inch of skin. I nose her hand and get no reaction. Indie circles to her face and touches his nose to her neck, searching for a pulse. He looks up, nodding. She's alive.

Bowing forward, I tug the bag strapped to my pack. It contains two outfits for restocking our clothing stashes. Indie shifts back and takes Lea under the arms, dragging her out of the water and laying her over the thick grass growing along the creek.

For a second, I have to focus on my humanity, and magic shivers over me until fur vanishes and I'm crouching on two feet. Hands shaking, I unzip the back and tug out clothes. Snow dusts the fabric within seconds. Biting my lip, I look up. The storm is coming in fast. "I don't think we can make it back on foot. There's no way she can walk, even if she wakes up."

"What about the safe house?" Indie asks.

Nodding, I step closer, holding out a shirt. "Yeah, it's close, I think. That's our best bet. We can get her there and one of us can go for help."

Indie shakes his head at the offered clothing. "Help me dress her." He glances down at her swollen, bloody ankle. "Probably just a shirt. Give her the bigger one."

"That way, you can wear pants and you won't be walking through the woods naked," I joke weakly. Together we tug the shirt over her arms and head. I support her head while Indie pulls on the pants, and then I dress in the second outfit.

Goosebumps cover Indie's arms as he scoops Lea up. "Lead the way."

Chewing my lip, I check the location of the sun and turn in a circle, relying on my natural sense of direction in the absence of a cell phone. "Not far, I think. Let's head southeast." Indie nods and pushes forward. Snow clings to his hair and shoulders and I brush it away the best I can.

"You should shift. There's no reason for both of us to be barefoot and freezing," Indie says, his words tight, not in anger but in discomfort.

"I'm not letting you suffer alone," I say, grinning. "What kind of best friend would that make me?" No way I'm leaving him to haul her dead weight all on his own. Moral support and all.

The cabin appears through the trees. We close the distance, my feet numb and calves stinging. With shaking hands, I input the code and shove the door open. Indie ducks sideways, carrying Lea in without smacking her head or feet on the doorframe. He pauses in the tiny living room, looking between the three doors.

"Left is the bathroom. Pick a bedroom, doesn't matter," I say, with an exhausted laugh. He disappears into the middle bedroom.

The stove in the corner is already full of kindling, stacked and ready to light. Grabbing a match from the shelf beside it, I strike it and toss it into the center. Scrunched up paper catches, followed by the thinnest kindling. Warmth creeps into the room. Sighing in relief, I turn to look for the radio.

"Bingo!" The battery-powered unit rests on a table in the corner. I didn't pay close attention when we were trained on these, but it seems easy enough. Holding down the button, I say, "Hello? Anyone there?"

Nothing happens.

Scowling, I look at the device and flip a switch. The screen glows and I try holding the button down again. "Anyone there? We're at the northeastern safe house."

"Who is this?" a familiar voice crackles through the line. Vale. Of everyone that could have been on duty, it had to be him. He isn't going to like this one bit.

"Vale! It's Bri. Indie and I were on patrol."

"Are you okay?" His question breaks off, disrupted by the growing storm outside.

"We are fine but we found someone." I hesitate. Here we go.

"Yes?" The word is sharp.

"It was Lea."

There is a beat of silence and I imagine his head blowing up. His voice is cold and measured when he responds, and that is so much worse than a snappy, irritated Vale. "What do you mean *found* her?"

"She was laying in the creek with a twisted ankle. Don't worry, I'm sure Indie can fix her right up, but she passed out so… yeah."

"She passed out?" Each word seethes and my heart leaps into my throat. That's about the reaction I expected.

"Yeah, she's gonna be fine. We are safe, warm, we have a first aid kit and a healer. I will keep you updated."

"The storm will knock out the radio soon. It's bad. Make sure you have enough wood because you won't be able to get more in an hour or so."

"Okay," I answer, drawing the word out into a question.

"Just stay put. Take care of her."

"Fine," I say. I'm not arguing with Vale when it comes to Lea.

Indie emerges from the bedroom, and I spy Lea on the bed with a blanket over her pulled up to her pale chin. "How is she?" I ask.

"Better than I expected, considering, but we need to get ice to get the swelling down," Indie says, his blue-green eyes darkening as the light in the room dims. It's not only the sun going down. The storm is rapidly becoming a blizzard.

"I don't think there is a fridge. Just the wood stove and the bathroom sink."

"Put some snow in a plastic bag. There should be zip closure ones in the emergency food bins." Indie pulls the cover back from her feet and frowns.

Hopping up, I head out of the room and follow his instructions, returning with a bag of snow. Indie lays it over the ankle gingerly.

"Do you think it's broken?"

He shakes his head. "Not that I can tell, but there's no way to know until the swelling goes down."

I study her pale cheeks. "When will she wake up?"

His mouth twists into a wry smile. "Geez, Bri, I don't know everything."

"Could have fooled me," I quip, gathering my hair and twisting it into a bun that unravels down my back when I release it. Indie watches me with that smile lingering. "What?"

"Nothing," he says, shrugging. "Let's go wait out there instead of standing around her bed all creepy." I have to cover my mouth to smother my giggle. He leads the way, and I tuck under his arm, letting him squeeze me against his ribs. He's the perfect height, two or three inches taller than me. We settle onto the solitary sofa and I rest my head on his shoulder.

"You got a hold of someone?" He asks, resting his cheek against the top of my head.

"Yup. Vale answered. He told me to stay here, so someone will probably come help in the morning when the storm breaks."

"So we're in for a long night," he says, almost a sigh. Wisps of my hair dance across my forehead with his breath.

"Not what you expected from agreeing to patrol with me?" I joke, tipping my chin up to grin at him.

"You owe me," he mutters. Rolling my eyes, I nestle against him for warmth.

II
SOUP BOWLS AND EX-BOYFRIENDS

LEA

Alertness comes back slowly, fading in and out, along with an aching pain. I can't remember why, but it's important that I get away. I need to hide and find shelter so I can make a plan. As that goal solidifies in my mind, I grab onto consciousness and drag myself from the depths of sleep.

A bang sounds, and I squint, trying to focus on my surroundings. It's a tiny bedroom in a cabin, and someone has put a shirt on me, though my legs are covered by only a blanket. I was naked when I fell, so that makes sense. Is this my new Intended's home in Ironcrest? No, it doesn't smell like Ironcrest. It smells like... familiar people... but I can't quite recall faces to go with the scent.

"Where is she?" I know that voice and it sounds angry. No way he is here.

The door swings open and Vale stands there, framed with flickering firelight that blazes across my eyes after waking in darkness. His chest is bare, and his hands tie the string of the sweatpants hanging on his hips. He seems bigger than I remember. His tall, thin frame holds new muscle that flexes as he crosses the room to loom over me.

"Vale," I say, my voice scratchy. Clearing it, I raise my chin which sends a dull ache through my head. "I didn't expect to see you here."

"What happened?" he asks, and I flinch at the cold fury in his tone. His eyes flare at my reaction, and he takes a deep breath. "Sorry, Lea. It's *upsetting* to see you injured." Each word seems to strain him. "Can you tell me what happened?"

My ankle screams at me as I push myself up and slide back to rest against the headboard. Wincing, I close my eyes and breathe in through my nose and out through my mouth as the pain fades. Vale is unmoving, glaring at my ankle like it personally offended him.

"Well, I fell and twisted my ankle." I nervously tuck the covers around my waist, trying to hide the fact I'm half-naked with my ex-boyfriend in the room. "But I'm not sure how I got here."

"Patrol found you and brought you here." He crosses his arms and leans against the door frame, his eyes still on my leg. It's starting to irritate me.

"Where is here?" My tone is insolent, but I can't help it. His eyes finally flick up to meet mine, and my lungs seize at the intensity there.

"A safe house for emergencies, such as the snowstorm we are currently experiencing." His arms tense, like he wants to come closer, but he stays firmly against the doorframe.

"Oh."

"Why were you in our territory?" His tone is neutral and it scares me. Am I actually in trouble? Technically, I broke shifter etiquette, but considering the circumstances... I was seeking refuge, I suppose. But he doesn't know any of this.

Drawing in a breath, I try to think what to tell him. Vale knows me too well. I can't lie to him. "I was in Ironcrest. My mother surprised me by arranging a mate for me."

He stares. Clearly this wasn't the answer he expected. Tipping his head back, he closes his eyes briefly. "So you have a mate now? How did you end up in the creek?"

I cringe. It seems he knows all the embarrassing details.

"After she informed me of the deal she made, I sorta ran away."

His eyebrows rise. "From Ironcrest and your mate?"

"Not my mate. I don't even know his name. The second I knew what was happening, I got the hell out of there."

"Will they come looking for you?" His voice is a growl that rolls over my skin, leaving a trail of goosebumps.

My hair flies as I shake my head emphatically. "Not until after the storm, I hope."

"Did *you* make any promises or agreements?" Each word is precise.

"No." I meet his anger with my own, eyes narrowing and lip curling.

For a long moment, he stares me down, dominant and demanding. He's different than I remember. His eyes are black in the dim room, holding me captive. He is no longer the slim, sweet boy that I fell for as a teenager. This man's dark hair has grown longer, curling over his temples and ears. The line of his mouth twists into a dignified frown.

Two figures fill the doorway behind him, a familiar heart-shaped face with long, dirty-blonde hair, and a taller man with a mop of reddish brown hair, millions of freckles, and an easy smile.

"Hey, guys," I say lamely. "Are you the ones who found me?"

Bri pushes past Vale, perching on the edge of the bed. "Sure did! You seemed to be in bad shape." She reaches out and twists a knob on a battery operated lantern, casting the room in a golden light.

"I appreciate the assist. Taking a swim in the creek during a blizzard is a bad idea, apparently," I joke. They smile politely. "So what's the plan? Wait out the storm and then send me on my way?"

"I don't know," Vale says. "We'll have to see how you're doing. But yes, I think we are all stuck here for the night, and it's getting late."

"We should see about some dinner," Indie says, rubbing his arms.

"Good idea," Vale says. "Lea, don't even think about getting up until the swelling goes down and we can wrap it up properly."

"Yes, sir," I mutter. He freezes, a rosy tinge to his ears. I would laugh if I wasn't in so much pain. Big, scary grown-up Vale isn't entirely immune to me.

"Come on, Indie, let's find some food," Bri says, grabbing his arm and pulling him from the room.

Alone again, Vale stares at me. The last time we were alone, I dumped him. The memory replays in excruciating detail - a track I watch often enough that guilt eats through me like acid. He may be having the same thoughts, because his brows furrow. Silence stretches until it's brittle, but we both stubbornly wait for the other to speak. It lasts until Bri returns with soup in a plastic bowl that I accept with a grateful smile. Vale mumbles something about leaving me to eat in peace, and then he's gone.

Disappointment unfurls in my gut, sour but comforting in its familiarity. But at least being here with my ex is better than getting claimed by some stranger back in Ironcrest. Even with the busted ankle taken into account.

INDIE

Bri peels away another can lid and plops the thick potato soup into the pot sitting atop the wood-burning stove. Aimlessly, I drag the ladle through the creamy soup as I listen for sounds from the bedroom. I don't mean to be nosy, but Vale seemed pissed and I'm dying to know what they're discussing. His dominance ramped up the moment I walked into the bedroom, obviously not wanting another male near her. I'm pretty sure he trusts me, but even so, I'm not looking forward to interacting with Lea again in his presence. I'm the healer here, so it's unavoidable. Hopefully, he will calm down once he sees that she is alright.

The door swings open wider and Vale stalks out, an angry scowl across his face. Bri holds up two more bowls and I ladle soup into them before offering one to Vale, who sinks into the armchair.

"Man, this tastes so good after being so freaking freezing," Bri murmurs, dragging her spoon out between her lips. I suspect she's still cold despite the fire so I wrap an arm around her shoulder and tuck her against my side. She sighs and I feel the slight motion against my ribs.

"So, what did you find out?" I ask quietly. Bri perks up, listening intently.

Vale shakes his head, disbelief written all over his face. "They tried to push her into an arranged mating."

"What? That makes no sense," Bri blurts.

"I had heard that Ironcrest was getting desperate, but this is surprising. Hazel and Ember won't like this one bit." Vale runs his hand through his hair, brushing it back from his forehead.

"You're right. Ember is going to be pissed," Bri adds. "She's worked so hard to get rid of the sexism in her pack's culture, but those ideas are ingrained in the older shifters." Her brother is mated to Ember, the Alpha of our neighboring pack to the northwest.

Our Alpha, Hazel, has done her best to help, and I know both of them will be outraged that Ironcrest is reverting back to the seventeenth century to solve their lack of females.

"How can we help her? She won't be able to walk for a few days." I ask.

"We can get help once the storm clears, and see what she wants to do at that point." Vale answers.

"Hazel and Slate will offer her sanctuary if she wants it. I mean, she could go anywhere," I say thoughtfully. Bri is staring at Vale, and I cock my head, trying to figure out why. There are wheels turning behind her eyes.

Vale sets the bowl on the small side table. "Okay, I'm exhausted. Running here through a blizzard really sucked. I'll take the sofa and you guys can fight over who gets the second bedroom."

"I'm not sleeping on the floor." Bri huffs, leaning heavily against my side.

"It's fine, I can," I say. "I don't mind. I've slept on the floor when we were attending patients overnight."

Bri shakes her head. "No way. We can share. It's plenty big, and we've taken naps together in hammocks and sofas. This is no different." She ducks under my arm so she can lean back and scowl at me.

A glance at Vale shows he is lost in his thoughts. I guess Bri has a point. "Are you sure?" I ask, my hand resting on her knee.

"Totally. Come on, let's go wrestle up more blankets. I have a feeling we are going to need them. She seizes my arm, wrapping her hands around my bicep and dragging me up when she stands. She bounces over to the cabinets, tugging blankets down so they land over her head. Chuckling, I gather them up. She turns, one draped over her hair and shoulders like a cloak. "Ready, snuggle buddy?"

She flounces off to give Lea and Vale blankets and I stand there clutching the last two, my mind stuck on her request to share a bed paired with the term *snuggle*. She may think it's no different, but I have to disagree. By the time I gather myself and turn to help, Vale has an arm thrown over his eyes as he lies stretched across the sofa covered in a single blanket. He has the warmth of the stove, so it's probably sufficient.

"Come on, I won't bite," Bri teases, glancing over her shoulder at me as she heads into the second bedroom. I carry our two extra blankets in. She hops on the bed and pulls the covers back so she can nestle under them.

After laying out our blankets, I follow her example and slide under the coverlet. We're both dressed in our oversized t-shirts and sweatpants, standard pack attire, but it feels like not enough fabric between us. My skin heats and I jolt when bare toes nudge against my calves.

"Bri, your feet are freezing," I whisper.

"Sorry," she mutters, her smile suggesting she isn't remotely sorry. She pulls the blanket tighter around her, but after a few minutes of silence, she exhales harshly. "It's so cold. The stove isn't cutting it. I feel like I'm going to die." Her teeth chatter to accentuate her point.

"Come here," I mutter, my irritation sounding shallow. It's not exasperation causing me to look away from her big blue eyes, but a brittle sense of losing my balance, teetering on the edge of a fall. Bri feels no such reservations and scoots closer until she's curled against my ribs. Her hands tuck under her chin. I want to turn on my side and wrap my arms around her to share as much heat as possible and ease her discomfort, but I stay flat on my back and stiff. Even so, she sighs contentedly and stills.

A tangle of dark blonde hair lies over the covers, her face tucked into my bicep with only a pink sliver of cheekbone and dark lashes showing. She wiggles, the icy tip of her nose rubbing against my skin.

"You really are a popsicle," I joke, my voice rough.

"And you're nice and warm. Help a girl out," she says, turning and seizing my arm and dragging it under her head until she can rest her cheek on my chest and my arm cradles her. Staring at the dark ceiling, I try to ignore the feel of her thin shirt as I press that hand against the curve of her back.

The soft, happy noise she makes is some sort of sweet torture. I'd do anything for her. She's my best friend, after all. When we were teenagers, for a while I hoped it would turn into more, but it never did. Regardless, this friendship is my most treasured relationship so I have no complaints. Her sweet strawberry scent fills my lungs as I rest my chin against the top of her head and finally close my eyes.

III
SPIN THE BOTTLE
VALE

Morning brings the same nervous energy that plagued me all night. Lea sleeps quietly in the nearer bedroom, and soft noises tell me that Briar and Indigo are finally getting up. I stir my instant coffee and take a bitter sip.

Hopefully we can get home today, though Briar and Indigo will have to go for help. Lea won't be able to walk for at least a couple of days, even with her accelerated shifter healing, and I'm not willing to carry her the dozen or so miles back through the snow barefoot. Perhaps we should have stocked boots in the cabin. Something to note for Hazel and Slate.

The door opens and Briar emerges. Her fingers drag through her long hair, untangling the mess of sleep. She moves to the stove, checking on the fire that is keeping us warm, but I've already added wood to it.

"Good morning," she says quietly, eyeing my coffee as she rubs her hands together. "Indie is still asleep."

"I bet he's tired," I mutter. Knowing Indigo, he probably laid awake half the night with Briar sleeping beside him. She seems well rested at least, her eyes bright and mouth curving into a small smile.

"Was the couch alright?" she asks, reaching for the pot to make herself a coffee. I hand her a packet that she shakes violently before tearing it open and adding it to her cup.

"Fine," I say, my attention already on the door to Lea's room. I thought I heard something, but it may have been her rolling over in her sleep or even a noise outside of the cabin. Another rustling noise comes from the closed door and I tense.

The door swings open and Lea balances against the doorframe, standing on one foot with a look of determination. Her eyes narrow when she sees me rise. "I'm fine," she snaps, "Just using the bathroom."

She takes a hop and reaches for the bathroom door. I'm across the room before I can think, my arms closing around her waist as she pitches forward. A collection of curses hiss from her lips as she's unable to pull herself back up and is forced to lean on me.

"Let me go," she says, her teeth gritted, shortening the words.

"I'll help you into the bathroom. There's nothing wrong with accepting help."

"I didn't ask."

"Would you rather I let you fall on your face?" I say, tightening my hold around her waist and supporting most of her weight.

"Yes," she growls, and I roll my eyes. Careful of her ankle, I half-carry and half-drag her into the bathroom until she can grip the sink and the edge of the toilet. She glares at me. "This is so humiliating."

"Don't worry about it," I say, heading to the door. "At least I wasn't the one who found you passed out and naked in a snowy creek." I close the door behind me. Turning, I freeze, listening to her soft grunts of effort as she maneuvers herself and sits down to pee.

Briar's eyebrows arch as she watches me. "What?" I hiss.

"You guys are cute." She smiles, taking a sip of coffee as she watches me over the rim of her cup.

Before I can argue, a loud thud comes from the bathroom followed by a string of curses. Privacy be damned, I'm not letting her get hurt worse. Twisting the handle, I step into the bathroom to find Lea with her bare ass on the carpet. Her shirt falls low, covering most of her while her sweatpants pool over her shins.

"Seriously? Get out!" She waves her arm, and I almost obey, but pain is written in every line of her beautiful face.

"Lea," I say. She bares her teeth at me - no, she's in agony, her ankle bent to the side. Without hesitation, I drop to my knees and stabilize her injured leg. Her next breath is slower and her face relaxes. Now I'm the tense one with my hands on her knee and calf when her pants are around her ankles. She pushes herself to sit up fully and I'm able to cautiously release her. As she moves, I see purple bruising dotted up her outer thigh.

"What happened?" I ask, my voice dropping low, my fingers skimming over the marks.

"What?" she asks, clearly focused on pulling herself up.

662

I take her hand to stop her from grabbing the sink. "Let me carry you, please. Now, how did you get those bruises?"

"Oh, probably falling when I busted my ankle," she muses, unconcerned as she turns her attention to dressing herself. "Look away, please," she commands and I comply. She has to lay back on the ground and push her hips up with her one good foot in order to tug the sweats on.

"Better. Now I can probably manage…" she starts to say. Scoffing, I scoop one arm under her knees and another behind her back to lift her against my chest. Her warm weight is familiar, sending me back half a decade in time. I was a different person back then, and I suspect so was she.

"Take me to the sofa. I'm bored in the bedroom and it's cold." she says. "Oh, I want some coffee too."

"Are you sure? It's pretty terrible," Briar says, grinning. She makes up another cup and hands it over. Lea takes a deep breath of the steam and smiles. That unguarded curve of her lips hits me in the chest and I look away, rubbing at my sternum absently.

"Morning," Indigo says, throwing his hand over his mouth as he yawns and stumbles to the sofa, plopping down on Briar's other side. His reddish brown hair stands on end, sticking out to the side. Briar reaches up and runs her nails through it, calming some of the wildness. He leans into her touch.

"I think there's oatmeal for breakfast," she says. "Sound good?"

"Sure," Lea answers.

My chest continues to ache as I watch her, so I busy myself with heating more water and making our breakfast. We eat quietly, but as Lea finishes her food, she purses her lips. "So, what's been going on the last few years? What's new?"

"Not much," Briar answers, stabbing her spoon into her remaining oatmeal. "Indie is healing people on his own now. Final stages of his apprenticeship." Pride fills her eyes as she leans her head on his shoulder.

"That's incredible," Lea says. "You'll be a full healer at, what, twenty-three?" Indigo nods. "What about you, Bri? Are you teaching?"

Briar shrugs. "That wasn't for me. I've been doing random jobs, but nothing has felt like a good fit."

"I'm sure you'll find the right position soon." She says it like a sure thing and Briar smiles back at her.

"What about you?" I ask.

Her expression cools and her eyes flash to me. "The same. Nothing new."

"Except being forced into an arranged mating," I say, my jaw ticking as I watch her reaction. Her lips thin and her lashes brush her cheekbones as she looks down.

"I think it stopped snowing," Indigo blurts, dissolving the tension. Everyone glances at the door, wondering. Bowls are set aside, and I approach the door. Taking a deep breath, I disengage the lock and tug it open. A wall of white blocks the light and sun.

"Holy snowdrift!" Briar joins me, gaping at the doorway.

Cold air rolls off the snow and a bit crumbles and falls at my feet. Grimacing, I shove the door closed and flip the lock.

Briar throws her hands up. "What do we do now?"

"Dig," I say dryly.

BRI

Vale leads the charge and the boys dive in. They try to avoid snow falling into the door, but it's unavoidable and soon a puddle of water forms. I use the two towels in the supply bins to sop it up, ringing them into the sink and then draping them over the arm of the chair nearest the stove.

After an hour, they give up. The sun shines through a two foot gap at the top, but I'm not exactly eager to get boosted up and shoved through that narrow space and then sink into four or five feet of snow. No, thank you.

Indigo and Vale shut the door and throw themselves down on the ground near the stove.

"How can I be this cold and sweating at the same time?" Indie says, using his shirt to wipe his neck. The movement reveals the bottom of his six-pack abs. I opened my mouth to respond, but it hangs open at the sight. When he looks up and catches my eye, he tilts his head curiously. Shaking my head to clear the image, I focus on making us some lunch.

"Hungry?" I hold up a bowl of instant macaroni and cheese. Vale takes one and passes another to Lea. Her leg is propped up across the cushions, so I settle on the floor beside the boys.

Indie takes his bowl, smiling that crooked smile I love. "Thanks."

Sighing, Lea stirs her pasta from her perch on the sofa. "I'm sorry you guys are stuck here with me. Not how you wanted to spend your weekend, is it?"

"This isn't your fault," Vale says sharply. When she stays silent, he turns to stare her down. Her lip drags through her teeth, but under his scrutiny, she nods in agreement.

I begin to reach to pat her leg but catch myself in time. "Don't worry about it. It's like a little vacation. In fact, if we are going to be stuck here another day, we should do something fun. We might as well enjoy ourselves."

Lea raises an eyebrow. "What did you have in mind?"

"Hazel insisted the cabin was stocked with some sort of entertainment, in case of this very situation. I'll see what I can dig up for us to do."

"Great," Vale says, rolling his eyes.

"Don't be a party pooper," I chide him.

He smirks, resting his temple against his fist as he turns to look at me. "Only you would make it into a party."

"I don't know, my sister would probably have decorated the cabin already and made everyone party hats," Indie mutters. A laugh escapes me. He's right, Marigold would make the best of it, and I'm determined to do the same.

"I appreciate your positivity," Lea adds, smiling sweetly at me. When her gaze moves to Vale, the smile changes. There's definitely still feelings there. I sensed it last night, but now the tension crackling between them is undeniable. It's been years since they broke up. Maybe this time together can give them closure… or maybe spark something back to life.

Indie washes out the bowls while I dig through the supply bins. A stack of books sits at the bottom, including crosswords, number puzzles, and those funny little stories with blanks to fill in.

"Look what I found!" I wave them in the air.

"What?" Lea asks, leaning to see the notepad. "Seriously?"

"Those are for kids," Vale mutters. He moves to the armchair and sips a cup of water, his eyes on Lea.

"Come on, it will be fun, especially with a bit of help." Grinning, I brandish the bottle of whisky I found tucked into the supplies. Unscrewing the top, I pour cups for Lea and Vale, plus a small one for myself. Taking a wip, I wince at the flavor.

"Want some?" I offer Indie, knowing he won't drink. He wrinkles his nose and shakes his head. Sighing, I sit against the sofa again, bumping my arm against his. He leans over to peek at the notebook. With a flourish, I pull the pencil from the spiral binder and turn the first page. "Alright, Lea, give me an adjective."

"Um, how about yellow?"

"Okay, yellow. Now a person, Indie?"

He scratches the back of his head, thinking. "How about Vale?"

"No," Vale groans, throwing his head back.

"Too late," I say, grinning. "But you can give me another adjective." He ignores me, but I press, "Come on, don't be the only one not playing."

"Stupid," he says, taking a swig of his drink.

"Very mature," I say, sticking my tongue out at him. "Now Indie, how about a place?"

My friends supply words and I giggle as I fill in the blanks, our cups steadily draining. Once it's complete, I clear my throat and brandish the notebook. "Ready? Here goes: It was a <u>Yellow</u> day, when the <u>Vale</u> decided to go to the <u>Stupid</u> <u>Cafe</u>. They visited the <u>Truck</u> and ate lots of <u>Foggy</u> <u>Strawberries</u>. Later, they were <u>Scared</u> so they went to <u>New York</u> and <u>Read</u>. They would always remember their <u>Fluffy</u> day."

Lea snorted, covering her mouth as she laughed. "That was ridiculous. Let's do another one." I waited for Vale to argue, but he has a small smile on his face as he watches Lea laugh. Oh, he definitely has feelings for her.

Two stories later, Lea winces as she shifts her weight, so Indie asks to examine her ankle. Vale hurries to get her a new ice pack, and I pull out the crosswords to keep us entertained until dinner. Already, my mind is spinning with ideas to make our evening interesting.

Dinner is canned chili. I enjoy the warmth in my belly as the cold creeps in. We add another log to the fire and check out the supply of firewood. It's good for at least three or four days, but hopefully we won't be stranded out here that long. Vale radios back, but it seems the entire pack is snowed in back at the compound.

The sun sinks below the treeline, plunging us into darkness, but no one seems ready to go to bed. We nurse a second cup of whisky, keeping that happy, tipsy buzz going. While the boys tidy up the dinner dishes, I gather up extra blankets and drag the chairs into place. Once Vale picks up Lea for a bathroom break, I grab the cushions from the sofa and toss my blankets over it.

"What is this?" Vale asks, standing in the doorway with Lea in his arms.

While he looks horrified, she grins. "Bri, did you make a fort?"

"Yup! Come into the snowy fortress!"

"I don't think…" Vale protests.

"Come on, you're twenty-six, not sixty. Get your ass in here," I tease, before dropping to my hands and knees. Feeling silly from the whisky, I wiggle my butt before crawling into my fort. Indie follows me, and his eyes are wide as saucers as he settles beside me. We squeeze against the sofa, making room as Lea crawls in. Vale comes after her, grumbling the whole way.

"Here, this will help," she says, grabbing the whisky bottle and topping off his cup. He scowls at her, and she tips his cup up with two fingers, giggling as he takes a sip while glaring at her.

Taking the bottle back from her, I set it on its side in the center. Now I have to hope everyone is relaxed enough to take a chance. Crossing my fingers, I announce, "Alright, we are playing spin the bottle."

Vale's eyes nearly pop out from his head, and Lea lets out a laugh.

"Bri, is that a good idea?" Indie asks softly.

"It's fine. What's a little peck between friends? And I'm guessing none of us got the chance to do this when we were younger, right? Vale was too busy being serious, I'm sure. So here is our chance to act like stupid teenagers again."

"I'm in," Lea says, a beautiful flush in her cheeks. "Why not? There's nothing else to do. It's too dark to do another crossword puzzle. Unless someone wants to start telling ghost stories, I say we do it."

"We can do that next," I say, winking.

Vale studies Lea and then nods. "Fine, but no pressure. Let's not make it weird." He frowns. "Even weirder."

"No promises," Lea chimes in.

INDIE

Bri's devious grin lights up the small space. Vale stares at the whisky bottle like it might bite him. Maybe he is right. With a little laugh, Bri gives it a spin. My breath catches as it spins and slows, passing me and coming to rest facing Vale. My heart drops.

He shakes his head, but Bri bounces up on her hands and knees and seizes his shirt, tugging him forward and planting a kiss on his cheek. "There, you survived," she says, sitting back.

"Unfortunately," Vale murmurs. "I'm going to need to drink more of this if I'm going to get through this." He twists the lid off and refills his cup.

"Share, please," Lea prods, holding out her own cup. He fills it. "Thanks. And don't forget, it's your turn." She grins into her cup as she takes a sip.

"Oh no," he groans. Covering his eyes, he tightens the cap and gives the bottle a spin, and it circles and circles, slowing until it stops with the top nearest to Lea. "Oh, no," he repeats.

"Am I that unkissable?" Lea asks, frowning at him, though her eyes sparkle.

"No!" Vale rushes to say. "You're beautiful." He blinks, his speech faltering. "It's just," he stops, unable to form thoughts. "Sorry." He leans toward her unconsciously while he mutters his apologies.

"Kiss! Kiss! Kiss!' Bri cheers, clapping.

Lea smirks and leans forward to meet him. Vale stays stiff and still as she places a peck on his cheek. "Well, that was life altering," she says sarcastically, sitting back. She grabs the bottle, giving it a spin. It slows and stops on Bri. I nearly choke.

Bri smiles and leans forward. Lea raises an eyebrow provocatively, her eyes on Vale, as she leans forward and kisses Bri on the lips. It's a quick peck, but I can't look away. Giggling, Bri grabs the bottle and twists it, sending it spinning. I haven't regained my senses when it stops on me.

Gaping at the bottle, I try to remember how to breathe, how to talk, anything but staring. Maybe I should grab the bottle off the floor and start drinking it, even though I don't drink. At least then I would have an excuse for gaping at her.

"Lay it on me," Bri says, squeezing her eyes shut and leaning toward me with her lips puckered. I blink. Her lashes flutter open. "Oh, come on. You can't possibly be scared."

"I'm not," I lie. I'm not scared of kissing her. I'm terrified of how much I want to. And that's not something a best friend should feel.

My mind flashes back to a memory, sitting in the meadow with our backs against a pine tree. Two fifteen-year-olds awkwardly pressing our lips together in an uncomfortable first kiss that had us laughing for weeks.

"It's not like it's the first time," she whispers. When my answer is to stare. She hasn't had any more whisky, and her eyes are clear. "Should I kiss someone else? You don't have to."

Not a chance. My hand shoots up, grabbing the back of her neck and pulling her to me. I should have kissed her cheek, but apparently I've lost my mind. Our mouths crash together, the feeling so unexpected I can't breathe. Her warm, soft lips slide against mine for a split second before I'm pushing away and covering my mouth. My breath comes in short pants.

"Sorry!" I splutter my apology, my face flaming.

Lea giggles. "Aw, you guys are cute, but your kissing needs work."

"Needs work?" Bri says, her voice pitching higher. "I'll have you know that was a life altering kiss. A kiss for the ages."

"We're just friends," I say at the same time, my words lifting at the end like it's become a question. Bri's eyes flash to mine and my blush deepens, my cheeks stinging with it.

"I mean, it's an important skill, I think," Lea says with a shrug. "Right, Vale?" Vale nods dumbly, but he would agree with anything she said.

Bri's eyes sparkle and her smirk returns. "Could we get a demonstration? Since you two have so much more practice and expertise?"

Lea throws back the rest of her whisky and slams the cup down. She waves to Vale in a sloppy invitation. "Let's show them how it's done."

"I think that whisky hit you pretty hard and it's time to go to bed," Vale says, moving to his knees to crawl out of their fort.

"A goodnight kiss then?" Lea asks, her shoulders shaking with silent laughter at Vale's horrified expression. "Fine, be that way." Sighing dramatically, she crawls out from under the blanket and allows him to scoop her up.

Bri grins, turning to press her forehead against my shoulder.

"So... what was that?" I whisper.

"They clearly still have feelings." Her eyes sparkle, her face flushed. She's loving playing matchmaker, but this is insanity. We're lucky it didn't blow up in our faces.

"You thought spin the bottle was the way to get them to realize it?"

She raises her face slowly, resting her chin on my shoulder until she's so close I can't turn my head without brushing our noses together. "I think it sorta worked. Do you have any better ideas? We can try something else tomorrow if this wasn't enough."

"Let them be adults," I say with a tired smile. "If it's meant to be, it'll happen."

"Unless they insist on ignoring their feelings. I mean, look at the last five years. They could have gotten back together, but he's too stubborn to reach out to her." Her sarcasm draws out her words. "Why do you think he's so grumpy? He misses her. Remember he wasn't that serious before he met her, and he was deliriously happy during their relationship."

"I can hear you gossiping about me," Vale says, and Bri jumps, her hand wrapping around my bicep. "Come on, I'm tired and you owe me a bed."

We crawl out and make quick work of reassembling the sofa. "Thanks," Vale says before flopping down.

"Goodnight," Bri chimes, looping her arm through mine. "Let's go, hot stuff." My brow furrows. She's never called me that before either. Vale's chuckle chases us from the room.

Passing through the doorway, I close the door and face her, unsure of what to say. But my heart is going a million beats per minute, and we should address this, shouldn't we?

"It's way colder in here. I swear, we should drag the mattress into the other room," Bri says, rubbing her arms. Goosebumps prickle over her tan skin.

Shaking my head, I cross the room and wrap my arms around her. "I don't think it would fit." She leans her head against my chest and I slide my hand down her back to tug her closer and share my warmth. "Come on, let's get under the covers and try to warm up." A flush creeps up my neck at the way my words could be taken, but Bri doesn't seem to mind.

I'm reluctant to let her go, and she's slow to move. We climb across the bed together and shimmy under the quilt. Bri shivers as she unrolls the extra blanket and tucks it around us before curling up in my arms again. It may be out of necessity, but it feels right having her against me, her silky hair tickling my neck.

"Do you want to talk about anything?" I ask.

"Like what?" Her words are muffled as she presses her face into my shirt. I can feel her hot breath through the fabric, and it sends a buzzy feeling across my chest and down my spine.

Clearing my throat, I try to think. "Um, like today, or your job thing," *or our kiss…*

She exhales roughly and pulls away enough she can look me in the eyes. "Ugh, jobs." She rolls onto her back and I resist the urge to drag her back against me. She turns her head to face me. "I'm frustrated and I feel useless."

"You're not useless," I insist. "You haven't found the right fit yet, and that's okay."

"Everyone else figured out their roles as teenagers during their internships, and I'm over here bouncing around jobs, no idea what I'm doing." She squeezes her eyes shut and scrunches her nose.

"When we get back, we will make a list of what you haven't tried. And if you don't like any of those, you'll get a remote job with humans. You have plenty of options."

She huffs, not liking that idea. I know she wants to contribute to the pack, but she shouldn't have to be miserable doing it. I touch my forehead to hers and close my eyes. We breathe in sync for a long moment.

"Indie?" she whispers, rolling back. When I open my eyes, we're nose to nose and she's all I can see. Her breath ghosts my lips. We're frozen, gazes locked, as I wait for her to speak. She hesitates, her eyes narrowing and brows rising minutely.

Her face tips up, nose brushing my cheek and her lips brushing mine softly, tentatively. I stay frozen, afraid to spook her. Her hand comes up, her fingertips lightly grazing my jaw. "Sorry," she mutters softly, pulling back and blinking at me. Pink colors her cheeks. "I shouldn't have done that."

"You're allowed to kiss me if you want to," I answer, my voice hoarse. "I can go get that bottle if you need an excuse."

Her frown melts away, a brilliant smile taking its place. She's so beautiful it hurts. Slowly, her face tilts up again and her eyes flutter closed, but she doesn't close the gap between us.

My arms tighten, pulling her closer, my fingers splaying over her shirt. I have no idea what I'm doing, but I'm not missing my chance. As I brush my lips over hers, she responds, kissing me back harder. She tangles her fingers into my hair, her body pressing into me. We kiss and kiss until her lips are swollen and her eyes are bright.

She tucks herself under my chin again and giggles. "That's one way to warm up, I guess."

I want to ask her what this means, what she wants, what the heck is going on but she seems content to nuzzle into my chest and go to sleep. Sighing, I reach over and flip off the lantern and close my eyes.

IV
DEFINE THE RELATIONSHIP

LEA

My ankle looks better in the morning. Thank you, shifter healing. I can stretch and sit up without any sharp jolts of pain. Shuffling to the end of the bed, I retrieve a fresh shirt from the trunk. It's the last one, so hopefully we will get out of here soon. The light through the narrow window seems brighter, so that's a good sign. In fact, I feel practically cheerful this morning, which isn't typical. Maybe getting away from my family and snowed-in with friends, and the ex, has been good for me.

Shoving off the bed, I hop to the doorway and grab the frame, swaying. When I push the door open, Vale jumps up. I wave at him with my free hand. "I've got it. I promise."

"Okay, but I'm here if you need help," he says, watching me work my way to the bathroom. I grip the sink and swing the door shut. Thankfully, I manage to use the bathroom without any disasters, which is good considering I'm hanging on to my dignity by a thread. There's nothing quite so humbling like falling off a toilet in front of your ex.

Vale waits outside the bathroom door when I pull it open. We stand face to face, and my stomach does a flip as I observe the gold flecks in his dark eyes. They're as familiar as my own heartbeat. He slides his hand around my waist and supports me as I limp to the sofa.

"Here, eat up," he says, handing me a bowl of oatmeal that warms my hands. The scent of cinnamon and dried apples makes my mouth water.

"Thank you." I hope he knows I mean thank you for more than the oatmeal. A million things are hanging unsaid between us. He nods and looks down at his own bowl.

"Lea," he says quietly, "last night, I hope you weren't uncomfortable," he trails off, raising his hand and dropping it.

I scrunch my face up as I shake my head. "It was fun. It feels like we're all friends again, and I missed that." *I missed you.* One side of his mouth pulls up in a smile. I should say more, but my courage slips away.

We sit together quietly until Indie and Bri emerge. I smile into my coffee, watching the two of them awkwardly move around each other, clearly hyper aware of touching.

"So what's the plan for today? Are we getting out of here?" Bri asks, digging her spoon into her oatmeal.

Vale glances at the door. "I think we need to get help today regardless of the snow. But it seems warmer today so I'm hoping by this afternoon, things will be easier."

"So what should we do this morning?" I ask.

"Not spin the bottle," Vale growls. I can't help my laugh.

"I saw a couple of puzzles in the bottom of the bin." Finishing her oatmeal, Bri stands. She digs through the supplies until she produces two boxes with wintery scenes on them. How appropriate. "There's two. Oh, why don't we have a competition?"

"Why does it have to be a competition?" I ask, looking between them.

Bri grins. "Because these two are competitive. Trust me."

"You are too," Indie mutters, rising and gathering dishes. She swats at his back and he laughs. The tension between them seems to be fading as they fall back into their best friends routine.

We settle onto the floor, Vale and I together against Bri and Indie.

The morning drifts by in a whirlwind of puzzle pieces. Vale is surprisingly good at completing puzzles, and I sort the pieces into color groups while he finds matches. I didn't know this about him. How much did I miss when we were together because we were young and stupid? How much has he changed?

He must sense my staring because he glances up, his dark hair falling over her forehead. I like it longer. He looks handsome. I reach out and brush it back, opening my mouth to tell him, but I remember our circumstances and stop myself. "You're pretty good at puzzles."

"Thanks." A small frown creasing his mouth. "Are you doing okay? Want to move back to the sofa? I can finish this alone."

"I'm okay. Besides, with my help, you're going to win this thing."

We reach for the same piece, our fingers bumping together. I'm reluctant to pull away, and his dark eyes connect with mine. It feels like he can see every piece of my marred soul.

Giggling interrupts us as Bri and Indie shuffle pieces back and forth. They have the outer edge complete, but not much else. I have a feeling they're distracted. Bri's hand rests on Indie's forearm and he's looking at her more than the puzzle. It's adorable. She leans in and whispers something, and a flush burns under his freckles.

"Done!" Vale sits back, grinning. It's the first true smile I've seen on his face in the last two days. My lungs seize, my stomach clenching. It's hard to remember how to breathe or think when he smiles.

"Finally," Bri says with a laugh. "I forgot that I hate puzzles. Let's get this cleaned up and see about some lunch."

"We're not going to finish it?" Indie asks, giving her puppy eyes.

"Vale, you're going to have to help him. He's not much better than I am," Bri says, hopping up. She works on lunch, and while Vale finishes the second puzzle, Indie pauses.

He frowns, looking at my ankle. "I think the swelling seems worse now than this morning. I think you should elevate it and apply another ice pack."

"Whatever you say, doc," I say, allowing him to pull me to my feet. Vale scowls, making me smirk as I throw my arm over Indie's shoulder and allow him to support me back to the bedroom. He retrieves a fresh ice pack and sits down to unwrap and inspect my ankle.

VALE

The moment Indigo and Lea leave the room, Briar turns to me. Her eyebrows rise, her mouth pinching into a tight line. I don't like that look.

"What?"

I appreciate all she's done to make Lea comfortable, but I could do without the scheming. Scowling, I cross my arms and wait for whatever she clearly wants to say.

Briar clicks her thumb nails together, her eyes narrowing before saying, "You're aware you're still in love with her, right?" A bone-deep tiredness washes over me. I do not have the energy for this conversation.

"It's obvious. And I know she dum..." I turn my head, my eyes flashing in warning. She changes direction mid-sentence. "Wasn't ready to commit to you back then, but things are different now and I see the way she looks at you."

Scrubbing my hands over my face, I lean back in the armchair and let my breath out slowly, filling my lungs again and trying to relax. Maybe if I ignore her, she'll go away.

"You should talk to her, romance her. She really wanted you to kiss her again last night." She continues on, ignoring my growing irritation. And there goes my last shred of calm.

"Bri!" I snap, "I don't think you're in a position to lecture anyone about relationships. You've been friendzoning Indigo for years."

Her mouth shuts, her teeth clicking. I should stop, let it go, but I've got five years of resentment built up over the situation and she stuck her nose right in the middle of it. "I don't know how you're deluding yourself into thinking you're just friends. And years from now when you both finally pull your heads out of your asses and realize you're meant to be mates, you'll regret all the years you wasted dancing around each other and avoiding a real relationship."

Briar flushes from her neck to her ears, her jaw tense and eyes wide as she stares at me. Before I can continue, she stands and walks away, straight into Indigo standing in the doorway to Lea's room. Ah, shit.

She ducks her head and breezes past him into their shared room, shutting the door in his face. He looks from the door to me, his mouth open. I want to justify what I said, but I know it was mean. I've made a mess of their relationship too, but hopefully they can salvage it. Sighing, I pass Indigo and slip into Lea's room. After forcing Briar and Indigo to deal with their feelings, it's only fair I do the same.

Lea looks up from her crossword puzzle. Icy sunlight paints her dark hair in a silver halo. It's mussy from two days in a cabin with no shower, but she still looks beautiful. She tilts her head, regarding me. "What's up?"

"Can we talk?" I hover by the door, wanting but scared to come closer.

"Are you sure you want to do that? It didn't go so well last time," she says dryly, patting the foot of the bed. Reluctantly, I sit, turning so one bent knee rests on the bed and I can face her.

Now that I'm here, I have no idea what to say. Exhaling, I blurt the first thing that comes to mind. "Have you figured out what you're going to do when we get out of here?"

She frowns, looking down at her hands. Her hair falls around her, brushing her cheeks. I'm aching to tuck it behind her ears, but I restrain myself. Sighing, she answers, "Find somewhere to hide, I guess. Eventually join another pack, maybe in Canada."

"Is that what you want to do?" I ask, tilting my head.

"Not particularly, but it's better than going home."

"What if you stayed with me?" I ask, feeling like I just pried open my ribcage and handed her my heart.

"What do you mean?" She tenses, shoulders drawing in and arms crossing defensively.

Rubbing the back of my neck, I try to find words that don't sound stupid. "What if we were mates? And then you could stay here, do whatever you want, and they can't force you into anything."

"But I'd be *your* mate."

"I'm not expecting anything," I rush to explain. She watches me warily, waiting for more of an explanation. "I'm not interested in seeing anyone else or finding a mate, so I can be that for you. And if you meet someone else later, we will figure it out."

"I don't want anyone else." Her words are quiet.

"Okay, well..." I wet my lips, hope rising up in me.

"Vale, I don't want you to be stuck with me. You deserve a loving relationship and someone who can be there for you. Not some faux-mate who you claimed out of pity."

"It wouldn't be like that."

"I'm sorry, it's not a good idea. I'm not going to do that to you." She sighs, tipping her head back and closing her eyes. "And I really don't want to argue about it."

Feeling utterly foolish, I search for any reasonable response, any reason for her to agree, and come up with nothing, so I say, "I understand," and walk out of the room.

B R I

Indie opens the door and slips into the room on silent feet. I refuse to look at him, hoping maybe if I pretend the last ten minutes didn't happen, we might experience some sort of Groundhog Day situation and I could try again.

Vale is crazy. He's never had a friend this close, so he has no idea what he's talking about. The wolf wouldn't know friendship if it bit him in the ass. He was projecting, or deflecting, or something.

"Bri?" Indie slides onto the bed beside me, resting his back against the wall and folding his hands in his lap. Usually, he would reach out his hand and rest it on my back or leg, and the lack of touch hurts. He studies me. "Do you think there's a chance Vale was right?"

I cover my face with my hands. "He's an idiot. He was just mad I was calling him on his feelings for Lea."

Silence stretches between us. I want to curl up and pull the quilt over my head. Indie is going to let me down, reject me, tell me I was stupid for what happened last night, that I'm ruining everything.

His voice is calm and gentle. "I mean, we kissed last night."

When I peek up, Indie's face is open, and it squeezes my heart. There's nothing to be scared of or ashamed of with him. "That was some sort of crazy cabin fever," I say, sounding a bit choked.

Indie bites his lip, his eyes flicking away like it's too intense to look in my eye while he says these things. I'm fixated on the way his teeth sink into his bottom.

"Really?" he asks. His throat works in a swallow and I follow the motion. "Because if I'm being honest, it's not the first time I've thought about doing that."

A nervous excitement fizzes through my blood. Is he serious? I mean, who hasn't thought about kissing their gorgeous best friend?

"I've thought about that too, but only because you're really handsome. I mean, have you seen yourself?" I joke.

He takes my hand, threading our fingers together. My breath stutters. Looking down, I trace lines between the pale freckles on the underside of his arm.

"Bri," he says softly. "I don't think that's normal." He tugs my hand over to rest on his leg, claiming my attention. "I'm not sure our relationship has been completely platonic for a while."

All arguments fall out of my head. Taking a slow breath, I venture, "Are you saying you've wanted to be more than friends?"

He reaches up and hooks two fingers under my chin, raising it so I'm forced to look at him. "If you want to return to being friends, we can make that work. I'm not willing to lose you. But if you want to try for more, I am interested." His voice drops, sending a shiver through me. "Very interested."

"Oh." I blink, letting his words sink into my soul. This is Indie. We've spent a hundred lazy afternoons together, nights under the stars. I can't imagine my life without him. "I gotta admit, it was pretty nice last night. I wouldn't mind more of that," I admit. "I already love you, but I'm not sure if I'm in love with you. I'm not opposed to the idea. Can we take some time to figure it out?"

His lopsided smile sends my heart into my throat. I've always thought he was perfect. Who wouldn't want to be with him? Tightening my hold on his hand, I gather my courage once more and ask, "Can we kiss again?"

"Yes, please," he says, launching himself at me. He kisses my jaw as I giggle. This is insane, making out with my best friend. He works his way to my lips and claims them with a new confidence that melts me. It's all I can do to hold on to his shoulder with my free hand as we tumble sideways. He stretches out our joined hands, keeping me in place as my lips part and his tongue tentatively explores my mouth. I suck in a sharp breath, overwhelmed with the way our mouths move together and his weight pressing me down.

He breaks it off, his breath coming fast. "Are you okay? Do you want to stop?"

"Absolutely not," I say, slipping my hand over his shoulder and under the neckline of his shirt, splaying my fingers over hot skin shifting over flexing muscles. He places a kiss on my jaw once more. My back arches when I feel his lips on the sensitive skin of my neck, right below my ear. He follows it with a soft bite that has me groaning.

"I've dreamed of doing that to you," he whispers. My breath hitches. Who knew my best friend could talk like that. Indie stops, dropping his face to my shoulder. "I'm sorry, that was too far." He pushes back and settles on his heels, facing me as I sit up, feeling disoriented and needy.

My fingers drag through my hair, untangling the mess we made. "I'm not complaining. I am game for all of that," I say, waving my hands to indicate everything.

Indie's cheeks tinge pink. "Yeah, but it's going to be hard for you to think things through if I'm mauling you."

I freeze. He's right. And until I'm sure I love him in that way, I shouldn't be sticking my hands under his clothing or licking every bit of skin I can reach. Not that I was thinking of doing that.

Groaning again out of frustration, I flop face down in the bed. Indie rubs his hand over my back. "Sorry."

Popping my head up, I glare at him. "Why are you apologizing? I'm mad you stopped and that you're right about needing to cool it."

He laughs lightly, stretching out until he's lying beside me, his fingers dragging lazy circles over my back. "If you wake up tomorrow and decide you don't feel anything, I want you to know it's okay. I won't hold it against you."

Sighing, I turn to rest my cheek on my forearm. "Is that what you expect?"

A beat passes. "Maybe."

"But that's not what you want," I ask, my throat tight.

"No."

"I don't want that either," I confess, shivering as his hand slides up under my hair and squeezes the nape of my neck.

V
FACING FAMILY
LEA

After the debacle with Vale, I stubbornly stay in my room until Indie comes to check on me. He lets me lean on him as I hobble out to the sofa. Bri stands from surveying the supplies, crossing her arms. "We are going to run out soon. This cabin is stocked for two for a week, but there's four of us."

She's right. We're burning through food fast, and the woodpile is getting low. That scares me more than the food supply. Laying in that freezing creek felt like dying, and I have no desire to repeat the experience.

"It's definitely been warmer today. We should check the snow," Indie says, glancing at the window. Pale sunlight streams through the hazy glass.

Vale sits in his armchair, brooding. At Indie's prodding, he snaps up. "Yeah, we've been here long enough." Stalking to the door, he pulls it open and surveys the wall of snow. It's compacted down, leaving a larger opening. "Briar and Indigo, are you up for a run in the snow?"

Bri nods, pursing her lips. "Yeah, I think we are up for it."

"Good. What do you need to be ready?" Vale says.

Indie shrugs, his hand drifting to Bri's lower back. "If you can close the cabin up, we can go now. We didn't exactly bring anything when we arrived."

Vale paces back, his expression tight. "Have some food and drink some water. I want you prepared for the run back through the snow." He's become a leader in the time we were apart. It looks good on him.

They obey, eating granola bars and draining cups of water. Bri rubs her hands over her arms, smiling at Indie. "Ready?"

"Be safe," I say, reaching up and beckoning her. Bri hugs me tightly, and Indie pats my arm. "I appreciate you guys rescuing me. Not sure I'd be alive otherwise. And for the great time the last couple of days. I owe you."

"Don't mention it," Indie says.

"We'll see you tonight." Bri says, winking. "Right?" I nod, wanting it to be true.

Indie boosts Bri up and she climbs over the compacted snow. Her legs are replaced with paws and a light brown tail that swishes before it disappears. Vale helps Indie up and he vanishes as well. A white and tan wolf face pokes over the edge. "Get going! We are fine," Vale assures him. Indie barks once and turns away.

The door shuts with a click and Vale turns back to face me. His perpetual frown is back.

"You okay?" I ask.

"Fine, don't worry about me," he says coolly, his eyes looking anywhere but at me.

His rejection stings, but isn't that what I did to him earlier this same day? Clearing my throat, I try to get his attention. "Vale, I'm sorry."

Vale shakes his head. "You don't owe me anything, Lea." He retrieves one of the small shovels and opens the door again, going to work on clearing more of an opening. That effectively shuts me down. Sighing, I nibble on one of the granola bars from the open package and watch his arms flex as he knocks away chunks of icy snow.

This man ran through a blizzard to get me. He offered to be my mate so my family couldn't force me into a mate bond with a stranger. I've rejected him twice now, and guilt swirls in my gut the more I think about it. He's selfless, dedicated, and way too good for me. I'd give anything to be good enough for him.

Vale freezes, shovel in hand and sweat on his neck. He cocks his head, listening. I stay silent, waiting for him to move. Slowly, Vale sets the shovel aside and closes the door, flipping the lock.

Without warning he strides to me and scoops me up. "What?" I whisper, leaning against his chest.

"Someone is coming and it's not my pack. Stay in the bedroom," he orders. He lays me down and tugs the curtains shut. When I reach for the lantern, he holds out his hand. "Don't."

He leaves the door open a crack and I crawl to the edge of the bed, trying desperately to listen. There's not much I can do to help, but I'll be damned if he gets hurt protecting me. My heart races, aching in my chest, as I strain my ears. Footsteps crunch in the snow outside, and I can practically feel Vale's tension.

A clanking knock echoes on the door. Vale ignores it, standing by the door with the shovel casually in his hand. The door rattles, the handle fighting against the lock.

"Open up, I know you're in there. We will break the door." The muffled yell is an unfamiliar voice. The banging sounds again. "This is your last warning."

Vale opens the door, facing them. Icy light illuminates the edge of his figure that I can see through the crack.

"Oh, it's you. I should have known," my mother spits. She always hated him and hated that Raven Pack had to be rescued by Bracken Creek Pack years ago. It didn't help that he encouraged me to be independent and stand up for myself.

"Hello, Camellia," he says, his tone neutral. Cold fury rolls under his words, almost a tangible thing brushing my skin. Anger on my behalf. I could kiss the man right now if I wasn't so frightened for him.

"My daughter is here, don't tell me otherwise, and she is coming home immediately."

"I'm sorry, you're mistaken. Best of luck locating her." He starts to close the door but it thuds against something blocking it.

"Don't bother with your lies. We tracked her here. I know she's inside and I don't mind going through you to get her."

"I wouldn't recommend it. My Alphas don't take kindly to trespassing or attacking their pack members." Vale's voice drops in warning, his anger no longer masked. "I would hate for you to break the peace we've had for so long."

"You're between me and my mate," a male voice says, matching his threatening tone. "I'm well within my rights."

"Lea is not your mate." Vale snarls, sending a shiver through me.

"The deal has been made, I am here to retrieve her and claim her properly." His arrogant words echo in the small cabin. "And if I get to maim her ex-boyfriend in the process, all the better. Your Alphas won't go up against both Raven Pack and Ironcrest Pack for a little beating." He sounds gleeful at the prospect.

"Just dispose of him," my mother says coldly. "They'll never know."

"Gladly."

"Don't touch him," I cry, pushing the door open and limping forward. Vale does not deserve to get hurt while sheltering me. Like he said, we don't owe each other anything. His lip curls, but he walks back and wraps his arm around my waist before I fall.

"Did you injure her?" the man demands.

Vale's answer is a growl. "She was hurt fleeing from you. So that makes it your fault."

"No matter. Azalea, come here. Your mate wants to take you home," my mother orders, snapping her fingers.

I hesitate, clinging to Vale. The man claps his hand like I'm a dog to call to heel. "Let's go, woman."

Before I can surrender, Vale tugs me closer until I am pressed up against his side. "You are not her mate. You cannot have her. She is already mine." His possessive words send heat through me. It might be an act, but it doesn't feel like one.

My mother's outraged cry is cut off by the man's haughty laugh. "I see no claim mark. Now give me my mate."

"It's common decency to wait until one's mate isn't seriously injured," Vale says, each word sharp. I wrap my arms around his waist, feeling his heartbeat against my palm. He raises his chin, challenging. "But the bond has already begun to form. I can feel her emotions, and she can feel mine."

My mother screws up her face. "Is that true, Azalea?"

"The magic is taking hold, and soon we won't be able to resist marking each other," Vale says quieter, more for me than my mother and the man. A mate bond between us? I don't know if it's true, but I hope so.

"Yes," I say, turning to face my pursuers.

"I will break it," the man says.

"You can't," I snap.

Vale growls. "She is now a part of our pack, and our Alphas will pursue her and if you claim her without her consent, they will kill you."

"Azalea, what have you done?" my mother shrieks.

"She's not worth this trouble," he says, throwing his hands up and walking away.

Anger pours off my mother, but I can't feel any of it through the pack bond. She glares at me. "Well, you've ruined things for the last time. Do not come crawling home when you make a mess of this. You're no longer a part of our pack or family," my mother declares before walking away.

If she meant to wound me, she failed. All I feel is blissful relief. My breath rushes out of me and I sag against Vale. He helps me to the sofa and goes to close the door.

VALE

Lea sits quietly and I wish she would yell at me, say something, anything. She folds her hands in her lap. I cross the small room to sit beside her, resisting the urge to reach out and touch her.

"You didn't have to lie for me," she says, "but thank you for getting them to back off."

It's time for complete honesty, no more holding back to spare her feelings. "I wasn't lying."

"What do you mean?" She asks hesitantly, obviously scared of the answer she already knows.

"I haven't looked at another woman since you. Have you been interested in anyone else?" She shakes her head and I continue, "I've tried to move on, but I've never been able to stop thinking about you, dreaming about you." I rub at my chest. "There's a hollow ache that eased when I came here and saw you again, for the first time in years."

"You acted like you were so angry with me," she whispers. "You seemed unhappy."

"Of course I'm unhappy. I've been away from you, living with this awful feeling instead of with the woman I love. It didn't matter how much I tried to suppress it."

She places her hand over mine. I wait for the rejection I know is coming. Maybe this time it'll pierce my heart and that will be the end. At least my suffering would be over.

"I don't know, but I think you're right," she says. I freeze, my breath shallow, afraid to break the spell. "I've been miserable the last few years. Since you asked me to be your mate. I wasn't ready then, and I'm sorry for that. Leaving you was my biggest mistake."

I shake my head. "I never want you to be unhappy or feel forced."

"I don't." She takes a slow, shaky breath. "When you showed up here to help me, I felt better than I have in years. I can't explain it."

"See? I think a bond took hold and we've been denying it, suppressing it with distance." She nods and my heart leaps.

"Can we try being together and see how it goes? I need a little reassurance before I commit to a lifetime with you." I raise my eyebrows and she lets out a shaky laugh. "I mean, it might be inevitable. Mate bond and all that. So I suppose we won't be able to resist each other eventually. Might as well let that run its natural course."

"I can't resist you now," I say softly. "You say the word, and I'm yours."

Her eyes widen and I feel her pulse pick up in her wrist. "I thought you didn't want a mate."

"I don't want anyone else," I correct, forcing myself to stay still. The way she licks her lips is delicious and I want to kiss her again so badly, but the confusion in her eyes is slowly dissolving into desire and I'm determined to banish the last of her doubts, so I force myself to be patient.

"Oh," she says, swallowing. "I feel the same." Her breathing grows shallow, her pupils dilating. It feels like a dream, like maybe that angry Ironcrest wolf hit me over the head and now I'm living in a delusion. I hope I never wake up.

Lea leans forward, eyes closing in a clear invitation to do something I've thought about every day for the last five years. My muscles strain, ready to snap under the tension. Gingerly, I cup her jaw, sliding my fingers into her hair as I lean in.

It's meant to be a soft kiss. A reintroduction. But she opens her lips and we are consumed in flames. Her hand tugs on my shirt, the other pressing against the back of my neck, urging me closer. I'm surging forward until she falls back on the sofa cushions.

"Vale," she murmurs, as I release her mouth and kiss down her throat, licking and sucking as I go. I can't get enough of her. She tastes like home. She gasps and stammers, trying to form words as I ravage her skin. "I don't think I ever stopped loving you."

Our mouths crash together, her tongue slipping into my mouth. Electricity races between us, lighting up every nerve across my body. She's everything I feel and taste. "Lea," I say, her name a prayer. Her response is a hum of praise as I slide my hand under the edge of her baggy shirt and run my thumb over her ribs. I need more of her, and from the way she claws at my shirt and bites my lip, she feels the same.

VI
COMING HOME

INDIE

We leap across compact snow, our journey slow as we sink into the white powder. Water soaks into our fur. I hate running through deep snow. Regardless, my tail has been wagging since we shifted. I would be embarrassed, but Bri's tail swishes back and forth ahead of me.

As we move south, the snow lessens and the trees thicken, and we are able to run along easily. Bri darts forward, bumping into my shoulder. I turn, snapping playfully. She leaps back and into a play bow, her tail waving high. We shouldn't be running and playing, but she takes off racing toward the compound, and I find my-self chasing her.

She's beautiful as a wolf, pale gray speckled with white over her back, light-ening to white along her belly and legs. Her movements are lithe, her blue eyes bright in the dappled sunlight reflecting off the snow.

With my longer legs, I close the distance easily and run beside her, matching her pace. As we weave through trees and come back together again, I rub my snout against the fluffy fur along her neck. She smiles, her tongue lolling out, as warm affection seeps through the pack bond.

The trees thin once more and we pass the first few cabins. Snow piles up around their windows and doors as well, but as we near the Alpha's home, the path has been shoveled. Leaping onto the trail, we follow it to the meadow. Paths lead

from the training building to the storage shed and down to the office, but it looks like most of the buildings are still blocked. Several packmates are working to clear a path to the diner.

Nudging Bri, I lead her to the training building. There is always plenty of spare clothes there, and it's a warm place to shift. It's blessedly empty. We trot to the lockers and shift back. Blushing, I turn away and focus on tugging on sweatpants. Somehow this feels more intimate than before I had my mouth on her skin. When I turn around, she's gripping the hem of her shirt, her eyes on my bare chest. My blush increases, but a pleased smile tugs at my mouth as I pull a shirt over my head.

"Ready?" I ask her.

Her answer is breathless. "Yeah."

She pulls the door open to see my father, Elm, approaching. "You're back!"

"Hi, Dad." He pats my back. "Vale is back at the cabin with Lea. She's injured and can't walk home."

"Back to Raven Pack?" He repeats, frowning.

"No, I think she's coming here," Bri adds, "Her and Vale were working things out."

"We'd better get the Alphas," he mutters, walking away.

"Do you think they're getting back together?" I ask her, ducking my head to speak into her ear. "Their talk the other day didn't turn out well. I'm pretty sure from his reaction that she rejected him."

She squeezes my hand. "Give them a chance. They're meant to be. Besides, there's no way he will let her go back to her birth pack after what they did."

She raises up on her tiptoes and brushes a light kiss over my lips.

"Oh!" A surprised Alpha Hazel stands in front of us, and I was so wrapped up in Bri, I notice our surroundings. Quite a few packmates are watching us, including Hazel whose eyebrows are raised. "Are you guys–? Never mind."

Her mate, Alpha Slate, places his hand on her back. A soft brown tuft of hair shows over the top of the baby carrier strapped to his back. He frowns at the sight of us, both scarlet. "Vale didn't tell us much before he left. What is the situation?"

Bri exhales and squares her shoulders, "Sir, we found Lea from Raven Pack injured in the creek on our border..." She summarizes the events of the last two days, beginning to walk along with Slate.

Hazel drifts closer to me. Swallowing, I fold my arms and look at the ground. "Your sister will be pleased," she says quietly.

"Why?" I tilt my head, frowning at her.

"She's going to win the betting pool." She laughs. My frown deepens and she explains, "We had a betting pool going on how long it would take you two to get together." She pats my arm. "I lost a long time ago, but Marigold thought it would be some time this year."

"Are you kidding me?" I blurt, pinching the bridge of my nose.

"But you'd better get Bri to tell Onyx before he sees you. He's going to be a sore loser. Not to mention he thinks Bri is way too young to date. He'd prefer it if you waited until you were thirty." She laughs, following Bri and Slate.

"Good idea," I say with a sigh. It'll be mere hours until the entire pack knows we got together. Hopefully Bri doesn't change her mind, because breaking up at this point would be a pack scandal. I had no idea so many people were invested in our relationship. A betting pool, of all things. Bri is going to laugh her ass off.

"You guys should go warm up. I'll take a group up to get them," Slate says. "Unless you want to lead it." He kisses Hazel's temple and she leans into him.

"That's okay. I know you need a good run after the last couple of days. Besides, I promised Rory we would come over for a playdate with the triplets once the snow was cleared."

Slate hands Bri the baby as he unstraps the carrier and passes it to Hazel. It takes her a moment to tighten the straps, but then she nestles the baby into it and kisses the top of his head. "It sounds like we are bringing home a new pack member. Do we have somewhere to put her?" Slate asks.

Hazel props a hand on her hip. "Well, I would think she'd want to stay with Vale. But if they're not ready for that, she can stay in the extra bedroom in Fisher and Clove's house. Right, Bri?"

Bri nods. The room used to belong to her twin brothers, both living in their own homes with their mates now. She grins at me, and I can picture our life together so clearly.

"Seriously, go warm up. Maybe eat something that wasn't canned," Hazel says, raising an eyebrow as she looks between us, staring into each other's eyes and smiling dopey grins.

"Yes, Alpha," Bri says, taking my hand. Hazel goes one way, and Slate the other, leaving us to walk home. We take our time reaching Bri's house. The scent of fresh bread fills the air, so her mother must be baking.

She stops at the front door and turns to face me, as reluctant to leave as I am. I rest a hand against the doorframe and lean over her, enjoying the way her pulse flutters and her lips part. She tips her chip and presses our lips together, setting off fireworks behind my eyes.

I could kiss her all day, but it's cold out here and she might want to shower after the last few days. "Hazel told me something," I murmur.

"What?" Her eyes widen in alarm, even as her hands slide around my waist and skim the hem of my shirt, her icy fingers brushing my skin.

"They had a betting pool on how long it would take us to get together."

"What?" she squeaks, pinching the skin at my hips.

Winching, I gather her hands and press them between mine. "Yup. Apparently my sister is the winner."

Scrunching her face up, she leans into me, hiding her face against my chest. "So are we the last to figure this out?" Her words are muffled.

"Seems like it," I say with a laugh. "You better go inside and warm up."

"Want to come?" she asks, fluttering her lashes.

Smiling, I kiss her once more. It takes all my willpower to let her go and not deepen the kiss. "You should talk to your mom. I'm sure she's been worried about you, and we shouldn't spring this on her."

"If you insist," she says, whining a little. When she presses closer and slips her hands under my shirt again, I can't resist one last kiss. Even if that kiss goes on far longer than it should.

LEA

Vale is everything I need. I didn't know it, but he is what my heart has been longing for. He feels like coming home. I work to pull his shirt off, and he gladly sheds it. My hands roam up his chest, admiring all of the muscle he's put on in the years we've been apart. He memorizes my face, touching every inch of me and following it with his mouth, sprinkling kisses over my cheeks, nose, jaw.

We turn, almost tumbling off the narrow sofa. Carefully, he lays on his back and holds my waist as I move to straddle him. My heart races, heat scorching through my blood. He looks up at me like I'm his salvation. Gently, he grips my hips and I bend to kiss him again. I'm lost to him, opening my mouth to welcome his tongue as his hands hold me firmly against him. My fingers trace his chest, dying to feel more of his skin.

Everything goes hazy and hot. I can't get enough of him. He must feel the same because his mouth is insistent against mine, his hands slowly exploring across my body. I'm rising up to pull my own shirt off when a knock sounds on the door. Instinctively, I duck down and Vale wraps his arms around me protectively.

"Are they back?" I whisper.

"It's probably my pack," he says gently.

"Are you sure?"

The knock sounds again and it's a familiar pattern. Vale smiles, silently reassuring me. I slide off of him and he pulls his shirt on before answering the door.

"Hey, Vale, how's it going?" Alpha Slate says, smiling at them. He's a handsome shifter, somewhere around thirty, with dark hair curling around the nape of his neck and startling bright green eyes peering at us. When I last saw him five years ago, he was preparing to welcome his first child. Now he has two, from what Bri told me.

"Alpha," Vale says, ducking his head. I wave from the sofa.

"Hello, Lea. I heard you might like to join our pack."

"She would like sanctuary for the time being, and the opportunity to join when she's ready, if that's what she decides," Vale says, and I could kiss him for being so considerate and respectful.

"Fair enough," Slate says. "You two ready to go?" He jerks his thumb back at a pair of snowmobiles.

Vale nods and returns to me. He leans over me, hand on the back of the sofa. I tip my chin up, some instinct hoping he kisses me, but instead he speaks softly. "Are you ready to go? Is there anything you need?"

Once I shake my head, he lifts me up. At the door, he transfers me to Slate, who is a gentleman as he carries me to the closest snowmobile to sit behind a woman I recognize. I'd prefer to limp along, but the snow is deep and I'm not a total idiot. Vale scrambles up, tugging the door closed behind him.

"Let's go!" Slate says.

On the drive back, I glance over at Vale riding on the back of the snowmobile behind Slate. I hold onto Aven's waist. She was Vale's teammate when we were together, but I don't know if they have the same positions now or not. I missed years of his life and I intend to make it up to him.

The snowmobiles noisily race back to their compound, past the outer cabins and straight into the central clearing. While Raven Pack is one large building with a few outliers, Bracken Creek Pack is many smaller buildings arranged around a meadow. It seems a better configuration to me, allowing everyone to spend more time outside.

"I'd like you to visit our healer, Sable," Slate says. He steps back, allowing Vale to support me. The snow has been cleared, so I limp along, my arm over his shoulder and his hand tight on my waist.

The older woman opens the door, ushering me inside. Vale lifts me onto the exam table. Sable rewraps my ankle and praises Indie's work. "You'll be good as new in a couple of days. Good job staying off of it. A lot of the healing is already done."

"Thank you," I say. "I'm lucky Indie found me."

"Indeed," she says, patting my leg. A smile wrinkles her severe face. "I'd like to see you in a few days, but you can go now."

Vale steps closer. "I've got her." Rolling my eyes at his protectiveness, I slide my legs off the table and allow him to support me as I stand. He speaks low and quiet into my ear. "Let's get you home."

I bite my lip. "And where would that be?"

"My cabin. Our cabin now," he says, closing the door behind us. Sunlight pours over him, turning his eyes and hair mahogany. He looks at me expectantly.

I smile at him, a flush rising up my neck. "That's presumptuous of you."

"I think I made my intentions clear." He kisses my temple. "Don't change your mind now."

"I like when you're bossy. You never took control like this before," I whisper, enjoying the curve of his lips as he smiles. His smiles are rarer now, more valuable, and I am greedy for them. Every one sends a thrill through me.

We cross the meadow, earning a few curious looks. Most of the faces are familiar, but no one approaches us. He's patient, allowing me to lean on him and limp along stubbornly. Once the cleared path ends and we are facing deep snow, he scoops me up, stomping through the snow until we reach his cabin. He sets my feet on the steps and pushes the door open.

Vale's warm scent envelops me. The cabin is homey and welcoming, and I press my hand to the stone counter as I hop inside and past his dark wood kitchen. Vale stays close at my back, his hands never leaving me.

An oversized gray couch fills half of the narrow living room, facing a television framed in bookshelves. Board games are stacked along the bottom shelves, and miniatures break up the expanse of books. I eye one that looks like a tiny spaceship. "Is this what you've been doing the last few years without me?"

His answer is hot on my neck. "Yes. Jealous?"

Laughing, I turn in his arms and fold my hands behind his neck. "I'm not jealous of a hobby. Actually, maybe I am."

"You have all my attention now," he says, gripping my waist and lifting me. Giggling, I cling to him as he walks us backwards until we reach the sofa. He's careful to not hit my ankle, even though it feels fine by now. As he looks down to make sure, I take the opportunity to kiss the side of his neck. He stills, groaning as I bite down softly. Slowly, he tips his head to the side, letting me run my tongue over the spot, reveling in the way his grip tightens.

Grinning, I tug on his shirt and lead him down onto the sofa. Once my back hits the cushions, his hands slide up my ribs, over my arms, and back down to skim the skin bared between my sweatpants and shirt. I squirm, pulling on his neck until our mouths crash together again. He grips my jaw, angling my head the way he wants.

"Be my mate," he whispers against my lips.

"I thought I already agreed to that. I mean, it's kinda inevitable at this point, right?" My words are breathless.

"I want you to choose it. Choose me." His nose drags up my cheek until his lips kiss my cheekbone.

"Needy," I tease.

"I want you. I didn't want you stuck with me, but I've always wanted you." I confess. He smiles, a full, true smile, and it's warmth across my skin after an endless, freezing night. "You're better than I deserve." I say, pulling back so I can look into his eyes.

"You are wrong about that," he says, "I'm lucky to have you, and I'm not letting you go. Not now that I know how you feel about me."

We pick up right where we left off, both unwilling to let go of the other for even a second. As he sheds his shirt, my eyes catch on something. "What is this?"

A cluster of flowers, each with five delicate petals framed in slender, dark leaves, is inked onto his ribs. I trace my fingers over the tattoo and look up at him. He smiles sheepishly. "I got it a few years ago. It felt right."

"It's beautiful." I purse my lips. "But how am I going to get a tattoo for you when your name is Vale? I'm not getting a tattoo of a valley. It's not a very practical name."

His rumbling chuckle vibrates through me as he dips his head and halts my speech with a searing kiss. "I'll change my name if you want, as long as I'm yours," he mutters. All ideas of teasing fade away as his hands ease under my shirt. Feelings locked away years ago break free as I open myself to him.

EPILOGUE
BRI

My trainees mill around, wiping sweat from their faces and draining water bottles. "Anything else before I let them go?" I ask my dad.

"What do you think?" he asks, smirking from his spot against the wall. It's the first week that he's observing me run everything on my own.

Crossing my arms, I survey the group. They worked hard during today's training session and it's almost dinner time. "Thank you all, you are dismissed," I say, raising my voice.

The group moves to their lockers and I turn to face my dad. He smiles, dimples hidden under his salt and pepper beard. "You did well. Why don't you head out too? I'll close up. I heard your stomach growling from all the way over here."

"Thanks. I'll see you later," I say, rising up on my tiptoes to kiss his cheek.

My stomach growls again, so I pull on my hoodie and head to the door. Late afternoon sunshine warms my cheeks as I jog across the meadow, past the supply shop and the school building. My brother's garden stretches across one side of our central compound, sprawling and green even this early in the spring. I pass under the trellis archway, walking toward the healer's cottage on the north end.

"Hey, Bri," Rory says, waving from where she perches on a stool, working on her latest painting. A rainbow of paint smudges mark up her hands and wrists, showing she's been painting all day. She's glowing, happy in her garden.

"That's really nice looking," I say, admiring the painting of the garden. "Will this go in your new collection?"

She shakes her head. "Nah, this is just for us." Sighing, she plops her brush into the jar of water and wipes her hands on a rag.

"Hey, Sis," Cedar says, emerging from behind a storage shed and holding a basket of carrots. He sets it aside and joins his mate, kissing her cheek. She beams at him. "We should go. Marigold is probably tired of dealing with our trio of gremlins."

I leave him to help pack up her painting supplies. Crossing the garden, I knock on the door of the stone cottage. Indie answers. He's wearing an apron, and I grin, wanting desperately to tease him about it.

"Get going, you'll be useless to me now with your mate distracting you," Sable calls.

"Thank you," Indie says to the healer, hanging the apron on a hook. The moment the door shuts behind him, he wraps his arms around my waist and lifts me. Giggling, I hold his face and kiss him soundly. "Good day?" he asks, setting me on my feet.

"Yeah," I say. Hands clasped and fingers intertwined, we turn south, passing Cedar and Rory. They've gotten distracted kissing, and I look away, not wanting to see my brother with his tongue in his mate's mouth.

The meadow is buzzing as the pack gathers to eat. My stomach growls again and Indie picks up his pace, tugging me toward the diner. We pause as a gaggle of four and five-year-olds race past, lost in their imaginary game. They're hazards, but young and cute enough to get away with it.

Lea and Vale stand in line for dinner. She's holding his hand with both of hers and as they talk quietly, she leans her head against his shoulder. The neckline of her shirt pulls sideways with the motion and her pale claim mark scars catch the light. I like to think I played a role in getting them back together, and I squeeze Indie's hand as we walk.

"Hey," she says, turning as we join them.

"How's it going?" I ask.

Vale wraps an arm around her shoulder. "She won't brag, but she finished scanning in all the old documents today - a feat no one else has been able to accomplish for years." He kisses her hair.

"Ah, yes, the very exciting tasks of an administrator." She rolls her eyes.

"Don't sell yourself short. Hazel and Slate rely on you. And I like having you so close." He's not wrong. Lea is an organizational mastermind, and once given autonomy and a healthy work environment, she loved getting the pack's office in order. Hazel sings her praises every chance she gets.

The line shuffles forward and the smell of soy and honey reaches me. "Oh, I'm starving!" I say, trying to peer over people's shoulders to see our dinner.

"Long day training?" Vale asks.

"My dad is relentless," I complain, smiling despite myself. Indie convinced me to try working with my dad. Being the pack's trainer is a family legacy and one I had little interest in, but he was right. It suits me perfectly. Babysitting and helping

Marigold teach set me up perfectly for the work, and the tougher environment fits my personality in a way childcare couldn't.

"At least you didn't send anyone to see me today," Indie says. "We were busy restocking after winter and doing a little spring cleaning."

We step into the diner and grab plates, loading them with sesame chicken and fried rice. Dessert is a fluffy sugar-coated donut, and I can't help sneaking a bite of mine as soon as we sit down at a picnic table together.

We laugh and talk while we eat, and even after we clear our dishes away, we sit and enjoy each other's company. I trace my fingers over Indie's back, up to the claim mark I gave him a few weeks ago, the night we moved into our new home. It still feels surreal. He glances over and smiles at me, and warm affection floods our mate bond. I tilt my head, silently suggesting we call it a night. I want him to myself so we can do things that aren't socially acceptable in the middle of a pack dinner.

"You guys look like you want to eat each other," Lea says quietly, scrunching her nose. "You're newly mated still. Don't worry about being polite, just go home. I know you don't want to be here with us any longer."

"Sorry," I say, trying to arrange my face to look like I'm not thinking about the things I'm going to do to Indie tonight. He looks at me, heat in his gaze, and I give up on socializing. He grabs my hand and we walk through the trees toward our cozy new cabin, both rushing to get home and get our hands on each other.

"I love you," he says, pausing on the steps. My answer is a kiss as I drag him inside. His foot kicks the door closed behind us before he picks me up and carries me to our room.

FAMILY TREES

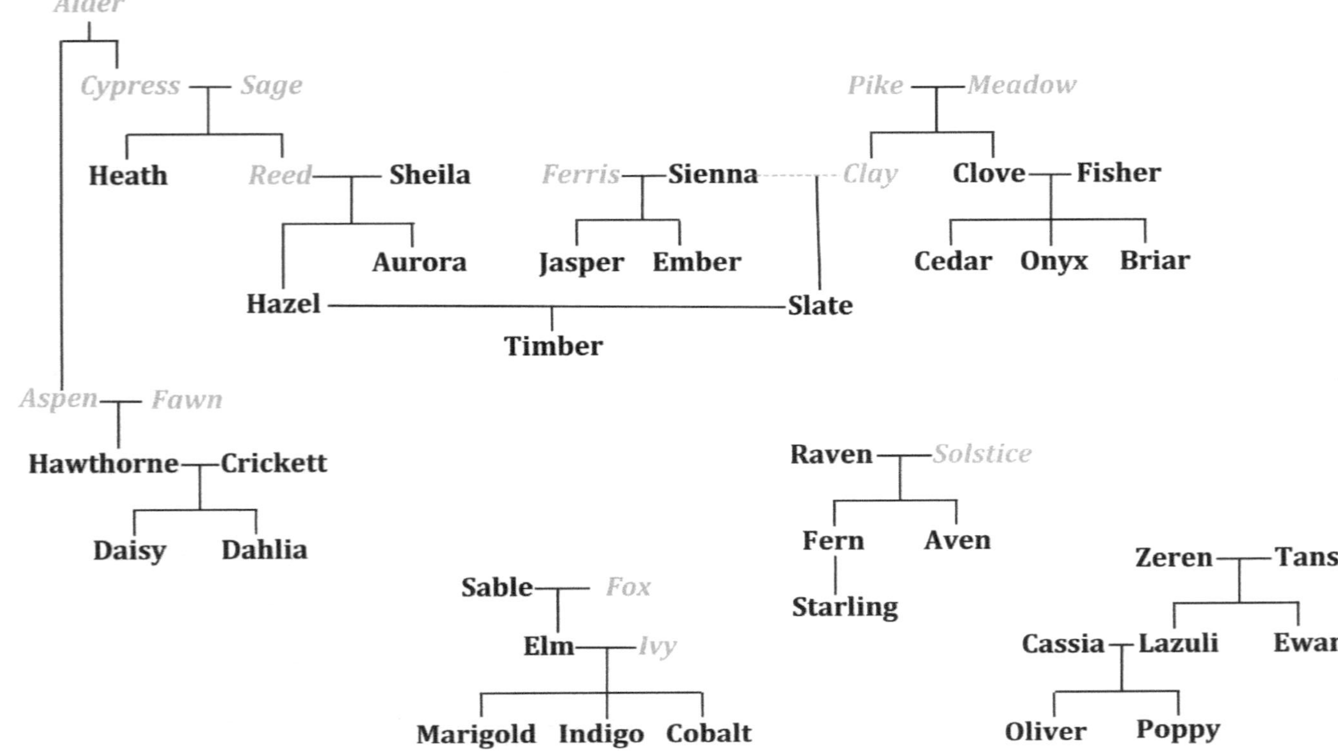

BRACKEN CREEK PACK

Alpha – Heath, later Hazel and Slate
Heir – Timber
Beta – Jasper
Gamma – Hawthorne
Delta – Fisher
Advisor - Heath
Zetas – Elm, Lazuli, Cassia, Onyx
Thetas – Vale, Aven
Healer – Sable
Business Manager – Linden
Supply Manager – Fern
Teacher – Marigold
Chef – Crickett
Baker – Clove
Gardener – Cedar
Others – Ewan, Ginger, Yarrow, Daire, Laurel, Violet, Briar, Indigo
Elders – Oren, Tansy, Raven, Zeren
Youth – Cobalt, Dahlia, Daisy, Elwood, Juniper, Oliver, Starling, Willow

IRONCREST PACK

Alpha - Zephyr
Beta - Beryl
Gamma – Dell

GRANITE RIDGE PACK

Alphas - Ferris and Sienna, later Ember and Onyx
Beta - Aries, and later Orion
Heir – Ember
Delta – Bear
Gamma – Aster
Others – Flint

RAVEN PACK

Alpha - Nyx
Others – Lea
Elders – Breeze, Heron

VALLEY PACK

Alpha - Cashel
Beta, Heir – Malachite
Gamma – Zinnia

His name was Shale in the 1st draft

yeah, probably...

Slate starts to respond, but I suspect it's going to be threats of violence against anyone who even looked in my direction during this ordeal, so I stop him the best way I know how. Grabbing his shirt, I yank him down and cover his mouth with mine.

Probably should have talked, but making out is good too!

Heat races through me, my skin tingling. I might be angry with him, but I need him more. He grips my ass and lifts me, my legs looping around his waist. Turning us, he presses my back into a tree. A thrill zings in my blood and I scratch my nails down his ribs. Kissing against a tree was a nonnegotiable plot point for this book.

He kisses down my neck. I recognize now that he is replacing the scent of his brother with his own. Claiming me again in this small way. Possessive!

xoxo

"Take me home," I rasp.

A throat clears, the noise cutting through my fog. Slate sets me on my feet so fast I almost fall, but his grip on my waist is steel.

Awkward!

The Alpha, my uncle, stands there. His hands are in his pockets and his eyebrows are the highest I've ever seen them. "Hazel, you're home," he acknowledges.

So I didn't know Hazel was a shifter until the 2nd draft!

During the drafting process, this first book was titled "Wild Claim" - so cringy!

He sighs. "I never stood a chance." His fingers thread through my hair. Tugging me down against his chest, he wraps me securely with both arms. When he speaks, I feel the vibrations in my ribcage. "I've heard pack members talk about meeting their mate. We don't date often, because when we finally fall for someone, that's it. It's like something clicks into place, or a bond that becomes unbreakable before you even realize what's happening."

I love this explanation- it's a choice, but also not.

Briar was always a favorite. She's ADHD and always trying new things, but she had to be tough with two brothers.

"Indie?" she whispers, rolling back. When I open my eyes, we're nose to nose and she's all I can see. Her breath ghosts my lips. We're frozen, gazes locked, as I wait for her to speak. She hesitates, her eyes narrowing and brows rising minutely.

one bed!

Her face tips up, nose brushing my cheek and her lips brushing mine softly, tentatively. I stay frozen, afraid to spook her. Her hand comes up, her fingertips lightly grazing my jaw. "Sorry," she mutters softly, pulling back and blinking at me. Pink colors her cheeks. "I shouldn't have done that."

"You're allowed to kiss me if you want to," I answer, my voice hoarse. "I can go get that bottle if you need an excuse." This feels so sweet to me ♡

Taking a deep breath, I nod. "So Cobalt was doodling peens on his notebook. Not the stuff he turned in, just the notes I wasn't supposed to see." Jasper shakes his head, his lips pressed together to suppress his grin. "Well, of course the other kids got in on it."

"So what happened?"

"Daisy turned a page in."

"Oh, no."

I nod. "I asked her what was drawn on the corner of her math quiz." I pause, enjoying his eyes going wide. "And she said it was a pickle."

I think Cobalt was about 12 in this book... I wish I could write him more. He's a wild child ☺

The pickle story really happened in my kid's 5th grade class, except it was a "stick figure eating a pickle".

I taught for 3 years and drew on that experience heavily when writing Marigold. Her selflessness and burnout is very teacher-coded.

Wolf jaws close over his arm, causing him to drop his hold on my hair. A white wolf drags him backwards and to the ground. Shocked, I push myself up and scramble over the back of the sofa to gain some distance.

Another wolf snarls and stalks closer to me while the man across the sofa screams. Spit drips from his bared teeth. *She's defending her students + already stabbed a guy!*

Weapon. I need a weapon.

There's nothing. I'll have to shift. My hands grapple with the tactical gear. I have to get it off or I'll be tangled up.

The dark wolf growls, its hackles rising, making it look huge. Another step, and my vision narrows as my heart races so fast my chest aches. My hand slips on the buckle, fear numbing my fingers.

The wolf lowers, its haunches bunching, preparing to leap. This time I can't help the shriek that tears from my mouth.

With a dull thud one of my daggers embeds into the wolf's ribcage, throwing him back against the wall. The body slides down to the wood floor, leaving a slick of blood on the old wallpaper. *screaming!*

"Don't fucking touch my mate," a voice growls. Slowly, I tear my eyes off the dying wolf and turn toward the gravelly voice. *this makes me feral*

Jasper stands on the other side of the sofa, naked with blood smeared across his mouth. *Jasper can be brutal when defending his family like at the end of Book 3!*

I think Jasper is objectively the best looking wolf boy... and Marigold is the most classicly beautiful.

vs Ember + Onyx are grungy, video games and concerts.

+ Cedar + Rory are all outdoorsy free spirit style.

(Hazel + Slate are the most average.)

"Why are you still here?" My arms cross over my chest. *Ember= black cat girlfriend*

"Maybe I'm drunk and horny and I like it when women are mean to me," he purrs. *Love this for Onyx lol!*

"You're pathetic. Find someone else to annoy." His eyes light up at my insult. I guess he was telling the truth about liking mean women. Then he's going to *love* me. *yes he will!*

I didn't picture Onyx with Ember until after I wrote Book 2, but the idea popped in my head + it felt so right. Nothing else would do.

We love a stabby girl!

His hand grabs my wrist, his thumb over my pulse. The contact of his skin scorches me. "Your heart is beating like a hummingbird."

"I'm considering all the ways I'd like to kill you," I bluff. "It's a very appealing idea."

He cocks his head, his eyes glittering with intelligence and mocking humor. "I don't think you are." His gaze drops down, to where my body has leaned into him. *Shit.* *when the enemies are bantering!*

He lowers his head toward mine and my lungs tighten. "I think you're thinking of *other* things you'd like to do to me."

"I'd settle for strangling, disemboweling, or a simple guillotine." I'm aiming to wipe the smile off his face, but instead it widens, pleased at my threats.

"We both know that isn't what you want."

His warmth is too tempting and it makes me dumb. He dips his head, lips near my ear. "I'm going to kiss you and you aren't going to stab me. Understood?" The touch of his breath triggers a shiver I try to hide.

Yes, Onyx makes really bad choices! But really, this story is about Ember healing + taking control of her life.

Book 4—"Onyx looks like someone who wore guyliner"

"Do you want clothes?" he asks.

What's the point? I drop my head again, the shock of my fight bleeding me out until I'm nothing but a husk.

"Ember," Onyx says. His voice is lower, darker. His shadow moves across me, and I don't realize until it's too late. His hand grips my shoulder as the other runs down my back over old scars from beatings. "What are these?"

I scowl at him, and even that seems to take too much effort. "I told you. When you do poorly at training, they beat you. Remember?"

He traces down to the scars on the sides of my thighs. "Can you tell me which wolves did this?" *Who did this to you?! Ahhhh!*

Honestly, Onyx is my favorite character ♡

Book 4 was the easiest to write. Freaking delightful!
(Book 3 was the hardest)

"Cedar!" she yelps, and I jolt forward, already reaching for her. "Look down there!" She points at the creek, her words squeaking with excitement.

Jasper Three wolves trail along the creek, the largest a dark gray *slate* followed by a solid white wolf and finally a smaller silvery wolf with bulging sides. Their forms are as familiar as my own. *Hazel*

"Oh, are those wolves? That one looks pregnant! That's amazing," Aurora says, creeping closer to the edge to get a better look.

"Woah, be careful," I say, grabbing her hand. Her fingers squeeze back, but she continues to lean forward to peer down at the creek. *Headed to see Ember + Onyx*

The white wolf bounds across the water and disappears into the trees. The darkest one turns to the little silver wolf and licks her muzzle. Together, they turn south and pad out of view. ♡ ♡ ♡

There were 2 magical concepts I loved exploring here—
1. The physical need to shift. Cedar keeps skipping his morning runs to be with Rory, + it bites him in the ass!
2. Plant magic! It was so fun to write Rory's magic as manipulating life force energy. But that's why she can heal.
♡ Rory + Cedar have a 3 year age gap, vs Ember + Onyx is 6! (18½ + 25)
  Marigold + Jasper are the only couple where the woman is older.

This happened hiking too!

When I try to step forward, my ankle catches on plants that have grown up and twisted around me. Their hold is so tight, I pitch forward and throw my hands out to catch myself.

My shifter instincts win out over the yelling in my head. One instant I'm a clumsy human falling, and the next second I'm a reddish-blonde wolf landing on four paws with the shreds of clothes drifting around me. *Whoops!*

Aurora lets out a scream so intense, my ears pop. Her hands clench into fists before she turns and starts sprinting through the trees.

I should run to get Hazel or Heath. What I really shouldn't do is chase her. So of course that's exactly what I do.

Predator instincts kick in and I'm racing after her before I can stop myself. The floral scent mingling with the chemicals of paint, something so uniquely Aurora, overwhelms my senses. I'm going to catch her.

This is one of my favorite scenes ever!
Gentle, controlled Cedar wolfs out and chases her!
This right after he rescues her from the mower/vines ♡

THANK YOUS

Thank you to my family for supporting my author journey.

Thank you to my editing team, Ilea and Anandi. There is no way Books 2-4 would exist without you.

Thank you to my author community, to **Tereza Kane** (Storm and Sea Saga) and **Harlie Kay** (The Lost and Found Duet) for publishing support, and **Harlowe Savage** (Monarchs of Eros) for being my writing buddy.

Also **Wren Jones** (Practical Potions Series) and **Vermilion H Baine** (Haunted Creatures Series) for sharing your experience and cheering me on.

And thank you to Laura at **Literally, A Bookshop** for bringing these stories to shelves.

I wouldn't have kept going if it wasn't for all of you.

ABOUT THE AUTHOR

Aly Hollis lives in the Southwest with her family, two blue heelers, two very judgmental cats, and an adorable turtle. She's written fiction her entire life, but never completed a novel until she attempted the book-in-a-month challenge in 2023. Four weeks later, she had a very angsty and repetitive version of Campfires and Canines.

Months and many rewrites later, she published her first book. But readers kept asking for stories for the other wolf boys, so soon Jasper and Onyx had their own books. A few months later, Cedar's story popped into her head. This is the end of the original series, but look for a prequel series coming soon.

Sisters Meara and Brenna have a quiet life as the daughters of the local apothecary in a queendom that hates and fears faeries. Meara spends her days forging for medicinal herbs in the forest, while Brenna works in the household of a noble family. But when an attack triggers elemental fire magic within Brenna, the sisters are forced to flee their home.

Reeling from the discovery they aren't human, Meara and Brenna find themselves in the Court of Autumn Harvest, under the protection of Cerne, a roguish fae lord, and his inner circle.

Brenna is enthralled by the beauty of the fae courts as she works to master her magic and discover the truth of their parentage. This search draws the obsessive attention of Emrys, a vampire prince of the High Court.

Scared for her sister and struggling to unlock her own magic, Meara finds herself caught between Cerne and his rival, the heir of the Summer Court, whose light draws out the shadowy magic within her. But as the conflict between humans and the fae escalates, the sisters must determine their loyalties and how far they will go to protect those they love.

Raven Rebel is an epic high fantasy, bringing you into fae courts full of inhuman faeries like nymphs, sprites, and puca. Join Meara and Brenna as they uncover new magic and experience the festivals, rituals, and politics of the fae courts.